The Henry Cecil Omnibus

The Henry Cecil Omnibus

ЯR

Ravette London

Contents

BROTHERS IN LAW

Contents

CHAPTER 1

Call to the Bar

'George Smith is acquitted by the jury at Assizes of a criminal offence. "You are discharged," the judge says to him, and then adds: "You were very lucky in your jury." Mr. Smith issues a writ against the judge claiming damages for slander. What are the first steps likely to be taken in Mr. Smith's action after the service of the writ?'

Roger Thursby looked round the hall where he was about to answer this last question in his Bar Final Examination. He was fairly well satisfied with his answers to the other questions and he had done most of them quickly. So he had plenty of time for the last. He looked at the pictures of past eminent judges on the walls. Surely, he thought, no judge would behave like the one in the question. He saw sternness in some of the faces, but no trace of the meanness which seemed to him implicit in the remark made by the judge to the prisoner. The jury had acquitted the man. Presumed innocent even before the verdict, he could not be thought less so after he had been found Not Guilty. Yet, after his acquittal, the judge, merely to gratify his own personal feelings, had strongly suggested that he was guilty. And the prisoner could not hit back. Or could he? That was the question. Well, there was plenty of time to answer it. How nice it was to be at the end of all his examinations. Roger was not an over-confident young man, but he knew that he had done well enough to pass at any rate. And soon he would be a barrister. Only twenty-one and a barrister. It was a great thought. There were not many young men who could be called to the Bar to-day at the age of twenty-one. A distant cousin of his had been called on his twenty-first birthday. But that was long before the days of military service. Roger had had to do a lot of work, and to give up quite a good deal, to be called before he was twenty-two. But he'd done it in the end. He had eaten all his dinners and had been pleased that this curious and pleasant custom was still retained as an essential qualification for admission to the English Bar. It must have been nicer still in the old days, he thought, when association in the Inns of Court with men of law and dinners with them in the evening took the place of examinations. He had enjoyed the dinners, meeting all sorts of different young men and women in the process. He had liked the sometimes quaint procedure and had been rather proud to drink a toast from a loving cup to the 'pious, glorious and immortal memory of Good Queen Bess'. And he had passed all his examinations, except this last, the Final. And now that was over, all but the last question. Well, the answer was simple enough.

'The judge,' he wrote, 'would, by the Treasury Solicitor, enter an appearance to the writ, possibly under protest, and would then apply to stay or dismiss the proceedings as an abuse of the process of the Court.' He paused and thought for a moment. Would it be too dangerous? Well, it wouldn't be fair to plough him for it. Here goes. And he wrote: 'Although I think the judge's application would be successful, as anything said by a judge in Court, however unfair or ill-advised, must be absolutely privileged if it in any way relates to the proceedings, all the same I think that the words "abuse of the process of the Court" should have stuck in that judge's throat.'

'I do hereby call you to the Bar and do publish you barrister.' The Treasurer of Roger's Inn had said the magic words and shaken hands with him, and Roger was a barrister. His optimism during the Final had been justified. Indeed, he had been placed in the first class, which he had not expected. And now here he was standing with the other newly-called young men and women. The actual ceremony was finished and the Treasurer was about to deliver a short homily to them before they sat down to dinner, the first dinner he would eat in his Inn as a barrister. Possibly one day he would be doing what the Treasurer was doing. He'd better listen to what he was going to say.

'Some years ago,' began the Treasurer, 'more than I now like to think, I was called to the Bar by a most learned Master of the Bench of this Honourable Society. He spoke to us as I am now speaking to you. What he said was excellent, but I am bound to admit that there can be too much of an excellent thing—even, for example, of the admirable sherry with which this Honourable

Society still provides us. Now I am not suggesting for one moment
that the length of the address and the sherry had anything to do
with one another—but the fact remains that he kept us standing—
and waiting for our dinner—as you are now, for the best part of
half an hour. Whether it was due to this I know not, but the custom
of making this address thereafter fell into desuetude and has only
just been revived. This brings me at once to the quality which I
strongly commend to you as the second most important quality to
be cultivated by you in your career. I will deal with the first in a
moment. The second is brevity. Don't confuse quantity with quality.
Say little and say it well. One might think that I was giving advice
to a newly-appointed judge, but it is almost as important for counsel
to know when to hold his tongue as for a judge. But the first quality,
without which no barrister ought to succeed, is a fearless integrity.
That quality needs no explanation. Fearless integrity. You will
nearly always know instinctively what is the right thing to do. Do
it. Finally, I commend to you the quality of good fellowship—"strive
mightily but eat and drink as friends". Which seems to me to be a
good note on which to end this address. I wish all of you the success
you deserve; I feel sure you will have it and I hope that thought
will not depress too many of you.'

And, after Grace had been said, judges, barristers and students
sat down to dinner.

CHAPTER 2

The Beginning

'For my next song,' said the baritone from abroad, 'I have chosen a German one. I shall sing it in the original language but, to help you follow it, I will first give you a fairly literal translation. "In the woods the birds sing and the other animals make their personal noises. But I sit by the disused well and weep. Where there once was up-drip now there is down-drip." '

'Drip's the word,' whispered Roger to Sally. 'Can't we slip out before he makes *his* personal noises?'

'Be quiet,' said Sally.

He had to endure that song and the next, which was called— Roger thought most reasonably—'Torment', and then he managed to persuade Sally to leave.

'It really is too bad,' he said when they were safely outside the hall. 'We're supposed to be celebrating my "call" and you have to drag me there. Anyway, we're out now. Let's *go* and celebrate. I can do with some down-drip.'

'We've missed mother,' said Sally.

'Was she going to sing too?'

'You don't imagine I'd have made you come otherwise. I told you about it.'

'I believe you did, now I come to think of it—but my mind's been so full up with my "call" that I haven't been taking in much else. Have we really missed your mother?'

'Don't sound so pleased. She hasn't a bad voice at all.'

'I'm sure it's lovely. Like you are. But, oh, Sally, I can't think of anything except that I'm a barrister, a real live one. I've been one for twenty-four hours. I could defend you for murder or shop-lifting. I could get you a divorce or appear at your inquest. Am I being very silly? Anyway,' he went on, without giving Sally a chance to answer, 'I haven't talked about it all the time. I did ask you to marry me, didn't I?'

'In a sort of way, I suppose—in the intervals.'

'Why did you say "no"?'

'It wasn't a definite "no".'

'It wasn't a definite "yes".'

'I suppose you'll be wanting everything "yes" or "no" now. You lawyers! Let me tell you one thing. You'll have to keep your law for the Courts. I'm not just going to be black or white. I'll be grey when I please.'

'I love you in grey. What'll you wear when you come to hear my first case?'

'First catch your fish,' said Sally. 'Besides,' she added, 'you said you'd thought of asking Joyce to marry you.'

'That was an alternative. Not both at the same time.'

'Look,' said Sally. 'You keep your beautiful legal mind for your unfortunate clients—if you get any.'

'I'm sorry, Sally. I didn't mean to be flippant—at least—I did. I am sorry, Sally. I don't know what to say. D'you think I'll ever grow up?'

'Well, twenty-one isn't all that old. Come on, cheer up. Now we *will* go and celebrate. I didn't mean to be beastly.'

A few minutes later they were drinking.

'Here's to Roger Thursby, barrister-at-law.'

'Here's to Roger Thursby, Esquire, Q.C.'

'Here's to Mr Justice Thursby.'

'Here's to us.'

When they parted later that evening Roger was very, very happy, though he was still uncertain whether it should be Sally or Joy. But he forgot them both when he went to sleep and all his dreams were of judges and barristers, beautiful clients and criminals. Sometimes they got a bit mixed up, but, even if they had not, they would not have borne much resemblance to the real thing.

The next day he kept an appointment at No. 1 Temple Court, the chambers of Mr Kendall Grimes, a junior of many years' standing with a substantial practice, to whom he had been given an introduction. His appointment was for 9.30 and he arrived ten minutes early and introduced himself to Mr Grimes' clerk, Alec Blake.

'Good morning, sir,' said Alec pleasantly. 'I'm glad you've come

early. Gives me a chance to put you in the picture. Don't suppose
you know anything about the Temple, sir?'

'I don't,' said Roger. 'Not a thing.'

'Well, there's lots to learn, sir.'

He might have added, as Roger soon appreciated, that the first
thing to learn on going into chambers in the Temple is the importance of the clerk.

'One thing, if I may say at once, sir,' went on Alec, 'is always to
be on the spot. Stay in chambers late. Come early. You never know
what may happen.'

As he made this last remark Alec sucked his teeth, and gave
Roger a knowing look. It was not that there was anything in his
teeth to suck, but it was a method, not entirely unknown in the
Temple, of indicating that the sucker knew a thing or two. Roger
shivered slightly. It was to him as cleaning windows is to some
people and much as he came to like Alec he could never reconcile
himself to this particular sound. On this, his introduction to it, he
was too thrilled at his first contact with chambers in the Temple to
be as affected by it as he became later. At that moment the telephone
rang.

'Excuse me, sir,' said Alec as he answered it. 'Hullo. Yes. Mr
Grimes' clerk speaking. Oh—Albert. Look, old boy, we can't do it,
really we can't. Must be thirty-three. What's that? Yes, of course,
I know they've a leader. I'm only asking for the junior's fee. I ought
to ask for the leader's by rights. Letting you off lightly. What! Now
really, old boy, it's a bit late to come that one. I dare say you don't
like the two-thirds rule—but it hasn't gone yet. What's that? If we
weren't on the telephone I'd tell you what you could do with that
Report. No, I can't send him in for twenty-five. All right, I *won't*,
if you like. Now look, old boy, what about a coffee and we'll talk
it over. See you over the way? About half-eleven? O.K.'

Alec turned to Roger.

'Sorry, sir. One of the things we have to do,' and he gave a loud
suck. Roger tried to look as though he didn't mind the suck and
had understood something of what had happened, whereas he had
not the faintest idea what it was all about, and he didn't like the
suck at all.

'It's most interesting,' he said. 'Is that Mr Grimes by any chance?'
he went on, pointing to a photograph of someone in uniform which
was hanging on the wall above Alec's table.

'It is, sir,' said Alec. 'He doesn't like my keeping it there, as a matter of fact, but I put my foot down. There were quite a number of people who stayed at home in 1914. He was in it from the start. Don't see why *I* shouldn't say so, even if *he* won't. Anyway, it's my photo and I can put it where I like. It's amazing, really, sir. You'd never think of him as a soldier. You wait and you'll see what I mean. But he went in just as a private, just as a private, sir—no pulling strings for our Mr Grimes, and how d'you think he ended up?'

'How?' asked Roger.

'As a sergeant-major, sir. If I hadn't seen him myself—I was a boy in the Temple then, sir—I wouldn't have believed it. Amazing. You'll see what I mean, sir. Mentioned twice in despatches he was, sir.'

'Jolly good,' said Roger.

The telephone rang again and just as Alec was answering it there was a noise on the staircase rather like a small express train coming up it and a second later Mr Grimes burst into the room, panting. Roger at first thought there had been an accident but he soon found out that this was Mr Grimes' normal method of entrance. Mr Grimes looked, panting, at Alec for a moment.

'It's Mr Brookes,' whispered Alec, putting his hand over the mouthpiece.

Mr Grimes nodded and then noticed Roger. He did not know whether he was a client or the prospective pupil or another barrister's clerk. So he gave him a 'Good morning' which would do for any of them and bolted into his room, which was next to the clerk's room.

Alec finished his conversation with Mr Brookes. 'Yes, sir. I'll have him there, sir. Don't you worry, sir. That's very nice of you, sir.' He turned from the telephone, obviously pleased at what Mr Brookes had said and, with one last violent suck, winked at Roger plainly indicating that there were no flies on Mr Alec Blake. Then with a: 'He'll see you in a moment, sir,' he went hurriedly into Mr Grimes' room.

Roger started to collate his first impressions of a barrister's chambers, with a view to telling Sally and Joy and his mother. It was exciting to be about to start his career, though a barrister's chambers looked very different from what he had imagined. It was not that they were clean. They weren't. Nor did he yet know that the lavatory was old-fashioned and that there was no hot water, unless you used a gas ring. He was as yet unaware that the system of cleaning was for a lady called a laundress to come in every morning, make herself a cup of tea and go on to the next set of chambers. It was just that he couldn't imagine, say, Crippen, being defended by anyone who worked in No. 1 Temple Court, which, it will be understood, was not one of the new buildings in the Temple. And Mr Grimes looked indeed very different from his idea of a busy barrister. He was tallish, thin, quite bald, except for two large tufts of coal-black hair which stood up obstinately on either side of the bald expanse and which equally obstinately refused to change their colour with the years. At the time Roger first saw him he also had bushy side whiskers which came half-way down his cheek on one side and not quite half-way down on the other. They, too, were obstinately black. Roger subsequently learned that he had once worn a drooping black moustache but that one day he had shaved it off and, like the disappointed witch in the fairy tale, it was never seen again.

There were other things, too, which Roger had yet to learn about Mr Grimes—that he was unmarried and lived near the Essex marshes with an old and feeble housekeeper who looked after him when he was not looking after her, that he kept bees, to which he was devoted, that his work, his bees, and his housekeeper appeared to be his only interests in life, that every morning he sat meekly in the driving-seat of a very fast car and drove it anything but meekly to the Temple, and that, on reaching the Temple, he jumped out as though his life depended on it and rushed to his chambers, with the result which Roger had just witnessed. His sight appeared to be extremely good, and it was said that the large horn-rimmed glasses which he wore in Court contained plain glass and were used by him simply because he found them useful for taking off when cross-examining a witness. Roger never discovered whether this rumour was based on fact or not, but he was quite satisfied that the story that Mr Grimes once appeared before the judge in chambers with each tuft of hair full of bees was entirely apocryphal.

Roger was still wondering at what he had just heard from Alec and seen in Mr Grimes when Alec came out and conducted him into Mr Grimes' room.

'This is Mr Thursby, sir.'

Mr Grimes held out his hand. 'How are ye, my dear fellow?' he said. 'How are ye?' He had a rather high-pitched sing-song way of speaking. 'So ye've come to the Bar, have ye? That's the way. Have a chair, my dear fellow. That's right, that's right.'

'Mr Milroy said you might have a vacancy for a pupil,' said Roger. 'Do you think you might be able to take me?'

'Do I think we might be able to take ye, my dear fellow? Well, my dear fellow, we might, you know, we might. Have ye been called?'

'Yes.'

'Who proposed ye?'

'Well, my mother knows Mr Milroy. He's a Bencher of my Inn, and he introduced me to Mr Sanderson.'

'When were ye called, my dear fellow?'

'The day before yesterday, as a matter of fact.'

'Just out of the egg, my dear fellow, just out of the egg. D'ye think ye're going to like it?'

'I'm sure I shall, but, of course, I don't really know much about it yet. I suppose the more important question really is whether it will like me.'

'Quite right, my dear fellow, quite right. Yes, I think we can take ye, I think we can take ye. When would ye like to start?'

'Straight away, if I may.'

'Of course ye may, my dear fellow, of course ye may. Take these papers and have a look at them. Alec will show ye where the pupils' room is. Ye'll find a couple of others there. They'll tell ye how the wheels go round. Now, off ye go, my dear fellow. Ask me anything you want to. Good-bye, my dear fellow—good-bye, bye, bye.' And Mr Grimes showed Roger to the door.

'All right, sir?' said Alec.

'Mr Grimes said I could start at once,' said Roger.

'Very well, sir. That's the pupils' room over there. I'll show you in. I hope you'll be happy here, sir.'

They started to go together towards the pupils' room door when Alec stopped for a moment.

'Oh, sir, would you make out two cheques, please. One for a hundred guineas for Mr Grimes and one for me for ten.'

'Now?'

'No—any time, sir, thank you.'

At that moment, Alec was sent for hurriedly by Mr Grimes.

'Would you mind showing yourself in, sir?' said Alec to Roger. 'I'm so sorry, sir,' and Alec rushed away.

Roger opened the door of the pupils' room and walked in. 'My name's Thursby,' he said. 'I'm a new pupil.'

'How are ye, my dear fellow, how are ye?' said a man of about thirty-three, giving a very creditable imitation of Mr Grimes.

CHAPTER 3

First Day in Court

There were two others in the room.

'Let me introduce everyone,' said the speaker in his normal voice. 'I'm Henry Blagrove. I live here. Professionally, you know. Expect you saw my name on the door. Been there seven years. Tell you more about myself later. You'll learn about me, if nothing else, while you're here. This is Peter Hallfield. He's been a pupil six whole months. A confident young man. Though, between you and me, I can't think why. And this is Charles Hepplewhite. He's just finishing. Another month, isn't it?'

'How d'you do?' said Roger generally. 'What do I do next, please?'

'Ye'll soon learn, my dear fellow, ye'll soon learn,' said Henry. 'It's up to these chaps to say where you're to sit. Nothing to do with me. I just come in here and waste your time when I've nothing to do of my own. Which, I may tell you in confidence, is pretty often.'

'Would this do?' said Charles, indicating part of a table in the middle of the room. 'Here's a chair.'

'Thank you very much,' said Roger. He sat down and put on the table the papers which Mr Grimes had given him. On the outside was written: 'Pennythwaite *v.* The Drum Bottling Co. (1948) Ltd. Instructions to Counsel to advise. 3 gns. Leatherhead, Frank and Compton, 4, Cockburn Buildings, E.C.4. Plaintiff's Solicitors.'

Henry looked over Roger's shoulder at the brief.

'Oh, that,' he said. 'You'll have some fun with that when you can understand it. Which is more than the Court of Appeal could. It's been twice to them and once to the House of Lords. All on a point of pleading. Now we're back where we started. Fortunately the Plaintiff's got legal aid and the Defendants are in liquidation. I don't suppose you understand what I'm talking about.'

'Quite frankly,' said Roger, 'since I arrived here I haven't understood a thing.'

'Then you've got a chance,' said Henry. 'It's people like Peter here who come to grief because they don't know a thing either but they think they do. I've done my best for him. Still do, as you can see, but it's a losing battle.'

'Henry,' said Peter, 'just because you're the most hopeless failure at the Bar and ought to have left it years ago, there's no need to be persistently offensive. He doesn't mean it, by the way,' he added to Roger. 'He just says things because he likes the sound of them. Does the same in Court. It amuses the judges, but they usually decide against him.'

'Too true,' said Henry. 'They ought to keep someone like me in every set of chambers as an awful warning.'

'Of what?' asked Roger.

'Of the result of talking too much and working too little.'

Roger soon learned all about Henry Blagrove, and one of the first things he found out was that Henry knew himself as well as any man can; that he knew, for example, that he could have succeeded at the Bar but probably never would. He was right in saying that he worked too little. He was incredibly lazy and, though sometimes he would do a great deal of work in one particular case, he would avoid hard work whenever possible. He loved the life and fortunately, or unfortunately, he had just enough work to enable him to stay at the Bar. He had a keen sense of humour and fun, he was highly intelligent, cheerful and generous, but he had no inclination for the sustained hard work which he knew was necessary to success. He had very keen perception and his judgment was excellent. He had very nearly a woman's intuition and knew almost at once which way a judge's mind was working—which occasionally was more than the judge did himself. He was indeed a tremendous asset to those of Mr Grimes' pupils who were sensible enough to listen to him. He had learned very quickly the secrets of success at the Bar; he had learned the tricks of the trade; he knew the ethics; he was popular with his fellow barristers, he never broke the rules. And he was a first-class mimic, though from force of habit he was inclined to imitate Mr Grimes too often. Working so close to him he found it difficult not to do so, and was far too lazy to resist the temptation. Roger did not, of course, learn all Henry's qualities at this first meeting, but one thing he found out very quickly. Henry loved to talk.

'What would you like to know to begin with?' he asked Roger, shortly after their introduction.

'There's so much. I don't know where to begin.'

'It really is rather extraordinary,' said Henry, 'that here you are, a fully-fledged barrister, licensed to lose anyone's case for him and you haven't had an hour of practical experience. Now a medical student has to watch a lot of butchery before he qualifies to dig for his first appendix. Yet your kind old Uncle George could send you a brief to-morrow. By the way, have you an Uncle George?'

'I'm afraid not. I don't think I know any solicitors.'

'Well, it doesn't really matter, because the ones you know are seldom much use. Whenever you meet a solicitor and he learns you're at the Bar, he'll murmur something about all his work being conveyancing or litigation not much coming his way. Still, at your present stage it's just as well. When you go into Court for the first time you'll have a nice white wig and a little theoretical knowledge, but, for the rest, you'll be supported by the love of your parents and the admiration of your girl friends. Which last, no doubt, you will do a good deal to cultivate, telling them the most thrilling stories of what you said to the judge and the judge said to you. You don't mind me lecturing like this, I suppose?'

'I'm most grateful.'

'I wish you'd shut up for a moment,' said Charles. 'I strongly suspect I'm going to be left in front of Nettlefold and I've hardly looked at the thing.'

Before Roger could begin to understand the meaning of this remark, he heard similar noises to those which he had heard when Mr Grimes had entered chambers.

'Heigh-ho,' said Charles. 'We're off.'

The next moment the door opened and Alec rushed in. Without a word he picked up the papers in front of Charles and rushed off again saying, as he went out: 'Court six first and then the Official Referee.'

'Come on,' said Charles, 'we're in this procession. You'd better make up your mind from the beginning what position you'll take up. Grimeyboy will run all the way with Alec trotting behind him. Peter, when he comes, usually goes a short head behind Alec. I walk. What'll you do?'

'Which would you advise?' said Roger to Henry. But before he could answer, Mr Grimes rushed past—while talking they had gone into the clerk's room—put a hand on Roger and said:

'Come on, my dear fellow, come on. Now ye'll see what it's all about.' And down the stairs he rushed, pursued by Alec and the pupils. On this occasion Roger felt he had better keep up with his master. He caught up with him just before he crossed the Strand.

'Should I wear my robes, d'you think?' he asked.

'Oh—yes, my dear fellow. Always wear your robes. That's the way to get known. Have ye got them with ye?'

'I've left them in chambers, I'm afraid.'

'Go back for them, my dear fellow. Ye've plenty of time,' said Mr Grimes as he rushed across the Strand with Alec hard on his heels.

Roger went hastily back to chambers to collect the bag containing his robes. It was a sack-like affair of royal blue cloth with his initials embroidered on it in white and it contained a wig in a box with 'Roger Thursby Esq.' painted on the lid in gold letters, three pairs of white bands and a gown. When he had ordered them he had thought that he would prefer a red to a blue bag. The assistant had coughed deferentially.

'I'm afraid that will come a little later, sir,' he had said. 'You start with a blue one.'

'What are the red ones for?'

'Well, sir, in a sort of way you get presented with a red bag, though it'll cost you a guinea.'

'What do you mean?'

'Well, a leader, sir, a Q.C., will give you one for doing well in a case in which he leads you. Then you give his clerk a guinea. I've never been able to think why. He doesn't pay for the bag. I hope you'll get one all right, sir.'

'Supposing I don't?'

The assistant had coughed. 'Well, sir,' he had said, 'there are people who never get a red bag, but between you and me, sir, if you don't get one in your first seven years, you won't have made much headway.'

Roger found his robes and hurried across to the robing room. Mr Grimes had already gone, but he found Henry there.

'It's easy to get lost,' he said. 'I thought I'd come and guide you. It's a bit hectic this morning.'

'That's awfully kind of you,' said Roger and robed himself as quickly as he could. 'Have you any idea what I'm going to hear?' he asked.

'Well, I believe the thing before Nettlefold is a running down case and then there's a building reference before the Official Referee. Normally you'll at least be able to look at the briefs before you go into Court.'

Henry led Roger to Queen's Bench Court 6, where they were just in time to see the judge arrive. Then Henry returned to chambers.

'Fisher against Mollet,' called the associate, the bewigged official sitting below the judge, and Mr Grimes at once got up.

'May it please your Ludship,' he began. He was one of the few counsel who still used that pronunciation of Lordship. 'I appear in this case for the plaintiff with my learned friend Mr Hepplewhite. My learned friend Mr Ferret appears for the defendant. Me Lud, this is a claim for damages for personal injuries.'

'A running down case, is it, Mr Grimes?' asked the judge.

'Yes, me Lud, on the Watford by-pass. My client was driving very slowly along the main road when the defendant suddenly came out of a side turning with no warning at all and there was a collision.'

'Why was your client going at such a slow speed? It is unusual on that road, to say the least of it.'

'Oh, me Lud, he was in no particular hurry and, if I may say so, driving most carefully.'

'So you say, Mr Grimes. But if he was going so slowly, one wonders why he couldn't stop before the collision. But I suppose we'd better wait until it comes out in the evidence. Is the special damage agreed?'

'Yes, me Lud, except for one item.'

'What is the agreed amount?'

'One hundred and twenty-five pounds, me Lud. That is for repairs to the car and loss of wages.'

'What is the item not agreed?'

'A pair of trousers, me Lud. I can't think why my learned friend won't admit it.'

'Let me see,' said the judge. 'You're claiming £7 10s. They were new, I suppose?'

'Oh, yes, me Lud.'

'You want to fight the pair of trousers, do you, Mr Ferret?' asked the judge.

'Well, my Lord, no bill has been produced nor have the trousers.'

'Well, I hope we're not going to spend too much time on them,' said the judge. 'If we do, one side or the other would be able to buy a whole suit with the amount expended in costs.'

'Oh, me Lud, I shall be very short about them. But if my learned friend wants me to prove the trousers, I'll have to prove them. I don't see why my client should make him a present of them.'

'I gather they wouldn't be much use now, Mr Grimes. Now, don't let's waste any more time. Is there a plan?'

'Yes, me Lud.'

'Thank you. Is there an agreed medical report?'

'Yes, me Lud.'

'Thank you. Very well—perhaps you'll call your first witness. I'll read the report in due course.'

So began the first accident case which Roger had ever seen tried. After the second witness had been called, Roger noticed Alec hovering close to the row in which Mr Grimes and he were sitting. Suddenly, Mr Grimes whispered to him.

'Come and sit this side of me, my dear fellow.'

Roger did as he was told. This brought Mr Grimes nearer to the end of the row. A moment later he had exchanged seats with Charles who now sat next to Roger. A moment later Mr Grimes was gone. There was a slight sound from the breeze caused by his gown as he rushed away through the door of the Court, followed by Alec.

'Ought I to follow him?' whispered Roger to Charles.

'Do what you something well like, my dear chap,' said Charles with unexpected asperity. 'I'm left with this ruddy thing and I haven't read half of it.'

'Yes, Mr, Mr—er, Hepplewhite,' said the judge, 'do you wish to re-examine?'

Charles got to his feet and cleared his throat—a sure sign in an advocate of nervousness, varying from the slight to the verge-of-tears variety. In Charles' case it was between the two. He no longer wanted to cry, only to run away. It is indeed somewhat of an ordeal for a young man in his first year at the Bar to be left with a case in the High Court. The fact that he has only looked at the brief and does not know it thoroughly does not make very much difference to the way he conducts it, but it certainly does not increase his self-confidence.

'If you please, my Lord.' He cleared his throat again and began: 'My learned friend has asked you whether you hooted. Are you quite sure that you did?'

Mr Ferret immediately got up, looked sorrowfully at Charles, said to the judge: 'Really, my Lord!' and sat down.

Roger, who had a vivid imagination, wondered what on earth he himself would do. Obviously the judge and Mr Ferret knew what was happening though the glances they exchanged conveyed nothing to Roger. He felt very sorry for Charles and hoped that he'd never find himself in the same position. The judge looked in a kindly manner at the white wig of Charles and said:

'Mr Ferret thinks that was rather a leading question, Mr Hepplewhite. I'm afraid I'm inclined to agree.'

A leading question, of course, thought Roger. But what on earth does one ask instead? Would 'Did you hoot?' be a leading question. Perhaps it would be better to say, 'Did you or did you not hoot?' A moment later Roger experienced a thrill of pleasure.

'Did you or did you not hoot?' asked Charles.

'He has already said that he's not really sure,' said the judge. 'Can you carry it much further than that?'

'If your Lordship pleases,' said Charles and sat down.

'Don't you want to ask him anything about the trousers, Mr Hepplewhite?'

'The trousers, my Lord?' said Charles unhappily. The judge appeared to have made it plain at the outset that he did not want to hear too much about the trousers. And now here he was inviting him to go into the matter. The fact was that the plaintiff had been somewhat knocked about in cross-examination over the trousers. The judge was not sure that he had done himself justice in his answers to Mr Ferret. The witness was a nervous young man and had been rather over-persuaded to agree to things to which the judge was not at all satisfied he intended to agree. A few well-directed questions in re-examination might have restored the position. But Charles was quite incapable of asking them.

'The trousers, my Lord?' he said again.

What on earth would I ask? thought Roger. This is a pretty nerve-wracking game. I wonder if I ought to have gone on the Stock Exchange.

Seeing that Charles was quite incapable of dealing with the matter, the judge himself proceeded to ask the necessary questions and a few others too, some of them leading. Mr Ferret grimaced. He couldn't stop the judge asking leading questions and he saw what was going to happen. Until Mr Grimes returned, the judge was in effect going to conduct the case on behalf of the plaintiff and by the time Mr Grimes did return, he would have got so used to it that he might have become unconsciously in the plaintiff's favour. Justice is a funny thing. It can never be perfect. Roger learned in due course that sometimes the poorer counsel wins a case just because he's so bad that the judge has to step in. So what seemed unfair to the one side becomes unfair to the other.

After the running down case had been going on for some little time, Roger felt someone touch his arm. It was Alec.

'Have you seen Mr Hallfield anywhere?' he asked anxiously.

'I haven't, I'm afraid,' said Roger.

'Well, would you come with me, please, sir,' said Alec. 'It's rather urgent.'

Roger went clumsily in front of Charles, brushing some of his papers to the floor in the process, got out of counsel's row and was soon trotting after Alec through what seemed like endless corridors. He wanted to ask Alec all sorts of questions but the pace was too fast. Eventually they reached a Court.

'In here, sir,' said Alec.

Mr Grimes was on his feet addressing the Official Referee.

'If your Honour pleases,' he said, 'I submit that in meal or in malt the onus of proof is on the defendant.'

'Why meal or malt, Mr Grimes?' said Sir Hugo Cramp, the Official Referee.

'If your Honour pleases,' said Mr Grimes with a deferential smile.

'Yes, but why, Mr Grimes? You're always saying in meal or in malt, and I can't think why, I really can't.'

'Just a phrase, your Honour, just a phrase.'

'Well, you've said it three times in half an hour. I made a note of it.'

Indeed, that was the only note that Sir Hugo had so far made. The stage for making notes had not yet arrived and he hoped that it never would—except for doodling and the like and making notes of Mr Grimes' stock expression. The case ought to be settled. So should all building references. And in Sir Hugo's Court they nearly always were. It was a good thing for everyone. It saved the parties expense and Sir Hugo time, and it resulted in the next litigants' cases coming on earlier for trial—or settlement.

'Take a note, my dear fellow,' whispered Mr Grimes to Roger.

'What in?' asked Roger.

'A notebook, my dear fellow—I'm sorry, your Honour. I was just arranging with my learned friend Mr—Mr Thorburn—'

'Yes, yes,' said Sir Hugo, 'but these devilling arrangements should be made beforehand. I take it that I'm going to be deprived of the pleasure of hearing your further argument, Mr Grimes.'

'Only for a very short time, your Honour. I'm on my feet before Mr Justice Nettlefold.'

Sir Hugo removed his spectacles and looked at Mr Grimes, with a puzzled air for a moment, 'Oh, of course,' he said. 'The prophetic present. Well, I mustn't keep you, Mr Grimes. Very good of you to have come at all and I'm sure your learned junior will fill your place admirably while you are away.'

'It's very good of your Honour,' said Mr Grimes and with a few whispered words to Roger—'Ye'll be all right, my dear fellow, just tell him the tale, just tell him the tale,' Mr Grimes was gone.

It had all happened so quickly that Roger had difficulty in realizing that he, Roger Thursby Esq., barrister-at-law, aged twenty-one, called to the Bar two days previously, had been left in Court to represent one side or the other (he did not know which) in a building dispute before a judge called an Official Referee, of whom he had only vaguely heard. He looked round the Court. There was not a face he knew. Something inside his head began to go round and round and the Official Referee's face started to approach him with alarming swiftness. He realized that he must pull himself together or faint. Sir Hugo addressed him:

'Now that 'Now that the wind has dropped, Mr Truefold, would you continue your learned leader's submission?' Roger wished he had fainted. He rose unsteadily, and looked blankly in front of him.

'Your learned leader was saying,' went on Sir Hugo who, without intending to be unkind, enjoyed this sort of scene immensely, 'let me see—what was he saying? Something about malt, I believe. Strange, in a building dispute. Ah—no, I remember—he was submitting that the onus was on the other side. No doubt you would like to elaborate the submission?'

Roger continued to look blankly in front of him. It was not that

the power of speech had left him, but he simply did not know what
to say. He had sufficient presence of mind to realize that, if he
started, 'Your Honour' and then paused, the Official Referee would,
after waiting a decent interval, say, 'Yes, Mr Truefold?' and then
he would either have to repeat, 'Your Honour' or lapse into silence
again. It was better not to break it at all unless and until he could
think of one sentence which meant something. The only sentence
he would think of was: 'I want to go home,' and that wouldn't do
at all. It flashed through his mind that he could pretend to faint
and he cursed himself for having resisted a moment before the
genuine impulse to do so. But he had a natural inclination to tell
the truth. This was sometimes embarrassing in his relations with
Sally and Joy, but they were a long way from his mind at this
particular moment. He remained standing and staring and thinking
for the thoughts which would not come.

'Come, Mr Trueband,' said Sir Hugo affably, 'it's quite calm
now. Shall we proceed?'

There was nothing for it. 'Your Honour,' he began—and then
came the inevitable pause. Sir Hugo looked enquiringly at him, and
so did counsel on the other side and, indeed, nearly everyone in the
Court.

The pause had already passed the stage at which it became
unbearable when Sir Hugo duly came in with the expected 'Yes,
Mr Truefold?' to which Roger replied with the only words he had
so far learned: 'Your Honour,' and again there was that terrible
pause. Eventually Sir Hugo broke it with: 'I suppose you say that
the defendants, having admitted that the work was done and that
it has not been paid for, it is for them to show that parts of it have
not been properly done?'

With relief which he could not conceal, Roger added a word to
his repertoire. 'Yes, Your Honour,' he said, and getting bolder—'I
do.' Then, 'Your Honour,' he added, in case the emphasis sounded
rude.

'An admirable submission, Mr Truelove,' said Sir Hugo, 'and
very succinctly put. But,' and he paused and frowned for a moment.
'But,' he went on, 'isn't it for the plaintiff in the first instance to
give evidence that he has performed his contract—and can he do
that without showing that the work was properly done?'

Roger's boldness vanished. The only truthful answer he could
make would have been: 'I don't know.' But that wouldn't do. So

he adopted his first line of defence, of standing and staring, keeping a 'Your Honour' in reserve for use if necessary.

'You can't very well rely,' went on Sir Hugo, 'on the maxim *omnia rite*, etc.—incidentally, I never can remember exactly how it goes.'

'*Omnia rite ac sollemniter esse acta prosumuntur*,' said Roger, thanking his patron saint for making him learn that legal maxim for his Bar examinations.

'Thank you, Mr Tredgold,' said Sir Hugo, 'thank you very much. But you can't rely on that maxim in a case such as the present, can you?'

At any rate, there was an answer to that which made sense.

'I suppose not, Your Honour.'

'Or *can* you, perhaps?' went on Sir Hugo. 'I'm not sure. Perhaps you could refer me to one or two of the authorities on the point.'

At this juncture, Roger's opponent could not resist getting up and saying:

'Surely, Your Honour, there is no presumption in law that a builder always does the right thing. If there were any presumption I should have thought it would have been the other way about.'

'Well, to whom does the presumption apply, do you think?' said Sir Hugo, mercifully directing his question to Roger's opponent. 'To Official Referees, perhaps?'

At that moment Alec came into Court, although Roger did not see him. Mr Grimes had managed to take over the reins from Charles in the running down case, not without a little obstruction from Mr Justice Nettlefold who disliked Mr Grimes' habit of chopping and changing and who, besides, was now running cheerfully along with the plaintiff. 'Mr Hepplewhite is deputising very satisfactorily for you, Mr Grimes,' the judge said quite untruthfully—except in the sense that, as the judge was doing all the work for the plaintiff, it was quite satisfactory from that gentleman's point of view. However, eventually the judge allowed himself to be persuaded and Mr Grimes took over. The plaintiff did not do quite so well after that. This was no fault of Mr Grimes'. It is just the way things happen. Once Alec had seen Mr Grimes safely into Court before Mr Justice Nettlefold he returned to the Official Referee's Court to see what was happening there, ready to send the junior clerk—who had now come over with him—sprinting round to fetch Mr Grimes if disaster seemed imminent.

'Anyway,' went on Sir Hugo, 'isn't there anything to be done in this case? Is there a Scott Schedule, Mr Truebland?' and he turned pleasantly and enquiringly to Roger. Roger was still standing and the relief when the Official Referee started to address his opponent was so great that he had begun to feel the warm blood moving through his veins again. But at the mention of 'Scott Schedule' it froze again. What on earth was a Scott Schedule? He thought of Sir Walter Scott and Scott the explorer. He thought of Scotland. Perhaps Sir Hugo had said Scotch Schedule. Just as people sometimes have an insane urge to throw themselves in front of tube trains, Roger suddenly had an urge to say: 'No, Your Honour, but I think there's an Irish stew.' That would be the end of his career at the Bar. Short and inglorious. But over. No more standing and staring and freezing and boiling. Which is worse, a cold sweat or a hot sweat? All these thoughts crammed themselves confusedly into his mind as he stood miserably waiting. Then he heard a voice from the ceiling of the Court:

'A Scott Schedule, Your Honour?' it said.

He knew that it was his voice really, but he did not feel himself speak and he never knew his voice sounded like that.

'Yes, Mr Trueglove. Is there one? Or perhaps Mr Grimes ran away with it.'

Roger endeavoured to smile, but it was very difficult. After what seemed an age his opponent came to his rescue.

'I'm afraid there isn't, Your Honour,' he said.

'And why not?' asked Sir Hugo. 'How am I expected to try this case without a Scott Schedule? How many items are there in dispute?'

'About fifty, Your Honour.'

'Fifty,' Sir Hugo almost screamed. 'This is intolerable.'

'It's the plaintiff's responsibility,' said Roger's opponent. 'He has the carriage of the proceedings.'

'I don't care whose responsibility it is,' said Sir Hugo feigning an indignation which he did not in the least feel. It was a first-class opportunity for browbeating the parties into settling the case. 'It's quite outrageous. You and your opponent had better put your heads together. I shall rise now for ten minutes and after that time I expect to be told that you and he are well on the way to a compromise. This is an expensive court, you know.' He frowned for a moment and then looked cheerfully at counsel 'It doesn't matter to me in the least,' he went on, 'whether you settle or not. If I don't try this case, I shall try another. I'm just thinking of the parties.'

Roger looked enquiringly at his opponent, who gave him a faintly perceptible wink.

'And in any event, I'm not going to try it without a Scott Schedule. The case will have to be adjourned anyway, but I'll give you a chance to settle it first.'

Sir Hugo rose, bowed to counsel and withdrew to his room. As soon as Alec had seen what was happening he had sent his junior at full speed to fetch Mr Grimes. Meantime, Roger's opponent, a man named Featherstone, turned to him and said:

'Well, my boy there we are. What shall we do about it? I'll give you a hundred and fifty. Not a penny more. You'd better take it, or you'll only have the costs to pay. You know what the old boy's like about costs. No Scott Schedule, indeed,' and Mr Featherstone rubbed his hands. 'No Scott Schedule, my dear boy. What d'you think of that?' and he laughed heartily.

'Would you very much mind telling me what a Scott Schedule is, please?' asked Roger.

'Haven't the faintest idea, my dear boy. Never come to this Court if I can help it. But it's something the old boy wants. No Scott Schedule, that's bad, isn't it? Well, what about it? Will you take a hundred and fifty?'

'I think I'd better wait till Mr Grimes comes back,' said Roger.

'Wait till he comes back? We'll be here all night. He's probably on his way to the House of Lords at the moment, just giving a friendly look into the Court of Appeal on his way. He won't be back. Not on your life. No Scott Schedule, now I ask you!'

At that moment Roger heard with a mixture of relief and distaste a sound he recognized. It was Alec giving a loud suck.

'Mr Grimes will be here in a minute. I've sent for him.'

'What'd I better do?' whispered Roger.

'Just hang on, sir,' said Alec. 'Don't agree to anything.' Alec emphasized this last remark in the usual way.

Roger turned to his opponent.

'Mr Grimes is on his way.'

'I've heard that one before. Well—I hope he won't keep us all night. P'raps he's gone to fetch the Scott Schedule. You're a pupil, I suppose?'

'Yes.'

'How d'you like it?'

'I only started to-day. I find it a bit hair-raising, I'm afraid.'

'You'll soon get used to it with old Grimes. I wish he'd be quick.
I'd like to go and have a cup of coffee. D'you know where he is as
a matter of fact?'

'He's doing an accident case before Mr Justice Nettlefold.'

'Is he, by Jove? Well—*he* won't let him go.'

At that moment in Queen's Bench Court 6 Mr Grimes became
aware that his junior clerk was making urgent signs to him. He was
in the middle of cross-examining a witness.

'I had no chance of avoiding the crash,' said the witness.

'So that's what ye say, is it? We shall see,' said Mr Grimes. 'We
shall see.'

'I wish you wouldn't make these comments,' said the judge. 'I
know they don't mean anything and that we may never see and
that, as there isn't a jury, it doesn't much matter whether we do
see or we don't, but cross-examination should be used for asking
questions and asking questions only. You can make your comments
when you address me.'

'If your Ludship pleases. So ye couldn't avoid the accident,
couldn't ye?'

'No.'

'Why didn't ye put on your brakes?'

'I did.'

'Oh, ye did, did ye? Then why didn't ye stop?'

'I did.'

'Oh, ye did, did ye? Then why did the accident happen?'

'Because the plaintiff ran into me.'

'Oh, he ran into ye, did he? I suggest ye ran into him.'

'It was the other way round. The damage to the cars shows it.'

'Oh, it does, does it? We shall see,' said Mr Grimes. 'We shall
see.'

'Mr Grimes,' began the judge, but he was too late. Mr Grimes
was on his way out.

A minute later he came, panting, into the Official Referee's Court.

'At last,' said Featherstone.

'I'm so sorry, my dear fellow,' said Mr Grimes. 'So sorry to have
kept ye. Now, what's it all about?'

'The old boy wants us to settle.'

'Oh, he does, does he? Well, that's simple enough, my dear fellow. You just pay and it's all over.'

'I'll pay you something.'

'That's very good of ye, my dear fellow, very good of ye. Ye've had all the work done and ye'll pay something! Ye wouldn't like us to build another house for ye as well?'

'Well, you'll need to, I should think. This one's falling down already.'

'Is it really, my dear fellow? Funny your clients are still living in it then.'

'Come on, let's go outside. We've got to settle it somehow. The old boy isn't going to try it.'

The upshot of it all was that eventually the defendant agreed to pay Mr Grimes' client £300 and all his costs, and there was then a rush back to the other case, where they arrived just in time to find the judge rising for lunch.

'Come on, my dear fellow,' said Mr Grimes. 'Come and get a bite while there's time. So good of ye to have helped me. Thank ye so much.' He led Roger at a fast trot to the restaurant in the crypt at the Law Courts. There Mr Grimes helped himself to a plate of meat and salad, asked for a cup of coffee and took it to a marble-topped table which was no different from any others, except that it bore a notice: 'The seats at this table, are reserved for Counsel from 12 o'clock until 2 o'clock.'

Roger felt very important sitting at such a table and even the ordinary nature of the food and the noise made by Mr Grimes in getting rid of his as fast as possible did not spoil his pleasure.

Between the bites and swallows, Mr Grimes asked Roger if he thought he'd learned anything and how he liked his first morning. Before Roger could reply, he went on to criticize Queen's Bench Judges, Official Referees and his opponents in each of the cases, finally ending up his criticisms with the pronouncement:

'But there you are, my dear fellow, they will do these things, they will do these things.'

Five minutes later they were off again, this time at only a very fast walking pace. They went to a place known as the 'Bear Garden' where Mr Grimes had a summons to dispose of before a judicial officer called a Master. It was to be heard by Master Tiptree. Before they went into the Master's room, Mr Grimes was joined by Alec and the clerk from the solicitors instructing him. Mr Grimes greeted

the clerk most affably and then proceeded to say something to him
in a low voice. Roger could only catch that it began with:

'I don't mind telling you, my dear fellow—' but what he didn't
mind telling him, Roger never heard. Fortunately they did not have
to wait long and soon they were in front of Master Tiptree. Roger
knew from his Bar examinations that various applications in the
course of an action were made to a Master, but he only had a slight
theoretical knowledge of such matters. A Master appearing in a
question in an examination paper is very different from an actual
live one sitting in his room.

'This is an application for discovery of specific documents,
Master,' began Mr Grimes.

'Where's the affidavit?' asked the Master.

'Oh, Master, before we come to the affidavit, I'd like to tell you
something about the action.'

'I dare say you would, Mr Grimes, but I want to see the affidavit.'

'If you please, Master.'

Mr Grimes obtained a sheet of paper from the solicitor's clerk
and handed it to the Master.

He glanced at it, threw it back at Mr Grimes and said: 'What
d'you call that, Mr Grimes?'

Mr Grimes looked at the offending document. 'I'm so sorry,
Master. It's the wrong affidavit.'

'I am only too well aware of that, Mr Grimes. I want the right
one.'

'Here it is, Master. I'm so sorry.'

Mr Grimes handed another affidavit to the Master, who read it
quickly.

'This won't do, Mr Grimes. It doesn't say the alleged missing
document relates to the matters in question.'

'Oh, but Master, if you'll be good enough to look at the pleadings,
you'll see it must be material.'

'I dare say, Mr Grimes, but Order 31, Rule 19A is quite definite
and has not been complied with.'

'Oh, but Master—'

'It's no good saying, "Oh, but Master," Mr Grimes. You know
as well as I do your affidavit is defective. D'you want an adjournment or shall I dismiss the summons?'

Mr Grimes' opponent then intervened.

'Master, I ask you to refuse an adjournment and dismiss the summons.'

'I dare say you do, but I'm not going to. You can have the costs thrown away.'

'But Master—'

'I've made up my mind. You can go to the judge if you don't like it. Now Mr Grimes, have you made up your mind?'

'Yes, please, Master. I ask for an adjournment to put the affidavit in order.'

'Very well.'

The Master started to write out his Order.

Mr Grimes whispered to Roger: 'Just stay and take the Order, my dear fellow,' and without another word he was off towards Mr Justice Nettlefold's Court.

The Master wrote for a few moments. When he looked up he saw that Mr Grimes had gone.

'Pupil?' he asked Roger.

'Yes, Master.'

'How long?'

'To-day.'

"Order 31, Rule 19A mean anything to you?'

'Not a thing, Master.'

'I should look it up when you get back to chambers, if I were you. It's the only way to learn the practice. You can't learn it in a vacuum. But if you look up everything that happens, you'll get a reasonable knowledge of it in time.'

'Thank you very much, Master.'

'Not at all. Good luck to you.'

Roger left the Master's room with the solicitor's clerk. 'Never heard Master Tiptree so agreeable,' said the clerk. 'He threw a book at me once.'

With difficulty Roger found his way back to the Court. The judge was giving judgment in favour of Mr Grimes' client. No sooner was it over than there was a frantic dash back to chambers, where Mr Grimes had several conferences.

Charles and Roger went into the pupils' room together. Henry was there reading *The Times*.

'Where's Peter?' asked Charles.

'He went off to the Old Bailey,' said Henry. 'Said building cases weren't in his line. Gosh!' he went on. 'You don't mean to tell me Thursby got landed with it instead?'

'He did,' said Charles, 'but he's still breathing.'

'Poor fellow,' said Henry. 'Tell me about it in your own unexpurgated Billingsgate.'

Roger told him.

'Well, well, well,' said Henry. 'He wins one case and settles the other and, knowing Grimeyboy, his client won't have lost on the deal. What I say is *fiat justitia ruat Grimes*, or, as the poet says,

"So justice be done,
Let Grimeyboy run".'

CHAPTER 4

At Home

Mrs Thursby, Roger's widowed mother, was, she hoped, making a cake when Roger arrived home after his first day as a pupil.

'Darling, how nice,' she said. 'You can give it a stir. I want to go and try on a new dress. Aunt Ethel sent it me. She's only worn it once. Just keep on stirring. I'm sure it'll be all right. Anyway, we can always give it to Mrs Rhodes. Oh, no, she doesn't come any more. Let me see, who is it now—'

'Mother, darling,' said Roger, 'I've had my first day in the Temple.'

'Of course, darling, how silly of me. Did you enjoy it? I won't be a moment. Just keep on stirring.'

And Mrs Thursby went to her bedroom. She was a young forty-eight. She had lost her husband soon after Roger was born. For some reason that neither she nor Roger, after he grew up, could understand, she had never married again. She was attractive and kind and plenty of men have no objection to butterfly minds. Roger's father, who had been a man of the highest intelligence and intellectual capacity, had adored her. So did Roger.

He stirred the mixture in the pudding bowl and as he did so he went over in his mind all that had happened during the day. Now that he was safely home it gave him a considerable thrill to think he had actually spoken in Court. He must tell his mother, though she wouldn't really take in the significance. But he must tell Sally and Joy. Which first? He stopped stirring and went to the telephone. It was Joy's turn really, he supposed.

'Joy—yes, it's me. Are you free this evening? I've quite a lot to tell you. Oh—what a shame. Can't you come and have a drink first? Yes, do, that'll be lovely. Come straight over. See you in ten minutes.'

He went back to the kitchen.

'Roger,' called his mother, 'do come and look.'

He went to her bedroom.

'It's lovely, isn't it? And I did need one so badly. I can wear it for the Fotheringays. Don't you like it?'

'I do, darling. D'you know I spoke in Court to-day?'

'Did you really darling? How very nice. What exactly did you say? Don't you like the way the skirt seems to come from nowhere?'

'It suits you to a T.'

'D'you really think so?'

'Of course I do. I didn't actually say very much.'

'No, of course not. They couldn't expect very much to begin with. I expect you'll say more to-morrow.'

'Joy's coming round for a drink. You don't mind?'

'Of course not. I think she's a sweet girl. It makes me look thinner, doesn't it?'

At last Joy arrived and Roger was able to tell someone all about his first day.

'I think you're wonderful,' said Joy. 'I should love to come and hear you. When can I?'

'Well, of course, I don't know exactly when I shall be speaking again.'

'Was it a murder case?'

'Well—no, as a matter of fact.'

'Breach of promise?'

'As a matter of fact, it was a building dispute.'

'It sounds terribly dull. Weren't you bored?'

The one thing Roger had not been was bored.

'You see, things which don't sound of interest to the layman are very interesting to lawyers.'

'I don't think I should terribly care to hear a building dispute. All about houses and things. Still, I suppose you have to start somewhere. Must take time to work up to a murder case.'

'Joy, dear, you don't work up to a murder case.'

'But surely, Roger, you're wrong. I've always understood you start with silly things like debt collecting and business cases, like your building dispute, I suppose, and eventually work your way into real cases like murder and blackmail and divorce and so on. Anyway, what did you say? Did you make the jury cry? It must have been very clever of you if you did with a building dispute. But then you are so clever, Roger, that I wouldn't put it past you.'

'They don't have juries with Official Referees.'

'Sounds like football.'

'Well, it isn't. An Official Referee is a judge. You call him "Your Honour". He's very important. This one was called Sir Hugo Cramp.'

'Well, what did you say to him?'

'Well, among other things—I quoted a legal maxim to him. He thanked me very much.'

'Did it win you your case?'

'Well, it wasn't exactly my case.' He paused for a moment. Then very seriously he said:

'Joy, d'you think I'll ever be any good? I was terribly frightened.'

'You frightened? I can't believe it. You're pulling my leg.'

'I'm not. Really, Joy, I'm not.'

'What's frightening about it? You just get up and say what you want and then sit down.'

'And suppose you don't know what to say?'

'Then don't get up.'

'But I had to.'

'But I don't see why. It's a free country. Anyway, next time make certain what you want to say, get up and say it and sit down.'

'You make it sound very simple.'

'Well, Uncle Alfred's a solicitor. Which reminds me—I suppose he might send you a brief one day. Would you like that, Roger?'

'Oh, Joy it would be wonderful.'

'What would you do if I get Uncle Alfred to send you a brief?'

'What would you like me to do?'

'There's something I'd like you not to do.'

'What?'

'Not see Sally.'

'Oh,' said Roger, unhappily. 'D'you think that's quite fair?'

'It's just as you like. I'm sure Uncle Alfred has got lots of young men to send briefs to. He'll bear up.'

'But, Joy dear, it's so difficult. And it wouldn't be fair to Sally.'

'That's right, dear—always the little unselfish one, thinking of other people. You're too good for this world.'

'Who are *you* going out with, anyway?'

'A friend of mine.'

'So I gathered. Do I know him?'

'Who said it was a him?'

'I did. Who is it?'

'D'you want to know all that much?'

'Not if you don't want to tell me.'

'Then why ask me?'

'Oh, Joy—don't let's quarrel. It's my first day at the Bar. And I want you to share it with me.'

'I'd love to share it with you—but not with you and Sally.'

'I rang you before her.'

'You went out with her last night.'

'How d'you know?'

'Now I know you did. Oh, Roger, why can't we just be married and live happily ever after?'

'We're so young, Joy. We don't any of us know our minds yet. I'd marry you both if I could.'

'Thanks very much. P'raps you'd like power to add to our number. It's George Utterson as a matter of fact.'

'That oaf.'

'He's not in the least an oaf. He's going to be Prime Minister one of these days. *He's* not frightened to talk in public. I heard him at a meeting the other day. He was grand. They applauded like anything.' She stopped for a moment. Then much more softly she said: 'Oh, Roger, if you'd give up Sally—I'd never see him again. I wouldn't even see him tonight.'

CHAPTER 5

Around and about the Law

The next day was calmer at No. 1 Temple Court. Mr Grimes was in chambers all day and, except for rushing out for his lunch and rushing back again, his presence in chambers was only noticed by the procession of clients who came for conferences and by the occasional sound of 'Good-bye, my dear fellow, bye, bye, bye' as he saw one or two of the more valued clients to the door. In consequence, Roger was able to ask Henry a number of questions.

'To-morrow,' said Henry, 'is an important day. I'm in Court. I have to appear before His Honour Judge Boyle at a County Court. P'raps you'd like to come with me. You won't see anything of County Courts with Grimeyboy.'

'D'you think Mr Grimes would mind?' asked Roger.

'Grimes, not Mr Grimes,' said Henry. 'I meant to tell you about that before. Once you're called you call everyone at the Bar by his surname.'

'Even a Q.C.?'

'Everyone. Even an ex-Attorney-General. The newest recruit to the profession will call the most distinguished of all plain Smith or whatever it is. And, while I'm about it, you might as well know how to talk to a judge—out of Court, I mean, or if you write to him. How would you address Mr Justice Blank if you ran into him in the Strand?'

'Well, I'd obviously be wrong. How should I?'

'Judge. "So sorry, Judge," or "do look where you're going, Judge." If he's in the Court of Appeal, call him Lord Justice.'

'And what about an Official Referee?'

'To be quite honest, I've never spoken to one—after his appointment. I suppose you could say "Official Referee," but it's rather a mouthful. "Your Honour" must be wrong. I don't care for "Sir Hugo" or "sir." No, you've got me there. The best advice is not to talk to them. There are only four anyway, so you should be all right. Now, what else can I do for you?'

'Sure you don't mind?'

'My dear boy, I'm only too delighted. Otherwise I'd have to look at these papers. I tell you, I'm bone idle. I'm delighted to have a good excuse for not working.'

'Well, yesterday I heard the clerk talking to someone on the telephone about something called the two-thirds rule. Something to do with fees, I gathered. Can you tell me what it is?'

'Indeed I can. I feel quite strongly on the subject. We had some pronouncements from a Committee on the subject quite recently. Up till a few years before the war if you or I or Grimes or any junior—you know that barristers are either juniors or Q.C.'s, and that a Q.C. has to have a junior?'

'That's just about all I do know.'

'Well, as I was saying, up till a few years before the war, if a junior was led by a Q.C. the junior had to receive two-thirds of the fee charged by the Q.C. So if you were lucky and led by Carson or F. E. Smith or someone like that, you might get a fee of 666 guineas for doing a case you'd have been perfectly prepared to do for a hundred, or even less. Doesn't sound very logical, you say?'

'I don't say anything,' said Roger. 'I'm listening. I must say, though, I like the sound of 666 guineas. Have you ever had that?'

'I have not, I regret to say. Well, a few years before the war it was agreed that the two-thirds rule should only apply to a fee of 150 guineas or less. Above that it was to be a matter of arrangement.'

'No more 666,' said Roger, sadly.

'Well, some solicitors were prepared to stick to the old rule. Of course some didn't. But there's worse to come. The Committee I mentioned has suggested that the rule should be abolished altogether. The point about the rule is this. By and large, barristers are not overpaid. Indeed much of their work is underpaid. This two-thirds rule is the cream which, when added to the skim milk, makes milk of a reasonable quality. The Committee, while recognizing that barristers are not paid too much, have said something like this: "This two-thirds rule increases the cost of litigation. If it's abolished, barristers will have nothing to make up for the lowness of their other fees, but none the less let's abolish it and good luck to you all." '

'What's going to happen?'

'If you ask me, nothing, but we shall see, my dear fellow, we shall see.'

At that moment Alec came into the room, took away the papers which were in front of Roger and replaced them with a large bundle.

'Mr Grimes thinks you'd better look at these,' he said, and went out again. The brief he left was about six to eight inches thick. Roger looked at it for a moment.

'D'you think I'll ever be able to cope with anything of this kind?' he asked. 'It makes me despair just to look at it.'

'Well,' said Henry, 'It all depends. If you take to the job and are good enough for it, you'll be able to tackle anything in due course. But it'll take time. Let's hope you only get little stuff to begin with. Otherwise you could come a nasty cropper. When I started I made the most awful bloomer with a case. The solicitors took it away from me in the end, but not before I'd done a lot of damage. Think of a medical student being allowed to play at pulling out a patient's appendix and grabbing hold of the wrong thing! I don't even know now whether I was stopped in time. As I said before, it's funny that we're allowed to do it. It's true that the public can't come to us direct as they can to doctors. But there are plenty of Uncle Georges in the world of solicitors—father Georges even—and, of course, brother Georges—their wretched clients don't know that it's your first brief.'

'But,' said Roger, 'one has to start some time. Every professional man has to have his first case, whether it's a doctor, accountant or a barrister.'

'Yes,' said Henry, 'that's true enough, but all professional men, except barristers, have had practical experience first. If a barrister couldn't address the Court until he's had, say, a year as a pupil, that'd be reasonable. Jolly good experience for you yesterday, but what about the poor client?'

'I hope he wasn't there,' said Roger.

'Of course,' said Henry, 'Peter ought to have been doing it, but he wouldn't really have been any better than you. Worse, probably. He'd have talked nonsense; you only said nothing. Neither of you ought to have been allowed to do it, but there you are, my dear fellow, they will do these things, they will do these things.'

'Was I what you call "devilling"?' asked Roger.

'Well,' said Henry, 'if looking unhappy and saying nothing can be called devilling, you were.'

'I suppose,' said Roger, 'that that's what Gilbert was referring to when he said:

"Pocket a fee with a grin on your face
When you haven't been there to attend to the case." '

'Yes,' said Henry, 'but it isn't entirely fair to the Bar to put it just like that. A chap can't be in two places at once and he can't tell when he first accepts a brief in a case that it's going to clash with any other. So there are times when he's got to get help from someone else. All I say is that pupils shouldn't be allowed to give it. Your case is certainly an extreme one and I don't suppose it has happened before or will happen again, but the principle is just the same. No offence to you, but during the whole of your year you won't be capable of handling a defended case in the High Court efficiently, even if you've read it thoroughly.'

'Then why didn't Grimes ask you to help him?' asked Roger.

'Well,' said Henry, 'that could be a long story, but I'll make it a short one. In a nutshell, I've got too big for my boots and I won't devil a brief unless I do the whole thing, or at any rate get half the fee.'

'Look,' said Roger, 'I don't mean to be rude, but you tell me an awful lot. How am I to know you're right?'

'Good for you,' said Henry. 'You can't know. And you're quite right to ask. Go on asking. Don't take anything for granted, not even Grimeyboy. In a month or two you'll think everything he says and does is right.'

'Isn't it?'

'It doesn't matter whether it is or it isn't, you'll think it is. Almost every pupil swears by his master. And it's often quite a long time before he realizes that his written work was bad, that he was only a very moderate lawyer and a poor advocate. I'm not saying any of that about Grimeyboy. It wouldn't in fact be true. But the point is, you must judge for yourself. Ask "why" the whole time. Oh, hullo, Peter. How's the Old Bailey? You know that Thursby had to devil for you yesterday?'

'Thanks very much,' said Peter 'I'll give you half my fee. Quite a good assault case, as a matter of fact. I'd have been sorry to have missed that. Oh, and there's a good one in the Court of Criminal Appeal to-morrow, I'm told.'

'D'you think I could go?' asked Roger.

'You certainly could,' said Henry, 'and if you want to become like Peter, I should. But if you're wise you'll get on with your work here. Popping off to the Old Bailey or the Court of Criminal Appeal to get a cheap thrill won't teach you anything.'

'I may decide to go to the Criminal Bar,' said Peter.

'If I were you, I should,' said Henry. 'Now I must go and work for once.'

Henry went to his room and Roger started to open a set of papers.

'Don't feel much like work this morning,' said Peter. 'Had a bit of a night last night. What are you reading?'

'I haven't started really,' said Roger. 'This is something called Biggs and Pieman.'

'Oh, that's quite amusing. Pieman's the M.P., you know. It'll never come into Court. It's a sort of woman scorned action. Neither side can afford to fight it. Wish they would. It'd be great fun. She's a very attractive woman. I saw her in the clerk's room before she saw Grimeyboy.'

'What's it about?'

'Well—it's a claim for money lent. To judge from the letters, Mrs Biggs and Mr Pieman used to see more of one another than they ought to have done—seeing that there was a Mr Biggs. Well, Pieman apparently needed money to start him on his political career and Mrs B. provided it. How much of it was Mr B.'s I don't know. Later on when the good ship Pieman was firmly launched he broke it off with Mrs B. She was very angry and asked for her money back. He wouldn't pay. So she sued him. He says it's a gift.'

'When is it coming on for trial?'

'I tell you, it isn't. Mr B. doesn't know anything about it, but if it came into Court he soon would. There are things in those letters most husbands wouldn't approve of. You read them. They're grand fun. She wanted to know if the action could be heard *in camera*. Of course it couldn't. So it's only a question of who'll give in first. Wouldn't do Pieman any good for his constituency to know that he'd been financed by another man's wife. Wouldn't do her any good for her husband to know she's been so kind to Mr P. Now, what else is there?'

Peter looked casually at the briefs lying on the table. He picked up one, opened it and read a little, put it back in its red tape and sighed.

'How can anyone be expected to get up any enthusiasm for drawing-pins? Consignments of drawing-pins. I ask you.'

He picked up another set of papers.

'This isn't much better,' he said. 'It's about wallpaper. I wish he'd have a breach of promise or an enticement action. He hardly ever does a divorce case. Had one the other day, though. Not bad at all. Cruelty case.'

He paused for a moment, trying to recollect some of the more lurid details.

'D'you know, he used to tie her up to a chair and then make faces at her. Now, what would he get out of that?'

'I can't think,' said Roger, but he said it in a tone which caused Peter to say:

'Sorry, old boy. Don't want to interrupt. Think I'll go down to the Old Bailey. Where's Charles?'

'I haven't seen him this morning.'

'Oh, of course. He's got a judgment summons somewhere.'

'What's that?'

'Oh—a summons for debt, you know. I'm not quite sure actually, but you get an Order sending them to prison if they don't pay, or something.'

'I thought that was abolished years ago.'

'So did I, old boy, but it's something like that. You ask Henry. He knows all the answers. Pity he's got no guts. Might have done well. Well, so long, old boy. May not see you again till to-morrow. Depends what they've on at the Old Bailey. I'll take my robes. Might get a docker.'

'A what?'

'Dock brief. You know, surely. I did before I was called. Any prisoner who's got a couple of guineas and the clerk's fee can choose any counsel sitting in Court. So if you just go and sit there you may get a brief. Look hard at the prisoner and hope you hypnotize him into choosing you. Henry's got a good story about dock briefs.'

'What's that?'

'Well, I might as well tell you first. Don't often get in in front of Henry. Well, there was an old lag down at the Bailey. He'd been there dozens of times, knew the ropes. Well, he was up one day for something and decided he'd like to have counsel to defend him. So he brought out his money and they took him up into the dock before the Recorder.

' "Can I have a dock brief, please, my Lord?" he asked, very politely.

' "Has he two pounds four shillings and sixpence?" asked the Recorder. The clerk informed the Recorder that the money was there.

' "Very well," said the Recorder. "Choose whom you like," and he pointed to the two rows of counsel sitting in Court. Some were very young, like me, and couldn't have had any experience. Others were very old and moth-eaten. At least one had a hearing aid.

' "What!" said the old lag in horror. "One of those?"

'The Recorder looked at the two rows of counsel and then said rather mournfully: "Yes, I'm afraid so. That's all we have in stock at the moment." '

'Well,' said Roger, 'I wish you luck. But if you did get a brief, would you know what to do with it?'

'As much as anyone else, old boy. Just get up and spout to the jury. Can't come to much harm. They're all guilty. So it doesn't really matter what happens. Feather in your cap if you get them off. Inevitable if they're convicted.'

'I wonder they bother to try them,' said Roger.

'Must go through the motions, old boy,' said Peter. 'And anyway, where would the legal profession be? Justice must not only be done but must appear to be done and, may I add, must be paid for being done. Bye, bye, old boy. Hope you like Mrs Biggs' letters. Some of them are a bit hot. I tried a bit on one of my girl friends. Went down very well. Breach of copyright, I suppose. But who cares? So long.'

For the next hour Roger was left alone and he devoted himself to the study of *Biggs* (*married woman*) v. *Pieman*. He found it enthralling—not so much in the way that Peter did, but because he felt so important to be looking into the intimate affairs of other people and, in particular, people of some prominence. Here he was, only just called to the Bar, and he knew things about a Member of Parliament which hardly anyone else knew. And then, supposing by one of those extraordinary coincidences that do take place, he happened to meet Mr Biggs! He might be a member of his uncle's club. And suppose his uncle introduced him and they had dinner together. He'd have to listen while Biggs extolled the virtues of his wife.

'A sweet little woman, though I say it myself who shouldn't,' Mr Biggs might say.

'I don't know whether you should or you shouldn't,' Roger would think to himself. 'Fortunately you didn't say good little woman.' Mr Biggs would go on:

'Pretty as a picture—but I'd trust her with anyone. It's not everyone who can say that, these days.'

'Indeed not,' Roger would think. 'Not with accuracy, anyway.'

At that moment, Mr Grimes came into the pupils' room.

'How are ye, my dear fellow? What are ye looking at? Oh, dear, dear, dear. That kettle of fish. Well, the fellows will be fellows and the girls will be girls. They will do these things, they will do these things.'

'D'you think the action will come into Court?'

'Oh, dear me no, my dear fellow. We can't have that, can we? Dear, dear, dear. Our husband doesn't know of our goings on and we don't want him to. We don't want him to, my dear fellow.'

'Then why did she bring the action?'

'Just a try on, my dear fellow, just a try on. He might have paid up. You can never tell, my dear fellow, you can never tell. There's only one motto I know of that's any good. "Never go to law," my dear fellow, "never go to law". And then where should *we* be, my dear fellow? We shouldn't, should we? So it's just as well they will do these things, isn't it, my dear fellow, just as well.'

Then Alec came in.

'Can you see Mr Wince, sir? He was just passing and wanted to have a word with you about Cooling and Mallet.'

Mr Grimes immediately left the pupils' room. It was not far enough to run but he went as fast as he could. Roger imagined that he would be pretty good at getting to the bathroom first in a boarding house.

'And how's Mr Wince?' Roger heard him say. 'How's Mr Wince to-day? Come along in, my dear fellow, come along in,' and then Mr Grimes' door closed and Roger heard no more. He wondered what Mr Wince wanted. What was Cooling and Mallet about? He looked on his table. What a piece of luck. There it was. He quickly tied up the bundle he had been reading and opened Cooling and Mallet. At that moment Alec came in.

'Mr Grimes wants these, I'm afraid, sir,' he said and took them away.

Roger went back to the sins of Mr Pieman and Mrs Biggs. Even at his age he found it a little sad to see how the attitude between men and women can change. The letters, which in the early correspondence started and ended so very, very affectionately, full of all the foolish-looking but (to them) sweet-sounding endearments of lovers, gradually cooled off. 'My dearest, sweetest turnip, how I adore you' became 'Dear Mr Pieman, if I do not receive a cheque by return I shall place the matter in other hands.' Is it really possible that I could ever hate the sight of Joy or Sally as undoubtedly Mr Pieman now hates the sight of Mrs Biggs? Perhaps it only happens, he thought, when the relationship has been that of husband and wife, or worse. At twenty-one these things are a little difficult to understand.

Roger had an hour more with Mr Pieman and Mrs Biggs when Charles returned. The Court he had attended was some way away, but he was still hot and flushed.

'Hullo,' said Roger. 'How did you get on? I hear you've been doing a judgment something or other. I wish you'd tell me about it.'

'I wish you'd asked me that yesterday. Then I might have had to look it up. As it is, I have lost my one and only client.'

'I'm so sorry. What happened?' asked Roger sympathetically.

'I'd learned the ruddy thing by heart. There wasn't a thing I didn't know.' He broke off. 'It really is too bad.'

'Do tell me, unless you'd rather not.'

'I think I'd like to get it off my chest. I was doing a j.s.—a judgment summons. That's an application to send to prison a person who hasn't paid a judgment debt, but you can only succeed if you can prove he has had the means to pay the debt or at any rate, part of it since the judgment. The debtor has to attend and my job was to cross-examine him for all I was worth to show that he could have paid. I went to the Court with my client and I told him the sort of questions I was going to ask and he seemed very impressed. "That'll shake him," he said several times. I was really feeling confident. And what d'you think happened? The case was called on and the chap didn't turn up. Well, that was bad enough, but it was after that that the trouble really began. After all, I can't know everything, can I, and I *had* read that brief. If the chap had been there I'd have knocked him to bits. But he wasn't. "Well," said the judge, "what do you want me to do?" Well, I ought to

have looked it up, I suppose, but I hadn't. I'd no idea what I
wanted him to do. Fortunately my client knew more than I did.
"Have him fined," he whispered. "Would Your Honour fine him?"
I said.

' "Your client wants his money, I suppose," said the judge.
"What good will fining him do?"

'I had no idea. Again my client prompted me. "If he doesn't pay,
he goes to prison."

'I repeated this to the judge.

' "But surely that isn't right," said the judge. "You've got to
prove means before he goes to prison."

' "Not in the case of a fine," whispered my client.

' "Not in the case of a fine, Your Honour," I repeated, like the
good parrot I had become.

'I was already beginning to feel extremely small, particularly after
the exhibition I'd given to my client in the train as to what I was
going to do with this judgment debtor. Here I was, just repeating
what he was feeding me with. But even that wouldn't have been so
bad if it had been right.

' "Nonsense," said the judge. "You can't commit a man for non-
payment of a fine unless you can prove he has the means to pay.
Do you know what is meant by an argument in a circle?"

' "I think so, Your Honour," I said.

' "A good example," said the judge, "is the law relating to judgment summonses. If a judgment debt isn't paid, the debtor can
only be sent to prison if you can prove he has had the means to
pay. Usually you can't do that unless he's present to be cross-
examined about his means. If he doesn't obey the summons to
appear, he can be fined, but you can't do anything about the fine
unless you can prove he has the means to pay it. But he doesn't
come. So you can't ask him questions or prove anything. So you're
back where you started. Of course, if he's got any goods on which
distress can be levied, it's different, but then you'd have tried
execution and wouldn't have bothered about a judgment summons
in that case."

'Meantime I'm standing there, getting red in the face.

"Well, Mr Hepplewhite, what would you like me to do?"

'Someone in the row—a barrister or solicitor—whispered to me.
"Ask for a 271."

'Again I did as suggested.

' "What on earth's that" asked the judge.

'Well, what could I say? The chap next to me might have been pulling my leg. I didn't know. I didn't know anything. So I said so. You can hardly blame the judge.

' "Really," he said. "This is too bad. Summons dismissed."

'My client said something to me about looking up the rules another time and added that he wouldn't be coming back my way. On the way home I started looking it up—and, blow me, if there isn't a thing called a 271. The chap was quite right. It was the only thing to do. Even the judge didn't know it. It's certainly a lesson to look up the rules another time. But it takes it out of you, a thing like that.'

'It must have been awful,' said Roger. 'But you can't look up everything before you go into Court,' he went on. 'How d'you know what to look up?'

'Well, I suppose,' said Charles, 'if you have a judgment summons, you ought to look up the rules which govern them. And I suppose, too, one ought to visualize the possibility of a man not turning up and find out what you can do then. I shan't forget 271 in a hurry. I feel like writing to the judge about it. After all, he ought to have known it.'

'What is a 271?' asked Roger.

'It's an authority to arrest the debtor and bring him before the Court if he doesn't pay a fine within the time he's been given to pay it. So it isn't an argument in a circle. You can get the debtor there. Funny the judge didn't know.'

'I suppose there are things judges don't know,' said Roger. 'Henry's got a case in a County Court to-morrow. D'you think it would be a good thing if I went with him? He said I could.'

'I should. You'll learn a lot from Henry. And, apart from that, he'll tell you stories on the way. He's got an unending fund of them. And they'll all be new to *you*. I expect that's one of the reasons he asked you to come.'

Roger spent the rest of the day reading the papers in *Biggs* v. *Pieman* and the case about drawing-pins. The evening he spent with Sally.

'It's amazing to think what's going on and no one knows it. I saw a case to-day about a Member of Parliament.'

'Who?'

'Oh, I couldn't tell you that. One of the first things Grimes told me was that anything I learn I must treat with confidence.'

'Then why did you tell me about the case at all?'

'You couldn't possibly identify the parties.'

'What's it about then?'

'Well, I suppose there can't be any harm in that. There are over six hundred M.P.'s and an infinite variety of married women.'

So Roger told her the facts as well as he remembered them.

'Humph!' said Sally. 'It *is* quite interesting. Sounds like old Pieman. I wouldn't put it past him.'

'What did you say?' said Roger, so horrified that he was unable to stop himself from asking the question, or from showing in his voice the surprise he felt.

'Roger—it is—it's old Pieman. Mother will be thrilled.'

'Sally, you're not to.'

'Then it is. How extraordinary.'

'The other thing I was looking at,' said Roger, lamely, 'was about drawing-pins.'

'It's much too late now, Roger. I know all about it.'

'Sally, you mustn't tell anyone. Promise you won't.'

'You didn't tell me in confidence, Roger.'

'But I learned it in confidence.'

'Then you shouldn't have told me in the first instance. Now, let's think who I've seen about with old Pieman.'

'Sally, you mustn't. How was I to know you knew him?'

'How were you to know I didn't.'

'I never thought for a moment—oh, Sally, please promise you won't tell anyone. I've done the most terrible thing.'

'I know who it is,' said Sally. 'A very smart woman—now what's her name? Let me think.'

'Please, Sally, please. I'm sure it isn't, anyway.'

'How can you possibly tell? I know, Anstruther, that's the name, Mollie Anstruther.'

'No,' said Roger.

'Roger,' said Sally, 'I'm sorry to have to tell you this—I do it more in sorrow than in anger and all for your own good—but it'll hurt you more than it hurts me all the same—you're an ass—an unmitigated ass. Why on earth did you say "no" when I mentioned Mollie Anstruther? That eliminates one possibility. Now I can try to think of someone else. I thought that was the sort of trick barristers played on other people.'

'Well, I didn't think it would be fair on the woman to let you think it was her.'

'Then it must be Dorothy Biggs. I've often seen them about together.'

Roger said nothing for a moment. Then:

'How on earth could I tell you'd guess?' he said miserably.

'What'll you do if I promise not to tell anyone?'

'I'll be more careful in future.'

'Is that all? You'll do that anyway, I hope.'

'There won't be any necessity. If you go telling people about it, it'll quite likely become known that it came out through me and then I shall be disbarred. After three days, too. I'm in your hands, Sally.'

'Don't be silly,' said Sally. 'Of course I shan't tell anyone.'

'You're a darling. I don't know what I should do without you.'

'Well, you'd have told someone else, I suppose.'

'Yes, I suppose I should. I am an ass. You're quite right, Sally. How lucky it was you.'

'Well,' said Sally thoughtfully, 'Joy might not have known the parties—but if she had—I'm sure she'd have done just what I did. Wouldn't she, Roger?'

'Yes,' said Roger, uncomfortably, 'I'm sure she would.'

'Well, that's settled,' said Sally brightly. 'Now you're going to tell me about the drawing-pins.'

'They were in confidence, Sally. You might have sat on one of them.'

'Too true,' said Sally. 'And does this mean that you're never going to tell me anything?'

'Of course not. I can tell you anything that happens in Court. And I can tell you about the people in chambers. Old Grimes is an extraordinary person. But he's got the most tremendous practice. And I gather his clients swear by him.'

'From what you told me yesterday on the phone, I thought you did most of his work for him.'

'I didn't put it as high as that. Oh, by the way, to-morrow I'm going to a County Court with an awfully nice chap called Henry Blagrove. He's quite brilliant, I think, but I haven't heard him in Court yet.'

'What's a County Court? Where they fine you for not having dog licences?'

'Oh, no. It's a Court for trying small civil cases—breaches of contracts, debts, accident cases and so on. And they have things called judgment summonses there. D'you know, they still send people to prison for not paying debts. I must say I thought that had been abolished after Pickwick Papers.'

'Are there debtors' prisons still then?'

'I don't think so. They go to ordinary prisons, I think. As a matter of fact, I don't believe many people actually go to prison. About a thousand a year, I was told.'

'I must ask mother,' said Sally. 'She sings at prisons sometimes.'

'That is good of her,' said Roger. 'She must go down awfully well. They like almost anything there—I mean, I mean—'

'Explain it to mother,' said Sally, 'here she is.'

Mrs Mannering came into the room a moment later.

'How are you, Roger? How nice of you to take tickets for Friday. I'm sure you can't afford it, as a poor struggling barrister.'

'I've been looking forward to hearing you,' said Roger. 'I was only saying so to Sally a moment ago.'

'How sweet of you. Walter Burr's going to accompany me. I've made him promise not to say a word. He's a brilliant accompanist but he's suddenly got the idea that he's a comedian too. And he always tries to introduce the songs and do a comic turn at the same time. Seems catching in the musical profession at the moment. Oh, who do you think gave me a lift home, wasn't it kind? Walter Pieman—the M.P., you know. I met him at Hilda's.'

Roger and Sally said nothing for a moment. Then Sally said:

'It only goes to show, doesn't it?'

'Goes to show what?' said her mother.

'That M.P.'s have their uses.'

The next day Roger met Henry at a tube station on the way to the County Court.

'I see you've a red bag,' said Roger. 'Have you had it long?'

'I was lucky,' said Henry. 'I got a brief with a leader in my second year and somehow or other it produced this. Lucky. It's much lighter than carrying a suitcase, particularly, if you've got a lot of books to take.'

'But why a suitcase?'

'Well—after a few years some people don't like to be seen with a blue bag. So they use a suitcase instead.'

'Who gave you yours?'

'Mostyn, as a matter of fact.'

'I say, that's awfully good, isn't it? He's one of the biggest leaders now, isn't he?'

'Well, he's made a lot of headway in the last year or two. Yes, I was lucky. Curiously enough, I actually earned it. I worked like hell.'

'Don't people always earn them?'

'As often as not it's done between the clerks. George meets Ernest in the "Cock." "D'you think you could get young Bolster a red bag, Ernie?" he says over the third pint. "I'll try, old boy," says Ernest. And if Ernest tries the answer is probably "yes." It's a funny custom. The only people who make anything out of it really are the people who make the bags. But it's a sort of milestone in a chap's career. The day he gets his red bag. You certainly won't find your way to the Woolsack without one.'

They discussed the other milestones in a career at the Bar; then they talked about County Courts.

'What's this judge like?' asked Roger.

'Well, fortunately,' said Henry, 'there aren't any others like him to-day. I don't mean by that that he's a bad judge. He isn't. But he's very inconsiderate. Furthermore, he's peppery, pompous and conceited, but he's quite a good judge for all that, though not as good as he thinks he is. Incidentally, one of the funniest things I ever heard happened in front of him. Like to hear?'

'That's one of the reasons I've come,' said Roger.

'Charles told you that, I suppose,' said Henry, and they both laughed.

There were three main characters in the story which Henry told Roger. The first was a barrister called Galloway, a well-intentioned, very serious and literally-minded man. The second was a former County Court judge called Musgrave.

'He's dead now,' said Henry. 'He was a nice old boy and quite a good judge when he tried a case, but he was a wicked old man and wouldn't sit after lunch. There aren't any others like him to-day, either.'

'What d'you mean?' asked Roger.

'What I say. He wouldn't sit after lunch. He spent part of the

morning either making people settle cases or adjourning them for
one reason or another and finally he tried what was left and rose
at lunch-time. Very rarely he came back after lunch, but usually
he made some excuse for postponing any case which hadn't finished
by lunch-time until another day. I liked him, but he certainly was
naughty. Well, one day Galloway had a case in front of Musgrave.
It was an accident case which would have been likely to occupy a
considerable part of the day. The judge had a medical referee sitting
beside him to advise. When I say sitting, well, it was arranged that
he should sit. The only question in the case was whether a man's
illness had been caused by the accident, but a good deal of evidence
would have had to be given about it. Before the judge sat he sent
for the doctors who were being called on each side and told them
to have a word with the medical referee. After they'd had a chat
for ten minutes or so, the judge went in to see them himself. Five
minutes later he came into Court, sat down and announced that
there would be judgment in the case for the defendants with costs.

' "But—" said the unfortunate Galloway, who was appearing for
the plaintiff.

' "But what?" said the judge, quite severely.

' "But—" repeated Galloway.

' "If that's all you have to say, Mr Galloway, I'll have the next
case called," and this was duly done.

'Well, of course, the plaintiff wasn't going to take that lying down.
His case had never been tried. The judge had no doubt acted upon
what the doctors had told him behind closed doors. It was a
complete denial of justice. So the plaintiff appealed to the Court of
Appeal and Galloway started to tell their Lordships all about it.
He hadn't gone very far with the story before the president of the
Court, Lord Justice Brand, said:

' "It's very difficult to believe that this really happened.
Naturally, I'm not doubting your word, Mr Galloway, but how can
it have happened as you say without your saying something to the
judge?"

' "I did say something, my Lord."

' "Oh—what was that?"

' "'But,' my Lord."

' "Yes, Mr Galloway?"

' "'But,' my Lord."

' "But what, Mr Galloway?"

' "Just 'but,' my Lord."

' "I'm afraid I'm out of my depth," said another Lord Justice. "Are you still addressing us, Mr Galloway?"

' "Yes, my Lord."

' "Then what did you mean when you said 'but' to my brother?"

' "That was what I said, my Lord."

' "I know you did, twice. But why?"

' "I couldn't think of anything else to say, my Lord."

' "Now, look," said Lord Justice Brand. "Let us get this straight. You didn't say 'but' to us—?"

' "Oh, yes, he did," said Lord Justice Rowe.

' "I know, I know," said Lord Justice Brand. "Please let me finish. The 'but' you said to us was the 'but' you said to the learned County Court judge, or to put it more accurately, it was another 'but' but the same word. 'But' is what you said to the County Court judge."

' "Yes, my Lord," said Galloway.

'Lord Justice Brand sat back in his chair triumphantly.

' "But," said Lord Justice Rowe, "if I may be forgiven the use of the word, but is that all you said to the learned judge?"

' "Yes, my Lord, just 'but.' " '

' "But it doesn't mean anything."

' "I didn't get a chance to say anything more, my Lord, and I was too flabbergasted."

' "Really, Mr Galloway," said Lord Justice Brand. "When I was at the Bar, I considered it to be my duty in the interests of my client to stand up to the judge and, if necessary, to be rude to him, yes, to be rude to him. I cannot believe that counsel of your experience would allow a thing like that to happen unchallenged."

'In the end, of course, they allowed the appeal and sent the case back to the County Court to be properly heard before another judge, but not before poor Galloway's mildness had been further criticized.

'A week later he had an accident case before Boyle—the judge you're going to meet. Galloway was appearing for the plaintiff. He got up and started to open the case to the jury, explaining to them where the accident happened and so on. He was just saying:

' "Now, members of the jury, at that juncture the defendant's car without any warning of any kind whatsoever—" when the judge interrupted:

' "Mr Galloway, might I have a plan, please?"

' "Be quiet," said Galloway and continued to address the jury. "And without any warning of any kind whatsoever—"

'Just as the Court of Appeal could not believe what was said to have happened in Musgrave's Court, Boyle couldn't believe he'd heard Galloway aright. Galloway was a polite man and his behaviour was normally impeccable.

' "I really can't follow this without a plan," said Boyle.

' "Will you be quiet," said Galloway and started to go on addressing the jury. But not for long. This time the judge had no doubt what had been said.

' "Have your taken leave of your senses, Mr Galloway?" he said angrily. "How dare you speak to me like that!"

' "Well, your Honour," said Galloway. "I was told last week by the Court of Appeal that it was my duty to be rude to the judge." '

CHAPTER 6

His Honour Judge Boyle

They arrived at the Court in plenty of time and went straight to the robing-room. It was crowded with solicitors and counsel.

'Hullo, Henry, are we against one another?' said a middle-aged barrister.

'I don't know. I'm in—now what's the name of it? Wait a minute, I can never remember.'

He opened his bag and got out the brief. 'Oh, yes, of course, Swift and Edgerley.'

'Yes, that's me,' said the other. 'We've got a hope. We're about last. He's got some judgment summonses, half a dozen possession cases and three other actions before ours. Any use asking him to let us go?'

'Not a chance,' said Henry. 'But all the same I should think we'd better try. The old so-and-so will never let anyone get away before lunch. I think he likes an audience really, to hear his wise remarks and his quotations from Birkenhead's famous judgment. Is anyone else going to have a crack at it? Let's get in before he sits and see what the form is.'

Counsel's and solicitors' row made an impressive sight for His Honour Judge Boyle as he walked on to the Bench. Henry was right in thinking that he liked an audience. The judge moved in and sat down slowly. He was a heavy man and not young. The first thing he did was to look at the pencils. He obviously did not approve of them. He tapped on his desk for the clerk to speak to him.

'Take these beastly things away,' he said, 'and get me some decent ones. I can't use those. How many more times have I got to say so?'

'I'm sorry, your Honour,' said the clerk.

'It's not your fault,' grunted the judge. 'It's what they send us.

I've complained about it dozens of times. They'll expect me to write with my thumbnail next.'

The clerk sent out for some more pencils.

A solicitor got up: 'Might I mention to your Honour,' he began.

'No, not yet,' said the judge irritably.

The solicitor sat down with a sigh.

'Cheerful mood to-day,' whispered one member of the Bar to another.

'The old idiot. I'd like to chuck the lot at him.'

'If people want to talk they must go outside,' said the judge.

'Charming,' said Henry, but quietly enough.

The new pencils were brought. The judge tried them. 'I suppose they'll have to do,' he said eventually. 'They're better than the last. Thank you, Mr Jones.'

'Shall I call the first application, your Honour?'

'Yes, please.'

'Mrs Turner,' called the clerk, and a small woman went into the witness box. She was making an application for some money to be paid out to her from a fund in Court. She was a widow whose husband had been killed some years before in an accident and the Court controlled her use of the damages she had been awarded.

'Well,' said the judge, after glancing at the papers in front of him, 'what do you want £10 for?'

He asked her as though she were a beggar at the back door when she was, in fact, the owner of the fund in Court. It was her money, but the Court had the paternal duty of seeing that she did not expend it too foolishly. The judge's manner was not in the least paternal.

'Please, your Worship,' the woman began—

'She's had it,' whispered a solicitor, 'calling him your worship.'

'It's a first payment for a television set.'

The judge's eyes gleamed. His remarks about television and other abominations of the modern age had frequently been reported in the Press.

'A television set,' he growled. 'What on earth d'you want with one of those things? Read a good book and get it from the library. Cost you nothing.'

'Please, your Worship, I can't read, not really.'

'What on earth have we been paying taxes for all these years? It's disgraceful.'

'Please, your Worship, I'm nearly blind.'

'Oh, I'm sorry,' said the judge. He thought for a moment and then added in a more kindly tone: 'But is a television set much use to you then? Why not have a wireless instead?'

'Oh, I have a wireless, your Worship.'

'I see.'

The judge hesitated.

'You think you'll get some pleasure out of a television set, do you?'

'Oh, yes, your Worship. Mrs Crane across the road has one and she can't see a thing.'

'Perhaps it's an advantage then,' said the judge. 'Yes, very well, Mrs Turner. You shall have your television set. Ten pounds I think you want. Very well. Can you pay the instalments all right? Good. They'll give you your money in the office. I hope your sight improves.'

'Might I now mention to your Honour,' began the solicitor who had tried before, hoping that the shock which the judge had just received might have put him in a more receptive mood.

'Certainly not,' said the judge just as fiercely as before, but not quite for the same reason. He was visualizing Mrs Turner's life without her husband and without much sight. 'And probably she hasn't much to think with either,' he was pondering, 'though p'raps it's as well,' when the solicitor had interrupted.

'Mr Copplestone,' called the clerk, and a young man went into the witness box. The judge glared at him. He had already glanced at his application.

'A motor bicycle,' he said. 'One of those horrible things. Why don't you use a pedal cycle or walk? Much better for you and safer. You'll go and kill yourself.'

'I'm getting married,' ventured the young man.

'You'll kill your wife too,' said the judge.

'I'm twenty-one next month,' said the young man, 'and we wanted the bike for our honeymoon.'

This was a young man who had been awarded damages when he was a small boy. At the age of twenty-one he would be entitled to all of it, but until then the Court had control.

'Why can't you wait?' asked the judge. He knew he couldn't keep the young man away from a motor bicycle for long, but he did not want to be a party to the transaction.

'We don't want to, your Honour.'

'I dare say you don't. Have you your parents' permission?'

'To have the bike, your Honour?'

'No, of course not. No one asks parents' permission for anything these days. You just go and do it. No—to marry, I mean. Still need it for that.'

'Can I speak?' said a man from the back of the Court.

'Silence,' called the usher.

'But it's all wrong,' shouted the man.

'Silence,' called the usher even louder.

'Let that man be brought forward,' commanded the judge. He required no bringing forward and came hastily to the witness box.

'Who are you?' asked the judge.

'I'm his father,' said the man. 'And I think it's a shame.'

'You've already interrupted the proceedings twice and if you speak like that I shall deal with you for contempt of Court. You'll either speak properly or not at all. Now, what is it you want to say?'

'I say, give the boy his bike. Why spoil the young people's pleasure? You only get married once.'

'Unfortunately,' said the judge, unable to resist the temptation, 'that to-day is not always the case, though I hope it will be in this instance. But if I let him have this horrible machine one of them at least will probably be killed.'

'They can't afford a car,' said the man. 'And they don't want to go for a honeymoon by bus or train. They want to be with each other. And I say they ought to be. My old woman and I went walking, but then we didn't have the luck to have had an accident and get the damages. Though it doesn't look as though that's going to be much good to him.'

'Will you be quiet,' said the judge.

'Why doesn't the Registrar do these?' whispered Henry to his opponent.

'Because the old fool likes doing them. He ought to do them in chambers, anyway. Pompous old idiot. Doesn't care two hoots how much time he takes up or how much he inconveniences everyone.'

The judge finished his applications, having very grudgingly given the young man his money. He realized that it would not be fair in this instance to refuse it.

'Now, does anyone want to mention any of the cases?'

The solicitor had a third attempt.

'Any member of the Bar,' asked the judge, ignoring the solicitor.

Henry's opponent got up.

'Your Honour is always so exceedingly considerate that I'm prompted to ask leave to mention the last case in your Honour's list,' he said.

'Let me see,' said the judge, 'Swift and Edgerley, is that it?'

'Yes, your Honour. My learned friend, Mr Blagrove, and I were wondering whether your Honour would give any indication of whether that case is likely to be heard to-day. I would not have mentioned the matter but your Honour is always so exceedingly helpful in these matters and as there are seven cases in front of us—' he paused and waited to see what effect his piece of hypocrisy had had.

'One does one's best, Mr Tate,' said the judge, 'but, as you know, it's very difficult with such heavy lists. Would it be a convenience to you if I said that I would not hear your case before the luncheon adjournment?'

'No bloody use at all,' said Tate in an undertone to Henry. 'Thank you very much, your Honour,' he went on. 'That is most kind of your Honour. Perhaps we might have leave to mention the matter again after the adjournment.'

'Certainly, Mr Tate.'

'If your Honour pleases,' beamed Mr Tate. 'The old so-and-so,' he added to Henry, 'he knows bloody well we can't get back to the Temple from here.'

'Any other applications from the Bar?' asked the judge. There was no response.

'Now, Mr Bloat, what is your application?'

'Would your Honour release my case too until after lunch?'

'If I release every case I shall have nothing to do. Are there any other applications?'

'But, your Honour—' began Mr Bloat.

'What is it, Mr Bloat?' said the judge angrily. 'It's quite impossible for me to help the parties in these matters if they don't accept my decision when I've given it. I do the best I can.'

'I think you're brilliant,' said Henry to Tate when they were in the robing-room again. 'It would stick in my gullet to talk to the old boy like that.'

'When you're my age,' said Tate, 'you'll never mind saying

"please" to anyone if it'll get you anywhere or anything—even if
you think you oughtn't to have had to ask for it—indeed, even if
it's your own. It costs nothing and sometimes it gets something. At
any rate we can have a smoke and plenty of time for lunch. He
only rises for half an hour.'

'But you perjured your immortal soul in the process.'

'If you feel so strongly on the subject, my boy,' said Tate, 'you
should have got up and disagreed when I said the old fool was so
exceedingly helpful. See how far that would have got us! Anyway
by keeping silent you adopted my lie and cannot now be heard to
complain of it. Estopped, my boy, that's what you are. And when
you get before St Peter, he'll have you for that. "You told a lie to
His Honour Judge Boyle," he'll say. You'll start to deny it. "We
can't have that," he'll say. "You told a lie to Judge Boyle all right.
Good for you. Come inside." '

Eventually Henry's case was heard and he and Roger left the
Court together.

'What sort of a clerk is Alec?' Roger asked him.

'Alec has, in my view,' said Henry, 'only one fault. This,' and
Henry imitated Alec sucking his teeth so successfully that Roger
winced. 'Cheer up—you'll have to get used to that,' said Henry,
and did it again. 'Some people,' he went on, 'would say that he
had two other faults. He doesn't drink or smoke. But that's a matter
of opinion.'

'Clerks seem to be most frightfully important,' said Roger.

'Well, you've noticed something. They are. A top-class man will
always get on, but a second-rater could be made or marred by his
clerk.'

'How does a clerk begin?'

'Usually as a boy in the Temple, at a very small wage. Then, if
he's no good, he goes to something else. If he does take to it, he
becomes a junior and then, if he's lucky, a senior clerk. D'you know,
Alec was making a thousand a year when he was not much older
than you are, and a thousand was a thousand in those days.'

'It's extraordinary. Of course, the method of paying them beats
me. I must say I like the idea of having my clerk paid by the clients.
Is there any other profession in the world where it happens?'

'I don't know of one—except, of course, that they're really paid
by commission and there are plenty of commission jobs. But they
are rather different, I suppose. Yes, it is a curious arrangement that

every time I have a conference my clerk gets five bob and the client pays him. But, of course, until you've got a practice you'll have to pay him a salary. And they're inclined to take the shillings in the guineas now as well from everyone.'

'What do they make these days?'

'Depends entirely on the chambers. But a clerk in a really good set of chambers might make two or three thousand a year, I suppose. And he's never read a law-book in his life, though he's carried a good few. All the same, the work he does is jolly important and the wheels wouldn't go round without him. Getting briefs, fixing up the fees and arranging it so that you're not in too many places at the same time. It takes a bit of doing. An intelligent and experienced clerk earns his keep all right.'

'What I like,' said Roger, 'is the sort of relationship which seems to exist between them and us.'

'Quite right!' said Henry. 'It's quite different from any other. There's an intimacy and understanding between a barrister and his clerk which, as far as I know, doesn't exist in any other job. And neither side ever takes advantage of it. But Heaven preserve me from a bad clerk. Alec does me proud—indeed, he'd do me much better if I'd let him, and I don't mind his little habit as much as you seem to.' And Henry repeated it several times until he saw that it really upset Roger. 'Sorry, old boy,' he said. 'I didn't know you took it to heart so. I'll try to remember,' and he just checked himself from repeating the process.

Shortly afterwards they parted. Henry went home and Roger went back to chambers. When he arrived there, he was greeted by Alec.

'There's a brief been sent down to you, sir, for next Friday.'

'For me?'

'Yes, sir. I thought you might know about it. The solicitors are something Merivale. Someone you know, I expect?'

'Gosh,' said Roger. 'Joy's uncle already.'

CHAPTER 7

First Brief

It was a divorce case. Roger picked it up lovingly. It looked so beautiful in its fresh pink tape with 'Mr Roger Thursby' typed neatly on it and almost as important, the fee—the fee that someone was going to pay him for his services. Seven whole guineas. He had never earned as much before in his life, though he had once earned a few guineas by tutoring a boy advertised as 'Backward (nothing mental).' He was a nice boy with a fiercely obstinate disposition and determined to learn nothing that his parents wanted him taught. He could recognize almost any bird or flower and many tunes from classical music. His parents were not musical, so he used to turn on the Third Programme. Funny, thought Roger, how one train of thought leads to another. Why should I be thinking of Christopher because someone's sent me a brief? A brief. His very own. Mr Roger Thursby. Five and two, total seven. And at the bottom 'Thornton, Merivale & Co., 7 Butts Buildings, E.C.4. Solicitors for the Petitioner.' The Petitioner. The life and happiness of one man or one woman had been entrusted to him. Man or woman, which was it? The outside of the brief, which was entitled 'In the High Court of Justice Probate, Divorce and Admiralty Division (Divorce). Newent E. *v.* Newent K. R.,' did not disclose whether the petitioner was to be a beautiful blonde. Perhaps it was an actress—Sally's mother might know her—no, that wouldn't do—it was Joy's uncle who'd sent the brief. What a pity it wasn't Sally's. He'd no business to think that. It was most ungrateful. How kind it was of Joy and she was really very pretty. Or was it a man, an admiral, perhaps, or a general or even a Member of Parliament? Well, he could soon find out. He opened the brief. E. stood for Ethel. His first petitioner was a woman. Poor thing! What a brute of a husband! Now she had Roger to protect her. It was Roger Galahad Thursby who looked eagerly at the rest of the papers. At the age of twenty-one

Roger found that rescuing ladies (in the imagination) occupied quite
a portion of his idle moments. At that age the pictures of such
events rather embarrassed him. He preferred her to be fully clothed.
Roger started to read the brief and was a little disappointed to find
that all that Mr Newent had done was to leave his wife—and, as
far as could be ascertained, not even for another woman. Roger
made the best of it, however, and soon imagined himself giving his
client words of encouragement and consolation which would stem
the poor girl's grief. Even this idea was slightly shaken when he
found that the poor girl was forty-five and that she was what is
called 'asking for the discretion of the Court.' But Roger steeled
himself to the task. He was broadminded. He did not in fact approve
of infidelity. He had attended several weddings and had always been
impressed by the words of the marriage service. He had difficulty in
reconciling them with the number of divorces which now take place.
But now he was face to face with an unfaithful wife—on paper
anyway, and he would soon see her. He could not help feeling a
thrill at the prospect. He had never to his knowledge met an—an
adulteress before. It was rather a terrible word. The newspapers
often covered it up. They talked of misconduct and infidelity. Adulteress sounded much worse. And then he remembered the great
words on the subject. 'He that is without sin among you—' Yes,
Roger would speak to this poor, fallen woman in a kindly, understanding way. She would never realize he was only twenty-one.
He would speak with such an air of knowledge, such a wealth of
understanding, that she would probably cry. And he would say:
'Madam, you and I have only just met—but I think I know what
you have been through.' He paused in his thoughts. What next?
Ah, yes, more sinned against than sinning. The lonely, slighted
wife, devoted to a husband who neglected her for his business and
his billiards. There she was alone at home, waiting, waiting—an
easy prey for the handsome seducer. Yes, more sinned against
than sinning, that was it. He read through the whole brief, the
correspondence, the petition and the discretion statement. This last
document was the one in which Mrs Newent disclosed how she
came to sin and humbly asked the Court—not to forgive her—but
to grant a decree of divorce just the same. Mr Newent apparently
was quite willing to be divorced and had not even entered an
appearance to the petition. This was a pity, thought Roger. It
was difficult to make an impassioned speech against someone who

wouldn't fight. And it was very clear that Mr Newent wasn't going to fight. His last letter to Ethel went as follows:

Dear Ethel

It is no good asking me to return. I told you when I left that this is final and it is. I had one year of happiness with you and five years of the other thing. You cared much more for your beastly boarding house and some of the boarders than you did for me, though I shall be surprised if you make more of a success of that business than you did of our marriage. 'Service with a smile' you used to put in your advertisements. Having regard to the charges you made and the little value you gave for them, I should have expected service to be with a smile, not to say a broad grin. If you don't treat your guests better than you treated me you'll lose them too. Most of them, that is. But then some people never learn. I have. And I'm not coming back to 'Sans Repos'—which is what it ought to be called. But you wouldn't understand. You can understand this, though, that I'm not coming back—no never—whether you divorce me or whether you don't. I hope you will because I'd like to be free. Not that I've met anyone else. I'll be darn careful about the next one, believe me. But if I can't be free, at any rate I'll be happy. I don't wish you any harm, Ethel. Maybe there is some man who'd be happy with you, but it's not

> *Yours*
> *Kenneth*

This letter had been written in reply to a very short one by Ethel which had simply said:

I'm writing for the last time to know whether you propose to return to me. If you do not I shall take such action as I may be advised.

The material parts of the discretion statement were as follows:

After I had been married to my husband for some years he ceased to take any interest in my business of a boarding house proprietress, although he knew when we married that I was very keen on my business and wanted to continue with it after marriage. He had agreed to this, but nevertheless he was always asking me to give it up and make a home for him. At last he refused even to look after the accounts, and one of the boarders, who had been with us for some years and who did a little accounting in his spare time, very kindly started to do them for me. As a result of this I got to know this gentleman, a Mr Storrington, rather well. One night he asked me to go to a dance with him, and, as at the time my husband was staying with his parents (one of whom was ill), I did not think there would be any harm in it. We went to a dance and unfortunately I had rather too much to drink. I am not a teetotaller, but very rarely drink intoxicating liquor. During the evening I had several drinks and though I felt all right during the dance, when we left I felt dizzy and faint. Mr Storrington very kindly offered to help me to my bedroom and somehow or other he came in and adultery took place. I felt very ashamed the next morning and told Mr Storrington that it must never happen again or he would have to leave. Mr Storrington promised that it would not occur again. Since my husband left me I have seen more and more of Mr Storrington and an affection has developed between us and, if this Court sees fit to grant me a decree of divorce, I wish to marry Mr Storrington and he is willing to marry me. Although Mr Storrington and I are living in the same house on affectionate terms adultery has not occurred between us except as aforesaid, nor have I committed any act of adultery with any other person. To the best of my knowledge and belief my husband was and is wholly unaware of my adultery.

It was a pity in some ways, thought Roger at first, that Mr Storrington was still about the place. For it meant that the petitioner already had a companion and friend. But Roger soon adjusted himself to the new situation, and decided that the poor little woman who had never known happiness with her husband should be given a new and happy life with her new husband, and it would be Roger who would be responsible for giving it her. After he had been through the papers several times Roger asked if he could see Mr Grimes, and eventually Alec managed to sandwich him in between two conferences.

'Well, my dear fellow, what can I do for ye?'

Roger mentioned that he'd had a brief for the petitioner in an undefended divorce. Might he ask a few questions about it?

'Of course, my dear fellow, of course. But ye won't have any trouble, my dear fellow. Not like it was in the old days. That was a very different cup of tea, a very different cup of tea, my dear fellow. Nowadays it's like shelling peas, my dear chap. In one door and out the other before you can say "knife." '

'This is what they call a discretion case. Does that make any difference?'

'Oh, that's all right, my dear fellow, just tell the judge the tale, tell the judge the tale.'

'As a matter of fact my client committed adultery before her husband left her. Does that make any difference?'

'Did he know of it, my dear fellow?'

'Oh—no.'

'Then that's all right then, my dear fellow. What the eye sees not, the heart grieves not.'

'I just wondered if it was desertion for a man to leave his wife if she'd committed adultery.'

'Oh, yes, my dear fellow, so long as he doesn't know, that's desertion all right. You look up *Herod and Herod*. That'll tell you all about it. And there are some later cases in the Court of Appeal. Now is there anything else I can do for you, my dear fellow?'

'No, thank you very much. It's most kind of you.'

'Not at all, my dear fellow. Very glad you've had your first brief. Had to wait much longer in my day. But everything's faster these days. I don't know what we're coming to. Judges on the Bench that haven't been called twenty years. I don't know, my dear fellow, I don't know. But there it is, they will do these things, they will do these things. Good-bye, my dear fellow, good-bye, bye, bye.'

Roger went back to the pupils' room, very pleased with life. But, easy though his task was going to be, he wouldn't leave anything to chance. First he would master the facts, then the law and then— then—glorious moment—he would have a conference with his client.

'Hear you've got an undefended,' said Peter. 'I think they're a bore.'

'Have you done one?' asked Charles.

'No, but I've heard hundreds. Simple as pie—but an awful bore. No, give me something a bit meatier for my first brief.'

'Haven't you had one, then?' said Roger.

'As a matter of fact,' said Peter, 'it's not a terribly good thing to have a brief too early in one's career. Might come an awful cropper. Of course an undefended's different. But I just don't care for the sound of them. Shouldn't want my friends to send me one of those. If that's all the use they've got for me I'd rather they went somewhere else.'

' "Said the fox,' said Charles, ' "adding to his wife, 'they always give me indigestion, anyway." " '

'I don't know what you're talking about,' said Peter. 'Anyway I can't afford to waste my time here. I'm going down to the Bailey.'

'Hope you get that dock brief,' said Charles. 'That'll be a start.'

'Well done,' said Charles when Peter had left. 'Who sent it you?'

'Uncle of a girl friend.'

'Good show. I never seem to be lucky that way. Are you going to have a conference?'

'I suppose so. It's marked on the brief—two guineas.'

'That doesn't mean a thing, as a matter of fact. They pay it whether you have one or not.'

'How odd,' said Roger.

'I suppose it's the same with every job. There are always things which are difficult to explain to people who aren't in it.'

'I suppose there are. But I think I ought to have a conference, anyway.'

'Is it sticky then?'

'Oh, I don't think so. I spoke to Grimes and he said it was all right. But I think I ought to ask her a few questions.'

'When'll you have it?'

'I don't know. What ought I to do about it? Speak to Alec?'

'Yes, I should think so. I've never had one yet.'

'You've never had a conference?'

'No, as I told you, we haven't all got girl friends with solicitor uncles.'

'I am lucky.'

'I should say you are. That'll make up for what happened on your first day. Very different going into a Court knowing all about it—with your own case too. What's it about?'

Roger told him and then went to arrange with Alec for a conference.

'You usually see them outside the Court, sir,' said Alec, 'but I can get them down here if you'd like.'

'Yes, I think so, please,' said Roger feeling very daring at giving orders to his clerk. Outside the Court did not seem to be the real thing.

After that he went to the Bar Library and read the case of *Herod v. Herod* and several other later cases in which it had been approved. It seemed clear enough. Then he looked up every other point of

law he could think of. He went back to chambers with a note of
what he had read. Then he went home.

His mother was out. So he went straight to the telephone to thank
Joy. 'It's terribly good of your uncle, Joy.'

'He's a dear old boy and if I give him a nice kiss, he'll do quite
a lot for me. Shall I give him lots more kisses, Roger?'

'Oh, please, Joy.'

'What'll you give me then?'

'We'll go and dine.'

'Lovely. Where? When?'

'Well, I haven't had the cheque yet. I wonder when they send
it.'

'I'd better give him another kiss, don't you think? I like talking
about kisses to you, Roger. Don't you?'

'Of course I do, Joy, it is sweet of you. I can't thank you enough.'

'Oh, yes, you can. And I'll expect you to try.'

'Of course I will.'

'Promise.'

'Of course.'

'Roger, darling—how lovely. I'll go and see uncle tonight and
we'll dine to-morrow. I'll lend you the money if the cheque hasn't
come.'

'Oh—I couldn't let you. But I can try mother.'

As soon as he'd finished talking to Joy, blushing slightly he
telephoned Sally.

'Oh, Roger, I am glad. What's it about?'

'Well, I'd rather like to talk to you about it, if I might. It's not
the sort of thing I can mention on the telephone.'

'Well, when would you like?'

'You couldn't come round now? I expect mother's got enough
food.'

'I'd love it.'

As soon as Sally had arrived Roger showed her the lovely brief,
but he covered up the names with his hand.

'You can't possibly know the people in this case and it must be
all right for me to tell you if you don't know their names. Even they
wouldn't mean anything to you.'

'All right,' said Sally, 'if you say so.'

'D'you mind if I tell you about the case as though I were
addressing the judge?' he asked.

'Of course not.'

'May it please your Lordship,' began Roger, 'my client who is a lady of mature years—'

'Stop,' said Sally, 'that won't do. How old is she?'

'Forty-five.'

'Well—she'd hit you over the head with her umbrella for that—out of Court if not in. Why mention her age, anyway?'

'I think it's important in this case, You see, Sally, there are things in this case which you and I wouldn't talk about normally—I mean—I know everyone does nowadays, but you're different. I do want you to understand that when I talk about—talk about this woman's—this woman's—er—behaviour—it's only because it's in the case.'

'Strictly professionally,' said Sally. 'I suppose you're trying to tell me she's committed adultery.'

'Yes,' said Roger, 'I am Sally, I'm afraid.'

'That's all right, Roger, it's not your fault; she did it, not you.'

'Quite,' said Roger. 'I'm so glad you understand. Now may I go on?'

'Please.'

'May it please your Lordship, my client who is no longer young—'

'No,' said Sally, 'if you must say anything about it, and I can't yet see why you should, say what her age is. She may not like that, but she'd prefer it to any of your phrases.'

'Oh, all right. My client who is forty-five is bringing this petition on the grounds of desertion. As your Lordship probably knows desertion is a matrimonial offence and consists of—'

'Just a moment, Roger,' interrupted Sally, 'I don't know anything about Courts and judges, but I suppose there have been a good many cases of desertion before yours.'

'Oh, Lord, yes.'

'Well—don't you think the judge might know what is meant by it then?'

'I said "as your Lordship probably knows—" '

'D'you think he'd like the "probably?" Some judges are pretty touchy, I believe.'

'All right then. As your Lordship knows—'

'Well, if he knows, why tell him?' said Sally.

'I'm sure I've read that they say things like that, Sally.'

'I expect that's when the judge *doesn't* know, Roger, and it's a

polite way of telling him. If it's something that he must know and
you know he must know it seems a bit odd to me telling him at all.
You might just as well tell him that the case is brought under
English law. I suppose every case is, unless it's a special one.'

'I say, you know, Sally, I do think you're marvellous. You ought
to have gone to the Bar. You're going to be the most awful help to
me. Oh—I could kiss you.'

Sally said nothing. Roger did nothing.

'Just another of your phrases, I suppose. Well, it's better than
saying I'm of mature years. Though I expect I shall be before—now
where were we?' she went on hurriedly.

'How would *you* start, Sally?'

'Well, I suppose, I'd say that it was a petition for divorce on the
ground of desertion and then say shortly what the facts were.'

'When would you mention the discretion?'

'What discretion?'

Roger explained what was meant by a discretion statement and
told Sally what was in it.

'But I don't understand,' said Sally.

'But I thought I'd made it clear. Where a petitioner has
committed adultery he or she has got to file—'

'Oh, no, I understand all that. What I don't understand is what
the husband has done wrong.'

'He left her and wouldn't come back.'

'Yes, but she'd committed adultery.'

'But he didn't know of it. It's all quite clear. It's in *Herod and
Herod*. I read it this afternoon.'

'Are you sure you didn't misread it, Roger dear? After all you
are fairly new to the game and I expect some of these things are
difficult to understand—'

'Now, look, Sally. I think you're awfully clever and all that, and
you're going to be an awful lot of use to me, if you will, but when
I say the law's so and so you've got to accept it from me. I've
looked it up.'

'But Roger, I'm sorry to seem so dense. Do try and make me
understand it. I gather the law disapproves of adultery.'

'Of course.'

'I suppose the law agrees that it's a breach of the marriage vows
or whatever the law calls them to commit adultery?'

'Certainly.'

'So if a wife commits adultery the husband is entitled to leave her.'

'Quite.'

'Well, that's what happened in your case.'

'He didn't know.'

'But surely, that can't make any difference.'

'Well, it does.'

'I still can't believe it,' said Sally. 'Look. Marriage starts with a husband and wife living together, doesn't it?'

'Yes.'

'And if one leaves the other it's desertion.'

'Exactly. That's what's happened here. He's left her.'

'Not so fast, Roger. Is a wife entitled to have her husband living with her if she commits adultery?'

'No,' began Roger—and then seeing where this admission was leading him to, he went on: 'Well, it depends. If the husband finds out he can leave her.'

'And are you really saying that if the husband doesn't find out—if the lady's clever enough to conceal it from him—then she has the right that he should go on living with her?'

'That,' said Roger, 'is the law of England.'

'I'm sorry,' said Sally, 'you know and I don't. You've just looked it up. You've taken all your Bar examinations. But I just can't believe it. You're saying that, provided a man or woman is a good enough liar, he or she can commit adultery as much as they like?'

'It sounds odd put that way, I agree,' said Roger.

'Well, isn't that what you were saying?'

Roger thought for a moment.

'I suppose it is really. I must say it does sound strange the way you put it. I didn't think of it like that, and I'm sure there's nothing in the cases I looked at about it. I think I'd better look at them again. I say, Sally, you really are a wonder. I could—didn't I hear mother?'

'You should know by now, Roger,' said Sally.

'Oh, no, it's the people next door.'

'Yes, Roger. You were saying?'

'Where was I now? Oh, yes—well, when do you think I should mention this discretion business?'

'Wouldn't it be a good thing to go and hear one or two undefended divorces yourself first, so that you can see when it's normally done?'

'How right you are. I will.'

'May I come and hear you do yours, Roger?'

'Of course—that is—well—'

'Well, of course, if I'll make you nervous, Roger—'

'It's not exactly that, Sally. You see—as a matter of fact—it's like this really—of course I'd love you to be there—but, as a matter of fact, well—Joy's uncle sent me the brief actually.'

'Well,' said Sally, 'that was very nice of him—and her, but why should that make any difference? Or have they taken the whole Court for the occasion?'

'No, of course not, but I expect Joy would like to be there—and I thought, I mean, mightn't it be a bit embarrassing? For both of you, I mean. And as it was Joy's uncle who sent the brief—'

'And Joy who helped you to prepare it?'

'That isn't fair, Sally. I won't ask you another time if you're going to throw it in my teeth.'

'I simply asked if I could come to hear you. I'm not throwing anything in your teeth. Joy and I won't tear each others eyes out, you know. We'd be sent to prison if we did. Which of us would you defend, Roger, if we were? You couldn't do both, could you?'

'I think that's a horrible question,' said Roger.

CHAPTER 8

First Conference

Two days later Roger had his first conference. Peter and Charles went into Henry's room so that he could have the pupils' room for the purpose.

Mrs Newent came with Mr Smith, a managing clerk from Messrs Thornton, Merivale & Co., who introduced himself and his client to Roger. He invited them to sit down. They did so. Mrs Newent was attractive in a cheap sort of way, rather overdressed and too much made-up. She had very shapely legs with sheer nylon stockings and she showed Roger much to much of them both. His eyes followed their movements, which were fairly frequent, as a rabbit's eyes follow a snake. From time to time with an effort he would look at the ceiling or out of the window or at the bookshelves, but it was no use. Back they had to come. He had never been so close to such things before. They revolted but fascinated him, and he simply could not help himself. He cleared his throat preparatorily to opening the proceedings. But Mrs Newent got in first.

'You're very young, if I may say so,' she said. She did not mean that she was in the least dismayed. Several of her friends had had divorces. One had to go through the formalities and that was all. Indeed, it was very nice to be represented by a pleasant-looking young man who couldn't keep his eyes off one's legs.

'It must be an awful responsibility,' she added.

Roger coughed. 'That's what we're here for,' he said eventually.

'I'm so glad,' said Mrs Newent, and recrossed her legs. 'I feel sort of safe with you.'

Even at that early stage and even with his inexperience, Roger began to wonder whether the discretion statement constituted the full and frank disclosure which such statements are supposed to be. He remembered, too, that the statement said quite a number of things about the husband and the dance and so forth, but when it came to the adultery it was disposed of in a very few words. The reason for Mr Storrington going into her bedroom was slurred over in the words, 'Somehow or other he came in.'

'Now,' went on Mrs Newent, 'was there something you wanted to ask me?'

By this time Roger had looked again at the cases and it certainly seemed as if what he had told Sally was right. It appeared that, in spite of Sally's doubts, the law was that, provided the adulteress was clever enough, she had the right that her husband should go on living with her. But there was just the point that it was for her to prove that her husband knew nothing about it. Roger quite rightly wanted to be sure of this.

'It's about your discretion statement,' he began.

'Mr Smith here wrote that out,' said Mrs Newent. 'I only signed it, you know. That's right, isn't it, Mr Smith?'

'I wrote it out on your instructions, Mrs Newent.'

'Instructions? I don't remember giving any instructions.'

'It's what you told me, I mean.'

'Oh, yes. What long words you lawyers use. If you'd said that at first I'd have understood.'

'I take it the statement is true, Mrs Newent?' asked Roger.

'True?' said Mrs Newent, recrossing her legs. 'Of course. Mr Smith wouldn't have written it down otherwise, would he?'

'There was only the once and you'd had a little too much to drink.'

'That's right. Gin and frenches all the evening. I felt on top of the world.'

'I thought you became dizzy and faint.'

'That's right.'

'After you felt on top of the world you became dizzy and faint?' asked Roger.

'That's right,' said Mrs Newent. 'You are a clever young man. I'm glad I've got you. D'you mind if I have a cigarette?'

'Of course not,' said Roger and offered her one and lit it for her. She guided his hand to the cigarette, much to his discomfort.

'I think you ought to do very well,' she said. 'I shall remember you appeared for me when I see your name in the papers.'

Roger blushed and coughed and tried to look at the ceiling.

'Now, there's another thing,' he said. 'Are you quite sure that your husband knew nothing about this and suspected nothing?' For

answer Mrs Newent put her first finger to the side of her nose and
winked.

'Are you sure?' repeated Roger.

'Not a notion,' said Mrs Newent. 'We were discretion itself, if
you'll pardon my using the word.'

'But,' said Roger, 'it only happened once and then you were faint
and dizzy. How can you have been discretion itself if you were faint
and dizzy?'

'Come now, young man,' said Mrs Newent. 'I'm not sure you're
as clever as I thought. I go to a dance. Right?'

'Yes,' said Roger.

'I drink too much. Right?'

'Yes,' said Roger.

'I go out into the cold air and as every judge knows—I should
hope—it hits me for six. Right?'

'You became faint and dizzy.'

'Exactly. So he helps me home. Now I'm hone. I'm still faint and
dizzy at the bottom of the stairs. Can't get up by myself. Right?'

'Yes.'

'He helps me up the stairs. We get to my room. Still faint and
dizzy. With me?'

'Yes.'

'Like the perfect gentleman he is he sees me into my bedroom.
All clear so far?'

'Yes.'

'Right. Well, when we get into the bedroom we take a liking to
each other—see, and I become less faint and dizzy. But it was too
late then.'

'How do you know your husband knows nothing about it?'

'Because he wasn't there and no one could have told him. As
soon as we took a liking to one another I sent Bert out of the room
to his own room, making enough noise that people in the next room
would have heard him go away within a minute or two of his
coming in. Then he comes back like a mouse. Didn't even hear him
come in myself. Didn't hear him go, either. I was asleep then. But
I know he was ever so careful.'

'When your husband came back, did he seem to suspect
anything?'

'Not a thing. He was just the same as ever. Cold as an iceberg.
A woman's got to get a bit of warmth from someone, hasn't she?'

'But it was only once?'

'It was only once,' replied Mrs Newent with emphasis. 'Because I know what's nice,' she added, 'that doesn't mean to say I don't know what's wrong. And with all the other boarders around you've got to be careful. People talk. Now what else d'you want to ask me? I'm getting a bit tired of this cross-questioning. I thought you were on my side.'

'Of course I'm on your side,' said Roger, 'but I have to ask you these questions.'

'Well, I can't think why,' said Mrs Newent. 'It's all plain and straightforward. I want a divorce, Mr Newent wants a divorce, what more d'you want? I don't know why there's all this palaver, anyway.'

'We don't have divorce by consent in this country,' said Roger.

'Well—who says it's by consent? He left me, didn't he? That's desertion, isn't it? Then you have this ridiculous business about discretion. I wouldn't have told you if I'd known there'd be all this fuss. Was I faint and dizzy? When did I stop being faint and dizzy? And if not, why not? You wouldn't have known if I hadn't told you and there wouldn't have been all this nonsense. I'll know better another time. I though one could trust one's lawyer.'

'We have a duty to the Court,' said Mr Smith.

'Fiddlesticks,' said Mrs Newent. 'A lot of old fools sitting up there, what do they care? They're half asleep, anyway. I went with my friend the other day. No fuss about hers. All over in five minutes. She didn't put in any discretion statement either, not on your sweet life. She couldn't have remembered for one thing. I'm too honest, that's my trouble. And what do I get for it? Asked a lot of intimate questions. I'd be ashamed if I were a man. It's not as though I'd done anything really wrong.'

'But I thought you said—' began Roger.

'All right, Mr Clever, not as wrong as all that. There are worse things. Murder, for instance, or blackmail. All right, I was wrong to let him in my room that night. All right, I've told you. There it is in black and white. You've got my ruddy discretion statement and I hope it chokes you both—and the judge. Now, is there anything else you want?'

The conference was very different from the one Roger had visualized and he was glad when it ended. He felt slightly sick. Mrs

Newent was not quite the sort of maiden he would care to rescue, even fully clothed.

CHAPTER 9

Joyce

That evening he dined with Joy. He had not had the cheque from the solicitors, but his mother had lent him the money.

'Of course, darling,' she had said. 'I't'll be an investment, really. You'll be able to keep me soon. Won't that be lovely? And I shan't have to look to Aunt Ethel for a new dress. I do think you're clever, darling.'

'It was Joy really, Mother.'

'But I'm sure the solicitors wouldn't have sent it to you if they hadn't heard of your reputation. I shall tell everyone about you. Fancy making a name for yourself in a week. But then I knew you would. It's your father in you. Not me, I'm afraid. Now that it's all right, I don't mind telling you, I've always been a little frightened that you might be a fool like me. I'm so glad you're not, darling. Shall we get a bottle of champagne and celebrate. We can pay for it next month.'

'That'd be lovely, darling, but I must go out with Joy tonight.'

'Oh, of course.'

'And you mustn't start talking about my having made a name for myself. I haven't done anything of the sort. I've been sent my first brief by the uncle of a girl friend and it's just an undefended divorce. I haven't even done it yet. I might make an awful mess of it.'

'Oh, no you won't, not you.'

'Well, I hope not, but—oh, darling, I'm appearing for the most awful woman. I'm so glad you're not like her.'

'Thank you, darling. So am I, if she's all that awful.'

'She's really terrible. It makes you feel uncomfortable to meet her. And the things she says. D'you know I felt quite sick after I'd had a conference with her. Don't tell anyone else. I suppose one's got to get used to that sort of thing, but I hope I don't get many

more like her. I'll be glad when it's over. Would you like to come
and hear it?'

'Darling, of course. When is it?'

'To-morrow.'

'You must tell me how to get there. Or will you take me?'

'Well, darling—you know I'd love to take you—but don't you
think it would look a bit obvious if we went in together? Rather
like showing off. Besides, I don't want it to look as if it were my
first brief. You do understand, don't you?'

'Of course, darling. I won't come at all, if you'd rather not.'

'No, I'd love you to.'

'I shan't make you nervous?'

'Oh no—once it's started, I shall be all right.'

'Well, you must tell me where it is. One of those places with blue
lamps outside them, is it?'

'Mother, darling, those are police stations.'

'That's right. Well, there's a Court next to them sometines, isn't
there?'

'Mother, this is the High Court of Justice, Probate, Divorce and
Admiralty Division. It's in the Law Courts in the Strand. It's the
most important legal place there is, except the House of Lords and
Privy Council.'

'Well, you mustn't be cross with me, darling. I don't know
anything about the law. And what did you say about Admiralty? I
thought yours was a divorce case. Does an admiral try it? I must
say, he'd look rather sweet with his cocked hat.'

'No, it's the Divorce Division, but that's linked up with Admiralty
and Probate for historical reasons. But it won't be an admiral in a
cocked hat. It'll be a judge in a wig and gown. And I'll be in mine
too. I'll tell you how to get there and which Court it's in. Now I
really must fly or I'll be late for Joy. Thank you so much for the
money.'

Joy was all ready for him, looking very pretty indeed. They went
to a Soho restuarant.

'This is going to be a lovely evening,' said Joy on the way. 'I'm
so proud of you, Roger. I know you're going to do terribly well.
Uncle Alfred's very impressed too. He says there's an awful shortage
of young men at the Bar and you're just what he's looking for. You
mustn't say I told you, but if you do this case all right, he's going
to send you a lot more.'

'Oh—Joy, it sounds too good to be true.'

'I gave him such a nice kiss for it. Right in the middle of his forehead. Funny, that's where he likes it. It's not my idea. But then an uncle's different. Oh, here we are. It's going to be a lovely evening, Roger.'

She squeezed his arm.

'Two, sir?' said the waiter. 'Over here, sir, if you please. Will this suit you, sir? Thank you, sir. And what about a little aperitif before dinner? Dry Martini, glass of sherry, anything you like, sir?'

'Do you think I should, Joy? I shall want a clear head in the morning.'

'Of course, silly. It won't hurt you at all. Buck you up. Stop you feeling nervous. I'll have a Dry Martini, please. You do the same, Roger. It'll be good for you.'

So they each had a Dry Martini and with their dinner they had a bottle of wine and by the middle of dinner, Roger, egged on by Joy, could see himself persuading judges, convincing juries and generally making a big name for himself at the Bar.

'Then you'll become a Q.C., Roger. I'm sure you'll be the youngest ever.'

'D'you really think so?'

'Of course I do. But then I expect you'll forget all about little me.'

'How can you say such a thing? It'll all be due to you really.'

'Then you won't drop me like an old sock when you're successful?'

'I'm not like that, Joy.'

'No, Roger, but you'll have so many people around you. I'm not very big, Roger. Sally's much taller.'

'Don't let's talk about Sally.'

Even older men can imagine a lot and forget a lot under the influence of a few drinks. At twenty-one all sorts of things can happen. To Roger, Joy seemed prettier than she'd ever been, really lovely, so that when she eventually said softly, looking down at her coffee:

'Roger, will you be a little loving to me tonight?' he was able to answer without any effort:

'Joy, darling, you know I will.'

'Roger, darling.'

Everything felt strangely unreal to Roger and it was very pleasant. He was going to be a great man and he had the prettiest girl in the

world opposite him. Life was very good, very good indeed. Then
he thought of his case in the morning. Perhaps it would be reported
in the papers. Oh, no, of course it couldn't be, except for the judge's
judgment. Thinking of the case he suddenly thought of his client,
Mrs Newent. It gave him a slightly unpleasant shock but, when he
mentioned her, Joy helped him by saying:

'But in a great career you're bound to come across nasty people.
Someone had to defend Crippen, didn't they?'

'Of course. How silly of me.'

They got up from the table. Roger felt slightly wobbly on his feet.
Suddenly he thought of his client again. 'Faint and dizzy.' Well, he
didn't feel faint or dizzy, but he did feel as though everything was
very easy to do. A lack of restraint, that's what it was. Had he
misjudged Mrs Newent? Perhaps she wasn't used to drink and it
had done something to her. He could understand stand it now. He
had never really wanted to kiss Joy before. But when she put herself
in his arms in the taxi, there was no difficulty about it at all.

'Darling, you're wonderful,' he said.

'Roger, I love you.'

'I love you, Joy.'

'Oh, Roger, I'm so happy.'

CHAPTER 10

The Divorce Court

The next morning Roger woke with a slight headache. There was a ring on the telephone. He got out of bed and answered it. It was Sally.

'Just to wish you good luck, Roger. I shall be there, but you needn't take any notice of me.'

'Oh, thank you, Sally. Thank you very much for ringing.'

He went back to bed for a few minutes. What had he said to Joy the night before? What hadn't he said? Oh, dear, how difficult it all was. And they'd both be there. Well, he mustn't think of that now. He must concentrate on his case. He had found out that you don't normally address the judge in an undefended divorce case before calling your evidence. Henry had told him and he'd been to hear some cases, as Sally had suggested. They certainly sounded simple enough.

He got to chambers early and found Henry there already.

'Who are you in front of?' Henry asked.

'Judge Crane.'

'Oh, that's good. You'll be all right in front of him. Bit of luck for you you're not before Judge Ryman. He's sitting to-day. He can be very difficult. He actually tries all his cases. It can be very awkward. Personally, I think he's right, but I'm in a decided minority. I think it's for Parliament to change the law if people want divorce made easier. But very few people agree with me. I expect I'm wrong, but there it is. Glad you're not in front of Ryman. That would have been a bit tough for your first case.'

At ten minutes past ten Roger, feeling rather self-conscious, walked across the Strand carrying his blue bag. He was on the way to the robing-room. At the entrance to the Law Courts he met his mother.

'Not late, you see, darling,' she said. 'Can you tell me where I go?'

'Would you mind very much asking an attendant? I've got to go and robe and I don't want to be late. We're sixth in the list, but you can never tell. Some of the people in the first five cases might not be there.'

He felt a little like he did in his first days at a public school when he was terrified his mother would call him by his Christian name.

He robed and went to the Court. He found Mrs Newent outside. She did not at first recognize him in his wig. She had recovered from her fit of anger in chambers and, feeling a little nervous herself, wanted someone to be nice to her.

'You look sweet,' she said.

Roger blushed and coughed.

'I don't think we'll have to wait very long,' he said.

'It's going to be all right, isn't it?' said Mrs Newent.

'Oh yes, I think so,' said Roger with reasonable confidence. Now that it was so near to the beginning of the battle, he was glad to think that Judge Crane was an easy judge. How nice of Henry to tell him. What a good chap he was. It made all the difference. He did in fact feel a little weak at the knees. He walked into the Court and at once saw Joy sitting at one end and Sally at the other. They were both attractively dressed. He tried not to let them see he had noticed them. His mother was sitting in the middle of a row. Counsel's row was almost full, but he was just able to get a seat at the end. A few minutes later the judge came in. The associate got up and called:

'Foster against Foster,' and then handed the papers in the case to the judge. Counsel got up and the case began.

'May it please your Lordship, this is a husband's petition on the grounds of desertion. Mr Foster, please.'

A man went into the witness box and took the oath. The following dialogue took place:

COUNSEL: 'Is your full name Ernest Edward Foster?'
THE WITNESS: 'Yes.'
COUNSEL: 'Where do you now live, Mr Foster?'
THE WITNESS: 'Apple Tree Lodge, Buckley, Essex.'
COUNSEL: 'And were you married on the 14th day of June 1930

to Elizabeth Foster, whose maiden name was Hadlow at the Register Office for the District of Bilcombe in the County of Surrey?'

THE WITNESS: 'Yes.'

COUNSEL: 'And there are no children of the marriage?'

THE WITNESS: 'No.'

COUNSEL: 'And after the marriage did you live at various places with your wife and finally at Apple Tree Lodge where you now are?'

THE WITNESS: 'Yes.'

COUNSEL: 'Now I think your marriage was quite happy at first, but after that did relations between you and your wife become strained?'

THE WITNESS: 'Yes.'

COUNSEL: 'And were there disagreements and quarrels and so forth?'

THE WITNESS: 'Yes.'

COUNSEL: 'And finally on the 14th June 1946 did she leave you?'

THE WITNESS: 'Yes.'

COUNSEL: 'Did she say anything before she left?'

THE WITNESS: 'No.'

COUNSEL: 'Nothing at all?'

THE WITNESS: 'No.'

COUNSEL: 'Didn't she say anything about never coming back to you again?'

JUDGE CRANE: 'I think that's a little leading, Mr Fox.'

COUNSEL: 'I'm sorry, my Lord. Did she or did she not say anything about not coming back to you again?'

THE WITNESS: 'She did.'

COUNSEL: 'What did she say?'

THE WITNESS: 'That she wouldn't come back.'

COUNSEL: 'And has she ever come back?'

THE WITNESS: 'No.'

COUNSEL: 'Now, will you look at these two letters. There are copies for my Lord. (*Letters handed to Witness.*) Are those letters in your wife's handwriting?'

THE WITNESS: 'Yes.'

COUNSEL: 'Your Lordship will see that in them she repeats that she will never come back to the petitioner again.'

JUDGE CRANE: 'Yes, I see.'

COUNSEL: 'Now may he see the acknowledgement of service?

(*Document handed to the Witness.*) Do you see a signature you recognize at the bottom of that document?'

THE WITNESS: 'Yes.'

COUNSEL: 'Whose is it?'

THE WITNESS: 'My wife's.'

COUNSEL: 'Thank you, Mr Foster. My Lord, if your Lordship is satisfied on the evidence I ask for a decree nisi.'

JUDGE CRANE: 'Very well, Mr Fox. Decreee nisi.'

The next case was called. The dialogue was very much the same, except that that case was, like Roger's, a discretion case. The petitioner was a man and, in addition to evidence very similar to that which had been given in the last case, the following passage occurred:

COUNSEL: 'May the witness see his discretion statement? (*The document is shown to the Witness.*) Now, Mr Brown, do you see a signature at the bottom of that document which you recognize?'

THE WITNESS: 'Yes.'

COUNSEL: 'Whose is it?'

THE WITNESS: 'Mine.'

COUNSEL: 'Before you signed that document, did you read it through carefully?'

THE WITNESS: 'I did.'

COUNSEL: 'Are the contents true?'

THE WITNESS: 'They are.'

COUNSEL: 'And have you committed adultery with anyone else or on any other occasions than are mentioned in that statement?'

THE WITNESS: 'No.'

COUNSEL: 'Thank you, Mr Brown. My Lord, upon that evidence, I respectfully submit that this is a case in which your Lordship can properly exercise your discretion in favour of the petitioner and if your Lordship is satisfied, I ask you to do so and to pronounce a decree nisi.'

JUDGE CRANE: 'Very well. I exercise my discretion in favour of the petitioner and grant a decree nisi.'

It was all very short, thought Roger. He would like, if he could, to make rather more of his case, if possible. He didn't want trouble, but this was, if anything, too easy. Mrs Newent, on the other hand, was very satisfied. This, she told herself, was exactly and precisely what the doctor had ordered. Her confidence now almost completely restored, she began to wonder where she and Mr Storrington should go and have a celebration that night. Just at that moment another associate came in and spoke to his colleague sitting below Judge Crane.

The latter, after a whispered conversation with him, stood up and spoke to the judge in an undertone. Then he announced:

'The following cases will be taken before His Honour Judge Rayman in Probate Divorce and Admiralty Court 4. Will the parties and their witnesses please proceed to that Court at once. Speed and Speed, Newent and Newent, Laver and Laver.'

As Roger got up to go counsel next to him said:

'Bad luck, old boy. Glad it isn't me.'

Roger felt his inside leave him for the floor. Why had he said to himself that he'd like to make a little more of his case? This was fate's revenge. He wondered what Ryman was like. Oh, well, there was nothing for it. And anyway he would see him try one case first, that was something. Fortunately Mrs Newent was quite unaware that there had been any change in her fortunes. She assumed that much the same happened in every Court. Roger started on his way to Court 4, with the managing clerk from her solicitors, and followed by Mrs Newent, his mother, Joy and Sally, who walked along together.

'So glad you could come,' said Joy.

'I'd have hated to disappoint you,' said Sally.

Roger went into the Court where Judge Ryman was sitting. After a short delay the associate called:

'Speed against Speed.'

Counsel next to Roger stood up and put his client, a woman, into the witness box. Roger looked at the judge. He noticed nothing particularly forbidding about his appearance and was grateful for that. Mrs Speed was petitioning for a divorce on the ground of cruelty. After counsel had asked the preliminary questions about the marriage, he started to ask about the history of the married life.

'Did he ever hit you?' he asked.

'Really,' said the judge, 'the Court of Appeal and the learned President have said more than once that leading questions should not be asked. This is a petition on the ground of cruelty. Please don't lead on any essential matters.'

'If your Lordship pleases. Well, Mrs Speed, did he or did he not hit you?'

'Really,' said the judge, 'that's just as bad.'

'With great respect, my Lord,' said counsel, who was a fierce little man with more ferocity than sense or knowledge. 'That was not a leading question. She could have said "yes" or "no." '

'I'm sorry to disagree, Mr Brunt,' said the judge. 'The witness could have answered "yes" or "no" to your first question, but it was none the less leading. So is this one.'

'Well my Lord, I've often asked this kind of question at the Old Bailey without objection.'

'I'm afraid I'm only concerned with this Court, Mr Brunt.'

'My Lord, I wish to be heard on this point.'

'By all means, Mr Brunt, if you think it of any value. You can always go to the Court of Appeal, you know, if you object to my ruling.'

'Think of the expense, my Lord. My client wants a divorce, not a visit to all the Courts in the country.'

'Please behave yourself, Mr Brunt. I can only say that if your client wants a divorce she must give her evidence without the assistance of leading questions. That is particularly the case in a matter such as the present one where, no doubt, the bulk of the evidence will be that of your client herself. I have to make up my mind whether I believe her or not. That's difficult enough anyway in most undefended cases. It's impossible if she only answers "yes" or "no." '

'Very well, my Lord. I have made my protest,' said Mr Brunt.

'Now, Mrs Speed, how often did these assaults take place?'

'Mr Brunt,' said the judge, 'I'm sorry to have to interrupt you again so soon, but that is not only a leading question, it is a double question and a most improper one in view of my ruling. The witness has not yet said that her husband did hit her.'

'Well, madam,' said Mr Brunt in a voice in which he did not conceal the annoyance, 'did he hit you?'

'Really, Mr Brunt,' said the judge. 'There must be a limit to all this.'

'Really, my Lord,' said Mr Brunt angrily. 'Your Lordship told me to ask the question and then your Lordship complains when I do ask. I agree that there must be a limit.'

'Mr Brunt, that was a most improper observation. I must ask you to apologize for it.'

Mr Brunt hesitated, made a quick appreciation, decided he had gone too far, though in his view not without extreme provocation, and said:

'I apologize, my Lord, but it is very difficult to know what questions to ask in front of your Lordship.'

'Well, please try, Mr Brunt,' said the judge. 'Only don't make them leading questions. If you would like me to suggest one, I will.'

'That would be most kind of your Lordship.'

'Perhaps you'd better ask her how her husband treated her after the first few months of married life.'

'Thank you, my Lord, I will.'

Meantime, Roger, who was not altogether able to make up his mind whether Mr Brunt or the judge was in the right, realized that what Henry had said had been only too true. He prayed that he would be able to aboid leading questions. It's very difficult if you don't really know what they are. Roger did not yet appreciate that the context or circumstances in which a question is asked may make it leading and that the question, 'Did he or did he not do so-and-so' may, according to the circumstances, be a grossly leading question or not a leading question at all.

'He treated me like a slave,' said the witness.

'In what way?' asked Mr Brunt.

'In every way.'

'Would you be a little more explicit, please, madam,' said Mr Brunt. 'Enumerate some of the ways.'

'En-enu-enum—?' said the witness, puzzled.

'Give some examples,' paraphrased Mr Brunt.

'It was always happening.'

'What was always happening, Mrs Speed?' asked the judge.

'Him treating me like that, your Honour.'

'Yes, but how did he treat you?' asked the judge.

'Oh, terrible.'

'Yes, but we weren't there, Mrs Speed. You must tell us what he did,' said the judge.

'It was all the time.'

'But what was all the time?' said the judge.

'What he did.'

'But what was it?' said the judge.

'Everything.'

'Tell me one thing he did,' said the judge.

'There were so many.'

'Then it should be easy to tell me one,' said the judge.

'It's a long time ago.'

'Well, Mr Brunt, you must see if you can elicit anything from the witness. I've tried, but with no success, I'm afraid,' said the judge.

'Madam,' said Mr Brunt, 'what did your husband do to you?'

'It was that time at Christmas,' said Mrs Speed.

'What happened at Christmas?' said Mr Brunt.

'No, it was Easter,' said Mrs Speed. 'You've got me all flummoxed.'

'Well, what happened at Easter?' asked Mr Brunt.

'You want me to tell the judge?'

'That's what I've been asking you to do for the last five minutes,' said Mr Brunt.

'I didn't half tell him off,' said Mrs Speed, 'but I don't think he heard me.'

'How long was this case supposed to take?' asked the judge.

'Fifteen minutes, my Lord,' said the associate.

'Well, it's taken nearly that to get this witness's name and address, which is about all we have got so far. Mr Brunt, would you like me to stand the case over to be started afresh another day before another judge? At this rate it will need at least an hour.'

'If your Lordship had let me ask the questions as I wanted to,' said Mr Brunt, 'it might have been over by now.'

'Equally,' said the judge, 'if I'd let you give the evidence. I thought possibly, Mr Brunt, you'd *like* the case to be stood over and heard *de novo* by another judge.'

'Yes,' said Mr Brunt. 'I think perhaps I'll accept your Lordship's kind suggestions.'

The case was accordingly adjourned and Roger, now on the high diving-board, waited for the word to go.

'Newent against Newent,' called the associate.

'May it please your Lordship, this is a wife's petition on the ground of desertion. I should tell your Lordship that it's a discretion case, Mrs Newent, please.'

'Are you putting in the discretion statement now, Mr Thursby?' asked the judge.

Do I or don't I, thought Roger. I don't know. Why hadn't I asked? Here I am, stuck before I started and mother's here and Joy and Sally. Oh, hell, why didn't I watch what they usually do?

The judge noticed the pause and Roger's white wig and said pleasantly: 'That's the usual course, Mr Thursby, unless there's some special reason for not doing so.'

'Very well, my Lord,' said Roger gratefully. 'I'll put it in now.'

'Very well, Mr Thursby, thank you,' said the judge.

That was better. It was good to be called Mr Thursby and now he was on an even keel again.

Mrs Newent was sworn and was asked by Roger the usual preliminary questions.

'And now, Mrs Newent, will you tell his Lordship how your married life went?' asked Roger.

'It was all right at first,' she said, 'but after that he started picking on me, said I paid more attention to my boarders than to him.'

'And did you?' intervened the judge.

'Not more than was necessary, my Lord. There's a lot of work to do running a boarding house.'

'Yes, Mr Thursby?' said the judge.

'And what happened in the end?' asked Roger.

'He left me,' said Mrs Newent.

It seemed very little to ask, thought Roger, but what more is there? Oh, yes, the letters.

'After he left you, did he write to you, or did your write to him?' asked Roger and then added, 'Or not,' in case it was a leading question.

The judge smiled.

'That wouldn't really cure it, Mr Thursby,' he said, 'if it needed a cure, but fortunately it didn't.'

'Thank you, my Lord,' said Roger.

'I wrote to him once or twice,' said Mrs Newent.

'What did you say in your letters?' asked Roger.

'Has notice to produce been given?' asked the judge.

'I don't know, my Lord,' said Roger.

'Well, perhaps you'd ask your client then.'

'Has notice to produce been given?' said Roger.

'Pardon?' said Mrs Newent.

'No, your solicitor client, Mr Thursby,' said the judge.

'I'm sorry, my Lord,' said Roger, suddenly realizing what he'd done. He turned to Mr Smith and asked him if notice to produce had been given.

'Of course. It says so in the brief, doesn't it?' said Mr Smith. He was an experienced managing clerk and did not like what was happening.

'Yes, my Lord,' said Roger.

'Very well,' said the judge. 'You can ask what was in the letters.'

'What was in the letters?' asked Roger.

'I don't really remember,' said Mrs Newent.

'So much for them,' said the judge. 'But what about the letters from the husband? Were there any?'

'Yes, my Lord,' said Roger.

'Well, you can put those to her,' said the judge.

'Did you receive these letter from your husband, Mrs Newent?' asked Roger, and then started to open his mouth to say 'or not' and just checked himself in time. He must remember to ask Henry about leading questions.

'Yes,' said Mrs Newent, 'these are in his handwriting.'

The letters were handed to the judge and he read them.

'Yes, Mr Thursby?'

'Has he returned to you, Mrs Newent?'

'No.'

'Or offered to return?' asked the judge.

'No.'

'Or to make a home for you?'

'No.'

For some reason that he could never make out, Roger then proceeded to sit down, as though the case was over. The judge seemed to realize what had happened and quietly said: 'Discretion, Mr Thursby?'

Roger jumped up, blushing.

'I'm sorry, my Lord. Mrs Newent, would you look at your discretion statement.'

He asked her the necessary questions about the statement, ending with:

'Have you ever committed adultery except as stated in your statement?'

'No,' said Mrs Newent firmly.

'What else, if anything, has taken place between you and the man named in your statement?' asked the judge.

'What else?' repeated Mrs Newent, a little nervously.

The judge nodded.

'Nothing.'

'But you say you are living on affectionate terms in the same house. Has he suggested further acts of adultery to you?'

'No, my Lord.'

'Why not?'

Mrs Newent was totally at a loss to answer the question.

'You're living in the same house and you want to get married. Presumably you're still attracted to one another. You've committed adultery once, so neither of you have any conscientious objection to doing so. I could understand your refusing, but I don't quite understand his not asking you.'

'Oh, I see what you mean, my Lord. Yes, he did ask me.'

'But you refused?'

'Yes.'

'Because you thought it wrong?'

'Yes, my Lord.'

'Thank you, Mrs Newent,' said the judge. 'There's only one other question I want to ask you. How long was it after your admitted act of adultery that your husband left you?'

'About a couple of months, my Lord.'

'Thank you, Mrs Newent,' said the judge.

Suddenly Roger thought he scented danger.

'Are you sure your husband never knew of your adultery, Mrs Newent?' he asked.

'Well,' said the judge, 'that is, I'm afraid, a leading question, but, now it's asked, she'd better answer it.'

'Quite sure,' said Mrs Newent firmly. 'He never knew or suspected a thing.'

'Did you treat your husband in exactly the same way, after your adultery with Mr Storrington, as before?'

'How d'you mean, my Lord, the same way?'

'Well, for instance, you say that you were ashamed the next morning. Your shame might have resulted in your treating your husband rather differently, don't you think?'

'I don't really know, my Lord.'

'You continued to share the same room?'

'The same room, my Lord, but not the same bed. We hadn't for some time.'

'Yes, Mr Thursby,' said the judge. 'Any further questions?'

Roger thought for a moment. He could not think of anything else to ask.

'No, thank you, my Lord,' he said. There was then a pause while Roger made up his mind what to do next. You ask for a decree, don't you, he said to himself. That's it, I think. Or is there anything else first? I'm not sure. Oh, well—

'Upon the evidence, my Lord—'

'Acknowledgment of service, Mr Thursby?'

'I'm sorry, my Lord.'

Of course, he would forget that. That made at least two things he'd forgotten, but thank Heaven the case was almost over. In a moment or so he would be outside the Court. It had been pretty bad, but it could have been worse. The witness identified her husband's signature on the document acknowledging receipt of the petition and then she left the witness box.

'Yes, Mr Thursby?' said the judge.

'Upon that evidence, my Lord, I ask your Lordship to exercise your discretion and grant a decree nisi with costs.'

There, he'd said it and his first case was about to be over. Not much credit winning an undefended case, but still—what was that? What was the judge saying?

'It's not quite as simple as that, Mr Thursby.' What on earth was he talking about? Surely he knew about *Herod and Herod*.

'You see, Mr Thursby,' went on the judge, 'your client committed adultery before her husband left her.'

'Yes, my Lord,' began Roger, with no clear realization of what he was going to say, 'but—but—' very tentatively he started to say, /Her—Herod—'

'But is it quite clear,' went on the judge, 'that *Herod and Herod* applies to a case where adultery is committed *before* the other spouse leaves? It strikes me as a bit odd that a wife who commits adultery should still have the right to the consortium of her husband, provided she's a good enough liar.'

Good Heavens, thought Roger, that's exactly what Sally said.

'How can you desert someone who hasn't the right to be lived with?' went on the judge.

'My Lord,' began Roger, but it was much too difficult. He wanted to say something about *Herod's* case, but had no idea how to put it. As if reading his thoughts, the judge continued:

'I know there's a passage in *Herod* which helps you, but is it more than a dictum? We'd better look at it, hadn't we?'

The judge sent for the case and for some others. After reading

several passages aloud and talking to Roger, who was almost unable
to say anything except, 'Yes, my Lord,' and 'No, my Lord,' the
judge eventually said:

'Well, Mr Thursby, much as I regret it, you have convinced me
that the principle must be the same in each case, although with the
greatest respect to the judges concerned, I cannot think that it is
the law of this country that the adulterous who can lie well enough
is entitled to the consortium of the other spouse, and that it is only
the less efficient liar who loses the right to be lived with.'

Roger was now extremely pleased. The judge had said—quite
untruthfully—that Roger had convinced him. They were words to
be treasured. And so he'd won his case after all. And there *had* been
a struggle, which made victory all the sweeter.

'Then, my Lord,' began Roger, 'I ask—'

'But I'm afraid,' went on the judge, 'that isn't the end of the
matter. *Herod* and all the other cases make it quite plain that it is
for the petitioner to prove that the adultery has not caused the
desertion. That's so, is it not, Mr Thursby?'

'Yes, my Lord.'

'Well—have you proved it?'

'The evidence is, my Lord, that the husband did not know of it.'

'I agree that is the evidence and though I was not much impressed
by your client, I'll assume for the moment that he didn't know. But
is that enough?'

Roger was now completely out of his depth. There was nothing
he could say.

'I don't know whether you're prepared to argue the point to-
day,' said the judge. 'If not, I'll give you an adjournment to enable
you to do so on a later occasion.'

'That's very good of your Lordship,' said Roger, having no idea
what the point was.

'The point is, Mr Thursby. I know that you can show me cases
where it has been said on high authority that, if a husband and
wife does not know of or suspect the other's adultery, that adultery
cannot be said to have caused the desertion. But, with the greatest
respect to the learned judges who have said this, is it correct? There
are many things which a husband or wife who has been unfaithful
may do or refrain from doing as a result of being unfaithful, and
any one or more of those acts or omissions may cause the other
spouse to leave. In such a case surely the petitioner would not have

proved that the adultery had not caused the desertion, even though it was not known or suspected. Now, Mr Thursby, d'you think you're in a position to argue that point to-day?'

Whether I shall ever be, thought Roger, is most uncertain, but one thing is quite certain, I can't do it now. I must get help.

'I should be most grateful for an adjournment, my Lord,' he said.

'You shall have it,' said the judge. 'It isn't at all an easy point. Adjourned for fourteen days if that's convenient for you and many thanks for your help to-day.'

CHAPTER 11

Post Mortem

The judge went on with the next case and Roger, very hot and very red in the face, gathered up his papers and went out of the Court. There he was joined by Mrs Newent.

'What's all that in aid of?' she asked. 'Why haven't I got my divorce? What's happened?'

'It's a little difficult to explain,' said Roger.

'There's nothing difficult about it at all,' said Mrs Newent. 'It's what comes of having schoolboys to do one's case for one. I ought to have known from the start. How old are you, anyway?'

The humiliation was so great that Roger could have burst into tears. He felt like throwing his brief at Mrs Newent, running to the Embankment and jumping into the Thames. What was the good of anything? He wished the earth would swallow him up.

'Well, how old are you?' persisted Mrs Newent. Even at that stage of his misery Roger remembered for an instant the image he had built up of Mrs Newent before he met her, the poor girl abandoned by her callous husband. Now he was all on the side of Mr Newent. He wondered how he had stood her for as long as he had.

'Lost your voice?' said Mrs Newent. 'Not very much to lose anyway,' she added.

This at last spurred Roger into action.

'If you're not satisfied with the way I am doing your case, madam,' he said, with as much dignity as red-faced twenty-one could muster, 'you can ask your solicitor to instruct someone else to continue it. I do not propose to stand here listening to your abuse. Good morning.'

He left Mrs Newent with Mr Smith and went hurriedly to the robing-room. He still felt it was the end of the world. But, as he went, he went over in his mind the way the case had gone before

Judge Ryman. What had he done wrong? Well, he had made mistakes once or twice, but they wouldn't have made any difference, surely? He had persuaded the judge that *Herod and Herod* applied— well, if he hadn't persuaded him, he'd at any rate mentioned *Herod* and the judge had gone into the matter. The judge had decided the first point of law in his favour. How on earth could he have imagined the second point would arise? Would anyone else have thought of it? Besides, the judge had thanked him for his help. He knew quite well he hadn't given any help, but the judge must think well of him to say it. But then the word 'schoolboys' started ringing in his ears again and he again had an urge to jump into the Thames.

'Warm, isn't it, sir?' said the attendant who helped him off with his gown.

'Yes,' said Roger. 'Very warm. Thank you.'

As he disrobed, he prayed that neither his mother, nor Sally nor Joy would be at the entrance to the Courts when he got out. He wanted to go and lock himself up somewhere out of sight of everyone. So this was the mighty Roger Thursby Esq., Q.C.! Called a schoolboy by his own client! He looked through the window of the door of the robing-room to see if the coast was clear. It seemed to be. So he went out hurriedly and rushed across the Strand in almost as fast a time as Mr Grimes usually put up. He went back to chambers.

'Get on all right, sir?' asked Alec.

'I don't know. It's been adjourned.'

'When to?'

'Fourteen days, I think.'

'Why was that, sir? Witness missing?'

'No—I think he wants some point argued further.'

'I understand, sir,' said Alec, an expression into which Roger rrad a wealth of meaning which was not in fact there. As he started to go into his room, Henry came into the clerks' room.

'Hullo,' he said. 'How did you get on?'

And then before Roger could reply, he went on:

'Like to come and have a chat with me about it?'

Roger gratefully accepted and went into Henry's room, where he told him as best he could what had happened in Court.

'My dear chap,' said Henry, 'I think you did damned well. Much better than I should have done at your age. I shouldn't have been able to open my mouth. Jolly good show. There's nothing to be depressed about. And you seemed to have got on with old Ryman all right. He enjoys an argument. All right, we'll give it him.'

'I shall never be able to argue,' said Roger miserably. 'I've made a mess of it. I'm hopeless.'

'My dear old boy,' said Henry, 'if you could have seen me coming away from my first County Court cases almost sobbing, you wouldn't worry half so much. I used to lose cases which quite definitely ought to have been won. All the way home I used to try to convince myself that there was nothing else that I could have done, but I knew darned well there was. As far as I can see, you did everything you could and you've got an adjournment to get ready for the argument. That's very much better than I did in my first case.'

'I can't think you did worse,' said Roger.

'I did indeed,' said Henry. 'Mark you, it'll happen to you too. Or you'll be extraordinarily lucky if it doesn't. My only point is, it hasn't happened this time. Your case is still on its feet. You can win it yet. Or maybe in the Court of Appeal, if necessary.'

'Me in the Court of Appeal?' said Roger.

'Why not?' said Henry. 'They'll be very nice to you.'

'They'll need to be,' said Roger. 'But what was your first case?'

'Just a simple little accident case. Absolutely plain sailing. One just couldn't lose it. The defendant's driver had turned down a street which had stalls in the road and had then hit one of the stalls, damaged it and some of the stock. After the accident he said he was sorry but he'd misjudged the distance. Said that to a policeman. So there couldn't be any doubt about it. He was prosecuted for careless driving and fined. It was a sitter. The only question was the amount of damages and there I'd got evidence to prove everything up to the hilt. It was given to me because it was reckoned it was a case that couldn't be lost. The only reason the defendants were fighting it was because the insurance company doubted the amount of the damage. And, as I've told you, I could prove every penny of the damages and I did. The judge was quite satisfied about the damages. Oh, yes, it was the perfect case for a beginner. Excellent experience and no one could come to any harm. You couldn't lose it.'

Henry paused for a moment. 'I lost it all right,' he went on. 'I lost that perfect, unanswerable, copybook case. I lost it. The defendant's driver does a man twelve pounds worth of damage and what does the plaintiff get for it? The privilege of paying about twenty pounds costs in addition to bearing the whole of his own loss. And why? Because he briefed *me*. That's why. Simple enough.'

'But how did you come to lose it?'

'You may well ask. I'll tell you. No one actually saw the collision. The plaintiff heard a bang, looked round and saw his stall on the ground with the lorry half over it and half the stock ruined. Counsel for the defendant objected to the evidence of what the defendant's driver said to the policeman on the ground that the driver wasn't the agent of the defendant to make admissions. I didn't know what that meant but the judge said it was quite right and wouldn't allow that bit of evidence to be given. I wasn't so worried because, after all, the lorry had run into the stall, hadn't it? At the end of my case counsel for the defendant got up and calmly submitted that his client had no case to answer. No one had seen the accident, the driver might have had to swerve to avoid a child or a cyclist or anything. It was for the plaintiff to prove that the accident was due to the negligence of the defendant's driver. Well, although it was my first case, I thought I'd done rather well, because I'd brought down a case to quote to the judge if necessary. It was called *Ellor and Selfridge* and in it the Court held that where a motorist knocked somebody down on the pavement that was *prima facie* evidence of negligence as motor cars don't usually go on pavements. It was, therefore, for the motorist to show how he got there.

' "What do you say to that?" said the judge to my opponent.

' "The answer to that it quite simple," was the reply. "In *Ellor and Selfridge* the accident was on the pavement. I agree that lorries do not usually go on pavements, but here the accident was on the roadway. Lorries do go on roadways. It's the only place they do go. After the accident the lorry was still on the roadway. I don't complain about the plaintiff having a stall on the roadway, but he has it there at his risk. If an accident happens to it while it's on the roadway, he's got to prove that the accident was due to someone's fault. The mere fact that the accident happened doesn't prove that. As I said, it might have been due to some emergency."

' "Well, what do you say to that?" said the judge to me. I stammered and stuttered and got very red in the face. I said everything I could think of. I knew that if I could ever get the driver into the witness box I was bound to win because he would have to admit that there wasn't any emergency and that all that had

happened was that he'd misjudged the distance. The thought that
the defendant was going to get away with it was horrible. I did not
become hysterical, but I felt like it. I said the same thing over and
over again. The one thing I did *not* say was that if a lorry runs into
a stationary stall on the highway, such an accident is normally
caused by the fault of the lorry driver and it is therefore for him to
explain how the accident happened, just as much as if the accident
had happened on the pavement. The same would apply to an empty
car which was standing stationary in broad daylight in the street.
If it's run into it's obviously for the person who runs into it to
explain how it happened. But I didn't say any of this, or think of
it, till I was half-way back to the Temple, I just talked nonsense
until suddenly the judge said:

'"Yes, I've got your point, Mr Blagrove. Do you want to add
anything?"

'Well, of course, I sat down on that and the judge proceeded to
give judgment against me.

'"Ask for leave to appeal," said the solicitor's clerk behind me.

'I did as I was told.

'"No," said the judge, "it's a plain case. I'm sorry for the plaintiff, but I can't let my judgment be blinded by sympathy. Leave to
appeal refused."

'Well, you should have seen the plaintiff outside the Court after
that. He was hopping mad at first. I don't blame him. And then
he said something which I've never forgotten—he said it just as I
was leaving him. He'd calmed down by then.

'"Hadn't you better do a bit more studying, boy, before you do
your next case?" he said.

'He said it in quite a kindly tone. That made it worse "I can't
think," he went on, "the law's such as ass as all that." Well, of
course, it isn't, but I was. And when I suddenly realized in the
train on the way home what I ought to have said, I felt like jumping
out on the line, I can tell you. Then, of course, I started to explain
to myself that it wouldn't have made any difference. One always
ends up that way, but I knew it would really.'

'I must say, it's a relief to hear that,' said Roger, and he then
told Henry what Mrs Newent had said.

'Of course, it is pretty dreadful for her to be represented by me,'
he went on, 'when one comes to think of it. And I do look so young,
too.'

'Well, you know my views on that,' said Henry. 'I don't think anyone should be allowed to address a Court until he's read for a year in chambers. But that isn't the case. And I'm quite sure you did as well as anyone with a first brief could have done. And you can still win, you know.'

'You've cheered me up no end,' said Roger. 'I suppose everyone feels like this to begin with.'

'Of course they do. We'll look up the point together if you like. I've nothing to do. Let's go and have lunch and then go to the Bar Library.'

Roger felt much better at the end of the day, but on the way home he wondered what his mother and Joy and Sally had thought of him. He found a note from Sally when he got home.

Well done, it said. *Can I come and see you?*

She ought to have been doing the case, thought Roger. She'd have told Mrs Newent a thing or two if she'd spoken to her like that. But then Mrs Newent wouldn't have spoken to her like that. There wouldn't have been any need to.

'You were simply perfect,' said his mother. 'I was so proud of you. You were quite the best-looking in the row.'

'How did you think I got on though?'

'Well, of course, darling, I don't know anything about law, but the judge seemed to do all the talking really. I suppose that's what he's there for.'

'I did say something, Mother, and, if you remember, the judge thanked me in the end.'

'Yes, I thought the judge awfully nice. I really would have liked to ask him to tea.'

'Mother,' said Roger in horror. 'You mustn't do anything of the sort. Promise you won't?'

'Of course, I won't, if you'd rather I didn't. But I would just like to drop him a note to thank him for being so sweet to you.'

Roger was very, very fond of his mother and he would never have cheerfully throttled her, but it was about the last straw. That's all she'd seen. The judge being sweet to him. And the worst of it was that it was no doubt true. The judge had been sweet to him and he looked like a schoolboy. All the good work done by Henry for a moment seemed to have been wasted. He was back where he started.

But then he realized that his mother might write to the judge. So he had to say something.

'Mother,' he said, 'you must promise not to do that either. The case is still going on. It would be most improper. You might get sent to prison and I might get disbarred.'

Just for the moment the idea of getting disbarred didn't seem to bad. He would go abroad and do whatever one does there.

'I was only joking, darling,' said his mother. 'You mustn't take everything so seriously. What a nice woman Mrs Newent seemed. I was so sorry for her.'

'Mrs Newent,' said Roger deliberately, 'is a bitch.'

'Roger!' said his mother. 'If that's the sort of language you are going to be taught at the Bar, I'm not sure that it's a good thing I let you start. Really, you quite took my breath away. It's not at all a nice word to use.'

'It's the only word,' said Roger, 'with which to describe Mrs Newent.'

'I can't think why you say that,' said his mother. 'Of course I didn't hear or understand half of what was said, but as far as I could make out, her husband had run off with one of the boarders. No, don't try and explain it, darling, I hate these legal technicalities and the sordid things that some husbands do. Not like your father, Roger. He was a very fine man. I thought you looked just like his pictures as a boy when I saw you in Court.'

'Thank you, darling,' said Roger. 'I'm so glad you were pleased. Now I must use the phone.'

He telephoned Joy.

'Roger, Roger darling. I was *so* thrilled. You were wonderful. I want to come right round now and kiss you. I'm so pleased. I never dreamed you'd be anything like that. You were quite perfect. And the judge thanking you at the end and everything. I'm so happy for you, I just don't know what to do. You'll have people coming to you to do their cases for them from everywhere. I'm sure Uncle Alfred will be terribly bucked. Oh, Roger—you are so clever. How do you do it?'

Knowing in his heart what the truth of the matter was, Roger did not take as readily to this eulogy as a young man might have been expected to do.

'Thank you very much, Joy. I don't think it was as good as all that, really.'

'Oh, but Roger, it was, it was. And, d'you know, the woman sitting next to me asked if I knew who you were. I said you were one of the most brilliant of the younger men.'

'Oh, you shouldn't have, Joy, really. What did she say?'

'Well, I didn't actually catch what she said. She had to speak awfully quietly, as you know, or we'd have been turned out. But I know she was impressed. Probably she's got a case coming on and she might even bring it to you. She was quite good-looking, Roger— but I shan't be jealous—not after last night.'

Oh, Lord! thought Roger. Last night. She hadn't forgotten. No, she wouldn't. But after all, I must be fair. She did get me the brief—this bloody, bloody brief, he suddenly said to himself. No, I must control myself. I wonder what Uncle Alfred thinks about it all.

At that moment Uncle Alfred, that is, Alfred Merivale, senior partner in Thornton, Merivale & Co., was having a word with his managing clerk, Mr Smith, who had been in Court with Roger.

'Don't make such a fuss, George,' he was saying. 'We'll just take in a leader next time.'

'Who's going to pay for it, sir?'

'Well, you aren't. So why should you worry?'

'Mrs Newent won't. She's livid, sir. Says it's our fault.'

'You are a miserable devil, George. I don't know how I've stood you for so long. Still we've got to have someone with a long face in the office. It's good for funerals and people drawing wills, I suppose. How d'you say the young man did?'

'He was quite hopeless, sir. I've seen some pretty good messes made of cases in the past, but that beat anything. My sympathies were all with the client, I can tell you. If I'd had someone appearing for me like that I think I'd have gone mad.'

'No one is appearing for you, George. And the case isn't over, anyway. Has he got a good presence, d'you think? You can't expect him to *say* anything yet.'

'Really, sir,' said George. 'I do think you ought to study the client a bit more. That case might have been lost to-day.'

'Well, it wasn't, George, it wasn't. I believe you'd have been pleased if it had been. No, I think I did make a slight mistake, but fortunately it's not too late to mend. We ought to have had someone to lead him in the first instance. After all, it was a discretion case and occasionally they go wrong. Yes, I ought to have thought of

that. But it's so seldom, that I'm afraid I took a chance on it. And
no harm's been done, George, no harm at all. On the contrary, I've
learned a lesson. We must give him someone to lead him each time
to begin with.'

'Why on earth d'you want to have him at all, sir?' grumbled
George.

'If a very old great uncle chooses to pander to his very sweet
little neice—at his own expense, George—at his own expense, what
the devil does it matter to you? It won't cost the client a penny
more and the young man will get a nice lot of experience and quite
a few guineas.' He paused for a moment and thought. 'Yes, George,'
he went on, 'you're quite right to be down on me for taking a
chance with this case, but all's well that ends well and only good
has come of it. He's very young at the moment. D'you think we'll
ever be able to send him into Court by himself?'

'He's quite well built,' said George. 'He could carry the books if
the clerk's missing.'

Meantime, Joy was continuing to compliment Roger on his magnificent performance and she went on so long and so ecstatically that
in the end Roger almost began to wonder if he had been so bad
after all.

'I can't manage just now, Joy, dear—but could we meet for a
drink or a walk or something about nine?'

'Where, darling?'

'The Pot-hole?'

'I'll be there, darling. Oh, Roger, I am so happy for you.'

A few minutes later he telephoned Sally.

'Thank you for your note, Sally. It was very sweet of you. Could
I come and see you?'

'Of course. Mother's out at present. Excellent opportunity.'

He went round at once. She opened the door to him.

'Glad you're still in one piece,' she said.

'What d'you mean?' said Roger. He was still under the influence
of Joy's remarks.

'Well, you did have a pretty rough time, didn't you? I thought
you took it very well. I'd have wanted to run away.'

'You think I was rotten, I suppose,' said Roger, a trifle sulkily.

'Oh, Roger, don't be silly. I tell you, I don't know how you stood
there at all. It was dreadful for you. Personally, I don't think it
should be allowed.'

The spell was broken.

'That's what Henry says,' said Roger.

'Who's Henry?'

'Henry Blagrove. A chap in Grimes' chambers. I've told you about him, surely?'

'Oh, that one, the nice one. Yes, you have. Well, I'm glad someone else agrees with me. I shall get quite swollen-headed soon.'

'You mean about what the judge said?'

'I must say I was rather pleased, after our little talk. But really, Roger, I thought you took it splendidly. I thought you were going to break down once, but you didn't.'

'Really, Sally, there is a limit, you know.'

'Be honest, Roger. Didn't you feel like dropping your brief and running for it?'

Roger laughed.

'Why are you always so right, Sally? I've never know anyone like you—not any girl, anyway. Henry's rather like you as a matter of fact—except—except—'

He didn't finish the sentence.

'Except what, Roger?'

'Oh, nothing—forget it.'

'Except that he's kinder, Roger? Was that it?'

Roger said nothing. She was right again.

'But you see, Roger,' said Sally rather sadly, 'Henry doesn't happen to be in love with you.'

'Oh, Sally,' said Roger, 'I wish I knew if I loved you, I really do. Why don't you tell me if I do? You're always right. I'll believe you if you tell me.'

'I don't want to be right this time. Roger,' said Sally.

Neither of them spoke for a time after that. Roger broke the silence with:

'D'you think I'll ever improve, Sally?'

'D'you want to know what I really think?'

'Yes, of course,' he said quickly and then: 'No—I'm not sure if I do.' He thought for a moment. 'Better get it over,' he went on, 'let's have it. I can always sort football coupons.'

'Roger,' said Sally slowly, 'I think you're going to be a great man.'

'Sally, you don't, you don't really?' he said, fantastically excited, and then he suddenly choked. He'd have wept if he'd tried to say another word.

'But,' Sally went on quite calmly, 'there's a long way to go yet and you'll have to work terribly hard. You'll have a lot of disappointments, particularly because you're so young and don't understand anything yet. But you will, you will—and, barring accidents, you'll go to the top. I shall be quite pleased I once knew you.'

'Oh, Sally,' he said and burst into tears.

He went down on his knees and put his head in her lap. She stroked it gently.

'I love you, Sally, I love you. I know I do.'

'You don't Roger, dear, though I love to hear you say it—and I'll always remember that you did—' She stopped for a moment as though deliberately pigeon-holing the memory—then she went on. 'Roger dear, dearest Roger, you don't love anyone at the moment—except Roger.'

They remained for a little while in silence.

'Am I as bad as that?' he asked eventually. 'Just a selfish cad not minding who I hurt?'

'No, of course not,' she said more brightly. 'But you're young and ambitious and you like a good time too. And that's all there is to it. And why shouldn't you be like that? It's perfectly natural. Now, dry your eyes and give me a nice kiss. I won't read anything into it.'

CHAPTER 12

Conference with Mr Merivale

The next day Mr Merivale himself made an appointment to see Roger.

'Good morning, young man,' he said after they had been introduced. 'I'm very grateful to you for all the work you've put into this rather troublesome little case of Newent.'

'Oh, thank you, Mr Merivale. I haven't done much good at present, I'm afraid.'

'Well,' said Mr Merivale, 'he's a difficult judge, she's a difficult client and it's not as simple a matter as I once thought. That's my fault, not yours. Quite frankly, young man, I think it was unfair of me to ask you to take the responsibility.'

'Oh, not at all. It was very good of you to send me the brief. I'm sorry I haven't done better with it. I imagine you'd like to give it to someone else now.'

'By no means,' said Mr Merivale, 'by no matter of means at all. I cannot think what could have put such an idea into your head.' He hesitated a moment and then said: 'You didn't see my clerk after the first hearing, I suppose?'

'No, I'm afraid I left in rather a hurry. Mrs Newent was rather offensive to me.'

'Well, that's all right then—I mean, I suppose she was a bit excited, but she shouldn't have been rude. But that's quite all right now. She quite understands the position and of course she wants you to go on with the case, of course she does. Be a fool if she didn't. I hear from my clerk that you put up a very stout performance— "for the ashes of your fathers and the temples of your gods." '

'I beg your pardon?' said Roger.

'Horatius, my boy. "And how can man die better than facing fearful odds—for the ashes of his fathers, etc., etc." Not that I'm suggesting you died, my boy. Far from it. Put up an excellent performance, excellent. Wish I'd been there to see it myself. I'll come next time, though, I really will.'

'I'm glad Mr Smith was pleased,' said Roger.

'Mr Smith was very pleased indeed,' said Mr Merivale. 'And I may tell you, young man, that Mr Smith is not a man who is easily pleased. Far from it. Far from it. Paticularly where counsel are concerned. No, I had a long talk with Mr Smith about you and I hope that in consequence we're going to see a lot more of you, my boy. We need young men like you these days. Fighters, that's what we want. Like your Mr Grimes, for instance. There are not many of them to-day. And there's a fighter for you. Never knows when he's beaten. D'you know, I've seen that man stand up in the Court of Appeal with the whole Court against him—all three of them—and battle with them for days. Another man would have sat down the first day.'

'And did he win, Mr Merivale?'

'No, my boy, I can't say that he won that particular case. But he went on three days and no one could have done more. Birkenhead himself couldn't have won it. Yes, that's the man for my money—my client's money, that is—a man who'll stand up to it, a man who's not frightened to tell the whole Court they're wrong—courteously, of course. But firmly and definitely and again and again, if necessary, until they almost have to throw him out by force. If a man's a fighter, I'll back him to the end. But they're very difficult to find to-day. Look at Marshall Hall, now, my boy. There was a fighter for you. Hardly knew a scrap of law, but it didn't matter. He'd thunder at the jury until they daren't convict his client. He'd never give up until the verdict had been returned. And, as often as not, it was in his client's favour. Of course, he couldn't win all his cases—no one could. Don't forget that, my boy, when you lose some. But fight, my boy, fight all the time. You don't mind an old man giving you a bit of advice, my boy?'

'I'm most grateful. I think it's very kind of you to take the trouble.'

'Now look,' went on Mr Merivale. 'This case of Newent. Between you and me, it's a tough 'un. It was bad of me not to realize it before. But we all make mistakes. That's how we learn. Now, I want you to do me a favour, my boy, a personal favour.'

'Why, certainly, Mr Merivale, of course I will.'

'It's just this. Newent's a case where in my considered opinion—

my considered opinion, and of course I've been at it now for a good many years—Newent's a case where I think two heads will be better than one. I remember the late Lord Atkin saying that to me in his junior days—we used to brief him, you know—yes, and Mr Scrutton, as he then was—oh, yes, and others too. I flatter myself I've always known how to choose counsel—that's why I was so pleased to hear of you, my boy. I remember Atkin saying: "Merivale," he said, "two of these," and he tapped his head, "are better than one."

' "Mr Atkin" I said, "there aren't two like yours in the world."

' "Well, then," he said, "get a leader with one as like it as you can find." He was a great man, a very great man, but d'you see, he decided in that particular case that two heads were better than one. You'd never have thought it possible that a man with his brain could want help from anyone, but, "this is a case for a leader, Mr Merivale," he said, and so a leader we had. And I'm going to make so bold in this case, young man, although I haven't the head of an Atkin—but just a few more years of experience than you perhaps, eh? I'm going to make so bold as to suggest that we have a leader in this case. Now, sir,' he added, 'now, sir, would you have any serious objection to our taking that course? If you have, say so, and it shan't be done. Mr Smith and I have absolute confidence in you, sir, absolute confidence. Those in fact were Mr Smith's very words. "Would you trust him again in Court, Mr Smith?" I asked. "I would," said Mr Smith, and he added—and mark this—"with something very heavy indeed." One doesn't often get remarks like that out of Mr Smith, I can tell you. And I don't mind adding, I was pleased, my boy, because I hadn't heard you myself. Now, what d'you say, my boy—you've only to say the word and we'll drop the idea altogether—but would you take a very old man's advice and—just as a favour to him—we get conceited, we old men, you know, and we like to think we're always right—would you, just to tickle my vanity—would you agree to our taking in a leader?'

'But, of course, Mr Merivale,' said Roger, who now had visions of a red bag, 'but, of course, I shall be only too pleased. As a matter of fact the judge said it was a difficult point—and now I come to think of it, Lord Atkin himself has said something about the matter.'

'Has he now?' said Mr Merivale. 'Has he indeed? Now that's most interesting. I shall study that with the greatest interest. Well,

I'm delighted to hear you approve of the idea, my boy, delighted. And now all we've got to do is to choose our leader.'

He held up his hand.

'No, my boy, I know what you're going to say. It isn't etiquette for you to suggest a name? I wouldn't dream of infringing the rules, wouldn't dream of it. Just a few words with your clerk and hey presto, I shall think of the name that's escaped me for the moment. Now, my boy, I think that's all I've got to ask you at present, and I'm most grateful to you for seeing me at such short notice. It was most kind.'

'Not at all, Mr Merivale.'

'Well, good-bye, Mr—Mr Thursby—good-bye, and I shall look forward to attending a consultation with you and—and—now what was the name I was trying to think of?' and opening the door he went into the clerk's room. A few minutes late he came back again.

'Forgive my intruding again. I was just wondering'—he coughed and hesitated—'I was just wondering,' he said again. 'I've got a young great niece called Joyce—I believe you've met her—I was just wondering whether you'd care to dine with us next Friday—not a party, you know—quite informal—but Joy happens to be coming and with my daughter, who looks after me, it would make up the numbers. I hope you don't think it's a presumption on my part.'

'Of course not, Mr Merivale. It's most kind of you. I shall love to come. Oh, and I don't know if this is the right thing to say, but would you please thank Mr Smith for the kind remarks he made about me.'

'I shall not forget, my boy, I shall not forget. Mr Smith shall be told.

And Mr Merivale left.

CHAPTER 13

Consultation

'Well, George,' said Mr Merivale when he was back in his office, 'that's settled. The young man took it very well.'

'So should I take it very well,' said George, 'if someone told me I was going to be paid two or three times as much for doing nothing. Who are you going to have?'

'Plaistowe, I think,' said Mr Merivale, 'if he can take it.'

'And what's that going to cost you?'

'I don't know and I don't care. When you're an old man like me, you may find other ways of getting pleasure, though to look at you, George, one would think that you'll be looking for something as unpleasant as possible, but I know what I like and if I can pay for it, why shouldn't I have it?'

'I don't like to see money chucked away, sir. Plaistowe will want at least thirty. That means you'll have to pay that bright young specimen of yours twenty, sir. Really, sir, it goes against the grain to give him anything at all—but twenty really is the limit. Why, we could have got any of the best juniors at the Divorce Bar to do it for fifteen at the most, sir.'

'I sometimes wonder why you trouble to call me "sir," George. It normally is a sign of respect which I find in your case is lamentably lacking. I won't say that's always been so. Forty years ago you used to behave yourself quite well. You were a little frightened of me, I think. But now all you say to yourself is—"the old fool won't be here much longer, doesn't much matter what I do say. Anyway, I'm much too much use to the firm for them to fire me. I'm part of the furniture—which is solid, meant to last, and ugly." '

'I've the greatest respect for you, sir, but I hate to see you making a fool of yourself.'

'Well, I'm not. If I choose to spend fifty pounds or whatever it is on giving my niece a bracelet I can do so without asking you,

can't I? Well, that's all I'm doing. Only she'll like this much more
than a bracelet. Now don't let's have any more nonsense about it.
Fix up a consultation with Plaistowe as soon as we know he can
take it. I should say you'd better not have the client there in the
first instance. He can see her later if he wants to. You'd better
attend it as you saw what happened in Court.'

'I did indeed, sir,' said George. 'I shall have great pleasure in
telling Mr Plaistowe all about it.'

'Now, George, you're to behave yourself. It's not young Thursby's
fault. It's mine, if you like. Well, you've taken it out of me, don't
try to take it out of him too. Come to think of it, I'll come with you
to see fair play. I'm not going to have him bully-ragged. Joy would
be very cross indeed and she'd be fully justified.'

'P'raps you'd like to go by yourself, sir,' said George.

'Now, George, don't sulk. Of course you must be there to put
Plaistowe in the picture. I'm only coming to see that you don't
make it too lurid.'

'As you please, sir,' said George. 'I'm only an unadmitted
managing clerk and I know my place.'

'Whose fault is it you're not a partner? You could have had your
articles years ago.'

'I knew my place then and I know it now. I don't believe in all
this partner business. My job's a managing clerk, I know it and I
can do it, and that's how it's going to stay.'

'By all means, George, but as that's how you want it, don't
grizzle.'

A few days later a consultation was arranged with Plaistowe, a
busy common law silk who did a certain amount of divorce work
and was known to be exceptionally able. His fees were extremely
moderate for a man of his ability and in consequence he was very
much in demand. Before the consultation began Plaistowe asked to
see Roger. They shook hands.

'How are you, my dear chap? I don't think we've met before.
You're in Grimes' chambers, I believe?'

'I'm his pupil, as a matter of fact,' said Roger. 'I've only been
there just over a week.'

'Got away to a flying start, eh? Good for you. I thought I'd just
have a word with you about this before we saw the clients. I gather
the lady's not here to-day. But she's given all her evidence—unless

we want something more out of her—so that's all to the good. I
gather we don't care for her very much.'

'No,' said Roger.

They talked about the case for a short time and then Mr Merivale
and Mr Smith were shown in.

'How are you, Mr Merivale? It's a long time since we met. Not
since I took silk, I believe.'

'Ah, I don't very often come to the Temple nowadays, Mr Plaistowe, but in this case Mr Smith—whom, of course, you know,
particularly wanted me to come. So, as I have to do what I'm told,
here I am and very pleased to see you again.'

Plaistowe shook hands with Mr Smith and they all sat down.

'I gather our clients a bit of a so-and-so,' said Plaistowe. 'D'you
think the judge believed her?' Plaistowe looked first at Roger and
then at Mr Smith. Roger cleared his throat.

'I think probably Mr Smith will know that better than me—with
all his experience.'

Mr Merivale looked at Mr Smith with something of an air of
triumph, which seemed to say, 'Not quite such a fool as you thought,
eh, George?'

'He won't believe her where he can help it, sir,' said Mr Smith.
'But I don't think he's going to down us on that. He doesn't like
the nearness of the adultery to the desertion, and he's not satisfied
that the mere fact that the husband didn't know is enough. Would
you agree with me, sir?' and he turned to Roger.

'It sounded rather like it,' said Roger.

'Well, do we want any more evidence from our client? What
d'you say, Mr Merivale?' asked Plaistowe.

'I think you'd better put that to Mr Smith. I'm really only here
as I've said because he asked me to come. I don't really know much
about it, except that your learned junior has so far done admirably,
as Mr Smith will confirm.'

Plaistowe caught Mr Smith's eye and quickly said:

'I'm quite sure he will. Well, what d'you say, Mr Smith? Is there
any point in trying to get any more out of our client?'

'Quite candidly,' said Mr Smith, 'the less we see of that lady in
the witness box—or indeed anywhere else—the better. He caught
her out in a thumping lie and although he hasn't said anything
about it at the moment, knowing Judge Ryman, I'm pretty sure it's
in safe keeping.'

'Then you think just argue the point of law that there must be desertion if there's no knowledge of the adultery?'

'Yes, sir,' said Mr Smith, 'that's my opinion, but, of course, Mr Thursby here may have different views. From what I gathered during his address to the judge, as far as I was able—'

'Yes, Mr Thursby,' interrupted Mr Merivale, 'and what is your opinion? My recollection is that, when I saw you in chambers, you were of precisely the same opinion as Mr Smith has just expressed, though Mr Smith won't mind my saying that I thought you put it rather better.'

'I wouldn't say that at all,' said Roger, 'but for what it is worth, that is my opinion.'

'I'm glad you confirm Mr Smith's view,' said Mr Merivale. 'It's always satisfactory to the lowly solicitor when counsel agrees with him. Alas, it is not often, I fear.'

'You're too modest,' said Plaistowe. 'I nearly always agree with solicitors—when they're right.'

CHAPTER 14

Sally

Sally's mother lay on a couch with her eyes closed. Sally came into the room but her mother took no apparent notice. Sally sat down and opened a paper and rustled it. Her mother's eyes remained closed. After waiting a few minutes, Sally said quite softly:

'Mother, darling, are you with Brahms?'

There was no answer and the eyes remained closed. So Sally went on reading. After a few minutes Mrs Mannering opened her eyes.

'No, Schubert, darling,' she said. 'What is it you want?'

'Could you bear to be separated for a moment?' asked Sally.

'He turned me out,' said her mother. 'Said he had an appointment with someone or other. I forget the name. No. I remember. George Sand.'

'That was Chopin, Mother.'

'My darling Sally, you must allow me to dream whom I choose. It was George Sand. As a matter of fact he said she was leaving Chopin.'

'Dates, Mother.'

'There are no dates in dreams, darling, not in mine anyway. But you look serious. What is it?'

'D'you think I'd be silly to change my job, Mother?'

'You're in love with that young man, aren't you?' replied her mother.

'Terribly.'

'How will changing your job help?'

'I thought—I thought,' began Sally and for once spoke with less confidence and started to blush as she said it:

'I thought of going into a solicitor's office.'

'I see,' said her mother, and thought for a moment.

'That certainly makes sense.' She paused again. 'But is it any good, Sally? Have you any chance?'

'Oh, Mother, darling, I just don't know. Not at the moment, certainly, not a hope at the moment. But you can't be absolutely sure. And I'd wait for years and years if need be.'

'You'd be very good for him,' said her mother. 'You'd make a nice pair. But he's terribly young, of course. Still, he'll grow. Of course, you're not all that old, though I agree that every one of your twenty-one years is equal to two of his. But that's usually so with girls.'

'I'm sure he's not really fond of Joy,' said Sally. 'She's much prettier than I am, of course, but she's such a little ass, he couldn't be.'

'I don't believe that's a criterion,' said her mother. 'There are lots of sweet little asses in the world, male and female, and highly intelligent people fall in love with them, marry them and live happily with them ever after.'

'I suppose that's right,' said Sally, 'but I'm not really worried about Joy. Except for one thing.'

'What's that?'

'She might buy him.'

'What a horrible thing to say. You can't love a man who'll hand himself over to the highest bidder.'

'He wouldn't know he was doing it. As you say, he's terribly young. He's very impressionable and—and very ambitious. If Joy can get her uncle to feed him with briefs—'

'Sally, this is really becoming unpleasant. You are actually proposing to start an auction. I realized it was something to do with Roger, of course, but I didn't realize you were seriously thinking of going into the market yourself.'

'Well—that's why I wanted to talk to you. Do you really think it's dreadful? If Joy didn't brief him, I wouldn't. But if she does, why shouldn't I? Why should she have such a huge advantage? Why, out of mere gratitude he might feel he had to marry her. That really is dreadful, if you like.'

'And suppose you send him bigger and better briefs than Joy— suppose you outbid her at every turn, two for each of her one, ten guineas where she sends five, the Court of Appeal when she sends him to County Court, the House of Lords when she sends him to the Court of Appeal—'

'Don't, Mother,' said Sally, 'there's no need to make it sound beastlier than it is. All right, it is beastly if you like. But I wouldn't let him marry me out of gratitude. I should know and I wouldn't. He did sort of ask me to marry him once, but I wouldn't say "Yes" then as I know he wasn't sure. I'll only marry him if he really wants me—but oh, Mother darling, I do want him to.'

'You certainly have got it badly, Sally.'

'You let Father accompany you, Mother, and it was torture. Wasn't that bidding for him?'

'You have a point there, Sally. That odious creature Nellie—what was her name? Thank Heaven—I've forgotten it. She used to let him play and she had a voice like an angel. What could I do? I wasn't in her class. But my wrong wouldn't make your wrong right.'

'But you weren't wrong Mother, darling. You were right. Look how happy you were—it can't have been wrong. He'd have been most unhappy with Nellie what's-her-name. You'll admit that, won't you? And you had all those years of happiness together and you produced a most efficient, intelligent, not too bad-looking—and entirely miserable little girl. I'm going to do it, Mother darling. You did and I'm going to. It's sweet of you to make things so clear to me. Now you can go back to Brahms, sorry, Schubert.'

She lifted her mother's legs on to the sofa again.

'Back you go,' she said. ''P'raps he's tired of George Sand by now.'

The same afternoon Sally obtained a secretarial job with Messrs Moodie and Sharpe to start in a fortnight's time when she had completed her period of notice with her employers.

'Have you any experience of legal work, Miss Mannering?' asked Mr Sharpe, the partner who saw her, after she'd given satisfactory proof of her shorthand and typing ability.

'Not really,' said Sally, 'but I've been to the Courts once and I've got a friend who's a barrister.'

'Oh, who's that?'

'Oh, you wouldn't know him. He's only a pupil. Just started. He's with a Mr Grimes.'

'Oh, I know *him* well. We brief him sometimes, as a matter of fact. That's very interesting. And why do you want to come to a solicitor's office?'

'I like the law and, who knows, I might become a solicitor myself in the end, if I were good enough.'

'And then you could send briefs to your friend—Mr—Mr—I don't think you mentioned the name?'

Sally blushed slightly.

'It's Thursby, as a matter of fact,' she said. 'Roger Thursby.'

'You needn't feel embarrassed, Miss Mannering. It's quite a normal thing. I advised a client of mine to send his daughter to be articled to a solicitor. She was going to marry a barrister. A jolly good partnership, I thought, unless they went in for more productive schemes. Even then they can sometimes be combined. Oh—no—you mustn't flatter yourself that you're the first to think of that.'

'Thank you for being so frank, Mr—er—Mr Sharpe.'

'Thank you, Miss Mannering, and would you like to start to-day fortnight? Good. You'll be working for me. My secretary's leaving to get married. No, not a barrister. Oh, by the way, I ought to warn you that I'm on the conveyancing side. I don't do any litigation.'

'I see,' said Sally. 'All the same, I'd like to come, please.'

'Excellent. I think we should suit each other very well. And don't worry too much about the conveyancing. I have a most understanding partner. But he won't send briefs to people who aren't any good. Has an old-fashioned notion about studying the interests of the client. Oh, there is just one other thing. I hope you won't mind or feel offended. It's purely a formality. I'd just like you to meet my wife first.'

'I see,' said Sally.

'It's much better that way,' said Mr Sharpe. 'She'll pass you without a doubt.'

'Indeed,' said Sally.

'She has an almost pathological aversion to blondes. That's all I meant, I assure you.'

CHAPTER 15

Newent *v.* Newent

In due course Mrs Newent's petition came on again for hearing. This time Roger was in a state of the happiest excitement. He was going to sit behind a Q.C. And he had only been called a little over a month. He wouldn't have to open his mouth in Court, but he'd be one of the counsel in the case, he was getting an enormous fee of twenty guineas, nearly three times as much as was marked on his original brief. He even wondered for a moment if he'd get both the seven and the twenty guineas, but he dismissed the thought as unworthy. Since the consultation he had spent many hours looking up authorities and he eventually had delivered a voluminous note to Plaistowe.

'Not at all bad, my dear chap. Difficult to believe you've only just been called.'

'I had a bit of help from a man in my chambers called Blagrove.'

'I see. Henry doing some work for a change. Never mind. Tell him I've marked it Beta plus. That'll shake him.'

Mrs Newent came to the Court to watch. Her anger had been assuaged by Mr Merivale and she was quite pleased at the idea of being represented by a Q.C. That would be something to talk about afterwards, particularly to her friend who'd only had a junior.

At 10.20 Roger was duly installed in Court waiting for his leader to arrive. Suddenly his inside dropped to the ground, just as it had done when the case had been transferred from Judge Crane to Judge Ryman. He had seen Alec and Plaistowe's clerk deep in conversation together. Then to his horror they approached Mr Merivale and asked him to come outside. Roger had by this time seen enough of the Bar to know that even a Q.C. cannot be in two places at once. And if, for example, a case in a higher Court in which Plaistowe happened to be involved had unexpectedly not finished he might have to stay on and finish it. Suddenly Roger

remembered having seen Plaistowe's name in *The Times* a few days
before in a case in the House of Lords. He broke into a sweat. He
was going to have to do it again. He hadn't even thought of the
possibility. He had at any rate seen the cases, but it was hopeless
for him to try and argue with a judge like Ryman. This time neither
Sally nor Joy nor his mother were present, but their absence gave
him no consolation. The Court was crowded and it would be awful;
even if it had been empty it would have been just as bad. He had
been so happy at the thought of sitting back and hearing how the
case should be conducted and now he was going to have to do it
himself—and, of course, he'd lose it. At that moment in his misery
Alec came into Court, reached in front of him, said: 'Excuse me,
sir,' and took away his brief. Fear was now replaced by utter gloom.
They were going to take the brief away from him. Not that he could
blame them, but that's what was going to happen. They'd already
done it. How terribly humiliating! As if he hadn't had enough
already. The fates were being very unkind. What would he say to
Sally and Joy? He'd look such a fool. Oh, well—there was always
sorting football coupons. He was interrupted in these miserable
thoughts by Alec, who replaced the brief in front of him. On it he
saw that what had once been marked as twenty guineas was now
thirty-three. All the conference between the clerks had been about
was an increase in the fee. Plaistowe's clerk thought that fifty
guineas would be more appropriate to the occasion than thirty. So
Roger had to have thirty-three whether he liked it or not. He sang
to himself:

'What was once down-drip is now up-drip'. He could have wept
for joy—and nearly did. A few minutes later Plaistowe arrived and
Roger's happiness was complete.

Then the judge sat and the case was called on. Plaistowe got up.

'May it please your Lordship, this petition in which I now appear
with my learned friend, Mr Thursby—' Those words sounded very
good to Roger. What a pity Sally couldn't have heard them. And
Joy too, of course. After all, it was entirely through her that it had
happened at all. And he'd have liked his mother there, too, though
she wouldn't have appreciated the importance of the occasion. But
he mustn't think of things like that. He must see how Plaistowe
dealt with the case.

'Yes, I remember, Mr Plaistowe. It was adjourned for further
argument. I'm very glad to have your help in the matter, though

this remark is not intended as any disparagement of your learned junior.'

'Thank you, my Lord.'

Plaistowe then went on to recall the facts to the judge's mind and then to argue on the point of law. He quoted every case which had any possible bearing on the matter. He laid particular emphasis on the passages which supported his contentions, and eventually when he could do no more, he sat down.

Judge Ryman arranged the papers in front of him and proceeded to give judgment. Among other things he said this:

'I am bound in this Court to hold contrary to my own belief that it is at present the law of England that a man or woman who commits adultery remains entitled to the comfort and society of the other spouse so long as the adultery is sufficiently well concealed. But although I am bound to hold in this Court that adultery does not automatically prevent desertion, the petitioner must prove that the deserting party would have deserted anyway and that the adultery had nothing whatever to do with it. In my opinion, where the parties are living together, the acts or omissions or words of an adulterous spouse may, without amounting to neglect or miscon-duct, set in motion a train of events which breaks up the marriage. The wife returning from her lover may, as a result of a guilty conscience, say something to her husband or may even look at him in a way which starts an altercation. That altercation may lead to further disagreements and eventually the innocent spouse may leave the other. How can it then be said that just because the deserting spouse did not know of or suspect the adultery, the adultery had nothing to do with the desertion? In a case where the adultery was many years previously and there had been a long history of a happy marriage with children being born thereafter, no doubt it could be said that, when twenty years later the wife left her husband, her desertion had nothing to do with the very remote act of adultery. But conversely when the act of adultery is close to the desertion, I should have thought that it would be very difficult indeed for a petitioner to satisfy a Court that the adultery did not cause the desertion. In the present case the adultery *was* very close to the desertion. It may be that it caused it. I do not say it did. I do not know. And that means that the petitioner has certainly not proved to my satisfaction that her adultery had nothing to do with it. In the result, I hold that desertion had not been proved and the petition must be dismissed.'

Well, thank Heaven, thought Roger, it wasn't my fault this time.

'Well, Mrs Newent,' said Plaistowe outside the Court. 'We shall have to consider whether to advise you to appeal. My personal opinion is that the judge is right, but, on the whole, I think that the Court of Appeal will take a different view.'

'That's all Greek to me,' said Mrs Newent. 'And I didn't understand what the judge was saying either. But I've lost my case, have I?'

'You have at the moment.'

'And I'm still married to that so-and-so?'

'Yes.'

'Well, all I can say is, I wish him joy of it. I've had enough of the law. *He* can try next time. I don't know what all the fuss is about. My friend got her divorce all right. So why shouldn't I? It isn't justice.'

'I'm extremely sorry, Mrs Newent,' began Plaistowe.

'Not half as sorry as I am,' said Mrs Newent. 'Cost me a pretty penny and what have I got for it? Nothing.'

She looked around for a moment as though trying to see whom she could blame. Her eye came to Roger.

'If you ask me,' she went on, 'it's all come about by employing schoolboys to do my case. If I'd had a proper barrister in the first instance this would never have happened.'

'You've no right to talk like that,' said Plaistowe.

'No right, haven't I? It's a free country and I can say what I like. Of course you all stand together. You would. But if you want my opinion you're all a bloody lot of twisters and that's straight.'

'Come along, my dear chap,' said Plaistowe to Roger. 'Good-bye, Mr Merivale, Mr Smith. Let me know if I can be of any further help to you.'

And so ended Roger's first case with a leader. He was secretly glad that Mrs Newent had started to abuse Plaistowe in much the same way as she had abused him, and that Plaistowe's reaction had been similar to his own. He wondered if Plaistowe would send him a red bag. He did not expect one, but it was nice to think of the possibility.

CHAPTER 16

Wrap It Up

It remained a possibility for a time, but not for very long. Plaistowe did in fact consider it but decided that it would be a bad precedent and possibly not very good for Roger, though he thought him a pleasant and potentially able young man.

After the tumult and the shouting about *Newent and Newent* had died down and Roger had told everyone about it, he returned to the normal life of a pupil with Mr Grimes. He looked at untold numbers of briefs. He went regularly into Court, he made notes in Court which sometimes Mr Grimes actually looked at. He turned up points of law in the Bar Library, he started to prepare those technical legal documents called pleadings as an exercise and then looked to see how Mr Grimes did them himself; he went and had coffee at Grooms, he lunched in the Crypt, in counsel's room in the Law Courts and very occasionally in hall. He often went to the 'Bear Garden' and he followed Mr Grimes about as fast as he could and he asked Henry innumerable questions. Sometimes he had that terrible sinking feeling in the stomach when he was in Court with Mr Grimes and saw Alec hovering about waiting to pounce on his master to drag him to some other Court, leaving perhaps Roger to hold the fort while he was away. But this did not actually happen for some months after his first day, though the fear of it was often there. Among other things he frequently went to the hearing of applications to adjourn cases. Mr Grimes often had to make such an application and one day, when it seemed as though he might be held up in the Privy Council and that no one else would be available, Roger was asked by Alec to be prepared to apply to the judge in charge of the non-jury list for a case to be stood out of the list. The application was consented to by the other side, but that did not necessarily mean that it would be granted. If cases about to come on for trial could be taken out of the list at will the lists would get into hopeless disorder. Some judges are fairly easy about granting applications which are consented to. Some are not so easy. Some are very difficult, particularly when the reason for the adjournment is simply that the parties are not ready. As usual Roger consulted Henry on the subject.

'Who is the judge?'

'Bingham, I think.'

'That's bad. He's the worst. You must wrap it up.'

'What's that mean?'

'Have you never heard of old Swift?'

'Only by name really. What about him?'

'I'll tell you. He was a judge with an attractive accent all of his own, though with a north country bias and a rather slow way of speaking. He would pronounce "Mister" rather like "Mistah" and "o" rather like "u" in "up". He was a very popular judge, though he was very much master in his own Court. No one could take liberties with Swift. He could be very awkward if he wanted to and he was naughtly sometimes. He could also be very helpful if he wanted to be, particularly to a young man. He had an amusing sense of humour. The story goes that one day Swift was hearing applications for adjournments when a young man called Croft with a very white wig got up and asked leave to mention the case of *Smith* against *Brown*.

' "What is your application, Mistah Cruft" said Swift.

' "It's by consent, my Lord, to take the case out of the list for fourteen days, my Lord."

' "On what grounds, Mistah Cruft?" said Swift.

' "Oh, my Lord, I don't think the parties are quite—"

'Before he could say any more Swift intervened.

' "Wrap it up, Mistah Cruft," he said.

' "I beg your pardon, my Lord?" said young Croft, completely mystified.

' "Wrap it up," repeated Swift.

'Croft just looked miserable—I believe you know the feeling—and thereupon Swift said rather sternly, but with a twinkle in his eye:

' "Sit down, Mistah Cruft, and listen to Mistah Andrew Pain. You have an application, I believe, Mistah Andrew Pain?"

' "Yes, my Lord—in the case of *Hatchett and Bellows* which is No. 1357 in the non-jury list."

' "What is your application?"

' "To stand the case out for a month, my Lord."

' "And the grounds?"

' "Oh, my Lord, the action is for a breach of an oral contract. One of the witnesses to the making of the contract is in Brazil and can't be back for at least three weeks. At the time the case was set down it was not known by anyone that he would have to go there, but unfortunately only recently the witness' aged mother who is staying in Brazil became ill and he had to go to her. Then, my Lord, another reason for the adjournment is that through no fault of the parties or their solicitors some of the documents in the case were burnt. They are vital documents and the solicitors are trying to reach agreement as to what they contained. Then, my Lord, another witness, or I should say a possible witness, has suddenly left his address and we haven't been able to trace him yet. Finally, my Lord, one of the partners in the firm of solicitors instructing me had unfortunately just gone into hospital for appendicitis and the managing clerk who was attending to the matter has gone to another firm."

' "Mistah Cruft," said Swift.

'Pain was still on his feet and his application not yet disposed of, so Croft, who was, of course, sitting down, thought he might have misheard and remained seated.

' "Mistah Cruft," said Swift loudly and sternly.

'Croft rose trembling to his feet.

' "Mistah Cruft, did you hear Mr Andrew Pain's application?"

' "Yes, my Lord."

' "That's what I call wrapping it up," said Swift.'

CHAPTER 17

Criminal Proceedings

Occasionally, though not very often, Mr Grimes appeared in a Criminal Court and Roger, of course, went with him. Peter always went on these occasions because, as he said, that was more in his line. On one such occasion Mr Grimes had a big conspiracy case in which he was prosecuting on behalf of a large company. Such cases always start in the Magistrate's Court and the day before the first hearing Roger mentioned it to Henry.

'I wonder if you'll be before old Meadowes,' said Henry. 'I hope so. He's an amusing old bird sometimes.'

'Come on,' said Roger. 'Let's have it—I can go to the Bar Library when you've told me.'

'Well, Meadowes had an old hand up in front of him who rather liked going to prison in the winter. He had a pretty hard life and he found prison more comfortable in the cold weather. So, regularly every October he'd commit some crime worth six months, do his stretch and come out in the spring. Well, one day this old boy came up in front of Meadowes. He pleaded guilty as usual, said he had nothing to say and waited for the usual six months.

' "Three months imprisonment," said Meadows.

'The old boy thought he must have misheard.

' "What's that?" he said.

' "Three months imprisonment," repeated the clerk.

' "But that's all wrong, your Worship. I always get six months for this."

' "Take him away," said the clerk.

'The old boy clung to the bars of the dock.

' "But please, your Worship, make it six. I always get six for this, straight I do."

'A policeman started to remove him from the dock.

' "Leave me alone, you something something," said the old man. "I have my rights."

' "Now, look," said Meadowes, who thought he had better take a hand, "If you don't behave yourself, I shan't send you to prison at all!" '

At that moment Alec came into the room.

'Mr Grimes would like to see you, sir,' he said to Roger.

'How are ye, my dear fellow,' said Mr Grimes when Roger arrived. 'Now look, my dear fellow, will ye very kindly keep this case in the Magistrate's Court back till I arrive to-morrow. It'll be quite all right, my dear fellow. I've spoken to Brunner who's on the other side and he's agreeable. All ye have to do is to tell the clerk before the magistrate sits, and then wait till I come. If by accident it's called on before I come, just ask the magistrate to keep it back.'

'You will be there, I suppose?' said Roger, who had learned a good deal now by experience.

'Of course I'll be there, my dear fellow, of course, I'll be there. What are ye thinking of? Of course I'll be there. Dear, dear, dear—not be there, who ever heard of such a thing, dear, dear, dear.'

'Suppose it is called on and the magistrate won't keep it back?'

'Just tell him the tale, my dear fellow, just tell him the tale.'

'But what tale?'

'Look, my dear fellow,' said Mr Grimes. 'if ye don't want to do it, ye needn't. I can get Hallfield to do it. But I thought ye might like it, my dear fellow, I thought ye might like it.'

'Oh, I should very much.'

'That's right, my dear fellow, that's the way, that's the way. Ye have seen the papers, have ye?'

'I've looked at them, but not very thoroughly.'

'Well, ye'd better look at them again now, my dear fellow Ye'll find lots of tales to tell from them, my dear fellow. Oh, dear, yes. It's a fine kettle of fish. Taking machinery from under their very noses. I don't know what we're coming to, my dear fellow, I really don't. They'll be stealing houses next and factories. They took half the contents of one in this case. And from under their very noses, under their very noses. I don't know, my dear fellow, but there it is. They will do these things, they will do these things.'

Roger took the papers away. The case was about a large conspiracy to steal. Roger wondered if he'd ever be able to master a brief of that size, though he had more confidence in being able to do so than he had three months previously.

The next day he went to the Magistrate's Court in plenty of time and saw the clerk before the magistrate sat.

'That's a bit awkward,' said the clerk. 'The lists are in a complete mess to-day. He's taking some summonses after the charges but there aren't many of them and they won't last long. Can't you start it?'

'I'd rather not,' said Roger.

'I thought that's how you got experience at the Bar,' said the clerk. 'When I was practising as a solicitor they used to play it on me like blazes. Sometimes I'd get the most awful damn fools appearing for part of the case when I'd briefed someone quite good. But it's jolly good experience for the young chaps who come down. Not such a pleasant experience for the solicitor sometimes, or easy to explain to the client.'

'Yes, it must be difficult, I agree. D'you think you'll be able to keep this case back, though?' asked Roger anxiously. 'I'm sure the solicitor will be furious if I do it. I'm only a pupil, you know.'

'Splendid,' said the clerk. 'I suppose it's the nasty part of my nature coming out. I love to see it happening to other people. Watch the client squirm while you make a mess of it—not that you'd make a mess of it, I'm sure, Mr—Mr—'

'Thursby's my name,' said Roger, 'and I can be guaranteed to make a complete mess of it. So if that's what you want, call the case and you'll have a whale of a time.'

Roger was surprised at his own self-confidence. The clerk laughed.

'Well, that's the first time I've heard counsel talk like that. Good for you, if I may say so, and if you don't mind an older man, albeit a solicitor, saying this—if you stick to that attitude of mind you'll have a darned good chance of getting on. It's these smart alecs and know-alls who come croppers. Good for you. Very glad to have met you. I'll keep the old boy back even if he starts dancing round the room.'

'That's awfully good of you,' said Roger. 'I'm most grateful. Sorry to have done you out of a good laugh though. One day p'raps I'll have a brief of my own and then you'll be able to make up for it.'

It was the first time Roger had been to a magistrate's court and he watched the proceedings with interest. First came the overnight charges, the drunks, the prostitutes, the suspected persons, and so forth.

'Were you drunk and incapable?'

'Yes.'

'Facts, officer.'

Facts stated.

'Anything known?'

'Not for this, your Worship.'

'Anything to say?'

Nothing.

'Ten shillings, please.'

And so on to the next case. The speed at which the magistrate got through his work astounded Roger and, after a morning at his Court, he thought that, if as he supposed, every Court had much the same amount to do, it was a great tribute to the care and ability of London magistrates that so few people complain of their cases not being properly heard. But he wondered what would happen if there were a concerted scheme on the part of the public to plead Not Guilty. It would cause chaos. As it was, most of those charged or summoned pleaded Guilty. It seems a pity- all the same, he thought, that criminal cases have to be tried at such a rate. He had started to work out in his mind what the cost to the country of a few extra magistrates and courts would be, when his attention was distracted from this calculation by the case of Cora. She was a demure-looking person and when she went into the dock she looked modestly down at her feet. The charge was read out and she was asked if she pleaded Guilty or Not Guilty. She started to say 'Guilty' when she looked up and saw who the magistrate was. Metropolitan Courts have at least two magistrates, sometimes sitting alternate days, sometimes in separate Courts on the same day. She had arrived late and thought that someone else would be sitting.

'Oh, no,' she said, 'Not Guilty. Not Guilty at all. I should say not,' and she added under her breath something which the gaoler could hear but the magistrate, who was old and slightly deaf, could not. What she said was: 'Not with you there, you old stinker.'

'What was that?' asked the magistrate.

'I didn't quite catch, your Worship,' said the gaoler, after a slight cough.

'Didn't know it was me, was that it?' asked the magistrate.

'Something like that, your Worship,' coughed the gaoler.

'Oh, I only wanted the sense, thank you,' said the magistrate. 'Very well. Take the oath, officer.'

Roger discovered the reason for the sudden change in Cora's attitude. Most magistrates fine prostitutes forty shillings and that's the end of the matter. They pay this about once a fortnight and the amount is only a trifle out of their considerable earnings. That is the maximum penalty that can be imposed. But there is power under an old Act—some six hundred years old—to call upon them to find sureties for their good behaviour with the alternative of a term of imprisonment. No prostitute can find such sureties, whether she is on her own or run by a man. If she is on her own, she would not normally know any who would stand as surety; if she is controlled by a man, the man who controls her would not mind losing his twenty-five pounds or whatever it was when the condition of the recognizance was broken, as, of course, it would be—but he does not want to advertise his relationship to the girl. In consequence in almost every instance of a prostitute being called upon to find sureties for her good behaviour, she goes to prison instead. Mr Meadowes was wont to adopt this course and, as often as not, prostitutes who were to appear before him simply did not turn up, but came on another day when there was another magistrate. Cora had made a mistake. As soon as she saw it she changed her plea to 'Not Guilty' just in time. Roger wondered whether the police would be able to establish, as they had to, that people who had been solicited by Cora had been annoyed. It could not be altogether an easy task, he thought, as none of the men solicited would be likely to give evidence. In Cora's case the material evidence was as follows:

POLICE OFFICER: 'At the corner of Regent Street I saw the accused approach a man. She smiled at him and said something. He walked away hurriedly. Five minutes later at about the same spot she approached another man. He spoke to her for a minute and then went away. He appeared annoyed. A few minutes later she approached another man. He apparently saw her coming and avoided her. I then arrested the accused. She said, "Take your hands of me, you filthy stinker. Why don't you go after some of the French girls. They drop you too much, I suppose." At the police station she was charged and said: "You're all a lot of stinking so-and-so's." '

THE CLERK (TO CORA): 'Do you want to ask the officer any questions?'

CORA: 'I'll say. That first man you say I spoke to, how d'you know I didn't know him?'

POLICE OFFICER: 'He didn't appear to know you. He walked off hurriedly.'

CORA: 'He may not have liked me.'

MAGISTRATE: 'Next question.'

CORA: 'You say the next man was annoyed, how do you know?'

POLICE OFFICER: 'He seemed annoyed.'

MAGISTRATE: 'How did he show his annoyance?'

POLICE OFFICER: 'He just seemed annoyed, your Worship.'

CORA: 'What at?'

POLICE OFFICER: 'Because you solicited him.'

CORA: 'How do you know that?'

POLICE OFFICER: 'There couldn't have been any other reason.'

CORA: 'I might have asked him for a light.'

POLICE OFFICER: 'He didn't put his hand in his pocket.'

CORA: 'Well, of course, he wouldn't if he didn't have a match, would he? You didn't hear what I said, did you?'

POLICE OFFICER: 'No, but you smiled at him.'

CORA: 'Is that a crime? Don't you smile at anyone?'

MAGISTRATE: 'You needn't answer that question.'

CORA: 'Well, I want him to.'

MAGISTRATE: 'I don't. Next question.'

CORA: 'That's all, your Worship, except that it's all lies what the officer says.'

MAGISTRATE: 'Is what you have said true, officer?'

POLICE OFFICER: 'Yes, your Worship. That's the case, your Worship.'

CLERK (TO CORA): 'Now, do you wish to give evidence on oath or make a statement from where you are?'

CORA: 'I'll stay where I am, thank you. I was just waiting for a girl friend. I didn't speak or look at anyone. The officer may have mistaken me for someone else. That man I was supposed to have spoken to, he spoke to me first. He asked me the time. I suppose he had an appointment and was late. That's why he hurried off. That's all I've got to say.'

The magistrate found the case proved and, on Cora admitting

her previous convictions, which were read out, he ordered her to find two sureties for her good behaviour in the sum of twenty-five pounds each or go to prison for six months.

'It's a stinking shame,' shouted Cora before she was removed from the dock, to which she clung for a short time. 'Why don't you have your stinking name put up outside your stinking Court?'

Roger was rather disturbed by these cases. The Galahad in him became very prominent. Couldn't something be done for these girls? he asked himself. He wished he could help. He couldn't very well offer to be surety himself. For one thing he wasn't worth twenty-five pounds and for another he didn't think it would look well. But he made a mental resolution that if and when he had the power or opportunity, he would do all he could to help these wretched creatures, many of whom are born into the world without a reasonable chance. A morning at such a Court for a kind and thoughtful young man of twenty-one is a very moving experience. And so Roger found it. He must tell Sally.

The charges went on and Roger became even more worried at the speed with which they were disposed of and at the reliance the magistrate seemed to place on the evidence of the police. But after all, he said to himself, he ought to know. He's been there long enough. But how does he know a policeman's telling the truth and that the other chap isn't? I should find it jolly difficult sometimes. And just at that moment the magistrate dismissed a charge.

'Quite right to bring it, officer,' he said, 'but I think there's a doubt. You may go,' he said to the prisoner.

When Roger saw the smile on the prisoner's face as he left the Court he was not at all sure that his first fears were justified. But how difficult it must be to decide so many cases rightly. And so quickly. He decided to speak to Sally about that too. 'The tempo's too fast,' he would say. Her mother would appreciate that.

The charges were finished and the summonses began. They were all petty motoring offences.

'You're charged with leaving your motor car on such and such a day at such and such a place, so as to cause an obstruction. Are you Guilty or Not Guilty?'

'Guilty.'

'How long, officer?'

'One hour, thirty-five minutes.'

'Anything known?'

'Fined ten shillings for obstruction at Marlborough Street Magistrates' Court on 3rd June, 1947.'

'Anything to say?'

'I'm very sorry, but I didn't realize it was as long. There was nowhere else to leave it.'

'I know the difficulties, but they must be overcome or the streets would be impassable. Pay forty shillings, please.'

Then came a few pleas of Not Guilty.

The car hadn't been there as long as the officer said. It hadn't caused any obstruction. Why hadn't the officer taken the number of the other cars there? They were causing more obstruction. Some of the defendants were angry, some pained and some resigned to their fate, but they were all found guilty that day.

One lady who was fined said: 'I'd like you to know that I entirely disagree with your decision.'

'You can appeal, if you wish, madam.'

'I think you twisted what I said. It isn't fair.'

'That will be all, thank you, madam.' He might have been bowing her out of a shop. She tossed her head and left and Roger could imagine her telling all her friends of the grave injustice she had suffered at the hands of Mr Meadowes. The fact remained that she had left her car in a busy street at a busy time of day when her car and any other vehicles which were left were bound to cause an obstruction. The fact also remained that she was fined no more than any of the others. But, of course, it was a grave injustice and the law is most unfair.

The summonses were finished and for once Roger did not feel alarmed as he did normally when the possibility of deputizing for Grimes drew near. The few kind remarks from the clerk made all the difference. Charles had told him of an experience he'd once had at a magistrate's court in the country. He had got to the Court early and he had had a long and pleasant talk with a man whom he believed to the clerk to the justices. This gave Charles tremendous confidence, until the justices came in and he found that his friend was the usher and the clerk himself extremely fierce. Roger had made no such mistake. His friend was definitely the clerk.

'Well,' said Mr Meadowes, 'What are we waiting for?'

The clerk whispered to him: 'Grimes isn't here yet. There's only a youngster holding for him. D'you mind waiting a few minutes? He won't be any time. It's a heavy case.'

'All the more reason for getting on with it. Why can't he call the first witness? He can always be recalled if necessary. I won't let him be bounced. But we'll never get through these lists if we don't get on.'

'I rather told him you'd wait.'

'Well, now you'd better rather tell him I won't,' said Mr Meadowes. 'Cheer up,' he added. 'I shan't eat him, you know.'

'But I rather promised.'

'Well, this'll teach you not to. Never make promises myself. Bad habit. Thundering bad.'

The clerk thought he saw an opening.

'D'you think so, really? We sometimes get some of our clients to make promises and occasionally they keep them. That does a lot of good.'

'Well, you're not doing any,' said Mr Meadowes. 'I'm going to start this case, promises or no promises. Now, will you tell them to get on with it or shall I?'

The clerk looked apologetically at Roger and nodded to the gaoler to bring in the prisoners. There was still no Mr Grimes. His solicitor rushed out to a telephone box.

'Where on earth is Mr Grimes?' he shouted down the mouthpiece.

'The senior's out, sir,' said a voice.

'I don't care where he is. Where's Mr Grimes? The case has been called on.'

'I'm afraid I don't know much about it, sir.'

'Give me patience,' said the solicitor.

At that moment a taxi drew up and out jumped Mr Grimes and Alec. The solicitor could see this from the telephone box and at once replaced the receiver. He rushed up to Grimes who was hurrying into the Court.

'The case has been called on,' he said excitedly.

'That's all right, my dear fellow,' said Mr Grimes. 'Here we are and now we shan't have to wait. So pleased to see ye, so pleased to see ye.'

And Mr Grimes dashed into the Court, panting more from habit than exertion, the distance from the taxi being much too short to put any real strain on the lungs. He slipped into counsel's row, bowed to the magistrate, whispered: 'Thank ye so much, my dear fellow,' to Roger and proceeded to address the magistrate.

'It's very good of your Worship to have waited,' he began.

'I didn't,' said Mr Meadowes. 'Too much to do.'

'If your Worship pleases,' said Mr Grimes and then opened the case to the magistrate. As Roger listened his admiration for Mr Grimes increased. He made everything crystal clear, every detail was in its right place, the story was unfolded efficiently, clearly and with overwhelming conviction. 'Will I ever be able to do it like that?' thought Roger. 'I can't believe it possible.'

As Henry had said, almost every pupil at the Bar thinks that his master does everything perfectly. Just as almost every juryman thinks a judge's summing up is brilliant. The point, of course, is, as Roger later learned, that, seldom having heard anything done professionally before, they have no standard to judge by. Mr Grimes' opening was certainly a perfectly proper, sound opening, but there was nothing spectacular about it and it was child's play to any experienced advocate who had mastered his facts.

The case went on for two hours and was adjourned for a week. It was some time before the hearing was completed, although the magistrate set aside several special days for it, Meantime, the men and women charged with the various crimes alleged had the prosecution hanging over their heads and some of them were in custody. That seemed to Roger rather hard on them if they were not guilty, though having heard what Mr Grimes had said about them, he could not conceive that any of them was innocent or would be acquitted. All the same, he thought, mightn't a few more magistrates and Courts be an advantage? He asked Henry about it.

'It's the Treasurey,' said Henry. 'Of course it's their job to fight every bit of expenditure especially at this time when the country has been crippled by two wars and public expenditure is enormous. Every suggestion of an extra judge or extra magistrate is fought by them tooth and nail. But you mustn't forget they've got other claims on them from every quarter. They have to satisfy the most important. We naturally think the administration of justice is most important. But what about health and education? Are they less? Who's to judge? I can't. But of course, I agree that there ought to be extra magistrates. I shouldn't have thought anyone would have disagreed. But when you say it'll only cost so many thousands of pounds a year, that doesn't mean a thing until you add up all the other thousands of pounds you've got to spend and see where they're all to come from.'

CHAPTER 18

Brief Delivered

'I'd like you to meet Sally,' said Roger to Henry one day.

'I'd love to meet her,' said Henry. 'She sounds out of the ordinary.'

At that moment Alec came in.

'Thornton, Merivale want you to lead Mr Thursby in a bankruptcy matter, sir,' he said to Henry. 'Will that be all right?'

'Who are they?' said Henry. 'Never been to me before that I can remember.'

'They're clients of Mr Thursby, sir.'

'Oh, Uncle Alfred, of course,' said Henry. 'Well, that sounds very nice. Thank you, Alec.'

Alec went out and Henry turned to Roger.

'Is this your doing, old boy?' he asked.

'I know absolutely nothing about it,' he said. 'I'm as surprised as you are.'

'Oh, come now,' said Henry. 'You mustn't be surprised at someone sending me a brief. I do get them occasionally, you know. Even a new client sometimes puts his head in the door.'

'I'm sorry,' said Roger. 'I didn't mean it that way. But it's jolly lucky for me. I'm so glad you can take it. Will I be a nuisance? I know nothing about bankruptcy.'

'You'll learn,' said Henry. 'Particularly if you fail at the Bar. I wonder when it's for. Hope it doesn't clash with Ascot.'

'Are you a racing man, then?'

'Oh, gracious no, but there are such lovely things to be seen at Ascot, some with two legs and some with four, and the whole atmosphere appeals to me. It's the only meeting I go to. Like to come? If you've got any sense, you'll say "no." You stick to your work. You've a hell of a lot to learn. But I'll take you if you want— and Sally too, if you'd like.'

'I think that's most unfair,' said Roger. 'Why did you have to ask me—and Sally? You know I'd love it. I hope the bankruptcy case prevents it. Anyway, what would Grimes say?'

'Grimes? He'd say, "Dear, dear, dear, going to Ascot are we? Going to the races instead of getting on with our work, are we? Dear, dear, dear. Have a good time, my dear fellow, have a good time. Good-bye, bye, bye." '

'Well, I shall consult Sally on the subject,' said Roger.

As he said that, the junior clerk came into the room and said that Roger was wanted on the telephone by a Miss Burnett. He went to the telephone.

'Hullo, Joy,' said Roger.

'Oh, Roger, Uncle Alfred told me he was sending you another brief—and I just wondered if you'd got it.'

'Oh, yes, Joy. I don't know if it's come yet, but I've just this moment heard about it.'

Joy was in her uncle's office at the time and it had all been arranged in her presence so that it was not exactly a coincidence that she telephoned when she did. She believed in striking while the iron was hot and she thought that Roger had a conscience.

'I'm so pleased for you,' said Joy. 'You are doing well. It seems ages since I saw you. I was wondering—' and she paused to give Roger an opportunity to do what any decent man, who'd had a brief from a girl, would do.

'So was I,' said Roger, with as much enthusiasm as he could muster. 'I'd love to take you out one night soon if you're free.'

'Any night, Roger. I'd put anything else off if it clashed.'

At that moment there was a knock on the clerks' door. The junior opened the door and in came Sally. Roger was just saying:

'Well, let me see, how would to-morrow do?' when he noticed her.

Sally had a brief in her hand.

'That would be lovely, Roger. Where and when?'

'Oh,' said Roger most uncomfortably. 'Anywhere at all.'

'Will you call for me, then?'

'Yes, certainly.'

'About seven?'

'Yes.'

'You sound awfully distrait all of a sudden. Is it another client?'

'I'd like to think so,' said Roger.

'How lovely,' said Joy, 'if it is.'

A remark which embarrassed Roger very much indeed.

He managed to finish the conversation with Joy and then turned to find Sally talking to the clerk.

'I've brought these papers down for Mr Blagrove,' she was saying. 'Mr Sharpe would be glad if he could have them back quickly. Hullo, Roger.'

'What on earth are you doing here?'

'My people have just sent a brief down to Mr Blagrove. No one else was available, so they asked me to bring it. Funny, isn't it?'

'I didn't know you did any litigation.'

'Oh, the firm does, but not the partner I work for. But this *is* from him. It's an opinion about a landlord and tenant matter. Mr Sharpe thought he'd like to try your Mr Blagrove. Have *you* had any more briefs lately?'

'I have, as a matter of fact.'

'From the same source?'

Roger blushed. He could not help it. 'Yes, if you want to know, but we oughtn't to chat here. It'll disturb the clerks. Come in and meet Henry.'

'Won't I be taking up too much of your time? Briefs and telephone conversations and things,' she added.

'Henry would love to meet you. Do come in.'

He took her to Henry's room and introduced them.

'I've heard so much about you,' said Sally, 'though you're not quite what I expected. That isn't meant to be rude. On the contrary, as a matter of fact.'

'Well, you're exactly what I expected, and knowing the source of my information, you couldn't ask for more than that, could you?' said Henry.

'I should like to think that,' said Sally. 'So this is where you decide how not to ask leading questions and whether to put the prisoner in the box and if the judge is likely to be prejudiced if you plead the Statute of Limitations?'

'You seem to know an awful lot about it,' said Henry.

'I've been with solicitors for three months. I've brought you a brief.'

'Me—you mean Roger.'

'I don't, my firm's pretty careful who it briefs. I hope I shan't have my neck wrung for suggesting you. It'll be Roger's fault. But he thinks you've the wisdom of a Lord Chief Justice and the power of advocacy of a Carson and he's managed to put it across to me. He doesn't always succeed.'

'Well, I hope it's something I can do. Your neck would be very much on my conscience. I'll certainly give it more than usual attention. Dispatch will oblige, I suppose!'

'Expedition specially requested,' said Sally 'is the form we use in our office when the papers have been overlooked for a week and the client is howling for that opinion we promised him.'

'Well—I've nothing to do—so—oh, yes, I have, though. Roger's getting me all my work.'

'I see,' said Sally. 'How nice. Does he get a commission? Or give one perhaps? Now I must go or I'll be shot. We've a lot to do in my office. Good-bye, so glad to have met you at last. Good-bye, Roger. We must meet some time out of working hours—if you have a spare moment.'

The truth of the matter was that for quite a little time Roger had been neglecting both Joy and Sally. He had been devoting himself almost entirely to work. Now he found it a little disconcerting to be subjected to this two-pronged attack. He saw Sally out and went back to Henry.

'Roger,' said Henry, 'if at any time you should commit yourself irrevocably to Uncle Alfred's niece, would you consider it a breach of good faith if I asked your friend Sally out to dinner?'

CHAPTER 19

The Old Bailey

In due course the conspiracy case came on for trial at the Old Bailey. It was likely to take a fortnight or three weeks and in consequence to interfere a good deal with Mr Grimes' other work. Roger had considerable qualms. He felt sure he would be left to do part of it. Peter, on the other hand, would have been delighted to be left with it. It was his ambition to stand up at the Old Bailey and say something, and he had the doubtful advantage that he would never realize how badly he had said it. He said to Roger that, if Grimeyboy went away in the middle, he thought that, as he was senior to Roger, he ought to have the chance of taking over before him.

'Of course,' said Roger and hoped that was how it would be.

'Since you came here,' said Peter, 'he hardly ever seems to use me. I don't think he likes me somehow.'

I wonder if that is it, thought Roger, or if I really am better.

It was an interesting day for Roger when he went for the first time to the Old Bailey. He was surprised at the smallness of the Courts. But the solemnity was there all right. He tried to visualize the murderers and other criminals who had stood in the dock. This was the Court in which, Henry had told him, five blackmailers had once stood to receive their sentences from the then Lord Chief Justice. The Lord Chief Justice awarded the first man he sentenced eight years penal servitude (as it was then called), the second ten years, the third twelve. It must have been obvious to the fifth man, the ringleader, what the judge was working up to, and slowly and methodically he worked up to it.

'And as this is the worst case of its kind I have ever tried,' he began in sentencing the ringleader, 'the sentence of the Court is that you be kept in penal servitude for life.'

'I'm told,' Henry had said, 'that it was an artistic, though not a pleasant performance.'

This, too, was the Court where the man who was said to have been a sort of Jekyll and Hyde had stood to receive his sentence.

'Counsel has argued eloquently on your behalf,' said the judge, 'that you are really two people, one very good and the other very bad. As to that, all I can say is that both of you must go to prison.'

Roger would have been spared some unnecessary worry if he had known that Mr Grimes had given his personal undertaking to be present the whole time throughout the case, and Alec had charged a fee to compensate for the results of complying with such an undertaking. Mr Grimes was there all the time, and Roger had the advantage of seeing him hold innumerable conferences on other matters with solicitors and managing clerks in the corridors of the Old Bailey. In the middle of a case involving theft of machinery, he discussed among other things a libel action brought by a politician, a claim for damages for being caught up in a sausage machine, an action by a householder against his next-door neighbour for nuisance by barking dogs, a claim for breach of contract on the sale of fertilizers, an action for breach of promise, some bankruptcy proceedings, an appeal to the Privy Council and a host of other things. A temperamental recording machine which decided not to record from time to time would have produced some surprising results if it had been placed by the side of Mr Grimes eating a sandwich on a bench in the Old Bailey, while client after client came and told his tale of woe, received expert advice and went away rejoicing. And Mr Grimes never put a foot wrong. A lesser man might have confused one case with another. But not he. Mr Grimes treated each client as though he were his only client and as though his case were his only case.

'Yes, my dear fellow. Don't ye worry, my dear fellow, that's quite all right. Just write and tell them the tale, my dear fellow. Good-bye, bye, bye.'

'Dear, dear, dear. You don't say, my dear fellow, dear, dear, dear, you don't say. Well, we'll soon put a stop to those goings on. Ye wait, my dear fellow, ye'll see. It'll be quite all right, quite all right. Good-bye, bye, bye.' And so on and so on, punctuated by bites of sandwich. Do this, don't do that, try for this but take that if necessary, apply to the judge, go to the Master, issue a writ, pay into Court, appeal, don't appeal, it's a toss up, my dear fellow, we

can but try; dear, dear, dear, they will do these things, my dear
fellow, they will do these things.

And so back into Court, stomach full of ill-bitten, undigested
sandwich, head, Roger would have thought, full of dogs, sausages
and fertilizers—but not at all. Mr Grimes examined a difficult
witness as though he had been doing nothing else but think about
his evidence. Roger was astonished at the number of watertight
compartments there must be in a busy barrister's mind. But then,
I suppose, he said to himself, it's exactly the same with everyone's
job. I don't imagine a surgeon often takes out the wrong part
because he's confused two cases or that a doctor, visiting a case of
measles, enquires about the big toe, which belongs next door.

The case went on day after day. Roger took voluminous notes,
Peter took a few, and from time to time when he found that his
services were not going to be required, wandered into the other
Courts where something more interesting might be happening.
Once while Peter was away, the judge said:

'Excuse me a moment, Mr Grimes. A prisoner wants a dock
defence.'

'Put up Arthur Green,' said the clerk and Mr Green was brought
up into the dock.

'You may choose whom you wish,' said the judge.

'That one, please, my Lord,' said Mr Green, and pointed to Mr
Grimes.

'I'm afraid Mr Grimes is engaged on a case,' said the judge.

'I thought you said I could choose whom I wish, my Lord,' said
Mr Green. 'I want him.'

'I'm sorry,' said the judge. 'Mr Grimes can't be in two Courts
at once.'

'I don't want him in two Courts at once, my Lord,' said Mr
Green. 'Just in mine.'

'Now, don't waste time,' said the judge. 'You can't have him,
though no doubt Mr Grimes is suitably flattered. Now, choose
someone else.'

'Oh, well, I'll have him,' and Mr Green pointed to counsel
defending the chief conspirator.

'I'm sorry,' said the judge. 'He's engaged too.'

'I thought you said—' began the man.

'I know, I know,' said the judge. 'But you can't have someone
who's engaged on a case.'

'How am I to know who's engaged on a case and who isn't, my Lord? Perhaps you could ask the gentlemen who aren't for hire to cover up their flags, my Lord.'

'Now, don't be impertinent,' said the judge quite genially. 'I'm sorry about this. Perhaps those members of the Bar who are not engaged in the case would be good enough to stand up.'

Three old, three middle-aged and three young men sprang to their feet with alacrity. This was a race in which youth had no advantage over age. Indeed a middle-aged man was first, though he ricked his back in the process. Roger remained seated.

'Get up, my dear fellow,' said Mr Grimes. 'Ye never know. Good experience for ye.'

So Roger got up a little time after the others, just as Mr Green had come to much the same conclusion as the old lag in Henry's story. The apparent reluctance which Roger had to join the race appealed to Mr Green.

'Him, my Lord, please,' said Mr Green, pointing to Roger.

'Mr—Mr—' began the judge, and then made a noise, half grunt, half swallow, three consonants and a couple of vowels. It was a work of art and had been cultivated by him over the years. It really sounded like a name and though no one could say what it was, no one could say what it was not. Whether a name began with a vowel or a consonant or a diphthong, the sound made by the judge was not unlike it, and, as he looked hard at its owner during the process, it never failed.

'Will you undertake this defence, please?' said the judge.

'If your Lordship pleases.'

Roger wondered what was the next move.

'Go and see him,' volunteered his next door neighbour.

'Now?' asked Roger.

'Of course.'

'Where do I see him?'

'In the cells. Bow to the judge and go into the dock and down the stairs. Quick. The old boy's waiting for you.'

Roger looked up and saw that his informant was right. 'Don't disturb yourself unduly,' said the judge. 'This case is going to last for weeks, anyway. What difference does an extra half hour make?'

Roger blushed. 'I'm so sorry, my Lord,' he said.

The judge gave him a friendly smile.

Roger walked into the dock rather self-consciously and went down

the stairs which led from inside it to the cells below. He was shown
to a room in which he could interview Mr Green who was promptly
brought to him.

'Afternoon, sir,' said Mr Green.

'Good afternoon,' said Roger.

'Funny weather for the time of year,' said Mr Green. 'Felt like
thunder this morning.'

'Yes, it did,' said Roger.

'But there,' said Mr Green, 'they will do these things.'

'What!' said Roger.

'He defended me twenty years ago,' said Mr Green. 'I haven't
forgotten. Nearly got me off too. If it hadn't been for the old judge
he would have too. Dear, dear, dear. Now we're starting to look
back. And that won't do. We must look forward, mustn't we? This
your first case?'

'Not quite,' said Roger.

'That's all right,' said Mr Green. 'I'll tell you what to do. It's
easy, dead easy. I'd have done it myself but it looks better to have
a mouthpiece. Can you sing?' he added.

'I don't know quite what that's got to do with it,' said Roger.

'Ah!' said Mr Green knowingly, 'but you haven't been at it as
long as I have. There's a lot of things you don't understand now,
aren't there?'

'Yes,' said Roger. 'I'm afraid there are.'

'Well, now that's agreed—can you sing?'

'No, I can't, as a matter of fact.'

'Never mind,' said Mr Green. 'As long as I know one way or the
other. Can't take any chances. Forewarned is forearmed. Many a
mickle makes a muckle. It's an ill wind and so on and so forth. I'm
not keeping you, I hope?'

'I'm here to defend you,' said Roger. 'My time's your time. My
services, such as they are, are at your disposal.'

'That's a pretty speech,' said Mr Green. 'Can you make lots of
those?'

Roger did not answer.

'All right,' said Mr Green. 'You win. Cut the cackle and come
to the hosses. Now, I'll tell you what we'll do. I've got it all laid
on.'

'But what are you charged with?' asked Roger.

'Oh, that!' said Mr Green scornfully. 'It's almost an insult. But

I suppose it's like everything else these days. Going down. You've only got to deration butter and all the places serve margarine.'

'I don't understand,' said Roger.

'Now, look,' said Mr Green. 'Have you ever seen an indictment before?'

Roger had not and said so. He would have admitted it anyway, but he made the admission a second before he realized that is was a pretty odd system under which a young man who had never seen an indictment could be employed to defend somebody who was charged upon one. Roger had read the charges in Mr Grimes' conspiracy case, but for some reason he had never actually seen the indictment or a copy of it.

'Well, now, look—this is an indictment—or it's supposed to be.'

He produced a typewritten foolscap document. All over it were pencil remarks made by himself.

'I call it an impertinence,' went on Mr Green. 'Do you know that I was once charged on an indictment containing thirty-three counts? Thirty-three. Now that's not bad, eh?'

'What happened?' asked Roger.

'Never mind what happened. That's not the point. But it's treating a chap with respect to bring in thirty-three counts. Shows you're frightened you might miss him here and there. Can't afford to take chances with him. I've had twenty-five, twenty and never less than ten or twelve. Oh, yes, I once had seven. And now look at this—I ask you—is it fair? Is it reasonable? I'm not so young as I was, I'm entitled to a bit of respect, aren't I? One count—one solitary, miserable count. They must think I've come down in the world. It hurts. That's what it does. If you've got a nice lot of counts to deal with, you've got something to fight. But this—this—it takes all the stuffing out of a man. I tell you—I had a good mind to plead Guilty and be done with it. One count! Two can play at that game. If they won't do the right thing, why should I? I've never pleaded Guilty in my life, but I tell you, I came as near doing it this time as I ever did. And then I remembered it was Ascot next week. So that wouldn't do. But if it hadn't been, I tell you—I'd have cut the ground from under their feet. Guilty, I should have said. That would have shaken them. There they are—counsel, solicitors, police, witnesses, judge, jury, ushers, flowers, herbs, spectators—everyone—and I say Guilty. I bet the clerk wouldn't have believed it. What was that? he'd have said. I'd have had a game with him. Not Guilty, I should have said. Oh, I thought you said Guilty, he'd have said. Yes, I'd have said, I did. Well, which is it, he'd have said, Guilty or Not Guilty. You choose, I should have said. I hate these parlour games. One of these days a judge will say—they look at TV all right, oh, yes they do, whatever they say—one of these days a judge will say—will the next prisoner sign in, please?'

'Now, look, Mr Green,' said Roger. 'I know I'm very new to the Bar, but you're paying me to help you. Hadn't you better tell me about the case? I love to hear your views on these other matters, but after all, if you want to go to Ascot next week the case is more important.'

'You'll do well, sir,' said Mr Green. 'You think of essentials. Ascot it is. I've never missed an Ascot yet—except when—well now I'm going back into past history. Dear, dear, dear. Now, let's get down to brass tacks. No beating about the bush. All fair and above board. In for a penny, in for a pound. Who laughs last, laughs loudest. You can't sing, I think you said?'

'Mr Green,' said Roger, 'this is a little difficult to say and please don't think I'm meaning to be offensive, but have you ever thought of pleading—that is—I mean—I hope you'll understand—putting up a defence of—of—insanity?'

'Cheer up,' said Mr Green. 'I always do this to begin with. Don't let it get you down. Helps me find out what sort of a chap you are. Now look. There's only one count against me. There's nothing in it at all. We're as good as out in the road already—only we're not. But don't you worry, we shall be. Now, d'you see what it says here?'

He showed Roger the indictment.

'Obtaining money by false pretences with intent to defraud. Well, it's ridiculous, that's what it is. It's laughable. It won't stick. They'll never wear it. Are you agreed upon your verdict? We are. Do you find the prisoner Arthur Green Guilty or Not Guilty. Not Guilty. Not Guilty, and is that the verdict of you all? It is. And out we go. Shame I couldn't get bail or I wouldn't have been inside at all.'

'Really,' said Roger. 'Times's getting on. You must tell me the facts. Have you a copy of the depositions?'

'That's a fair question. And here's a fair answer. Yes.'

'Can I see them, please?'

'Don't you think they might put you off?'

'Mr Green, if you're not mad and want me to defend you, you must let me see the depositions.'

'At last,' said Mr Green. 'Say it louder next time. I'm not sorry I chose you, but you're making me work. Don't you understand, young man, that at your game you've got to be able to shout down the other side, the judge, the jury and all? And what hope have you got if you can't shout me down? Eh? None at all. It's taken me ten minutes to get you annoyed even. Cone on, get tough, let's see some rough stuff. Tear 'em to pieces.'

'All right,' said Roger. 'P'raps you'd tell me what it's all about in as few words as possible, please.'

'Apart from the "please" that was all right. Good. I'll tell you. It's simple as pie. I'm charged with obtaining money by false pretences. How much money? Twenty pounds. A beggarly twenty pounds. How did I get it? By selling toffee. That's right, toffee. I get the money, they get the toffee. What's wrong with that?'

'Nothing as far as I can see—if they get enough toffee.'

'That's quick of you. Enough toffee. Well, as a matter of fact, they didn't, but they're not charging me with that. Look—you see—all it says is "by falsely pretending that a letter signed G. St Clair Smith was a genuine reference when in fact it was written by the accused himself." That's all, positively all. It's laughable.'

'Well—there is a Mr St Clair Smith then and he wrote it?'

'Be reasonable,' said Mr Green. 'Fair's fair and all that. But how would I get as far as this if there was a Mr Smith—St Clair or not?'

'Then there isn't anyone?'

'No idea. There may be for all I know,' said Mr Green.

'Then who wrote the reference?'

'Who do you think?'

'Well,' said Roger, 'if you ask me to be frank, I think you did.'

'Don't be bashful about it,' said Mr Green. 'Of course I did. Who else could have done—except Mr Smith, of course, and we're not sure about him, are we?'

'Well,' said Roger, 'if you wrote yourself a reference and pretended that it was written by Mr Smith, what's your defence?'

'They had the toffee, of course.'

'But not enough?'

'They don't complain that it wasn't enough here. They just say about the reference.'

'Yes, I see,' said Roger. 'But you had twenty pounds from them, didn't you?'

'Certainly.'

'How much toffee did they get?'

'At least a quarter of what they ordered. More like a third.'

'But you got the full price?'

'That's right.'

'Well, I'm bound to say it sounds pretty fishy to me,' said Roger.

'Of course it does. If it didn't sound fishy, I shouldn't be here, should I? I'll tell you something else. It was fishy. But that doesn't mean it was a crime. Oh, dear, no. It's a postal business I run. Cash with order, I say. Fair enough? And in my first letter I always offer a reference. What's more, I give them a reference whether they want it or not.'

'You mean,' said Roger, 'you write yourself a reference under another name?'

'I mean,' said Mr Green, 'precisely that. But this chap, like most of them, has too sweet a tooth, that's his trouble. He wants his toffee. So he doesn't bother about a reference and just sends his money.'

'Then I can't see why on earth you're charged if that's the only false pretence alleged. They've got to prove they relied on it and if they hadn't had it they couldn't have relied on it.'

'Smart boy,' said Mr Green. 'You saw the point.'

'Yes,' said Roger. 'But you did send a reference.'

'You bet I did,' said Mr Green. 'I always do.'

'And he must have had it before he sent the money,' said Roger, 'or the case wouldn't have gone on like this. You must let me see the depositions.'

'All right,' said Mr Green. 'As you are so pressing,' and he handed them to Roger, who read them for a few minutes.

'Well, it's quite plain from these that he had the reference first,' said Roger. 'I knew he must have done.'

'Well, he didn't,' said Mr Green. 'The quickness of the hand deceives the eye. I can prove he didn't.'

'How?'

'Elementary, my dear—I beg your pardon, sir. I shouldn't have done that. But it is too, too simple. Shall I explain?'

'Please do,' said Roger.

'How d'you catch mice?' said Mr Green.

'Now really—' began Roger.

'With bait,' went on Mr Green. 'I send my little reference on the 24th but I actually date it the 20th. What happens? Complaints are made by the public about my toffee. Not enough of it. Stale, bad, rotten toffee, and so on. Now, for one reason or another I didn't want the police prying into my affairs, looking at my books (if any), and so on and so forth. So, after I've had the money, I send this nice little reference in pretty obviously disguised handwriting. Aha, say they, we've got him. Handwriting experts and all that. His handwriting. And the date? Just before the customer sent the money. We've got him, they say. The customer doesn't want much persuading that he had the reference before he sent the money, particularly when the police point out the date. "You must have done," they say. "So I must," says he. So they don't bother to look into my affairs except quite casually. A false reference is good enough for them. Saves them a lot of trouble. He's in the bag, they say. But, you see, he isn't. That's just where he isn't. Proof of posting isn't proof of delivery, eh? But it's proof of *non*-delivery. I get a receipt for my letter. And here it is. Shows I sent the letter after he sent the money. I tell you he had too sweet a tooth. They all have. Of course, when they come and see me and show me Mr St Clair Smith's letter I pretend I haven't seen it before, but I look nice and uncomfortable when I say it and what with the date on it, my other letter and the handwriting expert, they're happy as sandboys.

' "Did you believe it to be a genuine reference, Mr Sweet Tooth?"

' "I did."

' "If you had not believed it was a genuine reference would you have sent the money?"

' "I would not."

' "Thank you, Mr Sweet Tooth." '

'Are you sure,' said Roger, 'that you only sent one letter to him at about that time?'

'Ah,' said Mr Green. 'I'm not so bad at choosing counsel after all. And you're not such a—now what am I saying? That's the one question you've got to ask. "Did you have any letter from the defendant?" I prefer that to "prisoner," but I don't really mind if you forget—"did you have any letter from the defendant at about the time you received the reference?" Well, he'll have to say "no"— but that's the one point you've got to be careful of. Once you've held him down to that, we're home. Out comes the receipt for posting and I can go and lose all the money I haven't paid you at Ascot. Right?'

'I see the point,' said Roger. 'I must think about it.'

Later that day when Roger returned to the Temple after completing his conference with Mr Green, he consulted Henry on the matter.

'You can never tell,' said Henry. 'If the chap admits that no other letters were sent to him at that time it looks like a winner. But don't you be too sure about getting that admission. And if you get the admission don't go on pressing him about it. That's a mistake beginners often make. They get the admission they need and they're so pleased about it they go on asking questions about it and before they know where they are, if the witness hasn't actually withdrawn the admission, he's what you might call blurred it, by adding words like, "Well, I'm not quite sure" or "perhaps I'm wrong" and "now I come to think of it there may have been another letter." Economy in cross-examination is very necessary.'

'Thanks very much,' said Roger. 'Yes, I see. I am grateful. Now, another thing. It won't arise in this case because I haven't any witnesses except the prisoner. But I always thought counsel wasn't supposed to see witnesses and I saw one or two counsel with a lot of people round them. I didn't hear what they were saying, but I should have thought some of them probably were witnesses.'

'Well,' said Henry, 'a good deal of latitude is allowed to counsel for the defence in criminal cases, but you're quite right in thinking that, generally speaking, counsel shouldn't talk to the witnesses except his own client or expert witnesses. But it's a matter for counsel's discretion, and in an exceptional case he certainly can. But don't you try to pretend to yourself that a case is exceptional when it isn't. We don't want you to get like old Ian McTavish, though I'm sure you won't.'

'Who was he?'

'He was a lovable old man, whom everyone liked, but he was an old rascal. The story goes that his opponent in a fraud case at a County Court found the old boy in the consultation-room surrounded by witnesses, saying:

' "Now then, boys, all together. 'We relied upon the representations.' " '

CHAPTER 20

Dock Brief

Roger had a difficult decision to make the day before the case of Mr Green came on for trial at the Old Bailey. Should he ask Sally, Joy and his mother, or alternatively one or more and which of them? He would dearly have liked his triumph—if it was to be one—witnessed, but on the other hand, suppose things went wrong and he made a fool of himself again? Eventually he decided to ask Sally her opinion.

'Roger,' she said, 'I should love to hear you, I really should. But d'you know, if I were you, I should wait until you've got more confidence. It's always possible the thought of one of us—never mind which—will distract or worry you. Then again—you might actually start to act for our benefit and that would be really bad. I'm doing myself out of a lot in saying this, because I'm sure my Mr Sharpe would let me go if I wanted to.'

'*Your* Mr Sharpe?'

'Roger,' said Sally, 'you're not jealous?'

'Of course not,' said Roger.

'No, I was afraid I must be mistaken.'

'Surely you don't want me to be jealous?'

'Oh, Roger, you are young. Never mind. Forget it. Will you ask Joy to go to the Old Bailey?'

'Of course not,' said Roger. 'I nearly always take your advice. I've never known you wrong yet.'

'Dear Roger, you're so sweet—and unformed.'

'You think I'm an awful ass.'

'I don't think anything of the sort. F. E. Smith was unformed once and all the others. You've lots of time. And d'you know—I think you've come on, even in the last six months.'

'Do you really? You're not just trying to be nice?'

'Have you ever known me? No, I'd really like to come to the Old Bailey to see the difference. I'm sure it'll be considerable.'

'Do come, Sally—I'd love you to be there.'

'Don't tempt me, Roger. It isn't fair. You tell me all about it when it's over.'

That evening Roger had an appointment to dine with Mr Merivale.

'My dear Roger,' said Mr Merivale. 'How very nice to see you. Very good of you to give me the time. You won't be able to go out in the evenings much longer. Nose to the grindstone, my boy. But that's the Bar. Either too much work or too little. How are things going?'

'As a matter of fact,' said Roger, 'I've got a brief at the Old Bailey to-morrow.'

'Dear me,' said Mr Merivale. 'For the prosecution or defence?'

'Defence.'

'Pleading Guilty?'

'Oh, no. I hope to get him off.'

'That's the way, my boy. Be a fighter. Ah, here's Joy. She'll have to give me a report on you. In case we have any big criminal cases.'

'Oh, what's all this?' said Joy.

'I've got a case at the Old Bailey to-morrow.'

'Oh, how lovely,' said Joy.

'And you're going to report it for me,' said Mr Merivale. 'I shall send you both in my car.'

'Oh, uncle—you are sweet,' said Joy and gave him a kiss.

'It's most kind of you,' said Roger, who did not see how he could possibly get out of it.

Roger did not tell his mother about the case. He decided to wait until it was over. It would be more effective and she'd be more likely to listen. On the day before the trial she was particularly difficult.

'Oh dear, oh dear,' she kept on saying. 'I'll forget my own name next.'

Roger was quite used to this sort of thing, but he asked politely:

'What is it, Mother darling?'

'If I knew, my pet, would I be asking? But there's something I've forgotten that I've got to do. And terrible things will happen if I don't do it.'

'What terrible things?'

'My dear, darling Roger, how should I know until they happen? Then it'll be too late. Of course if I could think what it was I had to do, they wouldn't happen. Be an angel and think for me. You know I don't do it very well.'

'I expect you've got to do something for Aunt Ethel.'

'No, I think it's more important than Aunt Ethel.'

'It must be serious then,' said Roger. 'I've got something important to do to-morrow too, but I'll tell you that later.'

'Another examination, Roger darling? Surely not?'

'Now Mother, really! You know I'm qualified. You've seen me in Court.'

'But you could still have examinations. Doctors do. The one who helped me with you said he wanted to be a gynæcologist. I was very flattered.'

The next day Mr Merivale sent Joy in his car to fetch Roger and take them both to the Temple and thence to the Old Bailey.

'Oh, Roger, I'm so excited,' said Joy. 'Now you really are starting. I'm sure no one as young as you has ever had a case at the Old Bailey. Oh, Roger—I do love you—and you do love me, don't you, Roger? It's at times like these when I feel it so terribly.'

She squeezed his hand. He squeezed hers.

'If I don't sound very affectionate, Joy, it's because I'm thinking about the case. A man may go to prison because of me —or be free because of me. It's a dreadful responsibility.'

'I'm so proud of you, Roger,' whispered Joy.

That morning Mr Sharpe sent for Sally.

'Sally,' he said, 'I wonder if you'd do me a small favour?'

'Of course,' said Sally.

'There's a young man I know—or know of, I should say,' he began.

'No, thank you,' said Sally. 'It's very kind of you all the same.'

'Now, how on earth d'you know what I'm going to say? I know a lot of young men—a very large number. I go to a boys' club among other things.'

'I hope none of them are where you're about to suggest I should go.'

Sally had told Mr Sharpe some days previously about Roger's case.

'Well, sorry,' said Mr Sharpe, 'if it can't be *volens*, it'll have to be *nolens volens*. As your study of the law of contract will have told you, an employee is bound to obey all reasonable orders of his or her employer.'

'Very good, sir,' said Sally.

'You will proceed,' said Mr Sharpe, 'to the Old Bailey with all convenient haste. You will there make enquiry as to where a gentleman called Arthur Green is being tried and you will go to that Court, mentioning my name if necessary, in order to get you in—and bring me a complete report of the case. Go along now. You know you're dying to.'

'But it won't be fair,' said Sally. 'I've stopped him taking Joy.'

'Good thing too,' said Mr Sharpe. 'I never did like the sound of that girl. You know the motto. Anyway, you can't help yourself, you're under orders. Get the sack if you don't. Then who'll give you your articles?'

'What was that?' said Sally.

'I said it,' said Mr Sharpe.

'Oh, oh—' said Sally about as excited as Roger had been when she told him he was going to be a great man. 'Oh—oh—I could kiss you.'

'I'm afraid,' said Mr Sharpe, 'that my wife would not approve of that even from a brunette. Pity. I should have liked the experience.'

'You are good. Why are you so nice to me?' said Sally.

'I'm not particularly nice to you. I like people as a whole. As for you—I think you've got more brains for a girl of twenty-one than I've ever heard of. You'll end up President of the Law Society— unless you go and get married or something. And even then—which reminds me—I believe I've just given you a job of work. Off with you. And a full report, mind you—not only the mistakes.'

Before he went to Court Roger had a final word with Henry while Joy stayed in the car.

'It's quite definite, isn't it, that I only get one speech,' Roger said, 'and that's after I've called the prisoner?'

'Quite definite,' said Henry, 'and make it a good one.'

Roger rejoined Joy and they drove to the Old Bailey, almost in silence, Roger becoming more and more nervous, like a runner before a race. They arrived at the Court and he took Joy through the main entrance. He decided to show her into Court before he robed. Ordinary spectators are supposed to go to the public gallery, but members of the legal profession can usually obtain admission for their friends to the body of the Court, unless the event is a very popular one. But the attendant at the entrance to the Court checks and sometimes stops the people who enter or try to do so.

'What do you want?' he asked politely but suspiciously of Roger.

'I'm Counsel,' said Roger with as much assurance as he could manage.

'Oh,' said the man, plainly taken aback. 'I'm sorry, sir. I didn't—' He didn't finish the sentence.

Roger showed Joy in and then went up to the robing-room. When he came back to the Court it was twenty past ten. His case was first in the list. Nearly zero hour. As he came into the Court a police officer came up to him.

'Are you Mr Thursby by any chance?' he asked.

Roger said he was.

'Your client wants to see you at once, sir,' he said.

He went hurriedly into the dock and down the stairs, wondering what it could be. Had he been more experienced he would not have been in the least surprised. Later he found out that old offenders, particularly those charged with fraud, often ask to see their counsel before and during the case and send them voluminous notes throughout the hearing. They are usually irrelevant and nearly always repetitive.

'Good morning,' said Mr Green. 'I hope you slept well.'

'What is it?' said Roger. 'There's only a few minutes before the case starts.'

'Now, don't get fidgety,' said Mr Green. 'When you've done this as often as I have you'll be quite calm and steady. Look at me. My teeth aren't chattering, are they?'

'No.'

'I'm not shaking like a leaf, am I?'

'No,' said Roger, irritable with nervousness.

'Now would you not say that I was in very good shape?' asked Mr Green.

'What has this got to do with it?' said Roger. 'I thought you wanted to see me about the case.'

'Look,' said Mr Green, 'you're my counsel aren't you?'

'Yes.'

'Well, I can ask my counsel questions, can't I?'

'Yes.'

'Well, I'm asking one. Would you consider that I was in very good shape? It's important, you know. If you thought I wasn't, You might want an adjournment. It's I who've got to go in the witness box and lie like a trooper, not you.'

'But you're not going to commit perjury?' said Roger, anxiously.

'Just a manner of speaking,' said Mr Green. 'I shall tell them much more truth than I gave them toffee. Now, how am I? Is my tie straight?'

'Really!' said Roger, and then said very seriously: 'You will tell the truth, won't you?'

'What d'you take me for?' said Mr Green. 'Anyone would think I was a crook. You'll hurt my feelings if you're not careful. And then where shall we be? Now, what about the tie? Does it cover the stud all right?'

'This is ridiculous,' said Roger.

'Come, come, sir,' said Mr Green. 'I'm playing the leading part in this show. You may think you are till it comes to going to gaol. Then you'll cheerfully yield pride of place to me. True, isn't it? You wouldn't go to gaol instead of me, would you?'

'No,' said Roger.

'Right, then, I'm the leading actor, and you don't send him on to the stage looking anyhow. He has a dresser, doesn't he? Couldn't afford one as well as you. So I thought you wouldn't mind giving me the once-over. Hair all right?'

'Quite,' said Roger. That was easy. There was none.

'Trouser creases all right?'

'Very good.'

'Pity I haven't got that gold tooth. I flogged it during my last stretch. Got some jam for it. D'you like jam?'

'I'm going back into Court,' said Roger, 'or I shan't be there when the judge comes in.'

'Don't be cross,' said Mr Green. 'You'll never do any good if you're cross. Give me a nice smile. Come on. That's better. Now take it easy. It's going to be perfectly all right. Next time I see you it won't be here. Won't be at Ascot, I'm afraid. Can't get into the Royal Enclosure any more. Even Mr St Clair Smith couldn't get me in.'

At that moment a warder came into the room.

'The judge is just going to sit, sir,' he said.

'Good luck,' said Mr Green. 'Chin up, head high, no heel taps, all's fair in love and war, dark the dawn when day is nigh, faint heart never won—oh—he's gone.' He turned to the warder:

'I almost threw that one back,' he said, 'but you should have seen the one that got away.'

Roger only just had time to get into the Court before the knocks heralding the arrival of the judge. The judge took his seat, and Roger, having bowed low, sat down and looked across at the jury who were to try Mr Green. As he did so two ladies came into Court and were shown to the seats behind counsel. But for the sight which met his eyes Roger might have noticed them. They were Sally and her mother. They had met outside the Court.

'What on earth are you doing, Mother?' Sally had said.

'Well, I thought, as you weren't going, I would. Now I see that I might have done some more practising. Well, as I'm here I might as well stay. Which way do we go in? I promise not to sing.'

The sight which had so shaken Roger was that of *his* mother sitting in the front row of the jury. At the last moment she had remembered what it was she had had to do. She sat cheerfully in the jury box looking interestedly at everything in the Court. Her eye travelled from the judge to the seats for counsel.

'That one looks a bit young,' she said to herself as she looked along the line. 'Quite like Roger really. Yes, very. I must tell him. Quite a striking likeness. Good gracious, it *is* Roger. Well, really, he might have told me. I wonder if he'll speak. Should I smile at him or won't he like it? Why shouldn't I? After all, I'm his mother.'

She beamed at her son, and waved her hand slightly.

Roger went red in the face. He adored his mother and hated to hurt her feelings, but it was very difficult to smile. And, of course, he couldn't wave. He turned round to see if people had noticed his mother waving to him. On his right was Joy where he had put her. On his left were Sally and her mother. He only had a moment to consider whose double dealing—as it must have appeared—was the worse, his or Sally's. But bringing her mother was really too bad. But now what was he to do about his own mother? The jury were about to be sworn. When was he to tell the judge? And in what language? How awful to have to get up and say, 'The lady's my mother,' like Strephon in *Iolanthe*. 'I suppose I'd better do it at once,' he said to himself, and very unhappily rose and looked at the judge, who simply shook his head at him and waved him to sit down. He did not feel he could speak to his next-door neighbour. It sounded too absurd. Being called by his Christian name at school was nothing. Oh, dear, this a nice way to start. Will I ever recover?

he thought. Now they were swearing the jury. He must do something. He got up again. The judge looked at him angrily. Even a laymen should know that the swearing of the jury must not be interrupted. Applications could be made after they had been sworn. Here was a member of the Bar not only getting up when he ought to have waited, but getting up again after he'd been told to sit down. He really must be taught a lesson.

'Yes, what is it?' he snapped to Roger. 'If you don't know the rules ask someone who does. I've told you to wait once.'

Roger remained standing, waiting to speak.

'Will you please sit down,' said the judge.

'My Lord, I want to mention—' began Roger.

'I've told you to wait,' said the judge. All right, if the young man wanted it he should have it. He turned his body slightly towards counsel's seats.

'In this Court,' he said, 'where I have had the honour to preside for a good many years I have never yet seen counsel behave in this shocking manner. Justice could not be administered at all unless directions from the Bench were observed by the Bar. Until this moment, I have never known—'

Roger had had as much as he could stand and subsided, his face scarlet.

'Thank you,' said the judge. 'Thank you very much. I am very much obliged. Now perhaps the swearing of the jury can be continued.'

Although the jury could in this particular case have all been sworn at once, it is the practice at the Old Bailey to swear them seperately. In due course it became Mrs Thursby's turn. It must be right to object. His client had been told that he must object when the jurors came to the Book to be sworn. Now was the time. He had a good mind to leave his mother on the jury. But then he supposed he'd be disbarred. Fearless integrity, the Treasurer of his Inn had said. That was all very well for him. He'd never had his mother on the jury. Well, he must do it, but there's nothing fearless about it, he said to himself. I'm terrified. He got up again. The judge could not have believed it possible. He was a choleric man, equally capable of bestowing immense and undeserved praise in fantastically flattering terms and of—figuratively—spitting like two cats. This time the cats had it.

'I do not know your name,' he began, thinking hard for the most offensive words he could find, 'but that,' he went on, 'in view of your extraordinary behaviour I do not find altogether surprising. Will you now do me the personal favour of resuming your seat. Otherwise I shall be under the painful duty of reporting you to your Benchers before whom it cannot have been very long ago that you appeared to be called to the Bar.'

As Roger still remained on his feet, waiting to speak, but not liking to interrupt the judge, from whom words poured steadily at him in a vitriolic stream, the judge said: 'I order you to sit down.'

Roger did as he was told and, from where he sat, said loudly and clearly—as though it were the last cry of a man about to be executed:

'I object to the next juror. She's my mother.'

There was an immediate and thrilling silence. It was broken by Mr Green.

'I don't, my Lord. In fact I like the look of the lady.'

'You be quiet,' said the judge, and thought for several seconds. During the time he had had the honour to preside in that Court he had seldom had to think for so long before making a decision. Eventually he tapped his desk with a pencil and asked the clerk for Roger's name. Then he spoke:

'Mr Thursby,' he began.

Roger did not know whether to get up or not. He'd been ordered to sit down. It would be contempt of Court to get up. Yet somehow when the judge was addressing him it seemed all wrong to remain seated. He did not know what to do until his next door neighbour whispered.

'Get up. The old fool's going to apologize.'

Roger took the advice and was relieved to find that he was not immediately ordered to sit down—indeed if the judge had told two warders to throw him to the ground he would not have been altogether surprised.

'Mr Thursby,' repeated the judge in dulcet tones after Roger had risen, 'I owe you a very humble apology, and I hope you will see fit to accept it. I am extremely sorry. By my haste I have placed you in a position which would have been horribly embarrassing for any member of the Bar and which for one of —if I may say so without offence—your limited experience must have been almost beyond bearing. You dealt with the situation with a courage and a patience which I shall long remember.'

A lump came into Roger's throat, and it was all he could do to prevent himself from breaking down. He tried to say:

'Thank you, my Lord,' but very little was heard of it and he sat down and looked at his knees. The judge then turned to Mrs Thursby.

'You had better leave the jury box, madam. I owe you an apology too, and I should like to say that you have every reason for being proud of your son.'

To someone like Peter this would have been simply splendid. But it made Roger feel distinctly sick. And then he thought of all the people listening to him. Sally, Joy, Sally's mother and his own. Not to mention all the rest of those in Court. He felt as he had felt after boxing at school and being roundly trounced by a bigger boy, when the headmaster came up to him and said in a loud voice:

'Plucky boy.'

It sent shivers down his back. He wondered if this sort of thing happened to everyone. They couldn't often have barrister's mothers on the jury at all, let alone in cases where their sons were engaged. Another juryman was sworn. The judge scribbled a note which the usher brought to Roger. It said:

So very sorry. I shall be so pleased if you will bring your mother to see me during the adjournment. S.K.

Roger did not know whether to answer it in writing or by bowing. He asked his neighbour.

'What do I do with this?'

'Just bow and grin.'

He did as he was told. The judge smiled back at him. The jury had now been sworn and were informed of the charge against the prisoner. They were told he had pleaded Not Guilty and that it was for them to say whether he was Guilty or not.

Counsel for the prosecution opened the case quite shortly and called as his first witness the man who had bought the toffee. His name was Blake. He was duly asked about his purchase from Mr Green and about the false reference.

'Would you have sent the money if you had not believed this document to be a genuine reference?'

'No.'

The moment arrived for Roger to cross-examine.

'You remember seeing the reference, I suppose?' he asked.

'Certainly.'

'Did you have any other letters about the same time?'

'Letters? Yes, of course.'

'From the defendant, I mean?'

'From the defendant? Only the one offering me the toffee.'

'How long was that before you received the reference?'

'Two or three weeks.'

'Quite sure?'

'Yes, I think so.'

That's what Henry meant, thought Roger. I shouldn't have asked that last question.

'Two to three weeks?' repeated Roger.

'Yes,' said Mr Blake.

This time Roger left it alone.

'Now, Mr Blake, you say you received the reference before you sent the money. Are you quite sure of that?'

'Certainly. Look at the date. The 20th. I sent the money on the 23rd. I must have received the reference on the 21st.'

'Got the envelope by any chance?'

'I don't keep envelopes.'

'So you're relying on your memory entirely?'

'Certainly not entirely. On the date on the reference as well.'

'So that if it hadn't had that date on it you wouldn't have known whether you sent the money before or after you received the reference?'

'I certainly would have. I sent it after I had the reference—what's the point of being offered a reference if you don't wait for it?'

'Does this in any way shake your recollection?' asked Roger holding up the receipt for posting to be handed to the witness. Mr Blake looked at it.

'Well?' he said.

'Does that shake your recollection at all?' asked Roger.

'Not in the least,' said the witness. 'It's just a receipt for posting a letter.'

'To you.'

'What of it?'

'It was given to the prisoner.'

'How do I know?'

'What is this document?' asked the judge. 'Let me look at it.'

It was handed to the judge who looked at it closely. 'This is dated the 24th,' he said. 'It shows that letter was posted to you on that date by someone.'

'Yes, my Lord,' said the witness.

'Well,' said the judge, 'it apparently came into the possession of the prisoner and if it was issued to him by the post office it shows that he posted a letter to you on the 24th.'

'Yes, my Lord?' said Mr Blake.

'Well—you've said that he only sent you one letter and that was two or three weeks before you received the reference.'

'Possibly I was wrong, my Lord.'

'Possibly anything,' said the judge, 'but what counsel very properly puts to you is this. If that receipt was issued to the prisoner are you still prepared to swear positively that you received the reference before you sent the money?'

'I must have, my Lord.'

'Then how is this receipt to be accounted for?'

'I can't tell you that, my Lord, unless I had another letter from the prisoner. I suppose I might have.'

'But you can't remember one?'

'I can't say that I do, my Lord. Possibly, my Lord, the prisoner got it from someone else.'

'Whom do you suggest?'

'I have no idea, my Lord. All I know is that I was offered a reference and, if I'm offered a reference, I'm sure I wouldn't send the money without getting it first. I know something about this mail order business.'

'You mean you've been cheated before?' said Roger all too quickly.

'Steady,' said Mr Green.

'Be quiet and behave yourself,' said the judge. 'Your case is being conducted admirably. It is a model of what such a cross-examination should be. Perhaps, Mr Thursby,' he added, 'that last question could be rephrased.'

'Have you in the past been cheated?'

'I have.'

'Toffee?' asked Roger with a flash of inspiration.

'Yes, as a matter of fact,' said the witness.

'You've a sweet tooth?' asked Roger.

'Well, I have as a matter of fact.'

'You like toffee, apparently?'

'I don't see why I should be ashamed of it,' said Mr Blake.

'No one's suggesting you should be,' said the judge. 'Counsel only wishes to establish the fact that you are fond of toffee.'

'Well, I am,' said Mr Blake, 'and I don't mind admitting it.'

'P'raps you decided not to bother about a reference on this occasion and chanced sending the money?'

'Well,' said the judge, 'what do you say to that?'

'I suppose it's possible,' said Mr Blake, 'but I don't think so.'

'It could have happened?' said the judge.

'I suppose so,' said Mr Blake reluctantly.

Eventually the case for the prosecution closed.

'Yes, Mr Thursby,' said the judge pleasantly. 'Are you going to open your case to the jury?'

What is this? thought Roger. He's inviting me to make two speeches. But I can't do that, surely. Henry said I couldn't, and I'm sure that's what it said in the book. But here he is inviting me to do so. It'll look rude if I don't accept his offer. He's being so nice to me. I mustn't offend him. P'raps it's a sort of consolation prize. Oh—well, here goes.

'If your Lordship pleases,' said Roger. 'May it please your Lordship, members of the jury, the evidence for the prosecution has been completed and it now becomes my duty to open the defence.'

How professional it sounded, thought Roger, as he said it. At that moment the judge suddenly realized that he might have misled Roger.

'Forgive me, Mr Thursby,' he said, 'but I assume that you are calling evidence in addition to the prisoner?'

'Oh, no, my Lord.'

'Well then,' said the judge, 'you can't have two speeches, you know. You address the jury afterwards.'

Well, I knew that, thought Roger. What's he want to make a ruddy fool of me for? Everybody will think I don't know a thing. Well, they're quite right but I don't want it advertised every moment. All right, here goes again.

'If your Lordship pleases. Mr Green, will you go into the witness box, please?'

'Certainly,' said Mr Green. 'With pleasure,' and he came out of the dock, and went into the box to be sworn. Roger asked him the necessary questions about himself and then asked:

'Who wrote the reference which was sent to Mr Blake?'

'I did.'

'I do.'

'Did you write any other letter to Mr Blake except this reference and the original letter which he has produced?'

'I did not.'

'Did you obtain that receipt for posting from someone else or is it in respect of the reference?'

'It's in respect of the reference.'

'Thank you,' said Roger and sat down. Counsel for the prosecution then cross-examined.

'Let me follow this,' he said. 'Do I rightly understand your evidence to be this? You offered to supply toffee to Mr Blake, and offered to send him a reference. He does not wait for the reference but sends the money. After you have received the money you send him a reference which you have written out yourself in a false name. Is that your story?'

'That,' said Mr Green, 'is not only my story but it happens to be true. I hope you don't mind.'

'Don't be impertinent,' said the judge.

'I'm very sorry, my Lord,' said Mr Green. 'I don't intend to be impertinent but I have a little way of talking sometimes which makes people think that I do. Perhaps I'd better apologize in advance for any false impressions I may—'

'Be quiet,' said the judge, 'you're not doing yourself any good by making these silly speeches. Behave yourself and answer the questions.'

'Well, then,' said counsel, 'will you be good enough to tell my Lord and the jury why you thought it necessary after you'd received the money to send the reference?'

'For good measure,' said Mr Green. 'After all,' he went on, 'it might make him happier.'

'Really,' said counsel, 'I completely fail to understand you.'

'Ah,' said Mr Green, 'there are more things in heaven and earth, Horatio, than are dreamt of—'

'Now, look,' interrupted the judge, 'I shan't warn you again. If I have any more nonsense from you I shall stand this case over to next session.'

'I hope your Lordship won't do that,' said Mr Green. 'I may get another judge and I like being tried by your Lordship. There's nothing like a fair trial, I say.'

'Well, behave yourself,' said the judge, not altogether displeased.

'Makes you feel good, even if you aren't,' went on Mr Green. 'I'm so sorry, my Lord,' he added quickly.

'Mr Thursby,' said the judge, 'I must really ask you to control your client. I shan't warn him again.'

'If your Lordship pleases,' said Roger, not knowing how on earth he was to comply with the direction.

Fortunately Mr Green was a little less irrepressible for the rest of his evidence.

'Now,' said prosecuting counsel, 'is this the language you used about yourself in this admittedly false reference? "I have known Mr Arthur Green for many many years." '

'Quite true,' said Mr Green. 'I had.'

'Wait,' said counsel. 'Does it go on like this? "And during that period I can say that I have given him credit for thousands of pounds." Was that true?'

'Well, I've trusted him all my life,' said Mr Green, 'and he's never let me down.'

'Has he ever been worth thousands of pounds?'

'He's worth more than that to me,' said Mr Green.

'Did the reference go on like this?' asked counsel. ' "In my view he is in a very substantial way of business and can be trusted for any amount. Knowing him as I do I cannot well say less." Were you in a very substantial way of business?'

'Well, it's a comparative term. I was getting a lot of orders.'

'By sending false references?'

'Oh, dear, no—I always sent the references afterwards. I told you already.'

'I cannot see the object.'

'I'm sorry,' said Mr Green. 'I've done my best to explain and got into trouble with his Lordship in trying to do so.'

'Do you say this was an honest transaction?'

'Certainly. I got the money and he got the toffee.'

'Not all he ordered.'

'There's nothing about that in the indictment,' said Mr Green.

'Never mind about the indictment,' said counsel.

'But I do. That's what I'm being tried on, isn't it? It says I obtained goods by giving a false reference. Well, I didn't. Isn't that the end of the case?'

'Don't ask me questions,' said counsel, 'and kindly answer mine. Did not Mr Blake get less toffee than he paid for?'

'That's possible,' said Mr Green. 'I had a very bad man doing the packing at that time. He made away with a lot of toffee. Must have had a sweet tooth too. So it's quite possible Mr Blake got too little. But that wasn't my fault. I can't stand over the man who's doing the packing all the time, can I? I've got other work to do. And I'd no reason to distrust him at the time.'

'Who was this man?'

'Well, the name he gave to me was Brown—without an "e"—but, of course, it might have been an alias.'

'Did you get a reference with him?'

'I don't much care for references,' said Mr Green. 'You see—' he added and waved his hand expressively.

'Are you sure there ever was a Mr Brown?'

'Of course,' said Mr Green. 'I can describe him if you like. Aged about thirty-five, middling height, brown hair, turned his toes in as he walked, small moustache—though, of course, he might have shaved it off now. Fond of toffee,' he added.

Prosecuting counsel paused.

'Yes, Mr Thackeray?' said the judge. 'Any more questions?'

'I suggest,' said counsel, 'that you sent the reference before you received the money.'

For answer Mr Green just waved the receipt.

'Will you answer my question?' asked counsel angrily.

'Well, Mr Thackeray,' said the judge, 'it is a pretty good answer, isn't it? Can you really do much more with this case? After all, it is for you to prove your case with reasonable certainty. No one likes false references—I don't suppose the jury do any more than you—but you've got to prove it was received before your client sent the money.'

'There is the evidence of Mr Blake,' said counsel.

'I know,' said the judge, 'but how far can that take you in a criminal trial? He was by no means certain about it—and here is the receipt. That is a genuine document, anyway. What the truth of this transaction is, I don't pretend to know, but the prisoner's quite right when he says he's being tried on this indictment which simply alleges one false pretence. I can't, of course, say there's no evidence—but it may be that the jury will say they have heard enough already.'

'My Lord, the question of attempting to obtain by false pretences could arise.'

'Surely not,' said the judge. 'How can he attempt to obtain money which he has already received?'

The judge turned towards the jury.

'Members of the jury,' he said, 'once the case for the prosecution is closed it is open for you at any stage to say you've heard enough and that you're not satisfied that the prisoner's guilt has been proved. You may think his methods of carrying on business are pretty odd—you may think that a little more investigation might have been made by the police into those methods—and such investigations can still be made. But there is only one charge against the prisoner and that has to be proved to your satisfaction. Perhaps you'd like to have a word with each other.'

The jury did as they were told and three minutes later they stopped the case and returned a verdict of Not Guilty.

'Thank you,' said Mr Green when the judge discharged him. 'May I say something, my Lord?' he asked.

'Well, what is it?' asked the judge.

'I should like to thank you for a very fair trial, my Lord.'

The judge said nothing, but he did not in the least object.

'Would I be out of order,' went on Mr Green, 'in inviting everyone to some mild form of celebration?'

'Be quiet,' snapped the judge. 'I've a good mind to send you to prison for contempt of Court.'

'Oh, that's different,' said Mr Green. 'I'd better go.'

And he left the dock. He went straight to Roger, shook hands with him and whispered:

'What did I tell you? Can you sing now?'

Roger said nothing.

'Would you like my card?' said Mr Green. 'In case I can be of any help to you in the future?'

'Good-bye,' said Roger. 'Good-bye,' said Mr Green, and started to go. Then he came back.

'Oh, if at any time you should want any toffee—' he said, and went again.

CHAPTER 21

A Jewel of a Husband

The judge rose for lunch immediately afterwards and Roger, as he had been bidden, took his mother to see him in his room.

'What do I call him?' she asked. 'I've never met a judge before. I don't want to do the wrong thing. I'd hate to disgrace you.'

'You call him "Sir Stuart," ' said Roger. 'I call him "Judge," I think.'

They went to the judge's room.

'I would like to congratulate you again,' he said to Roger's mother, 'on the very brilliant beginning your son has made. He will go a very long way and you should be very proud of him.'

'Thank you very much,' she said. 'I'm so glad he was able to be of some use.'

'Mother's never been to the Old Bailey before,' said Roger quickly.

'No,' said Mrs Thursby. 'I found it most interesting, and the flowers and herbs and things give it such a friendly, cosy air. Even the prisoner can't mind too much in such a charming atmosphere. It's more like a garden party really.'

'I'm not sure,' said the judge, 'that our invitations are always as welcome.'

'As a matter of fact,' said Mrs Thursby. 'I nearly mislaid mine and it was only by chance that I got here at all. Would you have been very angry if I hadn't come?'

'I'm afraid my mother doesn't quite appreciate the seriousness of a jury summons, Judge,' said Roger hurriedly. 'I'll make sure she knows next time. If I'd known this time, it wouldn't have happened. It was a dreadful shock for me when I saw her in the jury box.'

'Well, all's well that ends well,' said the judge. 'Is this your first visit to the Old Bailey?' he added.

'I've been coming here with Grimes for several days. I'm his pupil, Judge,' said Roger.

'Indeed?' said the judge. 'A remarkably fine piece of cross-examination for a pupil. Quite the best I've heard.'

'Thank you very much indeed,' said Roger, 'and thank you, too, for being so nice to me.'

'I'm not sure about that,' said the judge, 'but I'll try to make up for what happened earlier if you'll come and see me at the end of the day. I'll send these flowers to your mother.' He indicated the bouquet which went into Court with him. 'That is, if she'd do me the honour of accepting them.'

'Oh, Sir Stuart, that is most kind,' said Mrs Thursby. 'I shall be thrilled. I've never had flowers from a judge before. Oh, yes, I did once now I come to think of it. My husband knew one of the judges who gave licences and things to public houses. He sent me some carnations. I suppose you do that too.'

'Licensing justices,' said the judge, not entirely pleased at the comparison. 'No, that is rather different. Well, I'm very glad to have met you and once again I congratulate you upon your son,' and he got up to indicate that the interview was at an end.

None too soon, thought Roger. I wonder what else mother might have said. He took her out to lunch, then she went home and he returned to Court.

The first case he heard after lunch was a plea of Guilty by a woman who had run away from her husband and married someone else. She was charged with bigamy and obtaining credit by fraud from a boarding house where they'd spent their bigamous honeymoon. The judge sent the man to prison and then proceeded to deal with the woman. He was informed that her husband was prepared to take her back again.

'You're a very wicked woman,' he said to the weeping prisoner. 'You have a jewel of a husband—' he stopped in the middle. 'Let him come forward,' he added.

A moment later the prisoner's husband went into the witness box.

'A jewel of a husband,' repeated the judge. 'Now, Mr Grant,' he said, looking in the most friendly manner at the husband, 'I understand you're prepared to take your wife back in spite of everything. Magnificent. That is so, isn't it?'

'My heart's full,' said the man.

'Quite so,' said the judge. 'He very properly says that his heart is full. Most proper. A jewel of a jusband. But you are prepared to take her back?'

'My heart's full,' repeated the husband.

'Quite so,' said the judge still beaming at him. 'We all understand that. Very natural. But you are prepared to take her back?'

The man did not answer for a moment.

The judge's brow started to cloud ever so slightly.

'You are prepared to take her back?' he repeated.

'My heart's—' began the man.

'Yes, yes, I know. Very proper. But you are prepared to take her back?'

'Full,' said the man.

'Mr Grant,' said the judge in less kindly tones. 'Would you be good enough to answer my question?'

'Very difficult, my Lord,' said the man. 'My heart's full.'

'Look here,' said the judge, his patience rapidly becoming exhausted, 'are you prepared to take her back or not?'

'If you say so, my Lord,' said the man.

'It's not for me to say one way or the other. She's your wife and it's for you to make up your mind. If you don't take her back I shall probably send her to prison.'

'How long for?' said the man.

'Don't ask me questions,' said the judge.

The man remained silent.

'Well, which is it to be?' said the judge. 'We can't wait all night for you.'

Still no answer.

'Well?' the judge almost shouted.

Roger reflected that the case had now progressed some way from the 'jewel of a husband' stage.

'I don't think six months would do her any harm,' said the man, 'and it would give me time to think.'

'Now look,' said the judge, 'when you married this woman you took her for better or worse.'

'It seems to have been worse,' said the man.

'Will you be quiet while I'm speaking,' said the judge angrily. 'Have you never heard of charity?'

'Charity,' said the man, 'begins at home. She left home.'

'I'm not going to argue with you,' said the judge. 'If you lack all decent feeling, I can't give it to you, but, if you don't forgive her, it may be on your conscience for the rest of your life.'

'What about her conscience?' said the man. 'How would you like your wife to go running off with the lodger?'

'Take that man away,' said the judge, and the husband left the witness box.

'Now, Margaret Grant, I'm not going to send you to prison. Dry your eyes and listen. You've behaved very stupidly—yes—and wickedly, but the exact circumstances of your married life are known only to you, and the man who was just standing in the witness box.'

The woman opened her mouth as though to speak.

'Yes, what is it?' asked the judge. 'You want to say something?'

'Only this, my Lord,' faltered the woman.

'Yes?' said the judge in a kind, encouraging tone.

'He's a jewel of a husband, my Lord.'

I'm glad I stayed, thought Roger.

CHAPTER 22

Offer of a Brief

Roger left the Old Bailey feeling happier than at any time since he was called to the Bar. He had defended his first prisoner and he had got him off. The judge had praised him and congratulated him on his cross-examination. It was almost unbelievable. Mr Green no doubt had friends and perhaps he would send them to him. He could almost hear people saying already: 'He must have a chance, Thursby's defending him.'

He went back to chambers very elated, and at once went to Henry.

'Well, how did you get on?'

'I got him off.'

'Well done you. Jolly good. Tell me all about it.'

Roger told him everything.

'One thing perhaps,' said Henry, 'I ought to warn you about.'

'Oh?'

'Compliments from the Bench. You'll get them, you know, and you'll feel hugely pleased and think you've made your name and all that. For example, if you go to the Old Bailey again you will hear the old boy say: "Members of the jury, you have just heard what in my opinion is a model of a speech from counsel for the prisoner. Since I have had the honour to preside at this Court—" and so on and so forth. I'm sorry to have to tell you, old boy,' went on Henry, 'that it don't mean a thing. Indeed, when that stops happening from that particular quarter it means that you really have made a little headway.'

'Oh,' said Roger, a little disappointed. 'Then wasn't my cross-examination any good then?'

'I didn't hear it, but from what you tell me I should say it was very good. All I'm warning you about is not to be too elated when a judge plasters you with good things. There *are* compliments from the Bench which are greatly to be valued. But they are rare—and at your present stage you don't know which is which. You don't mind my telling you all this?'

'Of course not.'

'I'm only doing it because no one told me. And it was the most frightful disappointment to me after His Honour Judge Smoothe had lauded me to the skies—and incidentally decided against me—to find that clients weren't queuing up to brief me. Later on, if you look around any Court presided over by a judge who indulges in fulsome praise of counsel, you'll see looks being exchanged between experienced counsel and solicitors. The best judges and those whose praise is worth having don't do it. But cheer up. You got him off and that's the chief thing. Now I suppose you're going to celebrate with Sally. Or could I hope that it's Joy?'

'Quite frankly, I hadn't thought,' said Roger. 'Oh—hell,' he added. 'I'm in for a spot of trouble there. But I won't worry you with it.'

'Look,' said Henry, 'perhaps I shouldn't ask this, but would you very much mind if I did ask Sally to come out some time? I'll understand perfectly if you object.'

'Of course not,' said Roger. 'I think it jolly decent of you to want to.'

'I'm not sure that that's what I'd call it,' said Henry, 'but I'll try to behave.'

When Roger got home that evening he at once telephoned Sally. What had she thought of him? He was dying to know.

'Hello, Sally,' he said.

'Hello, Roger,' she said somewhat coldly.

He couldn't help that. He must know what she thought.

'Sally, what did you think? I'm longing to know. Was I any better?'

'As a liar, d'you mean?' said Sally. 'Yes, I think you've made quite remarkable progress in a very short time.'

'Oh, Sally—you must let me explain. You mean about Joy being there?'

'And you're so quick too.'

'Sally—you must let me explain. I'd no idea when I spoke to you that Joy was coming. Really I hadn't.'

'She just happened to come, I suppose? What with your mother being on the jury, the day was pretty full of coincidences for you.'

'Oh, Sally, please listen. I had to take her.'

'Oh, it wasn't a coincidence? You just changed your mind about taking her, was that it? Well, I suppose everyone's entitled to change his mind.'

'Which reminds me,' said Roger. 'What were you doing there? It was you who advised me not to have anyone there. And you not only come but you bring your mother too. The whole blooming outfit.'

'Don't you call my mother an outfit,' said Sally.

'Look,' said Roger, 'can't we meet and get things straight?'

So they met and everything was explained as far as it could be.

'It looks as though Joy's uncle is going to be pretty useful to you,' said Sally.

'It does, doesn't it?' said Roger brightly.

'And what other Herculean tasks d'you imagine he'll impose on you in return. Marrying Joy, d'you think?'

'Oh, don't, Sally. It isn't fair. I wouldn't be human if I didn't want to get on.'

'There are ways and ways of getting on. If you're in love with Joy, all right, splendid. Another excellent coincidence. Go ahead, marry her and let her uncle keep you.'

'You're being beastly.'

'Plain, if you like,' said Sally. 'If, on the other hand, you're not in love with Joy—well—what was the word you used—beastly, wasn't it? Oh, Roger dear, can't you get on without making up to Joy in order to get work out of her uncle?'

'It sounds awful putting it that way.'

'Well, how would you put it—if you're not in love with her? And if you go on doing it long enough you'll find you have to marry the girl.'

'I'm much too young to marry, anyway,' said Roger, 'and I haven't any money.'

'That's what I mean. If Joy's uncle provides the income—you can't very decently marry someone else on it—when you do marry.'

'I can't very well refuse the briefs.'

'If you stop taking Joy out, they'll stop too.'

Roger thought for a moment.

'You are right, Sally,' he said. 'At least I suppose so. You'd say it was rather like those men who—well, you know what I mean.'

'Oh, I wouldn't put it quite like that,' said Sally. 'But it does seem a bit mean.'

'All right,' said Roger, 'I'll stop. I'll tell Joy straight out that I'll never marry her. Then if her uncle still keeps on sending me briefs, that's his affair, isn't it? After all, the time may come when he briefs me for my own sake.'

'We'll drink to that,' said Sally.

And they did.

'Roger,' said his mother that evening.

'Yes, darling?'

'How long d'you think it'll be before you're earning real money? I mean, flowers are all very nice, but they don't pay the bills.'

'Oh, Mother—I'm afraid it may be an awful long time. I hope not, but it is a slow job, I'm afraid, unless one's awfully lucky.'

'What d'you mean by slow?' said Mrs Thursby. 'You wouldn't be likely to have two hundred pounds to spare next Thursday?'

'Mother—what do you mean?'

'Oh, well—never mind,' said Mrs Thursby. 'It doesn't matter.'

'Why, Mother darling, what is it?'

'I did rather a stupid thing, I'm afraid. I lent Elsie some money—to pay her bootmakers I thought she said. It seemed an awful lot for shoes, but still she's always so well turned out I thought she couldn't have paid them for some years. But it was her Scots accent. It was really her bookmakers. And now she's lost some more and can't pay me back when she promised. Oh, well—it only means the gas and telephone may be a bit cut off.'

'The telephone!' said Roger in horror.

'Well, we didn't always have them.'

'But I might have something frightfully urgent. Alec might want to get hold of me.'

'Oh, well, never mind. P'raps they'll forget to cut ours off. They must have a lot of others to deal with. Then if they do, we can always get an electric cooker. I've sometimes wondered whether I wouldn't prefer one.'

'But the telephone, Mother. We must find the money for that. How much do you owe altogether?'

'I never had much head for figures, but if Elsie had sent that two hundred pounds back it would be quite all right.'

'You didn't lend her two hundred pounds, Mother?'

'Well, she seemed to want it so badly. And I'd just had my

quarterly cheque. It was to come back in a month. And d'you know she said she'd add another fifty pounds. That was very nice of her, I thought. I'm sure she meant to. I'd trust her anywhere, if you know what I mean.'

'Backing horses is just lunacy,' said Roger.

'Not according to Elsie. She said it was only a temporary setback. She said she made a large profit every year.'

'So does everyone,' said Roger. 'That's why bookmakers smoke fat cigars. Oh, well—I suppose we'll manage somehow or other. But it is a bit of a blow.'

The telephone rang.

'Hullo, oh, hullo, Joy—yes—what—can't you say it on the telephone? It can't be as secret as all that. Oh, all right. I'll be along.' He turned to his mother.

'Joy's got something she must tell me. I suppose I shall have to go. Shan't be long.'

Roger decided to take advantage of the occasion and break the news to Joy as he'd agreed with Sally. Just as well to get it over. He went straight to her rooms. She was waiting on the doorstep.

'Oh, Roger, I thought you were never coming. Oh, Roger darling, I thought you were wonderful, getting that funny little man off and the judge apologizing to you and everything.'

'It wasn't too bad,' said Roger modestly. 'But one mustn't let things like that go to one's head. Henry said it didn't really mean a thing.'

'Well,' said Joy, 'see if this means a thing.'

'What is it?'

'It's so terrific you won't believe it. Oh, I am a lucky girl. You know the big sausage people—Baggallys?'

'Yes, of course,'

'Well, apparently somebody's been copying their sausages or something and they're bringing a huge action. I believe it's called a patent action.' She pronounced it like patent in patent shoes.

'Patent,' corrected Roger. He wouldn't have known it had a short 'a' if Henry hadn't told him.

'Well?' said Roger puzzled.

'Well, Uncle Alfred is their solicitor, and he's going to send a brief in it to you.'

'Me?' said Roger. 'But it's ridiculous. I don't know anything about patents. Even if I did I couldn't do a case of that size.'

'You won't be all by yourself,' said Joy. 'There are three other counsel in it besides you. There's, let me see, Sir George Pratt—Uncle Alfred says he's the chief man on the subject—and then there are two others and then there's you. So you'll get some help, you see. Oh, and Uncle Alfred's coming round to explain it to you himself. That's why you had to come at once. He'll be here in a moment.'

No doubt Roger ought to have acted at once on what might be called the Sally plan. But he could hardly be blamed for just waiting to see what Uncle Alfred said first. Anyway, there wasn't enough time to say to Joy what he had intended to say. He'd have to wrap it up a bit. And that takes time. And then Uncle Alfred arrived.

'My dear Roger, you must forgive this informality—but I hope that, now that I might say you're almost one of the family you will forgive me. Now, my dear boy,' he went on without giving Roger a chance to interrupt, 'I want your help, your personal help. And I want to have a word with you before taking official action. I don't know whether Joy has told you that we've quite an important action for Baggallys. Now—I don't want you to think I'm not satisfied with the counsel we've so far briefed in the case. I am indeed. But I can't help feeling that in a case of this kind an outside view from one of the younger generation would be a help. We've all eaten sausages for so long that we may have got into a rut with our ideas. So, to cut a long story short, I want you—as a personal favour to me—to accept a junior brief in the matter. I must apologize for not mentioning it to you at an earlier stage, but, to be quite candid, it was Mr Smith's idea and he only had it quite recently.'

'Well, it's most awfully kind of you, Mr Merivale.'

'And there is one other matter. And I hope you'll forgive my mentioning that to you personally too. I know that counsel and solicitors don't discuss fees together. As far as you and I are concerned it's done for nothing. It's the clerk who deals with the fees. But this is rather an embarrassing situation and that's why I'd be grateful for your help. You see, my firm's an old-fashioned one. We haven't moved forward like some of the others. Now, of course you're aware, my dear boy, of the two-thirds rule. Well, my firm have always stuck to that, even when the Bar Council agreed with the Law Society that we needn't. So that, for example, Sir George has got three thousand guineas on his brief, Wincaster two thousand and Soames one thousand three hundred and thirty-three.

Now quite frankly, my dear boy, we can't run to more than, say, four hundred for your brief. Not that you wouldn't be worth more, but we couldn't run to it. Now when Mr Smith approaches your clerk on the matter, your clerk who's used to our old-fashioned way will expect two-thirds of one thousand three hundred and thirty-three, and it would be most embarrassing for Mr Smith. So what I want to know, my dear boy, is whether you will very kindly have a word with your clerk in advance and ask him to accept four hundred on the brief—that's, of course, if you're willing yourself—and only if you're willing—I realize that it's rather a lot to ask, but I thought as a personal favour to me you might possibly be prepared to consider it. Of course, there'll be refreshers—about a hundred a day I should think—and I suppose the case ought to last about six weeks. So your total fees in the matter ought to be between three and four thousand pounds. That's, of course, in the Court below. It's bound to go to the Court of Appeal and probably to the House of Lords. Now, my boy, will you do it? I'm not pressing you at all—but it would be a kindness.'

Roger looked out of the window.

'It's terribly good of you,' he said. 'May I think it over?'

'I beg your pardon?' said Mr Merivale. 'My hearing isn't quite as good as it was. I didn't quite catch what you said.'

'May I think it over?' repeated Roger.

Mr Merivale put his hand through his hair several times. 'I only do this, young man,' he said, 'when I am surprised to the point of being astounded.'

'I want to ask advice,' said Roger.

'Advice?' said Mr Merivale. 'Advice is it? Well, my advice to you, young man, is that you should consult the nearest brain specialist. And another piece of advice is this: if you don't seize all the opportunities you're given at the Bar you won't get very far. I don't believe that there is any young man at the Bar who would have said what you did. Admittedly you have a very fine practice. But there must be days when you don't receive a brief marked four hundred guineas. Of course, the one thousand guinea briefs help to make up for it, but if what I'm told is true, there aren't as many of those as there used to be. And dock briefs—or should I say one dock brief at the Old Bailey—hardly seems to take their place. But no doubt you know best. May I take it then that you're too busy to accept the instructions? Or is it that you would consider it undignified to accept less than two-thirds of Mr Soames' fee?'

Roger looked out of the window again and then blood suddenly rushed to his head. He had had the experience before and he had it again several times later in his career. When blood rushes like that to a man's head he may win a V.C., commit suicide, marry the girl or say something he will regret or be proud of for the rest of his life. Roger did not know whether he would be proud or sorry, but he knew he must say it. When blood rushes like that to the head there is indeed no option. The thing has to be done or said. There is one course and one course only which has to be taken, whatever the cost. Through the window Roger could see a prostitute leaning against some railings.

'Yes, Mr Merivale,' he said. 'Undignified. That's the word.'

CHAPTER 23

Henry's Case

Three months later Henry was dining with Sally.

'You're the nicest man I know,' she said.

'You know what I think of you,' he said, 'and that by itself shows I'm not. I knew what would happen if I took you out to dinner. When you first briefed me in order to be near Roger I knew that, unless I took a very firm hold of myself, I should fall in love with you. So far from taking hold of myself I asked Roger if he'd mind. And here we are.'

'Yes,' said Sally, 'here we are. And there's nothing to be done about it.'

'P'raps it's as well,' said Henry. 'I shouldn't think very much of myself if you cared for me. As it is, it's all right. The only person who's in trouble is me. I must admit I rather like it.'

'I'm in trouble too,' said Sally.

'Ah, but you were before I met you. So I've no responsibility for that.'

'How is he doing? You think he'll get on, don't you?'

'I'm quite sure he will. He works like a black and he never believes anything anyone says to him until he's seen it's right. He's a certainty. How long it'll take before he really gets going, I don't know. But once it starts it'll come with a rush. And you'll see he'll develop. He's got all the right instincts. A certain degree of priggishness may be an advantage to begin with at the Bar.'

'Tell me another thing—you needn't if you don't want to. Have I a chance?'

'You tell me and I'll tell you,' said Henry.

'Don't be flippant, please.'

'I was not being flippant, I assure you. It's much worse at thirty-three than it is at twenty-one. I know. I've had both. You only know what it's like at twenty-one.'

'It's terrible, Henry. Do please tell me. I'd believe almost anything you tell me. But I shan't believe you if you say "no." Since he gave up Joy I thought something might have happened. But it hasn't.'

'Poor Joy,' said Henry. 'She overdid it.'

'That isn't an answer, Henry. Or is it intended to be the kindest way? You are kind, Henry. I'd trust you anywhere. Who'd think of asking an interested party like you?'

'It is a compliment, I agree. No, I've often tried to think what's the answer to your question. And the only one I can give is "yes." '

'D'you mean it, Henry?'

'Of course I do. But you mustn't be too optimistic; he's much too wrapped up in his work. He thinks of very little else. He hasn't had a brief since he broke with Joy, but he might have a large practice if one judged from the amount of work he does. He's still terribly young, but he's developing. And, of course, he'll fall in love. And it could be with you. He'll be a blithering idiot, if he doesn't.'

'Dear Henry—how lovely to be with you. You're the nicest man I know.'

'No chance of promotion?' said Henry.

Sally shook her head. 'I doubt it,' she said.

'Oh, well,' said Henry. 'No case is ever lost till judgment is given, and even then there can be an appeal.'

CHAPTER 24

The Stigma

Roger's year was nearly at an end when one day Alec came into the pupils' room. Peter had left by this time and there were two new pupils. Roger was now the senior.

'I've got you a brief, sir,' said Alec.

'Oh, Alec, how splendid,' said Roger. 'What is it?'

'It's only a judgment summons,' said Alec, 'but you never know what it may lead to.'

'Thank you very much,' said Roger and seized the papers eagerly. He found that he was in the comparatively unusual position of being briefed for the judgment debtor. Usually it is only the judgment creditor who is represented. For fairly obvious reasons. The debtor has no money to spare on engaging solicitors, let alone counsel. As always, Roger had a chat with Henry about it and in consequence he took Henry's advice and went to the County Court where the case was to be heard in order to see how the judge there, Judge Perkins, treated judgment summonses.

'They vary so tremendously,' Henry had said. 'Some judges don't seem to require any evidence of means worth speaking of and make committal orders right and left. Others hardly ever make them. I must say I think the whole thing's a bit out of date.'

At one County Court which Roger had visited the dialogue during the hearing of judgment summonses had usually been like this:

CLERK: 'British Loan Company against Brown.'

SOLICITOR: 'I appear for the judgment creditor, your Honour.'

JUDGE: 'Well, Mr Brown, have you any offer to make?'

BROWN: 'I'm very sorry I've got into arrears, your Honour, but—'

JUDGE: 'Never mind about that for the moment. Have you any offer to make?'

BROWN: 'Well, it's so difficult, your Honour, with the wife ill and being out of work myself—'

JUDGE: 'I'll go into all of that if necessary, but tell me first if you have any offer of any kind to make. This debt has got to be paid, you know.'

BROWN: 'I might manage ten shillings a week, your Honour.'

JUDGE: 'What do you say, Mr Worcester?'

SOLICITOR: 'I'll take that with a committal order, your Honour.'

JUDGE: 'Very well, then. Committal order for fourteen days, suspended so long as two pounds a month is paid. Now, do you know what that means, Mr Brown?'

BROWN: 'I have to pay two pounds a month.'

JUDGE: 'It means rather more than that, Mr Brown. It means that as long as you do pay two pounds a month all will be well—but, if you don't, then the bailiff will come and arrest you and take you to prison for fourteen days.'

BROWN: 'But suppose I can't pay, your Honour?'

JUDGE: 'I've told you what will happen if you don't pay. You should have thought of that before you borrowed the money. Call the next case, please.'

But Judge Perkins dealt with them differently. The first which Roger heard him dispose of was:

CLERK: 'James Brothers against Smith.'

SOLICITOR: 'I appear for the judgment creditor, your Honour.'

JUDGE: 'Any offer to make, Mr Smith?'

SMITH: 'A pound a month, your Honour.'

JUDGE: 'What do you say, Mr Bray?'

SOLICITOR: 'If your Honour will reinforce it with a committal order—'

JUDGE: 'You know perfectly well, Mr Bray, that I can't do that without evidence of means.'

SOLICITOR: 'But he's offered a pound a month, your Honour.'

JUDGE: 'That is simply a promise for the future. To my mind it is no evidence whatever that he has the money now or has had it in the past. Question him about his means if you wish.'

The solicitor questioned Mr Smith about his means but without much effect, and eventually the judge simply made an order for him to pay one pound per month, with no penalty attached for non-payment.

The dialogue in the next one was as follows:

SOLICITOR: 'Now Mr Davies, what do you earn?'

DAVIES: 'It varies.'

SOLICITOR: 'What does it average?'

DAVIES: 'Oh—seven to eight pounds.'

SOLICITOR: 'What about overtime?'

DAVIES: 'I don't do a lot.'

SOLICITOR: 'How much on average?'

DAVIES: 'I don't know.'

SOLICITOR: 'You must have some idea. If necessary, you know, your firm can be brought here to prove what you do earn.'

DAVIES: 'Last week I didn't do any overtime at all.'

SOLICITOR: 'What about the week before?'

DAVIES: 'I forget.'

JUDGE: 'Mr Davies, you must try to remember. You must know roughly what you average for overtime each week.'

DAVIES: 'Some weeks I don't do any.'

JUDGE: 'Mr Davies, if you persist in avoiding an answer to the question, I shall assume that you earn seven to eight pounds a week overtime.'

DAVIES: 'It's nothing like as much as that.'

JUDGE: 'How much is it, then?'

DAVIES: 'Not more than two to three pounds.'

JUDGE: 'Very well then. Your average earnings are about ten pounds a week.'

SOLICITOR: 'Possibly more?'

DAVIES: 'Not more.'

SOLICITOR: 'Whom d'you have to keep out of your ten pounds.'

DAVIES: 'My wife.'

SOLICITOR: 'Does she do any work?'

DAVIES: 'She does a bit.'

SOLICITOR: 'How much does she earn?'

DAVIES: 'I've no idea.'

SOLICITOR: 'You must have some idea.'

DAVIES: 'We don't discuss it. It's her business.'

JUDGE: 'No doubt it is, but I should have thought you might have taken sufficient interest in her affairs to know about how much she earned.' (*Pause.*) 'Well, don't you?'

DAVIES: 'She gets a few pounds, I dare say.'

SOLICITOR: 'What is your rent?'

DAVIES: 'Has this anything to do with the case?'

JUDGE: 'It certainly has.'

DAVIES: 'I don't pay rent. I'm buying the house through a building society—at least the wife is. I just guarantee the payments.'

SOLICITOR: 'How much are they?'

DAVIES: 'Eight pounds three shillings and four pence a month.'

SOLICITOR: 'Have you any other debts?'

DAVIES: 'That's my affair.'

JUDGE: 'You will answer the question. Have you any other debts?'

DAVIES: 'Not that I know of.'

SOLICITOR: 'Why haven't you paid anything off this judgment?'

DAVIES: 'Because it isn't justice. He hit me first.'

JUDGE: 'That matter has already been decided. There is a judgment against you. How much a month do you offer?'

DAVIES: 'Five shillings.'

JUDGE: 'You're just trifling with the Court. Is there anything else you want to say before I make an order?'

DAVIES: 'It doesn't seem much use.'

JUDGE: 'Mr Davies, you will be detained until the rising of the Court and I shall then consider whether to fine you or send you to prison for contempt of Court. Meanwhile, I shall deal with this summons. You will be committed to prison for six weeks and the order will be suspended so long as you pay five pounds per month.'

DAVIES: 'I can't do it.'

JUDGE: 'Then you know the alternative. I am quite satisfied that you could have paid off the whole of this debt by now and have deliberately refrained from doing so.'

In the next case before Judge Perkins the debtor admitted that he went in for football pools in a small way. The judge immediately made a committal order.

'You can't gamble with your creditor's money,' he said. 'It's not my concern whether you bet or not in the ordinary way, but if you could send half a crown a week to the pool promoters you could have sent it to the plaintiff, and you ought to have done so. Committal order for twenty-one days suspended so long as one pound per month is paid.'

The next case was an even worse one. The debt was due to a wine merchant and the debtor admitted that he had been going to greyhound racing regularly ever since.

'This is quite outrageous,' said the judge. 'You will be committed to prison for six weeks and I shall suspend the order for seven days only. If the whole amount is not paid within that time, the order for your imprisonment will be effective.'

'But I can't pay twenty-five pounds in seven days,' said the alarmed debtor.

'Then you will spend six weeks in prison,' said the judge. 'I have no sympathy whatever with you. You buy drink on credit, don't pay for it and spend the money you could have used to pay for it on going to the races.'

Roger went back to chambers feeling that he knew Judge Perkins' methods of dealing with judgment summonses fairly well. A day or two later he had a conference with his client, a cheerful gentleman called Starling. He came with his wife, who was also cheerful and was, in addition, an attractive young woman. They were brought by their solicitor, Mr Fergus Trent, who was an old friend of theirs.

'Well, here we are,' said Mr Starling. 'When's the party?'

'Next Tuesday.'

'That's awkward. 'Fraid we shan't be able to come. It's Lingfield that day.'

'D'you mean the races?' said Roger, a little alarmed.

'Don't be so prim and proper,' said Mrs Starling. 'Don't tell me you've never had a little flutter.'

'Well, just on the Derby, you know. I've never been to a race meeting, as a matter of fact, only to point-to-points.'

'Well, you ought to, old boy,' said Mr Starling. 'Do you a power of good. Champagne and brandy to begin with. Take a lovely girl with you. And you'll be on top of the world. I just take my wife. She's still pretty high in the handicap.'

'I say, you know,' said Roger, 'this is rather serious. I don't know if you realize it.'

'Serious, old boy? I'll say it is.'

'I'm glad you appreciate that,' said Roger.

'I meant if we couldn't go to Lingfield,' said Mr Starling. 'We always do well there.'

'Look,' said Roger, 'this judge sends people to prison.'

Mrs Starling laughed.

'Don't try and frighten us,' she said, 'that stopped a long time ago.'

'But he does really. What was this debt for?'

'Repairs to a car, old boy. Had a nasty smash in the Watford by-pass. Between you and me I was a bit pickled. But I got through the tests all right. And Sheila was a brick. Said she'd been with me all the evening—when she knew in fact that I'd been out with some of the boys. I told you she was class, didn't I? Real thoroughbred. Never have to ride her in blinkers.'

'The other way round sometimes, darling,' said his wife.

'I'm afraid I don't follow all this,' said Roger, 'but you're going to be in great difficulty before this particular judge. Let me see. The debt's forty pounds. Judgment was obtained three months ago. Now can you honestly swear you've lost nothing on horses since then?'

'Come again,' said Mr Starling.

Roger repeated the question.

'Old boy,' said Mr Starling, 'I can honestly swear, cross my heart and all that—I can honestly swear that we haven't *won* a penny. Otherwise, we'd have paid.'

'How much have you lost?'

'Is that fair, old boy? Don't rub it in. Why, Sheila actually sold a couple of dresses. Talk of taking the clothes off your back.'

'Mr Starling,' said Roger, 'I'm afraid this is going to be rather a shock for you. I know this judge, Judge Perkins, and unless you can pay the whole of that forty pounds within a week from Tuesday next, he'll send you to prison for six weeks.'

'You're not serious, old boy?'

'I am, absolutely.'

'But that's terrible. I couldn't possibly go to gaol. It's Sheila's birthday in a fortnight, and we're having a party to celebrate.'

'What with?' asked Roger.

'Oh, we can always raise a fiver or so.'

'Well, you'd better raise eight fivers,' said Roger.

'That's a different thing altogether, old boy. Just can't be done.'

'Then you'll go to prison.'

'But I'll lose my job.'

'Haven't you any furniture you can sell?'

'All on h.p., old boy. Only just started to pay for it.'

'Car?'

'Still in the Watford by-pass, I should think.'

'I thought you had it repaired?'

'That was the other fellow's.'

'Mr Thursby,' intervened Mr Trent, 'please don't think me impertinent, but are you quite sure about this particular judge?'

'Absolutely,' said Roger. 'I was down there last Thursday and he sent a chap to gaol for six weeks because he'd been gambling. Only gave him seven days to pay.'

'Oh, well,' said Mr Trent, 'I'm afraid there's nothing for it.'

'Come, come,' said Mrs Starling, 'you're not going to let us down, Fergie. Frank just can't go to gaol. I won't have it, I tell you. I'll speak to the judge myself and explain.'

'I'm afraid that wouldn't do any good, Mrs Starling,' said Roger.

'That's not very complimentary,' said Mrs Starling. 'I once got a bookie to give me five to one when he was showing four to one on his board.'

'I told you she was class,' put in Mr Starling.

'I'm afraid judges aren't like bookies.'

'Apparently he'll skin me just the same,' said Mr Starling.

'No,' said the solicitor mournfully. 'I'm afraid there's nothing for it.'

'Well, we can try,' said Roger.

'Try what?' said the solicitor.

'See if I can persuade the judge to give more time.'

'D'you think you'll succeed?'

'Quite frankly—I don't, but one can never be sure till it's happened.'

'No,' said the solicitor even more gloomily. 'There's nothing for it. I shall have to lend you ten pounds. It goes against the grain, but I shall have to. I wouldn't do it for you, Frank, but I've always had a soft spot for Sheila. So there we are. Thank you very much all the same, Mr Thursby. Sorry we shan't have the pleasure of seeing you at the County Court.'

'I'm afraid I don't quite understand,' said Roger.

He was quite prepared for anyone to withdraw instructions from him at any time, but in the first place he couldn't think what he had done to merit it yet, and secondly the solicitor's attitude was quite friendly. He was completely out of his depth.

'No alternative,' said Mr Trent.

'But ten pounds isn't any good,' said Roger. 'He'll need forty pounds and possibly some costs as well.'

'We'll just have to go bankrupt.'

Roger thought for a moment.

'But,' he said rather tentatively, 'don't you have to owe fifty pounds in order to go bankrupt?'

'Quite so,' said Mr Trent. 'Our friend only owes forty pounds. Quite correct. It costs ten pounds to go bankrupt. I lend him ten pounds. He then owes fifty pounds and has the funds necessary to enable him to go bankrupt.'

'Anyway,' said Mr Starling, 'I could rustle up some other debts if you really want them. I didn't know they'd be a help.'

'Will you excuse me a moment?' said Roger.

He left the room and went hurriedly to Henry.

'Look, Henry. Can you tell me something in a hurry?'

He then stated what had happened.

'Well, is that all right?' he asked. 'Will it work? What happens about the judgment summons if he goes bankrupt?'

'Yes, that's quite O.K.,' said Henry. 'Once a receiving order in bankruptcy is made against a man that's the end of the judgment summons, Incidentally he does not need to owe £50. Anyone who's unable to pay his debts, whatever they are, can file his own bankruptcy petition. But he does need £10 to do it.'

'And anyone can avoid going to prison under a judgment summons by going bankrupt?'

'Quite correct,' said Henry.

'Then why doesn't everyone do that?'

'Several reasons. Some people can't raise the ten pounds to go bankrupt.'

'So that a man with ten pounds can avoid going to prison and a man without can't?'

'Right again. Then people who are in business on their own account, or have furniture or property of their own, don't want to go bankrupt as it means the end of their business and the selling up of their property.'

'But if you're in a job and haven't any property, there isn't any snag about it?'

'Not normally, unless you don't like the stigma of bankruptcy.'

'I'd prefer the stigma of bankruptcy to that of gaol.'

'I quite agree,' said Henry. 'Of course quite a number of judgment debtors don't go bankrupt because they don't know that they can get out of their difficulties that way. But I gather your client does, now.'

Roger thanked Henry and went hurriedly back to his clients.

'I'm so sorry to have left you. I just went to make sure that there are no snags about Mr Trent's suggestion. I gather you've got a job, Mr Starling?'

'That's right. It's called a job, but between you and me, old boy, it's grossly underpaid.'

'And your furniture's all on hire purchase. Well, then, Mr Trent's idea seems an excellent one provided you don't mind the stigma of bankruptcy.'

'What's that?' said Mrs Starling.

'The stigma,' repeated Roger.

'Hold everything,' said Mrs Starling. 'Could we use your telephone?'

'Why, certainly,' said Roger, puzzled.

'What is it, old girl?' said Mr Starling.

' "The Stigma." It's running in the 3.30. We've just got time.'

'Good show,' said Mr Starling. 'Gosh—wouldn't we have been wild if we'd missed that? Could I use the phone, old boy? Won't be a jiffy. How much, old girl, d'you think? Half a quid each way?'

'Make it a quid, sweetheart,' said Mrs Starling. 'Then we'll have the doings to go to Lingfield.'

'O.K.,' said Mr Starling. 'Which way do I go?'

Roger showed him, and came back to his room whilst Mr Starling was making his investment.

'That's two pounds you've put on, is it?' he asked Mrs Starling.

'Yes,' she said. 'Wish I could have made it a fiver. You don't have things like that happening every day. It's bound to win.'

'D'you know anything about the horse?'

'Anything about it?' said Mrs Starling. 'What more d'you want? With a name like that it couldn't lose.'

Suddenly Mr Starling dashed in, almost like Mr Grimes.

'Look, old girl,' he said, 'There's an apprentice called Thursby riding it. Dare we risk a fiver?'

'Gosh, yes,' said his wife.

'O.K., old girl.'

And Mr Starling rushed back to the telephone.

'That's a bit of luck,' said Mrs Starling. 'You haven't a paper, I suppose?'

'I've a *Times*,' said Roger.

'Thanks awfully.'

She looked for the sporting page.

'It's in the twenty-to-one others. That'll mean one hundred and twenty-five pounds. How many runners are there? One, two, three, four—' she went on counting up to seventeen.

'Gosh, I wonder if he ought to do it on the tote. Some of it anyway. They might pay a hundred to one. Would you excuse me?'

She rushed to the door and almost collided with her husband coming back.

'Did you do any on the tote?' she asked excitedly. 'It's in the twenty-to-one others.'

'Relax, old girl,' said Mr Starling. 'Three quid each way on the tote. Two at S.P. O.K.?'

For answer, Mrs Starling kissed him.

'Oh, darling, I'm so happy. We'll celebrate to-night. Who'd have thought it? "The Stigma" with Thursby up.'

'And he gets a seven-pound allowance, old girl.'

'Can he get down to the weight?'

She took *The Times* and looked at the sporting page again.

'Yes—easily. It's in the bag.'

'Please forgive me, Mr Thursby. I don't suppose you understand this sort of thing. It means a great deal to us.'

'As far as I can see,' said Roger, feeling much older than twenty-one, 'you've just backed a horse and stand to lose ten pounds, a sum which you're about to borrow from Mr Trent in order to go bankrupt.'

'Old boy,' said Mr Starling, 'it does sound a trifle odd put that way, but Fergie understands. We put him on a good thing once, I say, old girl, you didn't happen to see if there's anything to double it with, did you? Quick, let's have a look.'

He took *The Times* from her, and started reading out the names of horses.

'My godfathers,' he shouted, 'excuse me. "Jolly Roger" in the 4.30. I'll see if I can get a half-quid each way double. Forgive me, old boy, I saw the name on the brief. Won't be a jiffy.'

He rushed out of the door and nearly crashed into Mr Grimes, who was about to make a telephone call from the clerks' room.

'So sorry, old boy,' said Mr Starling. 'Terribly urgent.' And took the receiver away from him.

Mr Grimes said nothing. For once he could not think of anything to say. Mr Starling might be a solicitor for aught he knew.

'Hullo, hullo—' said Mr Starling frantically. 'Is that Vulgans?

This is Frank Starling—Boozer. Are they off for the 3.30 yet? Oh, they are—damn—oh, well, can I hold for the result? Thanks so much.' He turned to Mr Grimes.

'Damned shame, old man,' he said. 'They're off.'

'Dear, dear, dear,' said Mr Grimes.

'Well, we'll get the result first anyway,' went on Mr Starling. 'Then we can put half the winnings on the next, can't we, old boy? That's better really than a double. Make sure we have a fat win, anyway. Not much in your line I gather, old man?'

'Oh, well, my dear fellow,' said Mr Grimes, 'it keeps the telephone operator busy, if nothing else.'

'I'm terribly sorry, old boy—what's that, what? Who between? It's a photo finish. Who? But of course you can say. No—that's too ridiculous. Excuse me a moment, old man. Don't hang up.'

Mr Starling rushed back to the pupil's room.

'It's a photo finish,' he announced excitedly.

'Who between?' asked his wife.

'Wouldn't say.'

'But that's absurd. They'll always tell you if you ask them. Excuse me.'

'You ask them, old girl.'

Mr and Mrs Starling rushed out of the room to the telephone in time to hear the last of Mr Grimes' remarks to Alec.

'I don't know what we're coming to, I really don't.'

Meantime Roger looked at the solicitor whose expression had hardly changed and who sat still, looking mournful.

'Odd,' said Roger, 'very odd.'

'Not when you've known them as long as I have,' said Mr Trent. 'They'd gamble their souls away if anyone would lay the odds. I'll bet—now look what they've got me doing. Until I met Frank I didn't know one end of a racehorse from the other. And now I can even understand the sporting edition of the evening papers. I actually read the stop press—to see how much they've lost.'

At that moment the door burst open and Mr and Mrs Starling rushed into the room.

'We've won, we've won, we've won,' they shouted, and proceeded to dance together round the room.

' "The Stigma" with Thursby up,' they shouted. 'Good old "Stigma," good old Thursby. Here, where's that silly piece of blue paper?'

He picked up the judgment summons which had been in front of Roger and tore it into small pieces.

The solicitor appeared quite unmoved.

'I'm glad they've won, anyway,' Roger said to him. Mr and Mrs Starling were too occupied in making frenzied calculations on Roger's *Times* to be spoken to. 'Aren't you?' he added.

'If you'd seen this happen as often as I have,' said Mr Trent, 'you wouldn't move a muscle. They'll spend it all in a week and then we'll be back where we started. Still, it's saved me ten pounds for the moment. But only for the moment,' he added sadly.

Mr and Mrs Starling continued with their calculations for a little time and then started to make suggestions to Roger for every kind of celebration. After just over a quarter of an hour of this Mr Starling suddenly said:

'Ought to be able to get the tote prices now, old girl. Would you excuse me?' He went out to telephone again. Meanwhile, Roger started looking at the sporting page of *The Times*. He glanced idly at the information about the meeting. A few minutes later the door opened slowly and a very dejected Mr Starling walked in. As soon as his wife saw him, she knew.

'What's happened, sweetheart?' she said anxiously. 'Objection?'

'Yes, confound it,' said her husband. 'By the stewards. Upheld. Upheld, now I ask you.'

'That's extraordinary,' said Roger. 'D'you know, I've just happened to see that the senior steward's name is Perkins.'

'Don't see anything funny in that, old man,' said Mr Starling gloomily.

'Well,' said Mr Trent, 'I said it was only for the moment.'

He looked at his watch.

'Now we've missed the Bankruptcy Court. Never mind, we can do that to-morrow.'

Sadly Mr and Mrs Starling and their solicitor left Roger. When they had gone, Roger said to Henry that he thought Judge Perkins must be quite a good judge.

CHAPTER 25

The End of the Beginning

By the time Roger had almost finished his pupillage he had certainly acquired a good deal of knowledge and experience and his confidence was correspondingly increased. He had earned the magnificent sum of sixty guineas. (It had, of course, cost his mother one hundred and ten guineas to enable him to do so.) He had opened his mouth sufficiently often in Court that he had long since ceased to hear his voice echoing above him. Although he still felt intensely nervous when left, or about to be left, by Mr Grimes to do part of a case in the High Court and although, as Henry had prophesied, he was still quite unfit to conduct a whole case there, he was in a very different condition from that in which he had started. He had learned a great deal from Mr Grimes and almost as much from Henry.

In a Magistrate's Court or a County Court he started to feel fairly comfortable and, although likely to be defeated there by more experienced advocates, he did not make nearly as many mistakes as most beginners make. He had taken Henry's and Charles' experiences to heart. A few days before his time was up Henry said to him:

'I'm sure that Grimeyboy will ask you to stay on here, if you want to. You're going to be very useful to him.'

'D'you really think so?'

'I've no doubt about it. There's another side to the question, though. How useful will he be to you? Well, you'll get a lot of experience and plenty of work. But unfortunately all his work is in the High Court and what you want is somewhere where there's plenty of smaller stuff about. Alec, no doubt, would do his best for you, but to get a County Court practice going in chambers where there isn't any small work is a pretty tough proposition. I think you'd do it in the end, but it'll be slow.'

'Then, what's your suggestion?'

'Well,' said Henry, 'something phenomenal has happened. I'm going to move.'

'You?'

'Yes, I've suddenly decided to try and do a bit more work. Sally's behind it, of course. I don't suppose it will last long. But she's persuaded me I ought to get out of this rut.'

'Where are you going?'

'Well, I know Mountview pretty well and his chambers are simply bursting with work. He said he'd like to have me there if I'd come. And I'm going.'

'I shall miss you,' said Roger. 'Can I come across and ask you anything when I want to?'

'You can come across altogether, if you want.'

'Move with you, d'you mean?'

'I do. I suppose you'll ask me what I advise. Well—' began Henry.

'I'm not going to do anything of the sort. If that's a firm offer, I'll accept. I know a good thing when I see it, even at my stage.'

He thought for a moment.

'It is good of you,' he added. 'D'you think Grimeyboy will mind?'

'Grimeyboy never minds anything,' said Henry. 'He takes everything as it comes. He's always been the same and always will be. Dear, dear, dear. I don't know what things are coming to. They will do these things, my dear fellow, they will do these things.'

On the day on which his pupillage ended, Roger and Henry and Sally dined together. Roger was in high spirits.

'I don't know where I should be but for you two,' he said. 'Floating in the Thames, I should imagine, if I hadn't been picked up by now. D'you know I actually addressed the L.C.J. the other day?'

'What did you say?' asked Sally.

'Well,' said Roger, 'as a matter of fact it was—"if your Lordship pleases." '

'I hope he took it well,' said Henry.

'He said, "So be it," ' said Roger. 'I thought that was very decent of him. Now let's have a drink. And what shall we drink to? The future? Everyone's future, that is. I know what I want mine to be.'

'And I know mine,' said Henry.

'Me, too,' said Sally.

'I wonder,' said Roger, 'whether any of us will get what we want.'
'We shall see, my dear fellow, we shall see,' said Henry.

FRIENDS AT COURT

Contents

CHAPTER 1

A Question of Silk

Roger Thursby was counsel for the defendant. The plaintiff was in the witness box. After Roger had cross-examined him for half an hour the judge asked the witness if he would like to sit down.

'Thank you, my Lord,' said the plaintiff, and sat down. But he would have preferred to run out of the Court, down the street, and into his mother's arms, or, at any rate, to someone kind and comforting. Even those who tell the truth in the witness box can have an uncomfortable time there, but the plaintiff had not even a clear conscience to cheer him. He wished he'd never started the action. He'd been warned that there were difficulties. Difficulties! That was a mild word. And now here was one of the ablest counsel at the junior Bar knocking him round the ring till everything was in a haze. If only he could go down for the count. At any rate it would be over then. He asked for a glass of water. That gave him a moment's breathing space—but only a moment, for the obliging usher brought it all too soon.

'He needs something a bit stronger,' said Roger's opponent, in an undertone. And then, as the witness braced himself for the next blow, temporary relief came to him in a manner he had not anticipated. For, just as Roger said:

'Come, Mr Frail, you don't really mean that, do you?' the judge intervened by saying:

'Just one moment, Mr Thursby, please.' The witness wondered if the judge was going to say—as he had said once before—in quiet but ominous tones: 'Mr Frail, I don't think you're doing yourself justice.' But the judge did not say that or anything like it. Instead, he began:

'Mr Leonard Seaforth Jones,' and, before the witness could even start to wonder what Mr Leonard Seaforth Jones had to do with the case, he went on: 'Her Majesty having been pleased to appoint

you one of her counsel learned in the law, will you kindly take your
place within the Bar.'

Mr Jones, ordinarily very large and even larger in the regalia of
his full-bottomed wig and Q.C.'s ceremonial dress, prised himself
with some little difficulty along the front row of counsel's seats until
he was approximately in the middle of the row, and bowed low to
the judge. He then turned to his right and bowed to a Q.C. who
was standing at that end of the row, then to another Q.C. at the
other end and finally he turned round and bowed to the junior Bar.
He was just about opposite Roger when he did this, and he and
Roger exchanged winks. Then Mr Jones turned round, faced the
judge, and sat down.

'Do you move, Mr Jones?' said the judge.

For answer, Mr Jones stood up, bowed again and then went, still
with some difficulty, along the row and out at the other end, to
wait patiently for his colleagues. When they had all gone through
the necessary motions in that Court, they would all go to the next
Court, where the same process would be repeated. And so on.

The witness eventually became aware that his torture was being
interrupted by the final ceremony in the taking of silk.

'Miss Drusilla Manville, Her Majesty having been pleased to
appoint you one of her counsel learned in the law, will you kindly
take your place within the Bar.' An extremely pretty woman, who
could not have been more than thirty-five, went through the formalities. As she bowed to Roger, her full-bottomed wig looking curiously old as it hung down her young face, he whispered: 'It suits
you very well, if I may say so.'

'Thank you, sir,' she said, as she turned to face the judge again.

Roger suddenly remembered that his mother was in Court and
would be wondering what on earth was happening. He scribbled a
note, which he sent to her by a junior clerk: 'I'll tell you all about
it afterwards.'

Ten minutes later he rose to resume his cross-examination of
the plaintiff. But by this time the unhappy man had regained his
composure sufficiently to indicate that he would like his seconds to
throw in the towel.

'When they reach the glass-of-water stage,' Roger told one of his
pupils later, 'there's at least an even chance that the end is near.'

Roger had been called to the Bar just over twelve years and in
that time he had made almost as much progress as it is possible for

a junior to make. During the ceremony of taking silk, another of
the new Q.C.s, when bowing to Roger, had said:

'You next year?'

Roger shook his head, but not very convincingly, either to the
questioner or to himself. He had, in fact, been thinking of applying
for silk for some little time. But it was not a decision to be made
in a hurry. The work that he had to do as a junior was of several
kinds. He did a great deal of paper work, writing opinions and
drafting the technical legal documents required in litigation. Then,
quite as important, he acted as midwife, wet-nurse and doctor to a
delicate baby case until it became strong and healthy, or, almost
as often, strangled it at birth, saying a few words of comfort to the
parents. 'Much better to tell you now why you won't win than to
explain later why you didn't.'

'But are you quite sure, Mr Thursby? You won't mind my saying
that our neighbour, who's a lawyer himself, said that he thought
we'd be bound to win and it was he who told me to come to you.'

'Well,' Roger had said, 'I can't deny that I think part of his
advice was excellent.'

The other side of Roger's practice as a junior was the conduct of
cases in Court, when sometimes he would be opposed by a Q.C.
and sometimes by another junior. Occasionally, if the case appeared
to be an interesting one, his mother came to listen. And so it
happened that, for the first time, she saw part of the ceremony of
taking silk.

That night, in trying to explain the ceremony to his mother,
Roger also discussed with her his own future. 'Discussed' is perhaps
not quite the correct word. Roger had inherited his father's brains.
He was devoted to his mother, but devotion could not blind him
to the fact that her intelligence was strictly limited. Nevertheless he
nearly always talked over his problems with her. He never analysed
his reasons for doing this, but there were really two. First, the
discussion was often more or less a monologue by Roger and in any
event it helped him come to a decision. Secondly, they both liked
the feeling that, whatever the problem, it was apparently shared
between them.

'You see, mother,' he said, 'a man may do awfully well as a
junior because his paper work is first-class and he's good enough,
though not spectacular, in Court. If he takes silk, he has to give up
his paper work and may be a complete failure as a silk.'

'Well, dear, why not just become a Queen's Counsel and give up this idea of taking silk?'

'Mother, how often have I got to tell you it's the same thing?'

'Then really, dear, I don't know what you're worrying about. If it were something different, you'd have to choose between the two, but, as they're both the same, it can't make any difference, can it, dear? Or have I got something wrong?'

'When you become a Queen's Counsel you have a silk gown, mother. That's why it's called "taking silk". Don't you remember? I really have told you before.'

'I know, dear. I really will try to remember this time.'

The next day Mrs Thursby was talking to a friend. 'My dear,' she said, 'Roger said something to me last night about taking silk.'

'I'm so glad,' said her friend, 'because now you'll be able to tell me what it means.'

'Well,' said Mrs Thursby, with some confidence, 'it means this.' She stopped for a moment. 'This is what it means,' she went on, with slightly less confidence, 'I'll tell you.' Again she stopped.

'I'm able to tell you,' she went on, after a pause, 'because Roger explained it all most carefully to me.'

There was another pause.

'When you're at the Bar,' she continued eventually, but as though she were repeating a lesson she had not quite learned, 'when you're at the Bar either you're a barrister—or you're not.' There was a moment's silence while Mrs Thursby's friend tried hard to look enlightened. 'That doesn't sound quite right,' said Mrs Thursby.

'Well, I did wonder,' said her friend.

'Because,' went on Mrs Thursby, 'if you're at the Bar you *are* a barrister, aren't you? I wonder what Roger meant, because I'm sure he said that, and it sounded so right when he said it.'

'I expect that's because he *is* a barrister,' said her friend. 'They're so convincing even when what they say is wrong.'

'Yes, I know,' said Mrs Thursby, 'but I'm sure Roger wouldn't tell me anything wrong. Just give me a moment, dear. I'm sure it'll come to me.'

Her friend gave her several moments. Suddenly Mrs Thursby's face lit up.

'I remember,' she said, 'there are two kinds of barrister. That's what I meant. When you're at the Bar you're either one kind or the other. D'you see, dear?'

'You mean—like with apples—either Cox's or Blenheims.'

'Oh—no,' said Mrs Thursby. 'There are lots of kinds of apples. More like grapes—either muscats or the others.'

'And which kind is Roger?'

'I'm afraid,' said Mrs Thursby, 'that's what I've forgotten.'

It was perhaps rather too much for Mrs Thursby to remember that barristers are divided into juniors and Queen's Counsel, and that, as a general rule, the work of a Queen's Counsel is mostly confined to appearing in Court. Roger had explained to her years before, in fact soon after he was called, that being a junior did not necessarily mean that you were young or inexperienced. 'Some of the juniors in the Chancery Division have beards, mother,' he had told her.

'Your father had a beard once, Roger,' his mother had replied. 'I'll find the photograph.'

'And some juniors become judges without ever taking silk, you know,' Roger had continued, while his mother was searching in a drawer.

'Here it is,' she had said a moment later. 'It was red—until he shaved it off—but, of course, the colour doesn't show there.'

About nine months after he had talked about silk to his mother, Roger talked very seriously to his clerk on the subject. Donald Pirbright had been his clerk for over eleven years. Roger had served his year's pupillage with a Mr Grimes and had then gone to other chambers. The clerk in the new chambers was Donald and, during the eleven years, there had grown up between Roger and his clerk the usual indefinable but close relationship which exists between a barrister and his clerk. Donald was an excellent clerk and, like all excellent clerks, he had his idiosyncrasies; they are not called faults in the Temple. When Roger arrived at his chambers in the morning, Donald would call him 'sir.' In the afternoon, after a visit or two to one of his favourite haunts, he would be more likely to say 'sir, sir,' or even 'sir, sir, sir,' and by the evening, as often as not, he called him 'Roger.' The discussion about silk was in the late afternoon.

'Well,' said Roger, 'what about it? Do I or don't I?'

'Next year,' said Donald.

'What's the point of waiting? Bullet and Angel are applying.'

'Sir, sir. Please don't mention Mr Bullet and Mr Angel. Not in the same breath as yourself, sir. Sir, really. Bullet and Angel. Sir, sir, sir.'

'Bullet's not at all bad,' said Roger.

'Bullet,' said Donald, '*Mr* Bullet, I beg his pardon, is bloody hopeless.'

'Anyway, he'll get it.'

'Sir, sir, sir, don't come that one on me. Of course he'll get it. He's an M.P. They get it automatically.'

'But why should I wait, anyway?' asked Roger. 'What's the advantage of waiting? Or are you frightened?'

'Now, sir,' said Donald, as sternly as his recent visits to The Feathers would allow, 'now, sir, my clerk's fees don't mean a thing. You know that. I'm surprised at you, sir. I really am.'

Every time that Roger received a fee his clerk received one too. It is not certain who invented the practice, but Roger had thought more than once that there should be a statue in the Temple to the man who had thought of the brilliant idea which resulted in a barrister's clerk being paid not by his employer but by the client. The clerks might perhaps subscribe to a second statue, nestling under the shadow of the first, to the band of heroes among the clerks who, after the 1939–45 war, successfully established the practice by which a barrister pays the shillings in his guineas to the clerk. The idea was not a new one, but it was only after the war that there was a concerted attack on the Bar by the clerks, who, without a shot fired, achieved their object. When barristers and clerks were reunited after the war they naturally discussed their respective adventures during the war and then, as it were by a prearranged signal, in every set of chambers the clerk would say in an almost off-hand way:

'Oh, by the way, sir, we now have the shillings in the guineas.'

A pause.

'That all right with you, sir? They're all doing it, sir.'

Victory was complete almost immediately. A few waverers wandered uncertainly and self-consciously about the Temple for a week or two, but they soon felt that they were being regarded as outcasts and within a very short time:

'Oh, Bernard, I've been thinking about the matter you mentioned the other day.'

'Matter, sir, matter?'

'You know—the shillings in the guineas.'

'Oh—that, sir.'

A pause.

'Well, sir?'

'All right, Bernard, I give in.'

'Thank you very much, sir. They're all doing it, really, sir.'

And they all were. And are.

When Donald said that his clerk's fee didn't mean a thing, he really meant it. Naturally he would have been sorry for himself as well as for Roger if, when he took silk, his practice declined and with it the clerk's fees and the shillings. But thoughts of that possibility were not uppermost in his mind and he was thinking almost entirely of Roger's interests.

'Well, why on earth d'you want me to wait, then? I'm working sixteen hours a day, week-ends included. I don't get time for a thing. I've about had enough. I haven't even had time to get married.'

'Sir, sir, sir,' said Donald. 'That's nothing to do with time. Find the lady and you'll find the time.'

'But I haven't time to find the lady. If I'm working for you all night and all day, how can I? No, really, Donald, it's not good enough. And anyway, you still haven't said what there is to wait for. I'm making ten thousand a year. If you think I won't get on as a silk at all, for Heaven's sake say so. I shan't take any notice, but do say so.'

'Get on, sir, get on? Of course, you'll get on. I'll tell you something else, sir. You won't be a silk for more than five or six years—that's if you want to go up. I'm not sure if I'd come with you myself if you go on the Bench. We'd have to ask Henry—Mr Blagrove.'

Henry Blagrove was the head of Roger's chambers. He was seven or eight years older than Roger and was as indolent by nature as Roger was energetic. But his charming and determined wife, Sally, had spurred him into a little more activity and he had eventually taken silk. He was extremely able and, as a silk, he had just about the size practice he wanted. Sally was a solicitor, but she had given up practice to have babies and Roger was godfather of their first. Theirs was a very happy set of chambers. If Roger became a High Court judge, Donald could have gone with him as clerk or stayed with Henry, and it was a difficult choice to make. However, that was a long way ahead at the moment.

'Well, if I'm going to get on as a silk, why not now? Tell me that.'

'All right, sir, if that's how you want it—now it shall be. All the same, I'd have liked to have seen another year's junior work behind you.'

'You wouldn't have to do it, Donald,' said Roger. 'You can play golf and take your wife out, while I sit sweating at home. Now we'll reverse the process. I can sit twiddling my thumbs while you search the highways and by-ways to find me a brief.'

'Search the highways, my foot,' said Donald.

'That's really all I wanted to know,' said Roger. 'P'raps you'd turn up the Law List and tell me all the people I've got to write to. How many d'you think there'll be?'

Roger now had the task of writing to every practising junior on his circuit, who was senior to him in call, to inform him of his intention to apply to the Lord Chancellor for the purpose of taking silk, so that they could apply also if they wanted to do so. It was a task to which he looked forward. It meant that he had made up his mind. It was a risk undoubtedly, but it was worth it. The only question now was whether the Lord Chancellor would give it him first time. He was certainly young—thirty-three—but there was no doubt about the size and quality of his practice. He did not think that he would receive—as some promising juniors had received in the past—a polite note with 'next time' on it. Anyway, if he did, the decision would have been made for him. That night he wrote a letter to the Permanent Secretary to the Lord Chancellor:

I shall be grateful if you will place before the Lord Chancellor this my application to be considered for appointment as one of Her Majesty's Counsel.

He showed it to his mother.

'How many Q.C.s are there, dear?' she asked.

'I don't know—altogether, I suppose, about three to four hundred, but I should say that only about half of them practise.'

'The Queen must have a lot of cases to need all those counsel.'

Roger did his best to explain.

'You make it all sound very clear,' said his mother.

'Good,' said Roger.

'But I'm afraid,' she went on, 'I still don't understand. All the

same, I'm glad you'll be one of them. But don't ask her too many
questions.'

Some little time was to elapse before the Lord Chancellor's
decision would be known and meantime Roger carried on with his
ordinary work. But he did so in a much happier frame of mind. He
could see the way ahead and there would be some time in it for
other things besides law. He was very cheerful when he lunched
next day at the Inn he used for the purpose. He usually sat with
the same people, though he could never quite think why. Probably
it was habit. They had been his neighbours when he first lunched
in that Hall some years ago before and it seemed rude to sit elsewhere. In any event, lunch did not take long. The conversation
during it was usually on the same lines. Arnold Carruthers, who
sat opposite him, was a barrister of a good many years' experience.
He found it helped him to discuss his professional problems with
other people and almost invariably he would begin, as soon as he
decently could—and sometimes before:

'Look, I'm an actress of uncertain age and not much talent. I get
knocked down by a bus. What's it worth? I couldn't act much
before the accident. Can't act at all now.'

Sometimes it would be a point of law. 'Look, the Court of Appeal
in *Lea and Moore* seem to have said that you can't try a case in the
County Court by consent unless it first started in the High Court.
I'm referring, of course, to cases which are outside the normal
jurisdiction. But they only looked at Section 43. They never once
referred to Section 65. Now, I think—' And Carruthers would
elaborate his point and try to obtain the opinions of those around
him. If he was lucky someone would point out that a new Act did
away with the effect of the decision.

Another of Roger's neighbours had a very small practice, a
reasonable private income, and a fund of undergraduate stories. He
began on this occasion with: 'D'you know this one? There was a
girl with a rather short skirt standing in a bus. The conductor gave
her a ticket, but she dropped it. "Will it matter?" she asked the
conductor. Have you heard it by the way?'

'Only once or twice,' said his immediate neighbour, 'and not for
a very long time.'

'Well, I don't suppose Thursby knows it. He's never heard any
of them.'

'No, I haven't, as a matter of fact,' said Roger politely, 'but it'll probably be above my head.'

'Oh, no—not this one. Well—the conductor turned to the girl and said—'

At that moment Carruthers arrived.

'Look, so sorry to butt in, but I've got rather a teaser. D'you mind? I'm a stable boy at a well-known racing stable—'

'Got anything for the Derby?'

'No, look, this is serious—'

'Then the girl said: "But how shall I know if it's the right ticket?" Then the conductor turned to the girl and said—'

'And while I'm out exercising a horse which I haven't ridden before—'

'Hullo, Roger, they tell me you're applying for silk.'

'But I've only just posted the letter—'

'Good news travels fast.'

'Then the girl turned to a passenger and said: "I wonder if you'd mind—" '

'Now this horse was well known to the trainer to be difficult, but I didn't know it. Now, while I'm on this brute—'

'Good news! If I get it first time, I expect I'll be in the bread line.'

'Rubbish—I hear Forsythe's applied.'

'Is there anything confidential you don't know?'

'Confidential be blowed. I bet you've written to at least thirty people on your circuit.'

'More, if you want to know.'

'Well, you can't expect them all to keep quiet about it.'

'Then the girl said—'

'As I fell on the ground the trainer arrived and cursed me. What he actually said was—'

And so on and so forth, what the girl said, how the conductor turned, why the stable boy fell, what the trainer called him, interspersed with the latest gossip and a few polite inquiries. And lunch in Hall was over.

CHAPTER 2

Retrospect

That evening Roger walked home from chambers. He thought first about the past, about his call nearly thirteen years before, his first miserable efforts in Court, the agonies he had gone through. How kind Henry Blagrove had been. He was sure he would never have got on but for Henry. It was not simply the encouragement Henry had given him, but he had shown him the only way to learn how to succeed at the Bar. I wonder if I've taught my pupils half as much as Henry taught me? Never accept anything without knowing why, Henry had always told him. Whether it's a matter of law or practice, you must know the principle behind it. When the judge says: 'But you can't do that,' find out why you can't do it, and very occasionally, in looking up to see why you can't do it, you'll find you can and that the judge was wrong. Yes, he owed nearly everything to Henry. He was glad that Henry owed something to him too—Sally. Roger found it difficult to remember himself and his girl friends without squirming. Who, outside of Dornford Yates, would have behaved as I did—or, indeed, as they did? Sally and Joy had both adored Roger. Roger at twenty-one, good-looking, ambitious, slightly priggish, wholly inexperienced was, to Roger at thirty-three, a somewhat nauseating spectacle. But he braced himself to the effort of looking back. And after all he had been very young. He thought of Joy, pretty and empty-headed. Well, perhaps not as empty as all that. She had sent her uncle to brief him, Uncle Alfred, that pompous elderly solicitor whom he had eventually insulted by refusing a three-thousand-guinea brief. How on earth had I the nerve? Three thousand guineas and we were very short of money at the time. But it would have meant marrying Joy. How right he had been. And as for Sally, who had more intelligence than any woman he had ever known, Sally adoring, rather lovely and rather sad. I wonder why I never wanted to marry her? I suppose because

I just didn't want to marry at all. Anyway, my loss, if it was one, was Henry's gain. He fell for Sally and eventually she capitulated. They were very happy. I am pleased about that, he thought. If it hadn't been for me, Henry would never have met her. That's something I've done for him. All the same, I could do with a home now. I wonder if I'll get one. I'll certainly get more spare time soon, at least I hope so. Well, I'm not going to waste it. Why on earth do I lunch with Carruthers and Co.? I joined Henry's Inn in addition to my own and I have to go and listen to that tripe. There were plenty of other people in Hall who seldom talked shop and never told dirty stories. I can't very well move somewhere else when I take silk. Oh—well I suppose I'm used to it by now. But that girl in the bus went on for ever. I don't even remember the end now. Perhaps I never heard it. I expect it was as old as the hills, anyway. His stories aren't just chestnuts—more like *marrons glacés*. Anyway, what am I worrying about? I'm going to take silk, marry and have a home. Life beings at thirty-three.

CHAPTER 3

Slograve, Plumb and Co.

'So Donald's letting you apply,' said Henry the next day. 'That's very decent of him. Of course, it'll ruin me, but don't let that worry you.'

'If I get any of your leavings, I shall be lucky,' said Roger.

'Leavings? I haven't returned a brief this year, but don't let it get you down. As a matter of fact, I'll exist quite well on *your* returns. You wait and see.'

'I haven't got silk yet.'

'You will. It's a foregone conclusion with your practice. Donald's a very lucky man. All he wants now is a junior who can take on your practice. D'you think Axford will hold it?'

Axford was older than Roger, but had not been in the chambers as long. He had started as a solicitor and then read for the Bar.

'I think he ought to keep some of it. He's a good lawyer and works like a black.'

At that moment Donald came into the room. 'Slograve, Plumb have just been on the phone. Want to come and see you at once. I said O.K.'

'All right,' said Roger. 'Any excuse for not getting on with some work.'

'It was Plumb himself. He sounded rather worried.'

'He's always gloomy. When you start a case he's worried to death that the witnesses won't come up to scratch and, if they do, that the judge won't. Then, if you win the case, he's terrified it'll go to the Court of Appeal and, if you win there, he has sleepless nights thinking of the House of Lords allowing the appeal. Then, when the Lords dismiss the appeal with costs, he's on tenterhooks that the other side won't have the money to pay. And when they've paid in full, he's pretty sure to point out that the amount he's had to charge his client is more than they've got out of the other side. And if you point out to him that he could have charged a bit less, that worries him more than anything—because it happens to be true.'

'I like your Mr Plumb,' said Henry. 'There's a richness about his gloom which I enjoy. One can almost pinch it as Mr Squeers pinched young Wackford. "There's oiliness for you." Don't forget me if they want a leader, Donald. Oh—by the way, I backed your confounded horse on Saturday.'

Donald owned two racehorses. He called one 'Conference' and the other 'Consultation'. He had bought them from a trainer for whom Roger had done a case.

'I didn't tell you to, sir. If you want to win on my horses, you wait till I give the word.'

'Sally and I are going to Alexandra Park on Saturday. Have you got anything for us?'

'I'll come back and see you when I've seen Mr Plumb in, sir. Conference is coughing at the moment. Consultation looks extremely well. The only trouble with that horse is that it doesn't like jockeys. Once it's thrown its jockey it goes like the wind. Almost flies you might say. I thought of suggesting to the Jockey Club they might try some riderless races. Have some corn beyond the winning-post. That'd stop them. Oh—there's the bell. I expect that's old Plumb. Excuse me, sir.'

'I'll go to my room,' said Roger.

A few minutes later Mr Plumb was shown in to him. He had a red face and a bald head, and whether it was hot or not he was continually wiping it with a handkerchief. He sat down rather ponderously, wiped imaginary sweat from his forehead, sighed, frowned and then spoke. He had a voice reminiscent of that of the Radio Doctor but lacking its cheerfulness.

'It's very lucky indeed,' he said in the gloomiest possible tones, 'very lucky indeed you're not in Court, Mr Thursby. It's a great relief.' He wiped his forehead again. 'I don't know what I should have done. There's no one else in the Temple I could go to.'

'It's very good of you to say so,' said Roger, 'but I'm sure there is.'

'But there isn't, Mr Thursby, there really isn't. That's what's so worrying. You may take silk one day and then where shall we be?'

'And, of course, I might be knocked down by a bus,' said Roger gently.

Mr Plumb said nothing.

'Well—I'll take all the care of myself I can,' said Roger. 'And we'll hope for the best.'

'Mr Thursby,' began Mr Plumb, and then stopped.

'Yes?' said Roger.

Mr Plumb hesitated.

'Well,' said Roger cheerfully, 'what's it all about?'

Mr Plumb again hesitated. He appeared to be in two minds as to what he wanted to say. Eventually one of his minds forged ahead, and he spoke:

'Well, Mr Thursby, I act for the proprietors of a seaside hotel. The Glorious at Westlea. It's a most respectable place, I assure you, terribly respectable. I've known Mr and Mrs Glacier—they own the place—for many years. They are very good clients, very good clients indeed.' As he said this, Mr Plumb looked so mournful that Roger really wondered whether he was going to burst into tears.

'They buy hotels all over the place and, I may tell you in confidence, the conveyancing is worth a very considerable sum, a very considerable sum indeed.'

Mr Plumb looked gloomier than ever.

'And what's happened? Have they stopped conveying?'

Mr Plumb wiped his forehead and was silent for a moment. Then his other mind came to the front and took command.

'Mr Thursby,' he said, 'my firm briefs you because I believe you to be without question easily the best junior at the Common Law Bar. I hope you will forgive my speaking plainly.'

'No one could object to such plainness, however undeserved,' said Roger.

'The plainness is to come, Mr Thursby. Because of our opinion of you, my partner and I accept your little bouts of facetiousness with as much goodwill as we can muster. But neither of us has much of a sense of humour, Mr Thursby. I know it is not fashionable to say so, but we have not. We are gloomy men, Mr Thursby, gloomy men.'

'I'm so sorry,' murmured Roger.

'Thank you,' said Mr Plumb, 'and would I be out of order if I asked you to add to your many kindnesses by not laughing at me too obviously too often? I'm consulting you about a most serious matter, very serious indeed, and while I shall quite understand if in the circumstances you ask me to leave your chambers, if you do not take that course I shall be grateful if you will at any rate conceal your amusement. No doubt sometimes you may indulge in a quip which, owing to my lack of humour, will go over my head and out of the window and maybe will rocket into the satellites. Pray do so, if you wish, so long as you are reasonably certain I shall not notice it.'

'I'm so sorry,' said Roger. 'I really am. Please don't take any notice of my flippancy. I apologise for it. It's very rude. I must confess, though, that, however serious a case, a light touch every now and then helps things along. I have even heard a judge make a joke in sending a man to prison.'

'And may I ask,' said Mr Plumb, 'did it send the fellow roaring with laughter to the cells?'

'A fair comment, Mr Plumb, and not one I should expect from anyone without a sense of humour. I think, if I may say so, you have one somewhere around.'

'It is of course possible,' said Mr Plumb with the utmost gloom. 'It is of course possible.' And he wiped his forehead.

'But to continue about my clients,' he went on. 'Mr and Mrs Glacier are Swiss by birth, but they are naturalized. They have lived here a considerable time. They started with very little capital and have worked up a magnificent business—magnificent. It is all very depressing.'

Roger restrained himself from asking what was depressing about that.

'Mr Thursby, solicitors have their feelings. I know that people are inclined to regard lawyers as soulless blood-suckers—but Slograve, Plumb are at any rate not without a soul.'

A little rhyme insisted on inserting itself in Roger's thoughts

> High-minded but dumb
> Slograve, Plumb

but he kept it to himself.

'I won't deny,' continued Mr Plumb, 'that the loss of their business would not mean a lot to us. It would. A very great deal.'

I convey, you convey, he conveys, went through Roger's mind.

'Indeed, such a loss could be a very serious blow to our business.'

Would that I may convey, would that you may convey, would that they (and in particular Mr and Mrs Glacier) may convey. May they convey, let them convey—consult Roger Thursby and they *shall* convey.

'But at the moment I am thinking not so much of our firm as of these two people. A man and a woman. My clients.'

Meet to be conveyed, considered Roger.

'Ruin, Mr Thursby. A life's work gone. Gaol. Naturalization cancelled. Back to Switzerland.'

How will they be conveyed? resisted Roger. Instead: 'How does it all arise?' he asked.

'It's absurd really,' said Mr Plumb, 'quite absurd. But, like so many serious matters, it arises from a small one. The licensing laws. The requirements with which licensees have to comply are very considerable and sometimes onerous, very onerous indeed. For example, there is no objection to a licensee giving a friend a drink after hours if he chooses. But who is a friend?'

'Who is my neighbour?' asked Roger.

'Precisely. An equally difficult question. A landlord of a hotel should be a friend to his guests.'

'It's a prosecution for a breach of the licensing laws?' queried Roger.

'If that were all,' said Mr Plumb, 'I should not have troubled you with the matter. That would be serious, but nothing more. It is far worse than that.'

He wiped his forehead several times. Roger was tempted to ask him if he would like a glass of water, but he refrained.

'You can imagine the shock it was to me when my clients came to me only this morning—you'll see I've wasted no time in coming to you—when they came to me and said they had been charged with bribery of the police. Bribery of the police. A conviction for that and they're finished in this country, apart from the fact that they'd probably go to prison. Mr Thursby, I don't ask you to take my word for it, but Mr and Mrs Glacier are charming and respectable people.'

And require a lot of conveyancing, added Roger to himself.

'I cannot for one moment think them guilty, but there it is, they're charged—under the Prevention of Corruption Act. Now, I believe in acting under counsel's advice from the word go—not, I may say, because that relieves us of legal responsibility, but because— provided you go to the right counsel—it pays—it pays us, it pays the client.'

And the client pays counsel, said Roger—again to himself. But he knew Mr Plumb was right. And, indeed, he encouraged his clients to come to him at an early stage. Many an action has been won or lost by the preliminary steps which have been taken long before it ever came into court.

'Now I might have gone to Mr Erswell of the Criminal Bar—a very sound man, if I may say so. But I wanted something better than that. Erswell is, if I may say so, excellent in Court, admirable at putting his case—when it's been prepared for him in an adequate brief—before judge or jury. But I have a feeling that this matter requires rather more imagination in its handling. So I've come to you and I hope—I earnestly hope you'll be able to help us.'

'I'll certainly do my best, Mr Plumb,' said Roger. 'Perhaps you'll tell me the facts.'

'I'd prefer to call them allegations, Mr Thursby. They are these. There have been rather late parties at the Glorious from time to time and apparently neighbours objected to the noise. I need hardly say that the parties were entirely respectable, but admittedly they were late and admittedly you cannot have a party without a noise. Apparently complaints were made to the police and, in consequence, somehow or other plain-clothes detectives attended one or two occasions. A few weeks ago an inspector and a sergeant from the local police station called on Mr and Mrs Glacier and informed them that they would be proceeded against for breach of the licensing laws. It is alleged that at that interview and again at a subsequent interview Mr and Mrs Glacier attempted to bribe the officers by handing them, on the first occasion, twenty pounds in one-pound notes and, on the second occasion, twenty-five pounds. It is alleged that the money was handed to the police to persuade them either to stop the prosecution or to make the offence appear to be a very trivial one.'

'I can understand your anxiety, Mr Plumb,' said Roger. 'What do your clients say about it? Do they admit giving the money?'

'Most certainly not,' said Mr Plumb. 'And I may tell you, Mr Thursby, that I believe them.'

'Well,' said Roger, 'I haven't met either of them and I haven't yet heard them tell their story, but I'll tell you quite frankly I shall be very surprised if their story is true. Now, please don't get excited, Mr Plumb.'

For Mr Plumb had started to brush his forehead very vigorously indeed.

'I'm not in the least excited,' said Mr Plumb, his red face redder and his handkerchief doing overtime. 'I'm not in the least excited, but am I to understand that you are calling my clients liars?'

'Certainly not,' said Roger, 'not yet. I tell you, I haven't seen them or heard them tell their story. Of course, I can't form a judgement on them yet. But just consider what it means if they're telling the truth. It means that an inspector and a sergeant—with very likely as many years of good character behind them as your clients—have put their heads together for no known reason to pretend that they have received money from your clients.'

'You're not suggesting, Mr Thursby, that the police never tell lies and never trump up cases?'

'No,' said Roger. 'It does happen occasionally, but there has to be a reason for it. And don't forget this. Those pound notes—forty-five of them, I think you said, are going to be produced at the trial. And I'll tell you who'll produce them.'

'The inspector and the sergeant, I presume?'

'Certainly not. Possibly even the local Chief Constable, and at least the Superintendent. After your clients handed these notes to the police officers—I mean after they *didn't* hand them to the police officers, these police officers on two separate occasions handed two separate bundles of notes to a superior officer. Now, of course, the Superintendent or the Chief Constable might be in the swindle, but I imagine you'll agree that that's going a bit far. So that, apparently, just in order to do down your clients, the inspector and sergeant laid their hands on forty-five pound notes and took them to the Superintendent or some superior officer, with a fraudulent story that your clients had tried to bribe them. Now it's one thing to invent a story. It's another to invent forty-five pound notes. They have to be obtained and they were obtained. Quite a lot of money, you know, for police officers to have. Much too dangerous to have drawn them from a bank or the post office. They must have kept them under the bed.'

The movement of Mr Plumb's hand had slowed down a bit.

'Mr Thursby,' he said, 'you shake me. But I still can't believe it. I'm sure there's some explanation.'

'I think perhaps,' said Roger, 'you'd better bring your clients to see me and we'll hear what it is. I'm in court all day to-morrow, but I expect Donald can fix a conference after 4.30.'

CHAPTER 4

Mr Grimes

Roger was in Court the next day dealing with a contract for the supply of machinery to Peru. The case was expected to last a long time. His opponent was Mr Grimes. The judge was Mr Justice Chance.

'How are ye, my dear fellow?' said Mr Grimes to Roger outside the Court. 'A little bird tells me ye've applied for silk. Good for you, my dear fellow, good for you. But—' and Mr Grimes shook his head, 'things aren't what they used to be, my dear fellow, not what they used to be. Ye'll find it a bit of a teaser, my dear fellow. Silks are two a penny, my dear chap, two a penny.'

'I'm going to charge twopence,' said Roger.

'That's the way, my dear fellow, that's the way, but I don't know what we're coming to. D'ye know, I've had a dozen letters from fellows on my circuit—they were only called yesterday—I don't know what they think will happen to them, but there it is, my dear fellow, they will do these things, they will do these things. Now, what about this case of ours, my dear fellow, my clients aren't at all inclined to settle it, ye know.'

'Nor are mine,' said Roger.

'Stubborn, my dear fellow, stubborn,' said Mr Grimes.

'It's dogged as does it,' said Roger.

'I beg your pardon?' said Mr Grimes.

'Nothing,' said Roger. 'But why should you want to settle? You've an unanswerable case and a hopeless opponent. What more could anyone want?'

'I can't understand your chaps fighting it, my dear fellow, I really can't,' said Mr Grimes.

'Nor can I,' said Roger. 'But it's lucky some of them will. Between you and me they're only doing it to keep me in practice.'

'Ye will pull my leg, my dear fellow, ye will pull my leg,' said

Mr Grimes. 'But all the same, my dear fellow, I think ye'd be wise to make me an offer. I think ye'd be wise.'

'If you'd said that twelve years ago I should have put my head on the block and invited you to chop it off.'

'Was it as much as twelve years ago, my dear fellow, was it really?'

'Well, you haven't changed. As young and bustling as ever. What's your record from the Temple to the Bear Garden?'

Mr Grimes never walked if he could trot and never trotted if he could run. Age had slowed him down a little, but only a little. The policemen on duty outside the Law Courts seldom needed to hold up the traffic for Mr Grimes; he was across the Strand almost before they'd seen him. It would have been an exceptionally skilled motorist who could have caught him. But he always complained bitterly: 'When they've killed a judge, my dear fellow,' he used to say, 'they'll put a bridge up or a subway. Till then one just has to take a chance. Good-bye, my dear fellow, so nice to have seen ye— good-bye, bye, bye.'

The 'byes' floated across the Strand as Mr Grimes dodged a bus, slipped behind a lorry, glared at a cyclist and cannoned into a pedestrian on the other side. 'So sorry, my dear fellow, it's these—' but by this time he was up the stairs leading to the Bear Garden and the pedestrian never learned what 'these' were.

'Oh, I don't know,' said Mr Grimes to Roger, 'one can't quite do what one used to do, you know, one can't quite do it.'

'Well, you seem to,' said Roger. 'I don't notice the slightest difference.'

'That's very kind of ye, my dear fellow, very kind of ye. Now, what about this case? Ye really ought to make an offer.'

'I said you hadn't changed,' said Roger. 'No, I think we'll see what old Chance thinks of the preliminary point. If he's against us on it, I might offer you something. Not much, mind you.'

'That's all right, my dear fellow, my people don't want to settle. Ye have a fight, my dear fellow, and see where it gets ye.'

As Roger said nothing and was about to go into Court, Mr Grimes added: 'Why don't ye offer something, my dear fellow?'

'You seem in a bad way,' said Roger. 'Let's see. You're claiming five thousand pounds. I'll offer you two hundred and fifty.'

'Two hundred and fifty pounds, my dear fellow, two hundred

and fifty pounds?' Mr Grimes almost screamed. 'That won't even pay the costs.'

'I don't suppose it will,' said Roger, 'but it'll be something towards them.'

'If that's all ye've got to say,' said Mr Grimes, 'we'd better go into Court.'

'I was just going,' said Roger, 'when you stopped me.'

'Why not make it one thousand pounds, my dear fellow? I might persuade my people to take it.'

'I'll make it guineas,' said Roger.

'A thousand guineas?'

'Oh—no . . . two-fifty.'

'It's ridiculous, my dear fellow. I tell ye it will only just pay the brief fee.'

'That'd be something.'

'The judge'll be coming in, my dear fellow, shall we ask him to stay out for a bit?'

'All right,' said Roger, who recognised the white flag when he saw it. He called for Donald.

'See if you can keep the judge back for a bit. It looks as though this is going to be settled.'

'I'll try, sir,' said Donald, 'but you know what this judge is like.'

Roger did know, and so did everyone else. Chance J. had a sweet smile and a melodious voice. He never raised it, he seldom said a harsh word to anyone. It is said that on one occasion he smiled so pleasantly at the prisoner he was about to sentence that the poor fellow couldn't believe it when he got ten years. He even appealed on the ground that it must have been a mistake. Chance J. always sat at 10.30 a.m. He had done it for years and proposed to go on doing so. He expected everyone else to do the same. He expected every case to be ready at the appointed time. If counsel was late he found his case struck out or at least put to the bottom of the list. And what made it worse, Chance J. was so nice about it.

'A traffic accident, Mr Peabody?' he had been known to say. 'I'm so very sorry. It must have been very difficult for you. No doubt you'll come by train next time. Much more reliable. I've had your case put to the bottom of the list. I doubt whether it will be heard to-day. I'm so very sorry. Please explain the matter to your client. I'm sure he'll understand. Yes, Mr Blank, I'll take your application for an adjournment now. It is refused. Thank you so much.'

However, Donald went hastily off to find Mr Justice Chance's clerk. They were old friends, played cricket together and had stood each other drinks at every bar within three hundred yards of the Law Court.

'Hello, old boy, what can I do for you?'

'Keep the old—back for a bit.' The—was in fact unspoken. That was out of respect for the Bench. You just looked the word, gave a momentary pause and the decencies were observed.

'Have a heart,' said the judge's clerk. 'I couldn't even keep him back for the Attorney. "I'll start the next case," he said when I asked him. "There isn't one," I said. "This is supposed to take all day." "Well, go and draw one from someone else. I'm sitting at 10.30." '

'Doesn't he ever remember he was at the Bar?'

'Now you've said something. Between you and me, I told him myself. "James," he said, "I used to wait hours when I was at the Bar. I didn't like it, but I had to. Now I'm not going to wait any more." But he said it all so nicely there was nothing I could say. Really, I daren't ask him, old boy. I'd do it for you if I'd do it for anyone. It'd be no good if I did. He'd simply give me a sweet smile. "Shall we go in, James?" he'd say.'

So at 10.30 a.m. precisely Roger's and Mr Grimes's case was duly called on immediately after Mr Justice Chance had taken his seat. Mr Grimes was whispering furiously to his clients, as the associate said:

'*Green, Rawhide, and Smithers* against *Confucios.*'

Mr Grimes rose: 'I wonder whether your Lordship would grant me a few minutes' indulgence?'

The judge smiled sweetly. 'Indulgence, Mr Grimes?' he said most amiably.

'Just a few minutes, me Lud. Your Ludship may not be troubled with the case.'

'But it's no trouble, Mr Grimes. That's what I'm here for.'

'But, me Lud,' began Mr Grimes unhappily.

'That's all right, Mr Grimes,' said the judge. 'Pray open the case. It has a South American flavour, if one may judge from the defendants' name. Oil, Mr Grimes?'

'Machinery, me Lud.'

'Ah, machinery. You'll have to treat me very gently, Mr Grimes.

Nice simple language, please. Is there a model in Court, I see something down there which—'

The judge put on his glasses.

'Oh—no, I'm sorry,' he added.

It was Mr Grimes's client.

'Now, I think we've wasted enough time, Mr Grimes. Shall we get on?' and he gave Mr Grimes the kind of beaming smile he had given the prisoner who had got the ten years. 'Now, please, Mr Grimes,' he went on without the slightest show of irritation—indeed still smiling—as Mr Grimes turned round and started murmuring feverishly to his client. 'Please, Mr Grimes, conferences afterwards. At one o'clock, shall we say?'

'I'll take five hundred pounds,' whispered Mr Grimes to Roger.

'Sorry,' said Roger. 'Two-fifty.'

'Guineas,' said Mr Grimes.

'Certainly,' said Roger.

'Mr Grimes,' said the judge, 'can you hear me?'

'Oh, me Lud, I beg your Ludship's pardon, but I'm glad to tell your Ludship that your Ludship will not be troubled —that me learned friend and I have come to terms.'

'A close thing, Mr Grimes,' said the judge. 'Do you want any order from me?'

'I suggest, my Lord,' said Roger, 'that the action should be stayed on terms endorsed on counsel's brief.'

'I think I should have a judgment, me Lud,' said Mr Grimes.

'Dear, dear,' said the judge. 'I thought I was told that the parties had come to terms. Either they have or they haven't. That's right, isn't it, Mr Grimes?'

'Oh—yes, me Lud.'

'Mr Thursby?'

'Certainly, my Lord.'

'I'm so glad we're agreed,' said the judge. 'Now, perhaps Mr Grimes would kindly open the case or tell me the agreed terms.'

'Won't you agree to a judgment, my dear fellow,' whispered Mr Grimes to Roger.

'I don't mind,' said Roger.

A few minutes later Mr Justice Chance started the hearing of the next case, and Roger and Mr Grimes left the Court.

'Tell me,' said Roger when they were outside, 'why did you crack like that? You hadn't such a bad case.'

'Ye're quite right, my dear fellow, I *hadn't* such a bad case at all—yesterday. But that agent fellow suddenly turned round and went back on his proof. So what could I do, my dear fellow, but still there it is, my dear fellow, they will do these things.'

CHAPTER 5

Mr and Mrs Glacier

With a long case out of the way, Roger was able to go back to chambers, and Mr Plumb was informed that he could have an earlier conference if he wished it. He jumped at the opportunity and telephoned his clients, Mr and Mrs Glacier, to meet him at Roger's chambers. They all arrived just before 3 p.m. and Mr Plumb asked to see Roger alone before he introduced him to the clients.

'How are you, Mr Plumb? Do sit down.'

'Very good of you to see us so soon,' said Mr Plumb mournfully as he sat down. 'I must say I'm more than ever glad I came to you in the first instance.' And he wiped his forehead. He waited a moment or two before speaking, and then: 'Mr Thursby, you were quite right, quite right,' he said.

'About what?'

'About the money. I put it to my clients just as you put it to me—about the actual notes being produced by the Chief Constable or the Superintendent or someone—and after a bit they asked if they could have a word together outside my room. When they came back they admitted that what they'd told me hadn't been true. It's most unsettling, Mr Thursby, most disturbing. But what's my duty? I don't pretend I don't want to keep them as clients—as I told you, the conveyancing—'

'Quite,' said Roger.

'But if you tell me to throw them out, I will,' said Mr Plumb. 'Slograve, Plumb have their reputation to think of. That comes first. We've never broken the rules yet.'

'Well, Mr Plumb, in a civil case I think that a solicitor or a barrister is fully justified in throwing out a client who deliberately lies to him. Often in a criminal case, but that isn't always quite so easy.'

'Mr Thursby, there seems to be a slight misunderstanding,' said Mr Plumb, mopping his completely dry brow. 'I don't want to throw them out. I want to know if I've got to.'

'I was coming to that,' said Roger. 'The mere fact that a client tells you a lie certainly doesn't make it necessary for you to refuse to act for him, particularly if he corrects it himself. But, subject to certain general rules, each case has to be judged by itself.'

'General rules, you say? Such as?'

'Well, I expect you know them as well as I do. Have you never been asked—how can you appear for someone whom you know to be guilty?'

'Yes,' said Mr Plumb, 'I have been asked that—more than once.'

'And how d'you answer it?'

'Well, Mr Thursby, to be quite candid, I change the subject. I find it much too difficult. You see, Mr Thursby, my firm doesn't do much criminal work, but, in every case we've handled, I've known the defendant to be guilty, and I feel a little awkward about it, particularly as we got two of them off.'

'D'you mean that your clients admitted to you that they were guilty?'

'Oh, dear me no, Mr Thursby, dear me no. Then it would have been quite simple. We'd just have pleaded guilty. But not a bit of it. They swore blind they were innocent and what's worse, they got away with it. In one case the magistrate swallowed it and in another case the jury.'

'I take it you didn't see them commit the crime yourself, Mr Plumb?'

'I beg your pardon, Mr Thursby? I don't quite follow.'

Roger repeated the question.

'See them do it myself? Of course not. What a question, if I may say so, Mr Thursby.'

'Well,' said Roger, 'if you didn't see them commit the crime and they denied to you that they'd committed it, how did you *know* they'd committed it?'

'Well—it was quite obvious in each case. The evidence was overwhelming.'

'Apparently the jury and the magistrate didn't think so. They're the people to judge, aren't they, not you? You say you *knew* your clients were guilty, but you didn't, you know, you only *thought* it.

The judges of the matter thought otherwise. So, as Dr Johnson once said, you were wrong and they were right.'

'I think I see what you're getting at, Mr Thursby.'

'You mustn't put forward what you *know* to be a false case but, subject to that, you must put forward whatever your client's case is, whether you believe in it or not.'

'You make me feel a good deal better, Mr Thursby,' said Mr Plumb, mopping his brow as though he felt a good deal worse.

'When you come to think of it, Mr Plumb,' went on Roger, 'hardly anyone would be defended if his lawyer had to believe in his innocence. If it's any comfort to you, in the few criminal cases I've had I haven't believed in my client's innocence yet.'

'You don't say.'

'I do—at least that's not quite accurate. When I was a very young man I was much more inclined to believe what I was told, and I did once appear for a motorist in whose innocence I passionately believed. She was very pretty, so I may have been prejudiced. It wasn't a very serious matter. She was fined forty shillings. I felt like paying it myself.'

'Well, Mr Thursby, I'd better say at once that I do not—and shall not—feel like going to gaol for Mr and Mrs Glacier—not for all the conveyancing in the world.'

'Hadn't we better have them in?' said Roger, 'or was there something else you wanted to tell me first?'

'Well, there was, but on the whole I think you'd better get it from them yourself. I wasn't very successful in the first instance.'

Roger rang the bell and Donald showed Mr and Mrs Glacier into his room. Mr Plumb introduced them. Mr Glacier was a small bearded man with a slight foreign accent. He had an extremely good command of English but, every now and then, he would use a perfectly correct expression in a manner which suggested that he was uncertain whether it was right. It might well have been an affectation. Mrs Glacier had obviously been very attractive when young. Her knowledge of English was not as good as her husband's—except as regards bridge terminology; she knew all the words necessary to be able to play the game regularly from 3 to 6 p.m.

'Mr and Mrs Glacier,' said Roger, 'I'm sure you'll understand that I'm only here to help you, but I cannot emphasise too strongly the necessity for your telling me the truth and the whole truth. If you don't, I may make things infinitely worse for you.'

'The truth,' said Mr Glacier. 'Ah—who knows it?'

'You and your wife do in this case.'

'Is the world round or flat?' asked Mr Glacier. 'Is the moon made of green cheese?' Mr Glacier paused to see if he had made an impression. Apparently he had. There was silence.

'At one time it was popularly supposed that the world was flat. If a boy at school had said it was round he would not have been telling the truth, as it was then known. Who knows—to-morrow the world may be flat.'

'It may indeed,' said Mr Plumb sadly.

'And green cheese,' continued Mr Glacier, 'is it impossible that it was once believed that the moon *was* made of green cheese? The truth—pah!' said Mr Glacier. 'When you English lawyers talk of the truth you make me—' and he looked round the room as though for a spittoon.

'Mr Glacier,' said Roger, 'I have not the time at the moment for a discussion as to the meaning of truth, but let us assume the earth once was flat and now is round, and that the moon was once made of green cheese and now is made of—I don't think you mentioned what the moon is now made of?'

'Brass,' said Mr Glacier.

'Brass?' queried Mr Plumb.

'No one has been there yet and brought away a—what is the word?—a sample. It could be. Or perhaps I should say you cannot prove it is not.'

'Scientists could,' said Roger.

'Scientists,' said Mr Glacier with an air of triumph, 'the best scientists of the day once were convinced that the earth was flat.'

'Very well, brass it shall be,' said Roger. 'And now shall we get down to the matter in question? All this arose because I wanted you to understand that you may do yourselves a great deal of harm by not telling me the unvarnished—'

'Brass,' put in Mrs Glacier.

'The inside of Holloway Prison is, I believe,' said Roger, 'no more comfortable than that of Wormwood Scrubs. Bribery of the police is a very serious charge. Anyone convicted of it is very likely to go to prison. Mr Glacier would start at Wormwood Scrubs and Mrs

Glacier at Holloway. I'm sorry to put it so crudely, but, unless you treat this matter seriously, you may be sorry later.'

'Very well, sir,' said Mr Glacier, 'put your questions. I will endeavour to answer them with a—how do you say?—a candour that will surprise us both.'

'You are both charged,' said Roger, looking at the summonses which Mr Plumb had given him, 'with two offences. It is said that on the 14th December Mr Glacier gave twenty pounds to Inspector Worcester as an inducement to persuade him to withdraw the licensing prosecution or to give false evidence. I understand that you did in fact give the inspector twenty pounds on that occasion.'

'No,' said Mr Glacier.

'But Mr Plumb tells me—' began Roger.

'No,' repeated Mr Glacier.

Roger looked at Mrs Glacier.

'I pass too,' she said.

'Mr Plumb,' said Roger, 'I thought you told me—'

'Ask them again,' said Mr Plumb.

'Did you not give the inspector twenty pounds?' repeated Roger.

'I did not,' said Mr Glacier.

'Either on the 14th December or on any other day?'

'On no occasion did I hand the inspector twenty pounds. My wife will confirm this.'

Roger looked at Mr Plumb, who sat quite calmly, only very occasionally mopping his brow.

'Ask him again,' said Mr Plumb.

'Really,' said Roger, 'I confess I'm getting a little tired of this. Mr Plumb originally informed me that you denied giving any money to the police, but after I had pointed out to him that the actual notes would be produced in Court he told me that you had admitted you had given the money.'

'Can I rely on the money we gave being produced in Court?' asked Mr Glacier.

'I thought you said you hadn't given any.'

'Can I rely on the money we gave being produced in Court?' repeated Mr Glacier.

'You certainly can,' said Roger rather crossly.

'I venture most respectfully to disagree,' said Mr Glacier. 'The money we gave will not be produced in Court—most assuredly it will not be. You may corroborate me, my peach.'

'I collaborate,' said Mrs Glacier.

'Ask me again the question,' said Mr Glacier.

'Did you give the inspector twenty pounds?'

'No,' said Mr Glacier. 'Definitely not.'

A sudden light dawned on Roger.

'How much did you give?'

'Thirty pounds,' beamed Mr Glacier.

'That was the first call,' put in Mrs Glacier.

'Correct, my angel,' said Mr Glacier.

'The second time you're supposed to have given twenty-five pounds,' said Roger. 'How much was it then?'

'Thirty-five pounds,' said Mr Glacier, with obvious enjoyment.

'I suppose there's no corroboration of your story?' said Roger.

'I collaborate,' said Mrs Glacier.

'Yes,' said Roger, 'but I'm afraid you're an interested party. You're charged with the offence.'

'But it's the truth,' said Mrs Glacier, adding, after a slight pause, 'this time.'

'Quite,' said Roger, 'but how is one to know? And if I believe you—and it doesn't matter whether I do or I don't —will the jury believe you unless there's something to show that you're telling the truth and the police officers aren't?'

'The jury,' said Mr Glacier, 'will not know of—how shall I say?— the way we first put it to Mr Plumb.'

'That's certainly an advantage,' said Roger.

'I'm afraid,' said Mr Plumb, 'that I'm a little out of my depth. Mr and Mrs Glacier are charged with giving money to the police. They admit it. What defence is it that they gave more than is charged against them?'

'I'll come to that in a moment,' said Roger. 'First of all, I wanted to see whether we'd be likely to establish that you had paid more than is alleged in the summonses.'

'Suppose you can? What then?' said Mr Plumb.

'I rather fancy,' said Roger, 'that the police would be much more interested in prosecuting their own black sheep than in securing a conviction against Mr and Mrs Glacier.'

'You're not suggesting we should tell the police what our clients have admitted to us?' said Mr Plumb, wiping his forehead vigorously.

'I certainly am,' said Roger, 'if it has any chance of being believed and quite likely if it hasn't.'

'Do I understand,' said Mr Glacier, 'that you intend to betray our—what is the word?—our confidences to the police?'

'Of course not,' said Roger. 'Until I know a lot more I don't know what I'm going to advise you. But if I advise you to instruct us to tell the police and you don't want us to do so, of course we shan't tell them. What you tell us is in confidence and if you don't want to take my advice you needn't. Is that plain, Mr Glacier?'

'Then would you explain why you should want at all to tell our case to the police? You will forgive me, Mr Thursby. I am not any longer talking of the earth being round or flat or the moon being made of green cheese or brass or cobalt or anything at all. What I am saying is nothing to do with the moon. Is that plain, sir?'

'Entirely.'

'Well, sir, I do not read many detective stories, nor do I read of very many cases in Court, but in my fifty-seven years I have read something of crime and I do not remember any case where a man's own lawyer has gone to the police—how do you say?—like a lamb to the slaughter—or perhaps I should say has led his client like a lamb to the slaughter.'

'Don't let's worry about detective stories or other cases, Mr Glacier, though, as a matter of fact, there are quite a number of cases where a solicitor has gone to the police with his client to make a confession.'

'I do not propose to make a confession. Why should I present it to them as you say on a plate—like a piece of cake?'

'As I've said before,' said Roger, 'until I know the full facts I can't say what I'm going to advise you, but, as you're so worried about this particular point, let me deal with it. Supposing I do advise you to go to the police and say what has happened, how will it hurt you?'

'*Mon Dieu!* The earth *is* flat,' said Mr Glacier. 'He asks how it will hurt me. You hear that, my cabbage. The moon *is* made of green cheese.'

'I collaborate,' said Mrs Glacier.

'Now listen,' said Roger patiently. 'Let's assume that you don't tell the police anything, what will happen? Both police officers will give evidence that you gave them twenty pounds on the first occasion and twenty-five pounds on the second occasion. Upon that evidence the magistrates are bound to commit you for trial at the assizes. When it comes to your trial the same thing will happen. The officers will give their story in evidence. If you don't give evidence in your own defence you will obviously be convicted. There'll be nothing to contradict the police evidence, and so the jury will believe them. Do you follow so far?'

Mr Glacier nodded in assent. Mr Plumb paused with his handkerchief in mid-air. He was puzzled and fascinated.

'If, on the other hand, you do give evidence,' went on Roger, 'you will then have to say what you've told me now. If it's got to come out then, how does it hurt you for it to come out earlier?'

This time Mr Plumb nodded in assent. But the effect on Mr Glacier was electric. He looked agonisingly upwards, he tugged at his beard several times, stood up, sat down, stood up again and threw out his arms, sat down and buried his head in his hands. Then he looked imploringly as for comfort to his wife.

'I collaborate,' she said.

'What's the trouble?' asked Roger.

'The world is not flat—it is not round—it is triangular—it is going round very fast indeed—now it is going to stop and we shall all be thrown off.' He cupped his hand to his ear. 'D'you hear those rumblings?' he asked. 'We shall be blown off any minute now.'

Mr Plumb, who had followed Roger's explanations of the situation with complete understanding and some pleasure, now began to mop his forehead vigorously again.

'Mr Glacier,' said Roger, 'I can only imagine that you're troubled at having to tell the truth to the jury.'

'Troubled?' said Mr Glacier. 'That is a good word. Troubled! It is we who rot in gaol, sir, not you or the amiable Mr Plumb—it is we, your clients. If we want to tell the truth to the jury, do we need a lawyer—two lawyers? Please do not think I mind the money. I like money, yes. But I pay your fees willingly if there is some point. But if all you say is go and lift up your chin so that it can be conveniently punched, or place your body in a position where it can be conveniently kicked—well, sir—I can do that without your assistance. I need no help to fall into the river. It is kind of you to offer to give me—how do you say?—a send off, but I can jump—and quite as far and as deep as you can push me—if I want to, sir— but—I do not want to, sir —*I do not want to,* sir. Do I make that plain?'

'I suppose,' said Roger quite calmly, 'that your idea is that we should invent a good story for you to tell.'

'What else is a lawyer for? When the truth is good, what need have I of a lawyer? I go to a lawyer when the truth is —how do you say?—inconvenient.'

'Well,' said Roger, 'there may be some countries where lawyers behave like that. And there may be one or two over here who'd do it for you, but not many, and they'd be kicked out pretty quick if they were found out.'

'There are not many such?' asked Mr Glacier.

'Very few,' said Roger.

'You have their addresses perhaps?' said Mr Glacier.

'I have not,' said Roger. 'I think perhaps Mr Plumb, the time has come—'

Mr Plumb said gloomily: 'I'm afraid Mr Glacier doesn't understand our ways. You see, Mr Glacier, although lawyers in this country have to help their clients, they have to do it honestly.'

'But of course,' said Mr Glacier. 'That is all I was asking.'

Mr Plumb and Roger tried hard to explain to Mr Glacier what are the duties and responsibilities of lawyers in this country. Roger even repeated part of his earlier advice to Mr Plumb. Mr Glacier tried hard to follow.

'But, let me ask you something,' he said after a little time. 'You wish your client to win the day, do you not?'

'But by proper methods,' interposed Mr Plumb.

'Quite so. But you want to do the best for him?'

'Certainly.'

'Well, gentlemen, let us suppose you have a client charged with murder and you think he has committed the crime. No —I have quite understood this afternoon's lesson—you only *think* he has committed it, you do not *know* it. Now, thinking he has committed it—do you say to him, as you said to me, now tell us the truth? If you are right in thinking him culpable—I mean guilty, of course— he will, will he not, have to admit the crime when he tells you the truth? And, if he tells you that he is guilty, I understand now from you that he will have to say the same to the judge and jury. Is that best for him, gentlemen? Is it even good for him? How hard do you try to persuade your client to tell the truth when you believe the truth will—what is the word?—will condemn him?'

'Mr Glacier,' said Roger, 'this is a very interesting discussion on the ethics of the legal profession, but I'm afraid I haven't time for very much more. If you want me to continue to advise you in your particular case, I will do so—provided you now understand and will stick to the rules. I must make it plain, though, that if you don't, I reserve the right to throw up the case in the middle.'

'I have read of that, now I come to think of it,' said Mr Glacier. 'I am interested to know what it means. I am sorry to have shocked you so much, gentlemen. I confess that you have shocked me. But I think I am, as you say, over it now and I would like you to proceed, if you please.'

'Well, then,' said Roger, 'I'd like you to tell me in your own words how you came to pay this money, what was said when you paid it, where you got the actual money from, and whether there's any means of proving that you paid sixty-five pounds and not forty-five pounds.'

Mr Glacier hesitated for a moment. 'As to proof—beyond my wife's and my own word—I shall have to think, but the rest I can answer now. We run a small club at the Glorious; our daughter is the secretary. The unfortunate matter of drinks after hours strictly concerns the club rather than the hotel. Our daughter, who is young and—you will forgive a father's pride—beautiful, has just become *fiancée*—engaged —unofficially. To someone of importance. It is perhaps not necessary at the moment to mention his name. If she had been prosecuted, it would have been most unfortunate—it might even have prevented the marriage—one cannot say where these things end. We were therefore extremely worried about the matter and, at the time the officers disclosed themselves at the party, the situation was in fact mentioned to them. No hint, I assure you, gentlemen, of money. We just happened to mention how unfortunate it would be if Melanie were charged. You can imagine then how pleased we were to find when the inspector and sergeant came to serve us with the licensing summonses that there was no summons for Melanie. We were overjoyed and we said so. The officers said they were only doing their duty and that Melanie did not—how did they say?—did not come into it. Now, the office in which we interviewed the police contains my safe where, during the day, a fair amount of cash is kept. I felt so pleased—so grateful that, without really thinking anything about it, I opened it, took out a bundle of notes and asked the inspector to accept it with our most distinguished compliments.'

'You say a bundle of notes. How d'you know there were thirty?'

'When I—how do you say?—balanced the cash.'

'You could have made a mistake.'

'Certainly not. Impossible. There is a check for everything. It balanced except for thirty pounds.'

'What did the inspector say?'

'He said it was very kind of us, but we were to remember he had only been doing his duty.'

'How did you come to give the next lot?'

'The inspector came again with the sergeant to prepare a plan of the premises for the Court proceedings. They chatted to us. It was all very friendly. They or I mentioned our daughter. Again we said how grateful we were. Again they said they were only doing their duty. Again I went to the safe. This time I knew it was thirty-five pounds I took out. There was a packet of twenty-five pounds and I took another packet of ten pounds.'

'Why?'

'Why does one do anything? I felt grateful. We are not poor. And then, too, I thought perhaps it was expected of me. The officers stayed rather longer than was necessary.'

'How did you account for the money in your books?'

'Entertainment expenses.'

'Well, I should like to see your books for the day and I'd like your accountant to go through the slips or checks for that day and let me have a report. What I want to find out is if there's any possible corroboration in your books and papers that the extra ten pounds passed each time.'

'To be quite frank with you, sir, I do not think there can be.'

'All the same I'd like it done, please,' said Roger. 'I'm bound to say I find difficulty in accepting what Mr Glacier says in its entirety—he will forgive me in the circumstances for saying so, I hope. If the officers were dishonest, I can't see why they should have put in a charge at all if they'd been given the money like that. They could just have kept it and no one would have been any the wiser. But suppose that what Mr Glacier says isn't entirely accurate. Suppose he did try to bribe the officers—it *is* possible that a dishonest policeman would try to get the best out of both worlds—by reporting the matter to his superior and keeping ten pounds on the way. He would argue to himself that Mr Glacier would probably deny everything—as indeed he did at first and would have done up

to the trial, if Mr Plumb and I hadn't intervened. He would feel
quite satisfied that at any rate Mr Glacier would never dare to say
he had given more than the forty-five pounds mentioned in the
summonses. Of course, after he had been convicted he might tell
everything, but it would be too late then. No one would believe
him. So, from a dishonest officer's point of view, it was pretty well
a certainty. If we'd got some corroboration and went to the police,
I believe there'd be a very good chance of their chasing their own
people instead of you. And if they didn't, as I've pointed out, you'd
have lost nothing. For better or worse, your story's coming out in
the end. Bring it out now and it may do you more good. I think
it's worth trying anyway, but we do want something more than
your word if we can get it. Mark you, in any event the fact that we
tell the police the story at all is fairly strong and will make them
think a bit.'

'So you advise?' said Mr Plumb.

'First of all, get someone on to the books at once. There must be
no delay at all. Then, in a couple of days I'd advise Mr and Mrs
Glacier to authorise you, Mr Plumb, to go straight to the Chief
Constable of the County and tell him everything—not in confidence,
mind you. Openly. Tell him he can use it as much as he likes.'

'Is that necessary, Mr Thursby?' queried Mr Plumb.

'In my view, yes. In fact, in criminal matters there can be no
such thing as without prejudice or the like and, although I've no
doubt the Chief Constable would respect your confidence as far as
he properly could—which incidentally might not be possible—you
can't go to a Chief Constable and say—between you and me, old
boy, and you won't let it go any further, but I've murdered my
grandmother—although he'd keep it in confidence if he could—
you've nothing to gain from his so doing and you may have something to gain from keeping it quite open. For example, we can tell
the jury all about it if they go on with the prosecution. But the
object, of course, is with luck to stop the prosecution. If we fail in
that, as far as I can see, we'll only have done ourselves a bit of
good. But it's up to Mr and Mrs Glacier. If they don't like the idea
that's an end of it.'

'Mr Thursby,' said Mr Glacier, 'I am beginning to entertain a
great respect for you if I may say so. I like the idea.'

'I collaborate,' said Mrs. Glacier.

CHAPTER 6

The Ancient Mariner

On his way home that evening, rather earlier than usual, Roger was stopped by one of the ancient mariners of the Temple. Their ages vary from something over forty to something under ninety. It is very difficult to get away from any of them, but no one likes to hurt their feelings. So they ply a flourishing trade. If Roger saw any of them far enough off and he considered himself unobserved, he would slip through an arch into another of the Temple's courts; but there are not many long approaches in the Temple and usually he, like everyone else except the really rude men of the Temple, had to submit to the inevitable. There is seldom anything sad about these ancient warriors. Few of them have ever had any practice and must have had independent means to enable them to continue at the Bar. None of them would recognise himself as one of their number and they are completely oblivious of the fact that their victims are wriggling and squirming to get away. Of course, sometimes they meet each other. That is excellent. All they want to do is talk, and they both talk and neither listens and a good time is had by all.

'Haven't seen you for a long time, old boy,' said Roger's captor. 'Done any sketching lately?'

'Not really had much time, as a matter of fact.'

'Ah, you're one of the busy ones—though between you and me I haven't met anyone who isn't. Everyone rushing off to or from a conference or consultation. Strictly between ourselves, old boy, I often suspect the conference is at the Cock and the consultation in the imagination. Not in your case, of course.'

'I'm going home, as a matter of fact.'

'And the best place, too. My home's here. Come up and have a glass of sherry and a yarn.'

'Well, as a matter of fact—'

'Come along, old boy—take your mind off all those briefs. Come on—it's only just up here.' He led the polite and unresisting Roger to his residential chambers.

'I like living over the shop, I must say. Saves an awful lot of time. I bet it takes you at least three quarters of an hour to get home.' Roger conceded that it did.

'There you are, you see. Takes me exactly three minutes. Have a chair. I'll get a couple of glasses.'

Roger waited patiently and wondered how long he would have to endure the punishment. He would refuse a second glass. That was definite.

'Here we are, old boy. Hope you'll like it. Rather a good line I've got from El Vino. I know the manager there rather well and he always lets me have anything rather special. Well—here's luck.'

They sipped the sherry.

'Not bad, eh?'

'Very good. Very good indeed.'

'I had Mervyn here the other day. Said it was the best he'd ever had. He ought to know. He was weaned on sherry. Well, what's the news? Who's going for silk? No one's written to me yet. As a matter of fact, they don't always, you know. I've seen a name or two in the paper—junior to me by years—but not so much as by your leave or with your leave. Oh, well—it's a sign of the times. Mind you, I don't believe anyone's applied just because they've had a note from someone else saying he is. Still I like these old courtesies. But courtesy's out of date, I suppose. Like me.'

'Nonsense,' said Roger. 'Didn't you have that robbery appeal in the Court of Criminal Appeal the other day?'

'Yes.'

'Jolly good,' said Roger, glad that he was right. 'You were successful, I gather?'

The ancient mariner's face fell slightly. 'As a matter of fact I was for the Crown, old boy, and they allowed the appeal. Between you and me I still don't know what they were talking about. Said I oughtn't to have asked one prisoner where he met the other.'

'Where was it?'

'In gaol, of course. How was I to know? Anyway, he only answered "In Devonshire, sir", and I don't suppose the jury knew it was Dartmoor.'

'Bad luck,' said Roger, 'but, as old Grimes would say—they will do these things, they will do these things.'

'Amazing man, old Grimes. Goes on for ever. Just as good as ever. Now *he* never has time for a sherry. But, of course, he hasn't. I don't know how he gets through it all. What you doing tonight? Theatre or something?'

'As a matter of fact, I've got a spot of work.'

The ancient mariner winked. 'I know, old boy,' he said. 'I could do with some myself.'

CHAPTER 7

Crabtree

Roger was in Court all the next morning trying to convince the Court of Appeal that one of its previous decisions had been made *per incuriam* or, as the layman might put it, by a slip of the tongue. He had little success. It is not particularly easy to convince a single judge that his tongue has slipped. It is naturally even more difficult to convince three judges that all their three tongues have slipped and all at approximately the same moment. During a lull in the proceedings, while his opponent was being asked a question, Roger—in a flash of genius—decided that, if one of the Lords Justices should be made a peer, his motto should be '*Per incuriam nihil*,' which, Roger thought, might be translated for the benefit of members of his family who knew no Latin as 'Always conscious of our bloomers'. He was interrupted in these thoughts by the Lord Justice in question:

'Well, Mr Thursby,' he said, 'I can't speak of my brethren, but personally I have no doubt about the matter.'

'My Lord,' said Roger, with a glance at the clock, 'I hope that after lunch I shall have the opportunity first, of infusing some doubt in your Lordship's mind and then, of satisfying your Lordship that my argument is sound.'

'You will require an extremely effective lunch,' said the Lord Justice.

'I'm afraid,' said Roger, 'I shall be lunching on a summons for interrogatories.'

'I hope,' said another Lord Justice, 'you won't seek to administer any interrogatories to us on our previous decision.'

'Oh, my Lord,' said Roger, 'no one is bound to answer any interrogatory which might incriminate him.'

And on that note the Court adjourned for lunch and Roger, with Donald, went hurriedly to the Bear Garden to do his summons.

'Who's against us?' he asked Donald on the way.

'Now keep calm, sir,' said Donald. 'It's Crabtree.'

'Oh—no,' said Roger. 'No—please not . . . anything but that.'

'Can't you agree it with him?' asked Donald.

'I'll certainly try,' said Roger, 'but I can never understand what he says.'

Miles Crabtree was an extremely nice fellow and everyone liked him, but he suffered from a most serious defect which made it difficult to understand why he ever received a brief. He was practically incapable of saying one complete sentence by itself. His cross-examination of a witness would usually run something like this:

'Now, Mr Sanders,'—and here he would point his finger at the witness and frown slightly in a rather learned manner —which at first terrified an untruthful witness and which was calculated to make any witness feel that some really difficult question was going to be asked; well, it was going to be difficult, but not in the way the witness thought. . . . 'Now, Mr Sanders, I want to ask you about—but so that your Lordship can follow the question would you be kind enough to turn to page 3 of the correspondence. Your Lordship will see there—in any event it's in the pleadings—would your Lordship look at page 2 of the defence—now, Mr Sanders, with regard to the meeting on the 20th January, but before I come to that would you be so good as to explain why—I don't want to trap you in any way—perhaps my learned friend would let the witness have a copy of the correspondence—would you be good enough to explain why—no, it's no good looking for assistance at the back of the Court, and I want a straight answer Yes or No to this question—your Lordship has found the passage? I don't want to be told afterwards you didn't understand the question, Mr Sanders, so I'll make it quite plain and if you've any doubt will you please say so now—will you kindly wait, sir, until I've formulated the question—you needn't think I'm going to be browbeaten as you browbeat my client—will you kindly give me your attention, sir. Have you—and tell me directly one way or the other—did you or did you not at that meeting in January—no, not the one in January—I'm so sorry, my Lord. I got confused with the correspondence—if your Lordship will turn to page 36—the last sentence but one—no, your Lordship is perfectly right—there is no page 36—there must be some mistake—oh, no—I have it, my Lord, it's page

26. And now, sir, I think you've had long enough, quite long enough, to answer the question. Will you kindly do so?'

'I'm afraid I haven't followed the question,' says the witness.

'So you haven't followed the question, haven't you?' begins Crabtree.

'I'm afraid I haven't either,' says the judge.

'Oh—I'm so sorry, my Lord. Your Lordship is very patient. If I may refer your Lordship to page 36—no, page 26 of the correspondence—your Lordship will see there—'

'Mr Crabtree,' says the judge, 'I think it would be better if you asked the witness a question—just one to begin with. I'll do my best to follow.'

'Your Lordship is very good. Very well then, Mr Sanders—you remember that meeting, the one I was referring to, not the one in January—that was a mistake on my part—the one in February, the meeting which is referred to in the correspondence. You know the one I'm talking about, there's no mistake about it, is there? Now, at that meeting there were three of you present. You, Mrs Bole, Mr and Mrs Meadowes—no, that makes four, I'm sorry. There were four people present and what I want to ask you, Mr Sanders, is did any of you at that meeting—any one or more of you, I mean you or Mrs Bole or Mr and Mrs Meadowes—I think there was no one else present—that's been admitted—your Lordship will see that in the particulars delivered on the 14th January last—no, I'm sorry, my Lord, it's in the defence itself under paragraph 7—oh, no, my Lord, I'm so very sorry—it *is* in the particulars of the 14th January after all—I had them in the wrong order in my bundle—I'm so sorry, my Lord. Now, Mr Sanders, this is very important, I shall make a note of your answer—did you, or Mrs Bole or Mr and Mrs Meadowes—any one of you, I mean—say anything like this—I don't mean the actual words—no one expects you to remember the exact words of a conversation all that time ago, but anything of the kind, I mean. I'm waiting for your answer, Mr Sanders.'

'Did who say what?' intervenes the judge.

'Oh, my Lord,' says Crabtree, 'I'm so sorry. I thought I'd asked the witness. Well, Mr Sanders, so that there may be no doubt at all about it I'll ask you again.'

And so on and on goes Crabtree, the most patient of judges eventually wishing that either he or Crabtree had never been born.

It was not, therefore, very surprising that Roger should be

dismayed at the thought of having Crabtree as an opponent. He had altogether fifty minutes in which to deal with the summons before Master Tiptree, and another one before Master Peabody and, if possible, to get something to eat. But, he reflected with some comfort, thank Heaven there'll be an end of all this if I get silk. He prayed that the Lord Chancellor would give it to him.

'Hullo, my dear fellow,' said Crabtree, as Roger came into the Bear Garden—so called because a lot of shouting goes on—though nothing like as much as there used to be.

The noise is comprised of:

First Attendant (in loud voice): First call—Counsel—G. to N.
George and The Glassbottling Co. Ltd.
Graham and Hurst.
The Gargantuan Co. (1953) Ltd, and Blowback, etc. etc.

First Solicitor's Managing Clerk (in loud voice):
Cosset and Green—Cosset and Green.
Anyone here from Cosset and Green?

Second Attendant (in loud voice): First call—Counsel—O to Z.
Orange and Mowbray.
Ostler Ltd and Jones.
Onapoulos and Deep Sea Fishing Co. Ltd, etc. etc.

Second Solicitor's Managing Clerk (in loud voice):
Briggs and Moulton—Briggs and Moulton.
Anyone here from Briggs and Moulton?

Add one more attendant for the cases lettered from A to F and any number of solicitors' managing clerks, and start them all up together, and you have the Bear Garden.

'I think we're against one another,' said Crabtree.

'Hullo,' said Roger. 'Yes, I'm in a bit of a mess, as a matter of fact. It may have to be adjourned, if we can't agree it. Will you agree to any of the interrogatories?'

'Look,' said Crabtree, 'I'd like to help you, but—well—if you take the first lot—I mean the first six, well five anyway —I don't personally see how . . . but no doubt I'm wrong, of course, but, if you ask me it seems to me—you see, on the pleadings it's quite clear—I mean if—'

'That's all right,' said Roger, 'we'd better let the Master decide.'

CHAPTER 8

Corroboration

A few days later Roger had an urgent call from Mr Plumb. 'I've had the most extraordinary piece of information,' he said. He wiped his forehead. 'I hardly know what to make of it. Look at this, Mr Thursby. I took this proof myself.'

He handed Roger a typewritten document. It was signed at the bottom: 'Albert Thrussle.' It began: 'Albert Thrussle, police constable in the Carpshire Police, will state:'

'Before you read it I'd better tell you how he came to see me. Yesterday Mr Glacier telephoned me and said that a policeman had called on him and he asked me if he might bring him along to my office. I said yes, of course, and they came. Mr Glacier then told the policeman to tell me what he'd told him and, after he'd told me, I made it into the form of a statement. I read it out to him. He said it was absolutely right and he signed it. He says he's quite prepared to swear to it.'

'I'd better read it,' said Roger.

He read:

I am a police constable in the Carpshire Police. I have been in the Force three years. I know Sergeant Warwick; I meet him sometimes in the police canteen. The other day he was drinking rather a lot of beer and we got chatting. Somehow or other we talked about cases of bribery and, after a bit, he said: 'I'll tell you a thing. If anyone tries to drop you anything—d'you know what to do?' 'Well, I think so,' I said. 'I bet you don't,' he said. 'Well,' I said, 'what is it?' He winked at me and said: 'They always deny it, don't they? O.K. Take a per cent for yourself. No one the wiser. Easy as pie. I've got one on now.'

'Well, what d'you think of it?' said Mr Plumb. 'There's your corroboration for you.'

'It certainly is,' said Roger. 'But why did he come to you, or
rather, to the Glaciers?'

'I asked him that. He said he'd heard about the prosecution and
he was so disgusted that anyone could behave like that he came
straight along and told Mr Glacier.'

'Why didn't he tell his superintendent?'

'I asked him that too. He said that he didn't like to. From what
the sergeant said, the inspector must have been in it too. He was
quite sure the superintendent knew nothing about it, but he was in
fact on very good terms with the inspector. He knew the inspector
and sergeant would just deny it, he thought the superintendent
would believe them, and he was frightened of getting into trouble.'

'Why isn't he frightened of getting into trouble now?'

'He says he simply had to do something and as he was frightened
of going to the superintendent he came to the Glaciers.'

'P'raps,' said Roger, 'he thought the Glaciers might do something
for him out of gratitude, if it became too unpleasant in the police
force. They're a grateful couple. We know that on their own story.'
He thought for a few moments.

'Did you happen to find out what beat P.C. Thrussle was on?'

'I didn't, as a matter of fact.'

'I hope that by coincidence it didn't take in the Glorious.'

'You mean?'

'Just that. Mr Glacier's moral sense is not exactly of the highest.
I said I wanted what Mrs Glacier calls "collaboration". We've got
it now with a vengeance. I hope it came of its own accord, and
without any assistance from Mr Glacier. I wouldn't put it past
them. One of us will have to ask them point blank. I will, if you
like; it sounds a bit offensive.'

'That's extremely good of you, Mr Thursby. I must confess I
should feel a little hesitation in asking my own client whether he'd
been—whether he'd been . . . well, whatever it is you think he may
have been doing.'

'I don't think one way or the other, Mr Plumb,' said Roger. 'But,
having regard to our previous experience of the Glaciers and their
ideas about the truth and what you go to lawyers for, it wouldn't
be right to act on this without taking every reasonable precaution
first. I'm not at all sure that I shan't make an exception and see

the policeman myself. I'll have to think that one out. I suggest you bring the Glaciers to me once again as soon as possible, and I'll let you know if I want the policeman as well.'

'Glacier's in London to-day, I know,' said Mr Plumb. 'I'll get his wife as well if possible—that's if you can see us.'

'I'll arrange it somehow.'

Mr Plumb left hurriedly.

'What *is* all this?' said Donald. 'I've got to fit in Fitcham and Grant some time. You seem to like the Glaciers. Sure you wouldn't like me to offer them a bed?'

'They're more likely to offer me one,' said Roger. 'They own a lot of hotels, in particular the Glorious at Westlea.'

'I've stayed there,' said Donald, 'when Consultation was running at Annington. Didn't care much for it. Too many visitors and they don't serve beer in the lounge. I'd have left, only we couldn't get in anywhere else. I'll charge them an extra con. for that.'

Donald was looking at the diary as he was speaking. 'All right, you can see them at six, if you like. How long are you going to be? Finish by to-morrow? D'you want me to wait, or will David do?'

'Oh—don't you wait, Donald. I don't suppose we'll be too long. If we are, I expect David can go too and I'll shut up. Tell him to give me a ring if he wants to get away.'

'Thank you, sir. Oh—that'll be old Park,' said Donald, as the bell rang. 'You'd better get back to your room. I want to have a word with him about a fee.'

Roger went back to his room, and Mr Park was admitted by the junior clerk and brought to Donald.

'How are you, Mr Park?' said Donald. 'He's all ready for you.'

'Remarkable,' said Mr Park, 'quite remarkable. The busier a set of chambers, the less you have to wait.'

'Organisation, sir,' said Donald modestly.

'Now, I used to go to—well, I won't say where—but somewhere else—and I never had a conference on time. I didn't so much mind myself as I used to send a clerk in the end, but it's the clients, you know, they don't like it. Some people think it impresses. So busy, we have to keep you waiting. Fiddlesticks! I'll tell you what impresses. Conference fixed for two o'clock, conference held at two o'clock.'

'I quite agree with you sir,' said Donald. 'It's just a little matter of arranging. Would you like to go in now, sir? I think you said the clients weren't coming?'

Donald made as if to take Mr Park to Roger—and then stopped: 'Oh, just one thing, as you're here, sir. I would have mentioned it to your clerk, but as you're here perhaps you won't mind. The fee in the Longworthy case, sir. I know the other side have only got seventy-five, but I really can't let Mr Thursby do it single-handed for less than a hundred and fifty.'

'A hundred and fifty?' queried Mr Park. 'That's a bit steep, isn't it? I could get a leader for a good deal less.'

'Of course you could sir, and between you and me, sir, I wish you would. It's putting a lot on Mr Thursby to do this by himself. He's got a great deal on at the moment.'

'Of course he has,' said Mr Park, 'but I want him to do this himself. Between you and me—apart from just a very few at the top—there isn't a leader to touch him. He'll be taking silk himself soon, I suppose?'

'Silk, sir?' said Donald. 'I don't know anything about that, sir.'

'If you did, you wouldn't tell me. Frightened of my taking my junior work away too soon, eh?'

'Well, I suppose he'll have to take it sometime, but he hasn't said a word about it to me at the moment, sir.'

'I believe you,' said Mr Park, 'though I can't think why.'

'Sir,' said Donald, in a tone of injured innocence. 'Well, would you like to go in, sir? That's all right about the fee, is it, sir?'

'Make it a hundred.'

'I couldn't really, sir. I'm having to return work as it is. I'll tell you what, sir, for old time's sake I'll make it a hundred and thirty.'

'That's a curious fee,' said Mr Park.

'I thought you might say that, sir,' said Donald. 'All right, sir. A hundred and twenty-five. That's settled then, sir. Will you come along now, sir?'

He showed Mr Park into Roger's room.

As soon as that conference—which was about a yacht—was over, Roger had to turn his attention to the comparatively simple matter of an accident on the Kingston by-pass. By six o'clock he was ready for the Glaciers. Only Mr Glacier came this time, accompanied by Mr Plumb.

'Now, about this policeman, Mr Glacier,' began Roger . . .

'Is it not magnificent?' interrupted Mr Glacier. 'From the gods it came, from the gods themselves.'

Roger checked himself from saying he hoped their name wasn't Glacier.

'You asked for corroboration—and there was none—and now—how do you say?—hey presto, you have the most beautiful exquisite corroboration—and all dressed in blue. Are you not pleased, Mr Thursby?'

'Mr Glacier,' said Roger, 'you must forgive my asking you this question, but I'm afraid it's necessary. This is a serious matter for you, and it's also a serious matter for the sergeant and inspector—very serious indeed. Before I'm a party to putting forward your allegations, I want to be as sure as I can that they're true.'

'Ah, we are back to the truth again—to the moon and the earth. I forget how we left them—brass or green cheese—flat or round.'

'I'm afraid that kind of thing doesn't impress me,' said Roger, 'not favourably, anyhow. What I want to ask you, Mr Glacier, is, first of all, whether Constable Thrussle was a complete stranger to you before he came to see you the other day?'

'A complete stranger? As far as I know, yes. I may have seen him in the street, just as I may have seen you in the street before—but I am not aware of having seen either of you.'

'Then you'd never spoken to him before?'

'Subject to the same—how do you say?—qualification, certainly not. I may have met him in a train and asked for a light, or on a country road and said "good evening"—just as I may have said either to you, Mr Thursby, but I am not aware of it in either case. You see how careful I have become since we first met.'

'So it was a surprise to you when he came to see you?'

'A complete surprise.'

'And presumably to your wife too?'

'Absolutely. We looked upon it as manna from heaven. But I assume from your question that you are wondering whether one of us put the manna there in the first place.'

'Perfectly correct,' said Roger. 'If it's true that you bribed two policemen you might easily bribe a third.'

'Logical, Mr Thursby, but fortunately not so. Why do you not send for the policeman and ask him questions? My English is not as good as his, my understanding of English ways is also not as good as his. Why not put your questions to him? After all, if he has been bribed by me we are both . . . both—what you call crooks—

and it should not take long for a man of your experience to find it out.'

'I had thought of seeing him, Mr Glacier, but it is not normally proper for counsel to see the witnesses in a case—except his own clients. I'm entitled to make an exception to the rule if I think there's a good reason for doing so. At the moment, in view of the advice I'm going to give you, I don't think there is. I've seen the officer's signed statement, I've heard from Mr Plumb how it was taken, and I think I must be satisfied with that.'

'And you are going to advise?'

'What I originally indicated. I think Mr Plumb should go and see the Chief Constable and tell him everything quite openly, and show him the policeman's statement. What happens after that will depend entirely on the Chief Constable.'

'You want me to go and see the Chief Constable?' asked Mr Plumb rather anxiously, and mopping his brow several times. 'I confess I should find that rather embarrassing. Would it by any chance be possible for you to accompany me?'

Roger thought for a moment. 'If you really want me to do so, I don't see any objection to it. It will be rather inconvenient, but I'll speak to Donald about it, if you like.'

'I should be most grateful if you would,' said Mr Plumb. 'I think it so important that a proceeding of this kind should start off on the right foot, and I might say something of which you would disapprove.'

'I'm sure you wouldn't,' said Roger, 'but, if it'll make you any easier, I'll try to come and start the ball rolling. Of course it may not roll.'

'I have a feeling,' said Mr Glacier, 'that it will roll.'

CHAPTER 9

Traffic Block

Roger agreed to go with Mr Plumb to see the Chief Constable on the following Saturday. They were to meet independently outside the Chief Constable's house, as Roger was coming from London and Mr Plumb from the country.

'It's a shame your having to leave so early on a Saturday,' said Mrs Thursby.

'I quite agree, Mother,' said Roger, 'but there it is—they will do these things.'

'I suppose they will,' said Mrs Thursby. 'What things?'

'Make work for lawyers. Just as well, I suppose. If everyone were reasonable and good there'd be no need for us.'

'Is the person you're going down to Westlea to see reasonable and good?'

'I'm going for two people really. Mr Plumb, I should say, was certainly good and moderately reasonable. Mr Glacier is logical, if not reasonable, but I suspect that he is pretty bad.'

'I can't think why you bother to act for him then, Roger. There must be plenty of good ones to defend.'

'I doubt it, Mother. Very few innocent people stand in the dock.'

'How horrible,' said Mrs Thursby. 'I'm glad I don't have anything to do with it. I could never defend anyone if I weren't sure of his innocence.'

'Lucky you didn't go to the Criminal Bar, Mother. You'd have felt the draught a bit. Now, I must be off. Bye-bye ... not sure what time I'll be back. I'll ring you if I'm going to be late for dinner.'

Ten minutes later he was on the way to Carpshire. It was not a very long journey, but it was a bad day for driving. Sporting events, roads up, experimental white lines being painted and the like made the traffic in places a seething mass. It did not worry Roger very much. There was plenty of time and it gave him a rest. He turned the wireless on and prepared to enjoy himself for whatever the length of the journey might be. He had just started to accelerate out of a prolonged traffic block when a small car came in fast from a side turning and would have caused a collision if Roger had not happened to have a reaction time quicker than the average mentioned in the Highway Code. The two cars stopped with half an inch between them.

'Really!' said Roger.

'So sorry,' said the girl driver. 'It was my fault. I'm always doing that.'

'You may not be so lucky another time,' said Roger.

'I really oughtn't to—' began the girl, when the sound of impatient hooters from behind made them both drive on. Ten minutes later they stopped next to each other again, but this time it was simply a traffic block. The girl noticed Roger first.

'—drive,' she said.

'I beg your pardon?' said Roger.

'I was finishing the sentence,' said the girl.

'How did it begin?'

'What a short memory you've got. Just as well, as a matter of fact.'

Roger now began to notice that she was attractive, about thirty and with a voice he liked.

'Well, remind me please, if it isn't a nuisance.'

'What I said was—'

Again hoots from behind put an end to the conversation. It was another ten minutes before it could be continued. As soon as they were stationary side by side again the girl went on. 'I really oughtn't to—' But this time they did not wait for the hoots, and it was another several minutes before she was able to add '—drive.'

'Why not?' said Roger.

'Well, it's like this,' said the girl, and they moved on again. About a mile later Roger said:

'Like what?'

'I'll tell you,' said the girl, and the traffic at once started off, this time rather faster than before and for longer. It was ten or twelve minutes before she was able to go on: 'I haven't the qualities of a good driver.'

Roger had time to say: 'I should think you must have a lot of others to make up for it,' before they went on again. Five minutes later: '—if I may say so,' he added.

'Thank you,' she said, and on they went.

At the next stop: 'Are you going far?' asked Roger.

'I'm going to—' but, though she said the word and Roger hoped it was Westlea, he did not really hear it. But she justified his hopes at a level crossing: '—Westlea.'

'So am I.'

'How curious.'

'Isn't it?'

'You wouldn't have—'

Five minutes later: '—lunch with me, I suppose?'

'It ought to be the other way round, really.'

'I shouldn't mind either way. But why?'

'As compensation for nearly running into you.'

'I'm very grateful to you.'

Prolonged hooting put an end to that part of the conversation. It was continued ten minutes later near a bridge which was being repaired. Roger had never been so pleased before to see the sign 'One-way traffic ahead.' He had never thought that he would have been on the look-out for any indication that was likely to produce a traffic block. It is a novel sensation for a motorist. But the girl in the car was giving him a novel sensation too.

'Have you ever picked anyone up in a traffic block before?' she asked.

'I've never even thought of it before.'

'Are you going to Westlea for the week-end?'

'Well no, as a matter of fact I'm going on business.'

'On a Saturday? How boring. I won't work on Saturday.'

'You're going for the week-end, I suppose?'

'Well—yes. My father lives there and I go down sometimes.'

'Where will you lunch with me?'

'If you really mean it—at the Glorious, I suppose. That's the best place.'

'Oh—' said Roger, 'isn't there anywhere else?'

'Why—don't you like it?'

'Well—I haven't been there, as a matter of fact . . . it's just —oh, well, I don't suppose it matters. My client owns the place.'

'Your client? You an architect?'

'No.'

'Solicitor?'

'No.'

'I give it up.'

The traffic moved on, and this time the high average speed it maintained was, for Roger's point of view, just too bad. 'Don't see why everyone's in such a confounded hurry,' he said to himself. 'Traffic blocks are good for people. This craze for speed, and getting on! It's absurd, and most inconvenient at the moment.' It was a long time before he had another chance, but it came in the end.

'One o'clock at the Glorious, then?'

'All right, if you really mean it. You will be there, I suppose?'

'I shall be there,' said Roger. 'Your father's retired, I suppose?'

'Do I look as old as that?'

'No—I meant . . . I mean—' Roger collected himself before he started talking like Crabtree. 'You said he lived down there, and I just assumed he'd retired. It was ridiculous, I agree.'

'He's the Chief Constable, as a matter of fact,' said the girl. 'Don't forget there's a fifteen-mile speed limit along the front—and he's very particular about it.'

CHAPTER 10

Colonel Madderley

Roger duly kept his appointment with Mr Plumb outside the Chief Constable's house.

'I was afraid you might be late,' said Mr Plumb. 'I'm told the traffic is terrible.'

'Oh, it's not too bad,' said Roger. 'Hope I haven't kept you waiting.'

'I always like to be a few minutes early,' said Mr Plumb, 'so I'm used to waiting, but I've had quite a pleasant little stroll—except,' he added, 'that I was nearly knocked down by a car.'

'Not by any chance a small grey saloon with a girl driver?' asked Roger.

'It was certainly a woman,' said Mr Plumb.

'Was she all right?' asked Roger, a little too anxiously.

'All right? All right? How do you mean?'

'I mean there wasn't an accident? The car didn't hit anything—or overturn or anything?'

'No, Mr Thursby—the only thing that was nearly overturned was me.'

'I'm glad it was nothing worse,' said Roger.

'So am I,' said Mr Plumb. 'If I could recognise the woman, I'd report her to the police. It was quite disgraceful. She came from a side turning . . .'

'From a side turning?'

'From a side turning,' repeated Mr Plumb, 'as though she owned not only that turning and the main road but part of the pavement as well.'

'Terrible,' said Roger, 'but you wouldn't be able to recognise her again, I gather? Too bad,' he added cheerfully.

'I didn't say so,' said Mr Plumb. 'I said *if* I could recognise the woman I'd report her. It's a small world, coincidences do happen. I might run into her somewhere.'

'Then you remember what she looked like?'

'You seem to take remarkable interest in this young woman, Mr Thursby.'

'Then you saw she was young?' said Roger. 'It's just in the blood, I suppose, Mr Plumb. We always cross-examine everyone when they tell us anything. Very bad form. I'm sorry.'

'Not at all,' said Mr Plumb, 'I don't mind your asking questions in the least. On the contrary, it helps to clear my mind; I'm not very observant, you know, and it's possible this little chat of ours will have helped to make the vision on my mind less blurred. You see—I can't describe the woman at all . . . I've no idea whether she was fair or dark, wearing a hat or not—or, indeed, anything about her, but if I see her again I may recognise her instantly. As a matter of fact, I'd started to think about the Glaciers and, if we hadn't had our little talk about it, the vision might have become too blurred to recognise again. But I have a feeling now that I shall be able to do it. Let's hope we meet her. Stranger things have happened.'

'Indeed they have,' said Roger. 'Don't you think we might go in now?'

The Chief Constable of Carpshire, Colonel Madderley, was ready for them. 'Sit down gentlemen, please. What can I do for you?'

Mr Plumb cleared his throat—the sign of a nervous advocate. Roger had done it for some little time twelve years previously and then suddenly, noticing it in other people, he found he did it himself. He stopped the habit instantly. If necessary he cleared his throat a moment or two before he got up to speak.

'Colonel Madderley,' said Mr Plumb, 'I act, as I told you when I made the appointment, for Mr and Mrs Glacier; and Mr Thursby is our counsel. I've asked him to be present at this interview and, indeed, to do the talking. In the special circumstances I thought it advisable. Perhaps, Mr Thursby, you wouldn't mind going on from there?'

'Certainly,' said Roger. 'Chief Constable, I want to make it plain at the outset that we are not asking you to treat in confidence what we tell you. As far as our clients and we are concerned, you may make whatever use you think proper of the information we give you.'

'Sounds very fair,' said the Chief Constable. 'Will you tell me the catch now or later, or do I have to find it out for myself?'

'There's no catch, Chief Constable, I assure you,' said Roger.

'Bait with no hook, eh?' said Colonel Madderley. 'You're not a fisherman, I gather?'

'Not to-day anyway, Chief Constable,' said Roger. 'The position is this.'

Roger then proceeded to tell Colonel Madderley the story told him by Mr and Mrs Glacier. As soon as he disclosed that more money had passed hands than was alleged in the charges, the Colonel's attitude changed and he became extremely interested. When this was followed by P.C. Thrussle's statement, he got up from his chair and walked up and down once or twice.

'Mr Thursby,' he said eventually, 'I don't trust your clients an inch. If you ask me—I don't expect you to agree—they're a couple of scoundrels. But scoundrels outside the police force are two a penny. Scoundrels inside the police force—and in particular the Carpshire police force—are very rare indeed. I'd sooner out one crooked policeman than convict fifty Glaciers. We're bound to get a bad hat in now and then, but, on the whole, the force is clean and, as long as I'm Chief Constable of Carpshire, the Carpshire force is going to stay clean.'

Mr Plumb cleared his throat. The Colonel, recognising the signs, held up his hands for silence.

'Forgive me, sir. I want to make the position plain. I wouldn't hang a dog on the word of your clients—forgive my language, and I don't expect you to agree—but it isn't just what *they* say . . . it isn't just what Thrussle says, though that's serious enough . . . it's the whole bag of tricks put together—it sounds right. I don't profess to be a clever man, gentlemen. I'm not; that's why they made me Chief Constable. But one gets a feeling in things—a sort of woman's intuition—and that's what I've got now. Don't misunderstand me— I may be quite wrong—and don't think that people in Carpshire get arrested because the Chief Constable thinks he has a woman's intuition. Not at all. When I get a feeling like this I follow it up— that's all; and if it leads nowhere, then I was wrong—that's all—and no harm done. I'm going to follow this up—and if I'm wrong I'll be damned glad, but if I'm right, we'll boot that inspector and sergeant out so far that they certainly won't be able to find their way back. Don't think I'm condemning them unheard; I'm not, but

. . . well, I won't say any more at the moment about that. Now, I'll tell you what I'm going to do, gentlemen; you may think I'm acting swiftly—well, I was brought up that way . . . shoot first and explain afterwards. I'm going to get straight on to Scotland Yard and, if they agree, as no doubt they will, with you and your clients' cooperation we'll deal with master inspector and master sergeant. Now, I think you wanted to say something, sir,' and the Colonel turned towards Mr Plumb—who had by now completely forgotten what it was.

'I'm sorry, sir,' said the Colonel, 'but you'll forgive me saying that if it was worth saying it was worth remembering. I'm a blunt man, gentlemen, as you'll find if you see much more of me.'

'My clients will certainly cooperate to the full,' said Roger, 'and so will Mr Plumb, I'm sure.'

'It's odd the Glaciers telling you to make a clean breast of it. That type doesn't usually. They lie like troopers, but I suppose you advised them to do so. Damned good advice, if I may say so. They're damned lucky.' He paused momentarily. In his mind's eye he could almost see the inspector and sergeant being flung out of the police force. 'Damned lucky,' he repeated, 'but I'd sooner your clients had the laugh of us than we kept one man in the force we couldn't trust. I don't care whether he's a flattie or a superintendent. You've got to be able to trust them. Same in the Army. But I won't bore you with that, gentlemen. Still, I did have a corporal once—now, really, I mustn't. My daughter keeps me in order when I'm off duty, but the superintendent doesn't like to. And I don't blame him. I'd give him hell if he tried.'

'Is there anything further you want of us?' asked Roger.

'Not at the moment, gentlemen, but, unless I'm very much mistaken, there will be. As soon as I've heard from Scotland Yard, I'll get in touch with you and let you know the plan of campaign. I won't anticipate what they'll suggest, but I've a very shrewd idea what it will be. Now, might I have your telephone number, please?'

'Mr Plumb will give you his,' said Roger. 'Mr Plumb wanted me to come down on this first occasion but, although I shall no doubt be advising him, I don't think it desirable that I should have any active part in any possible operations. Questions of giving evidence might even arise.'

'Mr Thursby,' said Colonel Madderley, 'you will not, I hope, think I am being fulsome when I say that I think Mr and Mrs

Glacier—and Mr Plumb—are very lucky to have your services. You seem, if I may say so, to think two jumps ahead.'

'That's very kind of you,' said Roger. 'I hope you don't still think there's a concealed hook.'

Colonel Madderley laughed. 'How do I know?' he said. 'The fish doesn't know until it's caught him. But, make no mistake, you'll find I struggle like hell—if there is one. Ever tried to catch a twenty-pounder? You'd know if you had.'

After a few more pleasantries, Roger and Mr Plumb left the Chief Constable.

'Magnificent,' said Mr Plumb, as they reached the street. 'Magnificent. I am most grateful to you, most grateful. I should never have put it like that—never. But, now that the ice is broken, I think I shall be able to manage quite comfortably.'

'I'm sure you will,' said Roger, 'but keep in touch with me all the time. If necessary, ring me at home. You know my number.'

'That's most kind. Now, will you do me the honour of lunching with me?'

'I should have loved to,' said Roger, 'but, as a matter of fact, I arranged to lunch with a friend.'

'Well—perhaps you'll have a drink with me before lunch? Where are you lunching, may I ask?'

'Well, as a matter of fact,' said Roger, blushing in spite of his efforts not to do so, 'it's at the Glorious.'

'Splendid,' said Mr Plumb. 'I was going to report to the clients there, anyway. I'm sure they'll want your lunch to be on the house. They'd be most ungrateful if they didn't. I suggest you bring your friend to the bar. I take it you've no objection to a glass of sherry before lunch?'

'That's most kind,' said Roger uncomfortably. Able as he was at getting clients out of difficulties, he did not see any way out of his own. He hoped that either Mr Plumb wouldn't recognise his aggressor or that, by a further coincidence, there was another girl in the area who drove like . . . 'Now—I wonder what her name is,' he said to himself.

'It's a girl, as a matter of fact,' said Roger, blushing again.

'Delighted,' said Mr Plumb, 'if you've no objection—and, of course, if she hasn't either.'

'I'm sure she'd be very pleased. Shall we meet in the lounge?'

They drove separately to the Glorious, but arrived almost at the same time. They parked their cars and went up the steps to the hotel together.

'Will she be there?' wondered Roger, not certain in the circumstances whether he hoped she would or wouldn't be. He soon knew. She was. He went straight up to her with Mr Plumb. 'Hullo,' he said, 'may I introduce—Mr Plumb, Miss Madderley.' He swallowed the name Madderley so successfully that Mr Plumb did not hear it. But the girl did. In a surprised voice . . . 'How—' she began, and then quickly altered it into 'do you do?'

'How d'you do?' said Mr Plumb and then, as Roger had feared he might, looked curiously at the girl.

'Surely we've met somewhere before,' he said.

'Then it was you,' she said. 'I'm terribly sorry. I nearly ran into you. I do hope it didn't give you an awful shock. There really ought to be some warning at the junction.'

'There is a kerb,' said Mr Plumb, recollection of his near escape and anger making him bold.

'Yes,' she said, 'there is, of course. I oughtn't to have gone over it. I am so sorry. I wonder why I do these things? Anyway, I'm so glad there are no bones broken.'

'Miss . . . I'm afraid I didn't quite catch your name—I'm only so sorry to have to say this to a friend of Mr Thursby—but—'

'Miss Madderley,' said Roger, 'is daughter of the Chief Constable of Carpshire.'

'Bless my soul,' said Mr Plumb. 'I see. I see. Oh, I see. Well—but . . . but you didn't appear to know her father.'

'I didn't until this morning,' said Roger.

'I see,' said Mr Plumb, 'but you didn't mention you knew his daughter.'

'We had other things to talk about, Mr Plumb, if you remember,' said Roger. 'What about that drink you promised us?'

'Of course, I'm so sorry,' said Mr Plumb, and led them to the bar.

'Have you been to see my father?' said the girl.

'I'm afraid I have,' said Roger and, as Mr Plumb was slightly ahead of them, added under his breath: 'I know it's a bit soon.'

CHAPTER 11

Paper Work

The next day—Sunday—Roger went to church. He had not done so on an ordinary Sunday for a long time.

'How nice,' said his mother, 'but is anything the matter?'

'Nothing unpleasant,' said Roger.

After church he spent an hour working before lunch, drafting Statements of Claim beginning with something like this:

> The plaintiff is and was at all material times the owner of a Jersey cow. The Defendant is and was at all material times the owner of a Standard motor car, index number 999 ZYX.

Somewhere in the middle of the Statement of Claim the two met. Animal lovers will be pleased to know that the penultimate paragraph showed that the cow completely recovered. The cost of convalescence, however, was considerable. This was explained in detail and a claim was made for all the expense to which the plaintiff had been put and for the inconvenience he had suffered, Jersey milk being unobtainable in the neighbourhood and the plaintiff having to be satisfied with something less beneficial to his health, as a result of which he had lost weight. Most people to-day would have given a small credit for this, but not so the plaintiff. It turned out that it was most important for him to maintain his weight. He did not claim for the loss at so much a pound, but included this claim under the general heading of 'damages'. The total amount was unspecified—such a pity if you claim too little—looks bad if you claim too much. 'Damages' covers everything from a farthing to a million pounds or more. Nothing was claimed for the inconvenience to the cow, unless this could be considered as coming within the last words in Roger's claim which were 'further or other relief'. He had asked for this in innumerable statements of claim, but he had never yet had a case in which they had done anybody any good. But it cost nothing to put them in and perhaps one day he would be glad they were included.

Having dealt satisfactorily and expeditiously with the cow and the motor car, Roger proceeded to draft a defence on behalf of a business man who was alleged to owe money to a company. Many and varied were the defences he raised. The money had never been borrowed or if it had (which was denied) it had been paid back; the company had no power to lend money; the money if paid to the defendant at all (which was denied) was really repayment of capital which was illegal and so much the worse for the company; and finally, having denied everything which was alleged against his client, he added 'Save in so far as has been hereinbefore expressly admitted'—and here it may be remarked that nothing whatever had been admitted—'the defendant denies each and every allegation in the Statement of Claim contained as fully as if the same had been herein set forth and specifically traversed.'

Having settled these two documents, Roger just had time before lunch to draft a letter for his solicitor to send in a case which involved carrots and linseed oil.

Then he had lunch, an hour's nap and back again to his paper work. And, of course, he must get ready for that non-jury case on Monday. What a pity he hadn't a leader in it. However, there it was—and, with luck, there wouldn't be too many Sundays on which he would have to do this again. He would be a leader himself—with time—with time for Anne.

CHAPTER 12

Conferences

A few days later Mr Plumb called on Roger with news of the Glacier case. He was almost cheerful.

'It's going very well, Mr Thursby, very well indeed. I've been down to see the Chief Constable again.'

'Well, what's happening?'

'It's been arranged that Mr Glacier shall be provided with marked notes with which he is to try to bribe the inspector and sergeant again. So as to avoid arousing their suspicion, the prosecution is to go on just the same but, if the officers fall into the trap, it'll be dropped.'

'Well,' said Roger, 'that's almost as good as we can get. When's the first hearing?'

'Next Friday week. I've arranged with your clerk for you to be there.'

'Who's prosecuting, d'you know?'

'Well—they're not sure. But I think they're going to take in a leader.'

'What's the object of that?'

'The Chief Constable says they did so in the last bribery case and he thought they'd better do the same again so as to avoid any possibility of the officers tumbling to what has happened. And I'll tell you two other things.'

Roger had never seen Mr Plumb so happily excited.

'Yes?'

'They're going to have plain-clothes detectives in and round the Court throughout the proceedings, in case our client gets a chance to give them something.'

'I shouldn't have thought they'd take anything like that. Still, I suppose they know what they're doing. What was the other thing you were going to tell me?'

'Most interesting. D'you know what he said to me?'

'The Chief Constable?'

'Yes. He said he'd suspected the inspector for a long time and would be damned glad to get him. They'd never had any evidence before.'

'That's useful,' said Roger. 'If things go wrong, we may be able to use that.'

'I'm afraid we can't,' said Mr Plumb.

'I think we can,' said Roger. 'I think it'll be admissible in evidence. But let's hope it doesn't arise.'

'But we can't use it, Mr Thursby,' said Mr Plumb. 'It was told me in confidence.'

'What do you mean?' said Roger, rather crossly. 'I told the Chief Constable from the start that there was no question of confidence on our side. Nor can there be on his unless he said so.'

'He did say so,' said Mr Plumb.

'Well—why on earth didn't you tell him there was no question of confidence either way?'

Mr Plumb brought out his handkerchief. 'I'm sorry if I've done the wrong thing, Mr Thursby,' he said, becoming mournful for the first time at the conference.

'It is rather aggravating,' said Roger. 'I thought I'd made it quite plain from the start. It's ridiculous that they should be able to use anything we say and that we can't use what they say. How did it happen?'

'It was like this,' said Mr Plumb, mopping away, 'it was like this. Nothing whatever had been said about confidence, I assure you, Mr Thursby. Then he told me what I've told you about his suspecting the inspector.'

'Well, where does the confidence come in?' asked Roger, brightening slightly.

'After he'd said it,' said Mr Plumb unhappily, 'he added "that's in confidence, of course".'

'And what did you say?'

Mr Plumb wiped his forehead vigorously and, after a few moments of this, looked hard at the ground and, in his most doleful voice, said: 'I'm afraid I said "of course".'

Roger sighed. 'Oh, dear,' he said.

'It took me by surprise,' said Mr Plumb. 'I never thought about it. He said "that's in confidence, of course", and I just said "of course". It's easy to be wise after the event, Mr Thursby, but I really don't know what else I could have done.'

'I agree it was difficult,' said Roger, 'but it is a pity you didn't remind him of what we'd said in the first instance; however, there it is. It's no use crying over spilt milk. And anyway, if all goes well it won't matter.'

'I'm sorry you think I did wrong, Mr Thursby. It shows how right I was to have had you there in the first instance. If you'd been there this time it would never have happened. I'm so sorry, Mr Thursby.'

'Never mind,' said Roger, 'most people would have done the same.'

'Then you don't think it amounted to negligence on my part?' said Mr Plumb. 'We'd better inform our insurance company, hadn't we?'

'Good heavens, no,' said Roger. 'Of course it didn't amount to negligence. At the most it amounted to an error of judgement. Some people might even say you were quite right.'

'I wish you were one of them, Mr Thursby.'

'Don't take it to heart, Mr Plumb. I've done far worse things in my time.'

'Thank you, Mr Thursby, that's very generous.'

'Well, I'll see you on Friday week then,' said Roger, 'at the Magistrate's Court. One thing I must know before then. Is it agreed with the prosecution that I should withhold my cross-examination altogether? Or am I to behave just as I should in the ordinary way? That's very important. I must know that quite definitely. I'll have a word with their counsel, of course, but I'd like to know before I see him what the form is.'

'You shall know,' said Mr Plumb. 'Oh, dear—I do hope I don't make any more mistakes.'

Mr Plumb went back to his office and Roger picked up the papers for his next conference—*Streak v. Broad*. He had just opened them when Donald showed in his solicitor, Mr Glade, and the client—a smart gentleman of about Roger's age.

'I've asked for this conference,' said Roger, 'because quite frankly I don't understand this case at all. Mr Streak apparently has some claim for commission against the defendant, but I can't follow what it is and I couldn't possibly draft a Statement of Claim on these instructions.'

'I shouldn't worry,' said Mr Streak. 'He won't defend; he can't.'

'I dare say,' said Roger, 'but I must know what you're claiming.'

'A lot of money, Mr Thursby,' said Mr Streak, 'and he's got it. I've seen it. And he'll pay. He'll have to.'

'But what is the commission you're claiming?'

'Oh—we had a lot of deals together. Just put in anything—he'll pay.'

'If I'm to draft a Statement of Claim I must know what the deals were, how they were made, what were their terms, and so on. We'd better take them one by one. What was the first?'

'This is really quite unnecessary,' said Mr Streak. 'Let me show you something.' Mr Streak opened an attaché case and brought out a number of documents. He handed one to Roger.

'What's this?' asked Roger.

'It's a photostat,' said Mr Streak.

'So I see,' said Roger, 'but of what?'

'Of the minutes of a board meeting which was never held for a company which didn't exist.'

'I don't follow,' said Roger.

'D'you see who was present?' said Mr Streak. 'Lord Mount, Sir Herbert Pennyfeather and the rest.'

'I wish you'd tell me what this is all about,' said Roger. 'I'm not surprised Mr Glade's instructions are unintelligible if this is how he had to get them.'

Mr Streak winked.

'That meeting was held in the imagination of Mr Broad only. That's his handwriting. He had five thousand pounds from Mrs Plant on the strength of that piece of paper. I bought it back from her for two thousand five hundred pounds—Mr Broad's money of course—and I gave it him back. But I took the precaution of having this made of it first. This is only one of them. I've got a lot more here. All forgeries. He made quite a nice bit out of it, anyway. He thinks they're all nicely burned. I saw him burn them. But when he knows we've got these, what can he do? He'll have to pay. It's a bit of cake, didn't I tell you? He'll have to pay. Just you put in anything, Mr Thursby. You won't need my help—any lawyer's jargon will do.'

'D'you call blackmail lawyer's jargon?' asked Roger.

'Now,' said Mr Streak. 'don't misunderstand me. I only want my fair share.'

'Your fair share, I should imagine,' said Roger, 'would be about five years, and I sincerely hope you get it one day. I'm sorry, Mr Glade, but I'm not surprised I couldn't understand these instructions. Perhaps you wouldn't mind taking Mr Streak away.'

'I'm so sorry about this' said Mr Glade. 'I'd no idea.'

'Of course you hadn't,' said Roger, 'but let's get rid of Mr Streak, shall we?'

As they left Roger's chambers, Mr Streak said to Mr Glade. 'But I don't understand. What did I do wrong, old boy?'

Roger sent for Donald. 'Who are Glade and Bream?' he asked. 'D'you know anything about them? I don't remember seeing them before.'

'No,' said Donald, 'they're new. All right, aren't they?'

'They may be, but their client isn't. I think you'd better give them a miss in future.'

'O.K., sir. Oh—you know you're going down to Westlea on Friday? I'm sorry . . . I couldn't get out of it. I did all I could.'

'Oh, that's all right,' said Roger. 'It'll be a change to go to a police court again.'

'A Magistrate's Court,' said Donald.

'Sorry,' said Roger. 'They were called police courts when I first heard of them.'

'Well, I'm glad you're not annoyed,' said Donald. 'I didn't expect you to take it so calmly.'

'Oh, well,' said Roger—but he blushed.

'Well, I'd got something to tell you to make up for it, but I needn't have troubled,' said Donald.

'Oh?'

'You'll have company on the way. Who d'you think they've taken in to lead for the prosecution?'

'Not Henry?'

'Right first time. Pity you can't settle it. That's the trouble about crime. It has to go all the way.'

'This one may not,' said Roger. 'It's out of the usual run.'

'No?' said Donald.

'Yes,' said Roger.

'Trust you to do a wangle,' said Donald. 'Blast,' he added suddenly.

'What's up?'

'It doesn't matter. I forgot to back something in the one o'clock.'

Wangle reminded me of it. But look, sir, I tell you what. You're
going to Westlea on Friday. The Annington meeting's on Saturday.
Why not make a week-end of it? I'll run Conference in the three-
thirty. I wasn't going to, but I will if you'll come. You've never
been to a race meeting, have you?'

'Only once,' said Roger, 'It doesn't sound at all a bad idea. A
week-end at Westlea. I've got a friend there, as a matter of fact.
She might join us.'

'Now I understand,' said Donald. 'Never known you take a brief
out of town like that before.'

CHAPTER 13

Crabtree in Charge?

Henry and Roger drove together to Westlea in Roger's car on the day fixed for the magisterial hearing. Sally was to join them the next day.

'This is a comic outing,' said Henry on the way. 'The prosecution and defence conspiring together to do down a couple of prosecution witnesses.'

'What troubles me a bit,' said Roger, 'is my cross-examination. It's been suggested by your people that I should cross-examine the inspector and sergeant on what they would expect to be Glacier's story—i.e., that no money passed. Well—I don't quite see how I can do that even if you agree to it, as no doubt you would.'

'Why not?'

'It doesn't seem to me that I can put to a witness who's giving evidence on oath what I know to be a false case—even with the concurrence of the prosecution. How can I properly invite a witness to swear to something which I know to be untrue? Suppose I say— "I suggest to you that no money passed between you and Mr Glacier," and suppose he agreed with me—after all it's my object to persuade him to do so—surely I'd be a party to his perjury? That can't be right.'

'I see your point,' said Henry. 'Not being as scrupulous as you are, I confess I hadn't thought of it before. But you're obviously right. You can't.'

'Of course I don't have to cross-examine at all—or I can just play about with them for a bit without putting my case to them. But either I must put my case to them or just ask them about their case. I can't put a false case to them.'

'Right as usual,' said Henry. 'What a lot Grimeyboy taught you.'

'It was by example then,' said Roger. 'You supplied the words.'

'Yes, I'm quite good at supplying words,' said Henry, 'if I don't

have to look them up. Well, that's settled then. I'll explain why
you're not doing what was suggested. With regard to the rest, it'll
just go its normal course, I suppose. I gather your client's pockets
are going to be stuffed full of one-pound notes, all marked. I can
never make out why they have to mark them as well as take the
numbers. I'm looking forward to meeting your Anne.'

'I hope you'll like her. I don't really know her very well myself
yet.'

'But looking forward to doing so, I gather.'

'Very much.'

'I seem to sense much the same happening to you as happened
to me when I met your Sally.'

'Stranger things have happened.'

'Good. I gather Donald's going to take us all to the races. He's
a very important person on a racecourse. He goes in by the "Owners
and Trainers Only". We just go where we're told. I like these
small meetings. They're much nearer to point-to-points. Friendly
atmosphere about the place and not so many toughs from London.'

'We represent the toughs from London this time.'

Eventually they reached the Westlea Court. Mr Plumb and Mr
and Mrs Glacier were already there, and Roger joined them outside
the Court. Henry met his junior—a Treasury junior named Digby—
and the representative from the Director of Public Prosecutions who
was instructing him. The Bench consisted of Mr Bragge, who kept
a large grocery store, Mrs Thwaites, who had once represented the
town as a Member of Parliament, the Chairman, Sir Henry Car-
stairs, who owned most of the land in the neighbourhood and had
once read for the Bar, Mr Pantin, who was on the point of retiring
because of old age, and Dr Spicer, who was a retired local doctor.
They were already sitting, but the Glaciers' case was timed to come
on later. Roger and Henry went into Court to see how matters were
progressing. They arrived in time to hear Crabtree cross-examining
a police surgeon. Crabtree's client was accused of being in charge
of a car while under the influence of drink.

'Now, doctor,' said Crabtree, 'I don't want there to be any
mistake about this. You've said that the defendant was unable to
pass three out of four tests through which you put him; well, it all
depends upon what you mean by pass, doesn't it? Some people
might think differently, mightn't they—no, doctor, that wasn't the
question, what I want to ask you is this—first of all you smelled

the defendant's breath and you say it smelled of alcohol; isn't it true that if you have any alcohol, however little, you smell of it—unless you've taken cloves or something, and would it surprise you to learn that my client always carries some cloves with him—his wife you know—you understand what I mean, doctor—well, if the defendant had wanted to deceive you, he could have taken one first, couldn't he—'

The doctor, having spotted the actual question, jumped in with an answer before Crabtree could continue. 'Certainly, if he'd been sober enough to think of it.'

'Really, doctor, don't you think that's rather offensive. I mean—' But the doctor, who enjoyed family games, suddenly thought of a new one—Get in with your answer. Perhaps he might suggest it to the B.B.C.

'Not in the least offensive,' he replied. 'You said yourself he deceives his wife that way.'

'Is that your answer?' said Crabtree. The doctor waited for a moment. It didn't seem possible. He was not aware that Crabtree's question was what may be termed a marking-time catch-phrase frequently used by some counsel when they are caught on the wrong foot by a witness. As Crabtree remained strangely silent, the doctor eventually answered.

'Yes, it is.'

'I see,' said Crabtree.

'Good,' said the doctor.

The Chairman decided to intervene in the rather uneven contest, and metaphorically told the doctor to stand away from Crabtree until he'd risen to his feet.

'I think,' he said, 'you should confine your remarks to answering questions, doctor.'

'I'm only too pleased,' said the doctor, 'when I can find one.'

'That'll do, doctor,' said the Chairman, administering a caution to the rather too lively doctor, who was apparently so full of fight that he was prepared to challenge the referee.

'Now,' said Crabtree, 'you complain that the defendant's tongue was furry, well what I want to know is, don't lots of people have furry tongues? Look at the medicines advertised—my tongue used to be like this—picture of an ermine coat—now it is like this— picture of a sirloin of beef—you know the sort of thing, well—'

'I've never seen that particular advertisement,' said the doctor. 'I think it's rather good. Which particular medicine does it advertise?'

Crabtree and the Chairman came in together. 'Don't ask me/him questions. You're there to answer mine/his.'

'Sorry, your Worships,' said the doctor, 'it slipped out. I'm sorry, Mr Crabtree.'

'Thank you,' said Crabtree.

'Thank *you*,' said the doctor.

'Next question,' said the Chairman. He felt that if he didn't get the doctor out of the box soon the proceedings might get out of hand.

'Now, doctor,' said Crabtree, 'you could only examine his tongue if he put it out, or at any rate if he opened his mouth—'

'Correct,' said the doctor. 'Full marks.'

'Dr Bulstrode,' said the Chairman, 'this is not your consulting-room, nor a music hall. Please behave yourself. You're in a court of law.'

'Well, unless you forced his jaws open—and I assume you didn't do that . . . well, unless you forced—'

'No, I didn't do that,' slipped in the doctor, and added—to himself—'I was a bit late that time.'

'Unless you forced his jaws open and you say you didn't do that, then you must have asked him to open his mouth and put out his tongue, and he must have done so—now, doctor—'

'I know what you're going to say,' said the doctor. 'Well, I'm—'

'Will you kindly wait till I've formulated the question, doctor,' thundered Crabtree. 'This is really too bad. The question I was going to ask you was this—if he did what you told him or, if you prefer it, what you asked him—if he did that—'

'He must have understood what I said and complied with my request? I take it that is your question,' said the doctor.

'Yes,' said Crabtree, a little crestfallen.

'That's all right,' said the doctor encouragingly. 'I thought it would save a little time if I answered before you asked it. And the answer is—he was not blind drunk or unconscious—he was just wholly unfit to be in charge of a car.'

'That was not the question I asked you,' said Crabtree.

'I thought it was what the case was about,' said the doctor. 'I'm sorry if it wasn't the answer you wanted.'

Roger whispered to Henry. 'This is going to go on all day at this rate.'

'They've had one day already,' whispered Henry. 'I read about it. The chap was as drunk as an owl, but there's a nice point as to whether he was in charge. Why don't you say something to him?'

'You try,' said Roger. 'He'll take it from you.'

Henry worked his way into the seat next to Crabtree and, just after the doctor had floored him for quite a long count, he touched his arm:

'I say, old boy, why don't you let the "drunk" go, and stick to the "in charge"?'

'D'you really think so?' said Crabtree. 'I mean to say—'

'Yes,' said Henry. 'I've read about it; I think you've got a jolly good run on it, but the "drunk" is as dead as a door-nail.'

'Thanks so much,' said Crabtree, rather relieved. 'No more questions, thank you, doctor.'

'But I haven't answered your last yet. I should like to.'

'Oh, very well,' said Crabtree.

'Would you mind repeating it?' said the doctor. It was what might be called a prize Crabtree, with hardly any beginning, no end and a sticky mess in the middle.'.

'Certainly not,' snapped Crabtree.

'But how can I answer it if you don't?' complained the doctor.

'I didn't ask you to answer it,' said Crabtree.

'But you did, really you did,' said the doctor. 'It began with— now, doctor, I want you to answer this question categorically, yes or no—I remember as far as that—it's the rest I've forgotten.'

'Then how can you answer it?' said Crabtree, feeling that something was required of him.

'That's what I should like to know,' said the doctor.

The Chairman intervened.

'Thank you, doctor,' he said. 'You may stand down. Is that the case for the prosecution?' he added, looking at the solicitor for the police.

'Yes, your Worships.'

'Very well then. Now, Mr Crabtree, are you going to call any evidence?'

'Submit there's no evidence of "in charge",' said Henry.

'I submit', said Crabtree, 'that ther's no evidence that my client was in charge of this car at the material time.'

'That's an interesting point,' said the Chairman, 'and we shall need the help of both you and your opponent over it. But, if you call no evidence, we shall be bound to come to the conclusion that your client was under the influence of drink at the material time. At least that's my view on the evidence so far given. I don't know about my colleagues.' His colleagues nodded assent. 'It seems that we're agreed on that then,' said the Chairman. 'So it's up to you, Mr Crabtree.'

'I'm entitled, am I not,' said Crabtree, after a whispered conversation with Henry, 'to have a ruling on my submission before I elect whether to call evidence or not?'

'We'll consult our clerk about that,' said the Chairman. There was a whispered conversation between the clerk of the Court and the Chairman. After a few minutes the Chairman said:

'Very well, Mr Crabtree, we'll hear your submission.'

'If your Worships please,' said Crabtree. 'Now, your Worships, I submit that for a man to be in charge of a car he must be *in charge,* by which I mean that it's no good for the prosecution to prove that he *might* have been in charge, they must prove that he *was* in charge, and it's no good for them to prove that he was in charge *before* the material time or *after* the material time, they must prove he was in charge *at* the material time. Now, what are the facts? The car was owned by my client. That's admitted. But he had a paid driver driving him. How can he be said to be in charge?'

'It all depends what "in charge" means,' said the clerk. 'If you can tell your driver to drive fast or slow or to stop or to drive here or there, or not to drive at all and to hand over the wheel to you, who is in charge of the car? The driver may be driving it as long as you let him, but why aren't you in charge?'

'It would be ridiculous if that were the case,' said Crabtree. 'A man who knows he's unfit to drive gets someone else to drive him home—what harm has he done? What harm can he do?'

'He can tell the driver to stop and hand over the wheel,' said the clerk. 'And if it's his car, the driver would presumably have to obey him. The only other course open to the driver would be to drive to a policeman or to get out and find one. He surely couldn't legally refuse to stop driving. It would be a trespass, wouldn't it?'

'If what you say is right, then a drunken man is allowed to be driven in his own car even if he takes no part in the driving, just because he may wake up and order the driver out of the car?'

Crabtree's unusually intelligent and intelligible replies were due to the fact that most of them were being pumped into him by Henry, who was now taking a personal interest in the case.

'Each case must depend on its own facts,' said the clerk. 'If the friend of a drunk man put him unconscious in his own car and drove him home, the position might very well be different. In such a case the owner of the car would not even know he was in it. I should have thought that, to be guilty of an offence while in charge of a car, a man must know that he is in charge. There must at least be some evidence that he did know. Then again, I suppose, if a man were too drunk to drive but could understand what was happening round about him, he could license someone else to drive on the express term that he could not determine the licence until he had been deposited at his home. I suppose in such a case you could say that the owner could not lawfully terminate the licence and order the driver out of the car until the journey home was over. In such a case it might well be said that the owner was not in charge. He would have temporarily parted with his right to be in charge.'

'If that can be done expressly,' whispered Henry, 'it can be done impliedly.'

Crabtree passed on the observation.

'I agree,' said the Chairman, 'but is that the case here? Let us consider the evidence. Your client had a paid driver. The driver in backing the car from behind another had a very slight accident and damaged a wing. Your client said: "Here, give me the ruddy key. You can't drive. You're drunk." At that moment—very fortunately—a policeman arrived. "Who's in charge of this car?" he asked. "He is," said the chauffeur, who was still angry at being told off. "Is that right?" asked the policeman. "He's my ruddy driver," said your client, "but he's not fit to drive. He's drunk." The evidence was that the driver was completely sober and that it was your client, if anyone, who was under the influence of drink.'

'The fact that he said his driver wasn't fit to drive didn't necessarily imply that he was going to drive himself. He might have been going for the police,' whispered Henry. Crabtree repeated it.

'And the statement made by the driver wasn't admitted by the defendant to be true. On the contrary, he said "He's the driver," ' went on Henry, followed by Crabtree.

'This case,' said the clerk, quite genially, 'seems to be involving a certain amount of outside professional interest.'

'We welcome such interest,' said the Chairman, who was profoundly grateful for Henry's assistance. 'Tell me, Mr Crabtree,' he went on, looking at Henry, 'do you say that a car need not be in the charge of anyone?'

Henry nodded.

'I do,' said Crabtree.

'If I leave my car on the highway, who is in charge of it while I'm away?'

Henry shrugged his shoulders, which was correctly translated by Crabtree into: 'It depends on the circumstances.'

Henry whispered to Crabtree, and a moment later Crabtree said: 'My client did not drive, he did not try to drive, he merely tried to prevent someone whom he thought unfit to drive from driving.'

'Well, Mr Crabtree,' said the Chairman, 'I think we'd like to hear what your opponent has to say.'

'A good deal,' said a small solicitor with a fiery red moustache. 'It will, in my submission,' he went on, 'be an encouragement to drunken drivers in the neighbourhood if the Bench finds there is no case to answer here. Here is a man obviously under the influence of drink who says to his driver, "Give me the keys." What for? To drive, of course.'

'Why not simply to stop the driver from driving?' asked the Chairman.

'Because someone has to drive the car!'

'Why?'

'To get home. Theoretically, I agree, the request to hand over the keys could be merely to stop the man from driving, but from the practical point of view what did it really mean? "Here, give me the keys." '

'May it not have depended on the emphasis?' asked the clerk. 'If he said—'here give *me* the keys'—that might suggest that he was going to drive. But if he said "here *give* me the keys" that could simply mean he was going to stop him driving. I confess my note does not show where the emphasis was placed. I don't know if any of their Worships remembers.'

Their Worships did not. At the time the question was asked the possible importance of the emphasis was not apparent to anyone.

'I suppose we might ask him again,' queried the Chairman.

'But he's heard all this argument,' said the clerk.

'I don't see why that should make any different,' said the prosecuting solicitor.

'I object,' said Crabtree. 'He has shown obvious bias against my client from the start, by which I mean that throughout his evidence—'

'We quite understand, Mr Crabtree,' said the Chairman. 'You object.'

'Yes.'

'All the same, unless my colleagues disagree, I think I'd like to hear the witness again.'

The driver was recalled. The clerk reminded him that he was still under oath.

'Perhaps I'd better ask the question,' said the clerk.

'Yes, please,' said the Chairman.

'Mr Mills,' said the clerk, 'would you repeat to the Bench please what the defendant said to you after you'd bumped the wing.'

'It wasn't my fault,' said the witness.

'Never mind about that,' said the clerk. 'What did the defendant say immediately afterwards?'

'He said: "Let's have the ruddy keys. You're drunk." '

'I thought you said that he said "Here, give me the ruddy keys." '

'So he did.'

'But you've just said he said. 'Let's have the ruddy keys." '

'So he did.'

'It can't have been both—or was it perhaps both?'

'I don't understand.'

'Did he say "Let's have the ruddy keys"?'

'Yes.'

'Did he say anything else?'

'Yes. "You're drunk." '

'Anything else?'

'No.'

'Then he didn't say,' went on the clerk, ' "Here give me the ruddy keys." '

'Yes he did. I've just told you so.'

'You've told us that he said "Let's have the ruddy keys." '

'That's right.'

'And that he said nothing else except "You're drunk." '

'That's right.'

'Then he didn't say "Here give me the ruddy keys." '

'I tell you, he did.'

'But "here give me the keys" isn't the same as "let's have the keys." '

The witness looked blank.

'Well?' said the clerk.

'Well what?' asked the witness.

'They're not the same, are they? They're different words.'

'I don't remember the *words* he said, only just *what* he said.'

The clerk turned to the Chairman.

'We shan't get any further than that, I'm afraid, your Worship,' he said.

'I should like to ask him some questions,' said Crabtree.

'I shouldn't,' whispered Henry.

'Very well, Mr Crabtree, what is your question?'

'I've changed my mind,' said Crabtree. 'No questions.' There was a whisper from Henry.

'But I should like to submit,' said Crabtree, 'that that evidence strengthens my submission. It shows that the sense of what the defendant said was that he wanted to prevent his driver from driving.'

'Well, what do you say, Mr Mountain?' the Chairman said to the prosecuting solicitor. 'You surely have to prove that the defendant was in charge of the car when the police arrested him— not just that it is possible that if the police had come a little later he might then have been in charge.'

'That is true, your Worship,' said the solicitor, 'but I submit there is at least evidence on which the Bench could decide that the defendant was in charge.'

'You have to prove your case,' said the Chairman.

'Not at the moment, with respect, your Worship. I only have to show that there is a case for the defendant to answer.'

'Surely,' said the Chairman, 'if at this stage we think the prosecution has not proved its case we can say so. A jury can stop the case after the evidence for the prosecution is over, can't they? If they can, why can't we? I'll ask the clerk if you like.'

He talked for a few minutes to the clerk. At the end he said: 'Thank you very much. I'm not sure that I'm very much the wiser— no offence to the learned clerk. I still think that, if my colleagues and I are not satisfied that the defendant was in charge of the car when he was arrested, the case ought to be dismissed.'

His colleagues nodded.

'Anything more to say, Mr Mountain?'

'It doesn't seem much use, your Worship.'

'No, I don't think it would be. Let the defendant stand up.'

A red-faced man stood up from where he had been sitting in front of the dock. 'Luke Halliday,' said the Chairman, 'we do not wish our decision in this case to encourage drivers of vehicles to think that they can drink with impunity. On the contrary, this Bench takes a very severe view indeed of drivers who are found guilty of being drunk while in charge of a vehicle. Only a few weeks ago we suspended such a man's licence for seven years. We shall not hesitate to do the same again. Let no one think that drunken, wanton, or even merely bad driving can take place in this area without the guilty party being in grave peril of fine, prison and, perhaps most important of all, of losing his licence. But in every case the prosecution has to satisy us by evidence that the offence has been committed. In the present case we are not satisfied on the evidence that you were in charge of the car when you were arrested. The case is dismissed.' The red-faced man stood still for a moment, swaying slightly; then he spoke.

'How much?' he asked before he was led away to have it explained to him by his friends.

'I thought you did that very well,' said Roger to Henry. 'We'd have still been there if you hadn't.'

In spite of Henry's intervention, however, their case could not start until after lunch. Before they went off to the Glorious, Roger saw Mr Glacier and Mr Plumb.

'I have arranged a magnificent lunch for you,' said Mr Glacier. 'I hope you will enjoy it, particularly your—how do you call him?— your opposite number. Perhaps when he comes to cross-examine me you might remind him that the *Sauce béarnaise* was specially made for him. Or does that too come under the Corruption Act?'

'It would if I weren't taking him to lunch,' said Roger. 'But tell me something much more important. What's happened so far?'

'As I have already told the good Mr Plumb,' said Mr Glacier, 'my pockets are—how do you say?—stuffed with notes—not this time taken from my safe—but from the public purse. I am to seek an opportunity of an interview with either the sergeant or the inspector. And then I have my instructions. I shall do it in much the same way as it is stated that I did it before.'

'Have you spoken to either of them yet?' asked Mr Plumb.

'No,' said Mr Glacier, 'I do not wish to be too—too obvious about it. I am learning, you see.'

'D'you know,' said Mr Plumb, 'that there are about thirty detectives inside and outside the Court, all watching the inspector and sergeant like hawks?'

'How lucky,' said Mr Glacier, 'that telepathy has not been brought up to modern standards of efficiency. When it is—when by a machine I can transfer my thoughts to you—when you by a machine can suck my thoughts from me—then I think the time will have come to go to one of the other planets. Let us hope that there will be a regular service by then. I cannot think of anything worse than that people can know what I am really thinking. Then the word truth would disappear. There would unfortunately be nothing else. How boring. But I am detaining you. Please make the fullest use of the hotel services.'

CHAPTER 14

Introducing Mr Trent

'I shall have a sherry,' said Henry. 'I suppose you'll stick to tomato juice, Roger.'

'Thanks,' said Roger. 'Must keep awake somehow during your opening.' 'Why bother?' said Henry. 'Ah, here are our clients. I'm sure they'll be sociable and join me. Mr Lockwood, sherry for you? Mr Plumb?'

Mr Lockwood, the representative from the Director of Public Prosecutions, said that a sherry would be very nice. Mr Plumb, in his usual mournful tones, agreed and had nothing to add.

'I gather my junior's had to go off somewhere else,' said Henry.

'He's left a pupil to represent him,' said Roger. 'A young man called Trent. Rather reminds me of myself. To look at, I mean. Hope he's not quite such an ass.'

'Where is he?' said Henry.

'I told him to be here,' said Roger. 'Perhaps he's in the lounge. I'll go and look.'

'Why should you look for my junior's pupils?' said Henry. 'I'll go.'

'You needn't,' said Roger. 'Here he is.'

Anthony Trent, aged twenty-three, bespectacled, arrived. 'I hope I'm not late,' he said in a rather fruity voice, which, like his appearance, seemed older than he was. 'Good of you to ask me,' he added. Roger glanced at Henry.

'Nice of you to come,' said Henry.

'I suppose I should be here really,' said Mr Trent, 'as I'm the sole personal representative of Digby. I think he's awfully good, you know,' he added.

'I'm sure he'd be very pleased to hear you say that,' said Henry.

'Now you're pulling my leg,' said Mr Trent.

'I wouldn't take such a liberty,' said Henry.

'What I like about the Bar,' said Mr Trent, 'is the fact that as soon as you're called you're equal with everyone else. People who didn't know would be amazed if they heard me call you, a silk of some standing—'

'Thank you,' interjected Henry.

'If they heard me call you just Blagrove. They'd think I was being uppish.'

'Extraordinary, isn't it?' said Roger.

'Which reminds me,' said Mr Trent. 'This is a most extraordinary case. But there was one point I thought I ought to mention to you, Blagrove. It's this—'

'D'you think it'll keep till after lunch?' said Henry.

'Certainly, if you'd prefer it. But it is rather important. As a matter of fact, I think that everyone's missed it so far. You see, under the Prevention of Corruption Act, 1906—'

'If you don't mind, we will wait,' said Henry. 'And, don't forget, our opponents are here in force.'

'Oh—it wouldn't matter their hearing,' said Mr Trent. 'It's a point which both sides appear not to have noticed.'

'And it's been left to—now, I quite forget your name,' said Henry.

'Trent. Tony Trent.'

'It's been left to Tony Trent to discover it.'

'Now you're pulling my leg again. I wasn't born yesterday, you know.'

'When were you called?' asked Roger.

'Ah,' said Mr Trent. 'That wasn't yesterday either. Three months ago, as a matter of fact. It's amazing what one can pick up in a short time.'

'Have you ever attended a conference with your lord and master?' asked Roger.

'I have, as a matter of fact,' said Mr Trent.

'Just one, I imagine,' said Roger.

Mr Trent looked mystified.

'You're quite right,' he said. 'But I expect there'll be another soon.'

'I shouldn't count on it,' said Roger. 'Did you happen to say anything yourself at the first conference?'

'Well as a matter of fact, I did just point out something they didn't seem to have noticed.'

'They must have been pleased,' said Roger.

'Well, to be quite frank,' said Mr Trent, 'I wasn't sure if they were.'

'Didn't they thank you?' asked Henry.

'Well, not exactly.'

'Shocking,' said Henry.

'There you go again,' said Mr Trent.

'Suppose we go and have lunch,' said Henry.

'I'll join you in a moment,' said Roger. 'I've just seen—' and, without finishing the sentence, he left the bar. He caught Anne in the lounge.

'Hullo,' he said.

'Hullo.'

'It is nice to see you.'

'And you too.'

'Look, will you come to the races with us to-morrow? My clerk's got a horse running. It'll be a sort of chambers party. I'd like you to meet them—that's if you care to at all.'

'I should simply love it.'

'That's a sweet little hat.'

'I'm so glad you like it. Shall I wear it to-morrow?'

'Please.'

A pause.

'I'm afraid I must go now. I've got this case on.'

'Yes, of course. Father's very worried about it.'

'I like your father.'

'I think he likes you.'

'Does he? Does he really?'

'Yes—I'm sure he does.'

'I am glad.'

A pause.

'And you?'

She nodded. 'I must go now. Where shall I meet you to-morrow?'

'Shall I call for you? We'll lunch at the course. About twelve do?'

'Lovely.'

'I'm so glad you can come.'

'So am I.'

'I must go now.'

'So must I.'

'Must you really?'

'Yes, really.'

'I should like to stay here talking to you instead of having lunch.'

'So would I.'

'Would you really?'

'But we can't. Anyway, it would look silly.'

'I suppose it would. But I shouldn't mind.'

'Nor should I really.'

'Wouldn't you really?'

'No, not really.'

'Really?'

'Really.'

'Darling,' said Roger, and hurried off to lunch. He found Mr Trent holding forth on the virtues and vices of some of the judges and silks he had come across in his three months' career.

'Now I think Swallow's really good,' he was saying. 'There's a top-class lawyer, if you like.'

'How d'you recognize one?' asked Roger.

'Oh—you can tell in no time,' said Mr Trent.

'I wish I could,' said Henry. 'You must teach me some time.'

'Now,' said Mr Trent, wagging his finger playfully at Henry.

'I don't know if it's the lobster cocktail,' said Henry, 'but I'm not sure that I don't feel a bit sick.'

'If it is,' said Mr Trent, 'you'd have a marvellous action for damages. We'd all be witnesses. Of course Thursby's client wouldn't have to pay. They're all insured, you know.'

'Is that really so?' asked Roger.

'Oh, yes,' said Mr Trent. 'You see, with all the possible claims by the public, all these places are insured.'

'I think, Henry,' said Roger, 'that we ought to find that out before you actually make a claim. I'm sure you wouldn't like my client to be out of pocket over it.'

'But you can really take my word for it,' said Mr Trent, 'they're all insured. It would be quite extraordinary if he weren't.'

'But extraordinary things do happen,' said Roger. 'Let me see,' he added, 'when did you say you were born—I mean called?'

'Just three months ago to the day. Exactly twelve years five months after you. I've turned you up in the Law List. I suppose you'll be taking silk soon. Blagrove took it three years ago. I like to know these things.'

'I wonder you find time to look in the Law List with all the other things you do,' said Henry.

Mr Trent smiled and waved his finger at him. Roger shuddered.

Mr and Mrs Glacier kept well out of the way during lunch. Usually they had a table in the restaurant so that they could keep an eye on things. This time they lunched in their private room. But the food they ordered for their legal guests was really superb. If only it had been dinner, thought Roger, I might have been able to do justice to it. I wish to-morrow would come.

CHAPTER 15

The Glacier Case Begins

'May it please your Worships,' said Henry, opening the case for the prosecution, 'I appear in this case with my learned friend Mr Digby, and my learned friend Mr Thursby appears for the defendants.'

Henry found someone pulling his coat. It was Mr Trent trying to remind him that he was representing Digby and that Henry ought to say either that he was appearing with his learned friend Mr Trent or at least with his learned friends Mr Digby and Mr Trent.

'Now look,' said Henry, turning to Mr Trent. 'Please keep your mouth shut throughout the whole of this case and leave me alone. If you can't be quiet, go and play in the street. And I'm not pulling your leg,' he added.

Mr Trent retired hurt for a moment. 'And I thought he was such a nice chap,' he said to himself. 'But I don't expect he means it. I suppose he's a bit nervous at the beginning of a case. That must be it. I'll help him by showing that I don't mind.'

'That's all right, Blagrove,' he whispered. 'But if you want my help, I'm here.'

'Shut up,' said Henry.

'The defendants in this case,' he went on, addressing the Bench, 'are the proprietors of the Glorious Hotel of this town; and this case arises out of a prosecution in respect of certain breaches of the licensing laws which are alleged to have occurred at that hotel and for which it is alleged that the two defendants are responsible. I should say at the outset that for the purposes of this case it does not matter one way or the other whether the defendants or either of them are guilty of those offences or not. I am quite prepared to assume that they are not guilty. The only material fact is that they were in fact served with summonses charging them with licensing

offences.' Henry then went on to explain to the Bench in some detail
the facts as alleged by the prosecution. It had been agreed between
the prosecution and defence to prolong the proceedings sufficiently
to ensure that there would be another day's hearing in the Magistrate's Court. This was in order to have an interval before the
magistrates committed for trial, during which the Glaciers would
have a further opportunity of trying to bribe the inspector and
sergeant. Should the plot prove successful, the prosecution against
the Glaciers would be withdrawn before committal. Accordingly
Henry took up a rather longer time in opening the case than he
would normally have taken. When he had finished he called as his
first witness the inspector—Inspector Worcester. After the usual
preliminary questions, Henry asked him about the licensing prosecution and finally asked him to deal with the interview when the
money was handed to him. The inspector cleared his throat.

'On the 14th December last, in company with Sergeant Warwick
of the Carpshire County Police, I called on the defendants at the
Glorious Hotel. I was shown into their private office. Both Mr and
Mrs Glacier were there. I formally asked them their names. They
were in fact well known to me. I then said "I'm afraid I have to
serve you each with these summonses", and I handed them each
two summonses.'

'I call for the original summonses served,' said Henry. Roger
handed them to Henry and the usher took them from him to the
witness.

'These are the four summonses,' went on Inspector Worcester.
'The first defendant read the summonses and then said—' The
inspector referred to his notebook and was about to read out from
it when Roger interposed with:

'How long after the interview were those notes made?'

'As soon as I returned to the police station,' said the inspector.

'All right?' said Henry.

'If you please,' said Roger.

'Go on, inspector,' said Henry. 'What did the first defendant
say?'

'He said,' continued the inspector, ' "Is this really necessary?" I
said: "I'm afraid it is." He said: "I really don't see why. There's a
perfectly good explanation." I said: "You will be able to tell that
to the magistrates." He said: "But I don't like the idea of appearing
in Court. The publicity's bad for the hotel." I said: "I'm very

sorry. There is no alternative." He said: "But surely there are ways of—how do you say?—of arranging these things?" I said: "I don't know of any and what do you mean by 'arranging these things'?" He said: "Oh—you know the sort of thing I mean, inspector, surely?" I said: "I certainly don't?" He then went to a safe in his room. I said: "What are you doing?" He said: "I'll tell you in a moment." Very soon afterwards he came back from the safe with a bundle of notes in his hands. I said: "What are those for?" He said: "To pay the fine, of course." I said: "you haven't been fined yet and, in any event, you can't pay it now." He said: "There are countries where people get fined on the spot for some things." I said: "This is not one of them." He said: "Don't these cases take a great deal of your time when you could be doing something more valuable?" I said: "They're my duty like everything else. If it isn't one thing it's another." He said: "Well, you'd do much better catching murderers and bank robbers and even some of the motorists who kill five thousand people every year." I said: "I do the cases that come into my hands, whatever they are, and this is one of them." He said: "If we're convicted how much d'you think we'll be fined?" I said: "That's a matter for the Bench. I can't discuss it with you." He said: "Well, it wouldn't be much for a first offence—particularly if you give us a good character." I said: "I know nothing whatever against you." That was true, your Worships.'

'I hope it's all meant to be true,' intervened Roger.

'I hope my learned friend will behave himself,' said Henry. 'Go on, inspector.'

'He then said: "Look, the fine wouldn't be more than this, would it?" and handed me the bundle of notes he was holding. They were one-pound Treasury notes, your Worships. I said: "I've told you I don't know what it will be." He said: "Well, keep them on account. You can give me back the change later." I said: "I can't do anything like that." He said: "Why not? Is it another of these red tapes I hear so much of?" I said: "It isn't a question of red tape. I've told you already that you haven't been fined and that, if you are, I don't know how much it will be. Whatever it is must be paid to the Court and not to me." He said: "Well, keep it anyway. I've plenty more." I then suspected that he might be trying to bribe me.'

'No!' said Roger.

'I really must ask my learned friend to refrain from these offensive and unnecessary interruptions,' said Henry. 'They serve no proper purpose and they are discourteous to the Bench, to the witness and to me.'

'I say,' Roger murmured faintly, so that only Henry could hear.

'Go on, inspector,' said Henry.

'My subsequent actions were based upon my belief that the defendant was endeavouring to commit an offence against the Prevention of Corruption Act 1906. I then said to the defendant: "What is this money for?" He said: "For you and the sergeant." I said: "What d'you expect for it?" He said: "Whatever I can get. If you can stop the summonses there's some more waiting for you. If you can't, you can make the evidence as friendly as possible." I said: "Very well. Thank you. I'll see what can be done." He said: "That's better. I thought you'd be sensible in the end. I suppose I went at it rather clumsily." I then said: "Yes, we do like it wrapped up a bit more." He said: "All right, inspector, if you get me out of this I'll wrap up the same amount again and a bit more." I said: "Thank you." Shortly afterwards the sergeant and I left. We went straight to the police station and saw Superintendent Rutland. I made a statement to him and handed him the notes. In my presence he placed them in an envelope which he then sealed with sealing wax and both he and I signed our names on it.'

'Is this the envelope?' asked Henry, and an envelope was handed to the witness.

'It is,' said the inspector.

'How many notes are there inside it?' asked Henry.

'Twenty,' said the inspector.

'Perhaps your Worships would care to open the envelope and a note can be made that it was opened in this court.'

'I think perhaps I'd better open it,' said the clerk. 'I could then give evidence of it later if necessary.'

'If you please,' said Henry.

'Any objection, Mr Thursby?' asked the Chairman.

'None, your Worship,' said Roger.

The clerk opened the envelope and counted out twenty one-pound notes.

'What happened next?' asked Henry.

'Acting on instructions from the superintendent, I called again on the defendants and again saw them in their office. Sergeant Warwick was with me. This was on the 27th December last. The following conversation then took place. He said: "Well, inspector,

have you any good news for me?" I said: "I may have." He said:
"Good. What's holding it up?" I said: "There are formalities, you
know." He said: "Of course—everything here is formalities. How
long will they take?" I said: "Well, I might be able to get it done
in a week." "What's holding you back?" he asked. I just said:
"Well—" and then he said: "Oh, of course, I see. It's I who am
the slow one this time." He then went to the safe again and got out
a bundle of notes. He came back from the safe and handed me the
notes, saying: "I suppose you'll see the sergeant all right." I said:
"Of course." He said: "You'll find twenty-five pounds there. I hope
you think that's all right." I said: "Thank you, sir." The first
defendant then said: "I can be sure this'll be the end of the matter?"
I said: "You leave it to us, sir." We left shortly afterwards and I
went straight to the superintendent again. I handed him the notes.
They were placed in an envelope and sealed with sealing wax and
both the superintendent and I signed the envelope.'

'Is this the envelope?' asked Henry. And the same procedure was
adopted with the second envelope. This one was found to contain
twenty-five notes. After this had been done the inspector continued
his evidence.

'Later, after the summonses in this case had been issued, I went
with Superintendent Rutland to serve them on the defendants. We
saw both defendants in the same office as before. The superintendent told the defendants the nature of our visit and handed each
of them summonses. The second defendant said nothing. The first
defendant then looked hard at me and said: "This is infamous."
The superintendent then cautioned him and the first defendant
said: 'I shall see my solicitor about this—it is infamous.' '

'Tell me, inspector,' said Henry, 'what part did Mrs Glacier play
at these three interviews?'

'She said nothing that I remember,' said the inspector.

'What was she doing when the first defendant was saying what
you have told us?'

'She was standing or sitting next to him.'

'But what was she doing? Was she reading or knitting or what?'

'She wasn't doing anything,' said the inspector.

'Could she hear what was said?'

'She could not have failed to do so,' said the inspector. 'Oh . . .
and I did forget to mention that the first time the male defendant

went to the safe he could not find his keys, and the female defendant looked in her bag and handed them to him.'

'Did she say anything?'

'Not that I can remember. She may have said: "Oh, here they are," but I'm not at all sure.'

'Two of the summonses had been handed to her?'

'Yes.'

'Charging her with licensing offences?'

'Yes.'

'When Mr Glacier was saying what you've told us, did Mrs Glacier do or say anything to show that she disapproved of what he was doing?'

'Nothing at all.'

'If what you say is true, the first defendant was asking you to procure the withdrawal of all four summonses—'

'I wish my learned friend wouldn't lead,' said Roger.

'He has already said it,' said Henry.

'With respect he has not,' said Roger. 'At no time did the inspector say that the first defendant referred to four summonses.'

'He said the summonses,' said Henry, 'and that meant the four.'

'It might have meant the two served on him,' said Roger.

'What, and leave Mrs Glacier out in the cold?' said Henry.

'I know it's all very amusing,' said Roger, 'but this is a criminal prosecution and my clients are charged with a very serious offence. Both of them. I entirely agree with my learned friend that it may well be that if the defendant said what is alleged—which I do not accept for a moment—if he said that, he may well have been referring to the four summonses. My point is that my learned friend must not add anything to the evidence himself.'

'Very well,' said Henry, 'how many summonses had been served by you in respect of the alleged licensing offences?'

'Four,' said the inspector.

'What was the first defendant asking you to do?'

'To procure a withdrawal of the summonses.'

'Did he say that he only meant the two served on him?'

'He did not. He just referred to the summonses.'

'Did Mrs Glacier at any time by word or deed show that she thought Mr Glacier was not asking you to procure the withdrawl of the summonses against her?'

'No.'

'Or that she did not want her husband to pay you the money?'

'No, she did not. On the contrary, on the first occasion she gave him the keys of the safe.'

'Thank you, inspector,' said Henry.

Roger then got up.

'I want to make it plain,' he said, 'that I do not propose to cross-examine at length in this Court. Should the Bench find there is a case to answer against either defendant, my case will be fully put to the witnesses at the Assizes. I don't want there to be any doubt about that. Now, inspector, I think you've said you've known the defendants for some time?'

'Yes, sir. Perhaps three or four years.'

'And you know them to be persons of the highest character apart from these recent incidents?'

'Entirely, sir.'

'It must have surprised you when they offered you money in the manner you say they did?'

'It did, sir.'

'When did you first consider that an attempt was being made to corrupt you?'

'When he told me to keep the money.'

'Did you not suspect it before then?'

'Yes, sir, I suspected it.'

'When?'

'Well, sir, his whole attitude suggested something of the kind from the beginning but, of course, one sometimes jumps to conclusions too soon?'

'May I put it this way? Almost from the beginning you smelled something?'

'Yes, sir.'

'And when the scent was conclusive, you decided to trap him?'

'Yes, sir.'

'You must have found that very unpleasant.'

'Very, sir.'

'But you have to do these things.'

'Exactly, sir.'

'Mr Glacier obviously considered that what you did was infamous?'

'Yes, sir.'

'What do you think he considered infamous?'

'Leading him on, sir, I suppose—and then charging him.'

'So you led him on?'

'He didn't require much leading, sir.'

'I was only using your own words, inspector. You led him on?'

The inspector paused for a moment. 'Yes, sir, I suppose you may put it that way . . . at a certain stage.'

'But it was you who put it that way, inspector. Let's not beat about the bush. From the moment you were satisfied he was trying to corrupt you and the sergeant, you led him on?'

'Yes, sir.'

'And lied to him in the process?'

'In accordance with my duty, sir.'

'Then the answer is yes, you lied to him?'

'At a certain stage, yes, sir.'

'How often do you lie to people to trap them into offences?'

'I didn't trap him into the offence, sir. He was already committing it. I merely had to obtain the evidence.'

'All right, I'll accept that for the moment. How often have you lied to people in order to obtain evidence?'

'I couldn't say, sir. Not often.'

'How often has anyone tried to bribe you before?'

'Only once, sir.'

'How long have you been in the force?'

'Twenty years, sir.'

'Starting as a uniformed constable?'

'Yes, sir.'

'D'you mean to say no one—not even a motorist—has ever—except on one occasion—expressly or impliedly tried to corrupt you?'

'There has only been one definite occasion apart from this, sir. I have had vague suggestions made before, but nothing definite enough to justify a prosecution.'

'I take it, then, that you've only been concerned in one prosecution for bribery before?'

'That is so, sir.'

'And is it right then that in no other case have you ever reported a case of bribery to your superior officer?'

'That is so, sir.'

'Have you done work in the West End of London?'

'Yes, sir.'

'There are some pretty undesirable types about there, are there not?'

'Yes, sir.'

'People who run disorderly houses and the like?'

'Yes, sir.'

'Have you been concerned in any prosecutions for that sort of offence?'

'Yes, sir.'

'How often?'

'I can't say exactly, sir. A number of times.'

'So many that you can't remember?'

'I wouldn't say that, sir, but on several occasions.'

'A dozen or more?'

'I don't think quite as many, sir.'

'Well, whatever the number, d'you mean to say that you were never offered anything by any of those gentry?'

'I was once, sir. That was the case I was referring to.'

'Well, that means that you were never offered anything by a motorist, a bookmaker, a barrow boy, or anyone else at any time in your career?'

'Not definitely, no, sir.'

'You must have moved in a very high class of undesirables.'

The inspector did not answer.

'At any rate,' continued Roger, without requiring an answer, 'you had to leave the motorists, barrow boys, bookmakers, and the scum of the West End and come to respectable people in Westlea before you had an honest-to-God case of bribery?'

'Except on the one occasion, that is so, sir.'

'A bit remarkable, isn't it?'

'I couldn't say, sir.'

'But you can, can't you, inspector? Take street bookmakers and keepers of disorderly houses . . . is it not within your knowledge that they often attempt to corrupt?'

'I have heard of cases, sir.'

'But only experienced one?'

'That is so, sir.'

'Now, let's come to another matter—Mrs Glacier. She never said anything you can remember except possibly "here they are"—referring to the keys?'

'That is so, sir.'

'She never offered you anything or gave you anything, did she?'

'No, sir.'

'When she offered the keys to her husband you didn't at that stage know that he was going to try to bribe you?'

'No, sir, not definitely. As I said, I was suspicious.'

'When he first handed you the money, you said that he said it was for the fine?'

'Yes, sir.'

'Well, at the time Mrs Glacier handed him the keys, there was no reason why she should not think that's what it was for?'

'I couldn't say, sir.'

'But you can, inspector. As far as you could see, had anything been said or done which showed Mrs Glacier that her husband was about to bribe you?'

'Nothing more than I've said, sir.'

'Well, then—even you, an experienced police officer, only suspected the possibility; can you suggest any reason why Mrs Glacier should even suspect that?'

'They might have discussed it before, sir.'

'Of course they *might*. Anything *might* have happened, but, as far as you can tell from what you saw and heard, they had not?'

'I couldn't say, sir, I certainly never heard them discuss it.'

'Didn't you really?' said Roger. 'Well, then, can you tell me why Mrs Glacier is charged at all?'

'That's not my responsibility,' said the inspector.

'But I presume you swore the information which led to the issue of the summonses?'

'That is true, sir, but it didn't rest with me who was to be charged. I simply swore to the facts, sir.'

'Are you opposed to her being charged, then?'

'Do you mean you want my personal views, sir?'

'What on earth have the inspector's personal views got to do with it?' interposed Henry. 'It will be for the Bench first, and later, if the defendants are committed, for the jury to express their personal views. I don't mind in the least what the inspector thinks. The object of evidence is to ascertain facts, not views.'

'Well,' said Roger, 'as my learned friend—and I don't blame him—feels so tender on this particular spot I won't aggravate the wound by pressing it.'

'I'm not in the least tender,' said Henry. 'If you like to ask me as representing the prosecution why Mrs Glacier is charged, I'll gladly tell you. All I object to is the wrong person being asked the question. The Director takes full responsibility for the charges in this case. I represent him, and I am the person to ask.'

'I can't cross-examine you,' said Roger.

'I shouldn't even mind that on this particular point,' said Henry. 'It's perfectly obvious why Mrs Glacier has been charged.'

'Not to the inspector,' said Roger.

'He hasn't been asked that,' said Henry.

'Well, I'll ask him,' said Roger.

'It's got nothing to do with him,' said Henry.

'I'm only trying to help,' said Roger. 'I gathered you wanted me to ask him.'

'Gentlemen,' interposed the Chairman, 'I'm sure you both know what's going on, but it's a little confusing for the Bench to have this altercation during the cross-examination of a witness. Do you think perhaps you could continue it outside the Court?'

'I was objecting to a question being asked by my learned friend,' said Henry, 'and I'm afraid that unless my learned friend withdraws it, I shall have to trouble the Bench to rule on my submission.'

'But I thought Mr Thursby said he was not going to press the question,' said the Clerk.

'I did say that,' said Roger.

'Then I cannot think what the argument is about,' said the Chairman.

'Can you?' whispered Roger to Henry.

He continued to cross-examine the inspector for a further half hour, and then Sergeant Warwick was called. His evidence was substantially the same as that of the inspector. Roger cross-examined him slightly, but not as fully as the inspector.

That was as far as the Bench would go that day and the case was adjourned for a week. Outside the Court Mr Glacier came up to Roger and Mr Plumb. 'I must see you at once,' he said.

It transpired that he had taken an opportunity of speaking to the inspector when no one else appeared to be looking—though in fact they were under the observation of detectives the whole time—and asked him if he would see him. The inspector had given him an appointment at the police station for the following Monday.

'Mr Plumb,' said Roger, when they had learned this, 'you must go straight to the Chief Cnstable and tell him. Er—perhaps you'd like me to come too.'

They went straight to his house and waited till he returned.

'Right,' said Colonel Madderley, when they had told him. 'This is it. We'll have a microphone installed and, if he takes the money, we'll catch him with the notes on him when he comes out.'

'But he might say he was going straight to the superintendent with the money,' said Roger.

'Of course,' said the Chief Constable. 'Stupid of me. We must arrange for the superintendent to be the first person to see him when he comes out of the room.'

'And might I suggest, Chief Constable,' said Roger, 'that he makes an excuse for taking him into his office? Anything will do. A friendly chat or another case. Otherwise he could say he didn't want to discuss it in any place where they might be observed.'

'Another bull's-eye,' said the colonel. 'You've missed your vocation. It shall be done. I've been watching this particular fish for months. We'll see if we can get a rise out of him this time. That's in confidence of course.'

Mr Plumb looked at Roger, who now had a very difficult decision to make. If it had been the first time the subject had been mentioned, he would have done what he had told Mr Plumb he ought to have done. But now the position was very different. Mr Plumb had already agreed to treat a similar statement in confidence. The colonel could rely on that promise to justify what was only a repetition of the statement. If Roger now stepped in and said it was not in confidence, the Chief Constable would not only be very annoyed but he might suspect double-dealing of some kind. On the other hand, if he simply said nothing he was, in effect, doing what Mr Plumb had already done. Silence in such a case must imply consent. If he was going to say at any later stage that the statement was not in confidence, he must say so now. It was all very difficult. In all the circumstances, he decided to do nothing, and he hoped more than ever that the inspector would be caught out and the prosecution of the Glaciers brought to an early end. He could foresee embarrassment and unpleasantness if this did not happen. And it did not help that he had already quite decided that, if she would have him, he was talking to his future father-in-law.

CHAPTER 16

Statistics

Roger enjoyed the next day more than he had enjoyed anything for a long time. He put the affairs of Mr and Mrs Glacier out of his mind; he decided to forget that he would have to do a day and a half's work on Sunday and that, in addition to a vast amount of paper work, he had a difficult non-jury case first in the list on Monday. This shall be a *dies non* he said to himself—or rather it shall be a Dies with a capital D. To the races with Anne. True, chambers would be there in force, but he would be able to see her alone from time to time, and anyway he would be able to see her and be near to her. This is it. Thank heaven she can't drive a car or I'd never have met her. As he shaved he thought more and more about her. What a lovely name. What a lovely face. What a lovely voice. I wonder what Sally will think of her. I do hope she approves. She's nearly always right. Anyway, I can't help it if she doesn't.

He fetched her in his car and they met the others—Henry and Sally, Donald and his wife—in the restaurant in the members' enclosure. Donald had already drunk three quarters of a bottle of champagne laced with brandy.

'Hullo, Roger,' he said, 'I feel we're going to have a good day.' Roger introduced Anne and spoke for a few moments to Donald's wife.

'Two bottles of champagne,' said Donald to a waiter. 'No, make it a magnum. There's a feeling about a magnum like a thousand-guinea brief. This is going to be a party.'

It certainly was. They all drank champagne and brandy. Before lunch was over Roger found he was holding Anne's hand. He looked at Sally. He could tell at a glance that she approved. It was all right.

After lunch they went to the paddock and on the way Sally took Roger by the arm out of earshot of the others. 'Well done,' she said.

'D'you mean it?'

'You know I do,' said Sally. 'I'm even a bit jealous. If you'd looked at me as you look at her I'd have been in heaven.'

'You make me feel most uncomfortable,' said Roger, 'I must have been awful. I think of myself sometimes and shiver. You're terribly happy with Henry, aren't you?'

'Who wouldn't be?' said Sally. 'I'm very lucky.'

'So am I—I hope,' said Roger. A sudden awful thought occurred to him . . . possibly he was assuming too much.

'You're all right,' said Sally, reading his thoughts. 'I saw the way she looked at you.'

'Hullo, Thursby,' said a voice. It was Mr Trent.

'Hullo,' said Roger, without much enthusiasm.

'I can give you something for the first race, if you like,' said Mr Trent. 'I know what I'm talking about.'

'That's very kind of you,' said Roger, 'but I don't know that we shall back anything in it.'

'Well, just in case,' said Mr Trent. 'Capsule. It's an outsider. But you'll see.'

'Thank you,' said Roger, and he and Sally moved on to catch up the others. They found them at the paddock. The horses in the first race were being led round. None of them looked very enthusiastic. Roger found Henry talking to another member of the Bar whom he knew slightly—Eagally.

'My dear chap,' Eagally was saying, 'I work it out on scientific principles. You just can't go wrong. What I mean is this. If a thing's always happened in the past it's going to happen in the future. That's fair enough, isn't it?'

'Very fair,' said Henry.

'Now, take this race,' said Eagally, looking at his race-card. 'There's a horse running that has never won a race. It's been out five times—not even placed. Now—and this is the point. This is a five-furlong race. I look at the breeding. I find that the sire was Fair Trial, a great sire of winners up to a mile. Now for the dam. The race-card tells you the name of the dam, but that's not enough. You want to know the name of the sire of the dam. I get that from here,' and he brought out a little book. 'You see, most racegoers are so stupid they don't know about this. Just imagine, the race-card itself—produced by people who are supposed to know about these things—not giving you the sire of the dam. But that's how

things are. Now I find that the sire of this horse's dam was
Panorama, one of the greatest sires of sprinters. So, on the one hand
you have Fair Trial and the other Panorama. A perfect combination
for a five-furlong race. But it isn't just that. I tell you, I go in for
this scientifically. If you look up all the horses which have been
sired by Fair Trial out of a dam by Panorama, you'll find that they
all win races sooner or later and nearly always sooner.'

'Suppose,' said Roger, 'the horse was sired by Panorama out of
a dam by Fair Trial. Would that be any good?'

'My dear boy,' said Eagally, 'you're getting the hang of it. It'd
be just as good—though, as a matter of fact, there does happen to
be one exception with that particular breeding. There is a horse of
that breeding which has never won a race—but, as far as I know,
only one. There must be the odd exception to every rule in racing—
but they're so rare you can disregard them.'

'But how d'you know it's going to win this race? You'd have said
the same for its fifth race, and it lost,' said Sally.

'Quite true,' said Eagally. 'I should have said the same, and I
should have backed it and lost my money. But don't forget, it's run
five races now. Past statistics show that, on an average, horses of a
particular combination of breeding win their first race within their
first three races. Accordingly, if they don't win in the first three
races, the chances of winning the fourth are greatly increased, the
fifth even more, and the sixth is as near to a certainty as doesn't
matter—unless it's going to turn out to be an exception to the rule.
Well, as I say, you're bound to get the odd exception, but you can
pay for it out of your winnings on the others.'

'What's its name?' asked Roger. 'Not Capsule, by any chance?'

'No, it's called Fair View. There it is. Not much to look at, I
agree. But if that horse doesn't win this race or the next, I'll eat
my hat.'

'Is it in the next race as well, then? It'll be pretty tired, won't
it?' asked Roger.

'No, I mean its next race. Anyway, I'm going to back it.'

'I was told that Capsule was going to win,' said Roger.

'Capsule?' said Eagally. 'I'll look it up. Let me see.' He referred
to his little book. 'By Trimbush out of a Tiberius mare. Now, this
is a good example of what I mean. That's a stayer. Perfect breeding
for staying. Anything from one and a half miles upwards. But not

for a sprint. Oh dear, no. Of course, it's only a two year old and they do win sometimes, but I wouldn't touch it.'

It was the general opinion of Roger's chambers that Eagally knew what he was talking about and they voted for Fair View and backed it. Then they went to the stands to watch the race.

'They're under starter's orders,' said the voice over the loud-speaker, and a moment later: 'They're off,' it said.

Fair View cannot have heard it. As soon as the tapes went up it turned round in the opposite direction.

'Hell,' said Eagally, 'w.r.s.t.n.p.'

'I beg your pardon?' said Sally.

'Tell you afterwards,' said Eagally.

The horses came towards them with more enthusiasm than they had shown in the paddock. About two hundred yards from the finish, one horse started to emerge from the others and it eventually won by a comfortable three lengths It was Capsule.

'So sorry,' said Eagally, when the race was over. 'It's just one of those things. It would happen to-day. It was a certainty if it had only raced. I couldn't tell it was going to do that, could I?'

'You were going to tell me what you said when it happened,' said Sally. 'I thought it might be a private swear-word.'

'Oh, you mean "w.r.s.t.n.p." That simply means "whipped round at start, took no part." I wish I knew when it was running again. It'd have to win. Couldn't lose, or my statistics are nonsense.'

'Have you ever considered that possibility?' asked Henry.

On the way down from the stands to the paddock, they met Mr Trent. He was talking to Mr Justice Kingsdown, whom he had waylaid, saying: 'Excuse me, Judge, aren't you Mr Justice Kingsdown?'

'Yes,' said the judge, who was a genial man. 'I must admit that. And who are you?'

'I don't suppose you would remember me, Judge,' Mr Trent had said. 'I was before you in chambers the other day—just as a pupil, you know. I didn't actually say anything. But I'd read all the papers. And I was quite sure you'd decide as you did.'

'How comforting,' said the judge. 'You don't happen to be quite sure who's going to win the next race, I suppose? Horses—I imagine—are less predictable than judges—though I have known a few decisions which could be classed as rank outsiders.'

At that moment Roger and his party were passing them.

'Hullo, Thursby,' said Mr Trent. 'The judge has just asked me for the winner of the next race. You can tell him I gave you the winner of the last. Hope you backed it.'

'Hullo, Thursby,' said the judge. 'And Blagrove. Quite a legal party. My daughter's somewhere about. I come to please her, you know. Doesn't mean very much to me.'

'The winner of the next race,' said Mr Trent, 'will in all probability be Cotton Wool—but it'll be a close thing between it and Madagascar. I shall back them both, if the odds are good enough.'

Eagally looked at his card. 'One and three-quarter miles,' he said. 'Now . . . the dam of Cotton Wool is by Gold Bridge—another great sire of sprinters. That won't do for one and three-quarter miles. It does occasionally happen with a very stout-hearted sire—Whiteway was an example—but normally if the dam's by Gold Bridge you can write off the horse as a stayer. Can't think why owners and trainers enter them for races of that distance. Now let's look at Madagascar. Sire of the dam was Sir Cosmo. That's almost as bad. No, I should write those off if I were you. Now, for a race of this description I'd choose something like—let me see—' and he consulted his little book.

'What about Roman Tour? By Tourbillon out of a Tiberius mare. Stay all the way from Land's End to John o' Groats. Let's see what it did last year.' He looked in another little book. 'Yes—not at all bad. Quite promising and, with that breeding, it'll stay for ever—that's the horse for my money.'

'Well,' said Roger, 'what's it to be?'

The prejudice against Mr Trent was so great that they voted for Eagally's choice. In due course they went to the stands to watch the race. Just before it started, Eagally said: 'There's only one thing I ought to have mentioned. There are only six horses in this race. That may mean that the race isn't truly run—isn't run at a fast enough pace. If that happens, it enables a horse which isn't a genuine stayer to win.'

'A horse like Madagascar, for instance,' said Roger, 'or Cotton Wool.'

'Could be,' said Eagally, 'but let's hope there's a smart gallop. I wonder who'll make the running.'

The race started and apparently no one wanted to make the running. The pace was rather like that of an underfed riding school going round Hyde Park. The crowd began to jeer and clap. But the funereal rate continued. It increased three or four furlongs from the end when two horses left the other four almost standing. They raced side by side for the last three hundred yards and made quite an exciting finish. There was no photo-finish apparatus, and the judge, after a moments's thought, awarded a dead heat—between Cotton Wool and Madagascar.

'What did I say?' said Mr Trent, as soon as he found Roger and Henry's party. 'Couldn't do much better than that.'

'Very good,' said Henry. 'Let's go to the paddock.' In the paddock they found Mr Justice Kingsdown wandering round rather uncertainly—as though he couldn't find something he was looking for.

'Hullo, Judge.'

'Hullo.'

A pause.

'Er—I suppose,' said the judge, 'you haven't seen that rather extraordinary young man about anywhere? I was just wondering—'

'He was by the stands a minute ago, Judge,' said Roger.

'Thank you,' said the judge—and a moment or two later was seen to be moving towards the stands.

'I could have told him something for the next race,' said Eagally.

'Another certainty?' asked Henry.

'Well,' said Eagally, 'you can't blame me for the last two races. If a horse doesn't start, it can't win, can it? And in the last race you heard what the crowd thought of the pace. If there'd been fifteen runners it would have been a different story. Now, the next race is another sprint—six furlongs this time. Now, this is where statistics come in. Fair View didn't win.'

'No, we noticed that,' said Henry.

'This horse is of similar breeding—I don't suppose it means anything to you—but it's by Denturius out of a Panorama mare.'

'I assume it's never won,' said Roger.

'You're right,' said Eagally.

'But how many times has it tried?' said Henry.

'Now that's the point. Five times. Just like Fair View. Now it's statistically impossible for both horses to fail on the same day—let alone at the same meeting. It can't happen.'

'Suppose,' said Sally, 'it w.r.n.s. or whatever the correct expression was?'

'W.r.s.,' corrected Eagally. 'Statistically it can't.'

'But I suppose it can physically,' said Roger.

'Of course it can physically,' said Eagally. 'Physically it could die or break an artery or fall down or throw its jockey or charge the tapes and injure itself—or even win and be disqualified on an objection. But statistically it will win. It can't help it. That's what's so extraordinary.'

'Do the bookmakers know this?'

'Of course not. They only know which horses are backed most. That's all they care about. There it is, by the way. Better looking than Fair View, I should say. In pretty good condition.'

'D'you think you could tell it not to w.r.s. if I back it?' said Anne.

'I tell you,' said Eagally, 'that it can't whip round at the start or do anything else except win. You can't go wrong with statistics. Admittedly very occasionally there's an exception. But I can count them on one hand. Which reminds me. I had one last week. Now, you couldn't have two in a fortnight. It's absolutely impossible.'

'Do tell that to the horse,' said Henry.

'I don't blame you for laughing,' said Eagally, 'but, at the end of the race—you'll see. Most chaps are a bit cautious about giving their tips—take the newspapers. "If so-and-so can give the weight to such-and-such I think it should win. But I'm a little afraid of what's-his-name, and they say that t'other-'un is in the pink of condition." You must admit that I tell you quite definitely that the horse will win.'

'And I'm afraid,' said Henry, 'you must admit that so far it hasn't.'

'There have been special reasons,' said Eagally.

'I hope there isn't going to be one this time,' said Roger.

'It's statistically impossible,' said Eagally. 'It's a bit of luck, really. I've never known a case where the odds were so strongly in my favour. Let's hope it'll convince you.'

'I'm hoping to be convinced,' said Henry. 'And, to prove it, I shall put one pound to win—what's its name?'

'Toothy Look,' said Eagally. 'Don't thank me now. Wait till it's won.'

'Very fair,' said Henry.

At that moment Donald arrived.

'Hullo,' he said and then, lowering his voice to a confidential whisper, he went on: 'My trainer says that Conference is bound to win if the boy can hold him in for the first mile.'

'What does that mean?' said Roger.

'Look,' said Donald, 'it's like this. By putting a boy on him he gets a seven-pound allowance—seven pounds less weight. Easier to run with less on your back, d'you follow?'

'Yes. That's very reasonable,' said Henry.

'Well, now, Conference is a little difficult for a boy to handle. He pulls like blazes, and if the boy can't hold him in he'll rush to the front and wear himself out. But if he can hold him in for a mile, he'll leave the others standing in the last two furlongs.'

'Well,' said Roger, 'what do we do about that?'

'I'll tell you. Some bookies will give you odds during the race. I'll put you near one or two who will. If Conference is in the rear at the end of a mile, put your shirt on him. But if he's right in front, leave him alone. He'll fold up in the last two furlongs and come in last. Got me?'

'Sounds plain sailing to me,' said Roger.

'Which race is it, the next one?' asked Henry.

'Now, Henry,' said Donald reprovingly, 'the next race is six furlongs. Eight furlongs make a mile. If he's to hold him in for a mile, stands to reason the race must be more than six furlongs.'

'Fair enough,' said Henry. 'Which race is it?'

'One after next,' said Donald. 'Now, don't forget. What are you doing for the next race? I saw old Kingsdown at the five-pound tote window.'

'He must have found Mr Trent,' said Roger.

'Come again,' said Donald.

'Mr Trent, in addition to knowing all the law worth knowing, knows all the winners worth knowing.'

'Who's Mr Trent?'

'He's the very learned pupil of my junior,' said Henry. 'He's worth meeting for a short time. I've no doubt he could give you a few hints.'

'Pity he's not your pupil, Roger,' said Donald. 'We'd teach him something.'

'My dear Donald,' said Roger, 'if Trent were my pupil I think I should retire from the Bar.' Then, in a slightly lower tone, he added: 'I'm doing that anyway, I suppose.'

'Don't come that one on me, Roger,' said Donald. 'See you later.'

Soon afterwards the chambers party and Eagally went to the stands to see the next race.

'They're under starter's orders,' was soon followed by 'They're off,' and this time Eagally's horse started with the rest.

'You see,' he said, 'no w.r.s. that time. It was statistically impossible. What did I tell you?'

'You said it would win,' said Henry.

'You'll see,' said Eagally. 'There it is—nicely tucked in on the rails—lying about sixth. Doesn't matter where it is. It's going to win.'

The horses charged towards the winning post. A furlong out Toothy Look was still lying sixth.

'I wish it would hurry,' said Roger.

'Don't you worry,' said Eagally. 'He'll make his effort any moment. But it doesn't matter whether he does or he doesn't—he can't lose.'

'He seems to have a very reasonable chance of doing so at the moment,' said Henry.

A hundred yards from home Toothy Look's jockey made a very fine effort indeed. Unfortunately so did all the other jockeys, and Toothy Look duly passed the post—still sixth. But it's true to say that there was not more than a length between all six horses.

'First—number ten, second—number three, third—number eight,' said the voice over the loudspeaker.

'But Toothy Look was number ten,' said Sally.

'What did I tell you?' said Eagally.

'But I don't understand,' said Henry. Nor did the crowd. There were groans and howls of various kinds. The race had in fact been won by the favourite, but the judge had mistaken the favourite's colours for those of Toothy Look; they were very similar.

'Toothy Look didn't win that race,' said Roger.

'His number's in the frame,' said Eagally, 'and, as long as it's there, he won. Now, in any other race there'd be an objection of some kind, but there can't be in this one. It's statistically impossible. Just listen to the crowd. It's no good. The judge's decision is final.'

And it was. As they went from the stands to the totalisator to collect their winnings, they met an extremely angry judge, talking to Mr Trent, who seemed quite calm and collected. Mr Trent had correctly informed the judge which horse would come in first—but not which horse would win. The judge had lost five pounds.

'This is quite outrageous,' he said to Henry. 'There should be some method of appeal. I've always been told that racing was a crook's game. Now I know it.'

Five pounds is quite a lot of money to lose in that way.

'I couldn't agree with that, Judge, with respect,' said Mr Trent. 'There's nothing crooked about it, if I may say so. The judge made a mistake. That's all. It must happen sometimes. After all, judges are only human.'

'Our mistakes can be corrected,' snapped the judge. 'So should this judge's.'

'But, Judge,' said Mr Trent, 'surely there are occasions when a judge's decision is final and conclusive. Take, for instance—'

But the normally genial judge had had enough. Without another word he turned his back on Mr Trent and walked away.

'It's a shame,' said Mr Trent. 'Still, on his salary, it shouldn't hurt him all that much. I'm glad to say I didn't back it myself. I had a feeling about the race. How right I was. Any of you get the first home?'

'Well,' said Roger, 'we backed number ten—which was rather better.'

Not long afterwards, Donald came up to the party and, in a somewhat conspiratorial manner, invited them to follow him. He led them into Tattersalls' ring and pointed out a large and beery-faced-looking man who was already saying in substance—in a loud and ugly voice—that he would lay ten to one the field bar one. Donald also pointed out a much smaller man with a pointed face, sharp nose, and small moustache. He was saying—in a more staccato manner—that he also would be pleased to lay ten to one the field bar one.

'What does that mean?' said Anne.

'Don't you worry what it means,' said Donald. 'I'll tell you later. Now—' he said, in his most confidential evening voice to Roger and Henry, 'either of these two will give you a bet during the race. You'll hear them offering odds. All you've got to do when the field reaches that point—d'you see?'—and he pointed out on the course a place a little more than two furlongs from the winning post—'all you've got to do is to say, "What'll you give on Conference?" But you'll have to be snappy, or you'll be too late. Come to think of it, you'd better do it a bit earlier. Say there—' and he pointed out a place about a hundred and fifty yards before the original one. 'Take whatever he offers, and put your silk gown on it,' he said to Henry.

'And you put your present one, Roger. You won't be needing it
much longer. But, of course, only if Conference is in the rear. If
he's in the lead, forget it and watch him come in last. Now—is
everyone clear?'

Donald surveyed his employers and their ladies rather like a
platoon sergeant giving instruction in musketry. Roger almost
expected him to say 'any questions'. Satisfied that they knew what
to do, Donald went hurriedly and erratically to see his trainer and
the apprentice who was to ride Conference.

Roger and Anne, Henry and Sally, and Eagally, who had become
one of the party, waited where they had been told.

'You haven't told us which one is statistically bound to win this
race,' said Henry.

'Statistically,' said Eagally, with authority, 'any horse could win
this race. That is why I haven't ventured to make any suggestions
for it. That's one of the things I forgot to tell you. With my system,
you can't back on every race. Oh, dear, no. You could certainly
lose money that way.'

'And would it be very rude to inquire how much you've won this
season so far?' asked Roger.

'Oh—I don't keep an exact account,' said Eagally. 'It isn't
necessary. Statistically I know that I must have won and that's all
that matters.'

'I should have thought it might have been worth having a check
every now and then to see if the statistics had gone wrong,' said
Henry.

'Statistics can't go wrong,' said Eagally. 'You've just seen a most
interesting example of that.'

Not long afterwards, the horses went down to the post. Conference undoubtedly seemed to be anxious to get down to the start
and indeed a good way past it. The boy on his back certainly was
going to have his work cut out to hold him in.

'Hadn't we better check up with one of those bookies that they'll
take a bet? Donald might have given us the wrong ones.' Roger
went up to the red-faced man. 'Will you take a bet during the race?'
he asked politely.

'What d'you think I'm something well here for?' said the bookie.
'Selling sweet peas, hokey-pokey penny a lump? Eights bar,' he
yelled.

Roger retired.

'I don't think I cared for him much,' said Roger. 'I think I'll try the other one.'

The sharp-nosed man, in reply to Roger's question, said: 'Any particular horse?'

'Conference,' said Roger.

'I'll give you a hundred to six now,' said the bookie.

'I don't want to back it now,' said Roger.

'How much d'you want to put on?'

Roger thought for a moment. There were four of them. 'About a fiver, I suppose,' he said.

'Well, you can try,' said the bookie. 'But it all depends what's happening. If Conference runs the other way, I'll give you a hundred pounds to a sausage.'

Not at all confident that Donald's plan would work, Roger returned to the others. 'We'll have to be pretty quick off the mark,' he said, 'or the race will be over before we've understood what they've said.'

A minute later the white flag was up, and then they were off.

'Oh, dear,' said Anne. And well she might. For the impatient Conference had virtually seized the reins out of the little boy's hands and was tearing for home as fast as he could go. He sprang into a two lengths' lead almost at once. This he increased to three, four, and, finally, to ten lengths—and by the time the vital point was reached he was still that much up.

'Tens bar,' shouted the red-faced bookie.

But the chambers party did not move. Round the bend came Conference with its little passenger—who had long ceased to try to hold him—looking rather like a little apple with a coloured cap.

'What a shame,' said Sally. 'It looks to me as though he's going to win all the same.'

By this time the jockeys on the other horses were doing everything they could to encourage their mounts to catch up Conference. They certainly made up some ground, but not enough, and, in due course, as though he knew where he was going, Conference safely delivered his little apple to the winner's enclosure. Donald was there to greet him—in a state of great excitement. His trainer was equally pleased. 'Sorry I couldn't hold him in,' said the little apple.

'If you win a race you're meant to win,' said the trainer, 'you don't have to apologize.'

The chambers party came to offer Donald their congratulations.

'How much did you put on?' he asked.

They stared at him for a moment. Then Roger said: 'Nothing, of course. You told us.'

'Sir, sir, sir,' said Donald. 'But I didn't tell you not to use your loaf, did I? It was obvious he was going to win.'

'You told me,' said Henry, 'that if he were leading at the spot you pointed out, we were not to touch him.'

'Sir,' said Donald, in what appeared to him to be a dignified manner, 'the trouble is you boys don't understand racing.'

'I think we can agree to that,' said Roger.

But it had been a good day, all the same, and he had found plenty of opportunity in between the races to be with Anne alone.

Donald, too, had had an exhilarating day. He had never won a race before. His wife put him to bed.

CHAPTER 17

A Question of Confidence

The next week was a particularly busy one for Roger. He was in court every day, had a large number of conferences, and had an infinite amount of paper work to do. But it all sat very lightly on him now. Towards the end of the week Mr Glacier and Mr Plumb came to see him to report progress.

'If you ask me,' said Mr Glacier, 'what you call a little bird must have spoken to the inspector.'

'The trap didn't come off?'

'I will tell you exactly what happened,' said Mr Glacier, 'and,' he added, 'you can be sure I am speaking the truth as everything which was said was recorded by tape machine.'

'Well, what happened?' said Roger.

'I duly attended the interview,' said Mr Glacier, 'and this is what happened. The inspector began:

' "This is all very irregular. What is it you want to see me about?"

'I said: "I hoped we might be able to come to an understanding."

' "About what?" he said.

' "You know what about, inspector," I said.

' "I certainly don't," he said, "and I must warn you that anything you say now may be given in evidence at your trial."

'Well, Mr Thursby, as you may have observed, I am not usually at a loss for words, but I was beginning to find myself—how do you say?—against a blank wall. It appeared obvious to me that any attempt to bribe him at the moment would have been quite hopeless. He was obviously on his guard. So I decided to play one more card—to see if at any rate I could take one trick. "I don't mind what you give in evidence, inspector," I said, "so long as it is the truth. Why did you not tell the truth about the money I gave you?" He did not answer for a moment. Then: "What do you mean?" he said. "You know quite well what I mean, inspector," I said, "You know I gave you thirty pounds and thirty-five pounds, not twenty pounds and twenty-five pounds. And perhaps you would be interested to know that the whole of our conversation is now being listened to by your superintendent." ' Mr Glacier paused.

'Good Lord! What did he say?'

'Nothing,' said Mr Glacier. 'Not only words failed him, but blood, or whatever it is, also failed him. He fainted. Fortunately he fell to the ground with a crash. I might perhaps have saved him, but I thought that we should then miss the noise of his fall in the microphone. So I let—how do you say?—nature take its course. He was not much hurt. But, of course, gravity will have its way and the inspector is a tall man.'

'What happened then?' asked Roger.

'Everything seemed to happen at once. The superintendent and Chief Constable who had been listening to the conversation rushed in to assist the inspector. At first they took no notice of me. But when they had revived the inspector and had put some plaster on the cut on his head, they appeared to notice me.

' "Can I be of any further assistance?" I asked most politely.

' "Kindly leave this station at once, sir, and don't come back," said the Chief Constable.

' "But really," I protested, "what have I done? Is it my fault if the inspector faints?"

' "You have been guilty of a disgraceful breach of confidence in telling the inspector that the conversation was being overheard."

' "You were never going to tell him then " I asked.

' "Leave the station, sir," said the Chief Constable.

'So, of course, I left and at once reported to Mr Plumb and he has brought me to you as soon as possible.'

'I have spoken to the Director's office,' said Mr Plumb, who had some justification for the mournful way in which he said it, 'and I'm afraid they don't like us at all, not at all.'

'Dear, dear,' said Roger. 'All is finished between us, I suppose, and the prosecution is going on as hard as ever. The armistice is over, the gloves are off, the detectives have gone back to Scotland Yard, and the fight is on.'

'You sound remarkably cheerful,' said Mr Glacier. 'I hope with reason. You will permit me to remind you once again that it is my wife and I who rot in goal, not you.'

'Well,' said Roger who, for reasons wholly unconnected with Mr

Glacier, was continuously cheerful, 'we shall do our best to prevent that happening. And I'm bound to say that, short of having the prosecution called off, we haven't done so badly.'

'You are satisfied then?' said Mr Plumb. 'I must say I never thought you would be happy about the present position.'

'Happier than either of you appear to be,' said Roger.

'Let me remind you yet again—at the risk of repetition,' began Mr Glacier, 'that it is—'

'No, I won't,' said Roger. 'I remember perfectly. It's you who'll go to gaol if you're convicted. Quite right. So it will be. As to that, all I can say is that I think you've a very good chance of not going to gaol, but, if you do, it's entirely your own fault for giving money to policemen.'

'Our little Melanie,' began Mr Glacier.

'Whether it was your little Melanie or not—and I doubt whether anyone will really believe that little Melanie came into the story at all—but, even if she did, you must have known perfectly well that to give sixty-five pounds to police officers is a wrong thing to do. None the less, I think you've a very good chance of getting away with it.'

'You think we will be acquitted?'

'I think it very possible. Nothing of course, is certain, but the case has got to be proved and, apart from your word and your wife's, we have three things in our favour—and there might have been a fourth. First, there's your police constable; secondly, there's the fact that we went to the police straight away and that they set a trap for their own people; thirdly, the inspector fainted. It's quite true that the sudden knowledge that his superiors sufficiently mistrusted him to make them set a trap for him might have been such a shock to him that he lost consciousness for a moment, but, of course, it's also posssible that your statement about the money, coupled with the knowledge that he was being listened to, had that effect. He, of course, will give the former explanation, but when you add the police constable's evidence to it, it'll shake the jury pretty considerably, I should say.'

'What is the fourth point that you might have had?'

'Mr Plumb,' said Roger, 'did you tell Mr Glacier about your conversation with the Chief Constable? The one you consulted me about?'

'Yes, I did, as a matter of fact,' said Mr Plumb. 'Before I told you about it. Shouldn't I have?'

'Am I to understand,' said Mr Glacier, 'that my lawyers have some doubt whether they should tell me something they have learned in the conduct of proceedings on my behalf?'

'It was said to Mr Plumb in confidence,' said Roger.

'Confidence,' said Mr Glacier. 'And when did I give you—how do you say?—authority to keep things secret from me?'

'Mr Plumb acted as many other solicitors would have acted. The Chief Constable said something to him and then added that it was in confidence and Mr Plumb agreed. Litigation could not be conducted if lawyers could not trust each other and say things in confidence to one another.'

'First,' said Mr Glacier, 'the Chief Constable is not a lawyer.'

'The principle is the same in this case,' said Roger.

'Very well,' said Mr Glacier, 'I will assume that it is. Is not litigation, as you call it, proceedings between two persons over some civil dispute? Is a prosecution where one side may go to gaol or, indeed, be hanged, litigation?'

'You may be right, Mr Glacier, that litigation strictly means civil proceedings. But criminal lawyers must be able to trust one another just the same.'

'I do not care two figs whether they trust one another or not. I do not mind what are the—I think you call them—the ethics of the legal profession. I who stand in danger of being sent to prison demand—yes, demand, I say—that all facts which are in my favour shall be used to help to secure my acquittal. Now I am right in thinking, am I not, that this fourth matter to which you referred is the statement to Mr Plumb that in effect the inspector was already a suspected person? I am right, am I not?' he repeated.

'Yes,' said Roger, 'you're quite right.'

'And am I further right in thinking that, in your view, if that further fact were brought to the attention of the jury, it would raise even more our chances of being acquitted?'

'That is quite true,' said Roger.

'Then,' said Mr Glacier, 'I demand that it be used.'

'Demand is a strong word, Mr Glacier,' said Roger.

'The occasion requires the use of strong words.'

'I told you,' said Roger, 'that I reserved the right to throw up the case if it was not conducted in a proper manner.'

'You, of course, have that right,' said Mr Glacier, 'and let me make it plain that I should be very sorry indeed if you did—how did you say?—throw it up. Indeed, I demand that unless I have done something wrong or require you to do something wrong, that you do not do so.'

'I wish you wouldn't keep on using that word "demand",' said Roger. 'I want to help you as far as I properly can, but whenever you say "demand" I feel like pushing you out of the room. You will please assume that I will do everything that is right and proper to secure your acquittal.'

'Do you not consider it right and proper that a fact which could affect the jury's verdict should be put before them? How can you have these so-called confidences in matters where a man's liberty— or, indeed, his life—the principle is the same—is at stake?'

'It is not an easy matter,' said Roger.

'I see no difficulty about it at all,' said Mr Glacier. 'Let us suppose for example, that you have a client charged with a crime and the counsel for the prosecution told you—in confidence—in absolute confidence—that, as a matter of fact, the prosecution knew that your client was not guilty but that, as they could not prove the case against the guilty man and the public wanted a—what is the word?—a scapegoat, they were going to try to secure a conviction against your client—supposing the charge were murder—the penalty death—suppose your client were convicted and hanged— would you think you had acted properly in keeping your learned friend's confidence or not?'

'Such a thing could never happen in this country,' said Roger.

'But suppose it did—strange things do occur—would you keep the matter told you in confidence?'

Roger did not answer at once.

'No doubt you would seek to be relieved of the obligation to keep the matter in confidence, you would see your opponent and endeavour to obtain a release from him and you would have sound arguments to urge him, but supposing all your efforts were in vain, what then? Would you keep his confidence—with a man's life at stake?'

'No,' said Roger, 'in a strong case like that I don't think I could. But that isn't this case. It is not a case of life or death and the statement made is nothing like so outrageous or unworthy of confidence as the one in the case you've suggested.'

'One thing at a time,' said Mr Glacier. 'You say it is not a case
of life or death. But is there any difference in what you lawyers are
pleased to call principle between loss of liberty and loss of life? Who
are you to say what the consequences of loss of liberty may be to
me or my wife? Prison may have a—what is the word?—a permanent effect on some people, it may kill others. This is not a criticism
of your prisons. I refer to loss of liberty. So first I say, how do you
distinguish between death and imprisonment?'

'There is obviously a difference in fact,' said Roger, 'but in principle you may be right.'

'Very well then. Now, as to the nature of the statement. You
pride yourselves in this country on the prosecution being fair. Is it
fair, do you think, to call as the main witness for the prosecution a
man whom you suspect of dishonesty, to put him before the jury
as a man of upright character and not to tell the defence of your
suspicions? Is that fair? And, if it is not, is the statement made by
the Chief Constable any more worthy of confidence than the one
that I suggested?'

'Mr Glacier,' said Roger. 'I'm bound to say you put your point
of view very ably. I shall have to think this one out. It's not at all
an easy decision to have to make.'

'I am quite sure,' said Mr Glacier, 'that you will consider the
matter most carefully before coming to a decision. Should your
decision be adverse to my interests, is it possible for me to consult
your society or institute on the matter?'

'The Bar Council, you mean?' said Roger. 'There would not be
time to get a ruling of the Bar Council before the case is heard. But
I would certainly speak to the Chairman about it, if you wished.
Indeed, I may do so in any event. I entirely see your point of view,
but the legal profession could not be carried on without rules and
the rules must be kept.'

'Even if the result is that innocent persons are hanged or sent to
prison? Permit me to say,' said Mr Glacier, 'that an amendment of
any such rules in a civilized community would seem to be highly
desirable. But, of course, no such amendment could be made before
the trial . . . you will say. You will, no doubt, send me a copy to
the particular prison where I am rotting.'

'I don't know why you're so convinced that you'll be convicted
if we don't use the statement. I should have thought that your clear
conscience would have made you more optimistic.'

'Who said I had a clear conscience?' asked Mr Glacier. 'You have already pointed out to me that it was wrong to give money to policemen.'

Eventually it was arranged that Roger should consider what course he was proposing to adopt and that he would let Mr Plumb know when he had made up his mind.

As soon as he could, Roger went in to see Henry.

'I gather we're enemies, again,' said Henry.

'So do I,' said Roger. 'But there's an awkward thing I want to talk to you about. D'you think you could get Digby over? It's rather serious.'

'O.K.,' said Henry. 'Are you sure you wouldn't like his able assistant Mr Trent as well?'

'I think we'll be able to manage without him somehow,' said Roger. 'We can always send for him if we get stuck.'

So a meeting took place the next day between Henry and his junior Digby, and Roger.

'So sorry I couldn't get down last time,' said Digby, 'but I feel sure I was most ably represented.'

'Incredibly so,' said Henry.

'I shouldn't have liked you to miss Tony Trent,' said Digby. 'He has to be heard to be believed. I confess he fascinates me. If I had the time I could listen to him for hours. Well, what's the trouble? Your Mr Glacier, if I may say so, is a pretty good stinker.'

'And a very able one,' said Henry.

'He's certainly that,' said Roger, 'whatever else he may be . . . as to which I don't feel called on to make any admissions.'

'The Chief Constable's hopping mad,' said Henry.

'I don't altogether blame him,' said Digby.

'I think you're being a bit unfair,' said Roger. 'No one had told him not to give the game away to the inspector. The Chief Constable wouldn't have minded if the inspector had been caught. What he, of course, is livid about is not catching the inspector and letting the inspector know that they'd tried to catch him. Must make it sort of awkward for him, I agree. But that isn't altogether my man's fault.'

'Yes—but look at the way he did it,' said Henry.

'Did what?' asked Roger.

'Look,' said Henry, 'if you ask me, old Glacier knew the game was up and that if he just asked the inspector why he said he'd received forty-five pounds when, in fact, he'd had sixty-five pounds the inspector would simply have denied it. So what does he do? He puts the question to him and, before he has time to answer, he fires at him point-blank about the Chief Constable and superintendent listening in. Well—he couldn't have known it'd be such a success and that the insepctor would faint, but he must have hoped that by following up the one question with the other he'd be bound to shake the inspector, and no doubt he hoped that he'd yammer for a bit. And even for the most upright inspector in the world it must be a pretty considerable shock to be told suddenly that a criminal is being used as a bait and that the conversation's being tapped. He'd no other cards to play, so he brought out that one.'

'Well,' said Roger, 'we shall see, my dear fellow, we shall see. No doubt you will ask Mr Glacier the question when he gives evidence. I promise you I won't tell him what to answer.'

'No need,' said Henry. 'He's quite capable of taking care of himself. I must say I don't blame the old Chief Constable. To blow the gaff like that was a bit steep.'

Roger suddenly had a horrible thought. 'I hope he doesn't think it was anything to do with me,' he said.

'Well,' said Henry, 'I must confess I don't think he likes you very much.'

'Blast and curse,' said Roger. I must see Anne and explain, he thought. Confound Glacier, confound everything. Why must Anne be mixed up in it? I hope she'll believe me. Oh—good Lord!— 'Where's the catch, Mr Thursby? Do you tell me now or later or do I have to find it out for myself?' 'There's no catch, Chief Constable.' 'Bait with no hook, eh? You're not a fisherman, I imagine.' Bait with no hook! Here was the hook with a vengeance. He'll never believe that I wasn't behind it all. Anne will believe me—I hope—but her father will think me a scoundrel. She might marry me just the same . . . but it would be horrible for her—she's fond of her father. Blast Mr Glacier—though, to be fair, I'd never have met Anne but for him. Oh, well—I shall have to do something about it.

'I hope you told him it wasn't anything to do with me,' said Roger.

'I haven't seen him yet,' said Henry. 'I got it from the Director.'

'Well—do tell him when you get the chance,' said Roger. 'It's rather important to me, as a matter of fact.'

'O.K.,' said Henry. 'I see. I'll do my best.'

'Is that all you wanted me for,' said Digby, 'as I've got to go to Brixton to see a friend?'

'No,' said Roger, 'that last bit made me forget what I really wanted to see you about. But that makes it worse than ever. I really don't know what to do. Look, this is the trouble.' He then told Henry and Digby what the problem was, putting all the arguments for and against the evidence being used.

'Of course,' he said, 'the Chief Constable shouldn't have said afterwards that it was in confidence. He ought to have said "I'll tell you this in confidence but not otherwise." That might have been different. But, however he did it, old Plumb said he would treat it in confidence. And if you say you're going to treat a thing in confidence, you've got to keep your word. It isn't like a contract. You don't have to have consideration for it. Moreover, if Plumb had said "You should have said that before, you didn't say it was in confidence and I'm going to use it," the Chief Constable would probably have cried off the whole thing. So by keeping silent Plumb in effect assured the Chief Constable that the statment would be kept in confidence. Then, like a blithering idiot, he goes and tells the client. That was a breach of confidence to begin with, but he didn't realize it. But let's assume he didn't tell the client. Let's assume only Plumb and I knew it, and we'd agreed to treat it in confidence—have we the right to do so if a man may be hanged or go to gaol if we do? I'm bound to say I think Glacier's right in saying there's no distinction in principle between death and prison. My natural instinct, of course, tells me that I can't use the state-ment—but then, as Glacier would say, it's easy for me. I don't have to rot in gaol. What do you each think about it?'

'I don't see any difficulty,' said Digby. 'It was said in confidence and that's an end of it.'

'What do you think, Henry?'

'I don't think it's as simple as that,' said Henry. 'As Roger says, it's easy enough for us. We stick to our rules and say what fine fellows we are, puff our chests out and say you can always trust a member of the Bar—good old Thursby—he'll never let you down; meantime, Mr Thursby's client is duly executed or sent to prison for life. I certainly wouldn't puff my chest out after that.'

'Confidence means confidence,' said Digby. 'If you can't trust a member of the Bar, you might as well shut up shop. That's where

it's different from business. You can rely on a reputable member of
the Bar not to do a dirty trick. If you couldn't, it'd be hopeless. I
don't know what you're worried about. It was said in confidence,
and that's an end of it. That's what I think, anyway; I'm not a
lawyer like you chaps, but I know the answer to that one.'

'If the charge were murder and you were in my shoes, would you
refuse to use the statement?' asked Roger.

'Of course I would,' said Digby. 'Shouldn't even think of using
it. Fight hard but fight clean, I say.'

'And you wouldn't worry if you hadn't used the statement and
your client were hanged?'

'Not in the least,' said Digby. 'He'd have been guilty ten times
over anyway if he were convicted. People make too much fuss about
these things, I think. They hardly ever get to the dock if they're
innocent and, if there's a chance in a million that they're innocent,
they get off. Even if I happen to be defending them. No—give them
a fair trial, I say, but no more. They're ninety-nine per cent guilty,
but I quite agree they should have a proper trial and, if there's any
loopholle, by all means let them get away with it. But don't lean
over backwards to push the guilty ones out of the dock.'

'Well,' said Roger, 'what d'you say to *this* point of Glacier's? You
say they should have a fair trial. If you have a witness who'd got
a previous conviction you'd tell counsel for the defence, wouldn't
you?'

'Of course.'

'Well—what's the difference in principle? You've got a witness
whom you distrust. The defence can't know that. So, unless you
tell them, the witness is put forward as a person of integrity.'

'If you haven't got anything against him, he *is* a person of integrity. Suspicion isn't enough. The Chief Constable suspected the
inspector. All right. But he may have been wrong. He'd no evidence.
If you had to tell the defence of every witness you weren't too happy
about, where would it stop? There's a limit, you know.'

'Has he convinced you, Henry?' asked Roger.

'I can't say he has,' said Henry. 'I'm glad I'm not in your shoes.
I'm hanged if I'd know what I'd do. I'm bound to say that I'm
inclined to think that, when the acid test is applied, there can't be
such a thing as confidence in criminal matters any more than there
can be "without prejudice" conversations or letters. I suppose the
answer is that, if anything is said in confidence in a criminal matter,

the confidence must be kept if it's possible. But, in the last resort, the man in the dock comes first.'

'I can only say,' said Digby, 'that with the greatest respect and all that I profoundly disagree. To my mind the seal of confidence is binding for ever and in all instances and there are no exceptions.'

'Well, there you are, Roger,' said Henry, 'the Court's divided. On the whole and without a great deal of confidence—no pun intended—I agree with you, Roger, that, if you think it absolutely essential in the interests of your client to use the statement, you must use it.'

'I can only repeat —with considerable confidence,' said Digby, 'that such a point of view, if adopted generally, would be disastrous for the legal profession.'

'There I don't agree,' said Roger, 'because this kind of thing will only happen very, very occasionally. It's never happened to you, I suspect, and you're at the Criminal Bar. It's certainly never happened to me before, and I'll be very surprised if it happens again. Well—I'm most grateful to you both. I really have to make up my own mind.'

'I'll be very rude to you,' said Digby, 'if you don't make it up the right way.'

'I don't care two hoots about that,' thought Roger . . . 'but Anne's father—oh, Lord . . . Anne's father.'

CHAPTER 18

The Missing Witness

Roger's other work fortunately prevented him from thinking too much of his pressing personal and professional problems. Among his minor activities in Court was an appearance in the Divorce Court to do an undefended divorce case of some difficulty. It was before a new County Court judge and, as Roger's case was fairly high in the list, he went there early to see how quickly that particular judge got through his list. He was an unknown quantity. Some judges can quite comfortably dispose of twenty or thirty undefended divorce cases in one day. Others have their work cut out to deal with a dozen. It rather depends on the approach. The approach of Judge Renfrew was not known. Roger found that Crabtree was in the first case and he arrived in time to hear him saying:

'Oh—my Lord—I'm afraid I shall be in some difficulty in this case—as an essential witness, who has been sub-poenaed—I can prove it, my Lord—is apparently not here, and I'm not sure how much I can prove without him . . . in due course I shall ask your Lordship to take steps against the witness but, in the meantime, my Lord, I was wondering—' He paused for so long that Judge Renfrew said:

'You were wondering, Mr Crabtree?'

'Yes—my Lord—I was wondering—'

'Quite, Mr Crabtree—but what?'

'I was wondering, my Lord—I was wondering—'

'So am I now, Mr Crabtree.'

'That's very good of your Lordship.'

'Not at all, Mr Crabtree. Were you perhaps wondering if I would hear such evidence as you have, and see how far it gets us?'

'That was it exactly,' said Mr Crabtree. 'It is very good of your Lordship.'

'Not at all, Mr Crabtree. At any rate it's stopped us both

wondering. Call your evidence and we'll see how far you can take it.'

Crabtree proceeded to call his evidence and, apart from proving that his client had duly married the respondent, that they had lived at various places and had no children, and that the photograph produced was a photograph of the respondent, and the signature produced was his signature—he proved practically nothing.

'And now, my Lord,' said Crabtree, 'I propose to prove that the missing witness was duly served with the subpoena and then I shall ask your Lordship to take steps.'

'Very well, Mr Crabtree.'

The process server was duly called and he duly proved that the witness had been served with the subpoena and provided with conduct money.

'And now, my Lord,' said Crabtree, 'I ask your Lordship to take steps.'

'Yes, Mr Crabtree, what steps?' asked the judge.

'Oh, my Lord,' said Crabtree, waving his arm as if to express something, 'oh, my Lord—' he repeated—'steps—against the witness.'

'Yes, Mr Crabtree—what steps?'

'Oh, my Lord,' said Crabtree, waving his arm again—'there must be steps.'

'No doubt,' said the judge, 'but what?'

'Oh, my Lord,' said Crabtree, and waited for inspiration. After it had failed to come for the space of about ten seconds, the judge said:

'Would you like a few minutes to consider the matter and I'll take another case in the meantime?'

'That is most kind of your Lordship. It would be most helpful.'

'Call the next case then, please,' said the judge, 'and let me know when you are ready, Mr Crabtree.'

'Thank you, my Lord,' said Crabtree, and went hurriedly to the Bar Library.

While Roger was waiting, Donald came up to him. 'You're all right in QB4 for the moment and you're quite safe in the Court of Appeal till this afternoon. You'd better wait here and I'll watch the non-jury.'

'Thanks,' said Roger.

Judge Renfrew had disposed of three more cases when Crabtree
returned and informed his Lordship that he was now ready.

'Yes, Mr Crabtree?' said the judge.

'My Lord, if your Lordship will be good enough to look at Rayden
at page 347, you will see that your Lordship can issue a warrant
for the arrest of the witness.'

The judge referred to the passage. 'Yes, Mr Crabtree, I see the
statement. Can you tell me under what rule of Court or statute the
power arises?'

'Oh, my Lord,' began Crabtree, 'oh, my Lord—'

'Yes?' said the judge.

'Oh, my Lord,' Crabtree repeated. 'I'm sure it wouldn't appear
in Rayden if it weren't right.'

'So am I,' said the judge. 'It is in the highest degree improbable.
But I must know the rule or the statute or whatever it is before I
interfere with the liberty of the subject.'

'But, my Lord, it says quite definitely here—' said Crabtree.

'I know, I know,' said the judge, 'but it gives no authority for
the proposition and, although I don't doubt it in the least, I must
know what it is.'

'Well, my Lord—'

'Yes, Mr Crabtree?'

'Well, my Lord—'

'Mr Crabtree, would you like me to put the case back again for
you to find out the authority?'

'That would be most kind of your Lordship.'

'Very well, Mr Crabtree. Let me know when you are ready.'

The judge continued with another case and several further cases,
including Roger's. As he finished Roger's case, Crabtree returned
and, as he had not yet been summoned by Donald, Roger waited
to see what would happen.

'My Lord,' said Crabtree, 'I've made an exhaustive search and
I'm afraid I can't actually find the authority your Lordship wants,
but I'm quite sure the learned editor of Rayden would not have
put it in unless—'

'So am I, Mr Crabtree, but, as I said before, I must be satisfied
before I have people arrested. I see that the subpoena itself says
nothing about arrest but only about forfeiting one hundred pounds.'

'Yes, my Lord.'

'Well, what d'you want me to do?'

'Well, of course, my Lord,' said Crabtree, 'if this came under the Rules of the Supreme Court, it would be quite easy to show your Lordship—'

'But it does come under the Rules of the Supreme Court, Mr Crabtree, subject to any modification by statute or the rules of this Division of the Supreme Court.'

'Oh, well, in that case, my Lord, I ask your Lordship to take steps—'

'But under what Rule of the Supreme Court, Mr Crabtree?'

'I'm afraid, my Lord, I haven't the actual rule in front of me— perhaps your Lordship wouldn't mind—'

'Certainly, Mr Crabtree, I'll take another case.'

The judge took several more cases and eventually Crabtree returned, looking rather dejected.

'I'm afraid, my Lord,' he said, 'that with such little time at my disposal I haven't been able to find—'

'Well, Mr Crabtree, wouldn't it be best if I adjourned this case for fourteen days for you to go into the matter? I should make it plain that I feel quite sure you are right in saying that, if a man deliberately disobeys a subpoena, he can be dealt with in an appropriate manner. Justice could not be administered if there weren't procedure to compel witnesses to give evidence. But I'm sure you'll understand that I must see the power under which I am acting before I deprive people of their liberty.'

'Of course, my Lord,' said Crabtree. 'It is very good of your Lordship, and I will gratefully accept your Lordship's suggestion of a fourteen-day adjournment.'

'Very well,' said the judge. 'Adjourned for fourteen days.'

Just as the judge was about to start another case, and Crabtree was about to leave the Court, a man, who had been there all the time, suddenly addressed the judge from a seat in the middle of the Court.

'May I speak?' he asked. 'I didn't like to interrupt before, but was it me you were talking about?'

It was the witness.

CHAPTER 19

Colonel Madderley's Opinion

The Chief Constable of Carpshire was talking to Anne. 'I'm sorry, Anne,' he said. 'I know how you must feel. If you're fond of him, there's nothing I can do, or would do for that matter, to stop you marrying him. And it won't alter you and me—I hope not—not as far as I'm concerned. But I can't have him in the house. I know I'm not a clever chap like he is—thank God I'm not—but I have a code. I dare say he laughs at soldiers and policemen. Blithering lot of idiots he thinks them. A lot of Blimps. All right, perhaps they are . . . and I'm one of them. But there are just certain things a chap doesn't do. And once anyone lets me down I'm finished with him. I'm not a fellow who wants revenge—I don't want my own back or anything of that sort—I just have nothing more to do with him. And that's all there is to it. I don't even say I'm in the right. If you like, he's in the right and I'm in the wrong. Be that as it may . . . when a chap does what he's done, I'm finished and that's all there is to it. I'm sorry, Anne, I really am. But that's the way it is and I'm too old to change now.'

'I understand, father,' said Anne. 'But why d'you blame Roger for it all? I'm sure he wouldn't do anything that was disgraceful or underhand for himself or anyone else. I don't know him well, but I'm sure he's not like that.'

'You don't know him well, Anne. You say so yourself. How can you tell? I judge by what a man does. It's the only way I know. Not the way he looks or what he says—but what he does. Simple, if you like, but it's the only way of judging a man that I've found any good. Your Roger could, I've no doubt, talk me into a cocked hat. He could play old Harry with me in the witness box—or in ordinary conversation if you like. I don't pretend to be any good at talking and he is—and if you ask me . . . I'm sorry to say this— he's a damned sight too good at it.'

'Father,' said Anne, 'please.'

'It's no good, Anne, and it's much better to face the facts. You and I always have. He sat in that chair you're in now. "Where's the catch?" I said. "There isn't one," he said. And then, when we'd had our chat, he said: "D'you still think there's a catch?" I trusted him, Anne, and his solicitor. The whole thing, if you ask me, was a thundering fraud. Clever, mind you—darned clever. It would take a clever chap to work that one out.'

'If I could show you it wasn't Roger's fault, father, you would change, wouldn't you?'

'My dear, dear Anne, of course I would. D'you think I like this between us—well, it isn't between us, because nothing could be—but interfering with us, hurting us both, of course I don't. But it's facts, Anne, facts. If you can show me facts are not facts, black is white and white is black—if you show it me, not by words or fine speeches but by things I can see and know—nobody will be better pleased than I shall be. But you can't do it, Anne. Facts can't lie. People can.'

Later that day Anne spoke to Roger.

'I'm sure if you came to see him, you'd make him understand,' she said.

'I can't during the case, Anne,' he said. 'He wouldn't see me anyway—and he'd be quite right at the moment. But, as soon as it's over, of course I will.'

And with that they both had to be satisfied.

CHAPTER 20

The Glaciers on Trial

The case of the Glaciers went on again the next week, but in a very different atmosphere. No cooperation this time between prosecution and defence, and no race meeting afterwards. Eventually the prosecution completed its case. Roger elected to call no evidence and both Mr and Mrs Glacier were committed for trial at the next Carpshire Assizes. They were both granted bail. Before the day of the trial they had a final conference with Roger.

'Well, Mr Thursby,' said Mr Glacier, 'have you made up your mind about this statement?'

'Yes,' said Roger. 'I have come to the conclusion that, if you require me to use it, it is my duty to do so—however much I may personally dislike doing it.'

'That simplifies matters,' said Mr Glacier. 'I require you to use it. I am extremely sorry for any inconvenience or embarrassment in which it may involve you. It is—how would you say?—just one of those things. And now, may I ask you yet again—what do you consider our chances are of being acquitted?'

'I think they're good,' said Roger. 'But naturally there's no certainty about it.'

'Ah, well,' said Mr Glacier, 'certainty is more than I could ask for, but I confess I should prefer to have certainty one way or the other.'

'You would prefer to have certainty that you would be convicted,' said Mr Plumb, in some amazement, 'than a reasonable chance that you will be acquitted?'

'We are on bail,' said Mr Glacier. 'The world is a large place. Now, please don't agitate yourself, Mr Plumb' he added hastily, when he saw Mr Plumb's hand and handkerchief starting up. 'I have no intention of—how do you call it?— jumping my bail.'

'It wouldn't be much use if you did,' said Roger. 'You'd only be picked up some time and extradited.'

'Do extradition treaties extend then to all countries and for all offences?' asked Mr Glacier. 'It is only what you would call an academic question,' he added.

'I don't know,' said Roger. 'I haven't looked it up.'

'As a matter of fact,' said Mr Glacier, 'I have made some research into the subject. I have surrendered my passport, but not my British Museum library ticket. It is, I find, a good thing to consider every aspect of a case. But pray do not be alarmed, Mr Plumb. I have the utmost confidence in Mr Thursby and, of course, in your good self, and, that being so, my visits to the British Museum can be considered of no practical significance. Though, of course, I am one who thinks that knowledge is never wasted.'

The case came on for trial very shortly after the conclusion of the proceedings before the magistrates. Mr Justice Kingsdown was the judge. There were two charges against each defendant. They pleaded Not Guilty, were given the usual permission to sit down, and the trial began. Henry, having informed the judge and jury that he appeared for the prosecution with his learned friend Mr Gerald Digby, and that the defendants had the advantage of being represented by his learned friend Mr Thursby, went on to tell them the facts, as alleged by the prosecution. He made no reference to the trap which had been set for the inspector and simply outlined the case as it had been before Roger and Mr Plumb went to see the Chief Constable. Before calling the evidence in support of his opening speech, Henry said this:

'Members of the jury, we pride ourselves in this country that corruption is rare and that, where we find it, we do all in our power to stamp it out. It is one of the most insidious of all evils, it is difficult to detect and, once it starts, no one knows how far it will go. No people are more likely to be tempted by corruption than the police force and it is vital that we should have a police force which is resistant to all such attempts. I venture to suggest to you, members of the jury, that—when you have heard the evidence in this case—you will come to the conclusion that it is a classic case of attempted corruption . . . by a rich man anxious to escape from the consequences of a breach of the licensing laws. Mr and Mrs Glacier no doubt find that money can buy them many things that poorer people cannot have and, in due course, I shall ask you to say that they tried to buy something which in this country is not for sale.'

Henry then called the inspector to give evidence. In examination-in-chief he said very much what he said in the Magistrate's Court. Then Henry sat down and he was cross-examined by Roger.

'How is your head?' was Roger's first question.

The judge and the jury looked surprised at the question, which, of course, was Roger's intention.

'It's better thank you,' said the inspector.

'A nasty bump, I'm afraid,' said Roger.

'Not too bad,' said the inspector.

'I take it,' said the judge, 'the jury and I are going to be let into the secret some time.'

'Of course, my Lord,' said Roger. 'You hit your head against a desk and cut it, I'm afraid?' he went on.

'Yes,' said the inspector.

'That was about three weeks ago, was it not?'

'Yes.'

'You were having an interview with the defendant, Mr Glacier, were you not?'

'Yes, I was.'

'The man who is supposed to have tried to bribe you?'

'Yes.'

'This interview was during the proceedings before the magistrates?'

'Yes.'

'A bit odd, isn't it, to interview an accused person after proceedings have started?'

'He asked for the interview.'

'I dare say he did,' said Roger. 'But why did you give it him?'

'I wanted to know what he was going to say.'

'Maybe,' said Roger, 'but he was represented by solicitor and counsel, and so was the prosecution. Did you ask any superior officer or anyone from the Director of Public Prosecutions Office whether there was any objection to your having the interview?'

'I told the superintendent I was having the interview.'

'That isn't what I asked you. Did you ask anyone whether it would be proper for you to have the interview?'

'No.'

'Have you ever done such a thing before?'

'I don't think so.'

'Then why on this occasion?'

'I wanted to know what he was going to say.'

'Do you mean that you thought you might get some more evidence?'

'Possibly.'

'I suggest that you thought you might get some more money.'

'Nothing of the kind,' said the inspector indignantly.

'Why so indignant, inspector?' asked Roger. 'Did you think it more likely that the defendant was coming for a proper purpose or an improper purpose?'

'I didn't know.'

'Of course you didn't *know*, but did you think it more likely to be improper or proper? Here was a man who had already given you money and he asks to see you in the middle of a case. Pretty irregular, wasn't it?'

'I told him so,' said the inspector.

'I know you did,' said Roger, 'and that's why I ask the question again. Was it more likely for a proper or improper purpose? More likely is all I ask.'

The inspector hesitated for a moment. Then:

'Improper, I suppose,' he answered.

'In what way improper?' asked Roger.

Again the inspector hesitated.

'May I help you?' said Roger. 'Possibly he was going to try to bribe you again?'

'Possibly,' said the inspector.

'Then why were you so indignant a moment ago when I asked you if you thought you might get some more money?'

'I thought you meant for myself,' said the inspector.

'Why did you think that?' asked Roger.

'From the way you asked the question,' said the inspector.

'Any other reason?' asked Roger.

The inspector did not answer at once.

'Come, inspector,' said Roger, 'is it such a very difficult question? You say that you thought my question meant that you expected to get some money for yourself. Very good. Now, was there any other reason except my manner of asking the question which made you think that?'

Again there was a pause. Then the inspector said:

'What the defendant himself said, I suppose.'

'And what was that?'

'He said he'd given me more than I'd put in the charge sheet.'

'You mean,' said Roger, 'that he said to you that he had given you more money than you handed over to your superior and that you had dishonestly kept the balance for yourself? That was the effect of what he said, was it not?'

'Yes,' said the inspector.

'And what was your reply?' asked Roger.

Again the inspector hesitated.

'You were very indignant with me a moment ago,' said Roger. 'I suppose you were very indignant with Mr Glacier and denied his wicked lies?'

As there was still no answer, Roger went on:

'Come, inspector, didn't you deny what he said?'

'No,' said the inspector, 'I didn't get the chance.'

'Oh—why was that?' asked Roger—in an interested inquiring tone.

'He said something else at the same time . . . and—and—'

'You fainted,' put in Roger, 'and banged your head?'

'Yes,' said the inspector.

'What else did he say?' asked Roger.

'He said that our conversation was being listened to by the Chief Constable and the superintendent.'

'Which was the greater shock?' asked Roger.

'I don't quite understand,' said the inspector.

'Was it a great shock to be told that you'd kept some of the money or that the conversation was being tapped—or was it a combination of both?'

'I don't know,' said the inspector. 'I suppose it was both.'

'It was true that the conversation was being tapped, wasn't it?'

'Yes.'

'It was also true, wasn't it, inspector, that you'd kept some of the money?'

'It was not.'

'On neither occasion?'

'Certainly not.'

'But you didn't deny it to Mr Glacier, did you?'

'I didn't get the chance.'

'You've heard the record of the conversation played over, haven't you?'

'Yes.'

'There was a pause between Mr Glacier's two questions, wasn't there?'

'There was a slight pause.'

'Why didn't you take advantage of it to deny the allegation?'

'It was a shock.'

'You mean that?'

'Yes.'

'But aren't you used to having accused persons making wicked and untrue allegations against you?'

'Sometimes.'

'It's quite frequent, isn't it?'

'It does happen.'

'Then why was it such a shock?'

'I can't say why exactly, but it was.'

'May I suggest a reason,' said Roger, 'that you were so surprised at Mr Glacier telling the whole truth about the matter?'

'No.'

'Didn't you think that he would deny ever having given you any money?'

'I didn't know what he would say.'

'Of course you didn't *know*, but didn't you *think* he would deny ever having given you any money? That's what you'd expect him to do, isn't it?'

'Possibly.'

'Well, of course, if he denies having given you any money he can't say he's given you more than you've handed over to your superiors, can he?'

'I suppose not.'

'So that, if you have been dishonest and if he's going to deny giving you any money, you're pretty safe, aren't you?'

'It didn't happen.'

'I didn't ask you if it happened,' said Roger. 'I asked if it seemed to you a pretty safe thing for a dishonest inspector to do?'

'I don't know whether it would be safe or not. I've never considered it.'

'I suggest,' said Roger, 'that you not only considered it but that you did it.'

'I did not.'

Roger then proceeded to put Mr Glacier's story about Melanie to the inspector. But he did not do it at any great length as it was a side of the story in which he did not have much faith.

Later the sergeant gave evidence, corroborating what the inspector had said in his evidence-in-chief. Roger then cross-examined him.

'You know P.C. Thrussle, do you not?' was his first question.

'Yes,' said the sergeant.

'An officer of good character?'

'As far as I know.'

'On quite good terms with you?' asked Roger.

'Yes—quite.'

'Any reason you can think of why he should tell a lie to injure you?'

'I can't think of any.'

'Do you meet him in the canteen sometimes?'

'Yes.'

'Chat about this and that?'

'Yes.'

'Ever speak to him about this case?'

'I told him we'd got it on.'

'Anything else about it?'

'Not that I remember.'

'Let me see if I can help you,' said Roger. 'Did you mention the amount that had been handed to the inspector?'

'I don't think so.'

'Didn't you? Just try to think.'

'It was only a casual conversation.'

'Drinking beer at the time?'

'I do drink it. Very likely I was then.'

'Tell me, sergeant, have you had any experience of bribery cases before?'

'I've had to do with one or two.'

'In each case the accused person denied he'd paid any money?'

'Yes.'

'That's what they usually do, isn't it?'

'I believe so.'

'That's what you'd expect them to do, isn't it?'

'I suppose so.'

'So that, if an officer wanted to be dishonest, he could keep part of the bribe for himself?'

'I suppose he could do.'

'Ever heard of such a thing being done?'

'No.'

'I suggest you have—and in this case too.'

'What do you mean?'

Roger explained what he meant and the sergeant denied that anything of the kind had happened.

When the sergeant's evidence was completed, the superintendent gave evidence. He told of the inspector approaching him in the first instance, of the money being handed to him by the inspector on two separate occasions, and he produced the actual notes and the envelopes which had been opened by the magistrates' clerk. He was cross-examined by Roger about the trap set for the inspector, and he identified as correct a transcript taken from the record of the interview. He also gave evidence of finding the inspector on the ground.

'Would you have been surprised if the inspector had acted dishonestly?' asked Roger.

'Yes, I would,' said the superintendent.

'Very surprised?' asked Roger.

'Yes, very.'

'You were completely satisfied of his integrity?'

'Yes.'

'Then why set a trap for him?'

'That was not my responsibility.'

'I see,' said Roger. 'So you throw that on to the Chief Constable, do you?'

'All I say is that it was not my responsibility,' repeated the superintendent.

'Is the Chief Constable going to be called as a witness, do you know?'

'That is not my responsibility,' said the superintendent.

Roger profoundly hoped, from his own personal point of view, that the Chief Constable would not be called. But from his clients' point of view he had to try to prod the prosecution into calling him. 'Is my learned friend going to call the Chief Constable?' he asked.

'Certainly not,' said Henry. 'My learned friend can call him himself if he wishes.'

'Thank you,' said Roger. 'I will consider the invitation in due course.'

'Mr Thursby,' said the judge, 'I think it would be better if you confined your cross-examination to asking questions.'

'If your Lordship pleases,' said Roger.

Not long afterwards the case for the prosecution was closed and Roger opened the case for the defence. Among other things, he said:

'Members of the jury, I entirely agree with my learned friend that corruption is a deadly disease and I say at once—whether my clients like it or not—that if you are satisfied that my clients or either of them are guilty, they deserve no sympathy whatever. I also agree with my learned friend that our police force is the most reputable in all the world. We rely on them and they seldom let us down. But there must be an exception to the rule from time to time, and it is my duty to suggest to you, on behalf of my clients, that this case has uncovered one of them—the case, it might be called, of The Fainting Inspector. I will deal a little later with the circumstances which led up to his unfortunate accident. At the moment I will only remind you that you are not trying the inspector; you are trying my clients and if, in all the circumstances, you are not satisfied as to their guilt, that is an end of the matter and they are entitled to be acquitted. Now, in most cases of this kind the defence can only rely upon the evidence of the man or woman charged with the offence. In this case, fortunately for the defendants, I am in a position to call before you another police officer who has nothing to gain—indeed, perhaps a good deal to lose—by giving evidence for the defendants.'

Roger then went on to outline what the police constable would say and, when he had finished, he called Mr Glacier as his first witness. He took him through the whole of his story, of how grateful he was that his little Melanie had not been charged, of the circumstances in which he came to give money to the inspector, and of the amount he gave. Finally, he gave evidence of the interview with the inspector. Roger then sat down, and Henry got up.

'Are you an honest man, Mr Glacier?' he asked.

'Ah,' said Mr Glacier, 'what is honesty?'

'Well what do you call it?' asked Henry.

Mr Glacier put his hands on the witness box. 'This is an opportunity I have been waiting for. I have often envied the person who,

without fear of interruption or contradiction, can express his views
to his congregation on all manner of subjects. Now—'

'Be quiet,' said the judge, 'and listen to me. You will give your
evidence properly or not at all.'

Mr Glacier raised his eyebrows. 'I am sorry to have offended
your Lordship. It was unintentional, I assure you.'

'Very well, then,' said the judge.

There was silence for a moment.

'Well?' said the judge. 'Are you going to answer counsel's question, or not?'

'My Lord,' said Mr Glacier, 'how do you wish me to answer it?
I am asked a—how do you say?—a metaphysical question. How
can I answer it except in the same—what is the word?—the same
idiom? What is honesty? It is a big—a very big question. I could
talk for hours on it. I assure your Lordship I will not do so,' he
added hurriedly.

'I can assure you you won't,' said the judge. 'Mr Blagrove,' he
added, 'it is rather a large question. Do you really need an answer?
I fancy the jury can judge what is meant by honesty from the
practical point of view.'

'If your Lordship pleases,' said Henry. 'Very well, then, Mr
Glacier. Whatever you yourself mean by honesty, do you count
yourself an honest man—as honest as the next man?'

'That rather depends upon who he is,' said Mr Glacier. 'I should
expect to be in a higher class than Inspector Worcester.'

'Very well, then,' said Henry. 'Do you consider it honest to bribe
the police?'

'Most assuredly not.'

'It is not a thing you would do?'

'It is most certainly not.'

'But you would give the police large sums of money?'

'I give the tax collector large sums of money, but I do not bribe
him.'

'Do you think it proper to give the police money at all?'

'I have been thinking about this,' said Mr Glacier, 'since these
proceedings were started, and I realise now that I was wrong to give
money at all. My motives might have been misunderstood—and in
fact, they have been grossly misrepresented. I shall not be so foolish
again.'

'Then you now consider that you acted improperly?'

'Yes. I regret it. But it was not a crime.'

'It was not the crime with which you are charged,' said Henry.

The judge intervened. 'Mr Blagrove, if you consider that the defendants' own story discloses an offence against the Prevention of Corruption Act, why didn't the prosecution charge them with it? They are charged with giving money to procure a favour in the future. Why weren't they charged with giving money for a past favour?'

'I can tell your Lordship that at once,' said Henry. 'It seemed to the prosecution, rightly or wrongly, that, if the jury accepted the story put forward by the defendant—and rejected that of the police officers—it would not be right to ask for a conviction for a crime which no witness for the prosecution alleges took place.'

'I understand,' said the judge. 'That seems eminently fair.'

'If your Lordship pleases,' said Henry, and continued his cross-examination. He led up to the interview during the magisterial proceedings. 'Now tell me, Mr Glacier,' he said, 'why didn't you give the inspector the chance of answering your allegation about the money before you went on to tell him that the conversation was being tapped?'

'Oh, Mr Blagrove, if I had your knowledge of the art of cross-examination, I might have acted differently,' said Mr Glacier.

'Mr Glacier,' said Henry, 'I do not propose to let you slip out of the question in that way. I consider it a very important one. Will you kindly deal with it seriously? Will you tell my Lord and the jury what possible object there could have been in telling the inspector about the interview being tapped before he answered the question about the money?'

'Sometimes,' said Mr Glacier, 'I have heard counsel ask two questions in one sentence. Can I be blamed if I, a layman, do the same?'

'Mr Glacier, I suggest to you that you put the two questions quite deliberately—that you knew what the inspector's answer would be to the first question and that you didn't want him to give it until you'd shocked him by disclosing about the tapping of the interview?'

'What is the question, please?' asked Mr Glacier. 'If I may say so, there seem to be at least two questions in that one. Even three perhaps.'

'Why did you want to disclose to the inspector that the conversation was being tapped at that particular moment?'

'Why did I want to do that?' said Mr Glacier. 'I do not know that I really did want to do it. I did it. I cannot say why. It just happened. Like so many things. I repeat in all seriousness that, if I had had your training, I might have done it differently.'

Henry finished his cross-examination. Roger did not re-examine, and called his next witness—Mrs Glacier. She said what was expected of her by both sides, and then the police constable was called. He stuck to his story, and though Henry tried to see if he could trace any connection between him and the Glaciers, he was unable to do do. He swore positively that the sergeant had told him that they had received altogether sixty-five pounds and were only putting forty-five pounds in the charges; that he was frightened to go to the superintendent and, not being prepared to leave the matter undisclosed, he went to the Glaciers. Finally, Roger called Mr Plumb to give evidence of his conversation with the Chief Constable. The latter was in court and his anger was so great that he had some difficulty in refraining from making an oututburst. He reserved that for later. Digby was sitting between Henry and Roger and, as Roger began to ask the questions which would lead to a disclosure of what the Chief Constable had said to Mr Plumb, he started a soft *obbligato* accompaniment—'in breach of confidence, in breach of confidence, in breach of confidence.'

'Shut up,' said Roger.

'In breach of confidence,' repeated Digby.

'I wish you'd control your little yapper,' said Roger to Henry.

'In breach of confidence,' repeated Digby, 'and I shall go on saying it until you've finished.'

'Don't be an ass,' said Roger. 'Do muzzle him,' he said to Henry, adding, 'if you don't, I shall have to ask the judge to do so.'

'What is happening at the Bar?' asked the judge. 'It is most inconvenient for me and the jury to have this noise going on. Please continue with the evidence, Mr Thursby.'

Digby eventually subsided and a very unwilling Mr Plumb proceeded to state what the Chief Constable had said—namely, that he had suspected the inspector for a long time and would be damned glad to get him.

'How is this admissible?' asked the judge.

'My Lord,' said Roger, 'is it not material that a party to litigation who calls a witness to support his case does not believe in the honesty of that witnesss? Could not a plaintiff be asked such a

question regarding his chief witness? And, if he could, is not the
Chief Constable in the same position? I, of course, appreciate that
the prosecution is by the Queen. But the Queen can only act
through agents and, if a person who has been responsible for the
conduct or initiation of the prosecution makes such a statement
regarding an important witness, it must—in my respectful
submission—be material for the consideration of the jury.'

'I see how you put it, but I'm not at all sure that it's right,' said
the judge.

'If a plaintiff or the Director of Public Prosecutions said of a
witness he is calling—"he is not a trusted servant of mine"—surely
that would be a matter proper for the consideration of the jury?'

'You can't call affirmative evidence to show bad character,' said
the judge.

'I respectfully agree,' said Roger, 'but the object of this evidence
is to show that the prosecution, through its agent—the Chief
Constable—has no belief in its case. Would it not be a proper
question to ask a party to litigation who has called a witness to an
important incident—"have you any belief that the incident really
happened?" '

'I should have thought not,' said the judge. 'The belief of the
plaintiff in his own witness has surely nothing tò do with it. It is
what the judge or jury thinks of the witness that matters. In so far
as the matter goes to the credit of the witness, you must agree it is
not admissible. And I must confess I can't see why the belief or
disbelief of a plaintiff or Director of Public Prosecutions in the
worthiness of a witness has anything to do with the matter. Obviously, if the Director knows anything specifically to the discredit of
the witness, he would probably inform the defence of the matter.
And, of course, the matter could be put to the witness in cross-
examination.'

'My Lord,' said Roger, 'I respectfully submit that, in a criminal
prosecution at any rate, the disbelief of the prosecutor—using that
term in the sense I have mentioned—in the honesty of an important
witness must be a matter for the consideration of the jury.'

'Well, what do you say, Mr Blagrove?' asked the judge.

'My Lord, whatever the strict legal position may be,' said Henry,
'I should not seek to exclude evidence which the defence desire to
tender unless it is quite unarguable that it is inadmissible. I would
respectfully agree with what has fallen from your Lordship, but, as

I concede that there is an argument to be put forward in favour of the evidence being received, I do not ask your Lordship to reject the evidence.'

'Very well, then,' said the judge. 'In these circumstances I will say nothing more—except that I have grave doubts as to its admissibility.'

'As the question of admissibility has been raised,' said Roger, 'I think it only right to tell your Lordship that, after the Chief Constable had made the statement, he said to my client—"That's in confidence, of course," and my client said? "Of course." Now, as your Lordship may imagine, in those circumstances it is with the greatest regret and consuderable embarrassment that I have felt bound to tender the evidence. If I could have avoided doing so, I should certainly have done so, but, if it is admissible in evidence, it seems to me that the defendants are entitled to the benefit of it. I hope your Lordship will think I have taken a proper course.'

'I am quite sure,' said the judge, 'that you have acted in accordance with your duty to your client. There can, of course, be no such thing as "without prejudice' conversations in criminal matters and, unfortunate though the matter is, it seems to me that, if the evidence is otherwise admissible, the Chief Constable's statement about confidence cannot have the effect of excluding it. Moreover, it seems to me that in a criminal matter different considerations apply from those which obtain in civil litigation. I do not think any other course was open to you.'

'I am very grateful to your Lordship,' said Roger, and hoped the Chief Constable was listening. He was.

'These lawyers always stick together,' he whispered to a friend in Court.

After Mr Plumb had completed his evidence, Roger addressed the jury—submitting to them that at the least the case for the prosecution had not been proved against either of his clients. Henry followed him on behalf of the prosecution and submitted that, on the contrary, the case had certainly been proved against Mr Glacier. As regards Mrs Glacier, if the jury thought she might have been under her husband's influence and was not a willing party to the bribery, he could not ask for a conviction against her. Finally, Mr Justice Kingsdown summed up. He reminded the jury of what the charges against each of the accused were; he spoke of the gravity of such charges, and then he went on:

'Now, members of the jury, in this country it is not for a prisoner to prove his innocence but for the prosecution to prove his guilt. Now, how must they prove that guilt? They cannot prove it with complete certainty—for you could only be completely certain of a prisoner's guilt if you not only were present at the commission of a crime but plainly saw it committed. In such a case you would be witnesses, not jurors. So you will see that justice could not be administered if complete certainty were required. But what is required is that the prosecution should prove the defendant's guilt with reasonable certainty. Suspicion is not enough—even strong suspicion. Before you can convict you must be reasonably sure that the Crown has made out its case. And when I say reasonably sure, you will understand—for the reason I have explained—that you cannot be expected to be completely sure. You must be reasonably sure. So much for the measure of proof. Now, what the prosecution have to prove with that measure of proof is this.'

The judge then explained the ingredients of the offence with which the defendants were charged.

'Whatever your view may be about the guilt or innocence of Mr Glacier, members of the jury,' he went on, 'you may well think that the case against Mrs Glacier has not been satisfactorily established. The law on the subject is as follows: there is no presumption that a wife acts under the coercion of her husband but, if the offence is committed by her in his presence, she may prove—if she can—that she was in fact acting under his coercion. If she does so she is entitled to be acquitted. The only evidence against Mrs Glacier is that she was present when the crime—if crime it was—was committed. She does not say her husband coerced her, but on the other hand it is his act that constituted the crime, and if she is liable it is only because he acted on her behalf. Now, in all the circumstances, are you reasonably sure that Mrs Glacier has committed any offence? If you are, you will, of course, find her Guilty; but you may think—it is entirely a matter for you—that it would be very dangerous on the evidence—and you are concerned with the evidence and the evidence alone—to find her Guilty of either of the charges against her. I need hardly say that, if you find Mr Glacier Not Guilty, you would, of course, find his wife Not Guilty also. But, up till now, I have dealt with the case of Mrs Glacier separately—in other words, even if you should find her husband Guilty, you may well take a different view of the case against her. I will now come to the much more difficult problem before you—the question of Mr Glacier. Counsel has quite rightly told you that you are trying him and not the inspector or the sergeant. That is absolutely true, but it will be impossible for you to come to a conclusion about the guilt or innocence of Mr Glacier without weighing up the evidence of the inspector and the sergeant. If you think they are a couple of scoundrels—that is an end to the matter. But if you are satisfied of that, you still have to be reasonably sure that what they are saying is substantially true before you can return a verdict of Guilty. And in that connection you have to weigh up the evidence of the police constable who gave evidence for the Glaciers.'

The judge then proceeded to go into the evidence in detail and, when he had done so, he said:

'Well, members of the jury, that is what these witnesses said. What do you believe to be the truth? If you are left in a state of uncertainty, the defendants are entitled to be acquitted. I have told you several times that, before you can convict, you must be reasonably sure that the truth is in the evidence given by the prosecution and not in that given by and on behalf of the defendants. What kind of an impression did the inspector and sergeant make on you? What kind of an impression did Mr Glacier make on you? Did he appear to you to be an honest man who was grateful to the police for not charging his daughter—or did he appear to you to be an extremely astute, exceptionally able man, who would be quite capable of inventing a plausible story to get himself out of his difficulties? It is of no importance what impression he made on me. What did *you* think of him? You may think possibly that that is the crux of the matter. If the story he is putting forward now is true, the inspector and sergeant are quite plainly wholly unfitted for their positions of trust. But, if it is false, then it is difficult to resist the conclusion that the evidence of the police constable called on behalf of the Glaciers is false also and—although there is no direct evidence to show that he has been induced by the Glaciers to give that false evidence—I think one must face that position, and, personally, I do not see how that inference can be resisted *if,* and only if, the evidence of Mr Glacier is untrue in the material matters. There it is, members of the jury, you are the judges, not I. I have told you the law on the subject and that you must take from me. If I am wrong in any of my directions, I can be corrected elsewhere. But the facts are for you and for you alone. If anything I have said about the facts does not commend itself to you, disregard it. It is your views which matter, not mine. I do not think there is anything further I can usefully add, members of the jury, and I will ask you to consider your verdict. I expect you would like to retire.'

CHAPTER 21

Mr Green

The jury retired, and Roger and Henry were about to leave the Court while the next case was called—when a prisoner who wanted a dock brief was put in the dock.

'Has he two pounds four shillings and sixpence?' asked the judge.

'Yes,' said the clerk.

'Very well, then,' said the judge. 'You can choose any counsel you like.'

'Ah,' said the prisoner, whom Roger seemed dimly to recognize, 'but not one who's engaged on a case, can I?'

'No, that's quite correct,' said the judge, a little surprised. 'You seem to know all about it.'

'I've been caught before, my Lord,' said the prisoner, and then added hastily, 'about choosing counsel, I mean, my Lord. It's such a disappointment when you choose a really brainy-looking—'

'Now don't start making speeches,' said the judge. 'Choose someone.'

'All right, my Lord,' said the prisoner, 'I'll have him,' and pointed to Roger.

'You can't have Mr Thursby,' said the judge. 'He's engaged on a case.'

The prisoner looked plainitively at the judge. 'That's exactly what I meant, my Lord. It would be fairer if they had a label on them.' He paused for a moment and looked along the line of counsel: 'Some of them might have an L on them too, don't you think, my Lord?'

'Behave yourself,' said the judge.

'Did I hear you say Mr Thursby?' said the prisoner.

'I told you you can't have him,' snapped the judge.

Suddenly Roger realised who the prisoner was. He had aged a good deal, but Roger recognised in him a Mr Green whom he had

once defended successfully at the Old Bailey while he was still a
pupil. In fact, Mr Green had done most of the defending and Roger
had long ago come to the conclusion that Mr Green's idea of L-
plates on pupils was not at all a bad one. They should not be allowed
to appear except in company with an experienced practitioner who
must sit next to them.

'My Lord,' said Roger, 'if it isn't too long a case, I'd be prepared
to take it for the prisoner.'

'That's very good of you, Mr Thursby,' said the judge. 'Is it a
long case, d'you know)' he asked. He was really addressing the
clerk, but Mr Green took it on himself to reply.

'Nothing long about it,' he said and added, 'I 'I hope.'

'Very well, then,' said the judge. 'Perhaps you'd like to see him
now, Mr Thursby.'

'If your Lordship pleases,' said Roger. Before going to see his
new client, he spoke to Henry. 'This is a chap I did a docker for
when I was a pupil of Grimeyboy. I hope he'll think I've improved.'

'I gather he hasn't,' said Henry.

Roger went to see Mr Green. He certainly had aged, but there
was still a good deal of the old sparkle Roger had noticed twelve
years before.

'Nice to see you, Mr Thursby,' said Mr Green. 'Nice to see you
any place, but I didn't come here for the purpose.'

'How are you?' said Roger. 'It is a long time ago. Things not too
good since then?'

'Mustn't grumble,' said Mr Green. 'Lose good conduct marks if
you do. Let me see,' and he thought for a bit. 'You were toffee,
weren't you?'

'That's right,' said Roger, 'it was a case about toffee. Glad you
got off. Sorry you're here now. What's it for?'

'Oh—don't let's spoil the party,' said Mr Green. 'Let's talk of
something pleasant. Haven't seen you for years. We can't get a pint
down here, I suppose?'

'I'm afraid not,' said Roger. 'We'll celebrate with one when we
get you off.'

The old man—at any rate he now looked one—shook his head.
His eyes grew a little moist. Then he brushed them with his hand
in an impatient gesture. 'Come, come, Mr Green,' he said, 'pull
yourself together. It's a long lane that has no turning. If you ask
me,' he added, 'it's going to be a ruddy long lane this time.'

'What's it all about?' said Roger.

'I've lost my grip,' said Mr Green. 'I'm slipping. Slipped, you might say. Nice to see you again though. Takes me back a bit. Toffee. That was good fun. We had 'em on the run, didn't we?'

'You did,' said Roger. 'I just followed behind you.'

'Well—you've made up ground since then,' said Mr Green. 'See your name in the paper no end. Nice to be able to tell one's pals—"I started that young man off." I've had several beers on that.'

'Well, it's quite true,' said Roger, 'and you deserved them. As soon as I recognised you, I decided to accept the brief—that's, of course, if it was offered to me.'

'It's a shame,' said Mr Green, 'that there isn't more kick in it. We could have had a high old time together—you and me. If I'd known you were going to be here—I'd never have done it. I shouldn't have, anyway. I told you I'm slipping. D'you know what I've done?'

'No,' said Roger.

'I've admitted it,' said Mr Green. 'Can you beat it? Signed, sealed, and delivered on the dotted line. I-have-been-warned-that-any-thing - I - say - may - be - used - in - evidence - and - I - make - this - state-ment - voluntarily - after - having - been - cautioned - that - I - am - not - bound-to-say-anything-unless-I-wish-to-do-so. And what makes it worse is—that's quite true. I was warned. It was voluntary. No cigarettes or cups of tea. I go and make a ruddy voluntary confession. Can't think what I was up to. Tired, I suppose. I'll get four years this time. That means three nearly—if you don't grumble. Three years to wait for a pint of bitter. Hard, isn't it? Pity I'm not on bail. We could have popped across and had one.'

'If you're pleading Guilty, why did you want counsel? You know the ropes as well as anyone, I should say.'

'Thank you,' said Mr Green. 'Experience teaches. Yes, I do. But I don't know this judge. Never seen him, never read about him. I thought I'd better get a line on him. It's worth four years, but not a penny more. And suppose this chap doesn't know the scale, he might give me five or six even.'

'It cuts both ways,' said Roger. 'He might give you eighteen months.'

'Can't see it,' said Mr Green. 'Had three years last time. It's a good idea though. If they halved it each time instead of doubling it. I'd only get nine months next time. Only four and a half the time after. Hardly worth going in for. But what d'you think this is good for?'

'You haven't told me anything about it yet,' said Roger. 'There I go again,' said Mr Green. 'That's what I did with you last time. Can't make bricks without straw, the labourer is worthy of his hire, who sups with the devil needs a long spoon—now, where had I got to? Ah,—the indictment. I used to call it in*dick*ment until you told me how to pronounce it. I've always remembered since then. Funny how one doesn't notice these things. The clerk says in*dite*ment all right, but I'd never noticed till you told me. I won quite a few bets over that. Pity there's no beer down here. Sorry to run on. But bets always remind me of beer. They sort of go together.'

'Well, you'd better let me see,' said Roger.

'The indictment?'

'Yes.'

'It's a scruffy-looking thing,' said Mr Green. 'Only two counts. But they'll be enough. Not so deep as a pint mug or as wide as a public bar—but they'll be enough—but I'll do the serving—worse luck.'

Roger looked at the charges against Mr Green, which were in substance that he had obtained one hundred and fifty pounds by pretending that he was running a genuine business called the Glenavon Chocolate Company.

'What was the total amount involved?' asked Roger.

'It says one hundred and fifty pounds there,' said Mr Green.

'I know,' said Roger.

'You are inquisitive,' said Mr Green. 'Do I have to tell you?'

'Not if you don't want to. But you might as well. The police will know. And it's better if I know what we've got to meet.'

'Well, as a matter of fact the business hadn't started long when something went wrong. I'm slipping, I tell you. I sent a man a cheque. If I'd just not paid him it'd have been all right. But I was feeling cocky. He'd written me a rude letter threatening all sorts of things. So I sent him a cheque.'

'And it bounced?'

'So high,' said Mr Green, and pointed to the ceiling. 'I hadn't an account, as a matter of fact, so you can't really blame the bank—though it was only for ten pounds and it wouldn't have hurt them to pay it. Still, there it is and here we are. What goes up must come down.'

'You haven't yet said how much is involved altogether.'

'Only about five or six hundred pounds. Hadn't had time to get started.'

'Don't you think you could get a decent job instead of this sort of thing?' said Roger.

'Now you've said something,' said Mr Green. 'That's what I say every time. To the judge too. I'll go straight, really I will. My Lord, if you will take a lenient view of this offence I promise you I'll never appear in the dock again.' He paused for a moment. Then he said, 'Tell me—how many times d'you think a chap can say that and still keep his self-respect?'

'It depends on the chap,' said Roger. 'But seriously, when you come out next time, why don't you settle down to something? After all, you're not making much of a success of this kind of thing, are you? You've had a good many beerless months in the last ten years, I should imagine.'

'You're quite right,' said Mr Green. 'I miss my beer and I've been without a lot of it, as you say. And I've had a bad season—too many bad seasons. Yes—you're quite right. But there's one trouble—and I don't know how you can get over that.'

'What is it?' said Roger.

'Well, between you and me,' said Mr Green, 'I don't like honest work.'

'It's lucky we're not all like that.'

'I certainly agree,' said Mr Green. 'It's very lucky indeed. Who'd run the trains and buses, who'd run Parliament, who'd run the Law Courts, the Stock Exchange, and so on and so forth? I can't really grumble, can I? I've lots of people working for me—the whole population nearly. And I get it all for nothing. Pretty good when you work it out that way.'

'Depends how long you have to enjoy it,' said Roger. 'When were you last inside?'

'Came out ten months ago. It was a Friday. Friday the thirteenth. That's a day to let you out. I suggested that in the circumstances they should make it the day before. They said they understood my feelings entirely and suggested the day after. So we compromised and I came out on the Friday.'

'Well, you'd better tell me something in your favour,' said Roger. 'How many honest days' work have you done in the last ten years?'

'I've just told you,' said Mr Green. 'I don't like it. Now, just

listen. If I took a job—item—I'd have to work regular hours. Well—
I just can't manage that. Then again you can't take holidays whenever you want to. You have people giving you orders. I'm not a
Socialist, Mr Thursby. I don't believe that all men are equal or
that everyone should have the same. Some people like being given
orders. They wouldn't know how to run my business. They're happy
in their little jobs. Start at nine, end at six. Half day Saturday.
Fortnight's holiday a year. Christmas and Easter extra. Sounds
lovely. So it is for them what likes it. I'm not one of them and I'm
too old to start now.'

'Well,' said Roger, 'it's a change to have anyone so frank, but it
won't be much use my telling the judge—that you'll do it again as
soon as you come out and that you're not in the least sorry you've
done it this time—only sorry you've been caught.'

'You don't think that would help?' said Mr Green. 'He wouldn't
say—this fellow's so honest, he must have some good in him, and
take off six months?'

'I doubt it,' said Roger. 'I doubt it very much. And the trouble
is—now that you've told me that you've no intention of going
straight and that you have never done so, I can't tell the judge the
opposite.'

'Oh—I can change all that,' said Mr Green. 'I could put on an
act, if you'd like me to. My Lord, I know I've done wrong, but I
promise you—'

Roger interrupted. 'It won't do, I'm afraid,' he said. 'I can't
deceive the judge.'

'No, of course not,' said Mr Green. 'It was very wrong of me to
suggest it. I apologise, I withdraw, least said soonest mended, no
broken bones, I hope.'

'Not at all,' said Roger. 'I'm glad we understand one another.'

'What would you advise then?' asked Mr Green.

'Well, quite frankly,' said Roger. 'I think you'd do better not to
have counsel at all.'

'You advise me to make my own plea?' asked Mr Green.

'On the whole, I do,' said Roger.

'Do you realise,' said Mr Green, with a twinkle, 'that I shall try
to deceive the judge?'

'You shouldn't do so, but I can't stop you,' said Roger.

'But you still advise me to make my own plea?' persisted Mr
Green.

Roger did not answer at once, and Mr Green went on: 'Because, if that's so, you appear to be advising me to deceive the judge.'

'Certainly not,' said Roger. 'I advise you to tell him the truth.'

'What, and get an extra five years?' said Mr Green. 'Is that you're best advice?'

'Perhaps not,' said Roger. 'You'd better say nothing at all.'

'But that won't do,' said Mr Green. 'He'll invite me to say something. And if I refuse—he'll fear the worst—and so shall I.'

'I don't see what else you can do.'

'Well, I do,' said Mr Green. 'I shall make an impassioned plea and promise that, if he exercises leniency, I'll never, never, never do it again. Never, never, never,' he rattled off quickly. 'Don't look so troubled. He won't be lenient and that lets me off the promise. Now, do you still advise me not to employ you?'

'I don't think there's anything I can do for you,' said Roger.

'Then, as they say upstairs,' said Mr Green, 'the answer is yes. But, as you know I'm going to tell a pack of lies to the judge, you're advising me to take a course which will result in the Court being deceived. How d'you get out of that one, Mr Thursby?'

'I don't know that I can,' said Roger. 'There's nothing whatever I can properly say in mitigation. So I'm bound to tell you that I can be no use to you. The result of that is that you'll defend yourself and I know that you'll lie in the process.'

'I suppose you couldn't get up in the middle when I'm saying my piece and tell the judge it's all lies.'

'Oh, good heavens, no,' said Roger. 'I couldn't do that.'

'I just wanted to be sure,' said Mr Green.

'Well, then,' he added, 'where do we go from here? Or perhaps that's a gloomy way of putting it. I think I'll solve your difficulty by withdrawing my instructions. That's the right expression, isn't it?'

'It is,' said Roger.

'Just before you go,' said Mr Green, 'tell me one thing for old time's sake. What's this judge like?'

'He's quite a good chap,' said Roger.

'Is he nice to young counsel?' asked Mr Green.

'Yes, very. Why do you ask?' said Roger.

'I just wondered,' said Mr Green. 'Now I suppose we'd better both get back,' he said. 'Look forward to our next meeting. Hope it won't be as long again—if it's in the right place,' he added.

Roger went back to Court and, at a convenient moment, Mr Green was put back in the dock. The jury in the Glacier case were still out.

'My Lord,' said Roger, 'the prisoner wishes to withdraw his instructions from me.'

'Very well,' said the judge. 'Do you wish to defend yourself then?'

'No,' said Mr Green, 'I'd like that one,' and he pointed to the white-wigged Mr Trent. The judge looked down at counsel's row and, for the first time, recognised his acquaintance of the races. 'Mr—ah Mr—' he began.

'Trent,' said Mr Trent. 'Anthony Trent, my Lord.'

'Mr Trent, will you accept this brief?'

'I shall be very pleased, my Lord. I will go and see the prisoner at once and let your Lordship know as soon as I am ready to proceed.'

The judge resisted the impulse to inform him that he would kindly be ready for the Court when the Court was ready for him. Mr Justice Kingsdown thought it most important in all proceedings, but particularly in criminal matters, that a client should not think he had done badly because of any deficiencies in his counsel. If—as he sorely wanted to do—he bounced Mr Trent up and down before the case began, it would be difficult for the prisoner to feel that he would have a satisfactory trial. So he contented himself with saying: 'That is very good of you, Mr Trent.'

'Not at all, my Lord,' said Mr Trent. 'I am only too anxious to assist the Court.'

I must find out where this young man belongs, thought the judge, and pass a word to someone in his chambers. He could think of some judges—more choleric than he was—for whom Mr Trent might be fatal.

While Mr Trent was interviewing Mr Green, the jury in the Glacier case sent a note to the judge. In consequence, the defendants were put into the dock again and Roger, Henry, and Digby took their places in Court.

'I have had a note from the jury,' said the judge, 'to this effect. "We are agreed about the case of Mrs Glacier, but not about the case of Mr Glacier. It might help if your Lordship would repeat what you told the jury about the extent to which the case has to be proved by the prosecution." I propose to have the jury back and

comply with their request, unless either of you have any submission
to make on the subject.'

Henry and Roger shook their heads. So the jury came back
into Court and the judge repeated to them at some length and in
substantially the same words what he had said before. He added
at the end: 'I hope that will solve your difficulties one way or the
other.'

The jury retired again. The judge dealt with the next two cases,
which were pleas of Guilty, and then Mr Trent returned to Court
and informed the clerk that his case was a plea of Guilty too. The
judge said he would take it at once.

'We must watch this,' said Henry to Roger.

Mr Green was brought into the dock. The two charges were read
out to him.

'Do you plead Guilty or Not Guilty?' asked the clerk.

'Unfortunately, Guilty,' said Mr Green. 'I should have liked to
have given my young counsel a chance to show what he's made of,
but I must stick to the truth and, as I'm guilty, I must plead Guilty.
I'm sure your Lordship would approve of that.'

'Be quiet,' said the judge. 'Your counsel will address me on your
behalf.'

'I only wanted to show willing,' said Mr Green.

Counsel for the prosecution then outlined to the judge the facts
of the case and called a police officer to state the character and
antecedents of Mr Green. He also read out a list of his convictions.
Mr Trent said that he had no questions to ask. That's something,
thought the judge, but his optimism was premature.

'Yes, Mr Trent?' he said. 'Do you wish to say anything in
mitigation?'

'If your Lordship pleases,' began Mr Trent. 'I will start by
reminding your Lordship of the duties of the Court in passing
sentence. First of the matters you should consider generally and
then of the matters you should consider by way of mitigating the
offence and then—yes—of the matters, if any, of aggravation. These
remarks of mine will, of course, be entirely general and by way of
what I may term preliminary submission and will not be concerned
with this case in particular.'

'I should prefer you to confine your remarks to this case, Mr
Trent,' said the judge, with as little grimness as possible.

'Oh, my Lord,' said Mr Trent, 'I have not made myself plain. I am so sorry. Of course my remarks will be relevant —if I may say so, they will be highly relevant—they concern every case where a judge is passing sentence and therefore they cover this case as well. They are remarks of general application.'

'So I gather,' said the judge, 'but I have had some experience of the duties of the Court in this respect.'

'I'm quite sure your Lordship has,' said Mr Trent, 'but I feel that it might help your Lordship in approaching this case if I brought some of the more salient matters to your Lordship's attention. Now, my Lord, in the first place your Lordship should consider the nature of the actual crime committed. Let me take an example. Supposing a man with many previous convictions is charged with a really trivial offence—'

'Mr Trent,' said the judge, 'I really cannot allow you to take up the time of the Court by reminding me of things I already know and which have been established for years. Pray confine your remarks to this particular case.'

'Then your Lordship is bearing in mind,' said Mr Trent, 'that, having first considered the nature of the crime, the Court's next duty is to consider—'

'Mr Trent,' interrupted the judge, with some heat, 'you have not been very long at the Bar and I am afraid you have a lot to learn.' The judge paused—not because he had finished but because he was saying to himself—you must tone it down, you simply must, or that wretched chap in the dock will think he's got an extra year because you didn't see eye to eye with his counsel. This gave Mr Trent the chance of saying:

'Indeed I have, my Lord. And might I say that I am most grateful to your Lordship for any instruction your Lordship sees fit to give me.'

This gives me a chance, thought the judge, but, before he could say anything, Mr Trent went on:

'Of course, I'm sure your Lordship will understand that I am here to act solely in the interests of my client, as I see them, and, supposing any advice your Lordship should very kindly give me should happen not to coincide with views I have formed after mature consideration—views, I frankly admit, which may be wrong—but I can only act on what I think right, for better or worse, can I not, my Lord—'

Something burst on the Bench.

'Mr Trent, be quiet and listen to me. When you are in my Court, you will do as I say. If you object to any of my rulings, you can go to the Court of Criminal Appeal.'

'Is your Lordship giving me leave to appeal?' asked Mr Trent blandly.

I can't stand much more of this, thought the judge. 'There is nothing to appeal from at the moment, Mr Trent,' he said with some difficulty.

'That's why I didn't follow your Lordship's observation,' said Mr Trent.

Never in his career had Mr Justice Kingsdown wanted to take off his wig and throw it at counsel, and to follow it up with the glass and bottle of water which were by him—and after that to run yelling blue murder through the streets, or to sit sobbing in his private room. 'This is intolerable,' he said. He had not meant to say it aloud, but it slipped out.

Mr Trent looked puzzled. Then a light dawned on him. 'Usher,' he said in a low voice, but one that could be heard, 'Usher—open some windows. His Lordship is finding the heat intolerable.'

'Mr Trent,' said the judge, in his sternest voice, 'are you intending to be funny?'

'Funny, my Lord?' said Mr Trent, 'certainly not, my Lord. I heard your Lordship say that something was intolerable and I could only imagine it was the heat, my Lord.'

'It was not the heat, Mr Trent—it was you,' said the judge. Again he had not meant to say it aloud, but he simply could not restrain himself.

'Me, my Lord?' said Mr Trent, in a surprised voice. 'I'm so very sorry, my Lord. Could your Lordship perhaps be kind enough to tell me what I have done to offend your Lordship, and then—subject, of course, to my client's interests—I will do all I can to remedy the matter.'

'Mr Trent,' said the judge, as calmly as possible, 'you can best remedy the matter by saying as shortly as possible what there is to be said on your client's behalf in mitigation of sentence.'

'But that's what I was doing, my Lord. No doubt, owing to my inexperience, I was doing it clumsily and not probably as your Lordship, when in my position, used to do it—but I do assure your Lordship that I am trying and trying only to urge on my client's behalf the various matters which are in his favour. But, in order to do that, it is necessary—in my view—and here I am sure your Lordship will forgive me if I cross swords with your Lordship—'

'Mr Trent,' said the judge, 'sit down.'

Mr Trent, looking puzzled, remained standing.

'Sit down, Mr Trent, sit down, sit down, sit down. If you don't I will have you removed by the usher.'

Mr Trent, quite bewildered, did as he was told.

'Arthur Green,' said the judge, 'the sentence of the Court is that you go to prison for eighteen months.'

Mr Green seemed stunned by the sentence at first—and then he turned to his attendant warders. 'Quick,' he said in a whisper, 'down the stairs before he changes his mind.'

Mr Trent was soon able to tell his friends—and others—that he got off an old lag with eighteen months after he'd only recently come out from doing three years for a precisely similar offence. And, indeed, the leniency was entirely due to Mr Trent. Mr Justice Kingsdown had ensured that the prisoner would not think that he had received a heavier sentence because of his counsel and that, although he had refused to listen to a speech in mitigation, the sentence he passed was not one which the Court of Criminal Appeal would reduce. Indeed, had Mr Green appealed they would doubtless have increased it. But there was to be no appeal by Mr Green, who went to goal almost singing. 'And what pleases me so much,' he wrote to Roger. 'and what I am sure must please you, is that we were able to affect his Lordship's mind without telling any lies or making any promises.'

CHAPTER 22

The Verdict

Eventually the jury returned to Court, agreed. They acquitted Mrs Glacier, but they convicted her husband. Roger was surprised. Mr Glacier was extremely displeased. The Chief Constable was slightly—only slightly—mollified. The judge sentenced Mr Glacier to nine months' imprisonment. Roger and Mr Plumb interviewed him after he had been sentenced.

'Mr Glacier,' said Roger, 'I think you should appeal. In my view the judge's summing-up was wrong in law on one important respect.'

'You will understand, Mr Thursby,' said Mr Glacier, 'that I do not place entirely the same confidence in your views. I do not mean by that that I think you conducted my defence badly. Nothing of the kind. I think your cross-examination of the inspector was—how do you say?—a masterpiece. But I should have enjoyed it more if I had been acquitted. No—I am grateful to you for your conduct of the case. But you will remember that you told me that I had a good chance of being acquitted.'

'So you had,' said Roger, 'and the jury took long enough to arrive at their verdict.'

'Not as long as nine months,' said Mr Glacier. 'But there,' he added, 'I must not yield to despair. I still have confidence in your ability. Is there really a chance of success in the Appeal Court?'

'Definitely,' said Roger. 'It's not altogether an easy Court, but I think you've a good point and, even if you lose there, I think there's a very good chance of your being able to get to the House of Lords. It's a point of great public importance, in my view.'

'And will it take more than nine months to get to the House of Lords?' asked Glacier.

'It certainly won't,' said Roger, 'but, even if it did, it would surely be worth your while to get rid of the conviction, even if you've served the sentence. And it's possible that, if the appeal took a long time, you'd get bail.'

'I must leave it to you and Mr Plumb,' said Mr Glacier. 'If you think I should appeal—very well, be it so. But may I say that I trust you will be quick over the matter as possible?'

'We shall lose no time,' said Mr Plumb mournfully. 'I'm so very sorry about it. Perhaps Mr Thursby would settle a notice of appeal at once. Meanwhile Mr Glacier and I had better discuss arrangements for his business and his wife—during his . . . absence.'

Roger left Mr Plumb and Mr Glacier together and then went to look for Anne. 'D'you think,' he asked her, very soon after he had found her, 'that it would be any good my seeing your father?'

'Not at the moment,' she said. 'I must say . . . I see his point of view.'

'You don't mean you agree with it?' he asked unhappily.

'Well—I don't know,' said Anne. 'I haven't really met any lawyers before, and I don't know their standards.'

'That's a horrid thing to say,' said Roger. 'It means you think I played a dirty trick on your father. I've done nothing of the kind. In the first place, I had no idea Glacier would give the show away at the interview with the inspector.'

'You used something father told your solicitor in confidence,' said Anne.

'I couldn't help doing it. I didn't want to—but I had to. The judge said I acted perfectly properly.'

'Yes, I know,' said Anne. 'Father told me.'

'Well, doesn't that make any difference?' he asked.

'Father says you all stick together—and that's true I suppose . . . like doctors and all professional men.'

'If you mean that a judge would say something was proper when it wasn't—just because he wanted to help a member of the Bar— that's absolutely untrue. He might say nothing, but he certainly wouldn't give his blessing to something he thought wrong.'

'Well, I'm glad you didn't do anything improper then,' said Anne, 'But you can't expect me to fall on your neck and kiss you for breaking a confidence. I think it's terribly important to be able to trust people.'

'So do I,' said Roger. 'Don't you trust me?'

'Well—ought I to after what you've just told me? Suppose I told you something in confidence now—and it became useful to you to use it for a client of yours—I shouldn't feel very safe with my confidences.'

'That would be quite different,' said Roger. 'That would have been learned privately . . . not in the course of acting for a client. Why can't you look at it from my point of view? Suppose you were acting for someone who was charged with murder, wouldn't you feel bound to use any material you had which might show that they weren't guilty?'

'Well, that would include my private confidences,' said Anne, 'wouldn't it? So I'm not really safe in telling you anything.'

'It couldn't happen like that,' said Roger. 'There's no reasonable chance that it could happen.'

'But if it did, could I trust you?' asked Anne.

'If you refused to allow me to use the information, I don't suppose you could really. If you'd told me something in the strictest confidence—privately, nothing to do with any case—which later showed that a client of mine hadn't committed a crime—and if I asked you to let me use the information and you refused . . . I suppose that I should have to use it. And so would most people, I think. Which is the worse —to break your confidence or let a man whom you know to be innocent go to gaol or be hanged? Which do you think?'

Anne did not answer immediately, and Roger followed it up with: 'Well, suppose it was your problem . . . suppose you could save someone's life by breaking a confidence. Would you do it—or not?'

'Well, I must admit that the loss of a life is more important than the breaking of a promise.'

'Well, then, what's the difference in principle between death and prison? Prison might kill a man. It is very likely to ruin him and his family. If he's a claustrophobic it might send him mad. What would you do? If you could save an innocent man from prison by breaking a confidence—would you do it?'

'Mr Glacier wasn't innocent.'

'Oh come, Anne, that won't do—really. He's presumed innocent until he's found guilty. He's only guilty now because the jury think he was.'

'You argue very well, Roger,' said Anne. 'I'm not surprised you've done as well as you have.'

'But what I say is right,' said Roger, 'it really is. Don't let it come between us—whatever your father thinks about me.'

'I do see your point of view,' said Anne. 'I'll see what I can do with father. But he'll be a tougher nut to crack than I was . . . but then, of course, that's rather different. I—' she trailed off.

'If only I've convinced you,' said Roger.

'I think you have,' said Anne, 'and I must say I didn't really want to win this argument.'

CHAPTER 23

Court of Criminal Appeal

Not long afterwards the case came before the Court of Criminal Appeal—consisting of Mr Justice Short, Mr Justice Rose, and Mr Justice Mellow. In opening the case to the Court, Roger, after a few prelininary remarks, said:

'My Lords, there is only one point in this appeal—a point of law but, in my submission, it is a very important one. This was a case where the jury took a considerable time to arrive at a verdict and, not only that, they expressly asked the judge to repeat his direction on what was the measure of proof required.'

'I have yet to learn,' said Mr Justice Short, 'that it is a ground of appeal that the jury took a long time to find the prisoner guilty.'

'It isn't,' said Roger, 'but if your Lordships will be good enough to hear what the ground of appeal is, I think your Lordships will find that the fact that the jury took a long time to arrive at a verdict is at least relevant in this case —though it is in no way essential to my appeal.'

'I don't know what your point is,' said Mr Justice Rose, 'but we've read the evidence. The jury obviously believed the evidence for the prosecution and not that for the defence. What's wrong with that?'

'Nothing, my Lord,' said Roger, 'if they were properly directed. I don't dispute that the jury were entitled to take the view they took if the summing-up of the learned judge was right in law.'

'Hadn't you better take us to the passages you complain of?' said Mr Justice Mellow. 'I'm bound to say it seemed to me a clear and admirable summing-up and not at all unfavourable to your clients.'

'My Lords,' said Roger. 'the misdirection of which I respectfully complain consists entirely of the way in which the learned judge directed the jury as to the burden of proof.'

'He said it was on the prosecution, didn't he?' asked Mr Justice Short. 'That's right, isn't it?'

'Yes,' said Roger, 'the learned judge said it was on the prosecution but, in my submission, he directed them wrongly about the extent to which the case had to be proved. It was because that is the sole point in this case that I ventured to draw your Lordships' attention to the importance which the jury apparently attached to this question of the onus of proof. That shows that—if there had been a different direction—they might have returned a different verdict.'

'If the learned judge had told the jury to acquit Mr Glacier, as he in effect told them to acquit Mrs Glacier, they might have found both of them Not Guilty, you mean?' said Mr Justice Short.

'No, my Lord, I don't mean that,' said Roger.

'Well, what is your complaint?' said Mr Justice Mellow. 'You concede that there's nothing wrong with the trial and nothing wrong with the summing-up, except this question of onus of proof. And the learned judge said it was on the prosecution. What more do you want? Didn't he say it often enough? Is that your complaint?'

'No, my Lord. My complaint quite simply is that, instead of saying that the jury must be satisfied beyond all reasonable doubt—'

'That's gone since *Summers*' case,' said Mr Justice Mellow.

'In my submission, my Lords, it has come back since *Hepworth's* case,' said Roger. 'But, even if I am wrong about that, the learned judge did not follow *Summers's* or *Hepworth's* case. He told the jury they must be reasonably sure of the defendants' guilt. In my submission, that is not enough. In *Hepworth's* case this Court at least suggested that "satisfied" is not enough.'

'Well, what should he have said?' asked Mr Justice Rose. 'I see that he did say that complete certainty was impossible and was not required. That's right, isn't it?'

'Yes, my Lord,' said Roger.

'Well, if you can't have complete certainty,' said Mr Justice Short, 'what can you have but reasonable certainty?'

'That is not the expression used in *Summers's* case, my Lord,' said Roger. 'The word used there is "sure" without qualification. The jury must "feel sure". That is repeated in *Hepworth*.'

'What do you say "sure" means?' asked Mr Justice Short.

'Frankly, I don't know,' said Roger. 'If "sure" means "sure"—it means "completely sure", which I agree is too high a standard. If it means something less than completely sure—how much less? I frankly don't know. But I do submit that the expression "reasonably sure" is putting it much too low. I'm reasonably sure I brought my watch with me means there may be quite a substantial element of doubt about it. With the greatest respect, my Lord, juries seem to have understood for many, many years the expression "satisfied beyond all reasonable doubt", and I should have thought that it was easier to explain that expression—if it requires explanation—than to explain what "being sure" or "feeling sure" means. I am sure I am addressing your Lordships. Have the jury to be as sure as that? No. Well, how far have they to be sure? If you tell a jury that they haven't to be absolutely sure but that they must be satisfied beyond all reasonable doubt—surely that tells them satisfactorily what is required?'

'I'm sure I brought my pen with me,' said Mr Justice Mellow reflectively, 'may mean . . . I'm beginning to have some doubt whether I brought it with me.'

'I respectfully agree,' said Roger.

'Reasonably sure,' said Mr Justice Short, 'does sound more like the balance of probabilities. Crime has to be proved with a high degree of certainty. How that is to be defined, I'm not sure; but reasonably sure does appear to me, on reflection, to be putting the standard too low.'

'And,' put in Mr Justice Rose, 'this was—as Mr Thursby has pointed out—a case where the jury were troubled about the onus of proof. And they were told more than once—that they must be reasonably sure. That doesn't seem enough to me.'

'I think we'd like to hear what your opponent has to say,' said Mr Justice Short.

Henry began at once to address the Court.

'My Lords, I respectfully agree that, if this appeal had come before your Lordships twenty-five years ago, I should have found it difficult to support the learned judge's direction. But in the last ten years the Lord Chief Justice has more than once said that he thought the expression "satisfied beyond all reasonable doubt" was only calculated to muddle a jury or, at any rate, that an explanation of it had that effect.'

'It seems to have served satisfactorily for a good many years,' interposed Mr Justice Mellow.

'And in *Summers's* case,' went on Henry, 'this Court approved the views of the Lord Chief Justice and said that that direction should not be given—and that the jury should be told that they should be satisfied of the prisoner's guilt so that they could feel sure their verdict was a right one.'

'I agree that the Court said that,' said Mr Justice Rose, 'but was it more than a strong intimation of the Court's views? It wasn't essential to the decision, was it? Moreover, in *Hepworth's* case this Court said that *Summers's* case may have been misleading and that the expression "beyond all reasonable doubt" would do. They also suggested that "satisfied" might not be enough.'

'That may be, my Lord,' said Henry, 'but there was *Kritz's* case in 1949, where this Court expressly upheld a direction by a judge that the jury must be reasonably satisfied of the prisoner's guilt. With respect, there is no difference between "reasonably satisfied" and "reasonably sure".'

'How is that to be reconciled with *Hepworth?*'

'I doubt if it can be,' said Henry—'although it was quoted to the Court during *Hepworth* and is mentioned in the judgement. But *Kritz's* case was a definite decision, not a mere expression of opinion and, if "reasonably satisfied" has been held to be good, I submit that "reasonably sure" is just as good.'

'We'd better look at that decision then,' said Mr Justice Short. A copy of the report was obtained for each of their Lordships, and Henry read it to them.

'That is in your favour,' said Mr Justice Mellow, 'but I'm bound to say for myself that I don't think it's a very satisfactory direction. But that case was a much stronger case from the prosecution's point of view than this one.'

Mr Glacier listened to all these arguments, in the place specially provided for appellants in the Court, attended by two warders. He found the arguments not uninteresting, but the result of success or failure was so important to him that he wished it didn't take so long to arrive at it—provided, of course, that the result was favourable. At last, after Henry had addressed the Court at length and Roger had replied, the judges conferred together for a little time and then Mr Justice Short proceeded to give judgement.

'The appellant in this case,' he began, 'was convicted at Carpshire Assizes of two offences under the Prevention of Corruption Act 1906, and sentenced to nine months' imprisonment. He appeals against the conviction. The evidence at his trial was as follows.'

The judge then went into the evidence in some detail. Mr Glacier who, in the short time he had spent in prison, had learned to be able to speak without noticeably moving his lips, whispered very quietly to one of the warders: 'How long does this go on for? We all know the facts. What we want to know is the decision.'

'Don't worry, cock,' said the warder, who, as a result of his prison experience, had become an amateur ventriloquist. 'You're O.K.'

'They allow the appeal, you mean?' said Mr Glacier.

'Thumbs up,' said the warder.

'Can I go now, then?' asked Mr Glacier.

'Better wait till he's finished. They like you to do that.'

'Certainly, if you say so,' said Mr Glacier.

'Thanks, mate,' said the warder.

Meanwhile, Mr Justice Short was concluding his statement as to the evidence. He then dealt with the judge's summing-up, with the return to Court of the Jury and the repeated direction given to them by the judge. He then stated what the ground of appeal was and elaborated the arguments for and against it.

'Personally,' he said, 'with the greatest respect to the learned Lord Chief Justice, I have always thought that the expression "satisfied beyond all reasonable doubt" was an admirable one—and it has served its purpose very well for many years. It is quite true that some judges have attempted to explain it at length and, in doing so, it is possible that they have confused the jury. But I can only say for myself that, if you tried to explain the extent to which a jury has to feel sure —having told them that they do not have to be completely sure—it would be just as easy to confuse them. Whereas, if you say to a jury—"you have not to be completely satisfied as to the prisoner's guilt, but there must be no real doubt in your minds about it, or, as we put it, you must be satisfied beyond all reasonable doubt," I should have thought a jury would have understood its duty well enough. On the other hand, if you use the expression "sure", I suppose you would have to say—"you must be as sure of the prisoner's guilt as you can be sure of anything which you have not plainly seen for yourselves." That may be putting the onus too high and *Summers's* case does not say that. But it does say that a judge should tell the jury they must feel sure. I ask myself "how sure?" Whatever "sure" may mean—bearing in mind that, as it does not mean "absolutely sure", it does not really mean what it says—because "sure" means "absolutely sure"—

unless it is qualified by some other word—I say again, whatever
the expression may mean—'

'For how long does this continue?' asked Mr Glacier.

'You'll get away in time to have lunch at the Ritz,' said the
warder.

'You will lunch with me, please?' said Mr Glacier.

'Can't, mate, thanks,' said the warder. 'Got to look after some
more of you blokes.'

'Perhaps if I explained,' said Mr Glacier.

'You'd get six months for contempt,' said the warder.

'You must come and see me at my hotel then . . . the Glorious
at Westlea. And bring your wife and family. I assume you have
one.'

'Thanks, cock,' said the warder. 'But once you're out you'll forget
all about me.'

'There you are wrong,' said Mr Glacier. 'I never forget a face or
a friend.'

'There's no need to be personal,' said the warder—who had kind
brown eyes but a large bulbous nose and a wart on the side of it.

'Forgive my English,' said Mr Glacier. 'I meant you are a
friend—unless you are wrong about this appeal.'

'Don't you worry,' said the warder. 'I don't know nothing about
the law. But you get to know what's happening when you've listened
as often as I have.'

They stopped for a moment as the judge said: 'I say again—
whatever that expression may mean, it is not the expression the
learned judge used in this case.'

'He rests still at the same place,' said Mr Glacier.

'That's nothing,' said the warder. 'I've heard 'em at the same
place all day, and then I've known 'em go on till the next.'

'Are you talking?' said the judge suddenly to Mr Glacier.

'No, my Lord,' said Mr Glacier, with the most innocent look on
his face which he could produce.

'Well, someone was,' said the judge.

'It was him,' said the warder to Mr Glacier.

Mr Justice Short looked severely at the prisoner and continued
with his judgement.

'His name's Short,' said the warder. 'Makes you smile.'

'Are they all like this?' asked Mr Glacier.

'Pretty well,' said the warder. 'But there are a few who say what the result is first, and give their reasons after. I think that's a bit fairer on the chap.'

'I collaborate, as my wife would say,' said Mr Glacier. 'It is good to think I shall be seeing her soon. You are right, I suppose? Let me see where he is now.'

'Now the expressions which the judge used . . .' Mr Justice Short was saying, 'were as follows—'

'No danger of him exceeding the speed limit,' said the warder. 'They don't, by the way. I used to be in the police force. And I've followed one old judge all down Constitution Hill and all along Birdcage Walk—twenty miles an hour exactly. Never more.'

'Perhaps he knew you were behind him,' said Mr Glacier. 'I should do the same in those circumstances.'

'Now, I wonder,' said the warder. 'I'd never thought of that.' He thought for a moment or two, which allowed Mr Glacier to hear Mr Justice Short say:

'now, these expressions are not to be found in *Summers's* or *Hepworth's* case.'

'But I don't think so,' went on the warder. 'I bet these old geysers stick to the law. It stands to reason. Dishing it out all day—wouldn't be able to do anything else.'

'But, as a change, do you not think?' said Mr Glacier. 'It must be so very—how do you say?—boring to keep to the law all the time.'

'You wouldn't know, chum, would you?' said the warder.

'That might be described, I suppose, as a leading question,' said Mr Glacier. 'Whatever that expression may mean.'

'Whatever that expression may mean,' went on Mr Justice Short—and for a moment Mr Glacier's heart went at double time.

'I thought he had heard me again,' he said, after he had recovered.

'The one that's talking can't usually hear because of his own voice,' said the warder. 'And the ones that aren't are so busy listening to what's wrong with the one that's talking says that they can't hear anything else. Or else', he added, 'they're asleep. With their eyes open, of course. That's one of the first things they learn on the Bench. Same as you learn to talk with your mouth shut in clink.' 'How do you know they sleep?' asked Mr Glacier, 'if their eyes are open?'

'By what happens when they wake up,' said the warder. 'They

don't actually yawn and stretch themselves. But they'd like to. You can see 'em. Look at *him* now.'

He pointed to Mr Justice Mellow. 'Why shouldn't he have a bit of shut eye? He's got nothing to do now,' the warder added.

'Then will he not speak as well?' asked Mr Glacier.

'Shows you haven't been before, chum,' said the warder. 'Only one of 'em speaks. Even if they disagree. But then the one that disagrees—he keeps awake listening to all the mistakes the other two have made. There, he's waking up . . . did you see that?'

Mr Justice Mellow had taken a glass of water.

'I expect he thought it was a cup of tea,' the warder added. 'Given him a nasty shock, look.'

They stared at Mr Justice Mellow sipping his water and imagined that they saw his Lordship give the suspicion of a jerk to his head.

'He nearly said: "What's the weather like, dear?" ' said the warder. 'But he's an old one. He was able to check it. They do say that before my time one of them did say something like it, but don't take it from me. I didn't hear it myself.'

'For myself,' said Mr Justice Short, 'I should be well satisfied to have left matters as they were before *Summers's* case. But, even accepting that case, I do not think that the direction in the present case can be upheld. Does "reasonably sure" mean more or less than "almost sure?" "Almost sure" would not satisfy *Summers's* case and "reasonably sure," if it is a stronger expression than "almost sure"—which I take leave to doubt—is certainly well below the standard of certainty required by "sure." '

'You are sure, I hope,' said Mr Glacier. 'Not almost sure?'

'Beyond all reasonable doubt, cock,' said the warder. 'It's about the only expression I know, but I've heard it so often it's stuck.'

'Completely and absolutely sure?' demanded Mr Glacier.

'As sure as he'll go on for another half hour,' said the warder.

'It is quite true,' went on Mr Justice Short, 'that in the case of *Kritz* cited by Mr Blagrove, this Court did dismiss an appeal where the judge had used the expression "reasonably satisfied". That case appears to us to be somewhat inconsistent with the later case of *Hepworth,* but, whether it was rightly or wrongly decided, it does not compel us to decide in this case that the repeated use of "reasonably" by the judge was a sufficient direction.'

'You seem to be right,' said Mr Glacier.

'Of course I'm right,' said the warder. 'Have you booked your table?'

'But why does he still continue?' asked Mr Glacier. 'He has said everything necessary to let me go.'

'Now Mr Blagrove has argued,' went on Mr Justice Short.

'He did not appear to argue as long as you,' said Mr Glacier who—though now very optimistic—was becoming impatient.

'Keep cool, chum,' said the warder. 'He's going to say it all—whether you like it or not.'

'So it seems,' said Mr Glacier.

'Some of 'em say it more than once,' said the warder.

'I have already gathered as much,' said Mr Glacier.

Almost exactly half an hour after the warder had said that it would go on for another half hour, Mr Justice Short paused for a moment and then said: 'For these reasons, we are all of opinion that the appeal must be allowed and the conviction quashed.'

The judge then looked towards the prisoner. 'Let him be discharged,' he said.

Mr Glacier bowed to the Court.

'This way, chum, said the warder, but when he let him out below the Court to freedom and shook hands—'Good-bye, sir, he said, 'and good luck.'

'And good luck to you,' said Mr Glacier. 'We shall meet again.'

'Not here, I hope, sir,' said the warder.

'You may be sure beyond all reasonable doubt that it will not be here,' said Mr Glacier. 'Thank you for making the time pass much faster than it would otherwise have done. If only that judge would come for a drink to my hotel on a really thirsty day, after a long round of golf, I should take the place of the barman—and I should mix the drink myself. First I should fetch the ice—lovely cool ice—the basis of the beautiful drink that the judge is going to have. I should put it in the mixer with a few polite remarks about the weather and what a thirsty day it is. Then I should find that each ingredient had to be fetched from the cellar. And when I had them, I should pour them in so slowly—oh, so slowly. All the time I should make polite conversation—always about the weather—and thirst—and what a difference a long, cool drink makes; no doubt about it, I should say . . . no doubt about it. And then, when at last I had the beautiful mixture all ready and the judge's throat is in that most exquisite state of—how do you say?—of anticipation,

when there is the certainty that the thirst is going to be—what is
the word?—slaked . . . certainty, did I say?—perhaps I should have
said reasonable certainty—then, at the last moment I should, by
an unfortunate accident, drop the mixer and have to start all over
again. First, of course, by clearing the mess—so very slowly.'

'I think that'd be a bit unkind,' said the warder. 'After all, he
did let you off.'

'But so should I let him have his drink,' said Mr Glacier, 'in the
end.'

Mr Glacier met Roger and Mr Plumb in the Law Courts and
thanked them for their help. 'But what a lot of time and money,'
he said, 'it has cost to arrive at the truth.'

'The truth?' said Roger. 'No one in Court said anything about
arriving at the truth.'

CHAPTER 24

Silk

For a variety of reasons there was unusual delay in the appointment of Q.C.s but, not long after the successful end to the Glacier case, the Lord Chancellor intimated to Roger that he was recommending Her Majesty to appoint him one of her counsel learned in the law. In due course, the necessary ceremony took place and both Roger's mother and Anne came to see him take silk. They saw the silks, one after the other, come to the Law Courts from the House of Lords and assemble to have some photographs taken in their glory—full-bottomed wig, silk gown, Court dress, ruffle, and the rest—and then go round to most of the Courts where the ceremony of calling within the Bar took place. When each judge was told that the new Q.C.s had arrived, he stopped the case he was trying and, one by one, he called them within the Bar.

Roger had explained to his mother a year before what it was all about, but he told her again. ' "Moving the Court" is, in effect, making an application to the Court,' he said. 'And when you take silk, the judge always asks you, as a matter of courtesy, "Do you move?"—which means, have you any application to make. To show that you are now a Q.C., he is inviting you, as a pure formality, to do something in your new capacity. Of course no one has any application to make, and you simply bow—which is the method of saying "No".'

'But suppose you wanted to make an application?' Mrs Thursby asked.

'You'd make it another time, mother. This is just a ceremony. I don't know what would happen if anyone taking silk proceeded to get up, when he was asked if he moved, and launch a motion. The judge would have a fit.' 'Then don't you, Roger,' his mother said. 'It would be very unkind.'

'I won't, mother.'

In due course Roger's turn came and he duly took his place, gave the necessary bows, and sat down.

'Do you move, Mr Thursby?' said the judge.

Roger bowed, went along the row, and left the Court.

The ceremony took a long time—nearly all day—but it was over at last and Roger felt a free man. They celebrated the event by having a dinner at which all the members of his chambers were present.

The next day he celebrated the occasion again by taking Anne out to dinner and, after dinner, they went back to his mother's house. She had quite enough sense to go to bed early.

'Anne,' said Roger, and stopped. It was not as easy to say as he had thought. Perhaps she would help him. She did.

'Mr Thursby,' she said, 'do you move?'

Roger moved.

SETTLED OUT OF COURT

Contents

CHAPTER 1

Nothing Like the Truth

'Take it easy,' said the warder, who led Lonsdale Walsh down the stairs from the dock in Court 1 of the Old Bailey, 'you can always appeal.'

The warder was a kindly man and realized that the prisoner was upset. He was not altogether surprised. A lot of prisoners became upset, even when they were convicted of lesser crimes than murder. Some of them shouted, some of them cried, some of them collapsed. Lonsdale Walsh did none of these things. He simply went very red in the face, very, very red. The warder rightly assumed from this that Lonsdale Walsh disagreed with the verdict of the jury, and he was preparing to add a few further words of advice about appealing. Not because he thought that an appeal would be likely to succeed, but simply out of kindness, to give the man some hope.

The warder had not been surprised that Lonsdale Walsh took the verdict badly, but he was most surprised and pained by the answer to his kindly advice. The convicted man was a very wealthy financier and, apart from the unfortunate matter of the murder, had never been in the hands of the police. Some prisoners have two warders to accompany them down the stairs, some even three. One should surely be enough for an otherwise respectable financier; but he was not. Lonsdale Walsh's answer was to turn round and knock out the warder with a well-aimed blow to the chin. Having thus relieved his feelings to a small extent, he then waited quietly for the inevitable to happen. But there was not much they could do to him. You can't add anything useful to imprisonment for life.

Later, Lonsdale Walsh arranged for £200 to be sent to the warder, with the result that that kindly man remarked to his wife that he wouldn't mind being knocked out again at the same price, preferably just before they took their holiday. It will be realized from this payment that Lonsdale Walsh had no grievance against the warder.

He had simply been compelled to lash out at someone, and the warder was nearest to hand.

It must be very unpleasant to be convicted of murder and even more unpleasant to be so convicted on perjured evidence. Any reasonable man would resent this. But there was a special reason why it was worse for Lonsdale Walsh than for anyone else. He was allergic to lies. Just as some people break out into a rash if they come near a cat or a strawberry, so a deliberate untruth had from his childhood revolted him. It was not a question of morality or religion at all. His devotion to the truth was like a purely physical complaint. No doubt he himself would have told a lie to save his own life or the life of someone for whom he had a sufficient regard, or to save his country, but he had never been put in the position of having to do any of these things. He had told no lies at his trial, not even to his own solicitors and counsel. And the evidence against him was almost entirely perjured from beginning to end. With the possible exception of their names and addresses, nearly everything stated by the chief witnesses against him had been untrue.

If this would be difficult for an ordinary person to bear, it was impossible for Lonsdale Walsh. And so the warder got his £200. Take it easy indeed!

Lonsdale Walsh was the child of well-to-do middle-class parents. They were very ordinary, decent people and, except to the extent that no one is absolutely normal, they were without 'isms' or allergies of any kind. Nor, curiously enough, did they notice anything wrong with Lonsdale until it was pointed out to them. But one day they were a little surprised to be asked by Lonsdale's headmaster to come to see him. They wondered whether the discussion was to be about the boy's career or whether he had got into trouble of some kind. They were not unduly alarmed. Lonsdale was a big boy for his age and good with his fists. But they could not think that he would be guilty of anything worse than a schoolboy prank. So perhaps it was his career after all. But, then, why ask them in the middle of term? Perhaps he had been bullying smaller (or even larger) boys. They knew that he was very determined to get his own way but, as he never told lies to his parents and never tried to knock them down, they could not imagine that he had done anything terrible. On the way to the school they discussed every possibility they could think of, but they were still somewhat mystified by the time they were shown into the headmaster's study.

'Nice of you to come,' he said. 'So sorry to have to trouble you, but we're a little worried about Lonsdale.'

The parents were relieved. This couldn't be anything very bad. You can't be 'a little worried' about a boy whom you're going to expel.

'Oh?' said Lonsdale's father.

'I thought you might be able to help us,' went on the headmaster.

'What's the trouble?'

'Well,' said the headmaster, 'you must know all about it, but it is becoming a bit embarrassing.'

'Embarrassing? I'm afraid I really don't know what you're talking about.'

'I'm sorry,' said the headmaster. 'It's this truth business, you know. It's really getting us down a bit.'

'Truth business?' said Lonsdale's father. 'I haven't the faintest idea what you're talking about. Has he been telling lies or something? It's not like him.'

'Lies?' said the headmaster, 'indeed no. I'm afraid I wish he would sometimes.'

'Look, headmaster,' said Mr Walsh, 'my wife and I are simple people, but I hope I may say of average intelligence. Would you kindly explain in plain intelligible language what your complaint is about our boy?'

'It's not exactly a complaint,' said the headmaster uncomfortably, 'but to put it bluntly, we think he ought to see a psychiatrist.'

'Who's we?'

'His form master, his housemaster and I.'

'Why on earth should he see a psychiatrist? He's a normal enough boy. He works well, doesn't he? He's good at games. Bit of a bully, perhaps, but that you can easily cope with at a school like this.'

'What you say is quite right, Mr Walsh,' said the headmaster. 'It's quite true that he is inclined to fight his way through, if he wants anything badly enough but, as you say, we're quite used to dealing with that sort of thing here. No, it's something much more unusual. Indeed, it's unique in my experience. But I can't imagine that you don't know all about it.'

'Well, I'm afraid we don't,' said Lonsdale's father. 'Will you be good enough to enlighten us?'

'Well, anyway,' said the headmaster, 'you must have noticed that he always tells the truth.'

'Really!' said Mr Walsh. 'I'm a very busy man and it's quite a long journey here. You haven't asked us to come and see you just because we've tried to bring our boy up decently.'

'Please don't be annoyed,' said the headmaster, 'I assure you that I have only the boy's interests at heart—and yours too, of course.'

'I'm sorry,' said Mr Walsh, 'please forgive me. But my wife and I would really like to know what you are driving at.'

'Well, as you don't seem to know,' said the headmaster, 'I'd better start from the beginning. Now naturally we like boys to tell the truth. But, of course, the normal boy doesn't always do so. Usually it's to avoid unpleasant consequences for himself or someone else. But occasionally it's simply out of kindness. Just as we don't hurt people's feelings by saying what we really think of them.'

'You find that Lonsdale speaks his mind too freely, is that it?'

'He certainly does, but that isn't it by a long way. Not only does he invariably say exactly what he thinks, not only does he invariably tell the truth, however unpleasant the consequences for himself or anyone else, but if he knows that anyone else is telling a lie, he . . . he . . . well I know it may sound ridiculous to you, as you don't seem to have noticed it at home—so let me say something else first. As I've said, we like boys to tell the truth, but equally, or perhaps even more important, we don't encourage sneaks.'

'You're not suggesting—' began Mr Walsh indignantly, but the headmaster held up his hand.

'Please let me finish,' he said. 'I am quite satisfied that your boy is not a deliberate sneak—that is to say, he never deliberately tells tales about other boys. I'm sure it's not deliberate.'

'What isn't deliberate?'

'Well, everytime Lonsdale knows that someone it telling a lie he—he goes red in the face, red like a turkey cock. In other words, if the truth is in question and Lonsdale knows it, the master has only to look at him to find the answer. I repeat, I'm quite sure the boy can't help it. He's got an allergy. Lies make him nearly burst. It isn't healthy, Mr Walsh. It doesn't so much matter here, but I'm thinking of his later career. Of course, truth is very important. We all realize that. And I must congratulate you on Lonsdale's truthfulness. But—but now—I'm not a psychiatrist, but, in my view, if he goes on like this without any assistance, if he goes into the world with this allergy, a world which unfortunately abounds with lies, he may very well find himself in a mental home. If you had seen the look on that boy's face sometimes when he knew the truth was not being told, you would understand why I am warning you. Now, of course, he may adapt himself to the behaviour of the world, I may have sent for you unnecessarily, but, in my view, I should be failing in my duty as his headmaster if I did not say that, in my opinion, your boy ought to be seen by a psychiatrist as soon as possible.'

Mr and Mrs Walsh said nothing for a moment. They simply looked at each other. Then Mr Walsh said:

'I must confess weve never noticed anything very peculiar. Now I come to think of it, the boy is very outspoken. But I've always liked that, and rather encouraged it. Are you sure it's more than that?'

'If you will treat the conversation as entirely confidential, then I'll send for the boy and ask him a question.'

'Certainly,' said Lonsdale's parents.

Lonsdale soon arrived and greeted his parents in the normal way. 'Tell me, Walsh,' said the headmaster to Lonsdale, 'what do you honestly think of Mr Thompson?'

'Bloody awful, sir,' said Lonsdale.

'There's no need to swear,' said his father.

'The headmaster asked me what I honestly thought,' said the boy. 'That was the only way I could express it honestly.'

'This Mr Thompson,' said Mr Walsh to the headmaster, 'what is your opinion of him? In confidence, of course.'

The headmaster coughed.

'He's a very good man,' he said eventually.

Lonsdale blushed furiously.

'May I go now please, sir?' he asked.

A month later Lonsdale was interviewed by an eminent psychiatrist, Dr Harvey McLong.

'Well, how's school?' began Dr McLong.

'All right,' said Lonsdale.

'I see,' said Dr McLong. 'Nothing more than that? Just all right?'

'Yes,' said Lonsdale, 'it's all right.'

'And what's it like at home?'

'All right,' said Lonsdale.

'No better than at school?' asked Dr McLong.

'It's different,' said Lonsdale.

'I see,' said Dr McLong, and there was a pause. 'I gather,' he went on, 'that you're happy both at home and at school?'

'Yes,' said Lonsdale.

'Nothing the matter?'

'Not that I can think of.'

'Why d'you think you've come to see me?'

'Because I'm growing up, I suppose, and you're going to tell me things.'

'I see,' said Dr McLong, and there was another pause. Then he decided he must get nearer the subject.

'Do you always tell the truth, Lonsdale?'

'As far as I know, I do.'

'Why?'

'Because I do.'

'Is there no other reason? Isn't it because you want to be trusted?'

'I've never thought.'

'D'you know the story of Cassandra, the Trojan prophetess, who had a curse laid on her that she should always prophesy the truth and never be believed?'

'That's a horrible story,' said Lonsdale, and went very red in the face.

'A thing like that upsets you?'

'Yes, it does.'

'Why?'

'How should I know? I don't like it, that's all.'

'You like the truth, don't you?'

'How d'you mean, like it?'

'Well, you always tell the truth yourself and you like other people to do so too.'

'I suppose so.'

'Why?'

'I don't know. I just do. Same as I like stewed apricots and not stewed prunes.'

'Good,' said Dr McLong. 'You've never thought of joining our profession, have you?'

'No,' said Lonsdale.

'Why not?'

'Because I think it's a lot of . . .' and Lonsdale then said a word which was seldom used in Dr McLong's consulting-room, except by men friends who happened to be calling on him for a chat, and a few women patients who wanted to show off.

'People used to make that sort of remark about a lot of things which have since proved to be very useful. We're a fairly new profession. You must be indulgent with us.'

Lonsdale said nothing.

'When I mentioned the story of Cassandra to you, you went very red in the face. Did you feel anything?'

'I felt hot.'

'Why?'

'Because I didn't like the story.'

'But you don't feel hot when you see stewed prunes, do you?'

'No.'

'Or when you see someone you don't like?'

'I suppose not.'

'Then why at the story of Cassandra?'

'Because I do.'

'And you feel the same if you hear anyone tell lies, don't you?'

'Yes.'

'Why?'

'Because I do.'

'It isn't really an answer to say that. We don't eat because we eat. We eat because we're hungry. That's right, isn't it?'

'I suppose so.'

'Then why d'you feel hot when somebody tells lies?'

'Because I don't like it, I suppose.'

'But you don't feel hot at everything you don't like?'

'No.'

'Then why at lies?'

'I don't know. I just do.'

'But you must realize that in a civilized society lies have to be told. Sometimes you have to lie to be kind to a person. If a girl asks you whether you like her dress, it wouldn't be kind to say you didn't, would it?'

'No.'

'Don't you want to be kind to people?'

'Sometimes.'

'Which would you prefer, to tell the truth and hurt someone's feelings or to tell a lie to avoid hurting them?'

'To tell the truth.'

'But that wouldn't be kind.'

'I didn't say it would.'

'What is your object in life?'

'To be a millionaire.'

'Why?'

'Because, if you're a millionaire, you can do lots of things.'

'What sort of thing?'

'Oh—I don't know, have swimming pools and yachts and things.'

'And girls all round the place?'

Lonsdale said nothing.

'Well, what are you thinking about?' asked Dr McLong.

'I thought you'd have got there before.'

'To girls you mean? You thought you'd come here to talk about girls?'

'Yes.'

'Are you disappointed that we haven't talked about them?'

'No.'

'Why not?'

'Plenty of time for them later, when I grow up.'

'What d'you like talking about?'

'Depends who I'm talking to.'

'What would you like to talk to me about?'

'Nothing.'

'I see,' said Dr McLong. 'You're not exactly cooperative.'

'What's that?'

'You're not trying to help me.'

'Help you do what?'

'Help you.'

'I don't want any help.'

'I think you do. D'you want to go through life getting red in the face every time someone tells a lie?'

'I don't mind.'

'You will.'

But it was many years before Dr McLong was proved right. Until his conviction for murder, Lonsdale was not personally affected by his complaint. Indeed, to a considerable extent, it stood him in good stead. During his career it became known by everyone with whom he had dealings that, though he would use every effort to get his own way, the lie was the one weapon he would not use. 'Walsh's word' became a synonym for the truth.

It was the other people who suffered, not he. He would not tolerate lies in any circumstances. Once, an office boy in a company of his started to take money out of the petty cash to put on horses. Eventually he had a lucky win and paid it all back. By a miscalculation, however, he paid back rather too much and his offences were discovered. His immediate superior, however, was so impressed at the boy's honesty in repaying the money that he tried to hush it up and told a lie about it. When this was discovered, Lonsdale immediately ordered the dismissal of the man who had covered the crimes of the office boy. The latter was allowed to remain.

Lonsdale's allergy only related to the spoken or written lie. Mere dishonesty was a totally different matter. He had no particular objection to the burglar, even if he used violence. But the woman who lied to the customs authorities in order to smuggle in some trifles provoked him to fury. He could have sympathy with a man who murdered his wife, but none with a man who tricked a woman into bigamy by pretending he was single. He never considered whether he over-valued truth at the expense of other qualities, any more than the average sufferer from one disease seriously considers whether he would prefer to have another.

CHAPTER 2

Discovery and Conviction

Lonsdale Walsh started his career as an accountant and he soon became deeply interested in finance. His parents left him a little capital and by careful, speculative investment he quickly increased it. By the time he was forty he was of importance in the City. By the time he was fifty he was a very wealthy man, and by the time he was convicted of murder, at the age of fifty-five, he was pretty well a millionaire.

His conviction arose as a direct result of the battles which often take place between financiers. Sometimes the contestants are on the same board, and it was so in this case. A great struggle was taking place for the control of the Anglo-Saxon Development Corporation Limited. This company had been nurtured by Lonsdale Walsh almost from its birth, and it had become one of the biggest and wealthiest companies in the country. Lonsdale was determined to retain control of it, but he had an equally determined opponent in Adolphus Barnwell, or more accurately, in Adolphus Barnwell's wife.

Jo Barnwell had been a singularly attractive girl and at forty-five she was as attractive a woman as Lonsdale knew. But there was no doubt at all that it was she who kept Adolphus at it. Probably he would have preferred to retire into the country and farm. But that sort of life was not for Jo. She liked to be at the centre of things. She enjoyed a fight. But though she did not lead her regiment from behind and would have been the first to admit her influence over her husband, she preferred to win her battles through him. So she never personally went on the board of any of Adolphus's companies. She contented herself with telling him what to do when he was on them. He gladly accepted her advice for two reasons. It was good advice and it made things easier at home. Once or twice in their early days he had made a mild protest at some of Jo's more outrageous suggestions, but she quickly put him in his place, and it must be said that, until he was murdered, he was very happy there.

Jo and Lonsdale often met and they each enjoyed those occasions. It was the attraction of opposites. Jo would tell a lie as soon as look at you, if it would serve her purpose, but she was highly intelligent and realized that, if you want to make the best use of the lie as a weapon, it should not be used too often. And it must be a good one. She was the one person whose lies had a fascination for Lonsdale. He loathed them instinctively but in her case they had the attraction which repulsive-looking objects have for some people. He would even try to provoke one on occasion, much as a person sometimes squeezes a painful sore to make it hurt more. No one is quite sure whether that is done because of the relief when the pressure stops, or whether there is something masochistic about it. Whatever the reason, Lonsdale enjoyed meeting Jo, and they danced many times together, while Adolphus sat quite happily in the background.

Lonsdale's wife had died young, and he had never remarried. But his relationship with Jo was completely blameless on the surface. Most of the time they fought, and in their words and actions towards each other there was never the slightest hint of the affection which may well have existed under the surface. Apart altogether from their verbal battles which were little, if anything, more than play, they fought in earnest behind the scenes. Had the opportunity arisen, each would cheerfully have made the other bankrupt. They asked each other for no quarter, and never gave it. The only difference between them was that Jo knew that she could always take Lonsdale's word, while he knew that he could never accept anything she said with any degree of assurance, unless it was on a matter of no importance to her.

The battle for the control of the Anglo-Saxon Corporation had only been in progress for a short time when the events, which were to place Lonsdale in the dock, started to take shape. In the course of gathering his forces together for the main attack, Lonsdale had exchanged a number of important and highly confidential letters with some of his associates. Knowledge of their contents would have been of the greatest possible value to the Barnwell forces. Jo indeed considered the idea of a burglary, but rejected it as too dangerous and too doubtful of success. She was quite right to reject the idea.

Lonsdale had taken sufficient precautions to deal with that possibility. He kept all such correspondence at his bank. So Jo had to think again.

One day Lonsdale received a letter from the Barnwell solicitors informing him that their client, Adolphus Barnwell, was proposing to bring an action for slander against him, and asking for the names of solicitors who would accept service on his behalf of such proceedings. The nature and occasion of the slander were mentioned, and Lonsdale knew that it was a pure invention. He was not unduly worried, although he had a vague feeling that there was more behind the threat than he could see. He went straight to his solicitors, Messrs Slograve, Plumb and Co., and interviewed Mr Slograve.

'What's this all about?' he asked.

'Did you say what the letter alleges?'

'Certainly not. I didn't even discuss the matter. What's behind it?'

'Let me think,' said Mr Slograve. After a moment or two, he said: 'I'm afraid I think I know what they're after. You're not going to be pleased.'

'What is it?'

'The Annual General of the Anglo-Saxon is in about nine months, isn't it?'

'Yes. But what's that got to do with it?' Lonsdale was becoming a little apprehensive.

'This slander action will be so framed that the correspondence we all know about and which Barnwell would dearly love to see before the Annual General, will be material to the action.'

'And?'

'Accordingly you will have to disclose it to them.'

'I'll do nothing of the kind.'

'I'm afraid you'll have to. You'll have to swear an affidavit saying what documents are in your or your agent's possession.'

'We'll destroy them.'

'Then you'll not only have to admit that fact but they can ask you what was in them.'

'My God!' said Lonsdale. 'It's that bloody woman. What can I do about it?'

'I really don't know,' said Mr Slograve. 'We could try to drag things out, but we'd never succeed in avoiding discovery before the meeting.'

'But the whole action's a fraud. It's just brought to get a sight of the correspondence.'

'I know. The more I think of it, the plainer it becomes.'

'But surely you can prevent a thing like that? It's an abuse of the process of the Court. Isn't that what you'd call it?'

'Certainly it is. But how can we prove it? All they have to do is to call their witness to say you said what's alleged.'

'But it'll be rank perjury.'

'But how can you show it to be? There's only your word against his.'

'It's an outrage,' said Lonsdale. 'Surely the law is strong enough to deal with a situation like this.'

'I'm afraid not,' said Mr Slograve. 'Of course, we'll go to counsel about it, to see if we can avoid disclosing the letters, but, as the whole object of the action is to look at them, I can't conceive that they won't frame their allegations so as to make any case for refusing to disclose them untenable.'

'So that anyone, who's unscrupulous enough, can just invent an allegation in order to look at someone else's private documents?'

'I'm afraid that is so, provided it's skilfully done and provided at least one person is prepared to commit perjury. Of course, we can fight them all the way, but in my view we shall lose, and, however much we appeal, we'll never keep the fight going beyond the meeting. We can only hope that Mr Barnwell had a coronary thrombosis before discovery.'

'What good would that do? That woman would carry on after him.'

'Well, she couldn't, as a matter of fact. A slander action dies when the plaintiff dies.'

'I thought the executors could carry on with an action started by a man who dies?'

'That rule doesn't apply to libel or slander actions. I don't pretend to be a great lawyer, but that's one of the things you can take from me.'

It was not long after this conversation that Adolphus Barnwell died, not from coronary thrombosis—but suddenly and violently. That was the end of the slander action, but not of Jo Barnwell. And, three months after her husband died, she saw to it that

Lonsdale stood in the dock charged with the murder. And the jury said 'Guilty', and the judge said 'Imprisonment for life'.

CHAPTER 3

Spikey Lee's Chance

For the first few days after his conviction Lonsdale was hardly sane, but he pulled himself together sufficiently to sign his Notice of Appeal to the Court of Criminal Appeal. He was present when his appeal was dismissed. Once again he had to be forcibly restrained. He was led away shouting unintelligibly.

After a few days in the prison hospital he recovered sufficiently to take stock of his position. His counsel advised him that it was impossible to apply to the Attorney-General for leave to appeal to the House of Lords, as there were no grounds for making such an application. So Lonsdale petitioned the Home Secretary and wrote to his M.P. for help. All his attempts to have his case reviewed failed, and the governor of the prison eventually told him that it was useless for him to batter his head against a brick wall and that he would be well advised to accept his sentence with resignation.

'But there wasn't a word of truth in the evidence for the prosecution, sir.'

'I'm afraid a lot of convicted people say that. Now, you're an intelligent man. Your sentence will be reviewed in ten years and any time after that . . .'

'Ten years!' said Lonsdale. 'That makes it a bit early to be measured for my coming-out suit.'

After a few months in prison, Lonsdale asked his only daughter, Angela, to visit him, and he was eventually allowed to see her.

'I want you to do something for me,' he said.

'Of course. What is it?'

'I want you to go round the Courts and find a barrister whom you consider to have intelligence of the highest class and to have a resilient mind. A chap who isn't hide-bound. A man who's prepared to consider new ideas or new situations, not just dismissing them because he's never come across them before. I don't mind if he's old or young, well-known or not, but he must have the qualities I've mentioned. He won't be easy to find, so go everywhere. Take your time. High Court, County Court, Sessions, Old Bailey, Magistrate's Court—but find me the right man.'

'Of course I will, Father, but what . . .'

'Never mind the reason. Find him. Now there's something else I want you to do. To some extent you can do it at the same time. I want you to find a High Court judge with the same qualities, someone of the highest intelligence but who's still prepared to learn. Will you do it?'

'Well, of course, Father, if it'll make you happier.'

'It will,' said Lonsdale, 'and, when you've made your selection, let me know their names and addresses.'

While Angela was making her tour of the Courts, her father was concentrating on the plan he had made. A person of his character must have something to live for, something in the not too distant future. By the time of his conversation with Angela, Lonsdale had completely recovered from the appalling shock of his conviction and the sense of utter frustration. At once his agile and determined mind began to consider ways and means of attaining his object before it was too late to be worth while. Neither the decision of the Court of Criminal Appeal nor the rejection of his plea by the Home Secretary, nor the governor's advice had in the least altered his resolve, which was to have the jury's verdict in his case set aside and, incidentally, to show Jo Barnwell that it was not as easy as she must have thought to put Lonsdale Walsh in prison for life. He gave her full credit for what she had achieved. It required ingenuity and boldness, and, if it had not also entailed the use of the lie from start to finish, Lonsdale might even have admired her handiwork.

Day after day and night after night he pictured the scene of his triumph and of Jo's anger, when he in spite of the apparently insuperable difficulties, he finally triumphed over her. But, though he allowed himself these dreams as a necessary entertainment during his drab prison life, he spent much time in working out, from the practical point of view, how he was going to attain his object.

His first step was to find a co-prisoner, due for release in a few months, whom he considered a suitable ally. He must be a man with many previous convictions, someone for whom crime was simply a means to an end and who had gone on too long in the business to become respectable, who indeed would consider himself a recidivist if he took an honest job. He must be a man who, as Becky Sharp might have been, would be honest on ten thousand a year. In other words, he must not be a man who enjoyed crime for its own sake and who needed the excitement involved. Such men are often exhibitionists and would be very dangerous to employ. Lonsdale needed a man for whom money and not notoriety was the spur. Eventually he chose Spikey Lee as someone who came nearest to his requirements. Spikey was a versatile criminal and was as prepared to go in for a long-term fraud as to climb up a drainpipe and tie up the lady of the house with her husband's pyjama-cord, preparatory to ransacking the bedroom. On one occasion, his calculations went wrong and the husband was there too, with the pyjama cord safely round him. He had also tried, not very successfully, a little forgery, and once (and he was heartily ashamed of this) a little blackmail.

'Honest, guv,' he said to Lonsdale (who was known in prison as 'The Guv'), 'honest, I wish I 'adn't. And that ain't 'cos I got five years out of it. It's the only time I meant it when I said I was sorry. The old basket didn't believe me any more than 'e did the other times. But I told 'im straight—"I'm sorry, my Lord," I said. "Straight I am. It's a dirty game, and I swear I'll never do it again. But the money seemed so easy," I said. "You see, my Lord," I said, "I take a lot of risks when I go climbing up a drainpipe. I may fall and break my blooming neck for one thing. And I may get caught for another. And there may not be anything worth taking in the end. And when I saw this easy money—with no drainpipes, no householders with rolling pins, nothing at all except to say 'more please' and out it comes all nice and easy, well I fell for it, my Lord. And I'd like to say to Mr X and Mrs Y and Miss Z that I'm really and truly sorry for what I done to 'em, and if I still 'ad the money I'd give it back." I can't say I really meant that bit, guv, but it just come out and it didn't make no difference as I'd spent it all long before. "I believe you're sorry," said the old basket— "you're sorry because you were caught." "Well, that's true, my Lord," I said, 'but I'm sorry for what I done too. I don't say I'll go straight when I come out, but I'll never do that again." "You won't get the chance for some time," he said. "Five years." It was quite fair, guv. It's a real dirty game and I don't 'old with it. Easy, though.'

And Lonsdale observed a look of regret on Spikey's face, as he savoured in retrospect the ease of the living which he had renounced.

It was not the renunciation which made Lonsdale think that Spikey was his man, but his obvious desire for ease. Here was the man who would work for money and who would certainly not exchange it for his picture in the Sunday newspapers and a pat on the back from the police. In other words here was a man who could be completely trusted so long as he was paid. And Lonsdale intended that he should be paid.

The whole prison population knew who Lonsdale was and accordingly Spikey could believe his ears when Lonsdale mentioned what he was prepared to pay for Spikey's cooperation. To Spikey it was the fulfillment of his life's dream. Always to know where the next pint was coming from and without having to work for it. It was like winning a football pool. For Lonsdale had promised Spikey a substantial lump sum and an annuity. And, once again, Lonsdale had the reward of his passion for the truth. Spikey really believed that he meant it. Anticipation is often sweeter than realization, and Spikey's last few weeks in prison were some of the most enjoyable he had ever spent in his life.

CHAPTER 4

A Tour of the Courts

Angela Walsh was a double First but she had the great advantage of looking and talking like a charming Third. She was as intelligent as her father, not quite so determined, and with an unexaggerated regard for the truth. She was devoted to her father but she had told him the normal lies which normal children tell normal parents, with this qualification, that from a very early age she never told him an untruth without being quite certain that she would not be found out.

She was deeply distressed at her father's predicament and anxious to do all she could to help him. She had but the vaguest idea of what was behind his request, and she did not attempt to find out. She knew that she would learn in the end and she simply concentrated on the task which her father had given her. Had the circumstances not been so tragic, it would have been a most interesting assignment and, even as it was, she was able to get considerable interest and even amusement from her tour of the Courts. At the end of it she could have written a most entertaining little book containing sketches of judges, barristers, solicitors, witnesses, and the other people who are involved in civil and criminal trials. It was a highly concentrated tour and, in the course of it, she reflected that it might be no bad thing if such a tour could be introduced into the curriculum of children about to leave school, or at any rate of university students. Although there would obviously be periods of boredom in such a course, it would for the most part, she thought from her own experiences, combine instruction with entertainment to such a high degree that even the dullest student must learn a good deal.

Although, in view of her father's wealth and previous position, she could easily have obtained introductions to solicitors or barristers to show her round, she thought it better, to begin with at any rate, to

go entirely by herself. She did not want her own judgement to be
affected by the views of lawyers of experience. She must make this
choice by herself. Once a well-known lawyer had advised her on
the subject, she would have difficulty in relying on her own inexperienced judgement. How could she tell whether the judgement of the
lawyer was right? Only the barrister she was looking for could have
given her the right advice.

So round the courts she went by herself. She heard impassioned
pleas at the Old Bailey, dry legal arguments in the Chancery
Division and incredible evidence by bankrupts, explaining how they
had managed to dispose of certain untraceable assets, explanations
which no one pretended to believe and which the bankrupts themselves sometimes put forward rather apologetically, as the best they
could do at short notice. She heard husbands' and wives' stories of
marital unhappiness, and motorists' protests at the diligence of the
police in prosecuting them for obstruction while armed robbers
remained loose, and so on. A little book! She could have written
several volumes. Sometimes she could not resist waiting, although
she knew that no one in the case was the man for her father. Very
sensibly she felt that she must have some relaxation and she used
such occasions for that purpose. And she would have been very
sorry indeed to miss such incidents as the cross-examination of a
witness by Mr Tewkesbury, that astonishing solicitor, who would
give a tight-rope walker points in the way in which he managed to
remain on the roll of solicitors.

Mr Tewkesbury's client was a lady of easy virtue. She chose to
be defended instead of pleading guilty because she had come before
a magistrate who was well known for his habit of exercising his
powers under a very ancient Act of Parliament. These powers in
effect enabled him to send prostitutes to prison, although the
maximum fine for the offence with which they were charged was
forty shillings. The method was to call upon them to find sureties
for their good behaviour. In default of such sureties being found,
the ancient Act entitled the Court to send them to prison. So Mr
Tewkesbury was from time to time, when he was sober enough,
pressed into service by these ladies. And excellent service he gave.
Magistrates in the districts where such ladies abound have very full
lists, and, if every one of them insisted on pleading not guilty, no
magistrate would be able to get through his list. Moreover, the
offences with which they were charged were not always easy to

prove, as it required proof that at least one member of the public had
been annoyed. As, normally, no member of the public is prepared to
come and give evidence that he was annoyed, the witnesses in such
cases almost invariably consist of policemen. Mr Tewkesbury knew
that, by spinning out the case to the greatest possible length, he
might eventually prevail on the magistrate to dismiss the charge,
not simply to put an end to the ordeal but because, in the course
of asking so many questions, it might well happen that some kind
of doubt might emerge. The lady in question was entitled to the
benefit of the doubt, and, after three-quarters of an hour of Mr
Tewkesbury, a magistrate could not be blamed for being in doubt.
Indeed, the endeavours to follow conscientiously all Mr Tewkesbury's questions and submissions sometimes made more than one
magistrate doubt if he was fit for anything else that afternoon.

It is not always appreciated by members of the legal profession
and the public that the conscientious judge is always listening,
listening intently, even when his eyes are half-closed, and it is an
extremely wearying ordeal to have to listen intently to arguments
which vary in infinite variety between the intelligent and the unintelligible. Interruptions in an effort to make a point clear usually
only succeed in making it even more obscure, and the business of
sorting out the various arguments and trying to make some reasonable sense of them occasionally almost reduces the listener to tears.
He does not actually cry, but his exhaustion is sometimes indicated
by a sudden exasperated remark from a judge who is noted for his
placidity.

Mr Tewkesbury's cross-examination during Angela's visit was
directed to the policeman's evidence that a man had been annoyed
by his client's solicitations.

MR TEWKESBURY: Now, officer, I want you to follow this next
question very closely.

CONSTABLE: I try to follow all your questions closely.

TEWKESBURY: And with what measure of success?

MAGISTRATE: You needn't answer that question.

TEWKESBURY: But, sir, with the greatest possible respect, am I
not entitled to an answer?

MAGISTRATE: No.

TEWKESBURY: But sir, unless I know the measure of success which the officer has in following my questions, it becomes more difficult for me to frame the next question.

MAGISTRATE: So far you seem to have overcome your difficulties most manfully. I have observed no lack of questions.

TEWKESBURY: Your Worship's courtesy overwhelms me.

MAGISTRATE (*to himself*): I wish it would.

TEWKESBURY: Is it now convenient, sir, that I should resume my cross-examination where I left off?

MAGISTRATE: Very well.

TEWKESBURY: Well then, officer, would you be kind enough to tell me the measure of success with which you have understood my previous questions?

MAGISTRATE: I've just said he needn't answer that question.

TEWKESBURY: But, sir, did I not understand you to change your mind and say I may ask it? If I may say so, the greatest judges change their minds. *Judex mutabilis, judex amabilis*, if I may say so.

MAGISTRATE: Mr Tewkesbury, would you kindly continue your cross-examination of this witness. I've fifty summonses to hear after this.

TEWKESBURY: I don't know how your Worship does it and retains your good humour.

MAGISTRATE(*quietly, to his clerk*): I've about had enough of this. Is he sober?

TEWKESBURY: Perfectly, sir. And my hearing is perfect too.

MAGISTRATE (*to himself*): Oh—God!

TEWKESBURY: Now, officer, I want you to follow this next question very closely.

CONSTABLE: I follow all . . .

MAGISTRATE: Be quiet, officer. That was not a question.

CONSTABLE: Sorry, sir.

MAGISTRATE: If you will confine yourself to answering questions, and Mr Tewkesbury will confine himself to asking material ones, we may get on.

TEWKESBURY: That would be an ideal cross-examination, if I may say so, sir. But (*shaking his head sadly*) *Non cuivis homini* something something *Olympum*.

MAGISTRATE: *Corinthum*, Mr Tewkesbury. *Contingit adire Corinthum.*

TEWKESBURY: Bless my soul, sir. I beg your pardon. I must be slipping. *Quantum mutatus ab illo Tewkesbury.*

MAGISTRATE: This isn't a Latin class. Please get on.

TEWKESBURY: If you please, sir. To resume, officer, when did you last see a person annoyed?

For a fraction of a second the constable looked at the magistrate and then hastily withdrew his eyes.

CONSTABLE: I'm not sure.

TEWKESBURY: Well, be sure, officer.

MAGISTRATE: How can he be?

TEWKESBURY: He can tell me the last occasion he *remembers* seeing anyone annoyed.

MAGISTRATE: That's a different question.

TEWKESBURY: Then I ask it. And remember, officer, you're on oath.

CONSTABLE (*after a slight cough*): I saw a pedestrian this morning annoyed by a motorist.

TEWKESBURY: How did he show his annoyance?

CONSTABLE: He shook his fist.

TEWKESBURY: Excellent, constable. He shook his fist.

MAGISTRATE: Don't repeat the answers, please, Mr Tewkesbury.

TEWKESBURY: I was savouring it, sir.

MAGISTRATE: Well don't.

TEWKESBURY: And when was the last occasion before that when you saw someone annoyed?

CONSTABLE: I cut myself shaving this morning.

TEWKESBURY: And what did you say, officer? You may say it in Latin if you prefer.

MAGISTRATE: You may not.

CONSTABLE: I said 'damn', your Worship.

TEWKESBURY: Excellent. Damn. I'm so sorry, sir. I was savouring again. And the time before that?

CONSTABLE: I can't be sure I get the order right.

TEWKESBURY: Of course not, officer. You couldn't possibly be expected to remember such things in correct order. *Lex non cogit ad impossibilia.* Well, constable, let us have another example of someone being annoyed.

CONSTABLE: I once saw someone slip and fall down in the street. He said 'bloody hell', as far as I remember.

TEWKESBURY: And the next? Your wife perhaps has burned herself in the kitchen, or dropped something?

CONSTABLE: I broke a plate the other day.

TEWKESBURY: And what did she say? You may write it down if you like.

CONSTABLE: She called me a clumsy lout.

TEWKESBURY: Admirable. And the next, please. Did your mother or father never hit you if you annoyed them?

CONSTABLE: I was smacked occasionally.

TEWKESBURY: You were a good child, no doubt, officer?

CONSTABLE: Normal, sir.

TEWKESBURY: And at school perhaps you have seen a master get annoyed?

CONSTABLE: Sometimes, sir.

TEWKESBURY: Can you think of any particular incident?

CONSTABLE: I saw one throw a book at a boy once. It missed.

TEWKESBURY: Thank you, officer. Well, that will do for the moment. You have given me six examples of people being annoyed. And now, officer, will you be good enough to tell me what the man did in this case? Did he shake his fist? Did he say 'damn' or 'bloody hell' or 'you clumsy lout'? Did he smack my client or throw a book at her? Did he do any of these things?

CONSTABLE: No, sir.

TEWKESBURY: But you say he appeared annoyed?

CONSTABLE: Yes, sir.

TEWKESBURY: Then I'm afraid I must trouble you for some more examples, officer.

MAGISTRATE: How long is this going on for?

TEWKESBURY: Well, sir, that depends on what the officer says. I am proposing to take him through every example of a person being annoyed that he remembers. And I then propose to ask whether the man in this case did any of those things.

MAGISTRATE: Why d'you say the man appeared annoyed, constable?

CONSTABLE: He just did, sir. The look on his face.

TEWKESBURY: But you had never seen the man before, officer, had you?

CONSTABLE: No, sir.

TEWKESBURY: Then he may have had a twitch? Or an itch? Or he may have just thought of something disagreeable. How can you be sure that he was annoyed? He said nothing, he did nothing, and you'd never seen his face before. you can't be sure he was annoyed with my client, can you?

CONSTABLE: I thought he was.

TEWKESBURY: But you're not absolutely sure?

CONSTABLE: Not absolutely.

TEWKESBURY: Then you're not sure?

CONSTABLE: I'm sure but not absolutely.

TEWKESBURY: I'm afraid that's impossible, officer. If you're sure, you're sure, aren't you?

CONSTABLE: I suppose so.

TEWKESBURY: You're sure, aren't you?

CONSTABLE: I suppose so.

TEWKESBURY: Well, if you're sure, you're absolutely sure, aren't you?

CONSTABLE: Not necessarily.

TEWKESBURY: Well, if you're not absolutely sure, you mean you're not quite sure?

CONSTABLE: I suppose so.

TEWKESBURY: Then the truth is that you think the man was annoyed but you're not quite sure. (*To the Magistrate*) I can go on for some time, sir, but I respectfully submit that I have now disposed of this little matter. If the constable isn't quite sure, your Worship certainly can't be.

MAGISTRATE: I think there's a doubt. Case dismissed.

TEWKESBURY: I'm much obliged to your Worship. (*In a whisper*) Don't be too annoyed, constable.

Angela tore herself away from Mr Tewkesbury with difficulty. The next call she paid was at London Sessions, where once more, she had to admit to herself, she stayed less on her father's mission than for relaxation. There she found Mr Sumpter Hedges in the full flow of his eloquence. She soon discovered that, although Mr Hedges had no difficulty in finding his voice, the barrister in John Mortimer's little classic, *The Dock Brief*, was much too near a reality for the liking of those who want criminals to be adequately defended. Mr Hedges was addressing the jury in a case where his client was accused—most properly—of receiving goods knowing them to have been stolen.

'Members of the jury,' Angela heard him saying, as she came in, 'you are men and women of the world. Suppose this had happened to you. Put yourself in my client's position. Not his present position in the dock. I would not suggest to you, members of the jury, that any of you would ever find yourselves there. But his position at 10 Elephant Road, when he came into the house and found these cartons of cigarettes in his room. Sixty thousand of them. What would you have done, members of the jury? My learned friend for the prosecution sneers at my client's explanation of what he did. But that is what the prosecution is for.'

CHAIRMAN: It is nothing of the sort.

HEDGES: Please don't interrupt.

CHAIRMAN: I shall always interrupt when you make improper remarks.

HEDGES: Then I shall leave the court.

CHAIRMAN: Continue with your address, Mr Hedges, and behave yourself.

HEDGES: I shall try again, members of the jury, but only for my unfortunate client's benefit. I was saying, when the Chairman thought fit to intervene, that my learned friend sneered at my client's explanation of what he did. Well, what would you have done? Why must the worst motives always be attributed to everyone? That is what the world suffers from to-day. Too little charity, too much suspicion. Why must every unusual action, every unusual event be presumed to be in bad faith? My client, who was once in the tobacco trade, finds these cigarettes in his room. Now, if you had once been in the tobacco trade, what would you have thought? It would have been different if they had been oranges and apples, or silk stockings. But they were not. They were cigarettes. And, members of the jury, I shall not be straining your knowledge of the world if I ask you to reflect that cigarettes form the bulk of the tobacconist's trade. Indeed that is admitted. Mr Jones, whom I cross-examined on the subject, agreed that, so far from cigarettes being a strange thing to a tobacconist, they are in effect his life-blood. Well, members of the jury, my client comes home and finds his life-blood on the floor. What more natural than that he should put it in the cupboard? My learned friend suggests that my client ought to have gone to the police. Why on earth, members of the jury? Why should he assume that there was something sinister about these cigarettes? What does a tobacconist expect to find on his premises? Iron bars, members of the jury? Flowers? Chimney pots? No, members of the jury, tobacco, and, above all, cigarettes. And now, if you please, members of the jury, the prosecution suggests that, because a tobacconist finds that a normal delivery of cigarettes has been made, he ought to assume that they have been stolen. At this rate no retailer could accept any deliveries without going to the police.

CHAIRMAN: I'm sorry to interrupt you again, Mr Hedges, but I cannot allow you in your enthusiasm to try to mislead the jury. The accused is not a tobacconist and never has been one. Twenty years ago he spent three months as a boy in a tobacconist's shop. He is not a shopkeeper at all. He is a window cleaner. He found the cigarettes, so he says, in the sitting-room of the house where he lodges. It is a private residence, not a shop.

HEDGES: Very well, My Lord, I shall retire from the case.

And, throwing his brief down on to the desk with a bang, Mr Hedges stalked out of court.

Angela waited to hear how the situation was resolved. The Chairman asked the prisoner what he would like to do—to carry on with the case himself, or to have an adjournment and a retrial with another barrister to defend him.

'I think I'll plead guilty and be done with it,' said the prisoner. 'I wanted to from the start.'

From London Sessions Angela went to the High Court, where she was relieved to find that the standard of advocacy was higher. First she sampled Mr Justice Storer's Court. The judge was speaking as she went in.

'I suppose you're relying on these cases, Mr Brownlow,' she heard him say, and then go on to mention the names of six cases dating from the eighteenth cnetury down to 1950 and to give all their references correctly. Angela could not, of course, be sure whether the cases were relevant or the references correct but, as counsel stood saying nothing, she assumed that they were. The judge then went on to refer to eight other cases and to quote from three of them. Counsel remained silent. The judge continued. Angela even began to wonder if she were seeing things and if the judge were really counsel and counsel were the judge. Certainly Mr Brownlow appeared to have one of the qualities which Angela had understood from friends was useful in a judge, the ability to keep quite quiet. Mr Justice Storer, on the other hand, appeared to be a remarkably good advocate. For, having put Mr Brownlow's case fully, as far as the law was concerned, he then proceeded to deal with the facts, and, there again, all Mr Brownlow ever said was, 'Yes, my Lord,' or 'If your Lorship pleases.' He once tried to say: 'Your Lordship is putting it so much better than I could have done,' but Angela could not tell that he was going to say that, as all the words after 'Your Lordship' were drowned in the further remarks of the judge.

Angela began to be extremely sorry for the other side, who, she gathered, was a lady called Mrs Perkins, represented by a young barrister called Space. But she soon found that her fears were quite groundless. For, as soon as Mr Brownlow had completed his almost entirely silent submission, and Mr Space had got up to reply, the judge proceeded to tell Mr Space what his argument was and to quote, Angela again assumed correctly, just as many cases as he had quoted in favour of Mr Brownlow. On Mr Brownlow's behalf the judge had certainly convinced Angela and had appeared to convince himself that the whole of English law and all the best English judges were ranged entirely against Mrs Perkins. But, once Mr Space was standing up, all the cases quoted by the learned judge appeared to show that the law was firmly established, by all the judges who mattered, in her favour. And, when it came to the facts, the same thing happened.

'And you would say, Mr Space, I suppose,' said the judge, 'that, unless your client is telling the truth, the evidence of the plaintiff himself doesn't make sense?'

'Indeed, yes, my Lord,' Mr Space managed to slip in.

'A very good way of putting it. Thank you, Mr Space,' said the judge.

Eventually, when Mr Space considered that the judge had nothing more to say, he sat down.

Thereupon, Mr Justice Storer gave judgement.

'I am most indebted,' he bagan, 'to counsel on both sides for their succinct and admirable arguments. But, if I may say so, each of them appears to have omitted several important considerations both of law and fact.'

The judge then began to refer to a dozen other cases which he had not so far mentioned, and to point out that it was really in those cases that the law applicable to this particular dispute reposed. He then proceeded to arouse that part of the law out of its sleep and, in a few well-phrased sentences (which, though of inordinate length, never got out of hand), he showed that neither Mrs Perkins nor her opponent really knew what was legally good for them.

'It is unfortunate,' he added, 'that the plaintiff did not plead this case in trespass. Had he done so, very different considerations might have applied. He could then have relied upon an entirely different line of authority.'

Having quoted eight cases in support of this proposition the judge, rather sadly, it seemed to Angela, sent them about their business with an almost curt:

'But, as I have said, that aspect of the matter does not arise.'

But, if the plaintiff had blotted his copybook by not pleading his case in trespass, the unfortunate Mrs Perkins had done no better. For she had failed to put forward the defence of 'leave and licence'. Had she done so, that would have temporarily resuscitated another eight cases. The judge referred to these, not, as he said, because they were really relevant to the matter he had to derermine but so that, if the case should happen to go to the Court of Appeal, that Court would appreciate that he had those cases well in mind.

By the time Mr Justice Storer had finished, Angela had come to the erroneous conclusion that she had heard the names of all the cases that had ever taken place in the English Courts. She was wholly unaware that Mr Justice Storer had only quoted a tiny percentage of the cases which his mind obstinately refused to forget.

Angela also formed a great admiration for the unbiased way in which the judge appeared to be determined, at one and the same time, that the plaintiff should win the case and that the defendant should not lose it. But, although she thought that this was a signal example of British fairness and of the complete impartiality of the English Bench, she felt somehow that Mr Justice Storer was not quite the man for her father. Judges, she remembered, were supposed to hear and determine cases. Admirably as Mr Justice Storer no doubt determined his cases, she did wonder when he actually heard them.

In the next court she tried, she arrived during counsel's closing address. He sounded an able man and seemed to have an extremely good case. He ended his speech with:

'And so, my Lord, with some confidence I ask you to find for the defendants.'

Whereupon the judge, without troubling counsel for the plaintiff to argue, gave judgement against the defendants for the full amount claimed by the plaintiff.

'Mr Barnstaple has, with his usual eloquence, endeavoured to persuade me to take a different view of the transaction. In my opinion there is nothing in his argument at all. Indeed, it is plain beyond a peradventure that the plaintiff's claim is made out. The only matter which has occasioned me any surprise is that the action was defended at all. The defence was doomed to failure from the start.'

Angela decided that Mr Barnstaple was not the barrister her father wanted. She realized that she was not able to judge of the merits of the case, but the point she took against Mr Barnstaple was his use of the words 'with some confidence'. If he did not know that he was going to lose the action, then, in view of the terms of the judgement, it showed that he must have a lower standard of intelligence than she at first thought. Alternatively, if he realized that he was fighting a hopeless battle, it was silly of him to use the cliché 'with some confidence', when he had in fact none.

Next she went into one of the Courts of Appeal which, at that particular time, was more like the Centre Court at Wimbledon, except that there was no applause. A singles match between two Lords Justices was in progress. Each was using Counsel rather like a ball boy, while the presiding Lord Justice acted as umpire.

'I suppose you say to that,' said Lord Justice Keen to Counsel for the appellant, 'that that point was never taken in the Court below and is not open to the respondent now?'

'I do, my Lord,' said Counsel, dutifully supplying Lord Justice Spenlow with the ball.

'What about paragraph 6?' asked Lord Justice Spenlow, making the chalk rise on the sideline.

'That quite plainly is only dealing with equitable estoppel,' replied Lord Justice Keen.

Before counsel could pick up the ball, Lord Justice Spenlow picked it up himself and returned it at speed with:

'Isn't that what we're talking about?'

'No,' said Lord Justice Keen.

By now the ball boys were standing almost idle, though ready to pick one up, whenever required.

'This is 1958 not 1872,' said Lord Justice Spenlow.

'Might I respectfully suggest,' said the presiding Lord Justice, 'that if we continue much more on this topic it will be 1972 before we reach the main point of the case.'

Lord Justice Keen immediately queried the umpire's decision, which can be done with more decorum in Appeal Court One than at Wimbledon.

'The rules of pleading must be observed,' he said.

'And the rules of common sense, fairness, and justice,' replied Lord Justice Spenlow.

Counsels' heads were now moving much like the spectators' at the side of the Court at Wimbledon.

'And those rules require that a party should put his case fairly into writing, so that the other side knows what he has to meet.'

'Personally,' said the presiding Lord Justice, 'it seems to me that that has been sufficiently done in this case.'

Angela translated this immediately into 'Fault called'.

She never learned what the case was about. She realized that it involved intricate matters of law, which laymen cannot be expected to understand. Nor could she judge of the ability or resilience of mind of the judges, as she could not follow the subject-matter with which they were dealing.

She went out into the corridor. She was standing there, looking a little disconsolate, when a young barrister in robes approached her.

'You look lost,' he said. 'Can I help you at all?'

'How kind,' said Angela. 'I wonder if you could.'

'What Court are you looking for?'

'As a matter of fact, I'm looking for a judge, not a court.'

'What's his name?'

'I've no idea.'

'That does make it difficult. Can you describe him?'

'Not physically. But he's the best you keep. Quiet on the Bench, quick, but not too quick, at understanding what's said to him.'

'By "not too quick" I suppose you mean that he doesn't interrupt counsel before he's finished a sentence, by saying: "I suppose you mean so-and-so", when, if he'd let him finish, he'd have found out that counsel meant nothing of the sort?'

'That's right,' said Angela. 'And he doesn't object to new ideas and doesn't ask questions if he knows the answers. In fact, as I said, he's the best judge you've got, full of learning but not parading it, courteous, kind, firm, with a mind of his own but ready to listen

to other people's views before he comes to a conclusion. In which
Court shall I find him?'

'Well,' said the young man, 'I'm not a judge yet, but meantime
I think Halliday's the man you want. He's in Q.B.3 to-day. I've
just done a case in front of him.'

'Would you mind telling me your name?' asked Angela. 'I might
want a barrister one of these days.'

'I'm sorry to hear that.'

'I've nothing special in mind, but one never knows. And you've
been very kind.'

'I'm afraid that doesn't necessarily mean that I'm any good at
the Bar.'

'Aren't you?'

'It's difficult to tell. I don't think I'm bad, but then I shouldn't
be much use if I did. I can't be good yet, as I haven't been going
long enough.'

'Well, if you can tell a good judge when you see one, that must
be a recommendation.'

'Oh, everyone knows Halliday. What he says to-day the House
of Lords says to-morrow. He's for stardom. The only question is
where and when.'

'That sounds like my judge,' said Angela. 'Could you tell me
which way to go?'

'I'll take you there, if I may.'

'It is good of you.'

'Not at all. I should like to.'

On the way to Court 3, Angela asked her guide when she could
have the chance of hearing him in action.

'I don't often come here,' he said. 'I'm mostly in the County
Court at present. Don't suppose you'd be interested, but I'm at
Hampstead to-morrow.'

'Could I come?'

'Well, of course, but I can't conceive why you should want to.
Now here we are.'

Angela found that the qualities of Mr Justice Halliday had not
been exaggerated to her. There was no doubt at all about it. This
was the judge her father wanted. He might have been made to
measure. She had succeeded in one part of her task. Now for the
other. She wondered about her companion.

'You haven't yet told me your name,' she said.

'It's Southdown as a matter of fact, Charles Southdown. May I be introduced?'

'I'm Angela Walsh. How d'you do? You've been a tremendous help to me. I am grateful. May I come to Hampstead to-morrow?'

'I'll call for you and drive you there if you like.'

'No, I won't let you do that,' said Angela, 'though it's extremely kind.'

She was not particularly anxious to disclose that she was the daughter of Lonsdale Walsh, and, as she still lived in his house, disclosure would in all probability be necessary if the young man called for her. It was not that she was ashamed of her father. He had told her that his conviction was based on perjury and she believed him implicitly. But it was sometimes embarrassing and she hated people being sorry for her.

They walked along the corridor. Charles pointed to a Court.

'Old Boniface is in there,' he said. 'He tried Lonsdale Walsh, you know. Oh, of course, your name's Walsh. No relation, I suppose?' he added with a laugh.

CHAPTER 5

Caught up in the Machine

When Lonsdale heard from Angela that she had found his judge and that she had considerable hopes that she had found a barrister too, he went into conference with Spikey and began to formulate his plans in greater detail.

Spikey listened with the happiest anticipation. When Lonsdale had finished Spikey said:

'Now, the bloke you want is the Boss.'

'Can he be trusted?'

'Now, look, guv. Do you trust me?'

'Would I be telling you all this if I didn't?'

'Right, you wouldn't. Then why do you trust me, guv?'

'Because I think you want the money and, provided there's enough money and not too much risk, there's no reason not to.'

'Right. Well, the Boss is the same. If he likes the job and the pay's right, 'e's safe as me aunt's grandmother and she died ten years back.'

'Good. Where is he now?'

'Well, unless 'e's 'ad a bit of bad luck, 'e's out at the moment; going straight they call it.'

'All right, Spikey. You go and see him as soon as you get out and tell him what we want. My daughter will give you all the money you need. I've already told her that you'll be calling on her when you get out and that she's to give you all the help you ask for. She'll understand that, but just to be on the safe side, try to smuggle this out with you.'

Lonsdale gave him a minute piece of paper on which he had written: 'And I mean all.'

'Angela will look after you and the Boss all right. Now, the only thing is, how are you to let me know?'

Spikey winked.

'You'll know all right,' he said, 'if your daughter understands this note. There ain't a prison wall which fifty nicker won't go through—and less,' he said.

'Right,' said Lonsdale. 'Well, I hope it won't be long now.'

Some little time before, Angela had gone to the County Court to hear Charles perform. She had formed an immediate liking for the young man and realized that she must guard against prejudice in his favour. She did not precisely know why her father needed his services, but she was quite determined not to recommend anyone just because she had a liking for him. Her father had said, however, that experience was less important than intelligence and mental resilience. So he was certainly a possible. But she was taking no chances and proposed to listen to him in action, even more critically than she had listened to the others.

She arrived at the County Court and sat in the public benches as near the front as possible. Judge Smoothe was presiding, an elderly man of a kindly disposition; not a profound lawyer, but with a keen sense of justice and a desire to do the right thing between the parties. Moreover, he was not simply anxious that the result of every dispute should be fair but that it should, as far as possible, also be satisfactory to both parties. In consequence he was known at the Bar as 'Old Settlement', for, in a very large number of cases, he persuaded the parties to agree to a compromise judgement. He did not always realize that, though such behaviour on the Bench may be of great value, it is a two-edged weapon. In a good number of the cases, where as a result of the judge's desire to satisfy everyone, the case was settled, the consequence in fact was that no one was satisfied. Judges and lawyers are good at trying to heal wounds and bring warring parties together and they are often successful, but it is important to ensure that this method of approach is not used or pursued to the end in inappropriate cases.

Sometimes Judge Smoothe would smile happily to himself, as he disrobed, about a settlement he had procured, and even make a remark on the subject to the usher who was assisting him.

'Very satisfactory, don't you think, Walters?'

'Very satisfactory indeed, your Honour.'

Naturally Mr Walters always agreed with his judge, but there was no sycophancy about it at all. He had been the judge's usher for many years and it was not strange that they began to think alike. Indeed, the usher could have given most valuable advice to the parties in many of the cases.

'Much better than fighting it out,' the judge went on. 'No one would have gained. A lot of mud slung, probably another day's costs incurred, and no one any the better off.'

'Very lucky they had you to try it, your Honour. I'm not sure that the parties always appreciate what you do for them.'

This was unconscious humour on Mr Walters's part, because at that very moment both counsel in the case were having the greatest difficulty in parrying the verbal blows of their respective clients.

'I came here to get my rights.' said the plaintiff. 'And what have I got? A bloody sausage.'

'Well, you did agree to the settlement,' said his counsel timidly.

'Of course I agreed. What else could I do with the old basket looking at me over his spectacles and telling me I'd bloody well got to?'

Judge Smoothe had not put it so indecorously, but unquestionably the plaintiff had got the point correctly. What the judge had in fact said was:

'Of course, if the plaintiff wishes me to try the case, I will do so. That is what I am here for. But I think he would be wise to bear in mind that no case is won until judgement is given, and, even then, it may be reversed on appeal. Moreover, even if the plaintiff should win, would it give him real satisfaction to live in the same house as a person over whom he has triumphed? Injunctions between neighbours do not make for good relationship. A friendly smile is worth far more than damages. I repeat that, if the plaintiff is prepared to take the risk of losing or of winning and finding it a barren victory, I will, of course, proceed with the hearing. But don't you think it would be wise, Mr Gathermore, if the plaintiff consulted you before taking the final decision?'

'Bloody well settle,' is certainly shorter but it is not the way judges talk.

On the day when Angela went to Judge Smoothe's court, Charles was appearing for the defendant in a case where a lady had somehow or other got her hair tangled in a washing machine. She complained that the machine was unsafe or alternatively that there ought to be a warning on it that people with long hair should tie it up before using the machine. Fortunately her hair was not torn off and her main complaint was the shock which she had suffered.

Her husband had come into the kitchen just in time and cut off the current. The plaintiff now said that she was too nervous to use the washing machine, and that in consequence she had either to do the washing in a tub, which took much longer, or send it out, which was more expensive. In addition she and her husband said that instead of being a happy, gay young woman, she had become moody and irritable.

'I hope,' said Charles, when he rose to cross-examine her, 'that I shan't irritate you too much. I shall try not to do so. Tell me, Mrs Small, do you feel irritated at the moment?'

'I feel nervous.'

'A lot of people feel like that in the witness box,' said the judge, 'and I'm not surprised. I'm only surprised at how calm most of them appear on the surface. Would you like to sit down while you give your evidence?'

'No thank you, your Honour.'

'What form does your irritability take?' went on Charles.

'I just feel irritable.'

'And how do you act when you feel irritable? Do you bite your husband's head off?'

'I wouldn't say that.'

'Well, that's something. Do you jump if you hear a bang?'

'Yes, I do.'

'And didn't you before the accident?'

'I don't know. I suppose I did.'

'Do you burst into tears suddenly for no reason?'

'I wouldn't say that.'

'Then what form does your irritability take? I've made a few suggestions. Can you help me at all about this?'

'I just feel irritable.'

'Could anyone tell that you feel irritable?'

'I don't know. I suppose so.'

'Why do you suppose so? Unless you do something to show that you're irritable, how should anyone know that you are?'

'I don't really know—now you put it like that.'

'Perhaps "irritable" is the wrong word. Perhaps you just have bouts of being moody and depressed? Is that right?'

'Yes, perhaps it is.'

'I suppose that happened to you occasionally before the accident, as it happens to most people?'

'I suppose so.'

'If you get a large award of damages in this case, do you think you will feel less depressed?'

Before the witness could answer, Judge Smoothe intervened.

'I don't think that's quite a fair way of putting it, Mr Southdown,' he said. 'The witness hasn't said she's depressed at the moment, only that she's nervous.'

'I'm sorry, your Honour,' said Charles. 'Do you feel depressed at the moment, Mrs Small?'

'It's all so strange here, I don't really know.'

'Did you feel depressed yesterday then?'

'Not all yesterday.'

'Then did you feel depressed at some time yesterday?'

'I think I did.'

'When?'

'I can't be sure.'

'Why did you feel depressed?'

'I don't know really.'

'Were you thinking about the case?'

'I may have been.'

'That depressed you?'

After a further short cross-examination about her shock and extra expense, Charles turned his attention to the question of liability. Within a very few minutes he had tied up Mrs Small in much the same way as the washing machine had tied up her hair. And half an hour later Judge Smoothe, in giving judgement for the suppliers and manufacturers of the washing machine, said this:

'There seems to be an impression to-day that, if someone is injured, someone else has got to pay. I cannot conceive any other reason for this action being brought. It was doomed to failure from the start. The accident was obviously due entirely to the plaintiff's carelessness. There was nothing whatsoever wrong with the machine. As for the suggestion that there ought to be a warning notice on the machine, you might as well suggest that the manufacturers of the machine should supply a nursemaid with every machine. If you bang your head against a wall it will hurt. If you hang your hair over moving machinery of course it may get caught up in it. The case is too plain for argument. I can only hope that the depression which may descend on Mrs Small as a result of this judgement may be of short duration. My advice to her is to forget all about it and to start using the washing machine again. But she should keep her hair up when she does so, charming as it must look when it is loose.'

At the close of her day in Court, Angela was satisfied that, in spite of his inexperience, Charles would do as well as anyone for her father. She wrote and told him so. Within a short time of his receiving the letter, Spikey was released and things began to happen.

CHAPTER 6

Invitor and Invitee

Spikey called on Angela the day after his release, and produced the note from her father.

'How much d'you want?' she asked Spikey.

Spikey told her.

'What d'you want all that for?'

Spikey told her.

'I see,' she said, 'and when is all this going to happen?'

'That depends on the Boss, Miss. 'Aven't seen 'im yet. 'E may have some other engagements. But I don't suppose 'e'll be long. 'E's got to get everyone organized, though. You can't rush these things.'

But, though things were not rushed, they happened, and, as a direct consequence, Douglas Broadwater received a telephone call which, though it pleased his wife, was a very great surprise to them both. Douglas had been Treasury Counsel at the Old Bailey for some years and he had in fact been one of those engaged for the prosecution against Lonsdale. Mary Broadwater was very anxious for Douglas to become a judge in due course, and she complained to him from time to time that he did not attend legal gatherings enough. She believed—quite wrongly—that, by associating regularly with the right people, Douglas would increase his chance of promotion to the Bench.

Douglas was not a particularly sociable person, and did not care for garden parties, cocktail parties, or the like. Indeed, he did not much care for going out to dinner. He was an able man at his job and had few other interests, except reading. He and Mary were very happily married and their disagreement on the subject of going out and about did not disturb their happy relationship. But Mary never stopped urging Douglas to do what she wanted.

They were both equally surprised at the telephone call, but Mary was delighted.

'You'll accept, of course,' she said, and on this occasion Douglas did not feel that he could refuse, though he was completely astounded at the invitation. He had answered the telephone and had been told that Mr Justice Halliday wished to speak to him. He had appeared before Halliday on a number of occasions but he did not know him personally and he could not conceive why the judge whould suddenly telephone on a Thursday evening. That was odd enough, but the conversation was even more odd. For Halliday had invited Douglas and Mary to come and spend the week-end with him. If he had not clearly recognized the judge's distinctive voice, he would have imagined that a practical joker was responsible. But there was no doubt about it. It was Halliday speaking. It was true that the judge apologized for the shortness of the notice and added that he had been wanting to invite them for some time but had never got round to it, but it was none the less one of the most extraordinary things that had ever happened.

'I just can't understand it,' he said to Mary. 'He doesn't know me. We don't belong to the same club. I don't think we've ever met out of Court. Why on earth should he invite us? It doesn't make sense.'

'Well, I don't know why it is,' said Mary, 'but it's a jolly good thing. He's just being sociable, I expect. Probably thinks that the Bar and the Bench should get together a bit more. You remember this when you're a judge. I'm glad I was in the room when he phoned, or I believe you'd have refused.'

'I must say he made it very difficult for me to say "no". It was almost like a Royal Command. What time shall we start?'

Mr Justice Halliday was a bachelor who lived in a house in the country called Howard House. It was not far from London. He had made a very large income at the Bar in the days when a man could retain a reasonable proportion of his earnings after paying income tax and surtax, and his attractive house stood in the middle of about ten acres of land. As Douglas and Mary drove up the long drive they were still discussing the possible reason for their visit.

'I wonder what a policeman's doing outside the front door?' said Mary, as they were driving up to it.

'I expect he's had a threatening letter or something,' Douglas suggested.

The judge opened the door to them himself and welcomed them.

'I'm afraid you must have thought it a bit odd being invited at the last moment, but I'm delighted you could come.'

He was about to show them to their room, when Douglas suddenly remembered an important telephone call that he needed to make.

'I'm so sorry, judge,' he said, 'but might I use the telephone?'

'Whom d'you want to phone?'

'A chap in London.'

'I'm afraid not,' said the judge.

Halliday had no reputation for meanness, but Douglas could only assume that he grudged the amount of the toll call.

'I'm terribly sorry to be a nuisance,' he said in a somewhat embarrassed voice, 'but the call is rather important and—and—of course, I'd want you to let me pay for it.'

'That's beside the point,' said the judge. 'I'm afraid you can't use the telephone, and that's all there is to it.'

'Well,' said Douglas, 'I'd better go down to the village and make it. It is rather important. I want my clerk to alter a conference for Tuesday.'

'Tuesday will keep,' said the judge.

'But I'd really like to let him know now, judge, and if you'll forgive me . . .'

'I'll forgive you certainly,' said the judge, 'but you can't go down to the village, and there we are. Shall I take you to your room?'

CHAPTER 7

The House Party

Miles Hampton, who was one of the witnesses for the prosecution at Lonsdale's trial, had had a varied life. He had never been very successful. Possibly his greatest success was in the witness box at the Old Bailey, where he withstood all the efforts of defending counsel to make him deviate from his original story. He came out of the box in the same good state and condition in which he went in. No sweat pouring down the face; no glass of water for him; he required no assistance from the judge. As calmly as his jerky method of speaking allowed, he told his story, and one juryman actually said quietly to his neighbour:

'Well, he's obviously telling the truth.'

And so it appeared. Yes, it had been a good day for Miles Hampton.

He did not have so many good days. He was the kind of man for whom no one is sorry, because he never appeared to need sympathy. One day he would be found in the Thames, or under an omnibus, and his friends and acquaintances would wonder why on earth he did it. Such a happy type. Not a care in the world. Up to a point they would be right. Apart from a desire to know where the next meal and the rent were coming from, Miles had few cares. But he took almost a childish delight in keeping up appearances. He certainly had no success at making money or love or any of the things which most people think important, but it was his ability to keep up appearances which made people think he had nothing to worry about. He wore well-cut expensive clothes, for which he sometimes paid. Usually by instalments ordered by the local county court judge.

'But really Mr . . . Mr Hampton,' Judge Knight had said to him, 'if you can afford to go to an expensive tailor, you can afford to pay him.'

'I'm afraid that doesn't follow, your Honour,' Miles had replied
blandly. 'I find it much cheaper to buy one really good suit than
several shoddy ones.'

'I've no doubt you do, if you don't pay for it.'

'But I shall, your Honour, given time. Unfortunately I have been
out of employment for the last three years.'

'What is your occupation?'

'I've told your Honour, none—at the moment.'

'But when you do get a job, what sort of job do you do?'

'Anything honest within my capabilities, your Honour. I have no
particular qualifications. I would take up bricklaying but I gather
it's a skilled occupation. I would do ordinary labourer's work, but
unfortunately I have a weak heart. I would sell newspapers but I
can't get a pitch.'

'What are your qualifications?'

Miles looked down at his feet inside the witness box and then up
again to the judge, as though making a swift appraisal of himself.

'I have had some administrative experience, your Honour. I was
a major during the war. For a short time I was a permanent
president of Courts Martial. I learned a little law then, but not
really enough to become a qualified lawyer.'

'What are you living on?'

'I sometimes wonder myself, your Honour. I have had National
Assistance, though I prefer to do without it when I can.'

'This is hopeless,' said Judge Knight to the creditor's solicitor.
'Your client had better forget it. Unless you'd like to make Mr
Hampton bankrupt. The debt is £60, I see.'

'I don't think that would do much good,' the solicitor had said.

'If only I could get a job I'd pay the debt at once,' Miles had
said, and he meant it.

At about the time Mr Justice Halliday was showing the Broad-
waters to their room, Miles was sitting in his room, wondering
how to spend the day, when his landlady sent a man up to him.

'Come in,' said Miles.

The stranger came in.

'You Miles Hampton?' he said.

'That's right.'

'Ever done any crowd work?'

'Films, you mean?'

'Yep.'

'Twice,' said Miles.

'Want a job?'

Miles repressed a choking feeling in his throat. He was a senti-
mental person and sentimentalized about himself. This incredible
answer to his needs made him want to cry. After a moment he said:

'Yes, I could do with it. How many days?'

'Three or four. Can't be sure.'

'When does it start?'

'Now.'

'How did you hear of me?'

'You're on the list.'

'Good Lord, I didn't know they were so efficient. Right. Where
is it?'

'Just out of London.'

'How do I get there?'

'I'll take you.'

'That's very kind.'

'Better bring a few things. It's on location. May have to stay
there.'

'O.K.,' said Miles.

Ten minutes later he was being driven towards Mr Justice Halliday's house. When they arrived, he pointed to the man outside the
door.

'Real policeman?' he asked.

'You bet,' said the man, and they went in.

The same afternoon Angela telephoned Charles's chambers, and
spoke to him. He was delighted to hear from her again.

'I'm afraid you'll think this very odd after our very short
acquaintanceship,' she said, 'but I wondered if by any chance you'd
be free this week-end. I've been asked to take someone to a week-
end party. I shall quite understand if you'd rather not, but could
you come?'

'I should love it,' said Charles. 'I shan't even look to see if I've
any other engagements, because, if I have, I shall cancel them.'

'How nice you are,' said Angela. 'I deserved a snub.'

'Nothing of the kind,' said Charles. 'How do we go? Shall I drive
you?'

'That would be lovely.'

They made the necessary arrangements and that evening Angela
and Charles drove to the house of Mr Justice Halliday.

'Why the policeman?' he asked on arrival.

'Your guess is as good as mine,' said Angela, a remark which would have made her father blush.

The party at Mr Justice Halliday's house was now beginning to take shape, but there were more guests to come.

One of the witnesses against Lonsdale was dead, and his widow was at home when a cheerful stranger called on her.

'Mrs Elsie Meadowes?' he asked.

'That's me.'

'Widow of the late Kenneth Meadowes?'

'Well, I was, but I'm courting again.'

'Glad to hear it, Mrs Meadowes. I've come just at the right time.'

'Why? Who are you?'

'You go in for the pools, don't you, Mrs Meadowes?'

'I do sometimes, but never 'ave no luck.'

'That's all changed, Mrs Meadowes. You've had some luck.'

'Me? I 'aven't won, 'ave I?'

'Not in the way you expected, but you've won just the same.'

''Ow much?'

'Well, I'm not sure, but I'll explain. Although we get a lot of winners on our pools, we want to encourage the people who don't win. So we've decided that a certain amount of the money will be set aside and a prize given out of it each week to certain losers selected at random. And you're one of the lucky losers, Mrs Meadowes. Congratulations.'

He held out his hand.

'Well I never. About 'ow much will it be?'

'Well, not less than a hundred pounds—perhaps more.'

'Well, if that ain't the best thing I've 'eard since Jimmy got the compensation. When do I get it?'

'Now—if you come with me. The first award is going to be made in person.'

Half an hour later they were on their way to Mr Justice Halliday.

''Ere, where is this?' said Mrs Meadowes. 'And what's a copper doing 'ere?'

'To see that no one pinches the stuff. Come along in, Mrs Meadowes.'

The late Mr Meadowes had had a good deal to do with judges, who had imposed varying sentences upon him, but he would never have imagined that his widow was actually going to be entertained in a judge's house.

The house party was now nearly complete. One of the prospective guests, Herbert Adams, was difficult to find, but he was traced in the end. He was on a bench in the park. Two men approached him.

'Herbert Adams?' said one of them.

'Well?' said Adams suspiciously.

'We're police officers,' said one of the men, 'and we want you to come along with us to answer some questions.'

'I ain't done nothing,' said Mr Adams.

'Then that's all the better for you,' said the man. 'Come along.'

And Mr Adams, without further protest, walked with the men to a car and was soon being driven to Mr Justice Halliday's house.

'Wot's this?' he said on arrival. 'This ain't a police station.'

'It's temporary,' said one of the men. 'While the other's being repaired.'

Jo Barnwell lived in an attractive house in the Regent's Park area. She was just leaving it when a small boy dashed in front of a car, narrowly missed it and then fell flat on the pavement and remained still. She at once ran to him. The boy was motionless. A fat man was getting out of the car. He helped Jo to lift up the boy. He seemed unconscious and his face appeared to be covered with blood.

'We'd better take him to the hospital,' said the man. 'I wonder if you'd mind helping?'

'Of course not,' said Jo.

Together they lifted the little boy into the car.

'I wonder if you'd mind sitting with him while I drive?'

'Certainly.'

The man got into the driving seat and drove off. He stopped at the corner and two other men got in. One got in beside the driver and the other in the back.

'Which is the nearest hospital d'you think?' the fat man asked Jo.

Jo told him, but her attention was mainly taken up with the boy. So she did not notice for a few minutes that the car was not going towards the hospital she had mentioned.

'You're going the wrong way,' she then said.

'I know the house surgeon at the hospital we're going to,' said the driver.

As Jo had not seen the small boy rehearsing his part that morning several times, and covering his face with red paint, she did not become suspicious until the car was nearly out of London.

'Where are you going to?' she asked eventually. 'This boy ought to be seen to at once.'

'He's O.K.,' said the man next to her. 'All right, Tommy, you can wake up now.'

Tommy sat up and grinned.

'Now don't make a fuss, madam,' said the fat man. 'You'll be quite all right, if you behave. But it's three and a half to one, and chloroform's a nasty business. We might give you too much.'

'Where are we going?' she asked.

'You'll see.'

And in due course Jo found herself at Mr Justice Halliday's house. She was momentarily relieved to see the man at the door.

'Officer,' she called.

'Yes, madam,' he said, coming up to them.

'I've been kidnapped by these men,' she said.

'Well, if you'll go through the front door and take the first door on the right, they'll take all particulars.'

Jo had not fully taken in this extraordinary behaviour by the policeman when her companions took her into the house.

One hour later another car drove up to the house, and Lonsdale got out and walked swiftly inside. A companion followed more slowly, after saying to the man at the door:

'That's the lot, I think.'

CHAPTER 8

Address of Welcome

Half an hour later the guests were all assembled in the drawing-room, when Lonsdale came in.

'I might have known it,' said Jo.

'Evening, Jo, nice to see you,' said Lonsdale. 'Now, if you're all comfortable, I'll explain. First of all, let me apologize to you all—particularly to you, Sir George, for the somewhat unusual methods I have been compelled to adopt.'

'I hope you realize,' said Mr Justice Halliday, 'that, although you are undergoing a sentence of imprisonment for life, you can not only be sentenced for your present crimes with a sentence to begin after your life imprisonment is over . . .'

'That is hardly a deterrent, Sir George,' interrupted Lonsdale.

'You know quite well what I mean. A sentence of life imprisonment is reviewed after ten years and normally the convicted person is released after serving anything from ten years to fifteen years. What I was going to add was that conduct such as yours will presumably result in your serving the maximum sentence for your original crime, in addition to the further sentence which I mentioned.'

'That is a risk I must face,' said Lonsdale, 'but let me say at once that, as far as most of you are concerned, I do very much regret the steps which I have had to take. But I venture to suggest that you must agree that there was no alternative open to me. Now, what are the facts? Eighteen months ago I was convicted of the murder of Adolphus Barnwell. I was convicted on perjured evidence. There is the woman who procured my conviction by that evidence.'

'There stands the man who murdered my husband,' said Jo.

'Don't interrupt please, Jo,' said Lonsdale. 'You'll have plenty of time to say your piece later. After my conviction, I appealed to the

Court of Criminal Appeal. My appeal was dismissed. I petitioned the Home Secretary, to no avail. I asked my Member of Parliament and other friends to have my case reviewed. It was hopeless. Nothing could be done. Now, Sir George, would you mind assuming, just for one moment, just for the purpose of argument, that in fact my conviction was procured as I have said. What other course was open to me? For most people there would have been no alternative but to suffer the sentence. But I was able to do something else. Admittedly I have had to break the law in order to do so. I have had to escape from prison and to induce all of you by one method or another to assemble in this house. You, Sir George, I have very regretfully had to make a prisoner in your own house. None of you I hope will suffer any more discomfort than is absolutely necessary. You will, I am sure, understand that every precaution will have to be taken to prevent you from communicating with the outside world. No one is going to come here looking for an escaped convict. But all the necessary steps have been taken to deal with friends and tradesmen who may call or telephone. None of you will suffer in the slightest degree, provided you make no actual or apparent attempt to get help. The judge has pointed out that my offences are already such that I have really nothing to fear from any further crimes which may be committed by me or on my behalf. So I do beg you all to be sensible and to make no show of resistance.

'Now, why are you here? Most of you will have guessed. We have the transcript of my trial, photostat copies of the documents, all the chief witnesses, except one, who gave evidence, and the lady who paid them. Now don't interrupt, Jo. You know you did. I am proposing, with the assistance of the two members of the Bar present, to go through the whole of the evidence at my trial in such a way as to satisfy the judge that what I have said is true. If, after this new trial, as I may call it, the judge is satisfied that my conviction was properly procured, I shall give myself up to the police and take the consequences of my actions. But if, as I am quite confident I can do, I satisfy him that hardly a word of truth was spoken at my trial, then I hope that in those circumstances the judge will take such steps as he thinks proper to put the matter right. I shall certainly surrender to the police, but I venture to suggest that no one can then fairly complain at my unorthodox methods of showing that the jury in returning their verdict of guilty

were grossly misled. How long this trial will take I naturally cannot
say, but in the intervals between the sessions every endeavour will
be made to make you as comfortable as possible. Now, are there
any questions?'

'What do you want us to do?' asked Broadwater.

'I should like you to be kind enough to conduct the case on behalf
of the prosecution, and your learned colleague, Mr Southdown, to
conduct the case on my behalf. I apologize for the absence of any
solicitors to instruct you but, in the circumstances, I'm sure you
won't mind interviewing the witnesses yourselves. It may be of some
help to you if I say that, while the witnesses whom Mr Broadwater
will see will tell him all manner of lies, I shall tell Mr Southdown
nothing but the truth.'

'Mr Walsh,' said the judge, 'if this affair is going to serve any
useful purpose. I should advise you to stop persisting in saying that
your case is right and the prosecution's is wrong. It doesn't impress
me in the least. Dozens of rightly convicted criminals say the same
thing, when they are trying to get off on appeal. It has no value at
all.'

'Thank you for your guidance, Sir George,' said Lonsdale. 'I will
try to benefit from it. But I hope you will understand that the
reason I emphasize these matters is because I feel very strongly
about them. I have been in prison for eighteen months as a result
of lies, and she knows it.'

'There you go again,' said Mr Justice Halliday.

'I'm sorry,' said Lonsdale. 'Now, I suggest that we have dinner
shortly and go to bed early. In the morning Counsel on each side
can get his instructions and by, say, twelve o'clock, they should be
ready to present the case to you, Sir George. Will that be convenient
to you all? Good. I take silence for consent. Spikey, could you
arrange about drinks?'

CHAPTER 9

No Escape

Later that evening the judge explained to Charles and Broadwater how the whole thing had started, as far as he was concerned. On the Thursday evening he had been dining by himself when his manservant informed him that a police inspector would like to see him. He was shown in at once.

'I'm so sorry to disturb you, my Lord,' he said, 'but the police have just received some urgent information. It may be a hoax but we don't think it is. I don't know if you remember sentencing a man called Thorowgood—an inappropriate name, if I may say so, my Lord—for robbery with violence? He got seven years.'

'You must tell me more about the case if you want me to remember. Names mean very little to me,' said the judge.

'Well, either at the trial or down below in the cells, he was heard to swear vengeance against you. He said it was an unfair trial and an unfair sentence and, to use his own words, he was going to get you.'

'I can't say that I remember anything about it,' said the judge, 'but convicted people do sometimes shout threats. As far as I know, no attempt has ever been made to carry them out.'

'That's right, my lord,' said the man, 'until tonight.'

'What has happened?'

'Thorowgood has escaped.'

'I've seen nothing about it in the papers, and there's nothing on the wireless.'

'I know, my Lord. In view of the information we had, it was decided not to assist the man in any way. You see, my Lord, when it's published that a man has escaped, something has to be put in the papers as to the steps being taken to recapture him. You know the sort of thing, my Lord—his house is being watched, or a search is being made in the woods near so-and-so, or it is believed that he escaped in a small blue car heading for the North; road blocks are being established round a wide area. That information may be true or false, but, whichever it is, it gives the man something to think about. Now, if nothing is said at all, it makes him jittery to begin with. The silence must worry him. Where are they searching? What are they doing? Indeed, has his escape been discovered yet? And so on.'

'Yes,' said the judge, 'but where do I come into all this?'

'My Lord,' said the man, 'there is another very special reason why we don't want to publish anything at the moment. We have pretty reliable information that not only is he heading in this direction with a view to carrying out his threat, but that he is going to be accompanied by several armed men to assist him. They're a very determined gang, and the police are very anxious to catch the lot. With your Lordship's assistance, I think we can. Would your Lordship tell me who lives in this house?'

'I live here with a cook and a manservant only,' said the judge.

'Trusted servants?'

'I've had them for years.'

'I don't want to alarm your Lordship, but we have information that two masked men were in Brocket Wood, five miles from here. What the police would like to do, if your Lordship will permit it, is to fill this house with plain clothes police officers, themselves masked, and wait until the attempt is made. We then hope to get the lot.'

'What's the object of the masks?'

'Well, my Lord, we believe that there are about ten or more men in this, coming from different directions. If one of them sees a masked man he will at once assume that he's one of the gang.'

'But mightn't it be dangerous for your own men, if one of them mistook one of his colleagues for one of the gang?'

'That's all been provided for, my Lord. They will wear a special type of mask and, of course, in addition there's a password.'

'I see,' said the judge. 'Well, it's all very odd, but, if that's what you want to do, I suppose I'd better let you do it. But I hope you won't make too much mess.'

'You leave that to us,' said the man. 'Thank you very much, my Lord. I'd be grateful if you and your staff would all go into one room above the ground floor, so that we can give you complete protection.'

'All right,' said the judge. 'When d'you want to start?'

Ten minutes later nine masked men were admitted into the judge's house, while he and his cook and manservant chatted in one of the bedrooms.

Not very long afterwards, the 'inspector' came into the bedroom.

'There's been a bit of a mistake,' he said. 'Thorowgood hasn't escaped after all.'

'Good,' said the judge. 'Then we can go downstairs again,' and he led the way to the drawing-room. In it were eight masked men.

'You might remove those things now,' said the judge.

'I'm afraid this is going to be a bit of a shock to you,' said the man who had fetched the judge, 'but we are not policemen.'

'Then who are you?'

'That doesn't matter,' said the man, 'but I'd better tell you what is going to happen. We are going to hold you and your staff prisoners and the house will be in a state of siege. But, provided you do what we tell you, no harm will come to any of you. On the other hand, if there is the slightest attempt to escape or call for help, I cannot be answerable for the consequences. Is that understood?'

'I hear what you say,' said the judge.

'Good,' said the man. 'Now, first thing in the morning, you will telephone to the Law Courts and say that you're not feeling very well and won't be able to sit that day and possibly not for a few days longer. If, in the course of that conversation you attempt to give the alarm in any way, it will be the worse for all of you. And you might bear in mind that none of us can be identified. You may have been surprised to notice that the uniformed man you first saw had a beard. Unusual in a police officer. And glasses. No doubt you'll be able to tell the police the colour of his hair and his approximate height. Any other information you give will be quite valueless.'

'What is the object of this outrage?' asked the judge.

'You'll learn in due course. The next thing you must do is to telephone to a Mr Broadwater, a barrister, and ask him and his wife to stay here for the week-end.'

'And if I refuse?'

'Don't,' said the man.

There was a slight pause, and the man turned to the cook and said in a somewhat menacing tone:

'You don't want him to refuse, do you?'

The cook thereupon fainted.

'You see,' said the man. 'She'd like you to telephone, and so should we. Shall I get you the number?'

'But I don't know him, or his wife.'

'You must make some excuse for asking him. After all, you're a judge and he's a barrister. He'll want to come. I expect he's appeared in your court from time to time.'

And so it came about that the judge telephoned and invited Broadwater and his wife for the week-end.

CHAPTER 10

Conversation Pieces

After the judge had explained what had happened, he lowered his voice and added:

'There is one thing we can do. I've done it already, as a matter of fact.'

'What's that, Judge?' asked Charles.

'Well, it's only a possibility, but it's worth trying. But it depends on the wind. I've written several notes calling for help, and, if there was a bit of a breeze, thrown them out of the window. One of them went quite a long way.'

'Did you see what happened to it?'

'I did,' said the judge. 'It was eaten by a cow.'

'We can all try it,' said Charles.

'Don't do it unless a wind gets up. Otherwise they'll just drop down and may be found.'

At that moment Lonsdale came into the room.

'I hope you're not finding things too inconvenient,' he said. 'If there are any urgent messages you want to send to anyone, I'm sure it can be arranged—provided you make no attempt to give an alarm.'

'How long do you propose to keep us here?' asked the judge.

'No longer than is necessary,' said Lonsdale. 'How long d'you think it'll take? The first trial took two days. This shouldn't take much longer. Perhaps not as long.'

'I can't think what good you imagine it will do you,' said the judge.

'Well,' said Lonsdale, 'without wishing to appear impertinent, you should. Supposing I did satisfy you that the whole case against me was a fake. What would you do?'

'I don't feel called upon to answer that question,' said the judge.

'Well, of course not,' said Lonsdale. 'There's no reason why you should answer. But I can't conceive that any judge, who was satisfied that there had been a verdict procured entirely by perjury, would do nothing about it, just because he only learned of the fact through completely unlawful means. You'd do something about it, wouldn't you,' he said, turning to Broadwater, 'if you were a judge? And you?' he added, to Charles.

Both of them took their lead from the judge and said nothing.

'Well, it doesn't matter,' said Lonsdale. 'I've enough faith in you all to make me think this is worth doing. You all loathe injustice, and I'm quite sure that, if any of you saw what you believed to be a gross piece of injustice you would take all the steps you could to have the matter put right. Almost anyone in the country would. And, whatever people may say about lawyers, I'm quite sure that they'd be the first to try to remedy an injustice they'd heard of, if they knew there was no one else who could do anything about it. Well, I mustn't detain you any longer, gentlemen. You know where you are sleeping, I think. I hope you'll have as good a night as possible.'

Lonsdale next paid a call on Jo. She was in bed reading.

'Forgive me for not knocking,' he said.

'I forgive you for nothing,' said Jo. 'Why did God make you such a bloody man?'

'My dear Jo, that's a line of inquiry which it would suit few people to indulge in. Even you, for instance. He'll have quite a lot of questions to ask you, when you get up there.'

'Thanks for saying "up".'

'I don't believe there's a down. We all go to Heaven. The only difference is that some of us won't like it. You, for instance, you won't find anyone to fight.'

'What about you? You fight hard enough.'

'That's only to get my way, not because I like it. You enjoy a fight for its own sake.'

'Perhaps I do. I'll put you back in gaol if it's the last thing I do.'

'You won't have to, Jo. I shall go back on my own, as soon as this is over.'

'I'll get you back before it's over if I can, and I'll see you stay longer when you do get back.'

'They may not ask you, Jo. Granted you put me there, it's not your business any longer. It'll be up to the judge then. It's up to

me at the moment. What does it feel like to be in my power? Do
you love every moment of it? It must be a new experience.'

'A very unpleasant one.'

'But you don't really dislike me—not really—any more than I
hate you.'

'That's all you know.'

'But I do, Jo. I do know. If I were standing on the edge of a
precipice you'd push me off as soon as look at me. But all the same,
if things had been different, you'd have pushed the other fellow off
instead. We'd have made quite a pair, you know. And I've never
pretended I didn't like you.'

'Funny way of showing it.'

'It's a funny world. But it's true. I like you very much, Jo. And
you like me.'

'I've a funny way of showing it.'

'True enough. May I kiss you?'

'I'm in your power, aren't I? What's to prevent you?'

'I shouldn't dream of kissing you by force. I told you, I hate
fighting. I only fight when there's something I want to get.'

'That's hardly a compliment.'

'I don't pay you compliments, Jo. Not that kind anyway. I *am*
paying you the compliment of having an extra guard outside your
window.'

'Why the window?'

'Just in case you thought of sending any little notes in the air.
We like to keep the grounds tidy.'

'You don't seem to have made much headway with the judge.'

'How could you expect me to, yet? But you wait.'

'I am waiting,' said Jo.

And they kissed.

At about the same time Angela was paying a visit to Charles.
She was very apologetic.

'You do see my point of view, don't you?' she said. 'I know my
father is innocent. He never lies. Wouldn't you have done the same?'

'I can't conceive the situation arising. But, when you say you
know he's innocent, how d'you know? Most wives who are fond of
their husbands believe them innocent. So would most children their
parents. The courts have found him guilty and the Home Office
can find nothing even to merit an inquiry. Why should they all be
wrong?'

'He would never have pleaded "Not guilty" if he'd been guilty.'

'There you are wrong. It isn't telling a lie to plead "Not guilty". It is simply calling on the prosecution to prove your guilt.'

'Well, anyway he's told me he's innocent and he's never told a lie in his life. I do want you to believe that.'

'How d'you know he's never told a lie?'

'Because I do. Because I've lived with him all my life and you can't live with someone without knowing these things. He just can't tell a lie. You're going to appear for him and I do want you to understand that.'

'Why? What difference can it make?'

'All the difference. If you don't believe in his case you may not bother.'

'Of course I will,' began Charles, and then stopped and laughed.

'What's the joke?'

'I said "of course I will" automatically, as though this were going to be a real trial.'

'It's going to be a very real trial,' said Angela.

'You don't understand. In an ordinary case in the Courts it doesn't matter to me if I believe my client innocent or guilty. I put up the story he tells me for better or worse, whether I believe it or not. And pretty well everyone does the same. If a criminal's counsel had to believe in his innocence before he could raise any enthusiasm for the defence, there'd be precious few enthusiastic defences put forward, and most of those would be put forward by pretty stupid advocates. If your father's were a real case, I'd do the best for him I possibly could, whether I believed him or not. But this case is different. So that really you're quite right about it this time. If I really believed your father to be innocent, I should try much harder to-morrow. In any event, of course, I'll try sufficiently hard to prevent one of your bodyguard knocking me on the head. But I suppose that's all I'm prepared to do. Now if I really thought he was in the right, I would have a go.'

'Well, thank Heaven I came to see you,' said Angela. 'You must believe me. Why d' you think he'd take all this trouble, spend all his money and risk getting many years of extra imprisonment, if he weren't innocent?'

'I'm afraid that argument can always be raised. It's sometimes said that there are two kinds of judges. One kind think that a plaintiff wouldn't spend the money on bringing an action unless he

thought he had a good claim and the other kind think that the
defendant wouldn't defend unless he had a good defence. And the
commonest cry by an obviously guilty thief in the witness box is:
"What should I want to steal it for?" No, I'm afraid that sort of
argument doesn't cut any ice with me, I'm much more impressed
with your obvious complete trust in your father. I say "obvious"
but I should say "apparent". I don't know you well enough. How
do I know that you're not putting on an act?'

'You're very frank.'

'No point in being anything else.'

'Well, I can only give you my word. Mark you, I'm not a truthful
person like father. I don't mean that I'm an inveterate liar. I'm
just normal. Like you, I expect. But father's not. He's quite
abnormal. He just never tells a lie, never, never. Please try to believe
me.'

'You certainly sound as though you meant it, but, if I accept
that, how can I tell that you're right?'

'Well, do I strike you as a fairly intelligent person?'

'Very.'

'Thank you. Well, then, if I am above average intelligence, surely
I'm either putting on an act as you suggest or I'm probably right?
Obviously I can't ask you to be certain about it. I can only beg of
you to think that what I'm saying may be true. You were quite
right. This is not a real trial. But it's vital to us, and, if you believe
in our case, it must be some help.'

'Well,' said Charles, 'I'll promise you this. I will go into it with
an open mind and then, if I find in the course of the case that you
appear to be right, I'll do my damndest. I can't say more than
that.'

'No,' said Angela. 'I don't think you can. Thank you for being
so sweet. Have you told the judge, by the way, that it's really your
fault that this is happening to him? I chose you myself, but, if you
hadn't told me to go and see the judge at work, I might never have
heard him.'

'Well, I haven't yet,' said Charles. 'I think I'll wait till it's over.'

'Tell me,' said Angela, 'if we are right, and if we satisfy the judge
that father is innocent, he will do something about it, won't he? He
won't just let father go back to gaol and say "serve him right for
making such a nuisance of himself"?'

'No, I don't think he'd do that. If you ask my honest opinion, I

don't believe for a moment that you'll do any good at all, but if
I'm wrong, and if you really showed that your father's innocent,
then I'm quite sure that the judge would do something about it.
We all would, if it came to that.'

'Father was sure of it.'

'It's the first hurdle you've got to get over. And I don't believe
you ever will.'

'But you will try?'

'I will, but you mustn't expect anything.'

'But I do.'

'Why are you so certain?'

'Because I think the truth's bound to come out the second time.
You'd say that it usually comes out, wouldn't you?'

'I don't know about usually, but often, certainly.'

'Well, I can't believe that it won't this time.'

'Well, good luck, anyway. At any rate I should never have met
you but for this.'

'Are you pleased?'

Charles paused.

'Yes,' he said eventually. 'In spite of being kidnapped and locked
up and threatened with I don't know what, I'm pleased.'

In what might be called the guards' common-room, Spikey was
holding forth on the beauties of a life of ease.

'No more cops,' he said. 'No more stir. I wouldn't 'ave believed
it if 'e 'adn't told me 'isself. Didn't know there was so much money
in the world.'

'How d'you know that he'll keep his word?'

''Ow do I know! 'E's done all right so far, 'asn't 'e? If we didn't
get no more we shouldn't do so bad. But I know 'im. 'E'll do wot
'e's said.'

The advantage of Lonsdale's infirmity of always telling the truth
was that he normally carried conviction with people, even in the
most unlikely places.

'Thou shalt find no ease neither shall the sole of thy foot have
rest,' put in one of the guards, known to his friends as Holy Hal.
He had spent many years in prison and the Bible had had a great
attraction for him there. Not from a religious point of view. He
simply enjoyed the language. He did not quote it either hypocriti-
cally or in order to moralize. Possibly he enjoyed showing off his
immense knowledge, but his real pleasure was to relate everyday

words and actions to phrases in the Bible for his own benefit. No
doubt saying it aloud and creating an impression among his friends
and acquaintances gave him added pleasure, but that was not the
real source of his enjoyment. It cannot be said that he ever deliberately went back to prison to devote more time to his study, but this
was hardly necessary. Like most habitual criminals, he was not
very successful and usually found his way back there soon after his
release. Some prison chaplains found his knowledge a severe test of
their own. One of them, in the hope that it might lead to better
things, actually played a sort of Bible chess with him. Everything
they said had to come directly out of the Bible from the beginning
to the end. Any failure to reply with a quotation lost two marks.
Any mistake lost one more. The parson had to confess that he
looked forward to his visits.

'Why not look on the bright side?' said another of the guards to
Holy Hal.

'We wait for brightness, but walk in darkness,' said Holy Hal.

'O.K.,' said Spikey, 'but it's round the corner. Me and the
missus'll go travelling, I think.'

'Do they put your previous ones on a passport, like they do on
a marriage certificate?' asked another guard.

They discussed the pleasures of life and the various ways in which
they would seek them out. Lonsdale had indeed put a very large
sum aside for the purpose of paying the men without whose help
he could not succeed. He was prepared to spend half his fortune or
even more on ensuring the success of his scheme. Angela had
already opened an account for the Boss, in which she had placed
£100,000 to be distributed among them all equally, with an extra
bonus of £10,000 for the Boss himself. Her father had promised
another £110,000 to be paid on the completion without interruption
of his new trial. Lonsdale did not consider that £220,000 out of a
million was a penny too much to pay for the chance of freedom.

Naturally suggestions of this kind were taken most seriously by
the Boss and his associates. Spikey had been quite right that the
Boss was the man Lonsdale wanted. The combination of a public
school and University with a prison education produced an interesting result in the Boss. He could mix happily in all circles. Among
criminals he was trusted because he never deliberately let them
down. His part in a crime was the organization. He seldom
appeared himself—except in the dock. One of the things his associ-

ates liked about him was that, if they were caught, he didn't try to wriggle out and leave them to take the rap. Naturally, if the police never came to him, he was not expected to go to them. But he did not do what so many receivers do when questioned by the police (and later in the witness box), throw the entire blame on his accomplices.

This tendency on the part of receivers is a great help to the prosecution in some cases. When there is a charge against a number of people of conspiring to steal, everyone knows that usually one of the accused is the receiver and the remainder are the thieves. The prosecution put the receiver first on the record, so that he has to go into the witness box first. He attempts to give a display of wide-eyed innocence and, without the slightest hesitation, he throws on the thieves any blame there happens to be going round. In their indignation the thieves trip into the witness box and sink themselves and the receiver. The result is that, even if there isn't much evidence against the receiver at the beginning of the case, there is at the end—all provided by the defence.

The Boss naturally tried to avoid conviction, if possible, but never at the expense of his friends. His public school had done something for him.

He was a kind of independent contractor in crime. Some hostesses, when giving a party, instead of employing direct labour and buying the food themselves, employ a caterer to do the lot. The Boss was the equivalent of the caterer. If you wanted, for example, to crack a safe, or carry out an important warehouse robbery, he would supply everything, the men, the materials and the method. Naturally, he only took on jobs of sufficient size. He didn't supply buns and cups of tea for the Mothers' Union Summer Party. He would do the equivalent of a small dinner party for six, if it was exclusive enough, but in round figures he would not touch anything if there was not at least £1,000 for himself, not subject to tax.

He was against unnecessary violence, but he recognized that neither banks nor ordinary citizens would part with their valuables without sufficient inducement. Accordingly, when an exploit could not be carried out entirely in secret, which he preferred, he authorized the use of enough violence to achieve the object. But he always emphasized the necessity for as much care being exercised as possible. For example, gagging can be a very dangerous operation, and he had two specialists (who had been male nurses) who

knew how to complete this delicate and sometimes difficult operation with as little discomfort as possible and no danger to the
patient.

When in funds, the Boss went to expensive restaurants, where
his cheques were gladly accepted. He never dishonoured a cheque,
though his bank manager did sometimes wonder where the cash
came from. Particularly did he wonder about this on one occasion,
a month or so after his own branch had been robbed of over £10,000.
Did Mr Bostock's payments-in come, as he said, from winnings at
the races? How lucky for the Boss that he was not like Lonsdale.
Otherwise presumably he would have had to tell the manager that
it would have avoided a lot of trouble if he had just transferred the
amount to his account before the robbery. It would have saved an
elaborate and quite expensive plan, and the temporary disablement
of a bank messenger and two policemen. It is sometimes difficult
for a bank manager to decide whether to open an account for a
man whom he knows to have convictions against him, or to keep
the account open after a conviction. Just because a man has been
convicted, he should not be denied ordinary services when he comes
out of prison. Obviously, if the account is considered unsatisfactory,
or there is something suspicious about the cheques paid in, the
account will be closed. But the Boss's account was always conducted
most satisfactorily. He never overdrew. On the contrary he normally
had a large credit. Any cheques paid in were from obviously satisfactory sources, and, though most of the payments-in were cash, that
is the case with many course bookmakers. And he always ascribed
these payments to winnings at the races. The Boss would never
have been so indiscreet as to pay in the proceeds of a robbery the
day after it had taken place. It would have given him some amusement to return to his bank, for the credit of his account, the money
he had stolen from it, the day after the robbery, but he had been
to gaol sufficiently often to curb his sense of humour on that
occasion. When he did pay in a large sum a month after the robbery,
the cashier did say to him:

'Had a good day, Mr Bostock?'

'One of the best,' the Boss had replied.

'I can't think why people bet,' said the cashier.

'People are very stupid,' said the Boss, 'fortunately for me.'

'Well, I suppose we all are if it comes to that,' said the cashier.

'If we'd been more careful we should never have lost that £10,000 a month ago.'

'I don't know what else you could have done,' said the Boss. 'Tell me, what other precautions could you take?'

'We're taking them, Mr Bostock,' said the cashier. 'But walls have ears, even in a bank, you know.'

'Well,' said the Boss, 'I expect they're unnecessary anyway. No one would go for the same place again so soon.'

'That's a comfort,' said the cashier. 'The messenger will be pleased to know that.'

'I hope he's all right,' said the Boss. 'I was very sorry to read about it . . . but there it is, it's a wicked world and these things will happen.'

'Well, it's nice to know they won't happen here again for a bit. I wonder what I'd do if a gunman suddenly walked in?'

'Now—what *would* you do?' asked the Boss. 'You ought to have a foot button you can press so that the doors close automatically and an alarm bell rings.'

'That's an idea,' said the cashier. 'Thanks very much. I'll pass it on. I wonder why we've never thought of that before?'

'Of course,' said the Boss, 'the chap might get cross and try to shoot his way out. I should just have the alarm bell if I were you and leave the doors open. But, you know,' he added, 'there's only one thing that will keep a really determined burglar out.'

'If it's not a breach of confidence,' asked the cashier, 'what might that be?'

'Don't have anything worth stealing inside.'

'Oh—that's an old one,' said the cashier.

'I know,' said the Boss, 'but it's the only one that works. Good morning.'

The Boss had made the arrangements for Lonsdale's escape and retrial with great care and efficiency. He had even gone to the lengths of arranging diversionary escapes at two other prisons, in the hope of providing employment for as many police cars as possible at the time of Lonsdale's escape. It had been a simple affair. Everything in these matters depends on exact timing. Three minutes were allowed for the whole operation. At the appointed moment a small car drew up to a particular place outside the prison wall. The street on which the wall abutted was not used a great deal and the precise spot which had been chosen could only be seen for about fifty yards in either direction. Between seventy-five and a hundred yards in each direction away from the place where the escape was to take place, two large lorries waited with their engines running, ready to block the road for a sufficient time at the crucial moment. At the appointed time two men got out of the small car and threw a rope ladder over the wall. Lonsdale was there, with a confederate to hold it while he made the descent. He went quickly up and down on the other side within a minute. The precise timing of the whole operation had been rehearsed most carefully several times to make sure that, as far as could reasonably be ascertained, they would have the necessary three minutes. The operation had been rehearsed without the rope ladder, so as to see that both sides were in the right place. Lonsdale was not an expert in climbing rope ladders but he made the journey safely, jumped in the car and was driven off. The two lorries never had to be used and drove away slowly behind the small car. By the time the alarm was given, Lonsdale was well out of the district, making direct for the judge's house.

The announcement of his escape was in the normal form. 'Lonsdale Walsh, who is serving a sentence of life imprisonment for murder, to-day escaped from Northwall prison. A special watch is being kept at all ports and airfields.'

But not at judges' houses.

CHAPTER 11

Out of Town Tonight

One of the few witnesses who was quite pleased to have been kidnapped was Miles Hampton. It was true that he was not to be paid as a film extra, but he was fed and housed and it was a new experience. His life had become increasingly dim and with little or no excitement in it. Now here was certainly an adventure which he would be able to retell over pints of beer. It hardly needed any exaggeration either. Indeed, it was so extraordinary that he doubted if people would believe it. That troubled him for a moment—until he suddenly realized with a thrill that, once it was over, it would make headlines in the newspapers. That thought quickly led to another. Perhaps he would be asked to write an article. He had heard that quite a lot of money could be made that way. Then again he might be interviewed on the wireless—or even on TV. They might even revive *In Town Tonight*. He visualized something of this kind:

THE INTERVIEWER: Tonight we have someone who will interest viewers tremendously, someone who actually took part in the incredible proceedings in Mr Justice Halliday's house, someone who was taken for a ride, literally, and forced to give his evidence over again before the judge, literally, at the pistol point. Has there ever been such an astonishing story as was unfolded after Lonsdale Walsh eventually surrendered to the police? It was, literally, breathtaking. But you have read all about the story for yourselves and you don't want to hear any more from me. You want to see the man who was made to take a part, and an important one too, in the astonishing events which fell, literally, like a thunderbolt on the legal world. So, without more ado, here is Mr Hampton. How d'you do, Miles, if I may call you that. Nice of you to come here tonight.
MILES: Not at all. I'm very pleased.

INTERVIEWER: I expect it will be a long time before you forget your extraordinary experiences?

MILES: Yes, I expect it will be.

INTERVIEWER: Nothing like that has ever occurred to you before, I take it?

MILES: No, that's right.

INTERVIEWER: Not the sort of thing that happens every day?

MILES: No.

INTERVIEWER: Tell me, what did you find the most interesting part?

MILES: The most interesting part?

INTERVIEWER: Yes, the part that interested you most.

MILES: In what way?

INTERVIEWER: In any way.

MILES: I don't really know.

INTERVIEWER: But it must have been very interesting?

MILES: Oh, yes, it was, very.

INTERVIEWER: And frightening too. I'm sure I should have been very frightened.

MILES: I wasn't exactly frightened.

INTERVIEWER: A little nervous perhaps?

MILES: Yes, I suppose so, at first.

INTERVIEWER: It must have been all very interesting.

MILES: Oh, yes, it was, very interesting.

INTERVIEWER: Didn't you wonder whether you would ever be rescued?

At this stage in the interview Miles suddenly realized with a shock that, if something went wrong, if a revolver suddenly went off, or someone hit him on the head with a blunt instrument, he might never be in *In Town Tonight*, or even in the world at all. The thought stopped his imagination for a few moments, and he spoke to his companion, Herbert Adams.

'D'you think we'll ever get out of this alive?'

''Ow should I know?'

'I thought you might have some sort of idea.'

'Well, I ain't, see. I been in worse spots and I been in better.'

'Well, you got out of them all right.'

'That don't mean we shall get out of this one.'

'It doesn't mean we shan't.'

'It doesn't mean we shall.'

'One doesn't want to be too pessimistic.'

His companion spat out of the window.

Miles returned to his thoughts.

Meanwhile Lonsdale was preparing for the trial in the morning. He chose the dining-room as the most suitable room, and it was arranged in the most convenient manner so that, while the proceedings would not be formal as in a court, they would be conducted with reasonable dignity. Angela had brought from his house three copies of the transcript of the proceedings at his trial, one for the judge and one for each barrister. He also had photographs of the exhibits. All these documents he had obtained for the purposes of his appeal to the Court of Criminal Appeal, and were brought by Angela together with notebooks and paper for the use of the judge and counsel. He had wondered whether the witnesses should be examined on oath but, after consideration, he saw no point in it; they had already committed perjury, so it was obvious that the fact of swearing on the Bible had no effect on them. And, whatever they said, they could not be convicted of perjury, as it was not a legal trial.

Finally he checked all the security arrangements and, after being satisfied that all was well and everything ready for the trial next morning, he went to bed. He slept reasonably well. He was happy in the thought that at last he was going to be able to prove that he was convicted solely by reason of a plot. The possibility of failure never occurred to him, even though he had no clear idea of how the prosecution's case was to be broken down. He had failed in breaking it down once. Why should he succeed the second time? The witnesses were the same, except for the man who had died. They would presumably tell the same story. Unless they were shown quite plainly to be lying, the judge would obviously believe them, and all his trouble would have been to no avail. But he did not believe this could possibly happen. He had not thought it possible at his trial. He had a different defending counsel then but, though he was sure Angela had made a good choice, it was not the change of counsel that made him so certain. It was the consciousness of right. Had he appreciated how gullible the jury would be on his original trial, he might have acted differently then. But now he knew that everyone was against him, everyone except Angela. That, he felt, made his task easier. He knew what he was up against.

Overwhelming prejudice. But that was at the same time his own strength. Everyone except himself and Angela would start the trial believing that it was little more than a farce. Once an inroad was made into the case for the prosecution, its fall would be all the greater, just because it had appeared originally to be impregnable. It would be a day of triumph. It must be.

CHAPTER 12

Retrial

The following morning Charles and Broadwater spent some time preparing for the case to begin. It was finally decided to have an early lunch and to start the trial immediately afterwards.

'You will, I hope, forgive a light lunch,' said Lonsdale, 'but I am anxious that none of us should feel sleepy.'

The judge did not feel called upon to comment, and Charles and Broadwater followed his lead. The cold ham and tongue and salad were eaten in comparative silence for about ten minutes. Spikey eventually broke it with:

'This ain't a funeral, is it?'

No one answered.

'Well—not if everyone behaves 'isself, it ain't,' he added.

Miles suddenly visualized himself being interviewed again. It was a most interesting lunch before the trial, he would say. Why? he would be asked. 'We had ham and tongue and salad' did not seem a very good answer. 'No one said anything' was not much better. Perhaps he could start something himself and make the lunch interesting.

'I have a feeling,' he said, 'that this has all happened to me before.'

'In that case,' said Jo, 'perhaps you'll tell us how it ends.'

'I don't actually remember if it did end. I can only seem to think of this part.'

'Well, pass the sauce, please,' said Spikey, adding: 'D'you remember that bit?'

They drank water or lemonade, and it was all over within half an hour, and then the proceedings began. Lonsdale opened them:

'I know that it isn't usual for the prisoner to start the ball rolling, except by pleading Guilty or Not Guilty, but I want to make one thing plain before we start. You know the object of this inquiry

and, in order to achieve it, it is quite unnecessary that the proceedings should be conducted as at an ordinary trial. For example, there
are all sorts of rules of evidence which normally have to be observed.
A witness mustn't say "what the soldier said". I dare say that
makes for justice as a whole. I don't know. Nor do I care. There'll
be no such rules here. There'll be no objections to evidence on the
ground that it isn't admissible. Everyone will have a free hand—
subject only to the judge's requirements. For example, I see no
objection to one witness being asked a question while another
witness is in the witness box. Mr A says something; the judge or
counsel can turn to Mr B immediately and ask him what he says
to that. The only requirement is that the proceedings should not
get out of hand and, if we all agree to do what the judge asks us
to do, that aspect of the matter should be sufficiently taken care of.
Does everyone understand?'

No one spoke.

'I take it from your silence that you understand what I mean,'
Lonsdale went on. 'It should be a new experience for you all.
Indeed, it might result in legal reforms being introduced. I won't
pretend that I'm interested in that aspect of the matter. All I'm
concerned about is to see that my original trial is fully investigated
by every means at your disposal. Now, shall we begin? Unless the
judge knows of some better method, perhaps Mr Broadwater will
start by calling his witnesses for the prosecution. You have, no
doubt, all read the evidence and know what the case is about.
Unless, therefore, the judge wants to hear, or Mr Broadwater wants
to make, a preliminary speech, I personally see no point in his
opening the case. But, of course, as I have already indicated, there
will be no objection to his intervening with an explanation or correc-
tion in the middle of the evidence. Indeed, all the things which you
can't or shouldn't do in court can be done here, if anyone thinks
they will help.'

Broadwater's first witness was a man who had been present at
the murder. He gave his name as George Allwinter. He was an
artist. He had been brought to the judge's house on the pretext that
he was to be commissioned to paint a picture. He said in evidence
that he was walking near Adolphus Barnwell's house, although he
did not know at the time that it was his house. He had heard of
Adolphus as a financier, but did not know anything more about
him or where he lived. As later evidence showed, Adolphus was on

the way from his house to the nearest pillar-box to catch the last
post, at the time when Mr Allwinter was strolling along the pavement thinking about a picture—or a model, he wasn't quite certain
which. He would probably not have noticed Adolphus at all in a
perpendicular position, but a large blue motor car came out of a
side turning, where it might have been waiting, and changed the
perpendicular to the horizontal. Mr Allwinter did not actually see
the impact. He had an idea of a car coming out of the side turning,
of a loud acceleration, a muffled exclamation (presumably of
protest) by Adolphus, and the next thing he knew was that the car
had disappeared and Adolphus lay dead in the middle of the road.
He was unable to take the car's number. He went across to see
what he could do for Adolphus, but saw that it was hopeless. He
went into the nearest house and telephoned for the police. They
were soon on the scene. He gave his account to a constable, and
that was really all he knew about it.

Charles then cross-examined him.

'You have known for a long time that my client is charged with
murder?' was his first question.

The judge interrupted.

'Southdown,' he said, 'I see no reason why you should call this
escaped convict your client. He is not your client in any sense. You
are doing what you are under compulsion.'

'I'm sorry, Judge,' said Southdown. 'It slipped out. I hope you'll
forgive me if it happens again. What d'you suggest I call him?'

'It is a bit difficult,' conceded the judge, 'but I must say that in
the circumstances I resent the expression "client". He is a thug and
a kidnapper.'

'I don't mind what I'm called,' said Lonsdale, 'provided you all
do your best to arrive at the right conclusion. I shouldn't take
offence if you repeated what the judge has said, and referred to me
as "the thug".'

'I'll try to call him "Mr Walsh",' said Charles.

The judge considered whether to suggest leaving out the 'mr'.
He was not one of those judges who refer to the prisoner by his
surname without any prefix. But this case was different. A prisoner
is presumed innocent, until he is found guilty. In the witness box,
he ought, therefore, to be treated like any other witness. But this
man had been found guilty. He was a convict with a number.

Lonsdale sensed what the judge was thinking.

'My number's 1074, if you'd prefer that,' he said.

The judge decided to leave the matter.

'Well now, Mr Allwinter,' went on Charles, 'you know that Mr Walsh has been convicted of murder?'

'Of course.'

'And have known it for a long time?'

'Quite.'

'And before he was convicted, you knew he was charged with murder?'

'Naturally.'

'How long after you saw the incident did you learn that the charge was not manslaughter, nor killing by reckless driving—but murder?'

'I don't know exactly. When it was published, I suppose. I saw it in the papers. About two or three weeks after he was killed. I can't be sure exactly.'

'From what you saw yourself, it might just have been an accident?'

'Why didn't he stop then?'

'He could have been frightened. Have you never heard of that sort of thing happening?'

'Yes, I have, but there's all the other evidence.'

'That's exactly what I meant,' said Charles. 'You've heard or read all the other evidence. If it weren't for that, this might in your view have been just an accident, mightn't it?'

Mr Allwinter hesitated.

'Well,' he said, 'there was no one else in the road and no other vehicle. There was no need to hit him, was there? The road was wide enough.'

'He might not have seen him.'

'Driving with his eyes shut?'

'Have you never done that?'

'Driven with my eyes shut? Of course not. If I've felt sleepy, I've stopped and had a rest. But anyway this wasn't long distance driving. This was in London.'

'I didn't ask you if you'd slept at the wheel. I asked if you'd ever driven with your eyes shut?'

'When I was awake? Of course not.'

'Haven't you?' said Charles. 'I should think again. Do you always stop your car before you sneeze?'

'I can't say that I do.'

'Well, when you sneeze, you shut both eyes. And it's for much longer than just a blink. Have you never thought of that?'

'I can't say that I have.'

'Well, I should,' said Charles. 'There are circumstances when it's very dangerous for a driver to sneeze when driving. We can test it if you like. Could we have some pepper, Mr Walsh, d'you think?'

Pepper was brought and the witness was induced to sneeze.

'D'you see what I mean?' asked Charles.

Not only the witness but everyone else could see that Charles was right.

'Well, Mr Allwinter,' he went on, 'how can you know that the accident wasn't caused by a sneeze?'

'Well, it didn't look like that to me,' said Mr Allwinter.

'But you didn't see anything until after it had happened, did you? You just had the impression of a car coming out of the side turning and the next you knew was that a man was lying on the ground and the car was gone?'

'But look at all the other evidence.'

'Exactly,' said Charles, 'that's what you've been doing, looking at all the other evidence. If it hadn't been for that, you'd have had no idea how the accident happened.'

At that stage Broadwater said that he felt he must intervene.

'All this talk of sneezing is very interesting, and may indeed be profitable for those of us who drive, but it was never suggested at the trial that this death was accidentally caused by a sneeze.'

'A lot of things may not have been suggested at the trial,' said Charles.

'I think we ought to know,' said the judge, 'if you are going to suggest that death was caused by an accident. Because, if you are, we might as well save our time. I have read the other evidence. The case for the prosecution was that this was a deliberately planned murder. Either it was or it was not. Sneezes do not come into it.'

'The point is, Judge,' said Charles, 'that the only person who the prosecution suggest may have wanted to kill Mr Barnwell is my—is Mr Walsh. If he isn't guilty of murder, it may have been an accident. Suppose Mr Walsh is right, and all the other evidence you're going to hear is perjured, the fact remains that the man was killed and killed by a car.'

'I see what you mean,' said the judge, 'but it doesn't matter to you how he was killed, so long as your—this man isn't responsible.'

'All the same,' said Charles, 'it's a little help—not much, I agree, but something, to show that accident is, apart from the other evidence, a possible explanation. Of course, if this other evidence is true, accident, I agree, doesn't come into it. It was a cold, calculated murder.'

'All right,' said the judge. 'I see what you're driving at. Shall we get on? Is there anything else you'd like to ask Mr Allwinter?'

'I'd just like to ask him about this once more. The dead man was found about the middle of the road, wasn't he?'

'About.'

'It's a good wide road?'

'Yes; he could have missed him quite easily. He could have driven either side of him.'

'If he saw him.'

Fortunately for Charles, at that moment Mr Allwinter sneezed. The pepper was still doing its work.

'Quite,' said Charles. 'Or, if he wasn't pay sufficient attention as he drove, he might have seen him suddenly and hesitated which side of him to go, in case the man went that way. You know, like two people bumping into each other in the street.'

'Then he would have stopped after the accident.'

'Most people would. But some people panic. And suppose this driver had previous convictions for dangerous driving, or suppose he was disqualified at the time he was driving, those would be reasons for someone not stopping.'

'I suppose so.'

'Then suppose he'd just stolen the car? That would be another reason, wouldn't it? You see, Mr Allwinter, you are not able to identify the car—or the driver—are you?'

'That's true. It happened too quickly.'

'So, for all you know, it might have been a thief, a disqualified driver or a man who sneezed and panicked. You have heard of hit-and-run drivers, haven't you? Why shouldn't this have been one of them?'

'But the other evidence,' began Mr Allwinter.

'Exactly,' said Charles.

'Suppose we get on to the other evidence,' said the judge. 'You've made your point quite clearly. If the other evidence comes to nothing, Mr Walsh should have been acquitted—but, if it's to be believed—as it was believed by the jury—he was plainly guilty, as you yourself have said, of a calculated murder.'

'If you please, Judge,' said Charles, 'I only wanted to establish that, apart from this other evidence, this might have been another of those cases where a driver doesn't stop after an accident.'

'Well, I think you've established that sufficiently,' said the judge.

'I respectfully agree,' said Broadwater.

'Good,' said the judge. 'As we're all agreed, we can get on. The sooner we finish, the sooner this outrage will come to an end. At least so the . . . the . . .'

The judge could not think of the right word. Lonsdale was not 'the accused'. He had already been accused and convicted. He was not 'the prisoner', as he was free. It was the judge and counsel who were the prisoners. He could not keep on calling him 'the escaped convict'. It was too heavy. To call him the 'murderer', when he was at least going through the motions of investigating the crime, offended his judicial sense. He was at a loss for a word. Eventually he went on:

'At least so the man who has brought us here has promised.'

'I keep my promises,' said Lonsdale. 'But I must make it plain that I should not feel called on to keep this one, if the investigation were conducted as a pure formality. I expect the case to be gone into thoroughly to the best of your ability. I apologize for being dictatorial in this matter. But it is the whole object of the exercise. Unless I get a fair hearing here I might as well have stayed in prison.'

'Are you saying that you did not have a fair hearing in the Courts where you were tried and where your appeal was heard?' asked the judge.

'No,' said Lonsdale, 'I'm not. As far as I could see, both hearings were perfectly fair. But mistakes have been made at fair hearings before and all I say is that my case is another example of such a mistake.'

'Very well,' said the judge. 'Your next witness, please, Broadwater.'

Jo came forward and sat in the seat which was being used for the witnesses. First of all she described her husband's position, and his relationship to Lonsdale.

'They were the leaders of opposing factions,' she said, 'and matters came to a head in regard to the management of the Anglo-Saxon Development Corporation Ltd. My husband had a very good chance of ousting Mr Walsh from his control of that company. Indeed, but for his death, I have no doubt that he would have obtained the necessary support for a resolution he was about to propose for the purpose of removing Mr Walsh from his position of Chairman and Managing Director of that company. Now, a short time before that meeting, my husband brought an action for slander against this man. In the course of that action Mr Walsh had to produce certain documents, but, shortly before the day fixed for the production of those documents, the action came to an abrupt end. It came to an end automatically because my husband was killed. And here is the man who was responsible for his death.'

'Let us avoid dramatics as far as possible, Mrs Barnwell,' said the judge. 'He has been convicted and sentenced, and there is no need for you to emphasize his guilt almost every time you speak. This is not the case of a man who is assumed innocent until he is proved guilty. He has been proved guilty and it is now up to him to show that the verdict of guilty was wrong.'

'I know him,' said Jo. 'He'll wriggle out of anything, if he gets the chance. Like he wriggled out of gaol.'

'I should hardly call it wriggling,' said Lonsdale. 'I climbed up a wall, not through a drainpipe.'

'Please,' said the judge. 'This bickering will not help the investigation.'

'Did your husband receive any kind of communication from anyone about a week before he was killed?' asked Broadwater.

'He did,' said Jo. 'He did indeed.'

'What was it?'

'He received a threatening letter warning him that, unless he immediately withdrew the action he had started, the consequences for him might be serious.'

'Have you still got that letter?'

'I produced it at the trial, and I have the photostat copy which Mr Broadwater has handed to me here.'

'Before you produce it, tell me this, Mrs Barnwell. Did your husband withdraw the action?'

'He did not—neither immediately nor at all.'

'What happened next?'

'My husband received a large parcel.'

'What was in it?'

'It was a road sign which had been dug up.'

'What sort of road sign?'

'It had YOU HAVE BEEN WARNED on it.'

'Did your husband pay any attention to it?'

'He did not.'

'What happened next?'

'He was murdered.'

'You mean he was run over by a car,' said Broadwater, his customary fairness as a prosecutor getting the better of him.

'I mean he was murdered,' said Jo, 'by being run over, and that man paid the driver to do it.'

'That is a lie,' said Lonsdale, getting very red in the face.

'It is the truth, and you know it,' said Jo.

'It is a lie, and you invented it,' said Lonsdale.

'Once and for all,' said the judge, 'I really cannot be of the slightest use, if this is the way you're going to go on.'

'She started it,' said Lonsdale. 'She has no respect whatever for the truth.'

'You have no respect for anything except yourself,' said Jo, 'but that respect is unjustified.'

'Will you please control yourselves,' said the judge. 'If this experience does nothing else, it shows the necessity for the Courts' power to maintain order. Nothing useful can be done if these interruptions continue. Surely you can see that?'

The Judge looked at Lonsdale as he said that.

'Yes, of course,' said Lonsdale, 'but I cannot stand listening to lies.'

'If your case is right,' said the judge, 'you will have to listen to a lot of them before this inquiry is over. How can I tell whether they are lies or not unless I hear them?'

'I will try to control myself,' said Lonsdale, 'but this woman deliberately tries to bait me.'

'If that is so,' said the judge, 'why do you give her the satisfaction of seeing her shafts hit the mark?'

'There are some matters on which I cannot conceal my feelings, but I will at any rate try to keep quiet until it's my turn to speak.'

'You kept Adolphus quiet all right,' said Jo.

This time Lonsdale said nothing.

Broadwater then resumed his examination.

'Now, Mrs Barnwell,' he said, 'a few minutes ago you said that you had a photostat copy of the threatening letter, which you say your husband had received. Will you be good enough to produce it?'

Jo handed to the judge the document. It was plain that the original consisted entirely of words and letters cut out of a newspaper or several newspapers and gummed together with transparent sticky tape. The sender was obviously taking no chances. Even the envelope, which was of a cheap kind obtainable in hundreds of shops, was addressed in the same manner.

'Had you any idea who had sent that letter?' asked Broadwater. Charles intervened.

'I don't quite know what course you want to take, Judge,' he said. 'If this were an ordinary trial I should, of course, object to such a question, which is plainly inadmissible, but in the circumstances perhaps you would prefer me not to object?'

'Well,' said the judge, 'there has been quite enough interrupting so far, I think; and in any event, when the procedure was laid down by our captor, he said that he did not want the rules of evidence to be observed. On the other hand, I really don't see how her answer is going to help me. We all know what she will say. But her saying it won't help to prove her statement or her belief true.'

'Very well,' said Broadwater. 'I won't press the question.'

'But I'd like to answer it,' said Jo. 'I knew perfectly well who had sent it. He had.'

And she looked hard at Lonsdale, with the obvious intention of provoking him to an outburst.

'Now—' said the judge warningly to Lonsdale, and Lonsdale remained silent.

'Was there anything which made you think that?' asked Broadwater.

'The substance of the letter,' said Jo. 'No one else had any reason for sending it. Although, of course, he had his lieutenants and associates—a lot of sycophantic sheep—none of them would have done such a thing, except on his orders. He was the real person who had an interest in threatening my husband. I must admit I didn't think he'd have the guts to go through with it. But he must have sent the letter, and we know from the other evidence that he did.'

'Don't let's worry about the evidence for the moment,' said

Broadwater. 'Let us confine our attention to the letter itself. Can you conceive by any stretch of your imagination any other person who could have wanted to send such a threat to your husband?'

'I cannot,' said Jo. 'And if I were twice as intelligent, and thought for ten times as long, I still couldn't. He sent it all right.'

And she again challenged Lonsdale by looking at him as she said it.

This time the judge said nothing, but merely looked at Lonsdale to see if he would rise again; he did not.

'I don't think I've anything else to ask Mrs Barnwell,' said Broadwater.

'Very well,' said the judge, and invited Charles to cross-examine her.

'Mrs Barnwell,' he began, 'it is obvious that you have the most profound dislike of Mr Walsh.'

'I haven't,' said Jo. 'I know him for what he is, that's all.'

'It is certainly obvious,' went on Charles, 'that you think he murdered your husband.'

'I don't think it—I know it,' said Jo.

'Well, you didn't see him do it, did you?'

'He didn't do it himself. He got someone else to.'

'You didn't see the other man do it, did you?'

'You know I didn't.'

'Nor did you hear him tell someone else to murder your husband.'

'The fact that I didn't hear him doesn't make it any the less certain.'

'How long have you been so sure that Mr Walsh was, if not the actual murderer, responsible for it?'

'From the very beginning.'

'So, from the time your husband was killed, you were satisfied that Mr Walsh was the culprit?'

'I was. And I was right.'

'When did you first learn that your husband had been killed?'

'Within a few minutes of his death.'

'At that time you had no evidence except that he had been knocked down by a car which did not stop?'

'I had the threatening letter.'

'Yes, of course, and the road sign. But, apart from those facts, you had none of the evidence which was given at his trial.'

'Of course not. What difference does it make? The evidence is there now and was given at his trial.'

'Well, that isn't quite right, is it, Mrs Barnwell? One of the witnesses is dead, isn't he?'

'That's not my fault.'

'Of course not. But, coming back to what I was saying, at the time of your husband's death you were quite satisfied that Mr Walsh was responsible, although you had no evidence against him whatever, except the threats which you believed he sent?'

'I knew he sent them.'

'Don't let's quibble about that. You felt sure in your own mind that he was the murderer from the very start. Is that right?'

'It is.'

'Now, Mrs Barnwell, will you listen to this question very carefully? You felt sure that Mr Walsh was guilty. You're a highly intelligent woman and you knew quite well that the mere production of the threatening letter and road sign would prove nothing whatever against Mr Walsh. You knew that, didn't you?'

'I never thought about it. I knew he was responsible.'

'But you also knew that he wouldn't ever be arrested, let alone convicted, if there were no other evidence against him.'

'I never thought about it. I assumed that the police would do their duty and bring the murderer to justice. And they did.'

'Did you know that all the witnesses we're going to hear about called on the police?'

'What do you mean? I don't understand.'

'I mean the police didn't find those witnesses. The witnesses came to the police.'

'What's wrong with that?'

'Nothing—if they were honest witnesses. Were they, in your opinion, honest witnesses, Mrs Barnwell?'

The judge intervened.

'What does it matter?' he said, 'whether she thought them honest? The jury obviously did.'

'I agree,' said Charles, 'that the jury believed them, but I assure you that it is material to ask this lady if she believed them.'

'All right,' said the judge. 'If you say it's material, ask her.'

'Did you believe the witnesses, Mrs Barnwell?' said Charles.

'When do you mean? In the witness box?'

'When else had you seen them?'

'I hadn't.'

'Then what else could I mean?'

'You ask so many stupid questions I've no idea what you mean sometimes. Of course I believed them. They were obviously telling the truth.'

'Were they?' said Charles. 'Are you sure?'

'Of course.'

'You would have done anything to bring the person you believed to have murdered your husband to justice, would you?'

'Of course I wanted him brought to justice.'

'That isn't what I asked. You'd have done anything to bring him to justice, wouldn't you?'

'The situation never arose. He was brought to justice.'

'Without your help?'

'I gave the evidence you know about.'

'Did you do anything else?'

'Nothing that I can remember.'

'You didn't by any chance see any of these other witnesses before you went to the police?'

'See any of the other witnesses?'

'That's what I asked.'

'Not to my knowledge.'

'Are you sure of that?'

'Of course I am. I may have seen you walking in the street before to-day, but I didn't notice you.'

'So that before these witnesses went to the police you had never spoken to any of them, so far as you know?'

'I spoke to Mr Allwinter.'

'But none of the others?'

'How could I? I didn't know of their existence, did I?'

'Didn't you?'

'I haven't got second sight.'

'But you knew, you knew—not thought but knew—that Mr Walsh had killed your husband?'

'You don't call that second sight, do you? That was a logical and obvious deduction.'

'And then,' went on Charles, 'without any prompting from you, the witnesses came along and proved you right?'

'Without my prompting them!' she repeated indignantly. 'Are you suggesting that I . . .'

'I'm not suggesting anything,' said Charles. 'I am merely asking you questions. Did these witnesses have any prompting from you?'

'I've already told you, I didn't know them.'

'The answer to the question may be easy,' said Charles, 'but I should like it none the less. Did those witnesses have any prompting from you?'

'Of course not,' said Jo.

'You lie,' said Lonsdale.

'Really,' said the judge, 'we were getting on quite well till then.'

'I'm sorry,' said Lonsdale. 'I tried to bite my tongue, but I just couldn't. This woman is an arrant liar.'

The judge sighed.

'She says you're a murderer, and you say she's a liar. Do you really think that's going to help me to form a view as to whether there was anything wrong with the jury's verdict? I'd better warn you that, at the moment, I have no reason whatever to believe that justice was not done at your trial.'

Jo looked triumphantly at Lonsdale.

'But, while I'm here, I will certainly go on inquiring into the matter. So do let there be an end of these silly interruptions. Now, Southdown, is there anything else you want to ask?'

'Not at the moment,' said Charles. 'But I may want this witness back.'

'She will be available,' said Lonsdale.

The next witness was Miles Hampton. He described how he had been sitting on a bench in Hyde Park, about a week or so before Adolphus was killed. A man, whom he took to be a down-and-out, was sitting on the same bench. While they were sitting there, a man of about the same height and build as Lonsdale, dressed in a morning coat and grey top hat, walked past them smoking a cigar. A little further on he stopped at a litter basket and threw something into it. The down-and-out (who was in fact Herbert Adams) got up immediately and went to the litter basket. Shortly afterwards he came back with a newspaper and the remains of a cigar. Miles could not say positively that Lonsdale was the man they had seen, but, from his general appearance, he might have been. Adams asked Miles for a light and proceeded to smoke the rest of the cigar and to read the paper which he had brought back with it. Miles noticed that the paper was curiously mutilated. It was not torn, but had many holes in it of different sizes where parts of it had been cut out. He thought nothing about it at the time, but remembered being slightly puzzled. After Adams and he had been sitting there for a further few minutes, they both suddenly noticed a grey glove which the well-dressed man had apparently dropped. Adams got up and fetched it.

'You can 'ave it for a bob,' said Adams.

'And what d'you think I could do with it?' Miles answered.

'Find the other 'arf,' said Adams, 'I'll make it a tanner.'

'No thanks,' said Miles. 'If I were you, I'd wait here for some time, in case he comes back looking for it. He might give you more for looking after it for him. Nothing more annoying than losing one glove, even if you're made of money.'

'Thanks, mate,' said Adams. 'I ain't got nothing special to do. I'll wait. Wot d'you bet 'e gives me? Is it worth 'arf a crown?'

'It's worth a good deal more than that,' said Miles. 'They're expensive gloves. But what he gives you is another matter. Some rich men are rich because they never give away anything.'

'I'll 'ave something to say if 'e don't.'

'I hope you get the chance,' said Miles.

But the well-dressed man never returned, and eventually Miles got tired of doing nothing in the park. So he got up and went to do it somewhere else. He had pretty well forgotten about the incident when he read in the newspapers about the death of Adolphus. The paragraph referred to the threatening letter and said that a man had brought to the police a newspaper and a glove which, it was hoped, might throw light on the matter. Miles, having nothing better to do, went to a police station and asked if he could help. It was soon established that the man who had brought in the paper and glove was Adams. Shown both articles by the police Miles had said that, as far as he could tell, they were the identical articles which he had seen Adams pick up.

All this evidence was elicited from Miles by Broadwater, and Charles then proceeded to cross-examine him.

'Have you ever seen this lady before?' was his first question, and he pointed to Jo.

'Oh, yes,' said Miles.

'When did you first see her?'

'When did I first see her?'

'Yes.'

'I can't be absolutely sure, but I believe it was at the police station. I think she was there, but I can't be quite sure. It may have been the police court.'

'Had you ever seen her or spoken to her before you went to the police station about this case?'

'Had I seen or spoken to her before?'

'That's what I asked,' said Charles. 'And what is the answer?'

'Before I first went to the police you mean?' asked Miles.

'That's right,' said Charles. 'Hadn't I made my question plain?'

'I just wanted to be sure,' said Miles. 'No, I'd never seen her before.'

'Or spoken to her?'

'Well, you can't speak to a person without seeing them.'

'What about the telephone?'

'Oh, of course, I'm sorry,' said Miles. 'No, I hadn't spoken to her on the phone.'

'Or communicated with her in any way?'

'I didn't know her.'

'Or communicated with her in any way?' repeated Charles.

'No,' said Miles. 'I didn't know of her existence before this case.'

'That may be,' said Charles. 'The case started with a man being killed, and what I want to know is, how soon after he was killed did you speak to Mrs Barnwell?'

'I don't know that I ever have spoken to her.'

'Do you say that you never have?'

'Well, I can't be absolutely sure. We were at the police court and possibly the police station together, and you know how it is when witnesses in a case are waiting in the same room. They may speak to each other. I may have done. I expect I did. But I can't be certain.'

'You do a little acting, don't you?' asked Charles.

'Yes, occasionally.'

'Are you doing any now?'

'Acting?'

'Yes.'

'Well, I haven't any engagements at the moment.'

'I didn't mean that,' said Charles. 'I meant are you acting at the moment—in this room?'

'Acting what?'

'Acting a part?'

'What sort of part?'

'The part of an apparently honest, entirely independent witness.'

'That's what I am,' said Miles.

'You really saw all this happen in the park?'

'Naturally, or I wouldn't say I had seen it. I may have made a mistake about a detail or two, but the substance is right.'

'What is your present financial position?'

'I can manage.'

'How much have you got in the bank?'

'I don't use my account much.'

'Is that because the bank won't let you?'

'Well, they do prefer me to have a balance before I draw a cheque.'

'When did you last draw a cheque?'

'I couldn't say. Some time ago.'

'What have you been living on during the period since Mr Barnwell was killed?'

'Oh—one thing and another, you know. I have managed.'

'Did you have a bit of luck, by any chance, just before or just after Mr Walsh's conviction?'

'A bit of luck? How d'you mean? What sort of luck?'

'Any kind of luck. Did you have a lucky bet on a horse, for example?'

'What horse?'

'Any horse. Is it a fact that at or about the time of the trial your financial position improved, if only temporarily?'

'My financial position always improves,' said Miles. 'It can't do anything else. Rather a pleasant position to be in really. Things can never get worse with me. They can only get better. How few people can say that. I find it very reassuring.'

'I gather from that,' said Charles, 'that there is no time when you would not find a present of £50 or so most welcome.'

'Well,' said Miles, 'there are about forty million people in this country, aren't there? There must be darned few of them who wouldn't find £50 useful at any time.'

'I take it you are not one of the few?'

'No,' said Miles. 'I could always find a use for £50.'

'Then you would have found a use for it at the time of the trial?'

'I tell you, I would have found a use for it at any time.'

'Did you in fact get some kind of payment at or about that time, either £50 or more or less?'

'From whom?'

'From anyone.'

'I can't recall it.'

'But, if it had happened, you could certainly have recalled it?'

'Indubitably.'

'Then why didn't you simply say you hadn't had it?'

'I did.'

'You said you couldn't recall it.'

'Precisely, because it didn't happen. If it had happened, I should have recalled it. As it didn't happen, I didn't.'

The judge looked at his watch.

'I don't know how long I'm expected to sit,' he said, 'but d'you think we could have a short adjournment now?'

'Of course,' said Lonsdale. 'I ought to have thought of it. Refreshments will be available in the drawing-room.'

CHAPTER 13

Interlude

'Ow d'yer think it's going, guv?' asked Spikey, after they had left the court room.

'It isn't going at all yet,' said Lonsdale, 'but then I never expected it would. But I like that young man who's appearing for me. I fancy he's shown two of the witnesses anyway a red light.'

'But 'ow are you going to show that they're telling a pack of lies, guv?'

'It'll come with a rush, Spikey. You'll see. They're telling lies and they know it, and they know we know it. One false step by one of them and we'll break the whole thing wide open. You wait, Spikey, you just wait.'

Meanwhile the judge was having a quiet word with Charles and Broadwater.

'There was a wind this morning,' he said, 'and with luck some-one'll pick it up.'

'I sent one too,' said Broadwater.

'Good,' said the judge. 'This farce has gone on long enough.'

'Judge,' said Charles, 'I'm not absolutely sure that it is a farce.'

'You're not at the Old Bailey now, old boy,' said Broadwater. 'No need to keep up appearances.'

'I'm not,' said Charles, 'but I shouldn't have gone half so far as I did to-day, if I hadn't thought that there mightn't be something in it. Admittedly, if this were a real trial I should have felt pretty uncomfortable at some of the questions I put, but I should have had to put them just the same. Something my client—I beg your pardon, Judge—something Walsh has told me has made me think very hard.'

'Don't overdo it, old boy,' said Broadwater.

'Oh, well,' said the judge, 'we shall see. And it's certainly good practice for you. How long have you been called?'

'Nearly seven years, Judge.'

'Have you really? Wish I showed my years as little. But you can't be thirty yet.'

'Not quite.'

At about that moment a small boy about a mile away from the judge's house had just picked up a piece of paper. It said in block capitals—SEND POLICE AT ONCE TO MR JUSTICE HALLIDAY'S HOUSE, HOWARD HOUSE.

It was signed by the judge himself. The small boy could not read but he entertained himself by tearing the small piece of paper into very much smaller pieces. Then, like Mr Justice Halliday, he threw them to the winds. Meanwhile, the piece of paper sent by Broadwater had stuck in a hedge in a lane.

Miles approached Jo while she was having a drink.

'How am I doing?' he asked.

'Don't ask silly questions,' she said sharply. 'There's no reason to suppose every word everyone says here is not being listened to. Not that it matters in the least. But it wouldn't take any time to secrete microphones here. Lucky we've clear consciences.'

'I see,' said Miles, rather abashed. 'I only meant . . .'

'Have you been to any good shows recently?' said Jo. 'Well, as a matter of fact, I don't go out a great deal,' said Miles. 'I find that as I get older I get more and more critical. Things that would have amused me ten years ago either bore me or irritate me now.'

'Theatre tickets are expensive,' said Jo.

'Yes, I suppose they are,' said Miles.

'I sometimes get free seats given to me,' said Jo. 'If they'd be of any use to you, I might let you have a couple from time to time.'

'That would be most kind.'

'I'll give you my address before we leave, that is, if we're ever allowed to go.'

A few minutes later a car drove up to the house, and the Boss arrived. He did not always pay visits to the site, but on this occasion he felt he should do so. He sent a message to Lonsdale to announce his arrival. Lonsdale excused himself from his guests and went to see him.

'Everything all right?' asked the Boss.

'I should like to congratulate you on the efficiency of your service,' replied Lonsdale. 'It has all gone like clockwork. Not a hitch from beginning to end.'

'Delighted to hear it,' said the Boss. 'Perhaps you can recommend me to some of your friends, if they ever have any delicate matters to be attended to.'

'Well,' said Lonsdale, 'I won't promise to do that. But I'll certainly keep you in mind myself.'

'Is there anything else I can do about this?'

'I don't think so,' said Lonsdale. 'The only possible danger now is from a stray caller, but I think your people have got that pretty well taped.'

'That's splendid,' said the Boss. 'I'll go home then. Spikey knows how to get in touch with me if I'm wanted. No casualties so far, I hope?'

'None at all, thank you,' said Lonsdale.

'Good,' said the Boss. 'I hate a messy job.'

CHAPTER 14

Direct Evidence

When the hearing was resumed Charles said that he did not want to ask any further questions of Miles for the moment. Herbert Adams was the next witness. He gave similar evidence to that given by Miles, and he identified photostat copies of the newspaper he had rescued.

'You will see from these pictures,' said Broadwater, 'that the threatening letter sent to Mr Barnwell fits exactly into the spaces in the newspaper. At the trial an expert was called, who demonstrated this beyond doubt. But really an expert isn't required. If one looks at it carefully it is reasonably plain to anyone.'

'Well, Southdown,' said the judge, 'you've seen the two exhibits. Do you agree that they're an exact fit?'

'Yes,' said Charles. 'I'm prepared to admit that.'

'What about the glove?' said the judge.

'You'll see about that from the evidence of the police inspector who interviewed the accused. I gather it was not considered necessary or politic to have the inspector here to-day. At least I take it he isn't here?'

'No, he's not,' said Charles.

'Well,' said Broadwater, 'in that case I might as well deal with his evidence now. He said that, when he interviewed the prisoner, he produced the glove which Mr Adams had found, and asked him if he had any like it. The prisoner produced a right-hand glove but said that he had recently lost the left. It was the left glove which Mr Adams and Mr Hampton had seen the man drop and which Mr Adams took to the police station. No one could, of course, say that it was the prisoner's missing glove, but he himself admitted that it was exactly like his own. He also admitted that he had lost it on the same day that Mr Adams found the glove. He did say that he had not lost it in the park, but he thought, at his club.'

'What d'you say about that, Southdown?' asked the judge.

'It's substantially correct, Judge,' said Charles. 'Mr Walsh did lose his glove and the one found was exactly like the missing one. I don't admit that it was found by Mr Adams in the way he suggests, but it may very well be the missing glove.'

'Very well,' said the judge. 'You'd better ask Mr Adams some questions about it. Because, if it is, your cl . . . —if it is Walsh's glove, it seems pretty clear that he was the man who threw away the newspaper from which the threatening letter was cut out. And if that is so . . .'

'Mr Walsh strongly denies that he threw away any newspaper into the litter basket. But he was dressed in a morning coat and grey top hat.'

'Then you'd better question Mr Adams about it,' said the judge.

'What time did this happen?' was the first question.

''Arf past two,' said Adams.

'Why are you so certain? Had you a watch?'

'I asked this gentleman,' and he indicated Miles, 'what time it was.'

'Why did you want to know what the time was?'

'It's important, the time is.'

'Why? You had nothing to do, had you? You were going to wait to see if the gentleman came back for his glove.'

'I like to know the time, see. Always 'ave. Not so important in the day as at night, but you get's the 'abit.'

'What d'you mean—not so important in the day as at night? You're not a housebreaker by any chance?'

'No, I ain't. But my brother was, if you want to know. And 'e taught me to be careful about the time. It was important to 'im. D'you want to know why?'

'Well, why?'

'Well, it's like this 'ere. My brother didn't like being pinched, but, when they found 'im on the job, that was a fair cop.'

'What's that got to do with it?'

'I'm telling yer. What 'e didn't like was to be pinched for nothink.'

'I can understand that, but what's that got to do with noticing the time?'

'Well, it's like this 'ere. My brother might think of a job ter do while 'e was dressing 'isself in the morning. But you can't pinch a man just for thinking, can you? Well, you can't anyway. I know

that much meself. It's a free country. You can think what yer like.
Now, if you 'appen to be carrying a jemmy or a screwdriver or
some skellington keys or somethink wot might be useful on a job,
they can't pinch yer for it before nine at night, see? You can go up
to a copper at half past eight and wave them in 'is face and say
"see these, chum?" and he can't do nothing to yer except tell yer
to move on. Unless he can read yer thoughts, and it ain't come to
that yet. But if it's arter nine o'clock 'e can pinch yer for carrying
'ousebreaking implements by night, see? And my brother didn't like
that. 'E didn't see why 'e should be pinched a mile away from the
job 'e was going to do, any more than 'e could be pinched while 'e
was dressing 'isself in the morning. It stands to reason, don't it? 'E
might change 'is mind on the way to the job and go 'ome. No, my
brother didn't 'old with being pinched for nothing. On the job was
one thing, but on the way to it was another. So 'e acted thoughtful,
my brother did. 'E made up 'is mind when 'e was going to do the
job, and then 'e'd take up the old instruments and 'ide 'em near
the place at about 'arf past eight. So they couldn't do nothing to
'im, unless they caught 'im on the job. And that suited 'im. 'E
didn't like being pinched for nothing, my brother didn't. So you
see, guv, if you want to be sure you're before nine o'clock, you've
got to make sure of the time. Guessing won't do. You got ter know.
And, once you get used to knowing the time, you sort of always
know it.'

'But this was your brother, I thought, not you?'

'Yes, but I used to have to find out the time for 'im, and that's
'ow I got into the 'abit. So that's 'ow I knew it was 'arf past three
when I saw the gentleman.'

'I thought you said half past two.'

'You got me all muddled. Yus, it was 'arf past two.'

'Sure it wasn't half past three?'

'I just told yer. It was 'arf past two.'

'Where's your brother now?'

'Dunno.'

'Sure you had a brother?'

"Course I'm sure.'

'Just the one?'

'Yus.'

'Any sisters?'

'No.'

'When did you last see your brother?'

''Ow should I know?'

'What time of the day was it when you last saw him? Before or after nine p.m.?'

'I think,' said the judge, 'we're wandering rather a long way from the subject. It's the glove you're challenging, not the time, I gather.'

'Well,' said Charles, 'we have strayed a bit, I agree, but my suggestion is that the whole of this episode has been invented, glove and all.'

'But a glove was produced,' said the judge. 'You admit that.'

'I agree,' said Charles, 'and I expect it was Mr Walsh's glove.'

'Then I don't quite see where this is getting you.'

'Suppose,' said Charles, 'this was a plot. The simple way of doing it would be to steal Mr Walsh's glove, while he was at his club or somewhere. Not very difficult for determined people.'

'You're assuming a most diabolical plot,' said the judge, 'and at the moment there is not the least evidence of it.'

'Perhaps not at the moment,' said Charles. 'Perhaps there wasn't one at all. But if my instructions are right, there was such a plot. And, if there was, there's at least a reasonable chance we shall be able to prove it.'

'All right,' said the judge. 'Have you anything more to ask Mr Adams?'

'Not at the moment,' said Charles.

'The next witness,' said Broadwater, 'is dead, but I can read his evidence from the shorthand note. His widow is present in case my opponent wants to ask her anything.'

Broadwater then read the evidence of the late Kenneth Meadowes. He admitted that he was a man of bad character with many previous convictions. He said that he was approached by Lonsdale three days before. Adolphus was killed, and asked if he could drive a car. He said he could. He was then asked if he'd do a job for Lonsdale, a job for which he would be very well paid. He asked what sort of a job it was. Lonsdale, he said, replied that it was easy enough and would only take a few seconds, adding that it meant 'driving a car and not stopping'. 'He told me,' Meadowes had sworn, 'that I was to wait round a particular corner with the engine running and that, as soon as a man whom he would identify to me walked into the road, I was to drive straight at him hard and then drive on until I was well out of the area. I was then to drive to a lonely spot in the country, to examine the car for blood or any other marks, clean it up as far as possible and do any first aid touching up necessary, and then leave it. He would arrange for it to be picked up. I did what he told me, ran over the man and drove away as he'd said and left the car in the country. I was paid £50 by the accused. I didn't take the number of the car, but it was a large blue car. It might have been a Humber. I was too taken up with the job I'd promised to do to notice much about it.'

In reply to further questions, Meadowes had said that he realized he was committing murder, and that anything he said might be used in evidence if he were charged with·the murder.

'Meadowes died a few days after the trial,' said Broadwater. 'Does my friend want to ask Mrs Meadowes any questions?'

Charles said that he did.

'I'm sorry to have to ask you these questions, Mrs Meadowes,' he began. 'I hope they won't distress you too much.'

'I never wanted to come 'ere,' said Mrs Meadowes. 'I'm supposed to be getting married next week.'

'Well, I hope we'll have finished in time,' said Charles.

'Well, I hope so, really, I do,' said Mrs Meadowes.

'Now, tell me Mrs Meadowes,' said Charles, 'your husband died of cancer, didn't he?'

'Yes.'

'Which he had had for some time?'

'Yes.'

'Had he been attending hospital?'

''E 'ad 'ad treatment, but they said there was nothing more they could do for 'im. So they sent 'im 'ome.'

'He could still walk about?'

'Oh—'e could walk about.'

'When did he finally take to his bed?'

'About a week afore 'e died.'

'They told him at the hospital that he was a hopeless case?'

'Yes, they told 'im.'

'Is that why he went to the police and confessed?'

'I don't rightly know. I didn't know nothing about it.'

'But you knew he went to the police?'

'Oh, I knew that.'

'And when he went to the police he was a dying man?'

'Yes.'

'So he had nothing to fear from any confession he might make?'

'I don't know about that.'

'Did anyone pay him anything to go to the police?'

''Ow d'you mean, pay 'im anything?'

'I mean what I say. Did anyone pay him anything to go to the police?'

'I shouldn't think so.'

'Did this lady ever call on you?' and Charles pointed to Jo.

''Oo, 'er?'

'Yes. Did she ever call on you?'

'I don't think so.'

'You don't *think* so. Don't you know?'

'We 'ad visitors from the 'ospital.'

'But she wasn't from the hospital.'

'Oh—wasn't she?'

'Then she did call on you?'

'Not as I knows of.'

'Mrs Meadowes, I'm sorry to have to ask you this, but your husband had a dreadful character, hadn't he?'

''E was all right to me, when 'e wasn't in the drink.'

'If someone had wanted a man to commit perjury, they couldn't have made a better choice than your husband, could they? He was a hardened criminal and he was dying.'

'A good man to commit a murder for you,' commented Broadwater.

'Had he ever been convicted of any crimes of violence?' asked Charles.

'Only for bashing me. But 'e was in the drink then and didn't rightly know what 'e was doing.'

'So, apart from a conviction for knocking you about, he'd never been convicted for violence?'

'Not really. There was 'is mother of course, but 'e only got three months for that.'

'Well,' said Charles, 'is it fair to say that he never hit anyone, except members of his own family?'

'Yes, that's right,' said Mrs Meadowes. 'I don't know if you count me sister-in-law as family. It was when 'e was in the drink. 'E was ever so kind when 'e was sober. Unless 'e was in one of 'is moods.'

'Oh, he had moods too, did he?'

'Well, not to say moods, but it didn't do to speak to 'im when 'e was in them.'

'So, apart from his family, including sisters-in-law, whom he sometimes hit when he was in a mood or drunk, was he ever violent to anyone?'

'Not wot you'd call violent. It didn't do to argue with 'im, of course, but a lot of men are like that. 'Is brother was just the same. Didn't like a argument. Now, I like one, all friendly, if you see what I mean. But 'e didn't. 'E couldn't abear a argument. 'E didn't say much, though. But if there was something lying 'andy 'e'd use it all right. No, 'e was a good 'usband as they go, but it didn't do to argue with 'im. Least, not if 'e was in a mood or in the drink.'

'And how often was he in a mood, or drunk?'

'Week-ends mostly—and Thursdays. I 'ad my 'arf day Thursdays. So we used to go to the boozer. 'E was all right for the first four pints. But after that 'e used to turn difficult. Couldn't please 'im no 'ow. Seemed to want you to argue, and, when you did, 'e bashed you. But 'e didn't mean any 'arm. Didn't know 'is own strength.'

'I hope your new husband will be gentler,' said the judge.

''E'd better be,' said Mrs Meadowes. ''E only comes up to 'ere,' and she indicated her shoulder. 'I chose 'im special,' she added. 'Laid 'im flat a week ago, if yer want ter know. Not taking any chances this time. But 'e wasn't a bad man, my Kennie, not to say bad. I known plenty worse. It takes all sorts, don't it?'

'I'd just like to get this clear, Mrs Meadowes,' said Charles. 'Your husband was violent to his family and when he was drunk or in a mood, but not otherwise?'

'Only to the police,' said Mrs Meadowes. ''E didn't 'old with them.'

CHAPTER 15

The Stable Doorkeeper

While Mrs Meadowes was being cross-examined by Charles, Colonel Pudsey-Pease, the governor of Northwall prison, was investigating Lonsdale's escape. The governor was a man who was never at a loss for a word. As far as quantity was concerned, he was a born small-talker. Some people dread cocktail parties. 'What shall I talk about?' plaintively asks the wife of the husband or the husband of the wife, as the case may be. Colonel Pudsey-Pease never had to ask such a question. He was equally at home with his convicts, his warders, and the ladies and gentlemen at the Lord-Lieutenant's garden party.

He would have chatted cheerfully to the Prime Minister about Britain's policy in the Far East or the problems of inflation, about which subjects he knew practically nothing. He once met a distinguished author of fiction. Almost immediately he said: 'I've got a plot for you.'

Wearily the author looked, not too obviously, for escape to some other part of the room, but, finding none, he said as politely as possible: 'Oh, really?'

'Yes, this should interest you,' the Colonel went on enthusiastically. 'There's a woman in my mother-in-law's road who only goes out on Thursdays. At least they've never seen her out on any other day. They call her "Mrs Thursday". And what d'you think her real name is?'

'Mundy?' ventured the distinguished author, who was fast becoming as distinguished for his good manners as for his own good books.

'No,' said the Colonel. 'Thursby. You could do something with that, I fancy. It's all yours. No charge.'

'That's most kind,' said the author, 'but you really ought to use it yourself. I'm sure you'd do much better with it than I should.'

'Well, I don't really write,' said the Colonel. 'Just a few scrib-blings. Not that I haven't had a lot to write about. Some of the fellows under my care are a book in themselves. Had a chap the other day who couldn't read or write. What d'you think he was in for?'

'Bigamy,' suggested the author. 'You don't require the G.C.E. for that.'

'Forgery,' said the Colonel. 'Would you believe it? Couldn't read a word, couldn't write a word. But, when it came to mere imitation of someone else's writing, he took a lot of beating. And bank-notes! I'd have fallen for them. Brilliant fellow. Such a pity. And some of the confidence tricksters I've had. You wouldn't believe some of the things they've done. Mark you, the public's gullible—and greedy. Or they wouldn't fall for it. But he thought up some pretty artful ones, I can tell you. Nearly fooled me once, but I just remembered in time who I was talking to.'

The Colonel would have been equally at ease discussing education with the headmaster of a public school, law with a judge, or ballet with Ninette de Valois.

But he was very worried by Lonsdale's escape.

'I'm determined to get to the bottom of this,' he said to his new deputy. 'When a man escapes, somebody in the prison knows where he's making for and I'm going to find out—if I have to put them all on bread and water.'

He had not the slightest intention of acting in this illegal manner, but he wanted to show how strongly he felt on the subject.

'We've got to get this fellow back,' he said. 'There've been too many of these escapes. And the trouble is, unless the fellow's dangerous, the public don't want him to be caught. Sentimental idiots. But just let them think that the wanted man might bump them off and they'll howl their heads off at the wicked prison authorities for not keeping him inside. I tell you, Maitland,' he went on, 'if you took a Gallup poll to-day, to find out how many people wanted Walsh caught, you'd find ninety per cent against it. But if we published that, since coming to prison he'd become dangerous, had knocked out two warders, half-killed a third, and was believed to be carrying a revolver, it would be the other way round quick enough. Blithering lot of idiots. They're only senti-mental when they're not afraid for their own skins.'

'I quite agree with you,' said Maitland. 'Who are you going to see first?'

'Well, the fellow we really want to see is a chap who was released not long before Walsh escaped. He shared a cell with him. Spikey they called him. I've told the police about him, but apparently they can't find him at the moment. So I think I'll see Jimmy Simpson first. If there's any mischief going on, he'll know about it.'

So Simpson was brought before the governor. He was offered a seat.

'Let me see,' said the governor. 'How much longer have you got?'

'You should know, sir,' said Simpson, 'better than me.'

'Come now,' said the governor, 'don't be foolish. Politeness costs nothing, but impertinence can be expensive here.'

Simpson said nothing.

'Another five years, isn't it?'

Simpson still said nothing.

The chief warder was about to tell Simpson to answer, when the governor held up his hand.

'The other day,' he said, 'the Home Secretary ordered the immediate release of a man who had still five years to go. Why d'you think he did that, Simpson?'

'Ask him, sir,' said Simpson.

'You—' began the warder.

'That's all right,' said the governor. 'I understand. We understand one another, don't we, Simpson? You think I'm going to ask you for information and that I'm hinting that you might get some remission if you gave it to me, not promising, mind you, but hinting. That's what you think, isn't it, Simpson?'

'I don't think anything at all, sir.'

'And you don't think it's right to split on your pals. That's it, isn't it? Well, think it over, Simpson. Five years is a long time. All right, you can take him away.'

As soon as they were alone, the governor said:

'Gently does it, you see, Maitland. I've had that type before. He's got plenty of time to think about what I've said. I believe in sowing the seed. But don't force it. Now let's see Everton.'

Everton was a very different type and was not offered a seat. He would have talked as much as the governor, if given a chance.

'You won't tell anyone if I tell you, sir, will you? Because, if you did, I'd be for it.'

'You will be fully protected, Everton.'

'Well then, sir, I can tell you where you'll find him. Ireland. That's where he is. He was going to lie low in London for a few days, and then off to Ireland.'

'Whereabouts in Ireland? It's quite a large place.'

'Well, of course, he may have moved, but he was starting in Dublin.'

'Any kind of address?'

'Oh no, sir. Don't suppose he knew it himself, sir.'

'And what was he going to do in Ireland? Any idea?'

'Now you have me, sir. Lie low, I suppose. He didn't need to work.'

'So you think that, if we look for someone lying low in Ireland, we might find him.'

'I was only trying to help, sir.'

'Then who told you all this?'

'Just prison gossip, sir.'

'Very well, thank you, Everton, you may go.'

Methodically the governor interviewed every prisoner who might have known something.

'I don't have to answer, do I sir?' asked one. 'I don't lose marks if I refuse?'

'No,' said the governor, 'you don't have to answer.'

'Then what'll I get if I do tell you something, sir?'

'I can make no promises.'

'Well, what's the inducement, sir?'

'The inducement,' said the governor, 'is the possibility—only possibility, mind you—of remission if you give me really useful information.'

'Possibility isn't much, sir. Would you make it probability?'

'I can't make it anything. You know perfectly well I've no power to do so. I can only tell the Home Secretary that you've been of use—if you have been. It's entirely up to him then.'

'What are the chances, sir?'

'I simply can't tell you, but, if what you tell me does really help, I'll certainly do what I can for you. I can't say more than that, and you'll have no right to complain if you get nothing out of it.'

'Very well, sir, I'll take a chance. I think you'll find he's staying with one of the judges.'

'What!'

'That's what I heard, sir. He's going to stay with a judge. No one will look for him there.'

'Don't be ridiculous. Take this man away,' said the governor. He had had a fruitless day, and he was really angry.

CHAPTER 16

A Different Light

'Look, Bert,' said Bert's young woman. 'Look what I've found,' and she showed him the piece of paper which had got stuck on the hedge. 'D'you think it's real?'

'Send the police to Howard House,' read Bert aloud. 'It's a joke, I expect. That's where his nibs lives. What'd he want with the police? Give us a kiss.'

She obliged.

'No, a proper one.'

She obliged again.

'But suppose it was real, Bert,' she said. 'Shouldn't we take it to the station?'

'Well,' said Bert, 'it wouldn't do any harm, I suppose. But there's no need to hurry ourselves. I like it here.'

'So do I, Bert.'

'We'll take it in when we go home then. That'll suit everybody.'

And Bert turned his attention again to what to him and his young woman on their half-day off were more important matters.

Meanwhile Charles, having finished for the moment his cross-examination of Mrs Meadowes, was inviting the judge to look at the evidence which had so far been tendered.

'All I can say,' said the judge, 'is that I can see no reason for disagreeing with the jury's verdict. It is perfectly true that the most important witness is dead, and was a man of bad character, but he did say on oath that he killed the dead man and was paid to kill him by the convicted man. Now it's obvious, I should have thought, that Meadowes had no personal reason for killing Mr Barnwell. Indeed, as far as I know, the only person who would have benefited from his death is your . . . is the convicted man. Well, now, of course, it's possible that Meadowes told a cock and bull story and was paid to do so. But there's no evidence of that at all. It's true that it is unusual for a man to confess to a murder in this particular way. But it would be equally unusual for a man to commit perjury in this particular way. Obviously the jury had to be warned that Meadowes was an accomplice and that his evidence ought not to be accepted without corroboration, but, of course, they were so warned. And now look at the corroboration. There was abundant evidence not only that your . . . that Walsh benefited by the killing of Mr Barnwell, but that he had sent the threatening letter and the road sign. Well, now, if the jury accepted that evidence, and I see no reason why they should not have done so, the position is that the convicted man threatened the deceased with unpleasant consequences if he didn't discontinue his action for slander, that the deceased continued with his action, that he was thereupon run over and killed, and the man who killed him said the convicted man paid him to do it. That was the evidence at the trial. What more do you want? As far as I can see, it was a perfectly proper conviction. Your suggestion is that the whole thing was a fake. I can only say that, at the moment, there is no evidence of that whatever.'

'I quite understand your present views, Judge,' said Charles. 'I propose to call Mr Walsh to see if he can change them.'

Lonsdale went to the witness chair and sat down. He described his financial affairs, in so far as they were relevant to the dispute with Adolphus Barnwell. He referred to the slander action and admitted that it was a grave annoyance to him.

'I go further than that,' he said. 'My solicitor told me that, unless Mr Barnwell died, the slander action would continue. I thereupon wished Mr Barnwell dead.'

'And he died,' put in Broadwater.

'And I agree,' went on Lonsdale, 'that, before he died, I sent that threatening letter and the road sign. But I didn't throw the newspaper into a litter basket in the park. I burned it in a grate in my house.'

Jo, who had been looking more and more triumphant as she saw the complete failure of Lonsdale's plan, could not resist a cry of triumph.

'I knew it,' she said. 'I knew it.'

The effect upon the judge of this uncontrollable outburst was remarkable. He turned towards Jo and asked immediately:

'What did you know, Madam?'

'You heard him yourself, Sir George,' said Jo. 'You heard him admit sending the letter and burning the newspaper in his grate. He's admitted it.'

For the first time since the inquiry had begun, the judge began to take a real interest in the proceedings. Up till that moment he had listened to the evidence and considered everything put before him with a fairly strong preconceived idea that there was nothing in it at all. Lonsdale appeared to him to be one of those self-righteous megalomaniacs who, though obviously guilty, almost think themselves into believing in their own innocence. In the judge's experience he would certainly not have been the first plainly guilty man who protested his innocence throughout his life. As the judge was compelled to investigate the trial, he had done so with reasonable care and, indeed, his judicial training had compelled him to conduct the proceedings as though he really wanted to inquire into the matter. But, until Jo's outburst, he had had no idea at all that there might be something in Lonsdale's allegation that he had been framed. He was glad that it was not a formal trial and that he could turn his attention to Jo at once.

'Mrs Barnwell,' he said slowly, 'why was it a surprise to you that the witness admitted sending the letter? You knew he'd sent it. You'd heard all the evidence.'

'I never thought he'd admit it,' said Jo.

'But he didn't admit the evidence given against him. He said that he burned the newspaper in his own grate. Whereupon you said: "I knew it, I knew it." And you said it in a tone of obvious delight.'

'Of course I was pleased,' said Jo. 'I want this man back in prison.'

'That you have made clear enough,' said the judge, 'but was not your pleasure at your *guess* that he sent the letter being right?'

The judge looked hard at Jo as he asked this question, and she could not continue to look at him. Nor could she immediately answer the judge's question.

'Now, Mrs Barnwell,' he went on, 'if what the convicted man says is true, those two witnesses who told this elaborate story about the park are telling lies. And there could be no possible reason for their telling lies unless they had been paid to do so. Of that there can be no doubt. So, if he burned the newspaper in his grate, someone persuaded those two men to put up their story. And someone cut out a newspaper so as to fit the letter which was in your possession.'

The judge paused and then added:

'And I suppose someone could quite easily have stolen his glove first.'

The whole atmosphere in the room had changed and everyone waited for the judge's next words.

'Mrs Barnwell,' he said, 'can you suggest anyone except yourself who might have persuaded those men to tell this story?'

'I certainly didn't,' said Jo.

'I didn't ask you that,' said the judge. 'Can you suggest anyone else who might have done so?'

'No,' said Jo, 'and I don't know why you should assume that they're not telling the truth.'

'It was you, madam, who first did that,' said the judge, 'when you said "I knew it" on hearing the witness say that he had burned the newspaper in his grate—the newspaper which was produced in court.'

'Does it matter how he did it?' said Jo. 'He sent the letter all right.'

'We shall see if it matters,' said the judge. 'I can imagine it mattering a great deal. Well, we'd better continue with your story, Mr Walsh.'

Lonsdale was not the only one to notice the 'Mr'.

'Tell me, Mr Walsh,' said Charles. 'Did you ever ask Meadowes to run over Mr Barnwell?'

'I did not,' said Lonsdale.

'Had you in fact ever seen Meadowes before you saw him in Court?'

'To the best of my belief I had never seen him before.'

As soon as he said that, Jo started to look feverishly in her bag. After a short search she obviously found something in it which pleased and surprised her. She at once got up and went across to Broadwater and whispered to him. Meanwhile Charles was still cross-examining.

'Did you attend a wedding one day in Bayswater?' he asked Lonsdale.

'Yes, I did, and Mrs Barnwell knew that I did. She also knew that it was at a church near to Hyde Park, and that I might easily have taken a stroll in the park before or after the ceremony. I probably did.'

'What about your glove? Did you lose it in the park?'

'I did not. I first missed it in my club. That was before I went to the wedding. I had not been near the park at that time. When I missed it I assumed that I had dropped it in the street and, of course, I may have. But now I believe it was probably stolen from the cloakroom in my club. It would be easy enough for a stranger to appear to walk in with a member. Indeed, for all I know, the thief walked in with me.'

'What about the road sign?'

'Yes, I sent that too. I wanted to scare him. I may add that I sent appropriate compensation to the Council to whom it belonged.'

'There's only one other thing I want to ask you,' said Charles. 'Why didn't you give evidence at your trial?'

'I wanted to, but my counsel was very frightened of the effect of the admissions I should have to make about the threatening letter and road sign. And he persuaded me not to. I can't pretend that I tried very hard to alter his view. If you employ an expert, you take his advice. He told me that it was safer to rely on the fact that Meadowes was not only a party to the crime on his own confession, but had a very bad record as well.'

'Thank you,' said Charles. 'That is all I wish to ask.'

Broadwater then started to cross-examine.

'I think you said that you'd never seen Meadowes before you saw him at the Magistrate's Court?'

'That is correct.'

'You're sure of that?'

'Certainly, so far as I know.'

Broadwater handed him a photograph which he half covered over.

'Is that a picture of you?' he asked.

'Yes,' said Lonsdale. 'Not a very good one, but it's me all right.'

Broadwater then showed him the rest of the photograph.

'And who are you talking to?' he asked.

'Good God!' said Lonsdale. 'Some people are never satisfied.'

'What on earth do you mean?' asked the judge.

'I mean this,' said Lonsdale, 'and, if anything will convince you of this woman's dishonesty, this will. This is a picture of me talking to the late Kenneth Meadowes.'

'I thought you said you'd never seen him before?' said the judge.

'I did,' said Lonsdale, 'and I meant it. And, in the sense I said it, it was true. I said I had never seen him before, as far as I know.

But, of course, one has seen all sorts of people in trains and in the street and in theatres and so on. And one doesn't remember them, any more than one remembers the man who stops you and asks for a light or to know the way. But people do ask for lights and do ask you the way. And I cannot tell you what Kenneth Meadowes was asking me when that photograph was taken. But I can say that I had never seen him before then—in the same sense as I've just mentioned—and I can say that I was not then asking him to murder Mr Barnwell; and I can say that it is very, very extraordinary that someone should have thought it worth taking a photograph of the two of us, and even more extraordinary that the photograph should be in the possession of that woman.'

'Yes,' said the judge, 'but there is something even more important than that. Why was this not produced at the trial? You were in the case, Broadwater. Do you know why?'

'Very simply,' said Broadwater, 'because the prosecution had no idea of its existence.'

'I see,' said the judge. 'Why didn't you give it to the police at that time, Mrs Barnwell?'

'I didn't think it important. I don't know why I've kept it so long. I only looked in my bag on the off-chance.'

'You didn't think it important,' said the judge, heavily underlining the words.

At that moment one of the guards came in hastily and spoke to Lonsdale. He thought for a moment and then said:

'Sir George, there's a police car coming up the drive. A real one, I mean.'

'I see,' said the judge, and he, too, thought for a moment. As a judge and a lawyer he knew that, from the point of view of arriving at the truth in Lonsdale's case, it was vitally important that he should go on with the inquiry without interruption. Although he could, no doubt, ensure that a further inquiry would be held later, the witnesses would have had time to think by then. If, as he was now beginning to believe, Lonsdale's complaint that he had been framed was justified, now was the psychological moment to go on with the investigation. Any serious delay might be fatal to the ascertainment of the truth.

'May I be allowed to go and interview the police myself?' he asked.

'Yes, Sir George,' said Lonsdale without hesitation.

The judge got up and went to the front door. The car had just arrived. An inspector and sergeant got out.

'I'm sorry to trouble you, my Lord,' began the inspector, 'but we've just had this brought in to the police station. I thought I'd better come down myself.'

The inspector handed to the judge the note which Bert and his young lady had found.

The judge laughed.

'Well, it's nice of you to come, Inspector. I'll let you know if I want you. Good afternoon. Forgive my rushing off, but I'm just in the middle of something.'

The judge went in.

The inspector looked puzzled.

'Extraordinary old boy,' he said to the sergeant. 'Didn't want to know what it was all about or anything. Practical joke, I suppose. Oh well—off we go.'

As they drove off, the inspector said to the sergeant:

'What's one of our chaps doing up here?'

'We haven't got one,' said the sergeant.

'Well, I'm sure I saw one going round the house as we drove up. Seemed to be in a hurry.'

'Must have been a mistake, inspector,' said the sergeant 'There's no one up here.'

'It's all very odd,' said the inspector, 'I could have sworn I saw one.'

'Helmet or cap?' asked the sergeant.

'Helmet,' said the inspector.

'Perhaps the judge is playing charades, inspector,' suggested the sergeant.

'From the way he behaved he might be playing anything,' said the inspector. 'Now what on earth are we going to put in the report book? Don't want to be had up for contempt of Court. It'll take a bit of thinking out. Any bright ideas?'

'I'd be an inspector if I had any,' said the sergeant.

The judge had meanwhile hurried back to the inquiry. There was a very different atmosphere prevailing. Lonsdale was full of expectancy. Jo was extremely worried but was grimly determined to battle on. The other witnesses were only dimly aware of what was happening or what might be in store for them.

'Now, Mrs Barnwell,' said the judge briskly, as soon as he had returned, 'you had this photograph in your possession at the time of Mr Walsh's trial, but you didn't think it important enough to show to the police. Is that the truth?'

'Yes,' said Jo.

'Did you expect the accused to plead guilty or not guilty to the charge?'

'Not guilty, I suppose.'

'Did you expect him to deny his guilt in the witness box?'

'He didn't go into the witness box.'

'You didn't know that he wasn't going to give evidence, did you?'

'No.'

'Then, before the trial started, you must have thought it at least possible that he would go into the witness box?'

'I'm not sure that I thought about it at all.'

'Are you saying that, before the trial, you never visualized the man you believed to have murdered your husband, and whom you accordingly and very naturally hated, going into the witness box and telling his story? Surely you must have thought about it? You're an intelligent woman.'

'Thank you,' said Jo, 'but I'm not a judge or even a lawyer. And we think about things differently from lawyers. You always think about things in terms of witnesses and evidence and so forth. Ordinary folk are different.'

'I dare say, Mrs Barnwell,' said the judge, 'but ordinary folk like you have their passions and one of the things you wanted was to see the man you believed to have murdered your husband brought to justice. That at least is right, isn't it?'

'Yes, that is right,' said Jo. 'And he was. He was brought to justice. He was found guilty—as he was.'

'I am beginning to have grave doubts,' said the judge, 'if he was brought to justice. He was tried, certainly, but the question of justice is another matter. Whether or not you considered the possibility of the accused giving evidence, you surely must have realized the possibility that he would deny having asked Meadowes to run over your husband?'

'I tell you, I never thought about it. I told the police all I knew, and there it ended.'

'Might I interpose a question, Judge?' said Charles.

'What is it?' asked the judge.

'Well, Judge, she was at the Maigstrate's Court, and must have heard the police officer, who interviewed Mr Walsh, given evidence that he denied ever having spoken to Meadowes.'

'Yes,' said the judge, 'thank you. Well, Mrs Barnwell, you heard what Mr Southdown said. It's right, isn't it? You knew before the trial at the Old Bailey that the prisoner was denying ever having spoken to Meadowes?'

'It's a long time now,' said Joe, 'But I suppose I heard it.'

'Then why on earth did you not at once produce this photograph and prove that his denial was false?'

Jo did not answer at once.

'Here was this man who had murdered your husband calmly saying that he had never seen or spoken to the man who actually did the murder. And here were you with a trump card in your possession. Why did you not produce it?'

'I can't really say,' said Jo. 'I didn't, that's all.'

'Where had you got this photograph from, madam?' asked the judge.

'I'm not sure. I think Mrs Meadowes gave it to me,' said Jo.

The judge immediately turned to Mrs Meadowes.

'Is that right?' he asked, 'did you give this to Mrs Barnwell?'

Mrs Meadowes looked blankly at the photograph.

'That's 'im,' she said.

'Yes, we all know it's your late husband,' said the judge, 'but have you ever seen this photograph before in your life?'

'I couldn't rightly say,' said Mrs Meadowes, 'but I'd know 'im anywhere. 'E was a 'andsome man, until the drink got 'im. But I've known worse nor 'im,' she added. 'And sober, too.'

'No doubt,' said the judge, 'but you don't remember ever giving this photograph to Mrs Barnwell, do you?'

'It wasn't the one on the mantelpiece. I wouldn't 'ave given 'er that. That was took on our wedding day.'

'Quite so,' said the judge.

'I'm keeping it there when I'm married again.'

'Yes, yes,' said the judge impatiently.

'That's all arranged. 'E didn't take to the idea at first, but 'e liked the frame. So that's settled,' said Mrs Meadowes happily.

'But this photograph was never in a frame, was it?'

'I never sold it, straight I didn't. 'E did all that sort of thing 'isself.'

'Mrs Meadowes,' said the judge, 'will you please try to follow what I'm asking you. Have you ever seen this photograph before?'

Mrs Meadowes looked at the photograph critically.

''Ave I ever seen it before?' she asked.

'Yes, have you?'

'Where?'

'Anywhere.'

'Ask 'er,' and Mrs Meadowes pointed to Jo, adding, ''ave I ever seen it before?'

'You know you gave it to me,' said Jo.

'That's right,' said Mrs Meadowes.

'Please don't interrupt,' said the judge.

'Why shouldn't I?' said Jo. 'This seems to be a free for all, with the police being sent away and everything.'

'That's my responsibility,' said the judge.

'I'll see that it is,' said Jo. 'Here am I, an ordinary citizen, kidnapped by a lot of thugs and, when I have the chance of being freed by the police, a High Court judge prevents it.'

'We'll deal with one thing at a time,' said the judge evenly. 'You can make any complaint you like later.'

'You can be sure of that,' said Jo. 'It's outrageous.'

'I'm not going to let your threats deter me from investigating what I believe may have been a grave miscarriage of justice,' said the judge.

'It was nothing of the kind,' said Jo.

'Mrs Meadowes,' said the judge, 'I suppose you couldn't tell me who took the photograph?'

'That I couldn't,' said Mrs Meadowes, 'but it's 'im all right. There weren't two of 'im. There aren't any of 'im now, but it takes all sorts, don't it?'

'Mrs Barnwell,' said the judge, 'when do you say Mrs Meadows gave you this photograph?'

'It's too long ago—I couldn't say.'

'And how did you happen to be seeing her?'

'I was sorry for her. I bore her no ill will. I knew her husband was dying, and I'd lost mine. There was a sort of bond between us.'

'Did you by any chance make inquiries at the hospital which he attended?' asked the judge.

'What d'you mean, make inquiries?' asked Jo.

'I mean "make inquiries". Did you make inquiries to find out how long Meadows was likely to live? It may be possible to check that, you know.'

'I may have at some time.'

'Did you know that Meadows had a very bad criminal record?'

'Of course I did at one stage.'

'Did you arrange for him to approach Mr Walsh in the street, and to have a photograph—this photograph—taken?'

'Of course not. It's ridiculous.'

'And did you keep the photograph in reserve for use if necessary?'

'Absurd. Why should I want to do that? If I'd had it taken specially, I would have produced it, wouldn't I? That's what you suggested yourself.'

'I asked you why you didn't produce it, and you've not given any satisfactory answer about that yet. Let me suggest a possible reason. Perhaps you thought that, if you added that piece of evidence, it might make the case too good to be true?'

'Nonsense.'

'Let us just see,' said the judge, 'and I warn you, Mr Hampton, and you, Mr Adams, to listen carefully to what I'm going to say. Mrs Barnwell felt sure that Mr Walsh had murdered her husband. But she had no evidence of any kind that he had done so. She had a threatening letter, which she felt sure he had written. And that was all. Now, I'm going to suggest what she might have done. I am not saying at present that she did it, but just that she might have done it. She makes inquiries to find out the name of a hardened criminal who is suffering from a fatal disease. That would not be difficult to ascertain under the guise of charity. She persuaded him, under promise of a payment of money either to him or his wife or both, to go to the police and make the statement which he in fact made. But, first of all, she arranges for the photograph to be taken. She then arranges for someone to steal Mr Walsh's glove. She next finds two characters who are prepared to commit perjury for money. She has the original threatening letter and cuts out a newspaper so that it will marry up with the letter. Now that may not be exactly what happened, it may not be what happened at all, but, if it did, it would account for the whole of this evidence, would it not? Can you suggest any flaw in my reasoning, Mrs Barnwell?'

'If you choose to assume that everyone's committed perjury, I can't stop you,' said Jo. 'But you could say the same in any case.'

'In other cases you don't find photographs withheld by a witness for the prosecution, nor do you find such a witness giving that extraordinary exhibition which you gave when Mr Walsh admitted sending the threatening letter. Which reminds me. Tell me, Mr Walsh, what did you intend by that letter?'

'I intended that Mr Barnwell should fear for his life I wanted to frighten him out of his wits, so that he should not go on with the slander action. I do not seek to justify my action, but that is what I intended.'

'It's a great pity you didn't give evidence at your trial,' said the judge. 'I should have thought your frankness, as compared with the hedging and show of indignation by Mrs Barnwell, would have stood you in good stead with the jury.'

'It is a great pity,' said Lonsdale, 'but, as I said, I had to abide by the advice given to me.'

'And do you still say that, apart from being asked for a Meadowes in your life?'

'I do,' said Lonsdale. 'Mrs Barnwell knows me well, and she knows that I never lie.'

'I know nothing of the kind,' said Jo. 'He's a liar and a humbug.'

Lonsdale went very red in the face. He must have relaized that everyone was looking at him.

'I'm sorry, Sir George,' he said, 'but I find it difficult to contain myself when such a deliberate untruth is told. Mrs Barnwell knows as well as anyone that I have never told her a lie in my life.'

'Do you still say that you never—either by letter or telephone or face to face or through a third party—requested Meadowes to run over Mr Barnwell?'

'I do. The whole story is a concoction from beginning to end.'

'Very well,' said the judge. 'I think the time has now come to ask Mr Hampton some more questions.'

Miles had now begun to realize what was happening.

'As a matter of fact, I was going to ask if I could be excused. I don't feel terribly well.'

'What's the matter?' asked the judge sharply.

'I just don't feel very well.'

'In what way?'

'Don't bully the man,' said Jo. 'He said he feels ill. Have you never felt ill? You don't have to have a pain or a temperature to feel ill.'

'You seem a little anxious that he shouldn't be questioned, Mrs Barnwell? Why?' asked the judge.

'I'm nothing of the kind. You just twist everything I say. I wonder they made you a judge. You won't be one much longer after I get out of this. It's an absolute scandal. I think I'm going.'

And Jo got up to go out of the room.

'I'm sorry, Jo,' said Lonsdale, 'you're not leaving here until this is over.'

'You'll be sorry for this,' said Jo. 'You're all going to be sorry for this.'

She went back to her seat.

'What about Mr Adams?' asked the judge. 'Is he feeling quite well?'

'I'm all right,' said Mr Adams.

'Good,' said the judge. 'Tell me, Mr Adams,' he went on, 'do you know what is meant by perjury?'

'Not exactly.'

'It's telling lies on oath.'

'Oh,' said Mr Adams, 'that's bad.'

'Have you ever done it?' asked the judge.

'Wot, me?' said Mr Adams, with a reasonable show of astonishment.

'Yes, you,' said the judge.

'Wot should I want ter do that for?'

'Money.'

'Oh.'

'What does that mean?' asked the judge. 'Why did you say "oh"?'

'I dunno. I just said it. It's all right, ain't it?'

'Have you ever been given money for telling lies?'

'That's asking something, ain't it?'

'I know it is. And what's the answer?'

'That'd be telling, wouldn't it?'

'Yes,' said the judge, 'and I want you to tell me.'

'Oh,' said Mr Adams.

'Well,' persisted the judge, 'when were you offered or given money to tell lies?'

'What'll 'appen to me if I tell?'

'Nothing,' said the judge. 'Nothing that anyone says at this inquiry can be used in evidence against him—or her—as the statements will have been made under duress.'

'What does all that mean?' asked Mr Adams.

'It means you can't get into trouble for what you say here.'

'Oh,' said Mr Adams. After a pause he went on:

'But what about what I said any other time?'

'What you say now can't be used in evidence against you.'

'Why should it be?'

'I can't be.'

'Oh.'

'Well, now, Mr Adams, tell me the last time you told lies for money.'

'The last time?'

'Yes.'

'I don't rightly remember. I can tell you the time before, though.'

'What! Has it happened so often?'

'Has what happened often?'

'Have you told lies for money so often?'

'Not to say lies. I did 'elp my brother once or twice.'

'How did you help him?'

'With the time like.'

'The time?'

'Yes. I said 'e was at 'ome.'

'And he wasn't?'

''E might 'ave been. I was asleep.'

'So it comes to this, that you used to give your brother an alibi every now and then?'

'That's right. But I stopped it in the end.'

'Why was that?'

'They didn't ever believe me.'

'You must have found it a refreshing change to be believed at Mr Walsh's trial?'

'Wot's that?'

'The jury believed you about the glove and the paper.'

'Oh.'

'D'you think they should have?'

''Ow should I know? That's their job, ain't it?'

'But you know if you were telling the truth.'

'It ain't so easy as that. I once said my brother was in bed at 'ome all night and 'e was. You could 'ave knocked me down.'

'They believed you that time then?'

'They didn't 'ave to. 'E'd 'ad the doctor in the night, but I didn't know. I wasn't there. They let 'im go that time, though. Stands to reason. 'E'd 'ad the doctor. It was someone else, as a matter of fact.'

'Not you by any chance?' asked the judge.

'They never found 'oo it was,' said Mr Adams, 'but it weren't my brother. 'E'd 'ad the doctor.'

'Did you tell the truth about the glove and the newspaper? Did you really see anyone drop a glove and throw a newspaper in the litter basket?'

'Wot would 'appen if I said I didn't?'

'Well, for one thing, Mr Walsh would probably be let out of prison.'

'E's out now, ain't 'e?'

'He'd be let out properly, through the gate, not over the wall.'

'And wot about 'er. Would she go in instead?'

'No,' said the judge. 'I doubt if anything could be done to any of you.'

'So nothing can't 'appen to me whatever I say?'

'Nothing.'

'All right,' said Mr Adams. 'I'm ready. What's the question?'

'Is what you said at the trial true?'

'Nothing can't 'appen to me?'

'No.'

'Right. Well,' began Mr Adams, 'I don't feel all that good. Feel queer like.'

'Was the evidence you gave at the trial true?'

'Near enough.'

'Near enough to what?'

'Well mostly.'

'What wasn't true?'

'It was near enough.'

'You leave it to me to say if it was near enough. How much of it wasn't true? Did you ever sit in the park at all next to Mr Hampton?'

'Oh, yes, I sat next to 'im all right.'

'And did a gentleman come along and drop a glove?'

'Oh, yes, 'e did that all right.'

'And put a newspaper in the litter basket?'

'Oh, yes, I saw 'im.'

'And you went and took it out?'

'Yes.'

'And picked up the glove?'

'Yes.'

'And later took it and the newspaper to the police?'

'Yes.'

'Well, everything you said at the trial was true then?'

'I said near enough.'

'You said it was a gentleman like that one there. Was it?'

'It was about 'is heighth.'

'But you wouldn't say it was him?'

'No, I couldn't say that.'

Charles then intervened.

'Might I make a suggestion, Judge? If my case is right, this was an elaborate plot and it would be much easier for these witnesses to give evidence, if the thing really took place as far as possible. There was nothing to stop Mrs Barnwell from arranging for these men to be on a bench in the park, and from sending someone of Mr Walsh's height, dressed in a morning coat and grey top-hat, armed with Mr Walsh's glove and the cut-out newspaper. It's much easier for witnesses to give evidence of something that really happened than to have to invent it.'

'Yes, I see,' said the judge. 'And that would fit in with Mr Adams's answers "near enough". But they'd have to be primed as to what was going to happen and what they must do afterwards, or it might all go wrong. So, if it was a fake, they'd have to be a party to it.'

'Yes, Judge, I think so,' said Charles. 'Perhaps you might care to ask them about it—if they're well enough?'

'Well, Mr Hampton,' said the judge, 'I don't know if you heard what Mr Southdown said—but was the whole thing a play in which you'd agreed to take part?'

'Well,' began Miles.

'The man's not well,' said Jo, 'leave him alone.'

At first when Jo had started to behave like this everyone had been very startled. Although the judge was not in robes and the room was not a Court, everyone knew he was a judge and the idea that he could be spoken to with impunity as Jo was speaking to him had not occurred to anyone. Nor did anyone else feel like trying it. But Jo proposed to use every weapon at her disposal.

'I don't believe there's anything the matter with him,' said the judge.

'You're not a doctor, not even a bad one—you're supposed to be a judge, though no one would guess it.'

'Mrs Barnwell,' said the judge, 'when this inquiry first started and when it appeared to me that Mr Walsh had been properly found guilty, you behaved yourself perfectly, just as though this were a Court. Do you not realize what a bad impression your altered behaviour is bound to make upon me? Don't you realize that it is likely to confirm my belief that you were party to a grave conspiracy?'

'That's no more than what I should have expected,' said Jo. 'As long as everyone licks your boots and says "Yes, my Lord" and "No, my Lord" they've got a splendid case. But, as soon as they speak their mind or hurt your dignity, you say they're guilty of conspiracy. I'm sorry for the people who have their cases tried by you.'

'Mr Hampton, do you feel well enough to answer a few questions?' asked the judge.

Miles hesitated.

'It rather depends on the questions,' he said eventually.

'I see,' said the judge. 'It's that sort of illness.'

'That's right,' said Jo, 'twist everything he says.'

'Well, then, Mr Hampton,' went on the judge, ignoring Jo, 'try this one. Before you went to sit in the park did you know that someone was going to come along and drop a glove and put a newspaper in the litter basket?'

'Well, I had an idea,' said Miles apologetically.

'And who gave you that idea?'

'It's rather a long time ago.'

'Yes, I know. But it must have been rather an unusual occurrence for you to go and sit in the park and wait for something which you knew was going to happen?'

'Yes, it was unusual,' conceded Miles.

'Then you should be able to tell me who asked you to do it. Such a thing has presumably never happened to you before or since?'

'I can't say that it has.'

'Well, then, can't you help me? Was it a man or a woman?'

'It's a little difficult.'

'It must have been one or the other.'

'Yes, I suppose so.'

'Then which was it? Come, Mr Hampton, I'm sure you want to help me.'

'The velvet glove,' sneered Jo. 'Come along, my dear little man, no one's going to hurt you. Just say what I want you to say and then you may go. It's lucky everyone doesn't know how judges behave.'

'Well, Mr Hampton,' said the judge, 'a man or a woman?'

'I really don't feel terribly well,' said Miles.

'You're quite well enough to answer that question.'

'I'm going to faint,' said Miles—and fainted.

'Well done,' said Jo. 'Now you can hit him on the head. He won't feel it.'

Miles was soon restored with a little cold water and, while he was resting, the judge questioned Adams again.

'Well, Mr Adams, did you know it was all going to happen and, if so, who told you?'

'Well, it was like this 'ere,' said Adams. 'A bloke came to me and asked if I'd like to make a bit. Naturally I wanted to know what it was all about. First of all I asked 'im if 'e thought I was me brother, because I wasn't in that line. 'E said no, 'e knew me brother and it wasn't in 'is line. So naturally I said: "Wot's in it for me?" and 'e said "Fifty nicker." So naturally I said: "When do I get it?" and 'e said "When you've done it." So naturally I said: "When I've done wot?" And then 'e told me.'

Mr Adams relapsed into silence.

'What did the man tell you?'

'I told yer.'

'No you didn't. You just said he'd pay you fifty pounds when you'd done it.'

'That's right. I told yer. That's what 'e said.'

'But what did he tell you you were to do for the fifty pounds?'

"E said it was dead easy. There wasn't nothing to it, 'e said. So naturally I said "if there ain't nothing to it, why do I get fifty nicker?" So 'e said: "'Cos that's the price; ain't it enough?" So I said: "All right. Wot is it?" And then 'e told me.'

'But what did he tell you?'

'Wot I 'ad ter do.'

'But what was that?'

'Wot I did.'

'You mean he told you to go and sit in the park and that a man would come along and drop a glove and throw a newspaper into a litter basket, and that you were to go and take them to the police?'

'That's right,' said Jo. 'Put the words into his mouth. Is he telling the story, or are you?'

'Is that what happened, Mr Adams?' persisted the judge.

'Near enough,' said Adams.

'And did you get your fifty pounds?'

'Oh, yes, 'e played fair all right. 'Arf on the day and 'arf later. Oh yes, 'e paid all right. Still don't know why 'e paid as much. But naturally yer can't turn down fifty nicker, can yer? 'E was quite right. It was dead easy.'

'Who was this man who paid you £50?'

'I dunno. 'Adn't seen 'im afore.'

'How did he get hold of you?'

'I dunno. 'E just came. Expect 'e 'eard that I did odd jobs for people.'

'This was about the oddest, I expect,' said the judge.

'I wouldn't say that,' said Adams, 'but it was paid the best.'

'Well, Mr Hampton,' said the judge. 'I don't know whether you heard any of that, but may I ask how much you got for sitting in the park and telling about it afterwards? All right, you needn't answer,' he went on hurriedly, as he saw that Miles was changing colour again.

'Now, Mrs Barnwell,' said the judge, 'are you still prepared to deny that, apart from the evidence of the man who was present when your husband was killed and the police evidence, you procured the whole of this evidence against Mr Walsh?'

'Of course I am,' said Jo. 'You can't bully or cajole me, as you have these other witnesses. I've never seen such a disgraceful performance. Witnesses fainting all over the place, evidence given at the pistol point, the police turned away, and then you have the impertinence to ask me if I deny having concocted a case which has been believed by a jury, believed by the Court of Criminal Appeal and believed by the Home Secretary. My case is the only true one, but your methods would twist any case, however true. You can do what you like about it, but so shall I. The newspapers and Members of Parliament and the Lord Chancellor will be told all about this. And there are too many witnesses here for you to deny it. You're almost worse than he is,' and she pointed to

Lonsdale. 'After all, he has got himself to look after. You can't so much blame a man for doing that. But you—you're so puffed up with your pride in being a judge that you love to interfere in other people's affairs, which are nothing whatever to do with you. The case has been decided. It's over. There was only one thing for you to do—hand this man and his confederates over to the police as soon as possible.'

'Mr Walsh,' said the judge, 'I shall have to consider most carefully what I am to do about this, but it is right to tell you now that, in spite of the unorthodox, unofficial manner in which this inquiry has come before me . . .'

'Unorthodox!' sneered Jo, interrupting.

'Unlawful, if you prefer it,' went on the judge. 'In spite of all that, I am quite satisfied that there was a gross miscarriage of justice at your trial. I am quite satisfied that the whole of the main evidence against you was fabricated by or at the instigation of this woman. I am quite satisfied that, had the true facts been known to the jury, they would unhesitatingly have acquitted you. I shall write to the Home Secretary to that effect, and give him my detailed reasons for my opinions. Unfortunately, as far as I can see, no proceedings whatever can be taken against Mrs Barnwell or any of her witnesses. They were brought here by force or by a trick, and their evidence has unquestionably been procured by threats and duress. What is to happen to you and your confederates for the methods you have seen fit to adopt, it is not for me to say. But, criminal though those methods have been, you are at any rate entitled to say that, as far as I can see, unless you had adopted them, your innocence could not have been made known. In these circumstances it may be that the Home Secretary will be able to take a different view of your behaviour and of that of your colleagues than seemed possible a day or two ago. But I must make it plain that that does not lie in my hands and that all I can do is to make the report which I have just indicated. I now call upon you to keep your promise to allow the police to be summoned and to give yourself up to them.'

'Certainly,' said Lonsdale, 'but, first of all, I am going to give those who have assisted me an opportunity of getting well out of the way. I see no reason why they should take any unnecessary risks, whatever view the authorities may eventually take. Spikey, tell everyone who wants to be off to go as quickly as possible. Any one who wishes may remain. I suggest we wait a quarter of an hour before summoning the police. Perhaps Spikey would produce some drinks for those who would like to wait. Forgive me for continuing to act as host for the moment, Sir George. I will hand over to you as soon as my assistants have left. And I should make it plain that we have brought our drinks with us.'

'I take it I may leave now?' said Jo.

'Certainly, Jo,' said Lonsdale.

'Just a word in your private ear before I go,' said Jo.

She took Lonsdale aside and whispered:

'Don't think you'll get away with this. I'll get you yet.'

'Perhaps we shall get each other,' said Lonsdale.

'I loathe you,' said Jo.

'You don't,' said Lonsdale, and much to the judge's surprise, he kissed her good-bye.

'You wait,' said Jo, and went hurriedly out of the room.

'All right boys, beat it,' said Spikey. 'I'll 'op it after the drinks.'

Within ten minutes no one was left in the judge's house except the judge and his staff, Lonsdale and Angela, Charles, Mr and Mrs Broadwater, Mrs Meadowes, Miles, Adams, and Allwinter.

'I'm most grateful to you, Sir George,' said Lonsdale, 'for the trouble you have taken over this matter, and I do apologize for any inconvenience you and your staff have been caused. I would also like to thank Mr Southdown and Mr Broadwater for their help and to apologize to them and Mrs Broadwater. I should include in my apologies Mr Allwinter, against whom I have no complaint.'

'Well,' said the judge, 'I don't think we'd better discuss the matter any further. It will obviously be the subject of a further inquiry by the Home Office. It will certainly give the newspapers something to talk about.'

In a corner of the room Broadwater chatted to his wife. 'What a bit of luck I insisted on coming,' she said. 'This is better than anything I could have hoped for. Think of the publicity.'

'My dear Mary,' said her husband, 'you're entirely wrong. Certainly I shall have something for my reminiscences but, if you think that the publicity in this case is going to advance me one foot nearer to the Bench, you're very much mistaken. Judges are not appointed by the number of times they appear in the paper or the number of cocktail parties they attend. In the old days undoubtedly politics had something to do with it, but fortunately to-day they

hardly enter into it. I'm not saying there aren't some bad appointments sometimes. There are. And that gives me a chance.'

'Don't be modest, darling,' said Mary, 'you'd be a very good
appointment.'

'That's a thing which no one can say. That's why there are bad
appointments. You get a man who's first-class at the Bar but makes
a rotten judge. And you get a man who isn't much of an advocate
and only has a moderate practice who'd make a first-class judge, if
only they knew it. On the whole, of course, you can get a fair idea
of whether a man is likely to be a reasonably good judge. In most
cases you might say it's a pretty safe bet. But there are always the
exceptions. Surprise appointments which turn out well and expected
appointments which turn out badly.'

'I don't mind which you are, darling,' said Mary, 'so long as
you're appointed.'

Angela was in the meantime chatting to Charles.

'I think you were wonderful,' she said. 'No, I really mean it.
Mark you, I take great credit to myself for having picked you out.
You fitted into the scheme of things so well. I'd no notion why
father wanted a barrister, but I can see now all right why he insisted
on the qualifications he mentioned. How right he was. And how
right I was both in my judge and my counsel.'

'I'd like to think I was your counsel,' said Charles.

'Would you really?' said Angela. 'You don't know me very well.
And my father's in gaol, or will be very soon.'

'You don't know me very well,' said Charles, 'but I can put that
right, if you'll let me.'

'You can start right now.'

'Will you dine with me this evening?'

'I'd love it. It's such a shame I shan't be able to dine with daddy.
But it won't be long now.'

'I think I ought to warn you,' said Charles, 'that it may take a
little longer than you think.'

Angela became anxious.

'You're not suggesting . . .' she began.

'Oh, no,' said Charles. 'I'm sure they'll give him a free pardon.
But a thing like this must take time. They don't just have a drawer
with free pardons in it, and take one out. Don't forget, the Home
Office knows nothing of all this, and though, with the weight of
Halliday's authority, I'm quite sure everything will be all right,

they've got to inquire into the matter. And that must take some time.'

'What do you mean by "some time"? How long?'

'Well, of course, I can't say with any certainty. But days at the least. Possibly weeks. I don't think more. But suppose the Home Secretary orders an inquiry. First of all he's got to appoint someone to preside at it. Then they've got to arrange about the place where to hold it, the witnesses who are to be summoned, counsel who are to be briefed. You can't rush important things like this. After all, your father has been convicted and his appeal dismissed. You can't scrub that out in a couple of minutes. Indeed, it's very fortunate for you that you've got someone like Halliday on your side. If it were one or two of the other judges I know, well, first of all, you might never have got to this stage; and secondly, even if you had, there would be less alacrity on the part of the Home Office to jump to it. No, you couldn't have had a better choice than Halliday.'

'You really chose him for me, but I chose you. I can take full credit for that.'

Mrs Meadowes, Miles and Adams had a little conversation with each other.

'Wot's it all about?' said Adams.

'Blessed if I know,' said Mrs Meadowes. 'When do we go 'ome? And 'ow do we get there? I'd come 'ere to win a football pool. Shan't go in for them any more, if this is wot 'appens. I don't know what my Ernie will say. 'E ain't all that partial to judges.'

'Personally,' said Miles. 'I wish I'd never had anything to do with it.'

'We'll get our names in the papers,' said Adams. 'And our pictures, I shouldn't wonder.'

'Yes,' said Miles, suddenly remembering his B.B.C. interviews, and brightening a little at the thought. 'Yes, there is that. Look,' he added suddenly, 'the three of us might give an interview on TV.'

Miles had originally thought of having a solo appearance but it occurred to him that the contrast between him and Mrs Meadowes and Adams might show him up to advantage.

'What d'you say?' he asked. 'You leave it to me, and I'll try and fix it up. We ought to get £10 apiece for it. What about it?'

'I don't mind,' said Mrs Meadowes, 'so long as they don't ask me a lot of silly questions.'

'I'm afraid that's inevitable,' said Miles. 'It's a very difficult job, you know, interviewing someone. People think it's dead easy. But it isn't, not by a long way. Suppose you were interviewing me now, how would you begin?'

'Well, I know that one,' said Adams. 'I seen it. I'd say "Good evening, Mr whatever your name is." That's right, isn't it?'

'Yes,' said Miles, 'that's all right so far, but how d'you go on after that?'

'I know that too,' said Adams. ' "So good of you to come tonight." '

'Jolly good,' said Miles. 'And after that?'

'Now you've got me,' said Adams. 'But then it ain't my job. But I didn't do so bad, did I?'

'It was just like the real thing,' said Mrs Meadowes.

'We got a new one coming when we're married. Ernie say's 'e can't abide those small screens. Can't see enough of the girls.'

'My brother made ours,' said Adams.

'He's a TV expert, is he?' asked Miles.

''E knows where to find 'em,' said Adams.

At this point the judge went to the telephone.

'Well, Mr Walsh,' he said, 'I think time's up. Your chaps have had ample time to get away now.'

'It's very good of you to have waited,' said Lonsdale. 'Which reminds me that I've never thanked you for sending the police away.'

'Well,' said the judge, 'I can't pretend I'm very happy about having done that. But it seemed to me that, if I didn't get to the bottom of things there and then, no one might ever do so. I took a chance. I hope I was right.'

'I'm sure you were,' said Lonsdale. 'But then, of course, I suppose I'm prejudiced.'

'Hullo,' said the judge on the telephone, 'can I speak to the inspector, please? This is Sir George Halliday speaking.'

'Hold the line, please, sir,' said the sergeant. 'Can you beat it,' he said to the inspector, 'it's the old boy on the telephone. I wonder what he wants.'

The inspector went to the telephone.

'Inspector,' said the judge, 'I have an escaped prisoner here. His name is Lonsdale Walsh.'

'Lonsdale Walsh!' said the inspector incredulously.

'That's right, inspector. Will you send for him at once? I don't think he'll run away, but come at once, please.'

'I *can* beat it,' said the inspector to the sergeant. 'He's got Walsh up there with him. If you ask me, he's had him there all the time. Now why on earth should he do that?'

'I'd be a superintendent if I knew,' said the sergeant.

CHAPTER 17

Public Inquiry

The same day Lonsdale was taken back to prison. He was almost immediately taken before the governor. The judge had given Lonsdale a letter addressed to the governor, who had read it before the interview.

'This is all very well,' said the governor, 'but you can't do this sort of thing. This letter says that in Mr Justice Halliday's view you were wrongly convicted. Well, I'm not a judge. I'm just a prison governor. There's no doubt you were lawfully committed to my prison and unlawfully broke out. As far as I'm concerned, everyone here is guilty.'

'I quite understand, sir,' said Lonsdale, 'but what else could I do? I had tried all the lawful channels, the Courts and the Home Secretary and my Member of Parliament. If you remember, I came before you, sir, and asked what I could do. You told me to wait ten years.'

'So you should have,' said the governor. 'It's unlawful to break out of prison.'

'It was a choice of evils, sir,' said Lonsdale. 'I had to break the law in order to have my conviction set aside. If I'd done nothing, no one else would. I should have rotted here.'

'Rules were made to be kept,' said the governor. 'There are a lot of people here who say they're innocent, but, if we let them all out to try to prove it, we'd have no one left in the end. They'd all say they wanted to prove their innocence.'

'Mine is rather an exceptional case, sir,' said Lonsdale.

'Exactly,' said the governor. 'Hard cases make bad law. You can't provide for every exceptional case. You've put everyone to an enormous amount of trouble and expense. D'you know that I personally have interviewed nearly every man in the prison to see if I could find out where you were going?'

'I'm extremely sorry, sir,' said Lonsdale, 'but, if you'll put yourself in my position, what else was there to do?'

'I refuse to put myself in your position.'

'At least I gave myself up when I was satisfied that something
would be done about my case.'

'Most considerate of you,' said the governor. 'D'you realize how
much you've cost the country up till now? I'm a human man, I
hope. But I won't stand for lawlessness. How did you get out
anyway?'

'I climbed over the wall.'

'Oh, you did, did you? That was an outrageous thing to do.'

'I couldn't very well walk out of the gate, sir.'

'Don't be impertinent. You had outside help, I suppose.'

'Oh, yes,' said Lonsdale. 'They threw a rope ladder over to me.'

'Then you needed some inside help as well.'

'Only one,' said Lonsdale.

'I imagine you're not going to tell me who he was.'

'No, sir.'

'Well, I don't grumble at that, but it'd be better for you if you
did. You've committed a number of offences now, whatever the
truth about the original charge. And you can be punished for them.'

'I must take a chance on that, sir.'

'Very well,' said the governor. 'I shan't deal with you myself. I
shall wait for the visiting justices, but I should make it plain that
personally I'm against you. What's the good of a prison if people
can escape from it because they want to prove they're innocent?
It's ridiculous. Take him away.'

The first announcement of Lonsdale's recapture was given some
prominence in the newspapers, but there was no hint in the first
news of the sensation which was to follow. At first there were only
rumours, and passages began to appear such as:

'It is said that there will be surprising developments when the
facts surrounding Walsh's escape are made public. It has been
suggested that for a time he hid in a High Court judge's house.'

Eventually there were so many semi-accurate and inaccurate
statements made that the Home Office issued an official pronouncement. But even this was in somewhat guarded language.

'Lonsdale Walsh, who recently escaped from prison and was
subsequently recaptured, during his period of freedom gave certain
information to Mr Justice Halliday, as a result of which a report

from the judge is now being considered by the Home Secretary. Certain other persons also gave information to Mr Justice Halliday.'

A crop of rumours then began to circulate as to the nature of the information given to the judge and the names of the people, in addition to Lonsdale, who gave that information. Finally, Miles went to one of the television authorities and offered to tell his story at an interview. The persons responsible for authorizing such an interview immediately communicated with the Home Office and asked if there was any objection to this story being published, to which the reply was received that the Home Secretary would much prefer that nothing was said in public pending a further official statement, which was being issued. The note added that the responsibility for any inaccuracies or mis-statements would be that of the television authorities. 'It is also possible,' added the note, 'that questions of contempt of Court might be involved.'

So Miles had to wait. But his visit certainly speeded up things.

Three days later the Home Office announced that the Home Secretary was proposing to appoint three Supreme Court judges to inquire into the circumstances surrounding the escape and recapture of Lonsdale Walsh, including any matters which might throw light on the question whether there was a miscarriage of justice at his trial for murder.

Soon after, Lord Justice Manners, Mr Justice Swann and Mr Justice Tennant were appointed, and the public waited with interest to hear and read what would transpire.

The result was beyond their wildest expectations, because one of the chief witnesses at the inquiry was Mr Justice Halliday himself. The whole of the circumstances of the house imprisonment of the judge and the kidnapping or enticing of the witness was made known. There were two main questions to be answered. The first was whether Lonsdale had been wrongly convicted and, if the answer to the first question was Yes, the second question was what was to be done about the methods adopted by him to prove his innocence.

The tribunal decided to go into the first question first.

'It is true,' said Lord Justice Manners, 'that in point of time the escape and kidnapping came first, but the unanimous view of the Tribunal is this. If we are not satisfied that there was any miscarriage of justice, then there is no real point in our inquiring into the other matters. The law must take its course and those responsible for breaking it, including, of course, the escaped prisoner, should be proceeded against for such crimes as they have committed. If, however, we are satisfied that Walsh's conviction for murder was procured by perjured evidence and ought not to stand, we must then proceed to consider what, in our view, in the public interest ought to be done about these other offences.'

Lonsdale was represented at the inquiry by Charles, while the Attorney-General appeared for the Crown with a Treasury junior. All the other people concerned were represented by counsel. In opening the case the Attorney-General said:

'Although this is not a rehearing of the case tried at the Central Criminal Court, I have considered it desirable, subject to the view of the Tribunal, to have present all the available witnesses who gave evidence there, and, of course, everyone available who was in Mr Justice Halliday's house. One thing I should make plain. It is the view of the Crown that nothing said in Mr Justice Halliday's house could be used in evidence against the person who said it, at any subsequent criminal proceedings against that person. They were detained by force in that house and undoubtedly that threat of force to some extent at least compelled them to make their statements. On the other hand, anything said now by any witness can, of course, be used in evidence for or against that witness in any subsequent proceedings. Accordingly, the Tribunal may wish to warn some of the witnesses that they are not bound to answer any questions which might incriminate them. Unless, of course, the Tribunal take the view that they should be compelled to answer such questions. In that case, of course, the answers would not later be available against them.'

Lord Justice Manners, after consultation with his colleagues, then announced that they were proposing to treat the proceedings for that purpose as a court of law and that no witness would be compelled to incriminate themselves.

The first witness to be called was Mr Allwinter. He gave similar evidence to that which he gave to Mr Justice Halliday and Charles was then asked if he wished to cross-examine. Before doing so he thanked the Tribunal for allowing him to appear at all.

'As I am a witness to what took place before Mr Justice Halliday, I should, of course, normally have refused this brief. Indeed, I should automatically have refused it had your Lordships not indicated that, in view of my client's very strong desire to have my services on this occasion, it would be proper in the exceptional circumstances for me to appear.'

He then proceeded to cross-examine Mr Allwinter.

'Mr Allwinter,' he began, 'a lot of water has flowed under the bridge since I last questioned you, has it not?'

'It has indeed.'

'And you yourself saw it first trickle and then burst into flood.'

'If you like to put it that way, yes.'

'Now, Mr Allwinter, all you actually saw of this occurrence was a vague impression of a car moving and then a man left dead after having been struck by it, and the car moving off swiftly afterwards?'

'Something like that.'

'When I questioned you last time, you were obviously of the opinion that it was a case of murder.'

'I was.'

'And when I pointed out the possibility of it being a hit-and-run driver, you referred to the "other evidence".'

'That is correct.'

'By the "other evidence" you meant the witnesses who made statements to Mr Justice Halliday, and the man Meadowes who died?'

'Yes.'

'You have now had the advantage of seeing their performances before Mr Justice Halliday?'

'Yes.'

'They were rather different from their performances at the Old Bailey, were they not?'

'They were indeed.'

'Are you still of the opinion that this was a case of murder or was it not just as likely, or indeed, much more likely, the case of a hit-and-run driver?'

'I feel quite sure now that it was a hit-and-run driver.'

'Thank you,' said Charles, and sat down.

'But I gather,' said Lord Justice Manners, 'that previously you were convinced that it was a case of murder.'

'That is so.'

'That was because you had heard other evidence?'

'Yes.'

'And now you are convinced that it was a case of a hit-and-run driver?'

'Yes.'

'So the truth of the matter is surely this, Mr Allwinter. As far as your own eyes and ears at the time of the occurrence are concerned, you haven't the faintest idea whether it was murder, manslaughter or no offence at all by the driver, except that he or she failed to stop?'

'I suppose that's right, my Lord,' said Mr Allwinter.

'That shows the danger of paying attention to other people's statements when you are supposed to be saying only what you saw and heard yourself.'

'It is only fair to Mr Allwinter,' said Charles, 'to mention that he didn't in the first instance say anything except what he had seen and heard. It was only when I questioned him that he showed what his views were.'

'In other words you say, Mr Southdown, that, as far as his actual evidence about the occurrence is concerned, Mr Allwinter did not allow it to become coloured by his opinion.'

'That is quite correct, my Lord.'

'Then I should congratulate Mr Allwinter,' said Lord Justice Manners, 'rather than criticize him. In most accident cases witnesses who have formed a view as to the cause, allow their evidence to become violently coloured by their views. Such evidence is pretty well valueless.'

'Please don't think I intend to be offensive to Mr Allwinter,' said Mr Justice Swann, 'but his evidence, dispassionately given as it is, is also pretty well valueless. We all know that the unfortunate man was killed by a car. And that is all he can tell us. Presumably his injuries and position in the road were such that this could have been deduced quite simply by his body being found in the road. That the car did not stop was plain because it was not waiting by the body.'

'It might have been a horse and cart,' put in Mr Justice Tennant.

'Or an omnibus,' said Lord Justice Manners.

'Or a motor-cycle,' continued Mr Justice Tennant.

'Or van,' said Lord Justice Manners. 'We have to thank Mr Allwinter for telling us that it was a car.'

'Does it help us much to know that it was a car?' asked Mr Justice Swann. 'What we want to know is whether the person in charge of the vehicle ran the man over deliberately or by accident.

As far as Mr Allwinter's evidence is concerned, the man might just have been found dead.'

'Surely,' said Lord Justice Manners, 'what we want to know is whether the vehicle, whatever it was, was driven by Meadowes. If it wasn't, that's an end of the first question we are invited to consider. Meadowes himself cannot tell us, and we have to find out from all the other evidence whether he was driving. Mr Allwinter, admirable witness though he is, doesn't help us in the least about that.'

Mr Justice Swann leaned back in his chair with an air of finality. His point had been established.

'Perhaps then, Mr Allwinter can be allowed to go home,' suggested Lord Justice Manners. 'Does anyone in the case want him to remain? Do you, Mr Attorney?'

'No, thank you, my Lord,' said the Attorney-General.

'Does counsel for any other party wish him to stay?'

One by one, counsel got up and said that his client did not require any further evidence from Mr Allwinter.

'Very well,' said Lord Justice Manners. 'Thank you, Mr Allwinter. We shall not want you any more. You may go away.'

'Do I have to?' asked Mr Allwinter. 'I'd like to hear what happens.'

The next three witnesses were very simply disposed of. They were Miles, Adams and Mrs Meadowes. One by one their respective counsel got up and said they had taken the responsibility of advising their clients not to give evidence. That is to say, they would, of course, go through the formality of going into the witness box and being sworn but, when it came to answering any material questions, they would claim privilege on the grounds that the answers might incriminate them.

'You talk of the formality of being sworn,' said Mr Justice Swann. 'From what you are saying, it suggests that your clients considered it a very unimportant formality.'

'If your Lordship pleases,' said counsel for one of those witnesses.

'I don't please at all,' said Mr Justice Swann. 'Your clients, having given vital evidence upon which a man was convicted of murder, now, if you please, haven't the courage to try to put right any wrong they may have done by their original evidence.'

'I don't please at all either, if I may say so,' said counsel, 'but, in all the circumstances, I think it the proper course for my client to take, and my learned colleagues take the same view.'

'This is tantamount to an admission that their original evidence was false,' said Lord Justice Manners.

'I cannot make any admissions,' said counsel.

'We are not asking you to do so,' said Lord Justice Manners. 'But, before we can relieve your clients of the obligation of answering the material questions, we have to be satisfied that to force them to answer might reasonably result in their incriminating themselves. You have not merely to admit that, but to assert it.'

'We all assert it, my Lord.'

'Very well, then. The only way in which your clients could incriminate themselves is by admitting that they had committed perjury at the original trial.'

'That is not the only way, my Lord,' said counsel. 'They might have to admit other offences as well.'

'You mean such offences as conspiring to defeat the ends of justice?'

'That is so, my Lord.'

'And you all claim privilege for your clients on the grounds that, if we compelled them to answer, they might render themselves liable to be indicated not only for perjury but for another offence or offences as well?'

'That is so, my Lord.'

'And you each make this claim of privilege on behalf of your clients, bearing in mind your responsibility to the Court as counsel and after careful consultation with your respective clients?'

'Yes, my Lord.'

'Very well, then,' said Lord Justice Manners. 'I repeat that this is tantamount to an admission by these witnesses that they endeavoured successfully to swear away a man's liberty by perjured evidence.'

'I am not in a position to say anything as to that,' said counsel.

The three judges conferred for a few moments. Then Lord Justice Manners said:

'We know that we can completely trust counsel neither to mislead the Court nor to make a dubious claim for privilege of this kind without disclosing the circumstances giving rise to the doubt. All three counsel have made it quite plain that, if their clients were compelled to answer the questions material to this inquiry, they

might well find themselves prosecuted criminally. No one is required
to give evidence himself in this way and we accordingly allow the
claim of privilege in reliance on counsel's statements and, of course,
on what we know of the case. But the witnesses will remain within
the precincts of this building until the inquiry has been completed.'

The next witness was Jo.

'I gather from your silence,' said Lord Justice Manners to Jo's
counsel, 'that your client does not wish to claim privilege.'

'She does not, my Lord.'

Jo then went into the witness box and gave much the same
evidence as she gave at the trial. She stoutly denied that she had
procured any of the witnesses and she repeated her explanations,
such as they were, for not producing the photograph earlier and for
her sudden exclamation before Mr Justice Halliday. In view of the
refusal of the other witnesses to give evidence, hers was an impossible task and she knew it. But at least she stuck to her guns and
made no admissions of any kind. When her evidence had been
completed, Lonsdale went into the witness box.

He gave his evidence well and frankly and appeared obviously
to be telling the truth. When he had finished, the judges consulted
for a few minutes and then Lord Justice Manners said:

'We have without difficulty come to a clear conclusion on the
first question we have been asked to consider. We will put our
reasons into writing, but it is right to say at once that we are all
firmly convinced that there was a gross miscarriage of justice when
Mr Walsh was convicted. We must now, therefore, consider the
second far more difficult question, which really comes to this. To
what extent are a man and his collaborators free from criminal
responsibility when they break the law in order to remedy an injustice? It is an extremely difficult problem. And perhaps I was wrong
to put it so generally. For example, it is plain that if a man charged
with capital murder is acquitted and subsequently confessed to the
crime, it would plainly be murder for someone to kill him, even
though he ought to have been executed. I think I must revise what
I said. We have to consider whether the steps taken in this case
were morally justified and whether, although amounting to crimes,
they ought or ought not to be visited with the normal consequences
of committing a crime.'

'There is, my Lords, a further question which I am instructed to
raise,' said counsel for Jo. 'I do so with some embarrassment, but

I am quite sure that it is my duty to refer to it, in view of my instructions.'

'What is the point?' asked Lord Justice Manners.

'It is the conduct of Mr Justice Halliday,' said counsel. 'With the greatest possible respect to the learned judge, he appears to have rendered himself liable, certainly to a civil action. Whether or not his actions amounted to a crime I leave it to your Lordships to say.'

'What on earth are you talking about?' said Lord Justice Manners, with some heat. 'The learned judge was in effect kidnapped, like your client, and forced to act as he did. He appears to have acted in a most courageous and balanced manner in very difficult circumstances.'

'My Lord,' said counsel, 'I don't dispute that for a moment. And up to a certain stage in the matter the learned judge was completely blameless.'

'When then do you say he incurred some kind of liability for his actions?'

'My Lord, when he deliberately sent away the police.'

'When he sent away the police? What are you talking about?' said Lord Justice Manners.

'My Lords, you have not yet heard the evidence, but the learned judge will himself tell you, I am quite sure, that at a fairly late stage in the proceedings, if I may so term them, the police arrived at the house and he sent them away again.'

'To prevent a pitched battle, no doubt,' said Lord Justice Manners.

'No, my Lord. It is perfectly true that only two police officers arrived and that they would have been heavily outnumbered and outgunned, but the learned judge did not send them away to get reinforcements, he sent them away so that he could proceed with the inquiry he had been forced to start. And the police will tell you, my Lords, that he gave them the impression that nothing was wrong but that he was busy.'

'Is that correct, Mr Attorney?' asked Lord Justice Manners.

'Substantially, yes, my Lord,' said the Attorney-General.

'Well,' said Lord Justice Manners, 'you have brought the matter to our attention and no doubt it falls within the scope of our inquiry. We had better wait until we hear exactly what happened.'

The Attorney-General then called Mr Justice Halliday to give his account of what happened. When he had finished, Lord Justice Manners conferred with his colleagues.

'We are a little troubled, Sir George,' he said, after a short consultation, 'about this matter of the police being sent away. As we understand the position, until that moment you were all held prisoner in your house?'

'That is so, my Lords.'

'But then you were permitted to interview the police inspector and sergeant and you could have asked them to bring help to release you. Is that right?'

'That is quite correct, my Lords.'

'In fact, however, you did nothing of the kind but put off the police as though nothing were the matter and went back to continue your inquiry.'

'Quite true, my Lords.'

'Well, Sir George, whatever the motives or reasons which prompted you to act in this way, didn't your behaviour identify yourself, to some extent at any rate, with your captors as far as the other captives were concerned? For example, Mrs Barnwell wished to leave the house but was prevented from doing so by the threat of force. If you had asked the police to bring up reinforcements, that would not have happened. May it not, therefore, be said that by your deliberate abstention from seeking help, when help could have been obtained, you became party to the false imprisonment of Mrs Barnwell?'

'My Lords,' said Mr Justice Halliday, 'while I am making no formal admission on the subject, I recognize that, as a pure proposition of law, that may be right. I had a very difficult choice to make. Shall I tell your Lordships why I acted as I did?'

'If you please, Sir George.'

'At the precise moment when the police arrived I had reached a critical stage in the inquiry I had been compelled to make. Your Lordships have now held that there was a gross miscarriage of justice at Mr Walsh's trial. At the time the police arrived I had come to the conclusion that that might have been the case, but I also realized that, unless I could pursue the inquiry at once, it might well be that it could never be satisfactorily concluded. It was a case of striking while the iron was hot. Three witnesses have before your Lordships refused to give evidence on the ground that they might incriminate themselves. Had the inquiry come to an end at the time the police arrived, it is at the very least possible and, in my view, probable, that those witnesses would have sufficiently recovered themselves and received sufficient advice and encouragement from other sources to prompt them to continue the conspiracy to defeat the ends of justice, which your Lordships have held they have impliedly admitted. Of course, my view may have been wrong, but I do not think it was. The position was, therefore, in my opinion, that, if I called for help from the police, it might never have been possible to establish the innocence of this man, and he would have had to complete his sentence of life imprisonment. The view which I held then, and which I respectfully adhere to, was that in such circumstances the sanctity of human liberty for such a length of time was more important than the comparatively short time for which our imprisonment would continue. If by my conduct I have rendered myself liable in damages to Mrs Barnwell or anyone else, if anything more than a nominal sum should in the circumstances be paid to them, I consider the money well spent. But I hasten to add that I think the Treasury ought to pay it. As far as crime is concerned, I entirely dispute that my action in failing to ask for police help amounted to any crime known to the English law. If it did, the law ought to be altered.'

'No doubt, Sir George,' said Lord Justice Manners, with the suspicion of a smile, 'the Attorney-General will address us on the law if necessary. Thank you for your explanation. Does anyone want to ask Sir George any questions?'

Jo's counsel got up. 'Sir George,' he said, 'you agree that Mrs Barnwell wished to leave the house and was prevented from doing so?

'I have already said so.'

'Did she not protest in the strongest possible terms about your conduct in sending the police away?'

'She did so, as you have said, in the strongest possible terms.'

'So that, in effect, you deliberately kept her in the house against her will.'

'I did not actually keep her, but I put it out of her and my power to get released.'

'Presumably you realized that you were doing this—that you were unnecessarily prolonging Mrs Barnwell's and your own imprisonment?'

'I did not consider that aspect of the matter at the time, I confess, but I agree that it was implicit in what I did. Perhaps I ought to add that it is possible that by my action I saved injury or life. I should make it plain that that was not the object of my sending the police away. I believed that, as soon as the inquiry was over, Mr Walsh would keep his word, send his men away and surrender to the police. But I also believed that he and his assistants were quite determined that the inquiry should be completed before his recapture. It is at least possible, therefore, that, had I called for help, there would have been a pitched battle between the police and our captors. I repeat that I had not that in mind. But your client may care to consider that it is possible that I saved her from injury or even death. Nor was she kept a prisoner for a moment longer than was necessary to complete the inquiry. I cannot conceive that the same thing will ever happen again, but, if it did, I think I should feel obliged to act in the same way.'

The judge completed his evidence and then Lonsdale gave evidence about his escape and the reasons for it. He refused to divulge the names of his associates and was not pressed to do so. Again he gave his account well and with obvious sincerity.

'The governor of my prison suggested that I ought to have waited in prison until I was released,' he said. 'I quite understand his point of view. No governor can view escapes with equanimity or, if I may say so, without bias. It was his job to keep me inside. It was my job to get outside. Had there been any legal method of achieving my object, I should, of course, have pursued it, but I had exhausted all legal methods. What else was there for me to do?'

That indeed was an unanswerable question. In order to have his case reviewed, he had not only to escape but to take the other illegal and dangerous steps which he had taken. When Lonsdale had finished his evidence, Charles took up the burden on his behalf.

'Your Lordships have now proclaimed my client to have been the subject of a disgraceful conspiracy and to have been wrongfully convicted. We know that occasionally such cases may occur, but this one had only come to light by reason of my client's illegal activities. It would, in my respectful submission, be an outrage if he were now prosecuted for the crimes he was forced to commit. I agree that there is less to be said for his accomplices who took on the job as one of business and for which they have been well paid. But my client has particularly asked that your Lordships should hold that no proceedings ought to be taken against any of them who can be found or identified. For certain it is that without their help my client would never have been able to do what he did. Their moral guilt may be rather more than my client's but, even in their case, they knew they were assisting in an attempt to prove my client's innocence. Whether or not they believed in it I do not know, but they may well have been impressed by the amount my client was prepared to spend on the undertaking.'

'Mr Southdown,' said Lord Justice Manners, 'I gather that most of your client's accomplices could not be identified, as they were masked.'

'That is so, my Lord.'

'Speaking for myself only, I must say that I should at least think it rather bad luck on anyone who was not so disguised being charged, while his associates got off scot free.'

'The same remark could apply to any burglary,' said Mr Justice Swann.

'Of course it could,' said Lord Justice Manners, 'but this is very different from a burglary. Indeed, the main object was not a felonious one at all. It wasn't a crime at all. The object was to procure an inquiry. That is all. The methods used to procure it were, of course, criminal, but no one was injured or more than inconvenienced as a result, and, as the object was a good one, I should have thought that the pursuit of the perpetrators would not be particularly desirable. Although public feeling is by no means always the right guide in these matters, there is no doubt whatever but that the public would be very much against the prosecution of any such proceedings. The only proceedings which, in my personal view, ought to be taken are proceedings against those who successfully sought the conviction of Mr Walsh by a criminal conspiracy. But there is obviously in law insufficient evidence to bring them to trial, however loudly the facts speak for themselves.'

Eventually the Tribunal completed its hearing and, in due course, its findings were published. They completely vindicated Lonsdale and recommended that no proceedings should be taken against anyone. Lonsdale had been released immediately after the public hearing. He received many letters of congratulation, including one from Jo.

'You've done very well,' she wrote, 'and I congratulate you. But don't think I'm going to let it rest at this. Love, Jo.'

Lonsdale smiled, and threw the note into the fire.

A little later on he had a visit from the Boss. He had asked him to call.

'How nice to see you again,' he said, after the Boss had been shown in. 'I do want to tell you how grateful I am for all you did.'

'Not at all,' said the Boss. 'It was a real pleasure and paid for handsomely. I wish all my customers were as forthcoming. D'you know, I've almost felt like retiring. But I should get bored, you know. I shall take a holiday, of course.'

'Why don't you write a book?' suggested Lonsdale. 'That's quite a recognized profession for retired crim . . . retired people to take up. I expect you could tell a few interesting stories. Change the names, of course, and alter them about.'

'I'm not much good with a pen,' said the Boss. 'I wasn't at school. My essays were dreadful. Always getting into trouble over them.'

'Oh, well,' said Lonsdale, 'it was only a passing thought. I'd hate to see anyone, who's been as useful to me as you, languishing in prison. I gather that they do catch up with you sometimes.'

'It has been known,' said the Boss. 'It's my own fault really. But I like to see a job's done really well, and that does mean paying visits to the site from time to time. But, after all, I shouldn't have got my practice together if I hadn't done that. So I can't really complain.'

'But you'll have to retire some time,' said Lonsdale. 'Why not make it now? You're still young enough to enjoy life.'

'That's the trouble. When I'm older I may not want the excitement I need now. You've no idea how thrilling it is to watch a well-prepared plan carried out. I got a terrific kick out of arranging yours. No mountaineer retires until he's past it. He just can't give it up. It'll be the same with me. However, let's hope I'm lucky. They haven't had me for some time.'

'They'll be on the look-out for you now,' said Lonsdale. 'I expect they know you were behind this.'

'I'm sure they do,' said the Boss. 'They know that no one else could have done it so well.'

CHAPTER 18

Counsel's Opinion

Two days after Lonsdale's release from prison, Jo walked into a solicitor's office. She had an appointment to see Mr Manage of Streak and Manage. As soon as she had sat down she came to the point.

'Mr Manage,' she said, 'would your firm have any objections to bringing an action against a High Court judge for conspiracy?'

Mr Manage brightened perceptibly.

'Mrs Barnwell,' he said, 'subject only to considerations of professional propriety, my firm would be delighted to bring an action against a High Court judge for conspiracy, bottomry, barratry or even for plain straightforward negligence. I personally should welcome the opportunity. Shall I tell you why?'

'By all means,' said Jo.

'I am only a humble solicitor, as you know. But in my humble capacity I have had the inestimable privilege of supplying barristers with briefs. You may or may not know that briefs are as necessary for a barrister as water for a fish. Neither can survive without a sufficient and continuous supply of, in the one case, briefs, in the other, water. Perhaps you knew this already?'

'I had some idea of it,' said Jo.

'So you know, too, that the legal profession in this country is divided into two branches. The superior, that is the Bar; the lowly and inferior, that is the solicitor's profession. But, humble and lowly as we are, we do have the great honour of being allowed to supply the superior branch with their neccessities of life, briefs. Naturally we count ourselves most blessed to be allowed to nourish such an admirable body of men and women as the Bar with their main source of existence. We do this from the moment the barrister is qualified. We help the young man, we bring distinction to the older man and, in a very large measure, we are responsible for the

promotion to the Bench of the most distinguished members of the
Bar. For you must know that judges are selected only from the Bar.
You might have thought that, in the circumstances, there would be
a measure of gratitude shown by the judge to the solicitor. Without
his briefs, he would never have become a judge. Indeed, while he
is still practising at the Bar, he usually treats solicitors not only
with the utmost courtesy and consideration, but you might almost
say that at times he shows actual signs of fawning on the hand that
feeds him. You must forgive this rather long introduction.'

'Certainly,' said Jo, 'If it means that you want to help me.'

'I certainly do. And I will now tell you why. As soon as many
of these courteous, polite barristers are elevated to the Bench their
attitude towards their humble brethren, the solicitors, appears to
undergo a marked change. "Where is the solicitor in the case?"
they say. "How comes it that he has done so-and-so and not done
so-and-so? While I am not trying an issue between him and his
client as to whether he has been guilty of negligence, I feel bound
to say that I can't see what answer he would have to such a claim."
On another occasion he will go so far as to make the solicitor pay
the costs personally, a horrible thing to do. In other words, he turns
and bites the hand that fed him. All our loving care goes for nothing.
Gone is the "Good morning, Mr Manage. How are you, my dear
fellow? So glad to see you. Thank you so much for your instructions
in the Wallaby case. They were, if I may say so, admirably drawn."
Instead, we have: "It's outrageous that this notice wasn't given or
this document not produced. What's a solicitor for?" When they
ask that last question I always want to say, "To brief the barrister
and that was once you, my Lord." But I don't. I should be sent to
prison for contempt of Court. So I must be content with muttering
to myself and telling my counsel to get up and stand up for me.
Now, I think it was a charge of conspiracy you wanted to bring.
That sounds admirable. I'd charge the whole lot of them with it, if
I got the chance. But, of course, I must first be satisfied that you
have a reasonable case. What's it all about?'

'Presumably you have read all about it, Mr Manage,' said Jo.
'Why shouldn't I sue Mr Justice Halliday and Mr Walsh for
conspiracy to detain me against my will? The judge knew that by
letting the police go I would be detained by Mr Walsh and he
intended that I should be.'

'It's a nice idea,' said Mr Manage, 'a very nice idea indeed. My only regret is that I can't say that Mr Justice Halliday has ever made me pay the costs personally. Indeed, he has been rather an exception to the rule I was mentioning. However, that can't be helped. It should be an example to the others. Let me think.'

Mr Manage was silent for a short time. Then he said: 'As a mere solicitor, my opinion on a matter of this delicacy is of little value. We shall have to approach the superior branch. In other words, we shall need the opinion of counsel. Do you mind the expense?'

'Not if it will get me anywhere,'said Jo.

'Very well,' said Mr Manage. 'We will approach the most suitable of these learned gentlemen who is available. My first choice would be Mr Trent. He is quite intolerable, but so are most of them in their different ways, as a matter of fact. At the same time, he appears to me to know his law as well as any of them. Not that that means very much. The standard of lawyers at the Bar gets lower and lower.'

'Well, if the Bench is recruited from the Bar,' said Jo, 'you can't think much of the Bench.'

'I don't, Mrs Barnwell,' said Mr Manage. 'I don't. Between you and me there are only six decent lawyers in the country. Three are in the House of Lords, one's an ecclesiastical lawyer, and the other two are dead. Mr Trent I consider to be the best of the extremely bad bunch which is available for your matter.'

'Then why don't you rely on your own opinion, Mr Manage?'

'That's quite simple, my dear Mrs Barnwell, quite simple. If I'm wrong, you could sue me. If I get counsel's opinion, you can't.'

'Even if he's careless?'

'Even, my dear Mrs Barnwell, if he is negligent to a degree which would justify the vituperative epithet of gross. The position is that, when your professional adviser, be he doctor, accountant, architect or humble solicitor, gives you the normal careless advice which the public have come to expect from him, you can take him to the Courts and his insurance company will pay you. But when the barrister is careless, far beyond the normal degree expected of him, you have no remedy against him and, of course, no remedy against the solicitor instructing him.'

'I must say it seems odd,' said Jo.

'It not only seems, but it is odd. I must make one qualification about my own position. If I took you now to a barrister who was a patent specialist and knew nothing about such things as Judges conspiring with escaped convicts and, if he were foolish enough to accept the instructions and gave you advice which might have been admirable if you had just invented a machine for making the tea and shaving you at the same time, but which was completely off the rails in relation to a claim for false imprisonment, then indeed I might be liable to you for going to an obviously unsuitable man. I am taking no such risk in going to Mr Trent. That he is intolerable, I have already told you. That he may insult you, I add now, but he certainly practises in those courts where judges who conspire with escaped convicts would be brought, if such cases were in the normal run of things.'

'Very well,' said Jo. 'Let us go to Mr Trent.'

So a conference was arranged with Mr Trent's clerk and, at the appointed time, Jo and Mr Manage arrived at his chambers. They were not kept waiting.

'On the dot, you see, Mr Manage,' said Mr Trent cheerfully, as he welcomed them in. 'I see no reason why a barrister, however busy he may be, should not keep his appointments punctually. I expect you to be here on time. You have a right to expect that I am ready.'

'That is most kind,' said Jo.

'It is not intended to be,' said Mr Trent. 'It is intended to be good business. Members of the Bar don't like referring to the word "business". They consider that it lowers their prestige. In my view, nothing lowers a barrister's prestige except inefficiency. And I venture to think you will find none of that here, Mrs Barnwell. You see, I don't even pretend not to know your name. I have taken the trouble to memorize it. You will find no affectation here either.'

'What we hope to find,' said Jo, 'is the answer to my problem.'

'That goes without saying,' said Mr Trent. 'I have read these papers and come to a clear conclusion in the matter. That's something I deprecate in many of my colleagues. They give you so many alternatives in their opinions, so many "ifs" and "buts", that you don't know what they really are advising you. My advice may be wrong—it isn't, but of course, you can't tell that—but it is always definite. The other day we won a case in the House of Lords. We had lost it before the judge of first instance. I had said that we should win it. "Should", mark you, not "would". I naturally cannot guarantee the correctness of every decision of a judge of first instance, even if I am appearing in the case. Some judges are so dense that you cannot penetrate their minds with any but the simplest propositions. I am not saying that was the case in the action I was telling you about. The judge was an excellent one, but unfortunately I was unable to accept the brief. The case was done by a very worthy and fairly able colleague, but, quite frankly, he wasn't up to it. So my client had to go to the Court of Appeal. There I would have appeared but, unfortunately, I was taken suddenly ill and had to return the brief. The case was lost again. You can imagine that at that stage my client must have been doubting the correctness of my advice. Four judges had now decided against my opinion. However, he came to consult me again and I advised him to go to the House of Lords. My advice was not that he "should" win there but that he "would" win. Provided, of course, that I was able to argue the case. I must say, my client took a lot of persuading to go on with the appeal. But, fortunately for him, in the end he agreed. I argued the case in the House of Lords and we won by a majority of three to two. The legal journals pointed out that that meant that six judges of high standing had decided in favour of my opponent and only three in favour of my client, and yet my client won. I pointed out, in a short and apt letter, that justice does not always go to the big battalions. I offer my apology for telling you all this. Mr Manage knows my reputation. That, no doubt, is why he comes to me. But you don't, Mrs Barnwell, and I always consider that the lay client—that is you, Mrs Barnwell—should get a fair idea of the man she is consulting.'

'I think you've given me an excellent idea,' said Jo. 'Apart, however, from what you have told me yourself, Mr Manage gave me a very good description of your qualities.'

'Did he?' said Mr Trent. 'He probably told you, then, that I was quite intolerable.'

Mr Manage blushed.

'So I am, Mrs Barnwell,' said Mr Trent, 'to most solicitors. Their abysmal ignorance and inefficiency is sometimes beyond bearing. I am not particularly referring to Mr Manage's firm, which is as good as any. Though, I am bound to say that isn't anything much. Now, most members of the Bar don't talk like this, Mrs Barnwell. They flatter their clients, usually without the slightest justification. You will gather that I don't. I tell them exactly what I think of them, and I am bound to admit that some of them don't come back for more. Indeed, if it were not for the fact that fortunately nature had endowed me with certain qualities which peculiarly suit me for this profession—I claim no credit for it, any more than one claims credit for having been born—if it were not for that fact, I don't suppose I should have a single client. I should have had to give up the Bar years ago. Fortunately, as you can see from the briefs on the table, that lamentable event did not occur. Solicitors have to come to me, whether they like it or not. I don't suppose Mr Manage likes it any better than most of the others. Now, shall we proceed?'

'Yes, please,' said Jo.

'You want to know whether you would have a reasonable chance of succeeding in an action for conspiracy against Mr Justice Halliday and Mr Walsh, the conspiracy being to imprison you falsely. The answer to that question is, quite simply, yes. If the action were tried by a judge, he would, in my view, if the case were properly argued in front of him, be bound to find in your favour. If the case came before a jury, I cannot predict with the same certainty what they would say. But, even if they decided against you, you would have a fair chance of upsetting their verdict on appeal.'

'Well, that's very good hearing,' said Jo. 'We'll start at once.'

'Wait a moment,' said Mr Trent. 'The two questions which would arise in your action are whether the claim is legally justified and, secondly, what are the damages. If, as I think it would be, the first question is decided in your favour, the second question arises. What are the damages? Now normally they might be heavy. But I am bound to say that, in the very peculiar and exceptional circumstances of this case, I think you would be lucky if you were awarded more than £5. That amount the defendant would certainly pay into court and, if you recovered no more, you would have the pleasure of paying the costs of both sides. Of course, you could accept the £5, but I rather think that would not appeal to you.'

'£5!' said Jo indignantly. 'Can decent citizens be imprisoned by judges without justification and only recover £5?'

'No,' said Mr Trent, 'I don't say that. But I feel quite sure that any judge or jury would hold that you were not a decent citizen, and that you were only detained in order that a wrong for which you were responsible could be remedied.'

'Are you on their side or mine?' asked Jo.

'I am on no one's side yet,' said Mr Trent. 'I am advising you to the best of my ability, which, as I have already indicated to you, is considerable. In the light of the Tribunal's report, any judge or jury would take the view that Mr Walsh was wrongly convicted and that you were in all probability responsible for that conviction.'

'He's a murderer,' said Jo. 'He murdered my husband.'

'Fortunately,' said Mr Trent, 'what you say to me is privileged and will, of course, be treated by me in complete confidence, but, if you are wise, you won't make statements like that outside these chambers.'

'That is where I am going anyway,' said Jo, 'and I shall say and do what I please there,' and she left the room abruptly.

'I'm sorry,' said Mr Manage to Mr Trent, 'but she feels strongly on the subject.'

'It is quite unnecessary to apologize,' said Mr Trent. 'I have only proved you to be right—in your advice to your client about me, I mean.'

'It's nice to be right for once,' said Mr Manage.

'I hope you won't have to wait too long for the next time,' said Mr Trent.

CHAPTER 19

All Square

Miles Hampton never had his interview on television. The best he could get was a ghosted article in one of the Sunday newspapers. It was called: 'Why I Refused To Give Evidence', and Miles received £100 for being a party to it. He read the article he was supposed to have written, and, though he could not fully understand the reasons, as stated, why he had not given evidence, he enjoyed seeing his name and photograph in the paper. He enjoyed the £100 almost as much. And, in the circumstances, he considered that, all in all, he had not done so badly. Instead of receiving anything up to seven years for perjury he had had an interesting experience, received a good deal of publicity, and been paid for it.

Mrs Meadowes duly married her new husband and both of them were good value, in the public houses which they frequented, for some months.

Herbert Adams went back to his bench in the park and waited for something else to happen.

Mr Allwinter went back to his art and had several ideas for pictures which he put into execution. One, a large canvas, called 'Mr Justice Halliday at home' and showing accurately the scene at the judge's house during the inquiry, was shown in the Academy. The judge bought it quickly, Mr Allwinter began another.

Angela and Charles began to see more and more of each other, with Lonsdale's entire approval.

Lonsdale himself, after taking a short rest, began to consider fresh financial ventures. About six weeks after his release he was taking, as he often did, a stroll in the evening near his London house when a large blue car ran into and over him in the middle of the road. He was fatally injured, though not killed on the spot. The car endeavoured to drive on, but somehow the collision had affected the steering and it swerved into a lamp-post. In the result, the

police, who were quickly on the scene, were able to take a statement
from the driver, after Lonsdale had been rushed to hospital. There
were no independent witnesses but the driver explained that the
injured man had suddenly rushed into the middle of the road in
front of the car, giving it no chance. The police might have had no
difficulty in accepting this statement as true, but for the fact that
the driver was Jo Barnwell.

As soon as they discovered her identity, they did all they could
to get a statement from Lonsdale before he died. A policeman sat
by his bed the whole time, night and day.

It was obvious that he would die, but a day after the accident
he recovered consciousness sufficiently to speak. He was asked how
the accident happened. Before he answered the question, he asked:

'Did the driver stop?'

He was told that she couldn't help it.

'Then you know who she is?' he asked.

'Yes,' said the police officer.

'What was her version?' asked Lonsdale.

The officer told him.

'Absolutely correct,' said Lonsdale, and closed his eyes.

'Nurse,' called the officer. 'Quick. He's gone almost purple.'

Later recovering consciousness again for the last time, he asked
to see Jo alone. She knew by then that he had confirmed her story.

'Why did you tell a lie?' she asked. 'You know I did it on purpose.'

'I know,' he said, 'but I've a great regard for you, Jo, and I
didn't mind that sort of attack. That was quite straightforward. I
ought to have thought you might try it. After all, it's only what I
did to Adolphus myself.'

'Then it was you, and you managed to lie about that too.'

'I didn't, Jo. I didn't have to, though I would have, if necessary.'

'You must have told your daughter you were innocent. I'm sure
she said you had.'

'I only told her and everyone else that I'd been convicted by
perjury. That was true enough.'

'So the only lie you've ever told was to save me?'

'Yes, Jo. I'm not sure that you deserve it. Fancy suggesting that
I'd let anyone else run over Adolphus for me. He'd have been sure
to make a mess of it. But I did better than you, Jo. I killed him
outright.'

'I did try, darling,' said Jo apologetically.

THE VICTOR CANNING OMNIBUS

THE PYTHON PROJECT is Victor Canning's most exciting thriller. The trail leads through Paris, Florence and Rome, to the sandy shores of North Africa.

'Canning in great form . . .' *Evening Standard*

'Beyond praise for inventiveness and wit . . .' *Punch*

A DELIVERY OF FURIES – Keith Marchant is a tough, free-wheeling ex-R.A.F. pilot who makes a precarious living transporting shady cargoes around the world. His plan is a bold one; he will hijack a cargo of six Hawker Sea Fury fighters on the high seas and deliver them to the sun-drenched Caribbean port of Acaibo, headquarters of Angelo Libertad, the fanatical Guevara-type leader of an island revolution, but he becomes caught up in the ruthless intrigue behind the revolution. Readers will enjoy this famous novel.

'**THE MELTING MAN** is well up to Mr. Canning's high standard of exuberant ingenuity, with the usual seafaring finale.' *Daily Telegraph*

'No one thrills like Canning can – and does.' *Yorkshire Post*

Mr. Canning is a professional thriller writer of high competence.' *Times Literary Supplement*

ANDREW GARVE OMNIBUS

MURDER IN MOSCOW – Verney had been sent to Moscow to report on changes in the Russian scene. When the leader of a British peace delegation is murdered, Verney discovers only too quickly the sort of changes that have occurred; the authorities produce a pseudo-criminal – and Verney soon sees why the truth doesn't make a scrap of difference.

'Convincing and fascinating.' *Illustrated London News*

'An authentic peek behind the curtain.' *New Statesman*

THE ASHES OF LODA – This is the story, told at a gripping pace, of how a man struggled single-handed and in alien surroundings to uncover events, intrigues and passions long buried in the 'ashes of Loda' – and of what he found.

THE CUCKOO LINE AFFAIR – When a highly respected citizen is accused by a pretty girl of assaulting her in a train, and two unimpeachable witnesses say they saw him do it, his position is serious. The incident was only the beginning of troubles for Edward Latimer, sixtyish, lovable and slightly quaint, on a journey to the Essex village of Steepleford by the ancient single-track railway known locally as the Cuckoo Line.

Andrew Garve is undoubtedly one of the most successful writers of detective-thrillers to emerge since the war. This is largely due to the vivid atmosphere he evokes from the varied and authentic backgrounds against which he sets his stories.

CHRISTOPHER LANDON OMNIBUS

ICE COLD IN ALEX – The thought of ice-cold lager, as served in Alexandria, haunted Captain Anson living on whisky – and his nerves – in doomed Tobruk. It became an obsession when he, his sergeant-major and two nurses set out in the ambulance Katy to break through Rommel's encircling panzers. Their desperate journey ran full tilt into action, excitement, personal drama – and Captain Zimmerman, who claimed to be a South African . . .

'The tension of this nighmare drive will grip you.'
Manchester Evening News

'Finely imagined, finely told.' *Birmingham Post*

'Wholly realistic and believable.' *Guardian*

DEAD MEN RISE UP NEVER is a novel of suspense with a dramatic courtroom twist and a tense finale aboard a sardine trawler off the coast of Spain.

THE SHADOW OF TIME – Anger, love and, above all, fear – these are the emotions that drive the characters in *The Shadow of Time* to their various fates. Christopher Landon is a master of suspence, and he keeps the reader on tenterhooks until the very end.